COLONY

ANNE RIVERS SIDDONS

HarperTorch
An Imprint of HarperCollins Publishers

Aknowledgment is made for permission to reprint: Excerpt from "Two Tramps In Mud Time" from *The Poetry of Robert Frost*, edited by Edward Connery Lathem, copyright © 1963 by Robert Frost. Copyright © 1964 by Lesley Frost, Ballantine. Copyright © 1969 by Holt, Rinehart and Winston. Reprinted by permission of Henry Holt and Company, Inc. Excerpt from "Ash Wednesday" in *Collected Poems 1909-1962* by T.S. Eliot, copyright © 1963 by Harcourt Brace Jovanovich, Inc., copyright © 1964, © 1963 by T.S. Eliot, reprinted by permission of the publisher.

This book contains an excerpt from the upcoming paperback edition of *John Chancellor Makes Me Cry* by Anne Rivers Siddons, copyright © 1975, Introduction copyright © 1992.

HARPERTORCH

An Imprint of HarperCollins*Publishers*
10 East 53rd Street
New York, New York 10022-5299

First HarperTorch paperback printing: December 2000
First HarperPaperbacks printing: July 1993
First HarperCollins hardcover printing: July 1992

HarperCollins®, HarperTorch™, and ❦™ are trademarks of HarperCollins Publishers Inc.
Avon Trademark Reg. U.S. Pat. Off. and in Other Countries,
Marca Registrada, Hecho en U.S.A.

Printed in the United States of America

Visit HarperTorch on the World Wide Web at www.harpercollins.com

30 29 28 27

For Stuart, Kelby, and Maggie Siddons
The next of us

Only where love and need are one,
And the work is play for mortal stakes,
Is the deed ever really done
For Heaven and the Future's sakes.

—Robert Frost
"Two Tramps in Mud Time"

Maude Gascoigne Chambliss

Prologue

Sound is queer here by the water, especially when the fog has come off Penobscot Bay, as it has now. It started in the middle of the afternoon, unusual for this time of year. Usually our late-summer fogs are only just beginning to drift in at this hour, so that walking home from drinks at one or another of the old cottages is still easy: pleasant, in fact, and quite lovely, with the edges of everything just beginning to soften and blur.

But people would not find the going easy this evening, would need their flashlights and sticks . . . if there were any people left to be going home in the fog. They're all gone now. I'm the last one left. It's a new experience for me, but not nearly so strange when you think about it. Someone has to be last.

And it is, after all, September.

I said the sound is queer here; by that I meant strange, with an otherness that can be quite disturbing until you get used to it. It bounces about so you can't tell where it's coming from, or how far or near it is, and it often mimics something else entirely. The rhythmic dripping of the downspout onto the porch shingles, for instance, and the wet riffles off in the birch grove opposite my cottage, when a little wind disturbs the branches, might well be the *twang-thud* of tennis balls and the polite spatter of applause from our little August tournament. It has been held every year since I have been coming to Retreat; I remember when the young men who played wore long white trousers and blazers, and few young women played at all. The snapping of sodden branches might easily be the little flat, popping starting guns for one of our endless regattas.

The creaking of the old twig rocker in the porch below my window, stirred by the rising night wind, sounds very much like the drying ropes on the sloops moored down in the little deep-water harbor at the foot of the lane—or lines, as I believe they're called. I never learned the proper sailing terminology; Peter was a passionate sailor, but from the first I disliked it, and to use the language without the object of it has always seemed to me both ostentatious and ridiculous. I have never thought myself either.

The mewl of the harbor gulls, now: that might be the questing cry of Amy and Parker Potter's old tabby tom, Widdy, or, years later, the baby that was born to Elizabeth in that house, prematurely and after all those ghastly long hours of labor—in darkness, too, for the dying lash of an August hurricane had knocked out the colony's power. The baby died that night, as I recall; Elizabeth could not get to the Castine hospital because a great fir was down across the lane, and there was no doctor in the colony then. I heard its crying all that endless afternoon, and into the evening, before it finally stopped.

I never liked the sound of the gulls after that.

Apparently Elizabeth didn't either. She never came back to Retreat after that summer, though I could not decide whether it was because of the sadness of the baby's death or the possibility of talk about its birth.

Probably the former. Elizabeth would not have cared about the latter. She would not have come to Braebonnie, to the family cottage, to have the baby if she had feared the tongues of the colony. Certainly not in light of the fact that the baby's father was in a nearby cottage with his own family that summer . . . or so we all heard. Such things may be discussed for generations in a small place like Retreat, with great enjoyment and with no proof at all. In this case, the proof lived less than twelve hours.

At any rate, Elizabeth never returned, and she never sold Braebonnie as we all thought she would, after Amy and Parker were gone. She simply rented it each summer, apparently to anyone in her curious and hectic world who had the price of it, and so the first chink in Retreat's armor, if you will, was breached.

We had never had renters before then. Amy and Parker would have died of shame, if they had not died of other things first. But I must admit that the renters of Braebonnie livened us up. One summer we had a world-famous composer who wrote his best-known work here, doodling and banging on the tuneless old Bechstein in the living room; and another summer a family of actors, Jewish, I believe, who alternately rehearsed their new play and excoriated each other every evening for three months. I should know; my upstairs bedroom windows face Braebonnie's living room and veranda, and, as I said, sound carries here at the edge of this cold sea. The noises from the Potter cottage have always rather annoyed me, except for the carefree back-and-forth calling Amy and I used to do when we were both young brides here. But tonight I would almost welcome the composer, or even the actors.

Not the sound of the doomed baby, though. Never that. Of all the sounds of birth and life and laughter I have ever heard down all these summers in Retreat, and all the sounds of quarreling and crying and even coupling, yes; and of all the sounds of diminishing and even of dying—please God, never again that one small and terrible sound, begun out of storm and anguish, ended so soon.

And yet, for me alone, never ended at all.

Chapter One

All places where the French settled early have corruption at their heart, a kind of soft, rotten glow, like the phosphorescence of decaying wood, that is oddly attractive. Seductive, even, if my mother-in-law, whose astonishing opinion that was, was to be believed. And she was always believed. The conventional wisdom of her day was that Hannah Stuart Chambliss would rather be burnt at the stake than tell a lie. I don't find that surprising at all. I think the Maid of Orleans role would have pleased Mother Hannah to a fare-thee-well, even the fiery martyr's death. Mother H had a streak of thespian in her as wide as her savage stratum of truth, and she employed it just as fiercely when the need arose. I never knew anyone who escaped those twin lashes except my husband, Peter. He alone might have profited from them.

She told me that, about the corruption and the seduction, on the evening I came to Retreat colony for the first time. It must have been in her mind ever since she first met me, the year before, when Peter took me to the big house in Boston to meet her and his father, but she had never voiced it until then. But it was plain to me—and, I suppose, to Peter—that it, or something like it, lay like an iceberg beneath her austere and beautiful surface. Oh, she smiled her carved Etruscan smile, all the years of our relationship, and hugged me lightly and kissed my cheek with lips like arctic butterflies, but none of us were fooled. I don't think she meant us to be. My unsuitability hung in the pristine air of the Chambliss drawing room like a body odor.

But it was not until Peter brought me as a bride to the old brown cottage on Penobscot Bay, in northern Maine, where the Chamblisses had summered for generations, that she allowed that particular little clot of displeasure to pass, and with it damned me and Charleston, and, indeed the entire indolent, depraved South to Retreat's own efficient purgatory. That she said it with a little hug of my shoulders and a small laugh, in response to something old Mrs. Stallings bellowed in her ginny bray, did nothing to mitigate its sting.

Augusta Stallings looked at me, small and roundly curved and black-eyed and -haired and brown with sun, standing in the chilly camphor dusk of the cottage's living room, and fell upon my utter alienness, in that place of fair straight hair and rain-colored eyes and long bones and teeth and oval New England faces, like a trout on a mayfly.

"Charleston, you say?" she shouted. "Gascoigne, from Charleston? I know some Pinckneys and a Huger, but I never met any Gascoignes. French, is it? Or Creole, I expect. Well, you're a colorful little thing, no doubt about that. You'll open some eyes at the dining hall, my girl."

And that is when my mother-in-law laid her long Stuart arm around my shoulders and made her light little speech about the French and corruption and seduction. My face flamed darker, but I doubt that anyone noticed. The cottage's living room was as dark as a cave because Hannah would rarely allow the

huge lilac trees that obscured its windows to be cut.
It was the first thing I did after she died.

Peter pulled me close, grinning first at his mother
and then at Augusta Stallings.

"The only French who settled in Charleston were
four hundred good gray Huguenots on the run after
Louis the Fourteenth revoked the Edict of Nantes," he
said. "Not a jot or tittle of corruption in the lot of them.
Or seductiveness either, I imagine. Unless, of course,
you meant that Maude was an octoroon, Mama?"

"Don't be silly, Peter," Hannah said, in a tone that
said she had indeed entertained the possibility. There
was my dark skin, after all, and the black eyes, and
the hair that curled in tight ringlets around my head.
And something about the nose. . . .

"You mean a nigger?" Augusta Stallings brayed,
peering more closely at me in the cold, pearly dusk.
The tumbler of neat gin that she held sloshed onto
the sisal rug.

"Oh, Augusta, really," Hannah said. "Of course
that isn't what I meant, and if I hear a word about it
around the colony this summer I'm going to know
where it started. Maude's family has been in
Charleston for two hundred years; they've had the
plantation almost that long."

"Oh, well, then," Augusta Stallings said, as if the
word "plantation" were a Rosetta stone that
explained the mystery of this overripe too-dark
southern daughter-in-law.

Peter laughed aloud, and I smiled, tentatively, and
the two older women moved away onto the sun
porch, where the drinks tray stood.

"We'll put a bone in your nose when we go to dinner tonight, and your career in Retreat will be guar-
anteed," Peter said, and I laughed aloud, as he had
intended. Peter could always make me laugh, even in
the worst times. Even though everyone and every-

thing in this strange, cold northern world was alien to me, and frightening, I would be all right as long as Peter was beside me.

"You don't want to pay too much attention to Augusta Stallings, my dear," my father-in-law said from the sofa in front of the vast fireplace. I jumped. I had forgotten he was present. He had said little since we arrived; he had said little, indeed, the few other times I had been in his presence. He was handsome and remote but somehow bleached out, a faded negative of Peter. He was kind, but he was simply, for me, not there. Every time I heard his voice, it was as if I were hearing it for the first time.

"It doesn't matter a bit," I said.

"Well, I hope not," Big Peter said. "Dreadful woman. Never see her that she's not half squiffed. Too much money and not enough to do. That's what's the matter with all these women. Too much money and not enough to do. Too many long New England noses in everybody else's business."

I smiled across the room at him, sensing an ally. With these two Chambliss men in my corner, how bad could the summer be?

I was wrong about that. I think my father-in-law might have been a formidable ally, if things had been different; I know I had his sympathy and liking. I had sensed that from the beginning. But I did not, then, know about the darkness inside him, the black place where he went for long periods of time and shut the door behind him. When he was there, in that place, there was no reaching him, and he did not reach out to anyone. Within days of our arrival he had slipped away into his dark room. Peter told me then that he spent most of his time in Retreat withdrawn from the world around him. I remember that for a long time I used to wonder why he came, when the place drove him into darkness.

"Well," Peter said once, much later, "it's just where we go in the summer."

And by that time, it was explanation enough.

We got to the old white-painted dining hall a little late, so that most of the assembled colony was seated, and perhaps a hundred eyes followed me as I moved along the aisle behind Hannah, feeling overdressed and gaudily corrupt and sleazily seductive and rank as spoiled fruit in my flowered silk dress. All around me pale linens and earth-colored tweeds and white coats and severe neutrals lay like old snow. All around me sandy eyebrows lifted over long noses and sharp, high cheekbones, and quiet murmurs swelled like well-bred bees. But there were smiles on every face, and thin fingers pressed mine in welcome. And for the first and only time, on that first night in Maine, I walked under the aegis of two powerful amulets: Hannah Stuart Chambliss and the great plantation that was my provenance. I knew most of the people present would have heard about that; Augusta Stallings was still at her appointed rounds, plying from table to table like a wallowing old tugboat.

Of everyone in the big hall that night, only Peter and I knew that the plantation was a myth.

I met him on the night of my first Saint Cecilia Ball. People always think it a romantic story, and in a way it is. I certainly thought so at the time; I nearly drowned, on that silver-forged November night, in the pure romance of it. Only Darcy caught the truth, all those years later. Darcy, with her entire ardent nature made for soaring and her wounded heart scarred shut against it.

"Oh, God, how awful," she said. "How unfair to you both. How could anything else ever measure up, after that?"

How indeed? But we tried. Our whole life together, Peter's and mine, was spent trying to live up to one enchanted night in the Carolina Low Country that began with a great armful of white hothouse lilacs—rarer in that place and season than diamonds—and ended with a kiss in the dark on the banks of a creek gauzed with gray moss and burning with moonlight.

On the main, we succeeded pretty well, I think. Sporadically, and at what cost only he and I knew, but there was magic in the marriage of Maude Brundage Gascoigne and Peter Williams Chambliss. There always was. Love and magic; I don't think the austere people in New Hampshire and Maine that I went to live among ever quite forgave us that. Or, rather, forgave me. In those dark hills they once burned women who made magic. Failing that, they tried other methods of immolation. But I kept the love, and some of the magic too; oh, yes, I did.

Decades later, when the musical *A Chorus Line* became thunderously popular, I was captivated with a bittersweet little ballad from it, "What I Did for Love." I hummed and sang it, and asked Darcy to buy me the album, and played it all that summer in the cottage at Retreat.

"Really, Grammaude, that's a harlot's song," she teased. "Well, maybe not a harlot, but a lady who's definitely been around the block a few times. Not suitable at all for a doyenne. What scandalous thing did you ever do for love? Tell."

I looked at her, blazing, that summer, in the fire and sun of her own first love. I had no doubt at all about the things she was doing for love, and knew she regretted none of them.

"I *will* tell you, I think," I said. "Only you. But not yet. You're a long way from ready to hear it."

"Oh, come on. Why not?"

"Because you're not woman enough yet," I said.

"And you are?"

"Oh, yes."

"I will wait," my red-haired granddaughter said, "with bated breath." She was laughing at me.

No matter. I would tell her one day, if she turned into the woman I thought she might. There were never any guarantees about that, but she had the raw material for it. If she used what life had dealt her already, I would tell her what I did for love. Of all the women I had ever known in that beautiful place on Penobscot Bay, my granddaughter Darcy Chambliss O'Ryan might, with luck, understand. And understand, too, the power of that love that was born on the banks of Wappoo Creek outside Charleston on a November night in 1922. . . .

The first time I heard his name was when my brother, Kemble, wrote to say he was bringing a Princeton friend home for the Saint Cecilia Ball, and I was to leave the sixteenth dance blank for him.

"Well, he's got his nerve," I said to Aurelia, who had brought me the letter at breakfast. I was eating it alone in the kitchen of the old house. My father had already vanished into the autumn swamp with his camera and field notebook, and the dining room had long since been closed off as unheatable and apt to collapse in mid-meal under the centuries-long kiss of dry rot.

"Who got his nerve?" Aurelia said.

"Kemble. He's bringing some total stranger home for the Saint Cecilia and ordering me to save the sixteenth dance for him. Fat chance."

Aurelia, gaunt and yellow and gold-toothed and loving, had been born and raised herself in Charleston. She knew as well as any Legaré Street matron or debutante that the sixteenth dance of a Saint Cecilia Ball was reserved by iron tradition for husbands or sweethearts. She also knew Kemble and me as no other living soul did, not even our father, having raised him from toddlerhood and me from infancy after our mother died.

"Like to be a fly on the wall at that dance when you all butt heads," she said. "That stranger gon' run all the way back up north, and you ain't gon' have nobody to dance that dance with. Prob'ly never will; prob'ly ain't never gon' get no husband. Prob'ly live out yo' life in the swamp."

Aurelia made no secret of her disapproval at the way my father had raised me, virtually alone in a ramshackle two-hundred-and-fifty-year-old house on a long-barren rice plantation on Wappoo Creek, that connected the Stono River to Charleston Harbor just where the Ashley River ran into it. It was a lonely place for a child, though I never minded that. When the first Auguste Gascoigne had cleared the land and planted the rice and built the big house and outbuildings and slave quarters, the swamp forests teemed with wild things that whistled and sang and slithered and screamed and bellowed and splashed; in 1923, when I was seventeen, they still did. But the house had slid gradually into disrepair, and the rice fields that had spawned a great fortune had long since grown over, and the fortune itself had dwindled over the years to barely enough to allow my father, Gus, the last of a long line of Auguste Gascoignes, to feed and clothe and educate Kem and me and pay Aurelia and her husband, Duke, while he immersed himself in the study of the flora and waterfowl of the Low Country like a creature with fins and gills himself. From the time I could toddle I followed him into the swamp. It became, for a long time, my passion too.

Our mother, a small, exquisite girl from a great old Charleston family, had died at my birth, thus fulfilling the prophecy of her grim-faced father that no good would come of her marriage to the last of the ragtaggle band of Gascoignes, and after that Kemble and I saw

little of our Brundage relatives. I know they sent
money for our schooling, and my father dutifully sent
Kemble to McCallie and Princeton and me, miserably, to Ashley Hall for what proved to be an
extremely short stay. I ran away so many times he
eventually gave up and let me stay home with Aurelia
and Duke and spend my days in the swamp forest
with a net and a notebook or a sketch pad, or in my
battered canoe with a waxed paper packet of sandwiches and a warm Coca-Cola, drifting along the
secret black surface of Wappoo Creek reading a
book. I had learned to read, early and prodigiously,
and I absorbed as by osmosis the classical music he
listened to in the evenings on the big Capehart, his
one major purchase that I can recall, and when he
remembered he tutored me in the long summer
evenings and the thick, dark winter ones. By the time
I was twelve I had read my way through the library at
Belleau, which was substantial and ran to whatever had been popular in the succeeding ages of
the Gascoignes; they could never have been accused
of being intellectuals. Going into my teens I knew
more of Life with a capital L than virtually any
other girl child between the Ashley and Cooper
rivers, albeit Life with a decidedly treacly, romantic
French accent; no one ever thought to take Balzac
and De Maupassant away from me. My father taught
me some geography when he remembered, and a
great deal of natural history and botany and
marine biology, and it never bothered anyone,
including me, that until I married I could do no sums
at all. Aurelia, who had grown up in the great
Brundage town house on Tradd Street until her marriage to Duke, at which time the Brundages sent her
with their daughter to Belleau, instructed me in the
delicate, vicious catechism of Charleston manners
and mores with less mercy than any mother would

have. Kemble taught me to dance. It was not, on the main, a bad education for that time and place.

But Aurelia considered me headed for a cold swamp-bound spinsterhood and my father culpable of virtual child abuse. I knew few of the chattering flock of Charleston girls who were my peers, and those I did, Ashley Hall classmates and a gaggle of Brundage and Gascoigne cousins, thought I was art-less, remote, boring, and tacky in the extreme. Of the boys of Charleston, I knew only my cousins and a few of Kemble's McCallie friends. They obviously thought the same thing. At seventeen, I had never been out with a boy. I can't recall minding.

From his first taste of life beyond the river swamp, Kemble knew the twentieth century was his natural habitat. He had dozens of wellborn friends from Mobile to Boston and visited them regularly, learned to play tennis and sail and do the new dances, acquired a taste for gin and cigarettes and politics, and, by the time he was in his third year at Princeton, owned two custom-made suits of evening clothes and several pairs of handmade shoes and a Dunhill cigarette case and lighter. He came home dutifully but briefly a few times a year, had one dinner with our father and me, and spent the other evenings in town with the Brundage young and their flock, looked thoughtfully at me a few times, and left again. Until the autumn I was seventeen, he never brought anyone home with him to Wappoo Creek.

"He got a name?" Aurelia said that morning in the kitchen.

I looked at the letter again. "Peter Chambliss," I said. "Peter *Williams* Chambliss. Of the Boston, Massachusetts, Chamblisses. Which means less than nothing to me and will no doubt remain so. Who does Kemble think he is? First he makes Daddy promise to take me to the stupid Saint Cecilia—I don't think Pa even remembered he belonged to the Society until old Kemble jumped in with his big feet and stirred everything up—and then he sends me a dress. Without even asking. Just assuming it would fit and I'd love it and that I'd go in the first place."

"Well," Aurelia said, pushing pancakes at me, "it do fit. An' it the prettiest Saint Cecilia dress I ever seen, an' I seen a lot of 'em, an' I spec' you do too love it, if you ain't too stubborn to say so. An' you *is* goin' to the ball. Yo' daddy know what's right, even if he do have to be poked up sometimes. I was fixin' to get on him about it if Kemble hadn't. Miss Caroline's girl goin' to the Saint Cecilia when the time come, ain't no two ways about that. Yo' granma and granpa come out here and git you and take you themselfs, if yo' daddy don't. You know that so. Look like you ought to be grateful to Kemble for gittin' you a dress like that an' gittin' you some boy to dance with. If he don't take care of you, what you think gon' become of you?"

"Why does anything have to become of me?" I said, cramming pancakes into my mouth. "Nothing's become of me so far, and I've been perfectly happy. If you mean I won't get married, or whatever, who cares? What's wrong with staying out here with you and Daddy and . . . all this? I love this place. I'd rather be here than anywhere else on earth. If you think I want to leave and go live with stupid Buddy L'Engle on Legaré Street, or stupid Tommy Laurence in his stupid *town house* on stupid Church Street, or with stupid Wenty Sterling in Bedon's Alley . . . and go to stupid teas and musicales and join the Historic Preservation Society . . . and have stupid little Charleston children who are cousins to everybody in town—"

"What else you gon' do?" she said, and her eyes

were worried and angry. "You gon' stay out here with the coons and the gators after me and yo' daddy is gone, run wild out in them woods till you eighty? Starve to death, fall and break yo' bones, lie in the swamp alone till you rot? Who you think gon' take care of you if you don't go to them balls and parties and git yo'self a husband?"

"Well, it's not going to be any stupid Peter *Williams* Chambliss of the Boston Chamblisses," I snapped. "I'll wear the dress and I'll go to the ball, because Daddy says I have to. But I'm not going to dance with any old Yankee Kemble drags home just to save his own face. Don't think I don't know why he's doing it. I won't dance the sixteenth dance with him or any other boy. I'll sit on the side and frown at everybody all night. But I will not dance with that damn Yankee."

"You sounds just like yo' mama," Aurelia said, grinning. "Stubbornest gal I ever did know. Ain't gon' go out with no Charleston town boy. Gon' go out with that boy from out to Wappoo Creek, and she don't care who say she cain't."

"And look where it got her," I said. I was having no succor from Aurelia or anybody else. Least of all my beautiful, unremembered, never-forgiven mother.

"Where?" she said.

"Dead," I said, and picked up my package of banana and peanut butter sandwiches and headed out into the morning woods.

One month later, on a still afternoon of sullen gray warmth, a great black Packard touring car with buttoned side curtains and a hood that seemed miles long came wallowing up the pitted gravel drive and stopped in front of the veranda. It was spattered with gray mud from the November rains, and yellow

leaves were plastered to its window glass. At the
wheel my brother, Kemble, in moss-green tweed,
grinned at Aurelia and me; we had hurried to the
veranda to see what sort of vehicle could be making
such a commotion. Kemble usually came in one of
Creighton King's spartan taxis from the train station.

From the front passenger seat, a long narrow face
with a long narrow nose and a shock of pale hair
grinned over a car-filling cloud of white lilac branches.
The grin was as white as the blossoms, but the rest of
the person was invisible behind flowers and foliage.
The flowers were like nothing I had ever seen, exotic
and impossibly perfect, incompatible with known
life. We do not have those great, swelling, spilling
trees in the coastal South. The face above the bouquet was as alien as the flowers. We do not have
those attenuated, gilded faces in the Low Country,
either. They are conceived, cell and matter, beside
colder oceans, in sharper air.

Strangeness and something else I could not name,
something breath-stopping and near to panic,
swamped me. I turned and ran into the house, banging the screen door behind me, and thumped up the
stairs to my room. I heard Kemble yelling my name
from the veranda steps, and Aurelia screeching at me,
and then I heard his voice—Peter's—for the first time
in my life, soft and full of the flat, atonal music of
Boston: "Please come back. I promise I'm harmless."

It sounded like "hamless." It was, in his accent, a
funny word somehow. It made me smile even as I
slammed the door to my room, cheeks burning angri-
ly at my own foolishness. It made him seem, indeed,
harmless. It made me able to come back downstairs,
smiling stiffly, neck and face still hot and red, and put
my hand out to him.

It was the first thing I fell in love with, Peter's
voice.

"I'm Peter Chambliss," he said, "and you can only be Maude. I'm glad to meet you, finally." He held my hand while he spoke. His was warm and dry and callused across the palm. From sailing, he said later.

"Whut on earth wrong with you?" Aurelia said. "Yo' comp'ny think you raised like a hog in the woods."

"I've seen 'em scream and faint at the first sight of Peter, but you're the only one who ever ran like a rabbit, Buckeye," Kemble said.

He hugged me, smelling of tobacco and aftershave and the rich leather interior of the car. My head came only to his armpit. It was why he called me Buckeye; I was little and round and dark. I hated the nickname.

"What'd you think, that the Yankees were coming to get you?" My brother had been laughing at me all my life, in precisely that tone.

"No," I said, stringing out the drawl until it was a caricature of all Charleston voices, thick and mindless, "I thought my drawers were about to fall off."

Aurelia screeched again, a wordless squall of outrage, and my brother stared at me with his mouth open, and Peter Williams Chambliss laughed with unfeigned delight. It was the youngest sound I could ever remember hearing.

It was the second thing I fell in love with, his laugh.

"When it's time for that," he said, "I'll let you know."

Aurelia screeched again, but it was a mock screech of indulgence and relief. She was as at home with this sort of drawing-room badinage as she was with the sweet, fluting Gullah that the blacks spoke down on Dock Street. This was how it was done; this was the ritual; this faintly sexual parry-and-thrust was the very glue of Charleston society. This long thin outlander was, after all, a gentleman, one of us. Fit for the only daughter of Miss Caroline Brundage of Tradd Street. I thought in that moment, listening to that honeyed screech, that Aurelia had glimpsed the future, hers and mine, and found it secure.

I glimpsed nothing but a pure shining-white void. Belleau and the swamp forest were not in it.

"No," I said. "I'll let *you* know."

This time they all three laughed. I felt a small frisson that was pleasure at a social sally well received, though, as I had never felt it, I did not recognize it then.

"The lilacs are for you, for the dance," Peter said. He put them into my arms. I could scarcely see over or around them; I saw his face through a dazzle of white petals, through a cloud of sweetness that made my throat close and my eyes tear. They were wet with the droplets from the old oaks over the driveway, which held the moisture from that morning's rain.

"Thank you," I said, thinking that no girl entering her first Saint Cecilia ballroom had ever held such a thing as that bouquet. I would be the talk of Charleston, coming in the company of a Boston Yankee from Princeton University and carrying such an extravagant explosion of alien Yankee flowers. Not the thing, not the thing at all.

Suddenly I loved the idea.

"Every old trout in town will be talking about them, and you too," I said, smiling at him. "You'll probably have to marry me and make an honest woman of me without ever laying a finger on me. These flowers will do it by themselves. Poor you."

My brother still stared at me open-mouthed. What vamping demon had slipped unseen into his unworldly little swamp rabbit of a sister? Aurelia frowned; enough in this vein was enough. Peter lifted his sandy eyebrows. His eyes were, I thought, the clear gray of creek ice.

"Are they . . . excessive?" he said. "Will they embarrass you? They came from the place in Boston we get all our flowers; my sister, Hermie, had them for her wedding. I brought them all the way down here on the train in a pail of water, with wet cheesecloth over them. But I assure you it won't hurt my feelings if you'd rather have something . . . smaller. We'll call your florist and I'll run in and get whatever you—"

"No," I said. "They're just right. They're perfect. They're beautiful. I never smelled anything so heavenly. How on earth did you think of lilacs?"

"Your name," Peter said. "You know, the old song, 'Come into the garden, Maude, where the lilacs spread their shade. . . .' I've always liked them best of any flower. We have two huge old trees in Maine, and in June you can smell them for miles."

"Come on in and let's have a drink before supper," Kemble said to Peter Chambliss. "Maudie is no doubt going to vanish upstairs to do mysterious things to her hair and face—at least I hope she is—and I'll bet anything Dad's still out in the swamp. Does he even remember tonight's the Saint Cecilia, Aurelia?"

"Prob'ly not," Aurelia said. "But he remember when he see that car. Where you git that thing, Kemble? You ain't bought it, is you?"

"Peter rented it from Rhett Gittings when we got here. What's the matter, don't you think it's grand enough for the Saint Cecilia?"

"Lawd God, Kemble, Rhett Gittings—" Aurelia began.

"Oh, he doesn't use it for funerals." Kemble grinned. "It belongs to his uncle from Savannah, who hardly ever uses it. Don't worry, ol' Buckeye won't go to the ball reeking of formaldehyde."

I began to giggle and then to laugh. I couldn't help it. First that outrageous, unseemly, magnificent acre of white lilacs, and then the undertaker's uncle's car.

"I thought, since we obviously couldn't get a horse and carriage out here, this was the nearest thing to a closed carriage that we'd find," Peter said.

I stopped laughing and looked at him. His long, tanned face was anxious. Kemble had undoubtedly been telling him some of the rituals and traditions of the Saint Cecilia, and he had remembered that one of the most cherished was to go to your first ball in a closed carriage, with a proper roof and doors that shut solidly. That substantial *thunk*, up and down the old streets south of Broad on Saint Cecilia night, was as right and proper a sound as the *chink* of softly burnished old silver, the *ting* of cloudy old crystal.

It was a tender, cherishing small gesture to bring me a carriage, one a mother might make, or a father . . . but my mother never could and my father never would have.

I smiled at Peter Williams Chambliss, standing there in the dim fustiness of my foyer on Wappoo Creek. This man was not, after all, a stranger. This man had come bringing with him lilacs from his family's heritage and a closed carriage from mine. Whatever he had come for, it was not to harm me. A wash of giddy joy swept me like a rip tide. Tonight . . . oh, tonight! Tonight would be all right, after all. Tonight I would know just what to do. . . .

"Aurelia, would you put these in water for me, please?" I said grandly, as if I had bidden her to do just that every day of my life. "I'm going to go up and . . . do some things. Peter, you and Kem make yourselves at home in the drawing room. Dinner will be about six-thirty."

"Dinner be whenever I gits it on the table," Aurelia said under her breath, but she took the flowers and went out with them, burying her face in their petals.

"Ummmm, *ummm*," I heard her murmur.

"Are there any spirits in the drawing room, Modom?" Kemble called after me. "Or shall I ask Jeeves to fetch some from the cellar?"

"There's enough left of that stuff you bought from Shem Waller over on John's Island to lay you up for three days, Kemble Gascoigne, just like it did last time," I yelled down at him from the stairs. Somehow I did not care what I said around Peter Chambliss. The afternoon was as bright and strange as if I had been drinking champagne. The last thing I heard as I slammed my bedroom door shut was Peter's laughter.

Oh, that night. It was, for me, the first of those moments that divide time, so that you think in terms of before and after. Was it before the war or after? Did it happen before the Saint Cecilia Ball or after? It was late that night, home once more and lying in my familiar white tester bed, staring up into the starched muslin canopy where I had stared for all the nights of my seventeen Novembers, that I first thought of time and life as anything but a smooth continuum. I had, I realized, thought about it, if I thought at all, as a kind of seamless brush-stroke arc, all the same color and value and thickness, stretching languidly from my birth to the faraway, unseen, unimaginable point of my death.

But now I saw clearly that life and time were like the readings of a seismograph; that life flowed—or careened, or plummeted, or soared, or perhaps merely slogged—forward from a series of spasms, or shocks, as clearly traceable as the activity of a series of quakes. And that it was entirely possible, many years later, to look back and see just where each quake had occurred and what sort of tracery it left . . . or what sort of damage. It was a frightening concept, and I shook with it as much as anything else that night as the moonlight on Wappoo Creek grew old: that I was and forever would be vulnerable to the random spasms of my life, great or small, and that tonight the first of the great ones had struck me. What pattern, what tracery, it left upon the graph was not up to me, and in any case it hardly mattered.

Just before I went downstairs that night I looked at myself in the cloudy old pier glass that had been my mother's, which stood in the corner of my bedroom. The fashion that year was for formal gowns cut to the knee in front but trailing out behind in a small train; they had dropped waists and were often so heavily beaded it was not possible to sit in them. Fortunately for me, girls at their first Saint Cecilia Ball wore floor length drifts of pure white cut in the chaste, full style of debutante balls everywhere and in all times; I would have looked, as Kemble said when he sent me the dress, like a chambermaid in a bad French farce in one of the current gowns.

But this dress was pure legerdemain. In it I looked . . . not real. Not me. Not round and low to the ground but tall and willowy and anchored to earth only by the white slippers that had come with the dress. This dress had thousands of tiny crystal pleats from neckline to billowing hem, cinched at the waist by a satin sash that spilled little crystal beads down the front, and a shallow boat neckline that flared into puffed, pleated sleeves but left my shoulders bare. The label in the dress and on its box said Fortuny; it did not shame me in the least that it was Aurelia, not I, who had caught her breath in recognition of that name when the package came. After all, she had had far more to do with ballrooms than I.

"Well, he know what it take to turn a mule into a race hoss," she had said that day, and I had scoffed and for a long time refused to try the dress on. But then one night after dinner I had, and saw what she had seen when she had first held up its spindrift stuff.

How had he known?

In the old mirror, its wavy greenish surface like looking into a forest pool, I leaned to meet this spectral woman who stood . . . or floated . . . in my childhood bedroom. Aurelia had come in while I was brushing my thick black hair, said, "No, not tonight," taken the brush from me, and silently piled my hair into a high coil that gave back light like lacquer. Then she had brought from her apron pocket a little velvet sack and taken from it a string of single pearls like sea water at dawn, perfect and luminous, and fastened them around my neck. Together and in silence we had looked at my image in the mirror, and then she said, "Your mama wore these at her first Saint Cecilia. Your granddaddy give 'em to her. She wore 'em at her wedding, too. She give 'em to me to keep for you not long before you was born; she say she 'fraid she gon' forgit, what with one thing and another, and she know as sure as she born yo' daddy would. I kep' 'em in with the string of beads yo' grandmama give me when Duke and me got married and come out here to yo' mama. Mine's jet; they looked real pretty together, them and these pearls. But not half as pretty as they look on yo' neck. You act as pretty as you look tonight, Maude, an' yo' mama and daddy be real proud of you."

"What about you?" I had said.

"I always proud of you," Aurelia said. "You know that."

I had hugged her, and she hugged me back and went out of the room. At the door she looked back.

"That Peter a nice boy," she said. "You behave yourself with him. You don't want him gittin' no wrong ideas about you."

I stared at her, affronted. "What ideas? I don't even know how to . . . give anybody wrong ideas."

She looked at me for a space of time and then pointed at the mirror.

"That girl know," she said, and went out the door and closed it.

I leaned now, in the low yellow lamplight, to the very surface of the mirror, so that the hair at my forehead touched that other hair, and my nose bumped that nose. Our breaths met and mingled, frosting the glass.

"Do you know?" I whispered. "Do you?"

"Let's go, Maude," Kemble shouted from downstairs.

And I touched the girl's cheek and said, "Yes, you do," and turned swiftly so that my dress billowed out behind me, and ran, lightly and in joy and terror, down the stairs of Belleau to meet Peter Chambliss.

"So it was perfect, huh?" my granddaughter Darcy said on that evening in Retreat, across a bridge of years and pain from me.

"Yes," I said, smiling into the birch fire that whispered on the old black stone hearth. "Yes, I think it was. Like a movie. Or, no . . . like a very good romantic play. One of Noël Coward's, maybe. With just that bittersweet edge to it, for salt. A perfect night."

"Nothing is perfect, Grammaude," Darcy said with the creamy assurance of youth. She stretched her pretty cat's body out to the dying warmth of the fire, slowly, so that all the muscles played and snapped back in sequence. It seemed newly ripe and fluid with love, that young body; I remembered that. The oiled sweetness echoed in my own limbs.

"Very few things, I'll admit, but that was," I said. It nettled me slightly to have that night so summarily dismissed by one too young to have had many such herself.

"Oh, nuts. I never figured you for a softie. You know as well as I do, there're thorns on the roses.

Blood and entrails in the pretty white snow. Tiny screams under the birdsong, and all that. 'Life is real, life is earnest.'"

Darcy was herself a child of woods and water and the wild, as I had been; she was right, and I knew it. Still . . .

"You sound just like your great-grandmother Hannah," I said. "I'll bet she said the very same thing to me a thousand times in the first few summers we spent up here. 'Life is real, Maude; it is not a silly child's fancy. Life is real.' I was a great trial to her."

"Hah," Darcy said. "She should talk. From what I hear of that old martinet and her crowd, life up here was about as real as tea with Helen Hunt Jackson. Morning calls with cards, and nature walks, and drives with rugs and parasols, and luncheons with linen and china, and servants and bridge and dessert parties and musicales: all of Retreat was a stage set for a play about country life. Still is. Look at it. Look at us. You're sitting in her chair and I'm sitting in one Great-grandpa brought up from Boston, and so far as I know neither one has ever been moved an inch. Or a pillow changed. Or a new picture hung. You could set the cast of some old Mary Roberts Rinehart play down in this place and they'd be able to pick up in mid-line. Real and earnest indeed."

I laughed. She was right about that too. Retreat is and always has seemed as timeless and lost to the world as a page from a Victorian novel. But under it, under all the careful rusticality, rocks lie, as cruel and tearing as the ledges on the outer islands in the little picture-book harbor, as the ice of winter in the black ponds. Well, Darcy herself surely knew that, and one day would know it even better.

"Maybe most things only seem perfect," I said. "But that night really was. . . ."

*　　*　　*

And it was. As far as human life can be, in one small arena of time and space, perceived through one pair of very young and human eyes, that night in November of 1923 at the Saint Cecilia Ball was perfect. It might not have been, undoubtedly was not, to anyone else there; I don't even think Peter found it perfect, though he came later to speak of it with me as though it were.

"Our one perfect moment"; we laughed about it many times later, when things went awry: when Petie cried through the fourth straight night with colic; when the hours dragged on and on and Happy did not come home or when Tommy O'Ryan came home yet another night stumbling drunk; when small Sean's screams of rage and terror left the colony heavy-eyed and thin-lipped.

"Well, we had our one perfect moment, anyway."

But no, I don't suppose Peter really thought it was. By then Peter knew about the dark places that lie even at the heart of light, even if he had not yet visited them. Even in the light places, even in the heart of love, the dark waited for Peter.

That night, however, Charleston brought out every trick and wile and enchantment in her arsenal for us, so that even my father, sitting bemused in his own father's greenish swallowtail in the front seat of the Packard with Kemble, turned to Peter and me in the back seat as we rounded the point of the Battery on East Bay Street and said, "Have they cleaned up downtown or something? It looks different."

"It looks just like it has for three hundred years, more or less." Kemble grinned at him. "When was the last time you were downtown at night, Papa?"

"I don't remember," my father said vaguely. "I don't get in to town much. I suppose it was the last time I went to a Saint Cecilia."

"And that was?" I teased him.

"Well, I don't think your mother and I were married yet," he said seriously. "I remember I had on this same coat, though."

We all laughed with giddiness and affection and joy at the sheer, flagrant, throat-tightening seduction of Charleston on a Saint Cecilia evening. Overhead the high white hunter's moon sailed above the great moss-shawled oak trees in Battery Park, and across the black harbor a string of lights picked out Fort Sumter and the tip of Sullivan's Island. Palms rattled in the warm wind off the sea, and gas lamps glowed yellow on the brick streets and on the lacy swirls of the wrought-iron gates and fences and balconies of the high old town houses. By day they were the ripe-fruit colors of the semitropics: yellow, pink, coral, green, cream, white, aquamarine. But in the moonlight of November they were all silver and pewter and gilt, and the night around them black velvet, and the stars above them diamonds of the very best quality. Down here, south of Broad, in the warren of old brick streets and alleys, where the oldest names of the city dwelt, there were few cars in sight and virtually none abroad on the streets, but there were fleets of shining-black horse-drawn carriages and, in them, glimpses of cloudy white dresses and flowers and correct black evening dress, and young faces blanched with expectation. Candles blazed in many windows, and from one, which I knew was the fabled Manigault House with its Sword Gates, a little liquid curl of Palestrina spilled like a handful of jewels flung out into the night.

"God, it's the most beautiful city in the world!" Peter breathed.

I turned to see if he was being sarcastic. He moved, after all, in the exotic streets of Boston and the East and, Kemble had said, Europe and South America. He wasn't. The smile he turned to me was that of a child at a wonderful party.

"It's completely out of any world I know. It's like a night in some fabulous Creole place a world away, centuries ago, or like a fairy tale. . . . Where are the cars? Where are the people going to the movies or to . . . to buy toothpicks and Sen-Sen?"

"They say that on the night of the Saint Cecilia, everybody who isn't invited puts the car in the garage and turns off all the lights and sits in the dark till dawn, so nobody will know they're home," Kemble said. "You're chopping tall cotton tonight, old man. I hope you're properly impressed."

"I am," Peter said. "By the dance and the town and the night and . . . everything."

In the darkness of the back seat my face burned, and my hands, when I clasped them together, were as cold as a dead woman's.

In the foyer of the old hall, standing at the edge of the red carpet with my arm through my father's and my heart bidding fair to buck out of my chest, I stopped for a moment, looking inside. In my terror and exaltation the great, graceful old room seemed a teeming swarm of candles and roses and gilt and faces turning toward us, faces over severe black evening clothes and dark silks and drifting cumuli of white, faces I did not recognize, though I almost certainly knew most by name. Music swelled and eddied and ebbed; voices and laughter murmured and rose. Was it at me? Surely it was. Surely it had always been. . . . My wrists and lips began to buzz horridly, and I thought I would surely vomit or faint. I tensed my muscles to turn and flee, and felt a hand on my shoulder, and heard Peter's voice in my ear.

"There isn't a woman in that room who can hold a candle to you tonight," he whispered. "Every one of them looks as if she'd like to stab you through the heart and grab that dress and go in the Ladies' and put it on and leave hers in the trash can. Drawers too, probably."

I took a deep breath that came out in a hiccup, and my heart jolted forward and into a deep, smooth groove, and laughter bubbled up from under my ribs, and I said over my shoulder to him, "Thank you," and to my father, "Let's go, Pa," and we swept into the ballroom and into the night.

From the beginning it was a triumph and I was a belle. I can say that now because it had never happened to me before and it never did again, and because I know full well it was Peter Chambliss who lit the fire that burned in me that night, who made the assembled friends and acquaintances and know-by-names and know-by-sights and cousins and aunts and uncles and grandparents and even old family servants believe that Caroline and Gus Gascoigne's strange brown gnome of a daughter had, against all odds, turned into a beauty. Because I was far from beauty, then or ever. Too darkly earthbound, too clearly a small creature of swamp and creek and old green darkness. But that night I shone like a tall taper, shimmered, burned. All because he stood beside me, and held me on the dance floor, and bent his head down to mine to laugh and whisper at supper.

It is a thing I saw people notice about Peter from the day I met him to the day he died: that impact on the eye, that almost physical clap of presence, as if some invisible concussion had left the very air shivering. He drew the eye like wildfire, or a wild animal. It was hard to look away from him. And yet, if you attempted to analyze it, you would come up with nothing that added up to that silent thunderclap. Peter was very nearly a plain man.

He was always too thin, and very nearly stooped with his height, and his features were long and sharp, a veritable caricature of wellborn New England. His chin jutted and his sandy eyebrows overgrew his deep-set gray eyes and his thick white-blond hair was usually down across his forehead, and his mother Hannah's vulpine white teeth were startling in the deep-water sailing tan he kept most of the year. But he moved with a sinuous, lazy cat's grace even when he shambled along at his slowest, and he was a wonderful and boneless dancer and an effortlessly good tennis player, and his smile was the very definition of the word sweetness. And there was that other thing about him, that caught and held eyes: a kind of goodness. A deep, bright aura of safety. Caring seemed to flow from him like wild honey. His father had it too, if more dimly. Poor Big Peter, poor Little Peter. No one could have lived up to that.

Everyone noticed and responded to him that evening. I saw it happen. I saw my Brundage grandparents and aunts and uncles and cousins in their accustomed places before one of the four great Adam mantels, where Brundages had stood to receive their friends since, I suppose, there had been any Brundages in Charleston, stop their flocking chatter and turn and look at him, and at me, and then at Kemble and our father, and I saw them nod and smile. And beckon us into their ranks. As we walked across the vast, shining floor to them, eyes burning like bees on my bare shoulders and neck, my father said in his soft, vague voice, "You know, Eulalie once told me I looked like an organ grinder's monkey in tails," and instead of a rush of rancor, or the accustomed sting of mortified tears, the new healing laughter came bubbling once more into my throat.

"She isn't going to say it tonight," I said. "And if she does, just tell her she looks like South America. Right down to the tatty little train on that dress. Aunt Eulalie could do with a little boning."

"Did I tell you how pretty you look tonight?" my father said. "I probably didn't. I think it often, but I never seem to get around to saying it. Your mother would be proud of you, little Maude. I am too."

"And I am of you," I said, finding the never-said words surprisingly easy on this magical night. "I've had a wonderful growing-up."

He looked at me and smiled, just before we reached our group.

"And now you're there, aren't you? I just never noticed."

"Neither did I," I said.

After that, I could never remember the particulars of that ball. I tried often; I would lie in the dark of many predawns, in cold New Hampshire nights or firelit Maine ones, trying to tell the details to myself like the beads of a rosary. But I never could. For me, once the music started and the dance cards were filled and the first waltz swelled, that night was a runaway carousel of flowers, candles, music, laughter, champagne, flowing motion and billowing skirts and fast-coming breath. My dance card filled quickly, with the names of boys I had known all my life but somehow never seen before; I smiled and laughed and chattered and flirted as if I had done it all my life, but through each dance that I did not have with Peter my eyes kept seeking him, and whenever they found him, whirling some newly blossomed nursery school or Ashley Hall compatriot over the mirror floor, his eyes met mine and he smiled. He danced five dances with me—unheard of in that day and place—and his was the name scrawled on the sixteenth line. We did not, that night, do the new, fast, jittering dances that were coming into vogue; the Saint Cecilia has never really yielded itself up to modernity. We swayed and dipped together to the ballads of that year, though: "My Wonderful One," "April Showers," "Whispering," "Three O'Clock in the Morning," "A Kiss in the Dark." And after the supper march and the never-varying feast of oysters and duck and turkey and wild rice and dessert and more champagne, we danced the last dance together, the sixteenth, to the traditional strains of "Auf Wiedersehen."

As we danced, he sang the words softly in my ear, and I realized somewhere in mid-dance that he was singing in German. Somehow it seemed to me the most romantic thing I had ever heard in my life: faultless, a perfect thing, a grace note to joy.

"I didn't know you spoke German," I said. It was a stupid thing to say; how would I have known?

"I don't," Peter said. "I'm a complete fool at languages. Kemble told me about this dance and 'Auf Wiedersehen,' and I went to the library and memorized the German words. God help me if you know German; you don't, do you?"

"No," I said, beginning to cry. "I don't."

I fell in love with Peter at that precise instant. I don't suppose many other women know the exact moment that the rest of their lives began.

Many years later, sitting out the terrible, howling hours while a hurricane lashed Retreat, I asked Peter why he had gone to the trouble to learn the German words of a song to sing to a girl he had never met.

"There was every chance that you'd think I was a total dud," I said. "Or that I would you. It was an awful lot of effort for a blind date."

I remember that the firelight picked out his forehead and cheekbones and teeth but did not reach his eyes. We had been in darkness for hours.

"Kemble had a picture of you at school," he said. "In a canoe by yourself on a black creek, with moss hanging all around you. I think you must have been twelve or thirteen. You had a great big armful of waterlilies and you were wet from head to foot and you were laughing. I always thought, long, long before I met you, that if I could catch you it would be like catching a mermaid. I thought a mermaid was worth a little German."

"And was she?" I said, my heart pounding with more than fear of the storm. There were many dangers abroad that night.

"Then and always," Peter said. "Then and always."

Very late that night, into the morning really, after we were home again and I lay in my bed thrumming like a stretched wire with fatigue and elation and triumph and a rising tide of something I could not name, I remembered that I had not put the lilacs back in water. Suddenly it seemed the most important thing in the world.

I got out of bed and put on my robe and tiptoed barefoot down the wide old stairs. Outside the window on the landing I could see that the huge white moon was flooding the woods and creek with cold silver radiance. But the house was dark and still. My father slept in his and my mother's big bedroom at the back of the house, and Peter and Kemble were in the twin beds in Kemble's old room, across from it. Both rooms were closed and silent.

I padded across the cold pine floorboards into the kitchen and put the lilacs, drooping sweetly now, into a bucket of water, and stopped to bury my face in them. I felt the foolish tears start again. I cried now with incompletion and an entirely new misery; after we got home Peter had said only, "Thanks for letting me take you to your dance, Maude. I had a wonderful time," and had gone up the stairs with Kemble, laughing at some foolishness of his. The door had shut behind them, and presently the laughter had stopped. They were to go back to Princeton on the noon train the next day.

I mopped my face and drew a sniffling breath and

went out onto the veranda. Peter sat in his satin-striped pants and white shirt, tieless and open-collared, rocking in one of the old wicker rocking chairs and smoking. I knew then that somehow I had known he would be there.

"What took you so long?" he said.

We danced on the banks of Wappoo Creek that night, Peter and I, danced in bare feet in the cold wet undergrowth while the moon poured its wild old silver down on us and the water ran black and ancient and the moss shone. We danced as Peter sang, softly, in his Boston baritone, "It's three o'clock in the morning, we've danced the whole night through. . . ."

When he stopped singing and we stopped dancing he kissed me.

"Tell me what you love most, Maudie," he said, holding me loosely against him. His chin rested on the top of my head. I could feel the warmth of his body through his shirtfront. I could almost taste the salt of his skin through the fabric.

"Dancing in the dark with damn Yankees," I tried to say lightly. My voice was an amphibian croak.

"No, really. What do you love best about your life? About living here, about Charleston?"

I thought. I thought of the slow yellow autumns in the swamp and the high honey sun of spring and the eternal silence of the marshes, and the shivering light on them, and the whisper of the spartina and sweet grass in the wind and the little liquid splashes of who-knew-what secret creatures entering that strange old place of blood-warm half earth, half water. I thought of the song of all the birds that I knew, and the soft singsong of the coffee-skinned women who sold their coiled sweet-grass baskets in the market and on Meeting Street. I thought of the glittering sun on the morning harbor and the spicy, somehow oriental smells from the dark old shops, and the rioting flowers everywhere, heavy and tropical and exotic. I thought of the clop of horses' feet on cobblestones and the soft, sulking, wallowing surf of Sullivan's Island in August, and the countless small vistas of grace and charm wherever the eye fell: a garden door, a peeling old wall, an entire symmetrical world caught in a windowpane. Charleston simply could not manage to offend the eye. I thought of the candy colors of the old houses in the sunset, and the dark secret churchyards with their tumbled stones, and the pure sweet bells of Saint Michael's in the Sunday morning stillness. I thought of my tottering piles of books in the study at Belleau and the nights before the fire when my father told me of stars and butterflies and voyages and the silver music of mathematics. I thought of hot, milky sweet coffee in the mornings, and the old kitchen around me, and Aurelia's gold smile and quick hands and eyes rich with love for me.

Oh, Charleston, I thought. Oh, my Charleston.

"I love it all," I said against Peter's shirt, knowing only then that it was true. "There isn't a single atom of it that I don't love."

"Could you leave it?"

"Yes," I said.

Chapter
Two

A summer colony is a tyranny of old women. At least that was and still is true of Retreat, and from what I have heard from acquaintances who summer at other family enclaves up and down the East Coast, it is largely true everywhere. Why this is, I have never fully fathomed; many of the men who came to Retreat and those other Maine oases of the day were great powers in the life and economy of their cities and, in some cases, the nation. Many were the heads of businesses and industries whose names shone on other shores than that rocky one; others were greatly distinguished in their professions or simply the heirs to large personal fortunes. I never met a "summer" man in Retreat or anywhere else in Maine who did not have extraordinary resources of some sort at his disposal, or the eventual prospect of them. And yet it was a world ruled totally and with little nod to democracy by the old women of the tribe.

None of those women would have admitted such a thing if their orderly lives had depended upon it.

"Why, I do everything for my Peter and yours," Mother Hannah said to me indignantly once, when I intimated that perhaps she and her friends were the kingdom and the power and the glory of Retreat. "From the minute I get up in the morning to the minute I lay my head on my pillow at night, my every thought and move is for the comfort and well-being of my husband and son. And every wife and mother up here feels the same way and acts it, and so should you, Maude. Our men work themselves to the bone for us all year. Their recreative weeks are a sacred thing."

And on the surface it was true. The men who sum-mered in Retreat lived days and nights of what seemed to me perfect carefree symmetry. You would see them on terraces and verandas in the cold blue early mornings, wrapped in woolen robes or heavy sweaters, drinking their coffee and looking out over the still, pink-flushed harbor. A bit later you would meet them on the silent paths through the birch groves or on the dirt road into the village, walking sticks to hand, striding through their morning consti-tutionals. By nine o'clock, in those long summer days, they would be on the little clay tennis court in correct white-clad quartets or sliding their big slender sloops and ketches and yawls out of the yacht club harbor or heading for the rough little golf course up at the Cove Club in the modest old cars they kept for the country.

The very young would be led about like downy ducklings by bored and restless village girls or nan-nies, down to the shore, to paddle in the flat calm off the pebble beach, or to the yacht club, where Amos Carter waited to begin the first wobbling lessons in the fleet of stubby little Brutal Beasts. The very old might pass mornings on terraces wrapped in steamer rugs, nodding or reading or visiting back and forth. But in all the years I came to Retreat, I saw few of them lift a hand to the running of that carefully rustic world. For that, there was the taciturn army of the natives—who made the bulk of their year's living serving the leisure of the summer people—and there were the young women.

And behind them all, like a corps of dark-clad gimlet-eyed generals, were the old women.

To me, in those first days, "old" was anyone the age of Peter's parents and beyond. But there were many younger women, platoons of them. Young wives and mothers like myself and yet so obviously and regrettably unlike me, an occasional unmarried young belle, many girl children, and a few aging daughters destined for spinsterhoods of starch and seemliness. All those women served. They served their own young husbands and families as the old women had taught them and continued to instruct them; they served the colony in its communal cultural and social endeavors; they served the little village and the surrounding townships, donating talent and money and long hours to benefit the hospital, the library, the free clinic, the Women's Self-Help League, the bake sales and the jumble sales and the flower markets. They poured out tea and coffee and made finger sandwiches and cookies and cleaned and redecorated the yacht club and saw that the children's playground was kept mowed and trimmed and comfortable for the nannies, and they hosted countless little luncheons and small cocktail parties and bridge evenings and desserts for their mother-in-laws' friends, and they marketed and drove to the egg and the vegetable ladies' houses every morning, and to the laundress's cottage, and to the fishmonger's truck down at the harbor, and to the nursery over in Lincolnville, to keep borders and window boxes on the old gray- and brown-shingled cottages bright and summery.

They cheered on their husbands and their brown

sons in tennis matches and regattas in the mornings, and visited around at other cottages in the afternoons with covered plates of fresh rolls and cookies and pots of tuberous begonias from the old gardens, and put toddlers down for naps and often oldsters too, and they bathed in the old claw-footed tubs in the cooling afternoons and dressed in their carefully simple cotton frocks and put pale cashmere sweaters around their shoulders and sprayed on little jets of 4711, and went down to stand behind the chairs of the old women, and fetch drinks and hors d'oeuvres and fans and canes and shawls for them, and to laugh at their deaf-loud sallies and oft-repeated anecdotes, and to help heave them from their chairs and give them their pale arms in to dinner. There were not many suntanned young women in Retreat. They were sunless and tired. Most of their eyes closed instantly in exhaustion when at last they got into their beds in small hot upstairs bedrooms, beside husbands who had long been stunned into sleep by fresh air and salt wind and alcohol. The young women of the summer colonies of the Northeast were the worker drones. Cannon fodder, Amy Potter, who was one, once called them.

But . . . and it was an all-important but . . . they were in training to be the old queens, and they knew it. One day they would sit on the porches and be driven about the countryside by their own daughters-in-law and have license to drink one drink too many at cocktail parties or say any outrageous and hurtful thing that came into their minds, and bully the servants and the wives of their sons and their grandchildren unmercifully, if they wished, and to break themselves any of the thousands of small, immutable iron rules that they laid down for the comportment of colony conduct, even while they enforced them for others. They could, as their elders did now, look back on their own days of servitude and obedience and extract the last full measure of flesh and spirit from their handmaidens. It was a self-perpetuating cycle, and in it lay and still lies power, absolute and fearsome. The men thought themselves outside it, and so laughed at it, but they lived every moment of their summers in Retreat by the sufferance of that power, and most never even realized it. It was the young women who knew the faces of their jailers and who had, or thought they had, no recourse but to smile into them even as their shackles were tightened.

The old women of Retreat . . . for my first few summers there, I came close to hating them. Now I am one, and here is Darcy, my dearly loved Darcy, fetching my tea and extending to me her brown arm to hold . . . brown, for Darcy, like me, never managed to be a success in her role as tender and cupbearer here. But still, here we are. Nothing really changes in Retreat. It is why, I think, that in the long run I came to love it so. It was stranger to me when I first came here than the back of the moon, but, like my own small old world so far to the south, my Charleston, it was eternal.

Hard, though . . . oh, in the beginning, it was hard. Even before I saw it for the first time, I was afraid of Retreat. I had only to think of a summer there in the big old brown-shingled house with Peter's father and his omniscient, omnipresent mother, and my heart froze in my breast. I, who before our marriage had confidently expected to love Peter's summer haven and be loved there, who had rapturously and loudly planned each slow, serene, sun- and ocean-washed day, knew before I passed through the old lilacs at the door that I was about as welcome as cholera. When we drove into Retreat from New Hampshire on that June day in 1923, in the smart little open Buick roadster Peter's mother had given him for graduation, I was staggering under a load of baggage I knew I would never put down.

When he left Charleston for Princeton after the Saint Cecilia, it was understood that we would marry. Or at least I understood it, and I thought Peter did too, though we had no formal agreement. But I knew; how could I not, after that night on Wappoo Creek? At the train, with Kemble pulling at his sleeve and the great wheels beginning to turn, Peter said only that he would write. And he kissed the top of my head and was gone. And I went home to Belleau, to weep with longing for him and to wait.

He did write. He wrote every day and sometimes twice a day, short funny notes and an occasional longer letter that was like he was: acridly witty, sweet-natured, introspective, full of unsuspected sensuality, wonderfully articulate. I got to know him, really, through those letters. Some were almost frighteningly intuitive; Peter seemed to sense each new doubt and anxiety of mine as it sprang to mind and addressed it in his letters.

You'll be fine in the East. You're smarter than most of the girls I've met up here, and what you don't know you can learn in a minute. I won't go off and leave you alone with any Yankees until you've learned the drill.

And in all my visits to Princeton that winter, he never did. To my own surprise, I did well enough with his clubmates and friends on that dreaming old campus. Perhaps it was merely that they all liked Peter so genuinely, but I was given just the proper modest rush by the other members of Colonial when I visited there, and I came home thinking that maybe I could, after all, make my way among the alien corn.

Your clothes are perfectly okay, he wrote another time. *Nobody expects anybody from*

Charleston to have a closet full of tweed and fur.
We'll get you what you need for the next winter.
What you have is like a bouquet of flowers after
all the plain summer cotton I see up here.

And:

   I spent this weekend in the Adirondacks at
Shoe Parson's family's camp, and saw deer,
pheasant, about a million raccoons, a pair of
gray foxes, and one skinny black bear. There's
enough wild in the East to last you all your life,
Maudie. I'll let you roam to your heart's content.
I won't pen you up in a city after Wappoo Creek.

And, in the spring of the next year, he wrote:

   It's time to come visit my folks. I've told
them I'm bringing you in April. Hermie and
the kids are coming up from Connecticut
then, so you'll get the whole lot of us at once.
You don't have a thing to worry about. They
love Kemble, and they will love you too.

But Peter was wrong about that. The Chambliss
family of Boston, Massachusetts, and Retreat, Maine,
did not love me like they did my brother, Kemble.
The female members of it, at least, did not; when I
walked into the tall, ivy-shawled brick house on
Charles Street at the end of that April, Hannah Stuart
Chambliss looked at me interestedly and said, "Well,
Petie, whom have we here?"

And the tall, stooped, fair-haired girl in the plain
water-colored linen who could only be Peter's sister,
Hermione, said, in a light, cool voice that was a caricature of Peter's, "I thought you said you were bringing Kemble, Buddy."

I stood in that dim old foyer, looking at them in the arched doorway of their dim old drawing room, feeling my rose-flowered chintz and pink cloche beginning to glow in the century-old gloom like rotting garbage, and felt a cold endless tide rolling toward me.

"I told you Kemble's *sister*, Hermie," Peter said fondly. "You too, Ma. What idiots you both are. Come and say hello to Maude Gascoigne from Charleston, about whom you have heard a great deal, and why you're behaving as if you hadn't I can't imagine."

The Chambliss women let a little space of time reverberate into the silence, and then his mother said, "Well, my dear, of course you're more than welcome. I cannot imagine why I thought . . . well. We'll have a lovely weekend getting to know Peter's charming southern friend. Peter, if you'd only told me, I could have gotten a few people together to meet . . . Maude, is it? Hermie, run ask Lorna to make up the room at the end of the hall and the bath across from it. I can't put this pretty child in that cubbyhole Kemble insists on when he's here. My goodness, I don't think I even knew he had a sister."

"Please don't go to any trouble on my account," I said faintly, my accent feeling as thick as clotted cream in my mouth. "Kemble's . . . the room Kemble uses will be fine. I'm really not used to big rooms."

I fell silent, heat flooding my chest and face. The edges of my hairline were suddenly wet. My room at Belleau was spacious and high-ceilinged.

Hermie gave me a slow smile, very like Peter's but without the sweetness. I saw that she would be considered, in her circle, a beauty, but she did not capture the eye as he did.

"I'm not sure you'd thank us for that," she said, "unless you relish the idea of listening to Peter snore all night. The rooms connect to each other, and the lock's broken. But maybe that's not such a liability?"

Her smile widened. Innocence and contempt fairly
radiated from it.

"Her*mi*one!" Hannah Chambliss said.

"You have a filthy mind, Herm," Peter said, grinning. But the grin did not reach his eyes. He put his
hand lightly on my shoulder.

"Is Dad around?" he said. "I want him to know
Maude; she's as nuts about birds and butterflies as he is."

"In his study," his mother said. "I'm sure he'll be
glad to see you . . . both. I'll just . . ." She gave us a crys-
talline smile and turned away toward the back of the
house, no doubt to alert the luckless Lorna. Over her
shoulder she said, "Don't bother with your luggage, my
dear; I'll have Marvin bring it up to you in a bit. You
won't need to dress for dinner; it will just be us. Unless
I can persuade Peter's father to take us to the club."

And she vanished into the all-pervading rich dimness. It was, I thought miserably, probably the dust
from much impeccable old money.

"Never mind, Ma, I'll get it," Peter said.

"I don't imagine Maude brought a lot just for the
weekend . . . unless, of course, you'll be able to stay
longer, Maude?" Hermione said.

"No," I said. "I have to go back on Sunday."

"Pity," she said, as Peter went out into the sunshine to fetch the heavy, scarred old leather case that
had been my grandfather's.

I looked brightly around the foyer and into the
drawing room and across into the enormous, vaulted
dining room and up the wide, polished stairs. Everywhere there was velvet and brocade and rich, dim
old figured carpets and acres of gleaming mahogany,
and dull gold shining softly from picture frames and
brass and copper trim. Ancestors—with those noses
and chins, they could only be Stuarts and Chamblisses—
lined the rooms and the stairwell. Their eyes, light
gray and cool on me, were no warmer than those of

the living Stuarts and Chamblisses in this house. I did not look at Peter, as he came in with my suitcase.

"What a stunning house," I said.

"Don't mind Mother," he said, hugging me briefly. "It's just her manner. Cold as a dead cod. She can't help it, it's pure Stuart. She treats Kemble the same way, and she adores him. Hermie, now, is being a bitch. She does it very well. I always thought she had a crush on old Kemble, even after she married William. Probably came hotfooting it up here to dump the kids on Lorna and get in a little flirting with Kem, and instead she gets his baby sister, and a gorgeous one besides. Herm is used to being the only beauty around here. They'll be straightened out by dinnertime."

"Peter, they really don't like me at all," I said in a near whisper. "I'd really and truly rather go to a hotel or something. . . ."

"Not on your life. They'll be straightened out by dinnertime. You'll see," he said, hugging me harder. "Come on, now, and meet Dad. He's the nice one of the family."

I followed him through that cold, silent house, thinking that I could always simply call a taxi and flee in full rout, if I had to, and wondering how in the world such a family had produced Peter.

Peter was right about his father. Peter senior was just the father I might have fashioned for my Peter: tall, fair-haired, handsome, with the same fine narrow head and features, the same commanding presence, even if, on the older Chambliss, considerably dimmer. And he was kind to me, and interested, then and always. He was knowledgeable, even quietly passionate, about his birds and wildlife, and his hunger to hear of those in my wilderness on Wappoo Creek was unfeigned. He smiled at me and called me "my dear" and said he was glad to have me in his house, that I brightened things up considerably in that cold, muddy Massachusetts spring and he hoped to see a great deal of me. And I thought he was sincere; it was simply that nothing about Peter's father truly . . . connected. He did not, in a sense, displace air. It was, I told Peter much later, like being entertained by the ghost of the original squire of that great old house.

"I know," Peter said. "Poor Dad. He just sort of faded out somewhere in my growing-up years. He went straight from Princeton into the bank—my great-grandfather's bank, really—and he's been there ever since. But I really think that all he ever wanted to do was watch birds and paint wildflowers. He's really good; it's what he does every day when we're in Retreat. When I told him that's pretty much what your father does, he said he thought your dad must be the luckiest man alive, and the wisest, and I ought to hang on to you. He's going to be the only ally I have when I spring my little bomb about Northpoint. Mother is going to blow sky high."

I looked at him, aghast. "You haven't told them yet?"

"Nope. I'm going to do it this weekend, when I tell them about us. That way most of the fuss about North-point will be mitigated by the to-do over the wedding. Mother's been waiting to get me married off since I could walk. We *are* going to get married after graduation, aren't we? I mean, I just assumed we were. . . ."

"Yes," I said. "I guess so, sure. Of course. But Peter, I don't think you're at all right about your mother. I don't think she's anywhere near ready for you to get married—not to me, at any rate. If you dump that on her on top of telling her you're not going into the bank . . . Lord, she'll think it's all my doing and never speak to me again. Really, I wish you'd wait awhile about the wedding. Tell them about teaching, maybe—in private, without me—but wait on the wedding."

And he said he would, to both those things. But that evening at dinner in the vast candle-flickering dining room, with spaces and unsaid words echoing between the four of us and the hovering Marvin looming large with tureens at our shoulders, he broke the news to his family after all that he would not be going into the family bank in September but had already accepted a position as American History instructor at a small, spartan boys' preparatory school in Northpoint, New Hampshire, and was going directly there from Princeton to settle into the cottage on campus that came with the position and get things set up to begin teaching in the fall. And his mother did, indeed, blow sky high.

When Hannah Chambliss blew, it was, instead of a white-heat explosion, a white-ice implosion. I came to know those outbursts well over the years, and the later ones were not one whit less wounding or terrifying than that first one. But it had the virtue of newness. I watched in anguish as she stared at her son, her face whitening and her eyes widening until they were ringed with white like those of a maddened horse, and then rose slowly from her seat and laid her hand across her dark silk bosom. Peter watched her too, warily, and Hermione with something near a smile, and Peter's father, with a sort of faint distaste mingled with distinct apprehension. Marvin took his tureen and left the room.

"You must do what you fancy, Peter," she said in a throbbing, strangled voice. Tears ran richly under it. "But know that if you do, you will not be welcome in your home again. You will break my heart if you do this, and your father's too, and disgrace your entire family . . . but it must be your decision. I have never interfered in your affairs, and I will not do so now."

"Thanks, Ma," Peter said, and picked up his fork once more. He turned his attention to the lamb on his plate, and his expression was mild, but I saw that his shoulders were rigid and the skin around his mouth and nose was white. Hermione and Mr. Chambliss both picked up their forks, not looking at either Peter or Hannah. Hannah stood like a woman of snow, or stone. I could not think where to look.

She turned her face to me.

"May I assume that you knew about this . . . decision of my son's, Miss . . . ah, Gascoigne?" she said. Her voice was like an iced lash across my face.

"Yes, ma'am," I said.

"And you approve, do you?"

"I think Peter should do what he wants with his life," I said, my voice quavering like a chastised child's. I could not imagine how I would get out of that awful dining room and away from there.

"Well, I submit that it is less your affair than anything I have ever heard, and your presumption in coming into my home uninvited and abetting my son in this . . . this . . . business is the very epitome of tastelessness, and—"

"It's very much Maude's business, Mother," Peter said, looking at her with eyes like dead glacier ice. "Because Maude is doing me the very great honor of marrying me as soon as graduation is over, probably in the Chapel that same afternoon, and will be going to Northpoint with me from there. We hope you will give us your blessing and your attendance, but we are going to do it anyway. And I hope I never hear you speak to Maude like that again."

Hannah Chambliss turned and walked away from the table and went up the stairs, her dark Grecian head held high, her spine straight, and I did not see her again until the day two months later that Peter brought me to Retreat. By that time she had made her apologies and what she must have considered adequate amends: a car, a van full of family furniture for our small stone cottage in Northpoint, some fine Georgian silver, a check for five thousand dollars "to start you off properly," and a letter to me in which she said that I must forgive her her outburst, as she had always been a woman of temperament and we had given her two very grave shocks, and that she was sure we would be the best of friends.

But I knew that first day, and Peter did, and probably his father and sister too, that the battle lines between us had been drawn and no tide on earth would really wash them away.

Peter's father looked at us and started to speak, then did not. Hermione said, "Really, Buddy, you do have the most awful sense of timing."

And Peter stood, held his hand out to me, and said, "Maude?" I took it, and we walked out of there, stopping only to pick up my heavy old suitcase, which still lurked in the foyer like a poor relation, and waited on the front steps in the chill twilight for the taxi Peter had called. When it came, we went to the train station and boarded a train to Elkton, Maryland, sat up in a dingy Pullman all night while the train plowed south, got off in the soft Maryland dawn, asked a taxi driver to take us to the nearest justice of the peace, and were married by 10 A.M. that morning.

I don't remember that Peter looked back at his home when we rode away from it.

We were happy during the few June days we spent in the little house on the edge of the Northpoint campus. It stood on the edge of a small birch wood, and I was enchanted with the ghostly silver gleam of the white trunks in the dusk, and the alien smells and sounds of these northern foothill forests, and the strange birds and animals that came close to our small veranda at evening. It was so totally unlike the woods and the swamp at home; the air smelled of pine wine, not sweet heat-heavy old earth, and nipped and bit, instead of pressing down; the nights called for fires and sweaters and piled blankets and the days for brisk movement. It was a minimal little cottage at best, the lowest rank of housing for the lowest rank of faculty, which Peter was, but we did not care about that. The old stone and brick school was nearly deserted in those cool June days, as the summer term had not begun and Peter's work would not begin until September. We were alone in those green-blue old hills except for the headmaster and his nice no-nonsense wife, who had us to dinner to see that we were comfortably settled in and then mercifully left us alone, and for a few of the custodial staff, small brown men in overalls. We arranged furniture and hung a few prints and pictures and ate the unspeakable meals I cooked and explored the campus and ranged farther afield into the hamlets and villages and up to Laconia and Lake Winnepe-saukee itself, twenty miles to our north. There, alone with Peter in a still green twilight on the shores of that beautiful old lake, I heard for the first time the neck-prickling, heart-swelling cry of a loon.

I turned a rapt face to Peter. He smiled.

"You'll get used to them," he said. "We have them in the harbor in Retreat."

I was silent for a while, and then I said, "I don't want to go, Peter. I'm afraid of Retreat. I'm afraid of everything there. I'm never ever going to be able to please your mother. You think because you can sweet-talk her out of any mood that I can too, but I can't."

He laughed. "You just have to let her know right up front she can't boss you," he said. "Who's ever bossed you, Maude? What have you ever been afraid of? You, who handle water snakes and paddle right up to gators and swim in that godforsaken black swamp water and stay out in the jungle by yourself for hours and days?"

I said nothing. I don't think Peter ever really understood the depth or quality of the fear I felt for his
mother and her world and the cost for me of accommodating to it all those years. He could always handle
her; she doted on him as I have never known another
woman to dote on a son, and her marblelike imperi-
ousness never daunted him as it did me and others. It
was useless to try to explain to him how I felt.

But I did say, "Why couldn't we just vacation
somewhere else this one summer and go to Retreat
next year? Along the coast here, or on this lake even;
it looks wonderful, and there are all sorts of cottages
we could rent."

"Because I don't start getting paid until September," Peter said. "And we have just about enough
money left to get us up to Retreat. We're pretty poor,
Maudie. We're not apt to have much money ever.
Even if I got to be a headmaster someday, somewhere, there wouldn't be a lot."

"I don't care about that," I said honestly. "You
know that. We've talked about it. I've never had any
money to speak of. I won't miss it."

"Well, I've had lots. Really lots. I probably won't
get any more, because it's in Mother's name and I
don't think she's going to part with any of it unless I
go into the bank. It's her last weapon; she's not going
to give it up. And I won't do that. I don't think I'm
ever going to want anything more than teaching here
or somewhere. I'm not very ambitious, my poor
Maudie. I just wanted to be sure you didn't mind."

"Lord, no," I said. "My mother's family never gave
us any of theirs either, not really. How could I miss
what I never had? Let's just make our own, enough
for the two of us, and tell the rest of the world to take
a hike. Crawl into bed and pull the covers up over us,
and never come out."

He smiled at me, and the sweet, thick warmth in

the pit of my stomach that stayed there most of the time began its slow coil up inside me once more. Sometimes I could scarcely breathe with the knowledge that for the rest of my life, whenever we wanted, Peter and I could lie down wherever we wished and do to each other the things that we did in the cool nights and pale dawns of Northpoint, New Hampshire. Who, I thought, reaching up to touch his face, cared about money when they could have that?

Peter put his hands on my breasts and pushed me back down onto the old blanket we had brought with us.

"You're going to have a hard time realizing we don't do this in Retreat," he said, putting his hands under my clothes. He ran the fingertips of one down my stomach, along the line of dark hair that grew there, and into the dark warmth below it.

I rolled over to face him, opening my legs.

"You're kidding," I breathed into his neck. It was hot, scalding.

"Oh, no," he said, easing over onto me. His hardness pressed against my thighs and then slipped down between them. "Nobody fucks in Retreat. Reproduction is accomplished by cell division, like amoebas. You'd be thrown out of the colony if they even suspected you did this."

He thrust, and thrust again. I felt the heat start up, up.

"Well, you shouldn't have corrupted me then," I gasped, arching up to meet him. "I can't just stop doing this . . . now . . . oh!"

"Or this?"

"No. . . ."

"Or this? Oh, God, Maude. . . ."

"Hurry, Peter, hurry. . . ."

"You'll have to give it up because the houses are so close together that you can hear . . . oh, Jesus, Maude . . . *everything*."

"Then," I said fiercely, riding with him up that long red crest, seeing lights explode behind my closed eyelids, "you'll just have to stuff a pillow in my mouth every time because I'm very surely going to scream—"

And did. And heard his whoop of laughter spill out with his climax.

I never tired of it, that long slide into red darkness, that shuddering up-spiral, that joyous outspilling. I would ride with him into hell on that, I thought. Bed and laughter, those two things, with Peter, would last forever, withstand anything. And despite what he said, we could do those things anywhere, including Retreat. Who would dare to stop us?

No matter that I came to feel the cold of Hannah Chambliss's mind reach out for me as the miles between us shortened, we set off for Maine on a blue-edged morning not long after that evening in an envelope of sensuality and laughter.

Retreat lies at the tip of Cape Rosier, a wild green stub of land fingering out into Penobscot Bay farther than any other land mass on that coast. Only the great islands of the bay—Deer Isle, North Haven, Islesboro—are more sea-locked and inaccessible. The seas around the cape, unbroken for many miles in their sweep up the Penobscot, are dark blue and empty for hours and sometimes days at a time of sail traffic, all but the enormous oceangoing sail yachts preferring the island-sheltered harbors around Rosier. There are many, teeming with sails and yacht clubs and summer homes and colonies: Bucks Harbor, at South Brooksville; Orcutt; Center Harbor, at Haven, near Brooklin; and the entire archipelago of small sheltered harbors around the tip of Naskeag Point into Blue Hill Bay and beyond into the great blue of

Frenchman's Bay. Here the truly wealthy have for a hundred summers nestled their enclaves like small succulent piglets nosing at the pure-cream teats of Bar Harbor and Mount Desert.

Over on that side of the long peninsula that juts out from Blue Hill down to Naskeag, the water is acknowledged to be warmer and gentler, the houses far grander and more accessible, the air sweeter and milder, and the blood far bluer. Cape Rosier is a wild place for mavericks, the conventional summer-people wisdom goes, for those who prefer their own society and don't mind the great seas and booming blue winds and howling storms; who don't care that the nearest good shopping town is elegant old Castine, some twenty miles away over horrendous roads (though, if you could go by water, it would be nearer five). The very small village of South Brooksville provides a general store and rental library and cemetery and infinitesimal post office; it is typical of Retreaters that they are proud that the post office was, until the early 1960s, the smallest in the United States. Surrounding farms provide produce, eggs, and milk; fishing boats bring in lobsters and haddock; tidal flats yield clams. A trip to Blue Hill or Ellsworth, for serious shopping and culture, is a half-day prospect, and a sojourn to Bar Harbor can still take the whole of a day, well into darkness. I once offered the suggestion to Mother Hannah that one saw the same faces year after year in Retreat because nobody else wanted to bother with it.

"I know we're supposed to be very careful who we let into Retreat," I said, "and I've heard for years how hard it is for outsiders to be accepted here. But for my money, it's because nobody but us could ever find the place, much less want to go to all the trouble of getting to it and actually living in it."

I was, by then, finally able to tease Mother Hannah

a little; I say finally, because it took me years to dare to do it. Mother Hannah never did come to invite it. But she seldom realized she was being teased, either, so I was fairly safe the few times I did.

"Nonsense," she said serenely, bothered not at all by any opinion I might have. "There are many people who would move heaven and earth to be a part of Retreat. But they're rarely suitable, and they wouldn't be happy here anyway. We're very plain-living people, you know, when we're up here. And often quite high-minded; most people are far happier in Northeast Harbor or at Bass Cove or Somes Sound. Places like that. Even Bar Harbor."

Her high-arched nose told me what she thought of those sinks of depravity and excess.

Peter, who was lying stretched full-length before the fire eating apples while one of our frequent June nor'easters moaned outside, said from the depths of an old Hudson Bay blanket, "'The soul selects her own society and shuts the door. On her divine majority, obtrude no more.'"

"Exactly," Mother Hannah said. "That's very cleverly put, darling."

"Emily Dickinson thought so," Peter's voice, suspiciously equable, said from the couch.

"Is she that strange little woman with the bicycle visiting Frances and English Sears?" Mother Hannah said vaguely.

"I doubt it," Peter said, laughter breaking through. "From what I hear, she never left her own back yard in her entire life."

"Really, darling, you know the strangest people."

"Don't I just," said Peter.

For whatever reason, mainly geographical ones, Cape Rosier and Retreat remain nearly as untouched today as they did on that long-ago day I first came here, and in a way it is a great pity, for this coast and the countryside around it are by far the most beautiful I have ever seen. But at first it frightened me. Stark, jutting, thickly forested with the graceful pointed firs whose silhouettes against the sky can break the heart, gray-spined where the great rock ribs of the earth break through, and bound at the sea's edge by huge pink boulders and fierce red ledges left by the last dying glaciers, the cape seems, at first, inimicable to man, inhospitable to life. The great blue skies and endless indigo seas—edged in a kind of crystal light when the weather is about to change for the worse, losing themselves altogether in the thick, silent, white sea fogs that sometimes roll in for weeks—seem to me to be deeper, purer, harder, vaster than anywhere else on that old coast. On the wind you can hear the cries of gulls all the way out on the big islands, or the fog buoy miles and miles away off Stonington on Deer Isle. On the days of high sun and still blue air, you can see the line of the Camden Hills across the entire great bay. Sight, sound, smells all have a preternatural keenness here.

It seems to me—and I remember it was perhaps the first thought I had when at last we jolted out of the forest and saw Retreat lying ahead of us in the sunset, at the end of that endless day—that Cape Rosier is about clarity. Simply that. There is nothing here shifting, seeping, insidious, seductive, smothering, soft, to blur the edges of anything. The sharp beauty cuts like a knife. Even the small rich green sweeps of the little sea meadows, thick with wild-flowers and rimmed with the black-green of the firs; even the undulating fringes of goldenrod and Queen Anne's lace along the dusty roadsides; even the riots of short-lived summer flowers in the yards of the most humble shacks—even these seem as sharply and clearly limned as the details of a Dali painting. To my senses, long lulled by the velvety morass that is the

Low Country, it looked that day a country of a million sharp and dangerous and beautiful sword points.

"I never saw anything so beautiful," I said to Peter finally, when it was obvious that he was waiting for me to tell him what I thought of this place he so loved. "And it looks like it could easily kill you. Peter, it's all so . . . *sharp.*"

He looked at me and smiled. "I know what you mean. But it's just what you'll come to love about it. It's . . . all open to you. It keeps nothing back. It shows you its teeth and spine and breath, and in the end something in you rises up to meet and match it. It never coddles you, but in the end it gets the best out of you. And it gives you its best. It clears away a lot of unnecessary stuff, this coast, this place. I guess what I mean is that it's possible to learn about absolutes here. You've never had that in Charleston."

I started to protest and then did not. He was right. That sinuous southern life, that oblique and slow and complicated old beauty, that warm thick air and blood-warm sea, that place of mists and languor and fragrant richness—it could soothe you and charm you and teach you much, but it could not cleanse and clarify. This place could. Perhaps that was what I feared most: that Cape Rosier and Retreat would ask of me a sea change that I somehow could not afford, or would fail to make.

"I don't think I'll leave this place the same person as I came here," I said obscurely, and he grinned wider and ruffled my hair and told me I was ridiculous, that I would be me, only more so, in Retreat.

All these years later, I still do not know who was right.

From the pitted county blacktop a sandy lane led off into the fir and birch groves that ran straight down to the sea, and there was an old gray wooden oar fastened to a post there that said, in letters faded nearly to invisibility, RETREAT COLONY, COVE HARBOR YACHT CLUB. The road was absolutely still and quiet, and the crystal-blue air was chilling as we sat there in the open car. I drew my sweater around me, shivering with more than cold. We might have been looking down into the dawn of time; no roofline or chimney or smoke rise broke the serrated line of the firs. No human voice cut the silence. Only the mewling cry of the gulls and, far away, a little hushing sussuration that I found later to be the gentle wash of the tide on the shingle beach.

"Well, let's do it," Peter said, and put the car into gear. I could not muster enough breath to reply. I was, at that moment, absolutely terrified.

Retreat has, instead of streets, a web of narrow, wildflower-fringed sandy lanes that wander through the dark woods, all of them leading one way or another to the water. The old houses are mostly gray- or brown-weathered cedar shingle, so that in the twilight all you can see of them at first is the flash of white trim and the blazing window boxes. Then your eyes adjust to the green darkness and you can pick them out, set back in that primeval forest from the lanes, bulking high against the lucent sky: tall and rambling, winged and elled old dowagers with many windows and porches, shouldering in among the great gray rocks that lie slumped like elephants on that rich black earth. All have views of the bay or the harbor, and the ones at the ends of the lanes have magnificent wraparound vistas; I often, in those early years, envied the families who had that largesse as a part of their lives whenever they chose to look at it. Liberty, our cottage, looked out to sea only over the shoulders of Braebonnie, the Potters' newer and larger cottage, which had been built on the very cliff overlooking the shingle beach. You could see the sea, but you did not have that wild, all-pervasive sense of it that Braebonnie and many other Retreat cottages offered.

"It's because Liberty is one of the three original cottages here," Mother Hannah told me that first summer. "In those days you could only come here by packet from Rockland, and it docked down at the foot of our lane. Peter's dear grandfather was thinking of his family's comfort when he built here. It was only a short journey up from the dock, you see. Easier on the servants too. Of course, no one in that original little group of settlers ever expected people to actually buy up the land between them and the water and build more . . . imposing homes. There was a sort of gentlemen's agreement among the originals. But of course Braebonnie was built much later by, I believe, some people from Connecticut. We didn't know them; they didn't care for Retreat after all and sold almost immediately to the Potters. I must say I've always been relieved to have them so close by; fellow Bostonians, you know. Even if the house is . . . a bit excessive for a simple summer colony."

Braebonnie was indeed large—it had perhaps twenty rooms—but it sprawled down the cliff in a weathered, mossy pile of shingle and stone so sweetly and unassumingly that it did not seem to me the least imposing. I loved it. I always have, ever since that first summer. So many of my happiest memories of Retreat were born in Braebonnie, when Amy and I were young together. I love Liberty too, of course; it is all I have of youth and Peter, and it is unquestionably home to me. But it is so somehow like Mother Hannah— square, upright, uncompromising—that I often fancy I can see her in the cedar-dark old rooms, straight-spined and austere and moving with her silent, sweeping tread, or hear her voice in the emptiness. As I said, sound is queer here by the water.

"Get out of here. This is my house now," I have said

to that disapproving shade more than once. And to exorcise her I have cut her lilacs down to size, and added a long sun porch that commands the sea, and enlarged all the back windows and added many, so that the sound of the water is the last thing one hears at night, and the dancing stipple of sea light on the ceiling is the first thing one's opening eyes see in the morning. She would absolutely have hated all of it. Mother Hannah was always more annoyed than exalted by the sea.

After the ritual of welcome, which never varied until Mother Hannah's death—the cool little kiss, the light embrace, the offered cheek smelling of talcum and smooth linen stored in cedar—she opened her arms to Peter and held them so until he came into them, and when she had him firm, she closed her eyes and rolled her cheek back and forth in the angle where his neck met his shoulder, smiling as rapturously as a nursing kitten. There were tears on her satiny cheek when she finally let him go and stepped back to look at him.

"You're far too thin," she said. "And you've lost your lovely tan. You shall have days and days in the sun simply vegetating, and Christina and I are going to feed you till you pop. If you're this worn out now, what on earth will you be when you start your position?"

Mother Hannah could never bring herself to say, simply, "teaching."

"I haven't lost an ounce, Ma, and I've been sailing every day for the past week at Northpoint," Peter said. "Winnepesaukee is right there. Stop fussing. Maude feeds me like a pig. She's turning into a great cook."

"I'm sure she is," Mother Hannah said, smiling her little V smile at me. "These pretty southern girls are born knowing how to please a man, I expect."

Both my neglect of her son and my overblown southern carnality hung in the air between my mother-in-law and me. I smiled brightly at her. She had forgiven Peter, I knew; the household appointments and the handsome roadster said as much. I also knew she had not forgiven me. The daughter-in-law she would present tonight to her world assembled at the dining hall was so patently not the one she would have chosen that it must have seemed in her wintry eyes grotesque.

"I'm trying hard," I said. "I never cooked at home, but taking care of Peter is number one now."

"Yes," she said.

Peter's father kissed me, I thought, with genuine pleasure and picked up my bags.

"The back corner, darling, please," Mother Hannah said, and Peter and his father looked at her.

"That room is an oven, Ma," Peter said. "And it's just got the one twin bed. I thought we'd have my old room."

"I know, sweetie, but Micah found dry rot in some of the floorboards in your room this spring, and he wasn't sure about the weight of two people."

Her eyes measured me. I flushed.

"Besides," she said, "it has much the prettiest view of the water. And I had Micah bring up the big bed."

She dropped her eyes and I flushed again. Peter's father vanished up a staircase of suicidal steepness and we followed him. I took a great deep breath, partly in relief at being out of her presence at last and partly of pure pleasure at the wonderful smell of old cedar holding the warmth of the day. The cottage has never been winterized, so that the exterior shingles of red cedar are also the interior walls, and the rafters and beams are of the same wood, and over the long years it has mellowed to a glorious, dark, fire-shot honey gold.

"The color," Amy once said, "of the world's most beautiful chestnut horse."

Our room, at the end of the upstairs central hall, was indeed tiny. The huge white iron bed dominated it. It was turned back, so that thin, lovely old white linen sheets showed their cutwork, and it was piled with crisp-slipped goosedown pillows and comforters and a thick orange-and-black Princeton blanket. I smiled, at the great bed and the blanket and at Peter.

"Old school ties," I said.

"There's one like it on practically every bed in Retreat," Peter said. "It was my grandfather and some of his club members who found this place and established the colony. For years afterward they only let in fellow Tigers, and then they started to have their own little tigers—conceived literally under the orange and black, you might say—and one thing led to another, and now Retreat is almost a Princeton alumni colony. You're going to get sick of 'Going Back to Old Nassau' pretty soon."

"No Yale? No Harvard?"

"Very few. They go to Northeast Harbor, or Bar, or somewhere. Or buy their own islands. Just Princeton. And virtually all of the Seven Sisters, of course."

"Of course," I said in despair. "Oh, Peter, I'm going to stand out like a sore thumb. No Boston, no New England, no tennis, no sailing, no Seven Sisters. Not even a college degree. Not even a year of college. What am I going to do?"

"You could always stay in bed and fuck your husband," he said. "You'd be the envy of every woman from sixteen to ninety. Like I said, nobody does it in Retreat."

"Well, how come there're so many of you?"

"Oh, we screw at home," he said. "That's what those long dark winters are for."

I looked at the huge bed. "It's hard to think about anything else, with that thing looming up like an iceberg," I said, grinning.

He laughed. For some reason, there was little mirth in it. I looked at him inquiringly.

"Well, think hard," he said. "Because it's apt to be what you do the most of in that bed."

"I don't understand."

"She's put us right over her head," he said. "This room is directly above the big downstairs bedroom they use, and this bed is directly above theirs. You could drop a pin in here, and they'd hear it down there. My old room is at the other end of the house; I've actually set off firecrackers in it and no one knew. Unless you like the idea of my mother and father lying there listening to every hump we hump, we're going to have to come up with something else."

"Well, let's just move back into yours."

"Dry rot," he said. "Remember?"

"Surely there are other places?"

"Yep. A nice room directly next to theirs where you can hear even better, and four bunk beds in a room up under the eaves where nobody could breathe from July on, and four hammocks on the upstairs sun porch. With huge holes in the screen. So that every black fly and mosquito in Maine would feast off your ass from now until September."

Red rage flooded me. "I don't care if she hears us every night," I said hotly. "She must know we do it. She must have done it at least once. Here you are, after all. I will not stop . . . doing that . . . just because she moved us in over her head. Peter, I know it was on purpose."

"Of course it was," he said. Laughter and anger warred in his long face.

"Well, are you going to let her stop us?"

"No," he said. "I'll figure something out. We could wait and do it when there's a thunderstorm. Or we could sneak up here and do it at midmorning, when she's out calling. Or we could do it over on one of the little islands; the moss there is as soft as a mattress. Or we could take the boat out and drop anchor around the point and do it."

"Peter! I think you're afraid to let your mother know you make love to me!"

"Not afraid of her. Just afraid she'll spoil it for us, if she catches us at it. I don't want that to happen."

I looked at him more closely. The laughter had left his eyes. He was serious.

"Well, she's not going to spoil it for me, and she's not going to catch me at it, as you say, and I'm going to do it with you whenever I please, and I please this very night, after we get back from dinner," I said indignantly. "The very idea!"

"Maude . . ."

"Hush. Don't say another word. You are as good as fucked right now, Peter Chambliss. You are at this moment a walking fucked man," I said.

"Well, since you put it that way," Peter said, and put his hands around me from behind and cupped my breasts. I felt the little point of flame lick at my groin.

"How long does dinner last?" I whispered, reaching around to stroke the hardness of him against my back.

"Too long," Peter said. "Way, way too long."

He was right. The rest of the evening, though it was essentially over by nine thirty, was too long. When we went back downstairs, Augusta Stallings was there working on a large martini and Peter's father had retreated to the long sofa before the fireplace and Peter's mother introduced me and made her destined-to-be-legendary remark about the French and corruption, and from then on the evening and night blurred into one long smear of hot-cheeked, blinded misery. It has remained so in my memory ever since. I can recall certain highlights— the memory of Mrs. Stallings sitting down in a low wicker armchair in the living room and missing and landing on her ample, corseted rump on the sisal rug, spilling not a drop of her third drink, is the most vivid, but there were others—but mainly, my first full evening in Retreat is a cipher, a void.

When I think back now, a low hum of seemly New England voices in the rustic dining hall rushes at me out of memory, and the warm fragrance of clam chowder and hot rolls, and the nodding of many narrow fairish heads, and the pressure of many cool fingers on mine, and the flash of many fine teeth, and the following wash of low conversation as we made our way on to our table. I get a sense of many young men and women who looked much like Peter reaching out to enfold him, not so much with their arms as their smiles, and thinking that I would never, never feel that welcome; I get a flash of several individual faces above cardigans and pearls or blue blazers. One—dark, clever, impish, framed in bobbed hair nearly the color of mine—stands out clearly: Amy Potter, the first time I ever saw her. I hear soft, flat voices asking me if I sailed or played tennis or bridge and assuring me I'd learn in no time. But there is no order and progression to the images. I was too tired and too cowed and, suddenly, too homesick for that other, warmer sea and the indulgent old city beside it.

When we got home, it was my mother-in-law who finally shooed us upstairs. Peter had lapsed into silence, sitting beside his father on the sofa with the birch logs snapping in the fireplace, and made no move to rise, and I would have died in my tracks rather than initiate any movement up to where that huge bed crouched. I sat looking at yellowing old magazines, my eyes growing heavier and finally drooping, until Mother Hannah came out of the rudimentary little kitchen and said, "You children should get some sleep now. You've had a full day, and you'll want to be out and around with the birds in the morning. Peter, Parker Potter said to tell you he needs a partner on the court at eight, and he'll wait until eight fifteen for you. Tina's making pancakes in the morning; she said to tell you. She brought you the first of the blueberry jam. Maude, dear, is there anything you need?"

Nothing but a long, hard, teeth-jarring, eyelid-rattling fuck from your son, I thought, getting to my feet.

"No, thank you," I said.

"Well, then, good night. If you should want anything, just call out. I'll hear you."

No, you won't, I thought.

But of course she did. Peter was reluctant when at last we slid under the heavy covers in the big bed, but slowly, and in total silence, I teased him with my fingers and then my hands, and then arms and legs and feet, and soon he had no choice but to roll over to cover me with his body, and only a moment after that he entered me. He was quieter than he had ever been before, and so was I; we strained and thrust together in total silence, our muscles clenching to keep from shaking the old iron bed. But it was no use. Both our climaxes were beginning when I heard her voice, as clear as a funeral bell, drifting up through the floor. "Peter? Are you ill, dear?"

He stiffened and lay rigid; I felt him slip out of me.

"No, Ma," he called, his voice tight.

"I thought you called out."

"No, Ma."

He lay beside me in the darkness for a moment, quiet and still, and then he said, "You still game?"

"Oh, yes. . . ."

And again, as the damp heat flowered deep within me and all of that secret darkness opened for him, came the voice.

"Peter? Petie?"

"Ma, I'm fine," Peter called back. His voice now was flat and furious. For some reason, I began to laugh. I laughed and I laughed, even as, inside, I ached for him, burned with incompletion. I could not stop. I stuffed the covers into my mouth, but the silent shaking went on and on.

"By God, come on, Maude," Peter said between clenched teeth, and got out of bed and jerked me after him, and caught up the Princeton blanket and pulled both of us into the tiny, freezing bathroom off the bedroom.

"What?" I whispered, doubled over with laughter. "What are you doing, you damned fool?"

He threw the blanket into the stained old claw foot bathtub and half pushed me in on top of it.

"I'm fucking my wife," he muttered. "I started it and by God I'm going to finish it and Mother can go kiss a quahog if she doesn't like it. This sonofabitch is bolted to the floor; if she can hear it thumping and squeaking she's a goddamn witch. Lie down, Maude."

I did. My head hung over one end of the bathtub and my feet over the other, and my stomach heaved with silent laughter. I looked at my tall thin naked husband, standing over me. He was shivering with cold and rage and his hair hung down in his slitted eyes, and he was fully and powerfully erect. I loved him absolutely. The laughter threatened to burst from my lips and sweep down the stairs and drown my mother-in-law.

"She *is* a witch," I gasped. "I could have told you that. She's turned me into a pig and you into a whooping crane with a hard-on."

And so it was that we made love for the first time in Retreat, Peter and I: laughing and wallowing in a cold porcelain bathtub on a black-and-orange Princeton University blanket, with a washcloth in my mouth to stop my cries and the sound of Peter's mother's voice over his laughter as he came: "Peter? Are you sure you're all right?"

I awoke the next morning to pale sunlight in a square on the bedclothes and the flickering wash of sea light on the ceiling. I was alone in the bed. Downstairs I could hear nothing at all, and I had no idea what time it was. Summer dawns come very early in Retreat; it could as easily be five thirty as nine. Peter might well be on the tennis court by now.

I lay still, not wanting to go downstairs after last night's bedroom farce. It was chilly in the little room, but my body still held the warmth of his. I might have him to myself in the nights, I thought, but each morning that dawned would draw him up and away from me and out into this place where he walked as surely and carelessly as a young king, where I did not think I could ever truly follow. I felt my throat tighten and my eyes begin to sting. I felt as abandoned and alone as I ever have in my life.

From somewhere close by I heard a voice, old and fairly quavering with malice, say, "If I had treated my husband's grandmother as badly as you do me, he would have divorced me. You are an ill-bred and thoughtless and self-serving child, and I shall have to tell Parker that you have forgotten my breakfast again for the third time in a week. He will not be pleased, Amy. Oh, no."

I got out of bed and went in my thin nightgown to the window and looked out. The morning was still and yellow and blue; the sea glittered. The big house just behind ours, Braebonnie, was undoubtedly the source of that malignant voice. The Potters', I remembered. The Potters senior and junior, and the senior Potter's old mother. It had to be her voice I had heard. And its target must be, had to be, the vivid dark-eyed girl I had met last night at the dining hall. Amy, young Parker Potter's wife. My heart actually contracted with pain for her pain at the old woman's hands, and knife-edged sympathy.

"Oh, poor Amy," I said aloud, but only just. "I know, I know."

And then, incredibly, I heard the sound of a young girl's joyous laugh. And that remembered voice, as cool and light as rain, said, "Oh, Mamadear, what an old fool you are! You had your silly breakfast two hours ago. You've forgotten again."

And a door shut and the voices trailed away. I got back into bed and lay there, watching the sun square creep across my comforter. I smiled. I knew, as surely as if I could see into the future, that in Amy Parker I had an ally and would soon have a friend.

Chapter
Three

The first week I was in Retreat I met three people who altered the channel of my life as surely as dynamite will alter a watercourse. The first, of course, was Amy Potter; before Amy I had never really had a friend; afterward she was the benchmark against whom all friendships were measured. The second was her husband, Parker. The third was a man who saved my life before I knew his name. They are all dead now. It is ironic that so often the stream outlives the cataclysms that shape it.

I met Parker Potter the morning of my first full day in the colony and by its end had come to wish the meeting had never occurred. Though he never in his life ceased to hug or kiss me in greeting, or to tease me with what seemed to be affection, I always knew he saw me through a scrim of enmity. Parker was as bad an enemy as his wife was a good friend.

When I came downstairs that morning the cottage was deserted. I had been unsure what one wore mornings in Retreat, and so had put on the dressing gown that Kemble had given me for a wedding present. It was a beautiful heavy satin that fell

like spilled syrup, coral piped in white, with handmade lace on the lapels. I walked in it through the
gloom of the downstairs and out onto the porch and
breathed in the sights and sounds of Retreat in the
morning, and my heart, despite its ballast of uncertainty and apprehension, rose up singing like a lark.
The air was crisp and damp and pine-scented, the
bay danced cobalt, white sails flitted sharply against
the faraway blue of the Camden Hills like butterflies,
and the crystal air swarmed with birdsong, so that it
seemed to rise up out of the very earth, seep from
the birch woods, pour from the rocks. There was a
whole web of sounds and smells that were alien to
me, and all of a sudden I was very happy. This entire
exotic northern world lay waiting for me to explore,
to come to know through my very pores, as I did the
wild country of the Wappoo Creek swamp forests. I
thought of the long lazy summer days ahead of me,
this and all the summers of my life, spent with Peter
deep in the woods or on the rocks of the shore with
a book or a sketchbook, or even on the calm sur-
faces of the little coves that I could see from the
porch, in a canoe. I smiled and stretched my arms
out as far as I could, and closed my eyes, and breathed
deeply.

"Good morning," two nasal voices called from the
path in front of the cottage, and I opened my eyes to
see, first, two ramrod-straight old ladies in many layers of starched cotton, gloves, and sun hats, and, second, that my lace lapels had lapped open and the
morning sun was shining on an unmistakable suck
mark on my left breast. One of the old ladies lifted a
lorgnette from her bosom and examined me. I pulled
my lapels together hastily and grinned, as Kemble
once said, like a possum in the middle of a cow plop,
feeling the heat flood up my neck to my hairline.

"Good morning," I called. "Isn't it a glorious day?"

"Very nice," said the first, averting her eyes delicately. "Please tell your dear mother-in-law that we'll call again when . . . you are more settled in," said the second. In her hand I saw, silver against the white glove, her card case at the ready. They marched down the path in lockstep, and into the road, and on toward the next cottage, heads together. I could just imagine the gist of their conversation. So much for dressing gowns in Retreat.

I crept into the kitchen, found it empty, and opened the old icebox door. It was nearly empty except for a blue earthenware pitcher of milk. I poured some into a tumbler and drank it, sweet and fresh, and then my eye fell on a note propped against the sugar bowl on the old scrubbed deal table in the very center of the slanting floor. It was from my mother-in-law:

Maude, dear,

Peter and Parker Potter from Braebonnie have gone sailing and will likely be out until dinnertime. I have taken Christina to the fishmonger's truck. We will be back about ten. I thought we would start our calls this morning, and then Mrs. Stallings wants us for a little luncheon. This afternoon I'll show you the cottage routine. A simple cotton morning dress will do nicely.

Love, Mother Hannah.

My heart fell to my feet. Calls? Luncheons with other old ladies . . . perhaps, even, the two I had just put to rout? The cottage routine? Why had Peter left me alone? Why had he not even wakened me? Last night had, in the end, been transcendent. . . . Suddenly, as clearly as if I had the Sight, I saw the shape of my days in Retreat.

"No, I won't," I said aloud. "Not today. Tomorrow, maybe, but not today, not until I've seen Peter and talked things over with him; not until I've seen the colony and the countryside and been down to the ocean. I haven't even been down to the ocean yet."

I flew upstairs and skinned into slacks and a sweater and tennis shoes, such as I might wear into the woods at Belleau in the autumn, and ran out of the house and down the dirt road that led, I knew, to the yacht club. I would pretend I had not seen the note. Time enough tomorrow to begin my sentence.

The Cove Harbor Yacht Club was then, as it is now, a rambling brown-weathered shingle Cape Cod, sagging porches spread around it like skirts, sunk gently into the long grass at the very tip of Cove Point. Early wildflowers nodded around it. On one side, that morning, the great empty bay stretched away toward Islesboro, which lay like a cloud in the middle distance. Beyond it the Camden Hills, that had been so sharp they seemed to vibrate in the eye when last I looked, were losing their definition in the dazzle of the sun. There was a peculiar softening to the edges of the nearer, smaller, dark green islands. It was hard to calculate the time of day.

On the other side of the point, Cove Harbor lay like a bite taken out of an apple, a sheltered half moon rimmed in great pink rocks, an enormous lone boulder standing on the shingle beach. The tide was far out; rocks and boulders wore beards of wet green moss and were pebbled with mollusks and barnacles. There were a few sloops and catboats bobbing at their buoys, canvases lapped tight and buttoned around their masts. A fleet of dinghies bumped at the foot of the long catwalk that extended like a finger out from the gray wooden dock. One boat, a long, low, racing sloop with lines like a deer in flight, stood ready to cast off, it seemed to me; its sails were up but loose, flapping gently in the little wind, and there were canvas bundles on the coaming, and a wicker hamper covered with cloth. But there was no one in evidence aboard her. The name on her transom read *Circe*. I peered around the harbor and saw no one. Peter was not in sight.

I stood still in disappointment, the stark beauty of the harbor and shore losing much of its impact. I thought perhaps Peter might be in the clubhouse, and went up the shallow steps and tried the door, but it was locked, and the salt-scummed windows were shuttered over. I turned away slowly. Peter and Parker Potter had evidently gotten clear away. There seemed no recourse but Mother Hannah and morning calls in the simple morning dress I did not own.

"Ahoy, there," someone called, and I turned to see a young man coming out of the clubhouse.

"Ahoy," I answered, shielding my eyes to look at him. The peculiar dazzle of the sun was directly behind him, and I could only see that he was short and stocky and had very red hair. The light on it was like live coals.

"You can only be the new Mrs. Chambliss," he said, coming down the steps into the shade of a great overhanging blue spruce. Without the light I saw that he was perhaps Peter's age, and had blue eyes screwed up into slits against the sun and a deep mahogany tan that was striking with the hair, until he came close enough for me to see that his entire face was a mass of freckles run together, like a mask. It should have been grotesque, but it wasn't; the snub nose and small white teeth gave him the look of a young boy, and a chipped front tooth added to the Huckleberry Finn aura. His hair hung in his eyes and his shirt sleeve was out at the elbow and there was a brownish stain on his white pants. Something in his bearing told me he was not a worker or an employee;

he just missed swaggering, with his barrel chest and short legs and rolling walk. Suddenly I knew who he was.

"Parker Potter, I'll bet," I said. "Oh, good; then you all haven't left yet. Is Peter in there? Oh . . . I'm Maude Chambliss. Well, but that's what you said, isn't it?"

"Well, but it is," he said, the smile widening. It stretched almost literally from ear to ear. His eyes all but disappeared into his cheeks, showing only a feathering of white eyelashes. His brows were nearly white too.

"No, Peter's gone to Micah Willis's boatyard up the bay, to see about getting the *Hannah* in the water," he said. "He thought you were going to sleep in. Said you were dead to the world when he left. I think he thought maybe his mother had plans for you."

Something in his slow voice and the way he said "dead to the world" made me redden from neckline to hairline again. The narrow eyes rested for a moment on my chest, as if he could, like the old women earlier, read the stigma of the night before through the stuff of my sweater.

"She does," I said crisply, "and I'd better get on back before she comes home. I just thought maybe . . . I've never done any real sailing and I thought Peter might—"

"Stay a minute," Parker Potter said. "I'd love to get to know you better one-to-one like this, instead of at the inevitable tea or whatever your mother-in-law or my mother or whoever will give for you. You're a surprise; old Peter never said a word about you. I can see why; I'd be tempted to keep you to myself too. He said you were something to look at, but he didn't say you were a fair knockout."

"I really can't," I said, acutely uncomfortable in his presence. Somehow he commanded the air around him. It was a different thing entirely from the power Peter had, and his father.

"Look," Parker said, "I didn't mean to scare you. I'm all bark. Peter's just about my oldest friend in the world; he'd have my hide if he thought I made his bride uncomfortable. Sit and talk to me while I stow some stuff on the *Circe.* I'd like us to be friends. My wife, Amy, met you for a minute last night and said how nice she thought you were."

I smiled at him. "I liked her too," I said. "She has a wonderful laugh. I'll stay for a minute. Maybe until Peter comes back. Do you know how long he'll be?"

"Well, until after lunch anyway," he said. "He was going to check the boat out with old Micah. It takes a while, after the winter. Tell you what, though. If you'd like, I'll sail you around there in *Circe.* It's not so far by water."

"Oh, I couldn't—"

"Come on. It'll be a nice surprise for Peter, and it's really a treat for me too. Not many women up here sail. I never met one who wanted to learn. I can't get Amy near my boat."

I looked at the slender white sloop swaying on the calm water. Sun danced on its brass fittings, and a little wind bellied its sails slightly. Far out the water looked as still as glass, and the hard, cold blue of the deep water outside the cove was going mild and milky. The air was stilling on my face, and the glare of the sun softened in my eyes. It seemed a lovely morning for a short sail, and I thought it would please Peter for me to appear at the boathouse already acquainted with his boyhood friend and already versed in the rudiments of sailing. It was, I knew, a passion with him.

"Well, if it won't take too long . . . ?"

"Have you home for lunch," he said. And grinned widely again. "You better do it while you can, Miss Maude. Once Peter's mother gets ahold of you, you can kiss mornings on the water goodbye. Ask my

Amy. She spends most of her mornings ferrying Mother and Mamadear around. It's not going to be much different for you."

"You convinced me," I said.

"Thought I would."

Outside the harbor the wind picked up, and the *Circe* heeled into it. At first it was only a gentle dipping, the slightest rolling wallow. But it accelerated rapidly. My heart tightened with something near panic. I felt absolutely certain that if the lee rail dipped an inch farther we would be precipitated into the water. Out here it looked terrible, deep and dark and lightless, the opaque indigo of endless night and cold. I clutched the railing with white fingers and grinned in terror at Parker.

"Does it usually get much rougher than this?" I said.

He smiled the face-eating smile again.

"Rougher? This is the calmest I've seen the bay in a long time. It's almost a flat calm, and we usually get those only in August. Hell, I've sailed *Circe* with the lee rail two feet under white water and all hands hanging perpendicular. Today will be like a stroll with your grandmother."

It didn't help much. I realized then that I would never sail with Peter. The sense of losing control and balance was simply too awful. It would happen whether there was a flat calm or a gale.

"It's better below," Parker said. "There's no fixed horizon to measure the roll against. Why don't you go down to the cabin for a little while? Look around, stretch out on one of the bunks. I think Amy put some hot coffee in a thermos too; it'll be in one of those ditty bags. We'll be there before you know it."

"Thanks, Parker," I said humbly. "I've only done Charleston Harbor sailing before now. It's not the same thing."

"I know," he said. "I won't tell on you."

I crept down the hatchway into the cabin of the sloop. It was dark and snug and friendly, like a warm teak womb. Everything was spare and neat and tucked and buttoned up, and the bunks—two fore and two aft—were covered in the ubiquitous Hudson Bay blankets and had small fat white pillows tossed about. The bags and basket sat in the tiny galley. I fished in them and pulled out a thermos of coffee and poured a cup and drank it sitting on one of the bunks. Parker was right; the rolling seemed less here. I peered out a salt-scrimmed porthole and saw the horizon tossing and swallowed hard and pulled the little curtain over the port. After that it was better.

"Okay below?" Parker yelled.

"Just fine," I called.

"I'll sing out when we've sighted the boatyard. I'm going to take her out into the bay a way so we can have a straight beat in."

"Fine."

I found a damp, curled copy of *Yachting* and leaned back in the bunk to look at it. It seems hard to believe now, but with the dimness and the rhythmic rolling and the close warmth, I was asleep inside five minutes. When I woke, the boat was not rocking any more, the slap of water against the hull had stopped, and I could hear no sound. I sat up quickly and banged my head on the bulkhead and straightened my slacks and sweater and groped my way up the companionway stairs. The light was peculiar, thick and white and lightless. Had I slept until late afternoon? Why had he not wakened me?

I put my head out into whiteness so dense and impenetrable that I felt it in my nose and mouth and on my face. I could see nothing. I could not see my hand at the end of my arm. There was no sound from Parker.

"Parker?" I cried softly, and my voice came out in a flat, treble squawk. It had no resonance, no dimension. Fog. Peter had said that sound was peculiar in the fog.

"Right here," Parker's voice replied, sounding at first far far away and then directly in my ear. I slewed my head around but saw nothing. Then I saw his dark shape bulking up out of the whiteness, almost at my fingertips.

"I'm sorry, Maude," he said. "I should have seen it coming. We hit it right off Orcutt, a solid bank. I think it'll probably lift soon. It's the nighttime fogs that last. I've dropped anchor and we'll just wait it out below and have some lunch. Don't worry."

I stepped back into the cabin and he came down, pearled all over with droplets, his red hair darkened with wet. He loomed large in the small space, and I could feel the damp heat of his body. I bumped into him a couple of times and finally retreated out of the way into the bunk.

"Is it going to make us terribly late?" I said. "Peter will be worried to death."

"I doubt it. When he finds the *Circe* gone and you gone, he'll figure it out. He knows the only thing to do in fog is drop anchor and wait. And he knows I'm the best sailor on the cape."

He reached past me for the basket, and I smelled a warm gust of whiskey. I looked closely at him. His face was flushed and his eyes glittered. He had, I thought, been drinking for quite a while. I had seen no bottle. Suddenly I was afraid.

It was in the inside pocket of his parka. He fished it out and poured a generous tot into two cups of coffee and passed me one. Then he leaned back in the opposite bunk and lifted his cup and said, "Cheers, Mrs. Chambliss," and smiled.

"I don't want any," I said. "I don't drink much."

"Time you learned, then. Everybody up here over

the age of twelve drinks. We'd go nuts in the evenings if we didn't. Come on, down the hatch. It'll take the fog chill out of your bones."

"I'm not cold. It's very warm down here."

He smiled. It was the same smile, but all the Huckleberry Finn had seeped out of it.

"It is, at that," he said. "Why don't you just skin out of that heavy damp sweater? There's bound to be something dry around here that'll fit you."

"I'm not wet, either," I said.

"Well, here's to . . . good sailing, Mrs. Chambliss. Maude. Pretty Maude from way down South." He drained the cup. "Whooeee. Just what the doctor ordered. You sure about that drink?"

"Oh, yes, thank you," I said. "Ah . . . how long have we been stopped? How long was I asleep?"

"Don't have my watch on and can't see the sun for the fog, but I'd say it was around midafternoon," he said. His voice was slower and thicker, and his eyes had drooped into slits.

"Midafternoon! Parker, we have to go back," I gasped. "Peter will be frantic, my mother-in-law will kill me—"

"Sweet thing, the only way we could possibly go back now is for you to go out on the bow with a long stick and lie down and hold it straight out so you could feel any rocks before we hit 'em, and for me to steer absolutely blind, going by just what I remember of this coast and what you tell me. I remember a lot but I ain't a genius, and you sure ain't a sailor. It's too dangerous. And it would take just as long as waiting it out here. So you might as well quit worrying and make yourself comfortable."

"I don't like this one bit," I said. I thought I might begin to cry soon.

"It doesn't have to be so bad," he said. "It could be fun. I can think of a way to make the time pass real quick."

I felt my cheeks flame and crossed my arms over my sweater. I knew that the wet fog had molded it to my breasts. I looked at the basket.

"You said something about lunch."

"Feel free," he said, not moving. "There's probably some sandwiches in there, if you can stand pimento cheese. You'd think after four years Amy would catch on to the fact that I hate pimento cheese. And there's sure to be apples. Old Amy never goes anywhere without apples."

"Can I get you anything?"

He held up the bottle. It was more than two thirds empty. He must have been drinking steadily ever since I came below the first time.

"Got everything I need," he said. "Almost everything, that is."

I ate my sandwich, looking interestedly around the cabin as if I'd never seen it before. How on earth was I going to get through the time until we could get under way again? Could he even *get* under way, after that much whiskey?

"Tell me about the *Circe*," I said brightly. "It's a beautiful boat."

"Damn right," Parker said. "Had old Willis custom make it for me. All custom, even the bunks. Softest bunks in the State o' Maine. Everybody says so. Come over here, Maude of my heart, and I'll show you how soft these bunks are."

"Parker . . ."

He got up off his bunk swiftly and came over to mine and dropped down beside me. Before I could even move his arms were around me, pinning me down, and his wet, loose mouth pressed hard over mine. His tongue probed at my teeth, and his right hand reached around under my sweater and cupped my breast.

I wrenched myself out from under him in one

motion, like a frantic snake, with strength I did not know I had. He was very heavy, and his arms were hard with muscle. I pulled my arm back as far as it would go and slapped him across the face so hard that my palm hurt badly. He stared at me, eyes narrow and unfocused, the white print of my hand livid on his face. A narrow thread of blood started down across his chin from his lip.

I picked up the heavy metal thermos.

"If you touch me again I'll hit you with this," I said.

My voice was without breath and ridiculous. My arms and legs shook badly. It was an entirely useless threat, and I knew it. He was much stronger than I, and I was trapped with him in this cabin who knew how far out on this alien white bay.

"I want you to take me home right now," I said. "If I have to lie out there with a stick for the next twelve hours I'll do it. Peter would kill you if he knew about this."

He smiled and straightened up, and I thought he was coming for me again and gripped the thermos harder, but he simply made a little salute and turned and went up the companionway.

"The lady wants to go home, home she shall go," he said. "I think you'll wish you'd stayed, though, Miss Maude. I wasn't kidding about that stick."

And he wasn't. The next few hours were the stuff of utter nightmare. I lay on my stomach on the bow of the *Circe* with a long bamboo pole tied to my wrist so that I would not drop it, making sweeps of the invisible water and air so that the pole's tip would strike any treacherous, protruding rock before the hull did. Parker had switched on the auxiliary engine, and we inched along in the blind whiteness with him at the wheel, leaning forward as far as he could to hear me if I cried out, "Stop." After thirty minutes I was wet through and shaking with chill, and my forearms ached. After two hours I was numb from cold and pain and not fully conscious. There was nothing in the world but whiteness and silence and the swish of the water as my pole sluiced through it, and the small, muffled cough of the engine. I hit rocks twice and we stopped and he steered out and around them, but Parker did not say another word to me. My universe closed down into one of cold and pain and fear. I had no sense at all of time passing. Later, Peter told me it was just past seven when we put into the dock at the yacht club.

But I never once wished we had stayed.

I was drifting, only half aware, when a muffled boom cut the thickness and a shower of colored lights arced and sizzled into the water close by. I jerked my head up and my arms, finally, gave way. The pole clattered onto the deck and slid into the water.

"What is it?" I tried to say. My voice could not get out of my raw throat.

"Fireworks from somewhere," he said casually, as if we were strolling in a park.

His voice was as clear and strong as when I had first heard it. There was no trace of whiskey slur. Hours in the cold salt air had taken care of that.

"What does it mean?"

"It means we're coming into somebody's harbor where they're waiting for us. I'd say it had to be ours."

I dropped my head into my arms on the deck and began to cry.

We heard voices then, the sound of men shouting and one or two women. There was urgency and even fear in them. I heard Peter's over the others: "Maude! Maude!"

Parker cupped his hands and shouted, "Out here! Coming in about ten yards off Cove Harbor Rock! We're okay, but hope you have blankets."

"Oh, Maude, thank God!" I heard Peter say, and all of a sudden we bumped hard into the dock and were home. As running feet began to pound down the catwalk Parker said, "You going to tell on me, Maude?"

I knew in that moment, clearly and roundly as an egg, that if I should do so, there would be those in this place who never would believe me, and others who would always wonder. I realized that I was not absolutely sure about Peter.

"No," I said. "But if you ever do it again I will."

"Your virtue is safe with me," he drawled. "It ain't worth the fuss."

When Peter's arms lifted me off the deck of the *Circe*, I was weeping with rage as well as with relief and deliverance.

When Peter had me fast in his arms, wrapped in a blanket, hurrying me, stumbling, up toward the cottage, Amy Parker came over to me and put her arms around me.

"I'm so sorry your first time out was like that," she said. "I know Parker's a great sailor and you were safe as a house, but it must have scared you to death."

"Yes," I said, my teeth chattering hard. "It did."

"I know," she said. "I hate it too. I absolutely will not go out again with Parker, and I'll bet you won't either. When you've rested I'll come over one afternoon and we'll go sketching down on the rocks. I do it often. If you'd like to, of course. Maybe you don't want to get that close to the water again."

I smiled fully and openheartedly at her. She was, with her artless chatter, absolving me of any complicity in the awful afternoon, and she was doing it in front of half of the colony.

"I'd love that," I said.

Peter was coldly and whitely furious, but it was with Parker, not me.

"Why in the name of God did you take her out?"

he shouted at his friend. "You knew there was fog coming in. It's why we didn't go; you said yourself you didn't want to get *Circe* out in that."

Parker, muffled to the eyebrows in Hudson Bay wool, looked at Peter in silence for a moment and then dropped his eyes. The effect was one of gallantry and forbearance.

"I know, I shouldn't have," he said. "But she wanted to go. . . . I could never stand a lady begging."

I took a deep breath and then exhaled. Let it go. As soon as I could be warm and in Peter's arms, nothing would matter. I was not, after all, worth a broken friendship.

But I knew that I would never be a friend to Parker Potter, nor he to me.

Mother Hannah was furious too, though she tried not to appear so, and there was no doubt that it was at me.

"It was extremely poor judgment," she said, as I lay wrapped in blankets before the fire in Liberty, shaking uncontrollably, sipping hot tea with brandy, with Peter rubbing my white chilled feet.

"I blame Parker, of course; he of all people should know better than to take you out alone, both because of the fog and the appearance of it. I shall tell Helen so, too. But Maude, I simply cannot believe you went aboard that boat without another woman present, or an older man—"

"I thought we'd just be an hour or less," I murmured. "He said he'd take me around to the boathouse where Peter was, and I thought it would be a surprise."

"Well, I'm sure it was that," she snapped. "We had the whole colony out. Big Peter called the Coast Guard; he had to call back and tell them it was a false alarm. Dr. Lincoln waited for four hours on that freezing dock in case you were injured, and him nearly seventy. Peter was beside himself. And his father and I—"

"Let up, Ma," Peter said, and his voice was cool and level. "Maude didn't know there was fog out there. That sail takes about half an hour, normally. Parker's the one who knew."

"Parker is too much a gentleman to refuse a lady when she . . . begs," my mother-in-law said. It had not, I thought miserably, taken Parker's lie long to fly up the lane from the dock.

"I doubt she begged," Peter's father said mildly from the couch.

"I didn't," I tried to say, but my sore throat closed around the words, and I felt weak tears threatening to spill. I was silent.

"Well, we'll say no more about it," Mother Hannah said. "Peter, you'd better get Maude upstairs and into a hot tub. I'll bring up a hot water bottle. Go straight to bed, Maude. I'm sorry you were frightened. I know you would not intentionally embarrass Peter . . . or his family. But you must remember that in a small place like this appearances are everything. Virtually everything."

"It would have solved everything if I'd drowned," I muttered to Peter just before he turned out the lamp and tiptoed out of the room. I was sliding swiftly into sleep, the awful shaking still at last.

"Don't even say it, baby," Peter said. "She was upset, that's all. I'm going to talk to her. She's always been stuck on appearances."

"Well, then, the appearance of me dead should gladden her heart immensely," I said, but he had gone and did not hear me. In another heartbeat I was asleep.

Mother Hannah kept me in bed the next day, though I felt fine, and Peter hung about the bedroom doing his best to entertain me, to stay at my side. He brought up the tray of chowder Christina fixed for my lunch and had his own beside me, spilling a good deal of it on the bedclothes, and finally settled down on the room's lone straight chair with a book. But the clear blue sky and the dazzling water out the window drew his eyes again and again, and finally I sent him away, saying that I thought I'd nap awhile. He kissed me gravely and tiptoed out, but his step on the stair was buoyant, and the *twang* of the screen door on the porch as he bounded out was jubilant. I knew he would head for the yacht club like a homing pigeon. I thought his anger at Parker would not last the day, with the great common chords of long friendship and the waiting sea between them, and I was right. When he came in that night, sunburn hectic on his cheekbones and nose, he said only, "Parker says to tell you he's sorry he scared you to death, and he's sure it's going to be his fault if you never set foot on a boat again. I think he means it, Maude. He was pretty contrite."

"Well, he's right about the boat," I said. "That was it for sailing and me. I hope you don't mind."

"No. Of course not. Not many women up here sail; you'd have stuck out like a sore thumb in a regatta. Oh, sometimes they crew for their husbands once or twice a summer, but it's not really a woman's thing. You'll find lots of things to do that will suit you better."

I stared at him for a moment; was this the man who had sworn we'd spend every waking moment in Retreat together? That there wasn't an inch of his summer world he was not eager to show me?

"I thought there might be some other things we could do together during the day," I said tentatively.

"Well . . . sure. We will. We'll go to Castine, and we'll go berrying, and clam digging, and over to Bar Harbor one day, and have dinner at the Astinicou Inn. I don't sail every day. Some days are just too wet or wild. Or foggy."

"Well," I said, trying to smile and thinking I had been a fool to believe he would break the ironclad tenets of this place for an outlander wife, "you can't accuse me of being a fair-weather friend. I'll love you just as much in foul weather as I would have in sunshine, and I'll see you at dinner at least."

His face fell. "I didn't think you'd mind if I sailed," he said slowly. "It's what I've always done up here. It's . . . sort of what the guys do, if they don't play tennis. Women have always seemed to like other things."

Like calling every morning on women they've seen every day of every summer of their lives? I thought, but did not say. Like putting on stockings and dresses and passing around deviled eggs and lobster sandwiches to old ladies every afternoon, while the men stand in the corner talking about sailing? Like driving a carful of blue-haired dowagers into the village or over to Castine to buy hair nets and kitchen towels and get permanents?

"I don't mind, darling," I said, feeling guilty at his crestfallen face and my own unbidden pique. Come fall he would be working like a slave for us, while I only kept a small house, and he would do so all the rest of his life. Let him have his days on the water. I would have his nights.

For the next two days Mother Hannah kept me busy with small household tasks, nothing taxing: sorting and folding the huge old double damask dinner napkins that had grown damp and creased over the winter; rinsing and polishing the ranks of blue and white Royal Copenhagen "summer" china and the breakfast Quimperware; polishing the candlesticks and bowls and flatware of heavy old English silver that had grown tarnished in the long cold months by the water.

"I really don't know why we use the damask and

silver here in the summer," she said once, fanning out a rank of twelve oyster forks. "They really are so hard to keep."

"Why do you?" I said. "I'd think pottery and pretty cotton might be better for a summer cottage."

She looked at me. Her blue linen morning frock brought out the chilly cobalt in her eyes, and I thought again what a beautiful woman she was, and how utterly unwarmed by humor or particularity. Her comment had obviously been rhetorical.

"We have always used these things in Liberty," she said. "None of the cottages have pottery and cotton. It is so easy in a summer place to let appearances slip, you know."

On my third afternoon of obedient domesticity, Amy Parker appeared at the screen door with a sketch pad and pencils. Christina led her out onto the sun porch, where Mother Hannah and I were making a list of things to be bought in Castine the next day. I nearly leaped on her and hugged her with joy and deliverance. I had begun to think her offer to take me sketching was merely polite talk, after all.

"May I borrow Maude, Mrs. Chambliss?" she said, kissing my mother-in-law lightly and dutifully on the cheek. "Parker says the weather's going to change again, and we're not going to have sketching weather for a while. I thought we'd go down to the beach just below Braebonnie. It's quiet and sheltered there."

Mother Hannah pursed her lips. "Well, I'd really thought Micah and I would show Maude about the borders and the picking garden this afternoon, and how to prune and trim. But I haven't seen Micah for days."

She looked up at Christina Willis. Christina was a short, square woman only a few years older than Amy and I, but there seemed a lifetime's difference between us. She had a pretty face, fair and serene, and thick, lovely taffy hair coiled up on her head, and her speech was that of an educated woman, though her accent was the flat nasality of Down East. The difference was more in her eyes; they looked as though they had seen a great deal, not all of it summer mornings and satiny old damask.

"Micah's been at the boatyard with his father, Mrs. Chambliss," she said. There was no apology in her voice. "Seems like everybody's wanting to get their boat in the water all at once, and Daddy Willis isn't as lively this summer as he has been. Micah said he'd be by this afternoon, but it would be late."

"Well, then, I suppose it's all right," Mother Hannah said. "It's nice of you to think of Maude, dear. She needs to know our young women. But don't stay too long, Maude; I think we're coming to your parents for cocktails tonight, aren't we, Amy?"

"Yes, ma'am," Amy said. "It's Mamadear's birthday. Hattie made lobster salad, and Parker is going to make champagne cocktails. They're her very favorites; she's so excited. And she has a new shawl Parker brought her from Hong Kong. It's really exquisite."

"Well, she *is* a wonder," Mother Hannah said. "So lively and interested, quite the undisputed queen of the colony, Maude, dear. How old is she now, Amy?"

"Ninety-six," Amy said, smiling.

"Extraordinary," Mother Hannah said, turning back to her list. Christina went back into the kitchen and I followed Amy off the porch and out into the pine-steeped crispness of the June day. It was like stepping into chilled champagne.

"Is she really ninety-six?" I said to Amy's narrow back. "That really is extraordinary."

Amy's back began to shake, and then she turned, and the lone dimple beside her wide mouth flickered and she began to laugh. It was the same sound I had heard on my first morning in Retreat, light, liquid, irresistible. I smiled.

"She is," Amy caroled, "an extraordinary pain in the ass, that's what she is. Pardon my French. Mamadear is the meanest old tyrant in the colony, and everybody knows it, including your mother-in-law. And there's simply no doubt that she's going to live forever. Meanness has preserved her like a salt mackerel."

I gave a startled gasp and then began to laugh aloud. We stood on the sunny path down to the beach below Liberty and Braebonnie, laughing so fully and helplessly that for a moment I could not get my breath. My chest pounded with joy and liberation and relief. I had been right about Amy Parker.

"I didn't think I'd ever laugh again up here," I said, when we had reached the pink ledge of rock that crowned the tiny half moon of shingle. The tide was full in and lapped hollowly in the crevasses. The entire blue bay lay before us like an indigo satin blanket, scarcely seeming to move in the dazzle of the high sun. Far out, Islesboro drifted, dreaming; beyond it the Camden Hills looked as if a Japanese brush had inked them against the sky. It was the same view I had had from Parker's boat, but this time I felt nothing but simple exaltation at its beauty and solitude. This would be mine always, this pristine, secret loveliness, this stark, pure joy. I could always come here and refill my emptiness.

"I know," Amy said, settling down on the blanket she'd brought for us and tossing her sketch pad aside. "There's precious little to laugh at in Retreat if you're young and female and you don't happen to adore counting out the grape shears once a week. You have to make your own things that tickle you. But now you're here, I don't have to go around pretending I know what all the old women look like naked dancing the Charleston. We can laugh with each other. I have a feeling we're going to do a hell of a lot of sketching."

"Suits me," I said, grinning at the image of my rock-corseted mother-in-law doing a wild naked dance. "I'm awful at sketching, anyway."

"Me too," Amy said. "It just gets me out of the house regularly. I always pretend I've got an important work in progress so I don't have to show anybody what I've been doing. I think Parker's poor mother thinks I'm getting ready for a one-woman show. She keeps talking about 'dear Amy's art.'"

"What will you do when she thinks the time has come for that?" I said.

"Lie again. Tell her I've decided I'm really not far enough along with it and need another year, at least. She won't know the difference. She's got too much on her hands with Mamadear and Parker's father."

"Is he ill?"

"Nope. Drinks like a fish. Mother Potter has to collect him off the lawn and haul him up to bed at least twice a week, and she lives in terror of what he'll do at cocktail parties. He got bounced out of the Maidstone Club for peeing in the punch bowl."

I rolled over onto my side, limp with laughter. I simply could not help it. This gentle, biddable girl, with her cloud of fine, dark hair and her piquant dimple, had a rebel heart the twin of my own and had found a way to live here on her own terms. In that instant I loved her like the sister I had never had. Then I wondered if she knew about her own Parker's drinking and stopped laughing. I thought, on the main, that she did not. She could not have been so cavalier about his father's, if she had.

"I wonder how long it's going to take me before I can handle all this as well as you," I said. "I'm never really going to be an insider here. I'm never going to be part of the young-wife-lovely-girl-happy-caretaker thing. At least you were born to that."

"Yes," she said, "but it doesn't mean I'm good at

it. I can't play tennis either. I don't give a diddly squat if Parker wins the Chowder Race or not. I couldn't care less if the silver tea service down at the clubhouse turns black as basalt. Imagine, a silver service in a one-room clapboard shack in the wilds of Maine."

She turned to me, and her face was serious.

"Two things, Maude, that you need to do. I'm not kidding, now. They'll be the saving of you here, until you're finally old enough to sit on the porch at the yacht club and boss everybody else around. Develop a chronic condition of some sort. Mine is migraines; at least once a month, and oftener if I need to, I get a migraine and go to bed and shut the door and read for three days. It's wonderful. And who's to know I don't have them? You can't see a migraine. I read up on the symptoms at the library after my first summer here. Now all I need to do is say something about an aura, and everyone packs me off to bed and leaves me strictly alone until I come out. I don't think you could get away with migraine, and I know Lolly Knox has dibs on cramps. I've been thinking, though; allergies might do for you. There's a girl at home who has them so badly to lots of things that she has to go to bed for days. You could suddenly become allergic to firs or shellfish or something."

"You mean other girls up here do that? Fake an illness to get away? Lie?"

"That's the other thing you need to learn," Amy said. "To lie like a bandit. Lie like a rug. Otherwise they'll eat you alive."

She wasn't kidding; I looked closely to see.

"I don't have any problem with that," I said finally. "Except that I can't lie to Peter, of course."

She looked at me for a moment and then looked away to the horizon. Her light brown eyes were the color of sherry, fringed with long, thick, gold-tipped lashes. She really was lovely.

"Your husband is the most important person you'll ever learn to lie to," she said.

I said nothing. I was not shocked, particularly, but I felt a heavy sadness, a kind of weariness of soul. I wished with all my heart that this ardent, generous girl did not have a husband to whom it was necessary to lie. But then, I thought, if you were married to Parker you'd undoubtedly find yourself lying without meaning to. Hadn't I already lied to protect him, on the very first day I had known him? Thank God I would never lie to Peter; I would never need to.

"Tell me about this beach," I said. "Whose house is that way up there on the point, which you can barely see through the trees? What's that little island out there called?"

"The house belongs to the Fowlers," she said. "From somewhere in Vermont, I think. It's called the Aerie. I don't know anything at all about them; they never go to any cocktail parties or anywhere else, and I don't think I've ever even seen her. She's got some kind of chronic illness for real, but I don't know what. It all sounds very mysterious and romantic. He's very protective of her; stays by her side literally all the time. They've been coming here for years and years, Parker says, and almost nobody knows them. They don't have any children, and apparently he does nothing but clip stock coupons and tend to her. I'd love to see that house; it faces its own little cove around the point that's supposed to have the best view on Cape Rosier. But I don't guess I ever will. Their property starts at the edge of our beach down there, and he's adamant about anyone setting foot on it, much less coming up to the house. Has it posted, even. He called the town South Brooksville police once when a gang of colony kids sneaked halfway up his hill."

"Are they old?" I said.

"I suppose so," she said. "At least, he looks kind of old. Thin and stooped and always a little sad. I see him sometimes at the general store, or at the market in Castine when I take Mother Potter there."

"I don't know but what I envy them," I said. "Her, especially. I'll bet she never has to count the damned damask if she doesn't want to. What about that island down there? The little one?"

She turned to follow my pointing finger, and said, "That's Osprey Head. There's been at least one osprey's nest there ever since Parker was little. He took me over and showed me, the first summer after we were married. It's right there above that—oh, God. There's a dog down there in the water."

"Oh . . . where?"

"There, just below the ledge right down below us. Oh, Lord, Maude, it's trapped in a crack and can't get out of the water, it's . . . no, it's a fawn! Oh, my God, poor little thing! Look, I think its leg is caught, it's struggling so."

I was on my feet and at the lip of the ledge in an instant. There, in the foaming white surf where the bay swept up into a narrow cleft in the lowest ledge, a small fawn struggled in the water, desperately trying to keep its drenched head out of the eddy. I could tell, from the way it was positioned, that a tiny foreleg was wedged into the rock. I did not think at all. I jumped up and stepped out of my shoes and was down the rock face and onto the lowest ledge before Amy could even scramble to her feet.

"Maude," she screamed, "come back! You'll fall; the undertow is awful there! Please come back; I'll go get somebody. . . ."

I flung myself down onto my stomach and reached as far down as I could toward the little shape. Spray stung my face and soaked my head and shoulders. It was incredibly cold, like being whipped with tiny iced lashes. I could not reach the fawn. For an instant its head came up and it looked straight into my eyes.

There was no fear in its huge brown eyes, only a kind
of terrible, intense, focused innerness. It was the will
to survive as naked and pure as I have ever seen it. I
saw the place where the miniature leg vanished in the
cleft of the rock; there was no way it could free itself. I
saw, too, that beneath it a pale shelf of rock lay flat,
like a platform, just beneath the transparent green surface. If it could only stand on that . . . or if I could. . . .

"Amy," I shouted, "go get help. Go get somebody
with a rope or something. I'm going in after it.
There's a rock I can stand on—"

"No!" she shrieked. "Don't go in there! People
drown in that cold before they even know it!"

"Go!" I screamed, and went over the ledge and
into the sea.

At first it was like plunging into fire. My skin
burned with it. And then the cold hit, and breath left
me, and I clung there rib deep, thinking I would
never get another breath, would die of suffocation
before drowning was even possible. And then the
fawn gave a tiny, despairing bleat and I clung to the
ledge and reached out my hand for it and touched it.
It scrambled and thrashed in terror at my touch, so
tiny that I could feel each birdlike rib, and the little
triphammer beating of its heart. It must be incredibly
tired. . . . I edged farther along the ledge toward it,
and finally found secure footholds against the dragging tide and reached out and put my hand beneath
its belly, so that it was borne up on my palm. Instantly, with a kind of shuddering sigh, it stopped its
struggling and slumped against my hand. Its breathing was ragged and deep, almost a pant. It could not
possibly have kept afloat much longer.

I tried to find the point where its leg entered the
crevice, but my other hand was so numb with cold
that I could feel nothing at all. Then I realized I could
not feel my feet, either. And it was becoming hard to

breathe. How long had I heard that a person could live in extremely cold water? Not long . . . it suddenly occurred to me that I truly might die if I did not get out of that water. And that I could not get out unless I let go of the fawn. And then, that perhaps I could not get out even if I did. With all feeling gone, I did not know where my toe and handholds were. I had no recourse but to cling to the ledge and the fawn and pray that Amy brought help fast. I could no longer hear her retreating cries.

Oddly, I do not remember being frightened. Not nearly so frightened, at any rate, as I had been earlier that week, on Parker's boat. I can remember whispering Peter's name, over and over, and saying to the fawn once or twice, "I'm here. I'm not going to let you go," and seeing it look back and up at me before its head dropped again. I remember thinking that I had always rather thought somehow that I would lie one day beside my mother in Saint Michael's churchyard, and that if I drowned off this lonely cape they might never find me at all. And a little later, I remember thinking that I was not cold at all any more, and that since I wasn't, this wasn't so bad and I could hang on indefinitely.

"We're going to be fine," I whispered to the fawn. It was probably the last thing I would have said to anyone.

I was very nearly unconscious when I felt hard, strong arms under my arms from above and heard a deep, nasal voice that was not Peter's saying, "Just a minute now. Hang on, dear. Just a minute more."

"Take the fawn," I whispered through numb lips. "Take the fawn. . . ."

"I've got it," the voice said, and the weight lifted off my hand, and in a moment more the arms pulled me straight up out of that killing cold and onto the top of the rock ledge. A heavy blanket went around me, though I could not feel warmth or anything else. Blackness flickered at the edges of my closed eyelids, and I knew it was going to take me down. I felt myself being swung up into someone's arms and held hard against a wide chest. Whoever held me set off with me at a run.

"Get the fawn," I whispered, trying to pound my fists against the chest. "Go back and get the fawn."

"I'll come back for it," he said. "It's all right; I've covered it up. I know what to do for it."

"Thank you," I managed, and let go, and the blackness took me under. From far above, as if on the surface of dark water, I could hear Amy Potter crying.

When I woke up for good and all, it was a day and a half later, and I was lying in the big bed in Peter's parents' room, weighted down with quilts and blankets, a hot water bottle at my feet. Peter stood at the foot of the bed, his face tired and white, his gray eyes puffed with fatigue. My mother-in-law sat by the fire that roared on the hearth, despite the thick heat in the room. Her spine was straight as a birch tree, and her face was white and set. Her lips were a thin sunless line of disapproval.

Peter hugged me and kissed me and said he was going down to bring the hot broth Christina had made up to me.

"Dr. Lincoln said for you to have it once every three hours," he said, trying to smile. "And he said a little shot of whiskey in it wouldn't hurt, either. For you *and* me."

He went out of the room. His mother and I looked at each other.

"Did I have the doctor?" I said weakly. My chest ached as if I had been hit there, hard. My voice was rasping and frail.

"Four times," she said levelly. "Including the middle of the night. Not to mention the minister, and every woman in the colony over the age of ten, with flowers and food and notes of sympathy. And Peter, who has not slept at all. And Amy Potter, who has slept only a little more. And, of course, myself."

"I'm—I'm sorry. . . ."

"You should be, Maude. You should be quite, quite sorry. You have caused everyone no end of worry, and of course you were very nearly killed. I wonder what it is going to take to keep you away from that sea."

"I won't go near it again."

"We all hope that is true. For our sakes as well as your own. Not to mention that of Micah Willis, who could easily have lost his own life trying to save yours."

"Micah Willis," I mumbled stupidly.

"Christina's husband. He'd just come in from the boathouse when he heard Amy screaming. You would be dead now if he had not. We owe him more than we can ever repay, of course."

I lay there, as miserable as I have ever been, will ever be again. She was right. Of course, she was right. There was nothing for me in that cold sea. That sea was nothing to me but the author of grief.

"Oh," I said. "The fawn . . . what about the fawn?"

"The miserable little creature is dead," Mother Hannah said coldly. "Its leg was broken. It couldn't have been saved no matter what you did. Micah went back down and shot it."

Chapter Four

For the next five days Dr. Lincoln and Mother Hannah conspired to keep me in bed, or at least sequestered on the sun-porch chaise, covered with quilts and throws and the omnipresent Hudson Bay blankets, and for once I was glad of the cover, if not the incarceration. One of the cape's notorious five-day fogs came ghosting in on the night of the incident with the fawn and held Retreat fast in its cottony manacles for nearly a week. Without the sun, the cottage stayed damp and cold all day, and I would have been grateful to stay in my bed upstairs, where a fire could be lit. But Mother Hannah put paid to that notion.

"With the fog and nobody being able to get out on the water, everyone will be calling on you," she said. "You can't get up yet, and this is the only faintly proper place I can think to put you where the men can visit. If it were only the women, I'd just bring them on up to you or put you in our bedroom. Of course, by rights this should be the week we called on them. Your little swim has upset more than a few applecarts, dear Maude."

"Well, Ma, you can't blame Maude for the fog, at

least," Peter put in cheerfully from the old Windsor chair at my side. He too was fogbound and seemed content to loll beside me in a heavy sweater, eating apples and reading course literature for his first classes in the fall.

"I don't blame Maude for anything, of course," Mother Hannah said, putting plates of Christina's warm doughnuts about the living room and sun porch. "I only point out that not many new brides have the entire colony come to them instead of the other way around. I can't recall its ever happening."

"Time it did, then," said Peter, snagging a doughnut. "Start a new tradition."

"Leave the doughnuts alone, Peter, please," his mother said crisply. "I don't want Tina to have to make more this morning. She's got her hands full with the laundry; it will never dry in this mess."

"There are enough doughnuts there to feed the entire county," Peter said lazily. "Who do you think is going to come out in this fog to eat them?"

"Everybody, of course," Mother Hannah said, and went into her bedroom to put on a suitable morning frock.

And they did. By ten-thirty the sun porch was full of the Retreaters who were in residence, muffled in sweaters and scarves and, in the case of the old ladies, hatted and gloved, sipping coffee and tea and munching Christina's delicate doughnuts with relish. Wrapped in a bright Spanish shawl of Mother Hannah's that she said had always overpowered her but suited my baroque coloring perfectly, I lay under layers of damp wool and shook hands and had my hot cheek kissed and murmured that I was perfectly fine and they were so kind to call until my head swam and I could remember no names and few faces. I had met all of them, I knew, in the dining hall on the night of my arrival, but it seemed to me that ages—eons—had passed since then. But of course it had scarcely been a week.

The occupants of Braebonnie came first, en masse, led by Parker's towering father, Philip, red-haired like his son and similarly boyish of face but altogether larger in scale and without Parker's compensatory slyness. Philip Potter was a mastodon of a man. He roared his greeting at me, thumped Peter on the back, grinned and kissed Mother Hannah on the cheek when she turned her head hastily to avoid being kissed on the lips, and stumped off in search of Big Peter and a glass of something decent for a foggy day.

"Don't have to wait for the yardarm when you can't see the damned thing," he shouted, and I heard, presently, the clink of the decanter that Peter's father kept on the desk in the little room behind the living room that served as his study, and men's voices mingled in the patterns of long familiarity. Parker, who came next with his timid, sparrowlike mother, Helen, kissed me on the forehead and whispered that I looked like a Cuban doxy in that shawl and vanished in search of his father and the decanter. Peter looked after him but stayed valiantly at my side to present his bride to his childhood friends and neighbors. I thought that in the close, chilly little sun porch, with only a yellow lamp for light and thick white fog pressing close against the small-paned windows, he was like a fire on an open hearth. People clustered around him as if for actual warmth. Men pounded him on the back and shook his hand in obvious liking; old ladies simpered; young women smiled widely and held his hand for perhaps a beat longer than I liked. I wondered, suddenly and for the first time, if any of them there that morning had hoped to be in my place one day. It seemed more than likely.

Amy came last, with Mamadear tottering fiercely on her arm. The old woman looked like a malevolent baby, muffled to the tips of her ears and chin with shawls and sweaters. She wore on her head, astonishingly, a sailor's watch cap, or what looked like one, rolled down until it sat atop her falcon's eyebrows, giving her the look, Peter whispered, of one of those coconut heads you get in Miami, carved to look like a pirate. Her eyes glared out from between strata of wool, yellow as an owl's.

"All she needs is a dagger in her teeth," Peter said. He said this aloud, to Amy, and I gasped in horror until I realized that Mamadear was deaf as a post, especially when swathed in wool. Amy grinned at Peter and kissed me.

"Forget the dagger," Amy said. "Her teeth are all she needs. The better to eat you with, my dear."

"What?" shouted Mamadear. "What are you whispering about, Amy? I can't stand it when you whisper; you do it all the time. I shall tell Parker."

"We're saying what a becoming cap you're wearing, Mrs. Potter," Peter said loudly, taking her savage little talons in his hands and smiling into her face. Incredibly, she stopped scowling and grinned back, an arch, terrible caricature of a flirtatious smile.

"Go on with you, Peter Chambliss," she shrilled. "I'm wise to your ways. Got them from your grandfather. Step back, now, and let me have a look at this wife of yours. Did somebody tell me she came from Egypt?"

"Charleston, Mrs. Potter," Peter said, his mouth trembling with laughter. Mine, too, quivered as I put up my hand to the old lady. Amy flushed brick red and turned away. Mamadear leaned over and peered into my face.

"Gussie Stallings said nigger," she said. "You certainly don't look it to me. Gussie never could tell the truth to save her life. But you surely aren't one of us, are you? Are you a Jew? Surely, Peter, you wouldn't bring a Jew here."

"Come on, Mamadear," Amy said, giving the old woman's arm a sharp jerk. Her face had gone from the pink of mirth to the white of anger. "Let's get some doughnuts down your craw. Shut you up for a minute, at least. I'm sorry, Maude. She yelled until Papa Philip said to bring her, and of course that meant me. . . . I'd say she didn't know what she was saying, but she does. So I'll just apologize for all of us, and you won't have to bother with her again."

"What are you saying?" the old woman shouted.

"I'm saying it's time to have some tea!" Amy shouted back.

"Is this the one that stayed out with Parker all night on the boat? That Micah Willis brought in wet as a drowned rat with no clothes on, carrying her right up in his arms?"

"Come *on,* Mamadear!" Amy dragged her grandmother-in-law away. The old voice floated back to Peter and me.

"She doesn't look like the kind of girl a Chambliss would marry, does she? Lying up there on that chaise, as la-di-da as a horse. I always thought he'd marry Gretchen Constable. Hannah always favored Gretchen. . . ."

I looked at Peter. His face was thunderous. I laughed. He grinned then, too.

"Gretchen Constable?" I said.

"One of the girls who grew up here summers. Married Burden Winslow the day he graduated from Princeton, just like they'd planned since they were thirteen. We were never anything more than friends, and that old harridan knows it as well as anybody up here. Mama never had any such ideas about her that I know about. Gretch is older and *lots* richer. God, somebody ought to throttle old women when they hit eighty; it's when the Cute Old Lady syndrome sets in. You know, where you can just say anything awful you think of, and do any damned spiteful thing you feel like, and people are supposed to say how you're so feisty and full of life. Or maybe it's just up here that it happens. Something in the water. I don't see how Parker stands it."

"I don't think he does," I said acidly. "I think it's Amy and Parker's mother who stand it. Mostly Amy, from what I can see. I don't imagine Parker and his father have had anything to do with her in years."

He gave me an odd look out of his long gray eyes and then turned to greet the next arrivals Mother Hannah was shepherding onto the sun porch. I sighed. It seemed to me that she was leading in a small army of people, and at their head stumped my first foe in Retreat, the redoubtable Augusta Stallings.

"Jesus," muttered Peter under his breath. "It's Stallings, Inc., with Grendel's Mother at the fore." He raised his voice. "Good morning, Mrs. Stallings. It's a lovely morning for ducks, isn't it?"

Augusta Stallings ignored him and came to peer down at me as Mamadear had done. I smiled tightly up at her, vowing silently that if I ever got to my feet no old lady in Retreat was ever going to be able to look down on me again. It was definitely a position of weakness.

"Well, my girl, not a week here and you've put the colony on its ear twice," she said. "Looks like you southern girls just can't stay out of the water. I was telling Hannah that we won't need to have concerts or musicales this summer; we can just put you in the water and watch the fireworks."

"They were accidents, Mrs. Stallings," Peter said levelly, and I knew that he was finally angry. "You know, like when you fell out of the chair here the other night? Just accidents. I know Maude regrets them as much as you do."

She rounded on him to say something, but one of the younger women who had come in with her took her arm and murmured, "Mama Gussie, did you fall and not tell us? What are we going to do with you?" And one of the men said, "Mama, you promised you wouldn't go visiting without one of the girls along."

I looked at them all. There were, besides old Augusta Stallings, four middle-aged men and four slightly younger women, and at first glance they seemed as identical to me as buckshot. The men were round and soft and short, like their mother, and had wet-looking black hair and hooded hazel eyes and full pink mouths, and the women looked remarkably like them except that their mouths were thinner and paler and their eyes more shadowed, as if with fatigue. All eight had a high color in their cheeks, and all wore prim, too-tight clothes under their sweaters, and all talked in the same loud, uninflected tones as Augusta Stallings, and all their conversation was of themselves: their cottages, their children, their servants, their boats, their activities back in Providence over the past winter, the state of their health. When old Augusta led them off toward the doughnuts and coffee, still talking at full bore among themselves about themselves, I turned to Peter and said, "I will never on this earth keep them straight. Except that they're all Stallingses, aren't they?"

"How could they be anything else?" he said, amusement and annoyance in his voice. "The Stallingses are our collective punishment for defrauding the natives of their land. They've been here since day one, and if nothing else they have heeded the Lord's dictum, 'Go forth and multiply.' They have God's own amount of money from the old grandfather's patent medicine, which I gather cured an entire nation of its hemorrhoids or something else unspeakable before it merged with Bayer, and since then they've never lifted a finger. Oh, the boys—that's Albert and John and George and Henry, whom you just met—sit on the board and go to offices back in Providence, but nobody pays any attention to them there. Here either, for that matter, but they never notice, since they stick together so and hardly ever mingle with the rest of us. For which we give silent thanks every day. They're duller than dishwater and dimmer than unlit bulbs, but they're too arrogant to realize it. They drive everybody nuts, but I think the only real harm they're capable of is voting in a bloc at the yacht club. As many of them as there are, they could turn us into a skating rink if they wanted to. Fortunately, they all live together, so you'll know how to avoid them, anyway."

"All together in one cottage?" I said incredulously. "It must be the biggest one in Maine."

"Well, the big house is, practically," Peter grinned in enjoyment. "It's enormous. 'Utopia,' the old man named it. Thirty rooms, I'm told. But old Gussie lives there by herself. Won't let any of the boys or her daughters-in-law or her thousands of grandchildren spend the night under the ancestral roof. The boys all have identical smaller cottages on the shore down from Braebonnie toward the club, clustered around the big one like baby pigs around a sow. And they and their ever-swelling broods are jammed in there just waiting for the old bat to kick off. There's going to be a fight for that big house when she does that will put the Civil War to shame when it comes to brother against brother."

"And these are the people whom the soul selects as her own society and shuts the door?" I said. "These are the plain-living high-minded people for whom Retreat, according to your mother, is famous?"

"To mother, the Stallingses are the horrible exception that proves the rule," he said. "And to give us our due, I don't think you'll find anybody else precisely like them here. The Winslows and the Conants may not be exactly plain-living, but they're about a million times higher-minded than Stallings *mère et fils,* which may not be saying a lot."

Dr. Lincoln and his wife came in then, and I smiled in genuine pleasure to see him. His had been a consistently kind face and voice to me during the past week, and I had found nothing but succor at his cool, gentle hands. He leaned over me as he had done many times already before, holding my hands in his, his long index finger automatically finding my pulse, and smiled his vague, sweet smile. Though I knew that he was near seventy, he looked nearer fifty, thin and erect, with a full head of only slightly graying dark hair and mild blue eyes with the soft cloudiness of myopia in them.

"I see our little mermaid is much recovered," he said, and I remembered through the fog of the past few days that his speech was gentle, formal, and nearly archaic, and his entire demeanor absolutely correct, if softened by a kind of otherworldliness. I had heard from Peter that he was a distinguished physician on staff at a number of fine Boston area hospitals, retired now; a classical musician of some note; father to three seemingly interchangeable pale aesthetes known in Retreat simply as "the boys"; and totally devoted to his piquant small wife, Mary. She stood beside him this morning, petite and very pretty and as seemingly untouched at sixty-odd years as a child or a doll, her porcelain face sweet and unlined.

"We've worried about you a great deal, dear," she said in a soft silver treble. "Such a terrible introduction to this lovely place. I was afraid you'd be quite put off. But Ridley said he thought you were made of sterner stuff, and I can see that he's right, as usual. You're looking very well and pretty. A fine choice, Peter."

"Thank you," Peter and I said together, and laughed. Dr. Lincoln straightened up and turned to his wife.

"Are you all right, my dear?" he said, and, to us,

"Mary is having trouble with her back this summer. We're sleeping on a board."

I bit back laughter and saw Peter do the same.

"I do hope it isn't serious," I said.

"Oh, no," Mary Lincoln said. "I think it's just the fog and damp. I do so look forward to July. Well, Maude dear, you must come over to Land's End and see us when Ridley says you can get up. I make a lovely lemon sponge on Tuesdays. And I'd love to see a bright young face in that dark old barn; the house belonged to his grandfather, and Ridley won't let me change a single thing. I'd have let some light in long ago, I can tell you. I think the dark and damp is one reason the boys don't come oftener."

"The reason they don't come oftener, dear heart, is that they all have jobs," her husband said fondly, with the air of one saying something he has said many times before.

"Oh, toot," she said blithely. "They could come if they wanted to."

The doctor rolled his eyes comically to heaven and led her back into the living room. I squared my shoulders and looked at Peter.

"They're all going to remember me as the girl who fell into the bay twice in one week and may be a darky to boot," I said. "But there's no way on earth I'm going to be able to remember all of *them*. You're going to have to help me."

"You're doing fine," he said. "Don't worry. I won't leave your side. And I'll fill you in on everybody; you'll have all summer to get them straight. Nobody expects you to remember so many people at once."

It was a good thing. Looking back, I cannot quite separate the ones I met that morning from those who came later that June, but of the stream of faces that emerged out of that first fog I recall especially Guildford and Dierdre Kennedy from Corpore Mens Sanos

(Camp Corpy) around the point, Philadelphians both, he a professor at Hamilton College, she a former suffragette, and their three daughters named, astoundingly, Clio, Thalia, and Calliope.

"They're eccentric as hell and terrifyingly athletic," Peter said later. "They do all manner of good works here and at home, are relentlessly hearty *and* hardy—I hear she swims naked in the open bay every morning, two miles exactly—and they're one-worlders with a vengeance. Dress up in some kind of international dress once a month and have a ghastly dinner party and serve the food of each chosen nation. I happened onto Japan last year and got, as God is my witness, squid and seaweed. They named the girls for the Muses, of course, but in poor Callie's case I think Calliope is a fair description. She sings at the musicales and sounds just like a merry-go-round whistle. And talk about high-minded: when you go there for bridge, he bids in Greek and she replies in Latin. It's a pain in the ass, but they're good sorts, really."

Next came the Valentine girls, two old maid sisters who lived in a vine-shrouded, falling-down cottage in the grove behind the dining hall, near the Compound, called Petit Trianon. One look told me that the Misses Charlotte and Isabelle Valentine from Baltimore, genteelly rich from their piratical papa's railroad fortune, were the two old ladies I had outraged with my coral satin on the morning after my arrival. The same white-gloved fingers raised the same lorgnettes, and the same old lips puckered into well-worn grooves of disapproval, and the same raptor's eyes took my measure as they had that morning. They had faint, exhausted southern voices and skin like finely wrinkled silk velvet, and smelt powerfully of some kind of jasmine bath powder.

"So sorry to hear of your misfortunes," Miss Isabelle (I thought) drawled.

"We've never been in that dreadful ocean our-selves," said Miss Charlotte . . . or, at least, the other one. "Papa always said bathing in northern water was too great a shock to the female system. Though he swam himself, every day, from the yacht club deck, didn't he, Sissy?"

"Not at all," Sissy said tartly. "Papa never went into the water here. That was at Rehoboth; you've forgot-ten again."

"Well, I have not."

"Yes, you have. You always do—"

Mother Hannah came in just then and lured them inside with promises of tea, and they marched away behind her, still in lockstep, still arguing.

"They'll be at it all day," Peter said. "It's what they come to Retreat for. I hear they never fight at home. I think it probably keeps them alive. Everybody goes nuts with it until they learn not to listen. They're like the Ancient Mariner; people run when they see them coming. I've seen grown men cut through the birch woods off the main road and sneak by on their hands and knees, rather than meet the Valentine girls head on. They visit around endlessly, and they gossip incessant-ly, and they're always getting themselves into some kind of mess, or breaking something, or losing it, and then somebody has to go bail them out and listen to them peck at each other all the while. They drive the Compound women wild. You're going to be their main target this summer, just because you're new. Don't let them monopolize you, or you'll spend the whole sum-mer taking them places and fixing things for them, instead of . . . whatever else you wanted to do."

Instead of running errands for my mother, I thought he was going to say. But perhaps, after all, he wasn't.

Next came three young women alone, slightly out of breath and with hair and clothes pearled with fog droplets and what looked like cereal. Two were the tall, fair, long-boned New Englanders I was growing accustomed to, and the other was dark and a bit overweight, but somehow they had a familial look to them.

"Ah," Peter said. "The Mary's Garden girls. Come and meet my wife, Maude. She is going to have need of the likes of you this summer."

"Hello," three crisp New England voices said in unison. Three tanned, capable hands shook mine firmly, and I felt, along each one, the ridge of callus on the outside of the palm that speaks of tennis rackets. Kemble had it. My own hand, with the nails I'd struggled so long to grow painted a delicate pink, felt puffy and effete in those serviceable hands.

"Priss Thorne, Jane Thorne, and Fern Thorne," Peter said. "Married, respectively, to Tobias, Clovis, and Phinizy Thorne. They live on the strip of beach just below Braebonnie; you can't even see 'em from the cliff top. They're here all summer with the children, and the guys come up from Washington in August. I don't know what anybody in Retreat would do without the Thorne girls. Whenever you need anything, from a tennis game to a pressure bandage to somebody to fetch bath salts for the Valentine sisters, you just stop by Mary's Garden and see who's there. They're the glue that holds us together."

"We're always glad to help out," Priss Thorne said. Her face was tanned like glove leather, and her hair was the straw blond of one who spends many hours in the sun. She had very blue eyes that crinkled attractively at the corners, and the long sculptured muscles of a young boy.

"If you ever need us and can't raise us at the Garden, just post a note on the tennis court bulletin board," Jane said. She was the other fair one, with strong, mannish features and hair cut in a straight bob around her long face.

"Do you play tennis?" said the one who, by default, must be Fern. She was square and resolute, really not at all pretty, and deeply tanned like the others. "We'd be glad of a decent partner. We can't seem to get any other of the younger women up here interested."

"I'm afraid I don't," I said, thinking they probably couldn't interest the other young women because they were too busy being handmaidens. How did these three manage enough free time for daily tennis? I had not yet met a young woman in Retreat who did not have an older woman attached.

"Well, we'll be glad to show you," Priss said. "I'll bet we could make a player out of you in one summer."

"I'll take you up on it," I said, sensing an activity that might spring me from Liberty periodically.

"We'll check back when you're feeling better," Jane Thorne said. "That water can be ferocious if you're not used to it."

Her tone was that of one who swam hours in that liquid ice. I felt cosseted and fussy, and hated it.

"Why aren't they at home taking care of Mommy-in-Law?" I said nastily to Peter. I was growing tired and wanted the stream of visitors to abate. But it showed no signs of doing so.

He laughed. "Because Mommy-in-Law cut out of here the minute old man Thorne died and deeded the Garden over to the boys and bought a place in Palm Beach. She always did hate cold water."

"So now the poor girls get to come up here every summer and mind children and take care of everybody else's mothers-in-law and all the widows, and the guys come in August and get waited on like kings," I said, seeing the shape of it all too clearly. When he did not reply, I said, "Sorry. I'm tired. Why is it called Mary's Garden?"

"Well, there are three cottages, all alike, side by side. The old man built them. He was a children's book illustrator, a funny, fussy little man, and there's a lot of family money, I think. He named the cottages Silver Bell, Cockle Shell, and Pretty Maid. You know, as in 'Mary, Mary, quite contrary, how does your garden grow?' Mary was their mother's name. But everybody just calls it Mary's Garden. How would you like to tell people you lived in Cockle Shell or Pretty Maid? They're three of the few cottages that have telephones. The boys had them put in the first summer the girls came alone with the children. Everybody goes over there to call. The girls really are the heart and soul of this place. They'll make good friends for you. Show you the ropes."

I doubted that but did not say so. I was watching a woman watch Peter. I did not particularly like what I saw.

She was a beauty. She always was. Gretchen Constable Winslow was one of the few Retreat women I knew when we were young who was truly a great beauty and kept her looks far into old age. Hers were the kind of looks born of perfect bones and teeth and a fortunate symmetry of all her parts; nothing about Gretchen did not match, or was out of scale or proportion, or failed to please. I don't think I have ever seen such clearly genetic loveliness. Most beauty depends in some part on animation or coloring or expression. Gretchen's never did; she had little of any of those. If you carved her in marble she would still look exactly as she did that morning standing living and real in the door of the sun porch in Liberty, staring at my husband with eyes that were the pale green of sunlight on marsh water.

He felt her gaze and looked up.

"Hello, Gretchen," he said, and smiled, and the woman came over and kissed his cheek lightly, and laid her hand along the other one for a moment before turning to me and giving me a small, polite smile. Her lips, cheeks, chin, and the dimples on either side of her mouth looked as if they had been chiseled there by a loving sculptor.

"I'm Gretchen Winslow, a very old friend of Peter's," she said, and her voice was cool and smooth, not New England but not anything else I could name, either. Like her face and hair and body, it had little color. Gretchen's hair was the pale gold-brown of sun-steeped tea, and her skin was only a few shades lighter. It was like looking at a woman created entirely out of warm, honey-toned Carrera marble.

"I'm Maude Gascoigne," I said mindlessly, and then added, I mean "Maude Chambliss, of course."

"Of course," she said. "We were all very surprised to hear about you. Peter never let on last summer."

"I didn't know her last summer," Peter said, smiling still. He still held her hand in his. "I only met her in November."

"And up and married her so soon," Gretchen said, laughing lightly. "Do you by chance have some news for us, Maude?"

"News?" I said, and then understood. "Oh. No. Of course not. At least, I don't think so. . . ."

Gretchen Winslow always could make me stammer.

"Well, soon, I'll just bet," she said, and dismissed me with her eyes and went back to Peter. "Listen, darling, I can't stay; that silly Nola didn't show up this morning, and the children are alone in the cottage. Burdie took his mother and father and Erica Conant over to the Sternhagens' house party in Northeast Harbor yesterday and can't get the boat back out of the harbor. Not that he's tried. So I'm all by myself with the wee ones until at least tomorrow. I know it's unpardonable gall, but I wonder if I could borrow you for a few minutes this afternoon or evening? Little

Freddie put his turtle in the toilet, and it sounds as though it's done something to the pump, and you know how I am about those things. . . . Maude, my dear, you wouldn't mind, would you? I'll send him home immediately with some of my toll house cookies. He used to love them."

"I don't mind at all," I said, hating her. Even if she had not been beautiful and arrogant and insinuatingly familiar with my husband, I would have hated her. It was as purely a chemical thing as I have ever felt, that first flare of enmity toward Gretchen Winslow. I knew she felt it too. You could see it in the chameleon-green eyes. If you looked at her closely you could tell that she was a good five or six years older than Peter. I thought, spitefully, that she was probably much nearer thirty than she wished to be thought.

"Then I'll see you later, Peter?" she said.

"Yeah . . . sure."

" 'Bye, then, sweetie. 'Bye for now, Maude. I'm sure I'll be seeing lots and lots of you."

"Depend on it," I said to her retreating back between clenched teeth.

"Listen, Maude," Peter began, but the last guest of the morning came up and gave him a sharp poke in the ribs, and he turned and caught her up and swung her around, laughing with pleasure. This time I laughed too.

She was very small, almost a midget, I suppose, and nearly perfectly round, and she looked as if she had been clothed by standing still in a room while people hurled cast-off garments at her. I never saw such an untidy woman. Nothing matched; everything trailed. Peter put her back down and I realized that I had seldom seen such a fat one either, at least for her height. Her flesh hung in pink folds and quivered and lapped and surged when she moved. Oddly, it was not, as it might have been, repulsive. Her smile was so open and delighted, and her laugh so young and free, and her blue eyes shone so, that nothing else about her, even the unmistakable traces of breakfast egg on her shawl, made any difference at all. I found myself wanting to reach out and touch her, as you would a pretty baby or a winsome pet.

"I'm Carlotta Padgett. Lottie," she said to me, and then I realized she was quite old but did not seem so because of the stretched, shiny pink skin. "I know you're Maude, and I wanted to come and tell you how glad we are to have you in Retreat. And my dear, how sorry I am about the fawn, too. It was a very brave thing you did, and I hope this nice boy is proud of you."

She looked at Peter.

"Yes," he said, startled. "I *am* proud of her."

"Then you tell her so. I'll bet you haven't," Lottie Padgett said. "And it's a sure thing that nobody else is going to. Listen, you pretty child, when they let you up off that silly chaise you come down to the Little House—that's what it's called—across the cove down there just under the Aerie, and let me get to know you. The kettle's always on, and there're always kittens and a puppy or two, and right now there's a baby raccoon I'm trying to raise. Some idiot shot its mother; I found it when I was picking mushrooms over on Osprey Head the other day. You are from the river swamps, I hear, and I'm from the piney woods, and I know a fellow animal lover and a wild heart when I see one. You come, now. There's lots I can tell you about Retreat that you need to know."

And before we could answer she was gone in a scuttle of skirts and a flip of draperies, trailing the thick scent of mothballs. Several people tried to stop her for conversation, and Peter's mother waylaid her in the door with doughnuts and coffee, but she waved them aside, shouted something over her shoulder cheerfully, and was gone out into the fog with a thud of the front door before I could draw a deep breath.

I looked at Peter. He was grinning after her.

"Did I dream that?" I said.

"No. She's the realest woman I know," he said. "Well, well. Lottie Padgett came to see you. You have been singly honored. Do you know, Maude, I don't think she's been in this house or many others in all the years I've been coming to Retreat? She lives down there on the shore in that little wreck of a house like a hermit, and talks mainly to the animals, and picks mushrooms and berries and stuff, and takes in strays and hurt birds and whatever, and nobody over the age of sixteen is ever invited in. But under that . . . God, her house is full of kids from dawn to dusk, all summer long. She's an absolute Pied Piper. I just flat loved her when I was growing up."

"Is she terribly poor?" I said.

"God, no. She's terribly rich. Her husband inherited oil wells, plural, in Oklahoma, which is where they were born, and brought her up here to visit a college friend—I think it might have been Sykes Conant, when he and Erica were first married—and she fell in love with the cape and the woods and made him build her that little doll's house down there. They had one son, the feckless Frankie, who is, I think, an Episcopal minister somewhere in California now. He was always ashamed of his mother. A real shit heel, was Frankie. He never married; I think he was, as they say in England, a bit of a poof. I don't think he's been up here since he left divinity school. Claude died about fifteen years ago. Except that she promptly gave a pile of money to start an animal shelter for the county over in Castine, I don't think Lottie has changed anything since she first came here. I know she's never bought any new clothes or furniture for the house. It looks like an animal pen. Which, for all practical purposes, it is."

"Do you still visit her?"

"I still do. Don't tell on me, though. She usually cuts you off when you reach sixteen."

"Well," I said, "I'd like to go. I liked her a lot. She's the only one who seems to care about that poor little fawn."

"I cared about it," he said gravely. "Do you think it pleased me that Micah had to shoot it? I was just so worried about you I forgot to say anything about it. You should go and see her; her friendship is a great honor. Only I wouldn't let Mother know, if I were you. She thinks Lottie is unsanitary, and crazy to boot."

"And do you?"

"Oh, yeah, no doubt about it. Both those things. But I love her for things other than her hygiene and her mental health. She has the gift of a purely loving heart. Sometimes I think that's a pretty rare thing in Retreat."

I looked at him in surprise. He smiled uncomfortably.

"I love this place," he said. "It's everything I ever knew of freedom and childhood and wildness. But it's a very small place. And its focus is very narrow. It's like a microscope: if you aren't careful, it can catch light from the sun and burn you. I'd be a fool not to know that."

"Peter, don't let it burn me," I said impulsively.

"Stick with me, lady," he said out of the corner of his mouth. "I'll see ya git home safe."

Soon after the last guest left I was upstairs in bed, deep under Princeton and Hudson Bay, fighting sleep. Peter fiddled restlessly about the room, staring out at the fog.

"You think you'll sleep?" he said. "You should; that siege must have exhausted you. I think I'll go over to Willis's and see if Old Micah's got his winch fixed yet. I'll be back before you wake up."

"Why don't you?" I said drowsily. "And are you going to go over to Gretchen Winslow's?"

He looked back over his shoulder at me. The strange, pearly fog light washed his fair hair to silver and put metallic planes on his high cheekbones. I really loved looking at Peter.

"Would you mind? It's bad business to be up here with no plumbing and two small children. I ought to see if I can get the turtle out, anyway."

"She usually gets what she wants, doesn't she?" I said, disliking my own tone.

He chuckled. "Winslows usually do. Been here longer than anybody but the Indians and some of the natives. Gretch's forebears came from Massachusetts around sixteen hundred something. She's one of the few colony women who has long ties on both sides. Sometimes she pulls rank a little. I won't go if you don't want me to."

"No," I said, burying my face in the pillow. "You do what you want to. I'm not going to start ordering you around, too."

I waited to see what he would say, but he said nothing, and I was asleep before he left the room. When I woke, the lamps were lit and the white fog had turned to black, and Mother Hannah was just coming into the room with a supper tray for me. Peter was behind her, his hair still wet with fog droplets, curling around his face. On the tray, beside the inevitable hot medicinal chowder and the rolls and butter, was a small plate of fresh toll house cookies.

"Did you find the turtle?" I said to Peter. He looked blank, and then said, "Oh. No. I didn't go over there. I stopped at Micah and Tina's and asked Micah to go. I couldn't have done anything about the damned turtle if I'd found it anyway."

Mother Hannah looked sharply at him. "You didn't go over to Gretchen's, after she asked you to? Really,

Peter. You can't just send a strange man into the home of a young woman alone; what on earth must she think of you? I thought you'd brought the cookies. I found them on the table."

"I guess she brought them over herself," Peter said, taking one and biting into it. "Hmmm. A mite dry. Gretch is losing her touch. Relax, Ma. Micah Willis is hardly a stranger. And he's been fixing colony crappers since he was sixteen; you know that. I'd have been a waste of time; she'd have had to get Micah in the end, anyway."

"You know what I mean," Mother Hannah said crisply, and turned and left the room. We both looked after her.

"I do, if you don't," I said, grinning. He grinned back.

"Well, you know. I think Ma always thought there might be something between Gretch and me. More of a merger than a relationship, I guess. The Winslows are stinking rich, and older than the Chamblisses by half a century. And they've always pretty much run the colony. Ma would love a crack at that. Freddie Winslow inherited the family merchant bank in Manhattan, and Burdie, Gretch's husband, will inherit it in turn."

"Your family has one of its own," I said. "Why does she care about theirs?"

"Well," he said, leaning over and unbuttoning the top button of my nightgown, "their bank is bigger than our bank. Feeling pretty good, aren't we?"

"What'll you give me to find out?" I said, drawing his damp head down to my breast. "But you know, I'm a little surprised that your mother cares about bettering her social position. That's not exactly high-minded. Ouch, Peter. That hurts."

He climbed into bed with me and drew the covers up over both our heads.

"She doesn't think of it as social climbing. To her it's keeping the bloodlines pure, or something. Ensuring suitable grandchildren. She'll back off once she has her own grandchild to spoil. Why don't we see if we can accommodate her, starting . . . right now?"

And we did.

"Peter?" Mother Hannah called up the stairs. "Is Maude all right? I thought I heard her fall. . . ."

The fog burned off the next day, and a spell of glittering, blue-edged days rolled in from the bay. Peter got the *Hannah* into the water at last and took to the sea like a gull, along with every other man in Retreat who was old enough . . . or not too old . . . to sail. When they came off the water, they flocked to the tennis courts; I could hear the *twang* of tennis balls, and shouts and applause, from the downstairs sun porch, where Mother Hannah allowed me to sit in the mornings, wrapped in afghans, sorting linens and copying out old family recipes for my own household file. I knew that I would make few of the creamy, molded, and bombéd things she thought suitable for brides' recipe files, but it kept her out of my venue, and in a day or two she seemed satisfied that I would not make a break for the water and commit some new outrage in her absence and began her morning round of calls and food-gathering again.

Big Peter was gone from morning till dusk that week, over on Rosier Pond, where the Chamblisses had a small cabin, cataloging his birds and sketching small creatures and writing in what Mother Hannah called his log and staring into God knows what dark, still recess of his own soul. In the few days we had been in Retreat, he had seemed to fade like ink script in the sun. I felt vaguely uneasy about him but no one else seemed to, and his absence meant I had the cottage to myself in the mornings. Christina Willis invariably accompanied Mother Hannah on her nuts-and-berries tours. I came to treasure those mornings as I have few others in Retreat. It was then, in those still first days, that the colony gave me its first and best gift, that humbling, rapturous, worldless sense of sea and sky and solitude. I still cannot really feel it unless I am alone.

But on the fourth morning I was beginning to fret from inactivity and sheer loneliness. I felt I had not seen Peter in daylight for a very long time. I was forbidden by both Dr. Lincoln and Mother Hannah to go out for another day or so, and Amy was incarcerated, that week, with her mother-in-law's house guests. I pulled out my sketch pad and messed about with charcoal sketches of the bay and the lane from the windows, but they were airless and stale; it was the real thing I wanted. I wandered into the living room and pulled an old volume of Sarah Orne Jewett from the bookcase, but the light in the room was so dim from the great old lilac trees pressing against the windows that I could not read. They were in full bloom, overwhelming clouds of white, so fragrant in the fog-damp air that you could literally taste their sweetness as well as smell it. I loved the smell; it brought that first magical night on Wappoo Creek stingingly alive, with a poignance that brought tears to my eyes. I thought I might, later, go out and pick a bouquet for our bedroom.

"What a long way from home I am," I said aloud. Only the untasted silence of an alien place answered me.

Just then the bushes outside the window began to thrash and shake violently, as if in a storm, and white blossoms began to rain down into the flower border and onto the lawn. I stood, staring; in a moment the room lightened and I found myself looking into the dark face of Micah Willis. He held a great pair of shears in his hand, and seeing me he touched his hand to his forehead and went on trimming. I hesitated; I had not seen him since he had pulled me from the sea on the day of the fawn and knew that my thanks to him were long overdue. I had tendered them to Christina, and she had smiled and said he was glad he got there in time; but I knew I should have written him a note. For some reason, I was embarrassed. The feel of his bare arms was still somehow warm on mine.

I went out the front door into the June sunshine, blinking like a cave creature. He had finished the trees on the left side of the doorstep and moved over to those on the right. The lawn was mounded with blossoms, like a summer snowfall. The cool air resonated with fragrance. A small boy, I thought about five or six, dark and vivid, apple-cheeked, gathered up armfuls of white branches and staggered with them to a mud-spattered Ford truck parked in the driveway and dumped them into the open bed, leaving a trail of white behind him. When I shut the screen door, man and boy stopped what they were doing and looked at me.

"I wanted to thank you for the other day," I said, hearing in my own ears the cloying syrup of the Low Country and thinking it must sound torturous to ears accustomed to crispness. "I should have sooner, but no one would let me outside. I feel like a runaway prisoner out here now."

He looked at me politely, the shears at the ready. The little boy came to stand solemnly at his knee, staring at me with his father's black eyes.

"Anyone would have done the same," he said. His voice was as low as I remembered, flat and uninflected.

"I hope you didn't . . . catch cold or anything," I said, knowing in despair that I was going to chatter. "That water is like nothing I've ever felt."

"Reckon it would take more than a dunkin' in the bay to give me a cold," he said, and the little boy giggled. I looked down at him and smiled.

"I'm Mrs. Chambliss," I said. "Who are you?"

"No, you ain't, then," the child piped, and Micah Willis did smile then, a flicker of white in the brown skin.

"The only Mrs. Chambliss he knows is your mother-in-law," he said. "Seems to him there's a mite of difference. This is Caleb Willis, my youngest and so far only. Say good morning to Mrs. Chambliss, Caleb."

"Good morning," the little boy said, staring at me. His eyes widened. "Daddy, she's the lady with the fawn, isn't she?"

"Yes," I said. "I'm the lady with the fawn."

I asked Micah Willis with my eyes if his small son knew about the fawn, and he nodded.

"Caleb knows I had to put the fawn down," he said. "He's as sorry as I am about it. You too, I expect. I told him you fell in tryin' to get her out."

"Her . . . ?"

"Little doe," he said.

He said no more, only stood there holding his shears, with his other hand on the top of his son's head, obviously waiting for me to go back inside and let him get on with his task. Instead, I said, "What are you going to do with all those lilacs?" and pointed to the truck bed.

His face froze. Not a muscle moved, but somehow it seemed to harden as concrete will.

"Mrs. Chambliss senior said it was all right to take them," he said.

"We gon' put 'em on the 'cesters," Caleb said helpfully. He looked from his father to me.

"Oh, please, I didn't mean I thought you were . . . taking them," I cried, reddening. "I just wondered what you would do with them—"

I stopped, miserable. Not only had I as good as accused him of stealing lilacs, I had intimated that I thought the natives had no need of gratuitous loveliness.

"I'm sorry," I whispered.

He did not smile again, but his face unfroze a bit.

"Caleb and I always take an armful to the cemetery when we trim Mrs. Chambliss's lilacs," he said. "All our people are there from the year one. Caleb knows almost every one of his ancestors by now."

"How lovely," I said. "How nice to be where all your people have always been. I think it's a wonderful idea. Thank you again, and please go on with your trimming."

I turned and went back into the house. Presently I heard the metallic snipping start again. Still hot-faced, I went back to Mother Hannah's Blueberry Bombe.

An hour must have passed before I heard the scream. It was the child; I knew that instantly, but the terror and anguish in it was electrifying, and I was on my feet and out the front door before it fairly ended. Micah Willis knelt on the grass beside his son, who was stretched out on his back, writhing and shrieking, while a fountain of bright blood arced through the air and spattered on the snowfall of lilacs around them. I saw that Micah had his pocket hand-kerchief pressed hard around the child's instep, but it had bloodied to slick limpness, and the fountain pumped on. I turned and flew to the linen closet and grabbed an armful of clean towels and ran back. Micah was just gathering the little boy into his arms, and the blood was still pumping.

"Here, hold it hard over the cut and don't let up on the pressure," I gasped, falling on my knees beside him. He grabbed the towels and wrapped the little foot in them, his face white under the tan. The boy screamed on.

"Who can I call?" I cried. "Is there a doctor in the village? I'll run down to the Thorne girls' and telephone—"

"It needs sewing," he said. "He needs the doctor over in Brooksville. It'll be faster to take him. Tell his mother where we've gone when she comes back."

He scooped the child up and ran for the truck, and when he did the awful bleeding started again.

"Wait!" I ran after him. "Somebody's got to hold that towel firm. Give him to me and you drive. I know first aid; we had to, in the woods back home."

He put the child into my arms in the truck and slammed it into gear. The old car coughed and wallowed up the lane and swayed out onto the dirt road toward the mainland. I held Caleb hard against me on my lap, a wad of towels wrapped tight around his little foot and held there with one hand. With the other I smoothed his hair and cheeks.

"Now," I whispered. "Now, then. It's stopping already, and we'll get you all fixed up, and maybe, if you're really, really lucky, you'll have a scar."

The child stopped some of his writhing and all of the sobbing and looked up at me. His face and blue denim clothing were spattered dark with his blood, and his eyes were huge in his bone-white face.

"A scar? You reckon, really?"

"Shoot, yes," I said, kissing the top of his head. "I can almost promise you a scar. Probably the best scar on Cape Rosier. You can charge people a penny to look at it."

"Aw, g'wan," he said, but he did not begin crying again. He slumped against me and closed his eyes. His father looked worriedly at him and then at me, but I could feel the strong beat of the little heart and the steady breaths on my arm.

"It's hard work making a scar," I said, more to the boy than his father. Both smiled, small smiles.

"Is it stopping?" Micah Willis said, and I nodded yes. Blood still seeped through the top towel, but it did not pump.

"What happened?"

"He stepped on the shears. I put 'em down to pull some witch grass and the next thing I knew he was screaming and bleeding like a stuck pig. I was some scared; I never saw him hurt like that before. His mother will kill me."

"It's not going to be so bad," I said. "There's an artery there, is all. That's why it bled so. It's close to the top; I'm almost sure it didn't go deep enough to cut a tendon. He couldn't move his foot like that if it had."

"Were you a nurse?" he said. He was still driving fast, the truck bouncing over the dusty corrugated ruts, but he was not literally flying now.

"No, but we lived in the middle of a river swamp miles from town, and my father made sure I knew what to do about cuts and snakes and things. I stayed out by myself a lot. And then I've read a lot of biology too. At least enough to know Caleb's going to be fine."

"We're beholden to you," he said formally. "I don't know that I could have managed without somebody to hold him. You're all over blood. Going to scare the bejesus out of your mum-in-law."

"Well, it may scare her, but it sure won't surprise her," I said. "After what I've put her through the last week, a little blood of somebody else's isn't going to bother her a bit. She'll probably wish it was mine, at that."

I looked at him sheepishly. This man was, after all, a virtual stranger, and the employee of my mother-in-law to boot.

"That was an ungrateful and ungracious thing to say, and I apologize," I muttered.

"Never mind," he said, and grinned outright. It soft-ened the sharp, dark face extraordinarily. "I heard about your outing with Parker Potter. Surprised you didn't knock him overboard. Good thing if you had."

I smiled too, suddenly shy, and said, "How much farther?"

"Through South Brooksville and on to Brooksville, about five miles," he said. "There's a full-time doctor with a surgery there."

"Oh—I plain forgot," I cried. "Dr. Lincoln was right there in the colony; he wouldn't be out sailing, and I don't think they leave the cottage until after lunch. We could have saved all this time—"

"This is better," he said. He did not look around at me. Something in his tone told me not to ask why. I was silent, holding the nodding child against my breast, until we pulled up at the doctor's gleaming white miniature Greek Revival, some twenty minutes later, and he did not speak either.

When he came out of the surgery carrying Caleb, washed and bandaged and drowsy with relief and anodyne, the little boy held his arms out to me as automatically as he might have to his mother, and I took him and held him against my shoulder and car-ried him back out to the truck. In the back, the mound of white lilacs looked incongruous, exotic, like a cargo of snow. They had scarcely wilted. We were halfway back to Retreat, Caleb sleeping limply, when I said, "It's a shame to let the lilacs die. Is there somewhere you can put them until you can get them to the cemetery?"

"Well," he said, "the cemetery's right on the way, just before we get to the general store. If you've got a little more time, I might drop them off there. Caleb's going to be disappointed if we don't. There's a spring and well there, too; might not be a bad idea if you cleaned up a tad."

I looked down at my hands and arms and the hem of my dress. They looked as if I had been assisting in an abbatoir.

"I'd like to see the cemetery," I said.

We turned into the little Cove Harbor cemetery through two leaning rusty-white marble pillars, long since naked of whatever arch they had supported. There was a dark screen of spruce and fir between the area of the graves and the road, but once past it you could see the tumbled old monuments, most blackened with age and weather and covered with moss, marching in irregular rows down to the saltwater meadow that fringed the bay. Wild grasses and flowers waved in the little wind off the sea, and the smell of salt hay drying down at the water's edge, and kelp, and lilacs, and the clean spruce smell of Cape Rosier itself was wonderful after the choking dust of the road. Butterflies danced above the grasses, and birds sang, and gulls mewled and wheeled overhead, and the dark fingers of the pointed firs scratched against the ringing blue of the midday sky. Without the racketing motor it was very quiet. The salt wind was damp on my hot face and neck.

"What a beautiful place," I said. "And what a lot of people are here. Is it very old?"

He paused from unloading armfuls of lilacs. We had laid the sleeping boy down on the front seat and covered him with the last of the clean towels.

"Goes back to about 1680. These up here are the newest," he said, indicating the nearest row of stones. "These are Allens; they got here in the late 1800s and had to take the slots nearest the road. The oldest are back down there, closest to the sea. My folks are back there. Christina's too. And the Murrays and the Bartletts and the Goodens. Got here first, got the best pews, so to speak."

"Your people have been here since sixteen something?" I said. "I didn't think anybody was here then but Indians. That's forever."

"Not really," he said, amused. "There've been people here since about three thousand B.C. Came from Spain and France. From what's been found of their artifacts, they were the same folks as the ones who did the paintings in the caves in Lascaux. Pretty stuff, very modern-looking. Then there were several ages of Indians, mainly the Abenakis, the Dawn People. Then old Leif Erickson brought his Vikings here and looked around; there are carvings on the rocks over on Monhegan and a couple of other places that they're pretty sure are Viking, and a paved highway buried deep at Pemaquid they're sure is. Then after that we had the English, and the Spanish, and the French, and the Italians—though they were mostly hired hands—and the English again, under Sir Walter Raleigh and his brother, and so forth and so on. The first permanent settlement was at Kittery, in 1616. My folks came over from Massachussets as soon as anybody knew about Maine. Never could stand not having our own piece of dirt, could the Willises. Christina's folks were Duschesnes, descendants of the French, the coureurs de bois, wild young rapscallions sent over here to live with the Indians and learn their ways. Wouldn't be surprised if there wasn't some Jesuit blood in the Duschesne family, either. Those old guys really got around in the name of God."

I looked at him, humbled. "I don't think many people know as much about their state or their family as you do," I said. "We do in Charleston, but only about our families. The rest of South Carolina might as well not be there. Do they teach you much history in the schools here?"

"Not too many of us go to school," he said matter-of-factly. "Most of us go to haul, or to apprentice with sails, or to the lumber camps or the land when we're old enough to wear long pants. There are precious few schools this far Down East. But we manage to learn. My family, now, is a great one for reading, so we learn that when we're tykes. That's what we do in the long dark winters, when it's too bad to get out. Others make music, or weave, or paint, or carve. Not many of us just sit there. And all of us tell stories to the rest of us. But there are formal educated people among us. Christina's brother is a biologist over in Bar Harbor, and her uncle plays a concert violin in Portsmouth. My own grandfather was a sea captain and my other one a teacher in Nova Scotia. I was set to go on to school and study, but Daddy lost the fingers of his right hand to frostbite and couldn't haul anymore, and he started a little old boatyard, and I've helped him, and now it's a right good little country boatyard, all told. Make nice wooden boats, if I do say so myself."

We reached the area where the Willises lay in their weathered ranks, and laid our armfuls of blossoms on their graves. We had enough left over for the Duschesnes too, and one or two more bunches for some of the neighboring graves. By the time he had shown me the little stone cistern over the spring, at the edge of the meadow under a great twisted spruce, and I had dabbed most of the blood off my face and my clothes, the sun was high overhead. We started back to the truck.

"Do you ever regret not going to school?" I said.

"Sometimes, I guess," he said, looking off to the water, a white glitter now in the noonday. "But usually not. Willises have always had some land and a house, whatever else they didn't have. We've always owned our own doorsteps. I don't think we could have kept what we had here if I'd left, and it wouldn't have been worth it to me in the long run. We're not too smart; we've always been willing to sacrifice anything we had, to keep our land and our homes. There'll be none of us rich. Maybe that boy up there will be the one to cut and run. But somehow I don't think so."

"You're just like my family," I said. "Or rather, mine is just like yours. My family has hung on to its big old place in the swamp since the 1700s too; you'd think land was the holy grail to us. Isn't that funny? I'm even French like your wife. My family's name is Gascoigne. I didn't think I'd ever find a soul up here I had anything in common with."

"You still haven't," he said crisply. "A French last name isn't enough, by a long stretch."

I was silent for a space, my face smarting with the sting of his rebuff. For a time I had forgotten we were employer and employee; we had been, in my eyes, only two people with a commonality, if a slender one. The ease had been palpable.

"You all don't like us much, do you?" I said. "Us summer people, I mean?"

"Well, it's mainly that you don't work, you see," he said seriously, and I thought he was sorry he had spoken sharply but would never tell me so. "We see you up here in your big houses and your automobiles and sailboats, but we never see you lift a finger. Mainiacs are keen on working."

"Well, most of us work the rest of the year," I said, wondering why I was defending these people who were, to me, such alien corn. "Some of us work up here. My father-in-law is working on a book on birds and flowers. My husband works on his lesson plans. Lots of the women work like demons in their flower beds."

"Flower beds. What kind of work is that? That's fussing around to make themselves think they're working. How do you suppose our women feel, seeing the way you live up here? Working for you in your houses? Saying yes, ma'am; no, ma'am? How do you think our men feel, seeing their women doing it? Or our children?"

"You don't have to do it, do you?" I said, annoyed.

"No," he said. "We don't. It's just that most of us are fond of eating in the winters. You cannot imagine what a winter here is like if you've never seen one. Or seen one in one of our houses, I mean. Big difference from staying over a few days in one of those big winterized jobs your folks have."

"They're not my folks," I said. "Not really. My folks are just as poor, and probably just as stubborn as yours are, if you want to play 'my poverty is nobler than your poverty.' I'm more like you than them. I don't think I ever really saw that until today. I don't know if I would have, if we hadn't come out here and talked to each other."

"Well, you'd do well not to make a habit of that, either," he said, looking straight ahead.

"You mean I can't talk to you any more? Or to Christina or Caleb?"

"It wouldn't go well for you if you did," he said. "Your mother-in-law wouldn't like it. None of those old ladies would. Probably not your husband, either."

"Don't you dump Peter in with those . . . women," I said hotly. "If you knew anything at all, you'd know he isn't like them, not at all. And I'll darned well speak to who I want to. That's one thing all the old ladies in the entire state of Maine can't stop me from doing."

He turned and looked at me. It was a long look, level and assessing. His eyes were very dark, and his mouth a straight line. He looked carved from dark marble. I remembered how warm his body had felt against mine when he had pulled me out of the water. I went suddenly scarlet and hot and turned away.

"You're not going to do well up here, Maude Chambliss," he said. "You see too clearly. You have a foolhardy heart."

"What do you mean?"

"That sail in the fog. The fawn. My boy."

"I don't understand you."

"That's true," he said. "You don't."

We got back into the truck and I gathered the sleeping child against me and we swayed on back down the road toward Retreat to deliver me to Liberty. Neither of us said much until we turned off at the place where the old oar beckoned beside the road.

He cleared his throat.

"We are mightily in your debt," he said. "It's for your own good that I ask you not to mention today to your family or any of your neighbors. I understand that you acted from a kind heart, and I thank you for it. But others here would not understand that."

"You mean just not say anything about the accident or any of it?" I said.

"That's what I mean. Your mother-in-law and Christina aren't usually back by now, and if you go and change your clothes there'll be no reason for them to know. Everybody else will be gone to lunch or out on the water. I'll let you off and go get this sprat to bed. That was good, that about the scar."

I nodded dumbly, and when he pulled into the driveway of Liberty I saw he was right; none of my family was about. The entire colony seemed deserted. But when I got out, rumpled and mussed and damp with spring water and still splattered with blood, Miss Isabelle and Miss Charlotte Valentine were just coming out of the cottage, their card cases in their gloved hands. I had a great desire to laugh, to shout, howl, double up with laughter, laugh until I rolled in the lane and choked on my glee. First coral satin and hickies, now rumpled, bloody, grass-stained clothes and Micah Willis's truck.

"Good morning," I said to them, as I had said on that other day that seemed a lifetime ago. "Isn't it a lovely day?"

Chapter Five

In early January of the next year I got pregnant, and so once again the summer world of Retreat narrowed, for me, to the slice of it I could see and smell and hear and taste from the sun porch in Liberty. That second summer we went there, Mother Hannah had me off my feet and under layers of wool almost before I had taken my hat off.

"I really think it most unwise of Peter even to bring you here this summer, but of course he never listens to his mother, and so here you are," she said, bringing me warm milk and Saltines on the sun porch. I have always loathed both.

"I'm fine," I said. "It's just five months. I may look like a blimp, but I've really never felt better in my life. My doctor at home says it's good for me to get moderate exercise."

"He's that young man from somewhere out west, isn't he?" she said smoothly. Dr. Canfield from St. Louis, whom Peter and I both liked enormously when I had my first appointment with him in Concord, seemed to diminish in my mind with the speed of light. Mother Hannah was outraged because I would not agree to come to Boston for six weeks before my due date and have the baby there.

"Missouri," I said, determined to be equable with her this summer. "And he looks far younger than he is. Really, Mother Hannah. I'm going to feel awful if I have to lie around all summer."

"We'll see what Dr. Lincoln says." She smiled thinly. "I've asked him to look in on you tomorrow morning. You cannot be up here in this wilderness in your condition without being under a doctor's care. I cannot take responsibility for you."

"I'm sure Peter will be happy to do that," I said, feeling my just-born equanimity die without taking a breath.

"Peter," she said, in fond scorn. "What does that happy-go-lucky son of mine know about expectant mothers? I've been in your condition twice up here, and Dr. Lincoln has attended me both times. Between us I think we can manage to keep you safe and sound. And that, my dear, means no more running around the cliffs or fooling around in the sea. Cemeteries either," she added, pointedly not looking at me.

"I knew I'd hear about that eventually," I said to Peter that night as we lay in our upstairs bed, properly tucked up under the Great Seal of Princeton. "I wondered why I didn't get both barrels last summer, when it happened. And as for Dr. Lincoln: Peter, he's ancient! They very probably *did* put pregnant women to bed for nine months in his heyday, but Dr. Canfield said—"

"I know," he said, patting my cheek and then letting his hand slide down my breasts to the mound of my belly.

The baby had been more active than usual that evening; the drive from Northpoint, though we took it in two days rather than one and stopped frequently, was still rough and tedious. His hand bucked with the baby's kicking.

"I promise you won't hear any more about oceans and cemeteries. Just give her and Dr. Lincoln their way for a week or two, and then I'll bet you anything they'll let up on the bed rest. Though to tell you the truth I'm not at all sorry Junior, here, will be keeping you out of graveyards and oceans this summer."

I looked at him sharply, but he said no more. He had said nothing about my careening trip to the village and the old cemetery with Micah Willis when it had happened last summer, except to tell his mother calmly that he'd just as soon not be married to a woman who would let a child bleed to death because it was a native. And when she said, "Well, of course I didn't mean that, I meant the appearance of it, being in that truck alone with Micah," he fairly snapped at her, so she rounded on him.

"Peter Chambliss, just because you're a married man now—"

Then Big Peter came out of his den, where he had been sequestered for the past three days, and said, "The appearance of a dead child on your doorstep would, I hope, distress you more, Hannah," and went back into the den and shut the door, and she turned and went upstairs. I heard nothing more that summer about the incident, but when we left for Northpoint, I felt as though I was coming out of a paradisiacal prison into blessed, ordinary air.

"Peter, can it possibly be good for me or the baby to spend an entire summer being bored and unhappy?" I said, knowing it was emotional blackmail, but not knowing how else to make my point.

"Maude, if you're truly that miserable up here this summer—if you really and truly are unhappy—we simply won't come again. That's a promise. I'm not going to torture you every year of your life. But give it another try this summer. It'll be different. She's going to lay off criticizing you; we had a talk about that. She's agreed to try, and she will. You try a little too. Try to think like she does, just a bit. She's worked hard to get where she is in the colony; she knows what the rules are. I truly believe she's trying to show you what it takes to fit in up here."

"What good is a place that won't let you be yourself?" I said sullenly. I was bested, and I knew it. "Do you want your child to grow up always straining to fit somebody else's mold? Do you want him—or her—to be so fenced in with rules?"

The silvery brows over the gray eyes knitted, and he looked at me, honestly puzzled.

"Why should he be?" he said. "I wasn't. I'm not. I've always been me up here."

I think I realized only then, clearly and without hope, that in Retreat the men's supernal freedom had always been bought by the sacrificial chains of the women. Peter truly did not understand what was bothering me.

"Then you better hope this baby is a boy," I said under my breath, rolling over in bed and trying to find a place in the spavined mattress for my belly. It was a long time that night before I slept.

At first it wasn't so bad. To no one's surprise, Dr. Lincoln agreed with Mother Hannah and decreed bed or sun-porch rest for me, but true to her word Mother Hannah did not chastise or instruct me further that summer, and if her company in the afternoons was not exactly stimulating, still, it was soothing and neutral and not unpleasant. She read aloud to me, during the cool clear June afternoons, from books she had read when she was young—*Penrod and Sam, Jane Eyre, Silas Marner*—and I was surprised to find I soon looked forward to those few hours before I was sent back up to bed for the nap I did not need. In the mornings, when she and Christina were on their errands, Peter sat with me on the sun porch, grading papers and reading over fall assignments. His vocation for teaching was a real one; he was endlessly interested in the minds of young boys and endlessly convinced of the importance of what was put into them. Sometimes we talked of the baby, but abstractedly, not as speculatively as one might think prospective young parents would. I know for Peter's part only that he was bemusedly charmed with the idea of parenthood but seemingly unconcerned with its reality. He would not talk of formulas and nurses and the logistics of living with a small child. He would talk, instead, of when the baby was grown: what work he would choose, what sort of man he would be, what his odd Boston-Charleston provenance would mean to him. And often he would say, looking at me and pantomiming lewdness, "That kid has pumped the old pillows up there pretty good, Mrs. C. Are you sure we couldn't, just once—"

"Dr. Lincoln says not," I would say.

"May Dr. Lincoln rot in hell. Easy for him to prescribe abstinence. He probably forgot what it felt like twenty years ago."

For my part, I simply could not see past the moment that my pains would start. It seemed to me somehow that I would have the pains and go to the hospital and there deflate like a balloon and come home and resume my old life once more. The fact that the rubbery, elastic mound in my stomach was going to turn us both into different people for the rest of our lives was simply, that summer, beyond my comprehension. I was still learning how to be a wife, still learning to be some sort of daughter-in-law. Surely the role of mother would not be asked of me as well. Not really. I worried endlessly, in those days, that I would be unable to love the baby.

Once I said as much to Peter.

"That's the silliest thing I ever heard of," he said. "Of course you will. It comes with the baby."

"Did you love Peter the minute you saw him?" I asked Mother Hannah.

"Instantly," she said. "It was the holiest rapture I have ever felt. We are given it with our children, I am sure of that."

But I was not sure. I would have given much to be able to talk to Amy about these doubts and fears, but Parker had taken her with him on a business trip to Hong Kong, and they would not be at Braebonnie until the middle of July. There was no one else I would dream of talking with in Retreat. Out of nowhere, once, the image of Micah Willis's dark face swam into my mind, and I knew that if I had had access to Micah I would not have hesitated to talk with him. But of course I did not, and would not. That much was understood after he brought me home under the eyes of the Misses Valentine last summer.

In our second week, Peter and Old Micah put the *Hannah* into the water, and after that I was alone in the sunny morning stillness of the sun porch.

"You sure you don't care?" Peter said, vibrating at the door in his eagerness to get out onto the dancing blue bay.

"No. Really. Go on. I'd far rather have you out there and know you're happy than stuck here. I can't go anywhere anyway."

"See you tonight," he said, and kissed me, and was gone. After that, the hours of confinement chafed painfully. I found myself wishing the baby would be premature, so that we could get it over and I could be on my feet again, and then I felt miserable and guilty about the wishing. It was, on the whole, beginning to be a bad time.

At the beginning of the third week my father-in-law came out onto the sun porch and found me crying.

"Maude, dear! What is it? Are you ill? Should I fetch Ridley Lincoln?"

I had never heard his voice so agitated. Poor man,
I suppose he thought he was alone with a woman
about to give birth. I gave him a watery smile and
shook my head.

"No, I'm fine," I said. "That's just the problem,
Papa Chambliss. I feel wonderful, and I haven't been
off this chaise for three weeks except to go to bed.
I'm sorry, I know everyone thinks this is the best
way, but I'm used to the outdoors. I miss the woods.
Oh, I miss the water so much—"

I stopped, feeling my voice break. I truly did not
wish to distress him. He had been silent and withdrawn much of June; I had scarcely seen him. I felt as
if a scene with me might be the feather that tipped
him irrevocably into his blackness.

He sat down and took my hand in his and
squeezed it absently, and I looked at him in surprise.
Except for ritual cheek kisses, he had never touched
me. He did not notice; he was looking out over the
water. The bay was calm and misted; you could not
tell where it ended and the sky began. It was warm
on the porch for June.

He turned his head back to me and smiled, and I
smiled involuntarily in return, he looked so much
like my Peter.

"Then you shall have the water," he said. "Tell me
where your sweater is; I'm going to take you for a little drive. It's a part of Retreat you haven't seen
before. I think you'll find it very lovely."

"But Mother Hannah—" I began.

"I will deal with Hannah," he said, still smiling.
"It's time I spent some time with my daughter-in-law,
before she makes me a grandfather again. It's not
easy to be a newcomer in Retreat, my dear. I wish
Hannah could remember that more often. She was in
your place once."

He brought out the big Marmon touring car in

which he and Mother Hannah motored to Maine each year and installed me in the front seat. We bumped out of Liberty's driveway and up the lane, past the cutoff down to Braebonnie and the smaller lane that led down to Mary's Garden, Fir Cottage, and Land's End. We were almost to the main road into the village when he stopped the car and got out and held back a great armful of leaning rhododendrons and unlatched a silver-weathered gate. There was no sign, no mailbox, no indication of any kind that another lane lay behind the sheltering rhododendron, but I could see that one did. It twisted away through the dense pine and spruce and birch forest, a mere ghost of a white sand ribbon in the green gloom. I would never have known it was there. I wondered how many people did.

"Where are we going?" I asked, as we bumped slowly down the lane. Vegetation leaned so close around the car that we literally pushed our way through it in the Marmon. My voice had dropped to a whisper. In that green stillness, a normal human voice would have seemed a shout.

"To see a very old friend of mine, who has the best view of the water on the cape and who will, I think, be interested in meeting you. I believe you'll like her too."

My father-in-law's face was calm and affable, but there was something in his eyes and voice, something of secrets and pleasure. It reminded me of a child's, near Christmas.

Suddenly I knew.

"It's the Aerie, isn't it?" I said. "I've seen just a glimpse of it from the rocks below Braebonnie. Amy told me about the people who live there: the Fowlers? She said Mrs. Fowler was an invalid, and that no one ever saw them—"

"It's the Aerie, yes." He smiled over at me. "Sarah and Douglas Fowler. Not many people see them, but a few do. I've known Sarah since we were children; the house was her family's. Douglas came here the summer they married and loved it, and when she got ill he just kept on bringing her back for the season. It seems to do her good. Sarah has always been passionate about the woods and sea."

"Does she . . . is she very ill?" I asked. I thought it odd that he would intrude on a sick woman, no matter how old a friend.

"It's hard to tell," he said. "Most of the time I can see virtually no change from the way she always was. Sometimes she doesn't talk, but she never did, very much. I know she is glad to see me; I wouldn't go if I thought she was not."

I said nothing; was he in the habit of visiting in this forbidden place, then? When did he come? I had thought he went in the mornings over to the camp on Rosier Pond, but perhaps I had misunderstood. My Peter had never mentioned the Fowlers.

He looked at me again, reading my confusion.

"Sarah's sickness is called schizophrenia," he said. "Or at least that's the name her doctors have for it. She lost three babies in a row, and after the third she just seemed to drift away inside her head, and she stays there a good part of the time. When she's . . . with us, she's almost as normal as she ever was, though she has a tendency to say exactly what comes into her mind, which as you may imagine is a perilous business in a place like Retreat. They could probably go out far more than they do, but Sarah always did hate the social part of our summers. I think on the main she lives precisely the way she wishes to."

"I hope I'm not going to upset her," I said anxiously. All at once, dealing with more nuance and uncertainty in this place seemed beyond me. Poor woman: all three of her babies dead, and me obviously, heavily, pregnant.

"No. She wants to meet you. I've told her a bit about you. She says she thinks you and she have much in common. She knows about your baby, if that worries you."

We came out of the tunnel of green and into a land and seascape that made me gasp. The great brown-shingled house sat on the very lip of a cliff, in a clearing surrounded by dense forest and looking straight out to sea. On three sides it hung in blue air, gulls wheeling above and below, and the wind, that had only teased fitfully down at Liberty, boomed in here like a whoop of joy. I had the swift, absurd notion that if you lived in this house, in this place, you would know how to fly. Far, far beyond us, Isle au Haut and North Haven dreamed, and beyond them the Camden Hills. Sails lay like confetti on all that wild, vast blue. One of them, I knew, was Peter's. Around the foundations of the house flowers rioted, and a railed staircase led over the cliff and out of sight. Everything was elemental: sun, sea, wind, rock. I wanted to cry for sheer joy.

"Is this enough water for you?" Big Peter said, smiling at my rapt face and open mouth.

"Oh," I said faintly. "Oh, it's glorious! Oh, my."

A man came down the steps toward us, an old man, I thought at first, and then saw he was no older than my father-in-law but was stooped and frail and seemed somehow bleached. But his smile was warm.

"You can see why we call it the Aerie," Douglas Fowler said, when I had been introduced.

"I'd call it heaven," I said honestly. "I don't think I'd ever leave."

And then I reddened furiously because, of course, they did not. But he only said, "Sarah feels the same way you do. The only time I've ever seen her cry is when we go back to Vermont every September."

Not even for her babies? I thought. But of course I did not say it.

Inside, a great room ran the length of the house and looked through a wall of many-paned windows out over a stone terrace and scrap of lawn and then the wild, all-dissolving blue. I thought you could do anything necessary to sustain life in that room, and they probably did: eat, sleep, work, play, love. At one end a huge blackened fireplace flanked by bookcases and window seats occupied an entire wall, with fat, spraddled sofas and chairs and ottomans grouped about it. At the other end stood a round oak dining table and chairs. An easel was set up by the window wall, and a little farther down a brass telescope trained out to sea. There were old black beams far up in the rafters, and a gallery all around the second story with, I assumed, bedrooms and baths off it. Bright rugs and cushions and afghans and books and papers and magazines were scattered everywhere, and flowers glowed from tables and the mantelpiece. A fire burned on the hearth, and on the shabby old plaid rug before it two massive Scotties dozed.

"When I die, this is where I hope I come," I said to Douglas Fowler, and he laughed, and so did someone else. I looked quickly around the room and saw no one, and then I did.

She stood behind the sofa table, at the entrance to the foyer through which we had just come, and the first thing I thought was, Dear God, she's a ghost. I have never seen anyone alive as pale as Sarah Fowler was. She was, in the gloom of the huge room, nearly transparent.

The second thing I thought was, But she's beautiful! And she was that, too. Tall and seeming taller because of her extreme thinness, she had the bones of a deer or a whippet and the face of a classical statue. You see that face on women on medieval tombs, a little greyhound curled at their feet.

"You brought your little runaway, I see," she said

to Big Peter, and smiled at me, and walked over and kissed him on the cheek. Her face was fine and blood-less and sweet, her eyes spilling light, her hair a wash of pewter watercolor down her back. She seemed all over silver. He put his hand lightly on her hair, just a touch, as if to brush it off her cheek, and suddenly I knew he loved her as a man does a woman—and had, for a very long time. With the swift prescience that comes at such times, I knew also that she loved him too, and her pale husband knew it, and none of the three would ever speak of it. I could not have said how I knew, but that sort of knowledge has come to me a few times in my life, as if on a very breath, and each time I have been sure past any certainty it was true, and it has been. I could have wept with the hopelessness of that kiss and that touch on the silver hair, there in the madwoman's living room.

But Sarah Fowler smiled in real delight, and took my hands, and said, "I asked Peter to bring you to me when I heard about Ridley Lincoln's putting you to bed. Old fool. Of course you must be up and out in the sun; of course you must have the sea. It's what healed me when . . . I was sick. It will keep you well. I want you to go down that flight of steps to the beach and just sit there and let it all wash over you, while I have a talk with Peter and Douglas runs into the village. When you're quite full up, come on back and we'll have a cup of tea."

"Sarah, I don't know about Maude going down all those steps alone—" Big Peter began, but she put her finger to her lips and he stopped.

"It's the solitude she needs, Peter. Believe me, I know. There is magic here, but it needs solitude to work."

"Please," I said, suddenly frantic to be off down the stairs to the sea, dying of my thirst for the water.

He nodded, and I was out the French doors and

across the terrace in an eye blink, into the stream of the wind. It caught me and washed over me like water itself, cool and damp and smelling of pine and salt and distance and dark, secret green places, and I threw out my arms and laughed aloud and rode the wind down the steps on the face of the cliff to the beach and the sea.

It was in all ways a secret beach, a perfect little half moon of sighing shingle, with great, beetling pink boulders shielding it on both sides and, above it, the cliff top and the house and the sky. No one not in that house would ever know you were there. No eyes or voices could follow you. No tongues could tell of your being here. I stood there alone, washed and washed with sea and solitude and the salt wind, and then I pulled up my skirt and waded into the water.

It was light green and cold as iced seltzer, bubbling and fizzing, and as terrible as it had felt to me last summer, it was that wonderful now. The shelf of sand beneath the water was level and gradual, and I waded and splashed and stooped and swooped cold water onto my face and arms, and I capered and kicked and sang.

"'Yes, we have no bananas,'" I shouted. "'We have no bananas today,'" and "'I been working on the railroad, all the livelong day,'" and "'It's three o'clock in the morning, we've danced the whole night through.'"

And suddenly I was a creature of lightness and grace again, a girl who might, indeed, dance the whole night through with the man who had brought her armfuls of lilacs. The sun was shining and the water lapped and dreamed, and I was young, and all things seemed possible. I will remember that morning on the beach below the Aerie as long as I live.

After I finished wading, I found a sun-warmed hollow in the great, tumbling pile of rock and sat down and closed my eyes and let the wind and sun and sea run into me through my skin, until no conscious thought was left and I could not have told where my boundaries were, or the sea's, or the sky's. The baby was very still, and there was a high humming in my ears that seemed the very music of the earth itself. I think I slept a little. When I heard my father-in-law calling me, the sun was a bit higher overhead and my cheekbones and nose were beginning to sting. Leaving that beach was one of the hardest things I have ever done.

We had tea and talked of nothing special, comfortable talk about who was in the colony and who would not be coming; about books and music and plays and Prohibition; about gardening and music and movies. We did not talk of my baby or of Peter or Mother Hannah or of Douglas Fowler, and I did not find that strange at all. When presently Douglas came back from the village with an armload of groceries, Sarah smiled with real fondness, and when we got up to leave, she gave me the same smile and said, "I think my hiding place has agreed with you. It's the one thing you need to know about Retreat, Maude: a few of us will always need a hiding place from time to time. I think you are one of those. I know I am. I hope my beach can be yours. Use it whenever you like, only remember that it really is a secret."

"I'd love that," I said, tears coming into my eyes and surprising me with their sting. "I really would. I've never seen a . . . better place."

"Come soon, then," she said, and turned to Peter. "You come too," she said, and put one finger on his cheek. "You come and bring Maude as often as you think you can."

Her voice was different when she spoke to him. I turned away to the car so as not to see her eyes, or his, murmuring my thanks over my shoulder. Douglas Fowler and the two Scotties walked me across the terrace.

"I hope you will come again," he said, in his

clipped New England voice. "She hasn't had a woman visitor in years, besides old Lottie Padgett. Only Peter. I think it's done her a world of good. I can tell she likes you."

"Well, I certainly hope I can," I said. "Thanks so much for having us."

"Good luck with your little one, Miss Maude," he said. "It's a lovely time for a woman. Enjoy it. Next summer you'll be running your legs off."

I thought of his own babies, never to be chased by the beautiful, transparent woman in the house on the cliff.

"Thank you," I said, my lips trembling. Just then Big Peter came, and we said our goodbyes and were off. We did not speak until we were nearly back at Liberty, but the silence was not oppressive.

"I go once or twice a week," he said, as if he were speaking of the weather. "It gives Douglas a chance to get to the village, and me a chance to see how Sarah is getting along. I suppose it's like running away; I'm sure the family thinks I'm at the camp. Not that Sarah would care if they knew, but . . . it's such a special place. I like feeling that I have one secret up here."

I knew he was asking me, delicately, not to mention our visit or that he came frequently, and had for many years. I knew I would not have anyway, not even to Peter. The beach was my secret now too.

"I can see why," I said. "To go there often would just be paradise."

"Then, my pretty Maude, we shall do just that, at least once a week, until you leave to go home and have your baby," he said, smiling at me. "After that I don't expect you'll have a snowball's chance in hell of getting loose to go driving alone with your father-in-law, but this summer will be yours and mine, to get acquainted with each other and let you sample the forbidden delights of solitude and salt water.

Nobody can object to the former, and what they don't know about the latter will never hurt them."

"Thank you," I said, and leaned over and kissed him on the cheek. "It isn't that I don't like being with . . . everybody. It's just that—"

"I know," he said. "I really do."

And so, once a week until mid-July, we left in the Marmon, my father-in-law and I, and drove decorously down the lane and headed for the Aerie like children out of school, and I will always be grateful for those quiet, sea-blessed mornings. They gave me back a measure of myself that summer, and they gave me all I would ever have of the man who was my husband's father. On July 18, Big Peter had a heart attack, swimming in the frigid water of Rosier Pond, and died before the hastily summoned sheriff could get him to the hospital in Castine. The first thing I thought when they came to tell us was, Who will tell Sarah? Oh, who is there who can do that?

If I had thought to comfort my mother-in-law, I soon found I was both mistaken and unnecessary. There is a drill for death in Retreat, an immutable ritual, and its name is Us. No one outside the ranks need apply.

It was Dierdre and Guildford Kennedy from Camp Corpy who came, with Dr. Lincoln in tow. The Kennedys had a small rustic camp over on Rosier Pond, as Peter's family did, and I learned later that Guildford had been swimming with Big Peter and had climbed out on the dock to take the sun only minutes before he heard my father-in-law call. He had dived in instantly, and pulled Big Peter to the dock, and shouted for Dierdre to call the sheriff and Ridley Lincoln. The Kennedys had ridden with Sheriff Carter to the hospital, holding Big Peter in their muscular arms and murmuring to him. The sheriff broke all existing speed records into Castine, but somewhere along the way, Dierdre Kennedy said, "I could tell he had left us," and Ridley Lincoln, who was waiting on the steps of the hospital, confirmed it. Mother Hannah sat as still as stone while they told her, white and silent, and I sank faintly to a chair in the sun porch, feeling the blood surge out of my arms and face. I knew that after the bloodless silence the grief would strike and would be terrible. I had come to love Big Peter, in those few weeks, very much.

There was a small, soft sound, like a sigh—only that—from my mother-in-law.

"Hannah, darling. Let me call someone for you. Maude's here, let me get Maude—"

"No," Mother Hannah said, and her voice was very old. "Peter. I want Peter."

"Oh, my dear," Dierdre Kennedy murmured, and I knew she thought Mother Hannah was talking about Big Peter. I knew also that she was wrong.

"My son," Mother Hannah said. "I want my son."

"Guild has already sent some of the men out after him," Dierdre said. "They'll have him in as soon as possible. But meantime, Maude—"

"I don't want Maude," my mother-in-law said. She was very calm.

And so, for a long while on that terrible day, I sat alone on the sun porch of Liberty and waited for both Peter and the grief to come, while the cottage filled up with women.

I am familiar with it now, of course; know in my own bones the resonance of the jungle drums, as Peter always called them, that announces to the women of Retreat that one of their own has been bereaved, even before the news of it comes. I still cannot account for it, but it has long ceased to surprise me. But on that day I was truly mystified. One by one, in the bright sun of noon, the women came. Helen

Potter from Braebonnie was first, holding Mother Hannah lightly and pressing her cheek to that marble one. Helen's eyes were closed and her face still, but I could read real grief in the tightness of her mouth.

"My dear Hannah, I am so sorry," she whispered.

Mother Hannah nodded, still silent. Her eyes were wide and white-rimmed and stared beyond Mrs. Potter's shoulder at nothing, but the awful composure held.

Mary Lincoln came next, twittering; then Augusta Stallings, carrying a bottle of something done up in tissue and looking ferocious; then cool Aurora Winslow, and pillowy little Erica Conant, and the Misses Valentine, peering suspiciously at me wavering in the sun-porch door before bearing down on my mother-in-law, arms outstretched, treble voices piping. Others came; in half an hour the cottage living room had filled with women, come to circle the wagons around Mother Hannah. A few men came with the women, but they did not come into the cottage. They stood on the lawn or the porch, smoking and talking in low voices, shaking their heads. There was sorrow in their group too, I knew; Big Peter had been popular, and these were his boyhood friends. But mainly they seemed merely diminished, a straggling herd of old males, their dwindling number down this day by one. It was the women who seemed to radiate strength, almost like body heat. And I saw then what I only came to fully realize much later: a man's death in Retreat does indeed diminish the men of the tribe, but it confers on his wife a new power. In Retreat, a new widow passes, literally in a heartbeat, from chatelaine to queen. And so it was with Mother Hannah.

I saw something else that day too: that in the great rites of passage here it is the old women whose place it is to come, to minister, to soothe, to witness. The young women stay behind to tend the children and the infirm. Peter said once, only half in jest, that when somebody dies in the colony the old ladies get first seating. I yearned for Amy but would have welcomed the interchangeable Stallings girls from the Compound, or the ubiquitous girls of Mary's Garden, or the featherheaded Clio, Thalia and Calliope Kennedy. I would even have been middling glad to see Gretchen Winslow. But for what seemed hours of anguish, while I sat or stood lumpenly on the sun porch waiting for Peter to come home, the young women did not come. Later, I learned, it would be their turn; all that evening and the next day, they would come and knock softly and hand in casseroles and cakes and armfuls of flowers from colony gardens with little cards affixed that said *Courtesy of Ella Stallings* or *Priss Thorne* or whoever the bearer happened to be. And they would hug Peter and inquire after Mother Hannah and ask if there was anything else they might do, and say no thank you, we won't come in just now, we must get back to the children, or dinner, or Mother Someone-or-other, and perhaps they would think to wave to me in my exile on the sun porch and perhaps not.

But until midafternoon I was alone. When I ventured into the living room where the women clustered, I was shooed out firmly and told to go and put my feet up, for goodness' sake; did I want to have the baby here and now on top of everything else? Or I was asked, politely and coolly, if there was anything I wanted, and when I said, miserably, no, they turned back to the circle in whose center Mother Hannah burned like a dark candle. Once Dr. Lincoln came in from the yard and put his fingers distractedly on my pulse, nodded, said, "Good, good," and went away again. After that, no one came until Peter did, finally. By the time I heard his running steps on the porch I was fighting tears with all my might. When I heard his voice they spilled over.

I flew through the living room to meet him, oblivious of the clustered women. I held out my arms and he came into them as naturally as a duckling into water, and I held him as hard as I could, my face pressed into his chest, and I wept, over and over again, "Oh, I'm sorry. Oh, Peter, I'm so sorry. . . ."

I could feel, rather than see, that he was crying too. His breath came in ragged gasps, and there was a fine trembling all through his torso and his arms. I could feel and taste the damp salt of the bay on his sweater and hear the galloping of his heart. I could not even imagine the awful sail home. He put his head down on top of mine, and then I could feel his tears scalding through my hair. But he did not speak.

Mother Hannah began to cry then. It was a strange sound, like a doll's silvery crying, or a very small child's. I had never heard her cry, could not even imagine hearing it, and so when she began I did not know what the sound was. Peter lifted his head and looked blindly around him, and I saw his face, and my heart squeezed as if someone had grasped it, beating, and wrung it. He looked smashed, ruined, destroyed. I don't think I would have known him if I had come upon him unexpectedly. I had never seen such grief.

"Peter, oh, my baby," Mother Hannah sobbed, and Peter's face cleared magically of grief and turned to marble. I saw it happen as I looked at him. I saw the wounded child Peter leave forever and the man Peter slip into the space that was left. He still stood, holding me, looking over my head at his mother. She stretched her arms out to him and wriggled her fingers at him as if she was waving goodbye. For a moment they looked at each other, mother and son, and I looked at them. Then Peter put me away from him and started toward her. The honor cadre of women parted and she stood up, swaying faintly, and then ran across the sisal carpet and threw herself into his arms.

"Petie," she sobbed, against his chest as I had, "Daddy's gone. We've lost Daddy, darling."

"I know, Mama," he said, rocking her back and forth in his arms as you would a child. "I know. I know."

"Maude, go in and get your husband a glass of whiskey," Augusta Stallings boomed from across the room. "I brought some in case you don't have it. Make it neat, and a strong one. And bring Hannah a glass of sherry while you're at it. Shock's wearing off." And, when I hesitated, "Well, go on, girl. You said you wanted to do something, then do it. Don't stand there gawping. Let them have some privacy, for God's sake."

My face burned and tears stung afresh. Privacy? From me? I was Peter's wife. His father was my father-in-law. I had lost this day too. I turned and went into the kitchen and poured out the whiskey and the sherry. But it was a moment before I could clear my eyes of the tears of anger and hurt, and in that moment I heard Mother Hannah say, "Petie, promise you won't leave me alone tonight. I'll be all right in the morning; Hermie will be here. But I've never spent a night in Retreat alone. Please don't make me do it now."

"No, Mama," Peter said. "I won't."

I took the tray of drinks into the living room and handed it to Augusta Stallings.

"Perhaps you'll take these for me," I said, and, not waiting for her reply, went upstairs to Peter's and my bedroom and closed the door behind me. I sat down on the bed and looked out the window over the rooftop of Braebonnie and saw, above the line of firs and spruce on the farthest point, high up against the sky, the chimney pots of the Aerie. I began to cry then. It was full dark before I stopped.

When I went back downstairs, cried out and ravenously hungry, the women were gone. There seemed to be no one in the living room, so I started there, and then I heard voices and soft laughter in the out-of-sight alcove by the fire. Though I had heard it only once, I recognized the laughter instantly as Gretchen Winslow's. I stopped on the bottom stair.

"Oh, there he is in that silly sombrero and serape Mother and Daddy brought him from Mexico," Gretchen said in a soft voice that mingled laughter and tears. "I was eight or nine, I think, and couldn't decide if I was in love with Big Peter or Little Peter. The sombrero definitely tipped the scales in favor of Big Peter."

There was answering laughter that I realized, incredulously, was Mother Hannah's. "He wore that hat and serape in the Chowder Race that year, do you remember, Petie?" she said. "Philip Potter said it was like being beaten by Ramon Navarro in a Friendship sloop. I must admit I thought it was all quite dashing."

"He wore the hat until one of the Stallings boys—was it Albert or Henry?—stole it and ran it up the Yacht Club flagpole and it got rained on and melted," Peter said, and began laughing too. There was a soft rustle of pages, and I realized that they were sitting by the fire looking at photographs in one of the big shabby old albums from the bookcase. Three people who had known my father-in-law most or all of their lives, beginning the slow slog through grief toward whatever healing they could find. Like a family. I turned away and went into the kitchen.

Micah and Christina Willis were there, sitting at the old deal table. A drainboard full of clean dishes and a sink full of soaking ones testified to Christina's presence, and a newly filled wood rack by the kitchen door to Micah's. Smells of baking curled from the oven, and vases and tin buckets full of flowers added their rich spice. Christina was cutting doughnuts out of yellow dough on the dough board, and Micah was carving an enormous brown leg of lamb into delicate, thin pink slices. Something in a big iron pot on the stove bubbled slowly. Fresh molasses doughnuts cooled beside the stove. I thought I would weep with hunger and hurt.

Micah looked up at me, a long look, unreadable. Then he pulled out a chair and motioned to it. Christina looked up and smiled.

"Sit," Micah said. "You look like something the cat dragged in. Get some food in you; I bet you haven't had anything all day. Everybody too busy mourning the dead to look to the living and the soon-to-be."

"Oh, you poor thing," Christina Willis said, concern clouding her smooth broad face. "I thought I hadn't seen or heard anything from you all day. I asked Peter, but he didn't know where you were. Have you not eaten, then?"

"I haven't been hungry till now," I said, not wanting to appear pitiful or deprived. "I've been upstairs until just a minute ago. Don't worry about me, for goodness' sake. And don't let me get in your way. I've been in somebody's way all day. . . ."

I hadn't meant to say that, and the tears welled up again. They must know that Gretchen Winslow sat in the living room where I should have been, comforting my husband and mother-in-law. I turned my head away.

"One of those doughnuts would be wonderful, though," I said. "And is that coffee I smell?"

"Sit," Christina said. "You'll have more than doughnuts, if I have my way. There's lobster stew from lobsters that Micah just brought an hour ago, and a lamb from his father's flock, and I've made some spoon bread. Your father-in-law always loved my spoon bread—" She stopped and flushed and busied herself at the stove, and Micah bent over his carving so that his face was hidden by the fall of his black hair. In the dim yellow overhead light, he looked older, carved and gnarled and worn, like weathered wood. He was all compaction; there was nothing of attenuation to him at all.

I realized that they had loved Big Peter too, in some manner, and were struggling to hide their grief as I was. It was for some reason an enormously warming and liberating notion. For the first time that awful day I thought I might speak of him without weeping.

"I'm going to miss him more than I can say," I said simply, looking from one of the Willises to the other. "We had just become real friends, he and I. He showed me . . . something precious of his . . . that I might never have known about. I'll never forget that he wanted me to share it. It's meant everything to me."

I had no idea why I was speaking so to them. It could not have been more inappropriate, I suppose, at least not by colony standards. And yet it felt completely natural, and wonderfully comforting. I smiled, inadvertently, at the thought of the big house up there atop the point.

"Ayuh," Micah said slowly, deliberately, not looking at me. "I reckoned he might take you along up to the Aerie one day. Seemed to me when you first came here you might be the one he'd show it to."

So he knew. But knew what? I looked at his dark profile and over at Christina. She did not look up from the plate she was filling for me. Knew everything, then. The Willises knew everything about my father-in-law and the beautiful and faded Sarah Fowler. It occurred to me they might satisfy my curiosity there, but I knew I would never ask, and they would not speak of it again.

I ate a plate of chowder and lamb and new green beans, and had two cups of coffee and a doughnut, and felt infinitely better. We sat at the kitchen table, Micah and Christina and I, and some subterranean bond that would hold us forever was born that night. It isn't often that you know the precise provenance of a love. I have always been grateful for that night of loss and beginnings.

Presently I said, not even wondering at the strangeness of asking the question of hired employees, "Will he be buried here?"

"You mean with us?" Micah said, and I knew he was seeing again the little silent sun-swept cemetery beside the sea and us there among his people, arms full of lavender flowers. "I don't know. I was going to ask you."

"I don't have any idea," I said. "I hope so. I think he'd love that. Are . . . any of us, any summer people, there?"

"It's public," he said briefly. "There's some that are. He'd be welcome there."

I thought, from his tone, that not many of us were welcome.

"You were fond of him, weren't you?" I asked.

"I was partial to him, yes. He taught me to sail."

There was something very near a smile on his face, but not quite. I wondered what it would take.

"To sail? Did he really? I thought the club . . . I thought your father would do that. Being a boatmaker, and all."

This time he did smile. He looked years younger. "You thought the club was private? You're right. It set the members on their ears something smart, I reckon. But they couldn't do much about it. He was commodore that year. I was nine, just a bit older than his own son. And that first summer I beat every colony tadpole up here in the Beast class. After that he didn't invite me to sail with the summer folks again; I reckon some of the women saw to that. But Peter and I used to have our own races, out of the boatyard harbor. Your Peter, I mean. He got so good he beat me half the time. Yep, I owe your father-in-law a lot, and sailing's not the least of it. He was teaching my boy, too. Reckon none of you knew that. Been coming down to the boatyard once, twice a week, all summer. I could have done it myself, but he was a better teacher. I wanted Caleb to learn from the best."

Sorrow flooded me afresh. I felt my face twist and pressed my fist hard against my mouth to keep it from contorting. I did not wish to weep in front of Micah and Christina Willis.

"I guess not all summer people are your enemies," I said thickly. "I guess there was one of us you called friend."

I was not looking at him and was surprised when, after a long silence, I felt his hand on my shoulder. It was a gentle touch. When I looked up, his face was gentle too. I had not seen it like that before.

"Only a fool talks in generalities, Maude," he said. "He *was* my friend. He had a lot of friends among us natives. There've been a few of you who did. Likely there'll be others. It just isn't a policy with us. But more than the Retreat folks will grieve for him. I think we'd all be honored if he rested with our own."

But it was not to be. The next morning Hermione arrived from Connecticut, straw-pale and cold-faced and red-eyed, and set the cottage to ringing with the tempest of her grief and anger. It was the fury of the abandoned child; even I knew that. But it fairly howled. The first object of that bereft rage was Peter's suggestion that their father lie in the little churchyard by the sea. I heard the explosion from the stair landing, as I was coming down for a late breakfast, having lingered as long as hunger allowed me in the bedroom where I had, for the first time, slept alone. True to his word, Peter had sat up all night beside his mother. Once again I turned and went back upstairs and took refuge in the little cubicle overlooking the bay. I thought at this rate I might never eat a meal in Retreat in company of anyone but the Willises again. I closed the door firmly, but I could still hear Hermie's hot, bitter words.

"No! Not while there's breath in my body," she shrieked, strangling on tears. "He will not be all the way up here with all these country bumpkins where we can't come see him; I won't have him in that common little . . . mudhole! This is not our place; Boston is our place! Our people have always been buried in Boston! I never got to see him at all in the summer after I was married because he was stuck up here, and I will not let him stay up here forever! I won't! Mama, I will not!"

Her voice spiraled up and up, until she was actually keening, and I heard Mother Hannah's voice murmuring to her, and Peter's, strong and hard with his own anger. I had not seen him at all since the afternoon before, but I was relieved to hear that iron in his voice. It had not been there yesterday.

There was a hissing, spitting row, an ugly chewing thing that no door could have shut away from my ears, and I could only sit and listen miserably while my husband and his sister fought like starved dogs over the body of their father. Somewhere in it, Hermie rounded on Peter about his refusal to come home and take their father's place at the bank. She called him, among other things, a traitor to the family and the indirect instrument of their father's long depressions. Mother Hannah began to cry.

"You probably killed him too, on top of everything else," Hermie shrilled. "It was all that worry over you that weakened his heart. I've always known it would."

There was a ringing silence, and then the sound of a slap, a gasp, fresh wails from Hermie, and the slamming of the front door. I doubled over the hard melon of my baby, nearly blind with misery. I simply could not cope with the storms of two women who had lost their mainstay, two women who did not, in any case, want comfort from me. I could not do it alone. I knew that Peter would head for the water. The only thing I did not know was when he would return.

I spent another day in my room. At midafternoon

Christina brought me a tray and said that Mother Hannah and Hermie had gone over to the funeral home in Castine to take the things Big Peter would wear home on the train to Boston.

"You ought to come down and get some air," she said, putting her work-reddened hand over mine. "You look some peaked. Dr. Lincoln has stopped in twice to ask about you, but both times he's had to see about Mrs. Chambliss and Miss Hermie. They're taking it real hard. He asked me to look in on you. All this stir-up really isn't good for you, you know."

"I'm all right, Tina," I said. "I have books, and I know you're not going to let me starve. I think I'm probably better off up here for at least one more day. The family has some things they need to work out."

"Looks to me like Miss Hermie has already worked everything out," she said primly.

"I guess they'll be taking him back to Boston, then," I said. "Do you happen to know when? And . . . did Peter say when he was coming back?"

"They're going home with him tomorrow on the noon train from Bangor," she said. "The funeral home is taking him straight to the train, and Micah is going to drive them over and bring the car back. Don't you worry about Peter. I've been watching him run away to sea for lots of years. He'll be back."

She smiled at me, and despite my anguish I smiled too. Odd that in only twenty-four hours she and Micah had become my constants in this place. I had always thought Peter would be that.

To my great relief, I did not see Hermione at all during her visit. I was drifting near sleep when Mother Hannah came up to my room that night and sat down on my bed. Hermie was not with her.

"I put her to bed," Mother Hannah said. "She's had a dreadful day. As I have. And, I suspect, you too, Maude. You've been very sensitive to us in a trying time, and we are grateful. You must forgive us for abandoning you; I knew that the Willises would look after you, but we've quite ignored you, and I know you were fond of your father-in-law. When we return from Boston we shall make it up to you, Peter and I. Meanwhile, I think it would be much the best if you stayed quiet and didn't try to come with us. I'd much prefer that you stay here where Dr. Lincoln can keep an eye on you. I've arranged for you to go to the Potters for the weekend. Amy is going to come over for you early in the morning and put you straight to bed, and Dr. Lincoln will be by a bit later. The best thing you could do for Big Peter is keep his grandchild safe."

I nodded, knowing I was bested. In any event, I did not want to be part of that sad cortege to Boston. I wanted to stay in Retreat and keep what I had of Big Peter here with me.

"Is Peter . . . have you heard . . . ?"

"He'll come home in time to go with us," she said, smiling fondly. "He's just upset. Go easy on him, Maude. He always comes back in time."

He did, of course. He came in at dawn and tiptoed up the stairs and climbed into bed with me, and I turned over and put my arms out to him, and he crept into them. We held each other in silence. His skin was cold and damp, and his heart beat in slow, dragging thuds. There seemed nothing to say, so I said nothing. Presently, when I thought he must be asleep, he murmured, "Are you all right?"

"Yes. Are you?"

"I will be, when I can get all this over and get back here to you. Maude?"

"What, love?"

"I want the baby to be a boy. I want you to have a boy so he can be Peter Williams Chambliss too."

"Well, then, I'll do that," I said, and kissed him. "Go to sleep."

"You're the only thing that makes any sense," he mumbled, and then he did sleep. After a while, I did too. When I woke, Amy Potter was standing by my bed with a breakfast tray and the sun was high, and they had been gone with Micah Willis in the Marmon for over an hour.

For the rest of the summer Peter was someone I did not know. He was silent and distracted, and away more than he was there. When he and Mother Hannah got back from Boston he spent one night prowling restlessly about the cottage and then took the *Hannah* out for three days. Busy with her stream of visitors and thank-you notes and the minutiae of her new queenship, Mother Hannah hardly seemed to notice his absence. She thrust me smartly back into quarantine on the sun porch and left me with embroidery and yellowing novels, and without my husband or my father-in-law I had no friend at court to help me escape the chaise and the blankets. I lay there, as lonely and alien as I have ever felt, out of the mainstream of the constant flow of women, and wondered if there would ever be anything in this beautiful, sharp-edged place that was mine alone.

"I miss Peter," I said to her once, when she asked if I was all right.

"Well, you'd better find a way to accept these little trips of his," she said. "He's always handled his difficulties like this. He's sensitive and needs his time alone. His father did it too. We must remember, we women, that this place is really for the men, to help them find the strength they need for their work. When you look at it like that, I'm sure you won't mind that he goes for a little sail by himself every now and then."

But I did mind. Peter's little sails became more and more frequent and lasted longer and longer. I grew larger and clumsier and tireder and unhappier, and the baby dropped low, waiting, I thought, to be born. I told myself that soon it would be time to go home to Northpoint, and in the fall my baby would be born, and then I would surely have Peter back, and all would be well again. I had only to wait. Only to wait. . . .

But I did not wait long enough, it seemed. On the second week in August, while Peter was away on the *Hannah* far around Naskeag Point and up into Blue Hill Bay, I went suddenly and violently into labor, and it was Micah Willis who drove me those endless jolting miles to the Castine hospital instead of my husband, and Mother Hannah who held me in her arms in the back seat, bracing me against the bumps, Mother Hannah whose voice told me, over and over, "It will be all right. I'm here."

It was a long grinding labor, and I was blinded with sweat and pain and fear. I knew it was too early. The baby would be too small. I could not seem to help; the pain came in sucking red tides, and I could have no ether because of the prematurity. I tried to push but my body seemed paralyzed; I tried to breathe shallowly and fast, as I was told by the sweating, distracted house physician and the tired nurses to do, but I could not seem to do that either. There seemed for an eternity only pain and pressure and more pain; nobody had ever told me that pain could be like this. This pain was past monstrousness and consumed the world.

Toward nightfall I thought my mother was in the room with me. I could see her plainly beside the bed, small and dark and lovely and smiling, her hands on my face, her voice soft with the honey and smoke of Charleston. I began to cry with sheer relief.

"Oh, Mama, I can't do this," I wept. "Tell them. I can't make them listen to me, and Mama, I really can't do this. . . ."

"You can do it," she said, but her voice was changing; it was not hers any longer.

"I can't," I wailed. "Not without Peter, I can't. He's left me by myself and I can't do this without him. Oh, Mama, I hate him!"

The words rose up and up and became a scream, and the scream went on and on. Through it the woman leaned near me and brushed my wet hair off my forehead and held my hands hard, and I knew it was not my mother, after all, but my mother-in-law.

"You can do it," she whispered to me. "You can and you must. You must forgive Peter and go on. At all costs we must keep things even, we women. This is up to us. And we will do this together."

And we did. At four that morning my son Peter Williams Chambliss slid into the world, tiny and red and roaring with life, and the awful love that caught and whirled me away when they laid him on my stomach was as strong and old as the earth and would, I knew dimly, abide as long. Even as they lifted him out of my arms and I slid finally into sleep, I whispered, "Mine. Mine. Mine."

The first thing I saw when I opened my eyes the next morning was a nurse with an armful of silken anemones, as perfect and incredible as butterflies' wings. She handed me the card.

From your lady of the secrets, it read in a slanted black backhand. *To this very newest Peter. With all the love left. S.*

Chapter Six

I t's almost uncanny, isn't it, the way our lives seem to run in parallel?" Amy Potter said to me on a June morning of my third summer in Retreat.

We were sitting on the beach below the Little House, watching the straggling remnants of one of the colony's Saturday regattas toil out of sight around the point toward Little Deer Isle. They would circle Birch Island and come home again; this race would last all day. Peter had gone ahead early in the *Hannah;* we had watched him take her past the beach nearly on her lee rail. There was a streaming wind from the east that meant rain tomorrow or the next day. Parker Potter was only now struggling past in *Circe;* we could see the blaze of his red hair under the high sun. He was laboring with the mainsail, which was luffing badly. Amy sighed. It was not a good summer for Parker.

Petie lay beside me on a blanket, face reddened from the crying fit that had slid him, finally, into exhausted sleep. His small knotted fists still stirred restlessly, and a bubble formed between his red lips and burst. I adjusted the parasol that covered my small furious son and looked over at Amy.

"You mean because of the baby and being up here so close to your time?" I said. Amy was pregnant that summer, vastly and miserably. Her baby was due in late July, and Parker had promised to take her home to Boston in a couple of weeks. Like mine, the summer before, her mother-in-law thought she should not be at Braebonnie at all and allowed her out of the cottage only for Saturday outings with me, and only after my promise that we would come straight to old Lottie Padgett's tiny house on the shore. I knew that Helen Potter, like most other colony matrons, thought Lottie eccentric and unsanitary but a veritable good witch with children.

And it was true. If worst came to worst, Lottie Padgett could probably deliver babies as well as any midwife. So Amy and I came to her each Saturday morning, me with flailing little Petie, Amy with her troublesome burden. She had been sick most of her pregnancy and was still nauseated from time to time. Lottie Padgett fussed over us and fed us herbal tea and spice cookies and settled us in the sunshine on her beach, or by her fire if the weather was bad, and swept us into the untidy and beguiling circle of visiting animals and children as if we had been one of them. I felt tension run out of me like water here in this arcane doll's house, and Amy seemed soothed and lightened, and even Petie stopped his crying and slept. This morning Lottie was off down the beach gathering mussels with the tow-haired children from Mary's Garden and one or two Compound youngsters, and a nest of orphan red squirrels chirred in cotton wool beside her banked fire. I think I have seldom known such utter, seamless peace in Retreat as I did on those few June Saturdays at the Little House.

Amy pushed her hair off her face and grimaced as her baby kicked. It was a terror for kicking; I had seen her stomach literally dancing with its force all summer. I thought it must keep her awake, that and other things. Her dark, impish face was pale and thin that summer, so that the lone dimple beside her mouth seemed a hole poked in the flesh, and her eyes were deep-shadowed. And most startling of all, her dark bob was threaded all over with strands of silver. It had happened over the winter. They had not been there the summer before. I remembered she had told me that her mother was completely white-haired by the time she was thirty, so I was not altogether surprised. But the effect, on Amy, was not that of heredity but of illness and depletion. She seemed exhausted that summer, and very frail.

"Well, the baby, yes," she said. "And then Father Potter dying so suddenly, like Big Peter did. And Parker being . . . disturbed, and everything. I know Peter went through a pretty bad time after his father died."

"It *is* uncanny, isn't it?" I said. "Just be sure you don't have your baby in the Castine hospital. Then I'll be afraid that anything bad that ever happens to me will happen to you too." I saw her tired eyes darken and added hastily, "Not that having Petie was a bad experience. But I'd rather have done it at home, with Peter there, and I know you would too. And you will."

It was odd, that summer, that I, the younger and more inexperienced of us, in all ways the initiate, seemed older than she did. I thought again how very wide was the gulf between a woman who had borne a child and one who had not.

"I hope so," she said, and her voice was thin and old. "I hate to say it, but I can't seem to make Parker get serious about going home. Or much of anything else. Half the time I think he forgets that this is a baby in here. His baby, at that. He told Gretchen Winslow the other day that if I got any fatter and sloppier he was going to divorce me. With me and both the Valentine sisters standing right there."

"Oh, God, I'll bet Gretch the Wretch adored that," I said, anger at Parker flashing hotly through me. It was not the first small cruelty I had seen him deal Amy that summer.

"Probably," Amy said. "Especially since she's lost another million pounds and gotten a gorgeous tan. Oh, Maude, tell me it'll be better when the baby comes. It was for you all, wasn't it? Didn't it make Peter sort of . . . start to put his father's death behind him? I don't know what will happen if Parker doesn't."

I know what will happen, I thought grimly, but did not say. He'll drink himself to death and you'll be stuck with his mother and his grandmother and his baby for the rest of your natural life.

"It'll be better, you'll see," I said, patting her hand. Its bones felt like a bird's under mine, light and impossibly fragile. "Peter got himself together when Petie was born. He doesn't go off on the boat for days; he's not distant any more. He stands up for me to his mother. He's my old Peter; we're closer than ever. And Parker will change too. Besides the change that comes with being a father, it's sort of the other side of the coin of death. A birth so soon after a death makes everything seem . . . natural, a part of something much bigger and older. A cycle of the earth. It doesn't take the grief away, but it takes the worst of the pain."

"I wish I thought so. . . ."

"I know so."

Philip Potter had died on the Brookline Country Club golf course the previous April, of the secret red flower of an aneurysm that, the doctors said, had probably lain dormant there all his life and bloomed only at that moment. It had been lightning quick; he had been dead by the time he hit the fairway. A mercy, everyone told Helen and Parker. He was simply not the sort of man who could have borne being ill or crippled. And that was true and, for Helen Potter, seemed to afford a great deal of comfort. As so many of the older women of Retreat did, she appeared to gain enormous strength, almost power, at the death of her husband. She who had never made a decision in her life, never even voiced a strong opinion, became overnight a woman capable of running a firm and selling the vast ancestral seat and finding a smaller and more modern home in Brookline and telling her mother-in-law, who had been wailing for forty-eight hours like a banshee, to shut up. It was Mamadear who could not handle the death of Philip Potter. Mamadear and his only child, Parker. Parker got drunk the night his father died, and few people had seen him entirely sober since.

He had always been a hard drinker, and to an extent the colony was used to his escapades. But mostly they had had a kind of sophomoric exuberance about them, a bad boy's panache. They were funnier, in the main, than they were destructive. It was widely considered that Parker was trying to get his red, roaring father's attention, to be seen by him as an equal or at least a proper heir apparent: a cub trying his claws on an old lion.

But this summer there had been nothing amusing about Parker Potter's behavior when he drank, which was virtually every day. He lost his fine athlete's edge on the tennis court and at the helm of the *Circe,* and blundered and erred and stumbled and fell, and lost matches and races, and when he did he bellowed and cursed and threw his racquet and kicked the flanks of his boat and blamed everyone and everything but himself. He became so abusive on the tennis court that courteous Guildford Kennedy, who was his doubles partner, reprimanded him publicly, and Parker threw his racquet at Guildford and gashed his large, fine nose. He roared at a young native waiter in the dining hall when his coffee came to him cool, and dashed the liquid over the boy and told him to get out and not come back. When Amy tried to reason with him, he told her to shut her damned flapping mouth and stalked out, overturning his chair and leaving her to struggle with tears as she made excuses for him. He ran Erica Conant's chauffeur off the road into the village in his Mercedes roadster, severely shaking the furious Erica and her visiting bridge club from Beacon Hill. And, Peter told me on coming in from the water one afternoon after a regatta, no one would sail with him any more. His temper was simply too bad and his seamanship too erratic to be safe in deep-water races. I remembered the red-faced, savagely smiling young man who had faultlessly navigated miles of killer fog even when half drunk only two summers before and thought what a long, sad way Parker had come from that day.

"And he dumped God knows how much whiskey in the punch at the yacht club tea this afternoon, and you know there are always old ladies and children who drink that stuff," Peter said. "It wasn't at all funny. Burdie Winslow is talking about suspending his club privileges, and Guild Kennedy has spoken to the tournament committee about barring him from court play for a while. I've never seen anybody behave this badly in the colony, and there've been some pretty high-spirited members before him. His father, for instance, raised more hell than anybody in living memory, but somehow he was never really offensive. It's the liquor. He's turned into a bad drunk this summer."

"Where does he get it?" I asked. "I know there's always been a little liquor at Braebonnie, but no more than any of us have, and that's surely not enough to get drunk every day on."

Peter looked at me quizzically. "Do you really not know?" he said. "He gets it the same place we all do. We buy it up here. There's more whiskey smuggled into these coves and inlets on dark nights than the rest of the Atlantic coast put together. Best stuff, too. Up here, if a guy has a lobster boat, you can be fairly sure he's smuggling. Retreat has three or four 'official' sources. I'm not going to tell you who they are, but Micah Willis didn't get that Ford truck hauling, you can bet on that."

"Micah . . . oh, I can't believe that," I said. "He has a family, a business—are you sure? I thought the liquor in the cottages was just sort of . . . what everybody had left when Prohibition started. Peter, you know as well as I do that Micah Willis is one of the most *moral* men we've ever known."

"I agree," Peter said, grinning. "And if he thought he was doing anything immoral, he'd stop and turn himself over to the sheriff. He thinks, like most of the natives, that it's the law that's immoral. That the government's got no business telling a man what he can drink and what he can't. I'm not so sure he isn't right, either."

"Is it dangerous?"

"You bet your bottom dollar it is," he said. "And that's all I'm going to tell you about smuggling or Micah or anybody else. And you'd do well not to mention it to him or Christina or my mother. She still thinks our stock is Dad's leftovers."

"I'm not a fool," I said crisply. And of course I did not mention it to Micah Willis or to anyone else. But forever after that, when I caught a glimpse of Micah's solid shape pruning shrubbery or carrying the ladder around the house or swinging easily into the kitchen with a load of wood, I saw behind him, as if in a kind of pentimento, the dark shapes of silent skiffs on moonless water, and cloth-muffled oars resting in oarlocks, and the still forms of waiting men peering through the black for a single flash of light far out in the bay and straining for the low throb of idling engines. And something old and dark in my own blood leaped to meet those images.

"Maybe it would be better if nobody would sell Parker liquor," I said to Peter, but he shook his head.

"Micah and some of the others won't now, but there's always somebody down bay who will. If Parker wants booze he can get it easily enough. I really thought when his dad died he'd shape up, but it's gotten a lot worse."

"Of course it is," I said. "He can never win, now. He can never on this earth show his father how tough he is, or how grown up. He'll drink more and more and act worse and worse, and he still won't be able to get his father's attention."

Peter skinned out of his salt-damp sweater and came and put his arms around me. I buried my face in his smooth, cool, damp chest. I licked his skin lightly; it tasted of salt and the sweetness of his flesh. He kissed the top of my head.

"How come you're so smart?" he said.

"I'm not," I said. "I just know how it feels to go around having an eternal one-sided conversation with a dead parent. I railed at my mother for years, for going off and leaving me to grow up without her. And . . . I think that's sort of what you were doing when you went off in the boat last summer, after your father died. You were furious at him, and so you ran away from home."

"Don't make excuses for me," he said into my hair. "I was a jerk. A louse. It still makes me cringe to think about it. Leaving you alone to cope with all that shit after he died, and then to have to go to the hospital to have our baby with only my mother and the hired man.

Christ! I wonder you even let me back in the house."

"Well, I knew how upset you were," I said, nuzzling him. "And after all, the baby wasn't supposed to come for almost two months. And I could do worse than have your mother and Micah around when I had a baby. And after all, you're back, aren't you? You haven't run away to sea once since then."

He pulled me with him down onto the bed. It was tumbled and warm, and outside the clouds that the east wind presaged were streaming in, sucking the heat from the last of the sun. I was still a bit sleepy from the nap his homecoming had interrupted. Downstairs, Petie slept in the old wicker crib that had been his grandfather's, watched over by pretty twelve-year-old Polly Willis, Micah's brother's child. Mother Hannah had hired her expressly to mind Petie this summer, and she was good at it. She minded several small siblings and cousins at home. I knew that if Petie woke in one of his small red rages, Polly could soothe him back to sleep. I burrowed into the warm bed and curled up into Peter's side.

"What would I do without you?" he said, sleepy himself, into the curve of my neck. "What if you were somebody else and not you, somebody I couldn't talk to? What if you didn't understand me like you do? What if you were stuck up or mean-spirited or stupid?"

"Then I'd know you married me for my looks," I said, eyes closed. After the distance and trouble of the past summer, Peter's body against mine felt doubly precious, doubly comforting. I'd told Amy the truth that morning; I did indeed have Peter back and could not imagine ever feeling estranged from him, shut away. But I had.

"What if I couldn't . . . do this?" he said, turning me to face him and wrapping his long legs around me. "Or maybe this. . . ."

I let myself go limp against him but said into his ear, "You may want to reconsider. It's not the best time for this unless you want another baby—"

"Christ, no," he said, propping himself up on one elbow and running his hand over his face. "Not until this one shapes up."

I was silent against him. Yes, I had told Amy the truth about Peter that morning, but not the whole truth. The other part of that truth was, this summer, the first great wedge between us.

For Peter could not seem to make contact with his son, not on the terrible subterranean level where I felt my kin with him; indeed, not in any essential way. It was not that he ignored Petie. He played with him in the mornings and held him when he was awake, and fresh from his bath, and fed; he carried him about the colony when we first brought him there and showed him to all the friends of his youth and seemed, at those times, to be every inch and every fiber the proud young father. And I think he was, at those sweet times. It was just that he could not sustain the bond through the bad times, and there were plenty of those with Petie. Then he gave him back to me or to Polly and, if the crying did not stop, went into his study or back into the big bedroom to talk with his mother or, less frequently, down to the water, to the boat. At home in North-point, he seemed more patient with the baby, and more sympathetic with my struggles to calm and quiet him. There, he seemed, if not smitten with Petie, at least moved by his tiny son's war with the universe and sometimes softly amused by it.

"That's right, little guy," he would say. "Go after that windmill and give it hell."

But in Retreat, he seemed to distance himself from the baby and to slide over into his mother's stern and implacable camp. "That child needs to shape up. Let him cry, Maude. He'll never hush if you run in there and pick him up every time he opens his mouth."

"You sound exactly, precisely, like your mother," I said early on that summer. "Spare the rod and spoil the child. Children should be seen and not heard. What happens to you up here? You don't sound like that at home. Shape up, indeed. He's a ten-month-old *baby,* Peter! You sound like you want to put him in military school."

"It might not be a bad idea," Peter said grimly above the baby's outraged howls, and I picked Petie up, love and pain at his pain twisting me inside from my throat to the pit of my stomach. Peter Williams Chambliss IV had been born furious, as if racked with helpless rage at being tumbled early from his secret sea, and was, these ten months later, still an angry and inconsolable baby. He fought, he cried, he raged, he hungered, he thirsted, for something we simply could not give him. At times he frightened me badly; at others he angered me in my turn. He seemed insatiable, a ravenous little organism, a living, breathing need. He was dark and simian and red and flailing; I knew that in his grandmother's eyes, and to a lesser extent in his father's, he was the very graven image of the dark, low-to-the-earth aliens of the swamp South who were my people. There was nothing in little Petie, in those early days, of his father's long-boned, flaxen, northern tribe. I think Peter only saw that clearly when we were in Retreat, among those people; saw what Mother Hannah saw and pursed her mouth at. At home, Petie was more his son and less exclusively mine.

Mine, mine . . . yes, he was mine. Every ounce and bone and eyelash and fingernail and tooth and shriek, he was mine. I shook all over with love for him; I wept, often, at his intractable, furious pain. I felt every tremor in my own flesh. I know they thought I spoiled him badly, my husband and my mother-in-law.

"Maude, I worry so that he'll be spoiled beyond reclaiming, and nobody will want to be around him, and then what sort of life will he have?" Peter said once, as I rocked the baby in the middle of yet another sleepless night. After that, I tried not to go so often to my crying child. I would do anything to spare him the loneliness of alienation.

But in the end I could not let him cry alone. I knew about outcasts and pariahs. I had cried in the night at Retreat, too. My child would be loved here in this place, if only by me.

A week or so after Amy and I had our talk on the beach of the Little House, Peter took me over to Castine for an outing. We went alone, for once, Mother Hannah having an afternoon bridge game at the club with Erica's visiting friends. Petie was asleep in his crib when we left, and Polly Willis sat beside him reading *Anne of Green Gables*. I had found her, when she first came to us that summer, a proficient reader and starved for books, so I had dug out the best of the cottage's library for her and borrowed others I thought she would like from the little village library. I had even taken her there one afternoon and helped her get her own junior library card. Miss Prudence Comfort, the librarian, told us she was the youngest person in the library's history to have one, and Polly was as proud as if she were writing books instead of merely reading them.

"She's ruined for sure," Micah said when he brought her to us that morning. "Not a jot of work can anyone get from her now, nose always in a book."

But his face as he looked at his niece, reading beside the sleeping baby, was gentle.

"You don't fool me, Micah Willis," I said. "I know

you sit up nights and read Greek by lantern light, or something impossibly esoteric. Runs in the family, I'll bet."

"That's all you know, Maude Chambliss," he said, going out the kitchen door. "It's Latin, not Greek. I'll pick you up at four, Pol," he called back to his niece. "Your Aunt Christina won't be here today; gone to old Mrs. Waldo's funeral. But if you need me, call the store and send down to the boathouse."

"I'll be fine, Uncle Micah," she called back, not lifting her taffy head. Micah and Peter and I all smiled at her. Polly had that effect on people. She had a child's generous, trusting heart in the ripening body of a young woman. It made an appealing combination.

"We'll be home by four too," I said, and she smiled again, and Peter and I got into the Marmon and left. As we drove out of the driveway I noticed again how tall the lilacs had grown, once again shutting the windows away behind a wall of green and white. It seemed only days since the day Micah had cut them, not years. The smell of them was almost dizzying.

It was a near-perfect day. The air was cool and fresh and smelled of the kelp and salt that streamed in off the bay at the full of the tide. The sun was high in the tender vault of the sky, and the thunderheads that would sweep in late in the day were still only white marble puffs at the margins of the sky, solid and silver-lined. There was a blue clarity about the horizon and the distant hills that spoke of a weather change, but not for another day or two. Along the meadows' edges, as we drove past, I saw pink clover and purple lupine, hawkweed and wild daylilies. Brilliant pink wild azaleas, called lambkill here, flickered like wildfire in the birch groves. Daisies, buttercups, wild columbine, and the purple flags of wild iris starred the roadside. Behind them all was the eternal dark of the pines and firs and spruce thickets and, between those, the glittering indigo of the bay. I took a deep breath and put my head back on the seat.

"This is what Maine is," I said. "The sky, the ocean. Wildflowers and black fir and spruce, and rocks and gulls and always the smell of pine and salt in your nose. Nothing else really matters; everything else is just . . . tacked on. Just noise."

"Me too?" Peter said. "You too? Are we just noise?" But he covered my hand with his and squeezed it, and I knew he knew what I meant.

We had lunch on the porch of the ornate wooden Pentogoet Hotel, surrounded by flower boxes full of begonias and geraniums with butterflies dancing above them, overlooking the sail-speckled harbor at the foot of the steep street. The great three-masted schooner that was the official training vessel of the Maine Maritime Academy atop the hill lay at anchor, her sails furled, small blue-clad figures moving about her decks. The packet for Islesboro wallowed at the dock, and a small crowd of soberly dressed people waited for the arrival of the great steamer, the E.S.S. *Belfast,* that had plied the bay from Boston to Bangor since near the turn of the century. The street and harbor had the air of a resort village or a European working port; it seemed exotic, far removed from the stark gray, green, and cobalt terrain around Retreat. From where we sat, we could not hear the noise of the harbor, but there was still a tingling feel of holiday in the air. A fat yellow cat came out of the hotel and settled down to doze in the sun, and a perfect blanc mange with a daisy on it arrived for dessert. Old ladies and crying babies and frightened young wives seemed light-years away. I stretched in the afternoon balm and smiled at Peter and felt very young again, and as free as a leaf in a lazy river.

"It's going to be hard to go back," I said dreamily. "I feel eighteen again, with everything still ahead of us."

"Not off by far, since you're only twenty." Peter grinned, his eyes closed against the sun. Then he opened them and looked at me. In the light they looked more like clear ice than ever, ice over cold depths untouched for centuries. His face and forearms had already gone the deep red-gold that the long days on the water burnt them, and the shock of hair had whitened. I smiled at him, simply because he looked so fine sitting there. My husband. My first love.

"Is it really so hard for you up here, Maude?" he said softly. "This beautiful place: does it really make you feel as if everything good is behind you? Because that's not true."

"No," I said. "I know it's not. I do know that. It's just that . . . now I know the outline of everything ahead. I didn't, when I was eighteen."

"And you don't now," he said. "Don't be so eager to get your life all settled. Nobody can see ahead."

"Can't you?" I asked him, truly surprised. I would have thought that he of all people could see the shape of all that waited ahead for him, especially in Retreat. In that place where time had long since jelled.

"Of course not."

We were mostly silent on the drive home. It had been a wonderful runaway day, and I was content to bask in its afterglow, knowing that when we reached the cottage Petie would be awake and probably howling and the magic of the last few hours would disperse. But we could always go again. There would be days and days for that, years and years. . . .

It was well after four when we turned into the driveway of Liberty, and Micah's truck was already there. But instead of being neatly drawn up to the back door, as it always was, it was skewed across the drive with two wheels on the front lawn, blocking our entrance, and the front door lay back against the cab as if it had been slammed there with great force and left. The front door of the cottage stood open too, and I could see dim figures behind the sheltering screens on neighboring porches, looking toward Liberty.

"Petie," I breathed, my heart stopping the breath in my throat, and was out of the Marmon and running across the lawn before Peter had completely stopped it. I heard him slam the car door and start across the lawn behind me, calling my name, and then a high red keening that I realized later was my own blood began in my ears, and I heard nothing else. When the screen door burst open and a figure tumbled backward out of it, I did not even hear the noise of that. I stared at the man who somersaulted down the front steps of Liberty and lay in a boneless heap on the white gravel walkway with deaf ears and stupid, uncomprehending eyes. Only when Peter arrived and bent over him and said, in disgust, "Oh, Christ, Parkie!" did I realize that the man was Parker Potter and that he was very drunk and bleeding from the mouth. Sound came flooding back, and even as I raced into the cottage I heard my child shrieking, and a softer sobbing, and the cold, furious voice of my mother-in-law saying, "Get out of my house this instant. I am going to call both the doctor and the police, and at the very least you will not set foot in this house again."

Inside, in the lilac-spawned dimness, Micah Willis stood in the middle of the living room floor, breath coming in tearing gasps, one hand cradling the other, white as death beneath the tan of his face. His eyes stared past Mother Hannah toward his niece, who sat curled in a wing chair, face buried in her hands, crying softly. There were white rings around the irises, and his mouth was a slit scraped from granite. Mother

Hannah, in her dressing gown, something I had never seen her wear outside her boudoir, had a great brass Chinese candlestick in hand, as one would hold a club, and her face was mottled with rage and slicked with cold cream. In his crib, Petie bleated on and on. I went to him and picked him up automatically, even before I fully took in the scene in the room. Behind me, Peter said, "What in hell is going on here?"

Micah said nothing, only slowly moving his eyes over to Peter, and Mother Hannah advanced a few steps and took Peter's arm and said, in the same cold, outraged voice, "I heard this terrible commotion, and then the children crying, and I came in and found him simply beating Parker Potter to a pulp, right there on the floor! He threw him out the door; I'm sure everyone has seen and heard it. Peter, call the sheriff; I want him arrested. I will not have this in my house—"

"Hush, Mother. What's this about, Willis?" Peter said. His voice was a carbon of his mother's; I had never heard it before.

Micah took a deep breath and shook his head. Polly Willis caught a ragged sob, and he looked back at her and then to Peter again.

"Came to pick Polly up and found him all over her out on the sun porch," he said. His voice was tight and flat. "Had his hands all over her, one hand over her mouth . . . she was backed up against the windows white as a sheet, fighting him, couldn't breathe. . . . I pulled him off her and knocked the living hell out of him, and if your mother hadn't come in I would have killed him. I still may. He's drunk as a skunk and has been, this summer long. If you folks want to put up with him, that's your business, but if he lays a finger on one of my own again he's a dead man. And I mean that. That child is one month over twelve years old—"

"You came into my home and hit a guest here," Mother Hannah shrilled suddenly. I shook my head to clear it. I had never heard her raise her voice before.

"He was trying to rape my niece," Micah said.

"Do not use such language in this house! You are dismissed as of this instant—"

"What are you saying?" I heard my own voice screaming at my mother-in-law. "He comes in here and finds that . . . that oaf crawling all over his twelve-year-old niece and you stand here and tell him not to use bad language? You think Parker Potter came into your house as a guest this afternoon? Do you let your guests rape twelve-year-olds? Where were you all this time?"

She whirled on me. "You hush your mouth! You know nothing about . . . about the way things are done here! You never have! I might have known you'd stick up for—for trash, against one of us. . . . I was asleep; I had no idea anyone was here but Polly and the baby."

I stared at her, speechless, and then turned to Peter. He stood silent, looking from me to his mother.

"*Peter!*" I cried. He shook his head.

"Mother, shut up," he said levelly. "If you can't be quiet, go back to your room. He did the right thing; he couldn't stand there and let Parker . . . *Christ!* What a mess. Thank God he got here when he did. Micah, wait until I get him home to Braebonnie, and then we'll talk about this. Of course you're not fired; I hope you don't think—"

"I don't think anything that's not true," Micah Willis said, his voice colder even than Mother Hannah's and perfectly calm. "You better get him on home. I didn't hit him hard. Didn't have to. The whiskey did the rest. You can probably walk him, if you feel like getting that close to him. And don't bother firing me. I quit."

Peter looked at Micah, started to speak, and then

turned and went out the front door. I stood silent,
Petie snuffling in my arms, one hand on Polly Willis's
trembling head. I knew I should comfort her, but I
could not look away from the dark, dead-eyed man in
front of me. He looked back at me, also silent. I saw
his chest begin to slow in its heaving and heard his
breath go nearer normal. Outside, I saw Peter come
past the windows, half carrying Parker.

"Polly, can you walk, child?" Micah said then. I felt
her nod her head.

"Then let's get you home."

He came over to her, and put his arm around her,
and lifted her out of the chair, and walked her to the
door. He did not look back.

"Micah, wait," I called after him.

He kept going. The screen door banged behind
him.

"Micah, I want to talk to you. I want to tell you . . .
please come back a minute. Let me help with this.
Micah, this is *me* . . ."

He turned to face me, dark and hard in the sun of
late afternoon. Polly sat in the truck, staring straight
ahead.

"No," he said. "Don't you understand? You are not
one of us. I want nothing from you or your family. Or
any of the rest of you."

"But we're not like that! That's not us, that was
Parker."

"It only takes one of you," he said. And he got into
the truck and shut the door. I sat down in the wing
chair where Polly Willis had huddled in her terror,
and bowed my head over the struggling form of my
child, and cried. Petie cried too, and I rocked him
back and forth in my arms, but I did not stop crying,
and I did not lift my head.

After a time I sensed rather than saw a presence,
and looked up, and Micah was there, standing silently

beside my chair. His hand rested on Petie's downy head, and the baby had stopped crying and was looking solemnly at him. He still said nothing, only stood there touching the baby and looking down at me.

"You were there when he was born," I said, tasting salt. "You were there for his start; you were part of it. Please. Don't punish us all for what Parker did. I wanted . . . I want Petie to know you when he's growing up."

He sighed.

"I was wrong," he said. "Not to hit him. I should have done that, and probably more. But wrong to say I was quitting. I wanted to tell you that. Polly can't stay, of course, but Christina and me, we'll stay on, I reckon. If she'll still have us, and if Peter says so, she will. But it isn't for her we'll stay. It's for your father-in-law. And this little tad, that's at war with everything, like you were. And for you, I suppose. No . . . you're not one of us. But you could have been. That's the difference. You still fight it, all this, don't you? Lord, I smell the smoke of your battles all the time. You're some fierce, Maude Chambliss."

"Thank you," I said, smiling a watery smile at him. He grinned in return, unwillingly.

"It wasn't a compliment."

"Thanks, anyway . . . Micah."

"You're welcome . . . Maude," he said, and left again, this time for good.

After that, things were almost as they had always been in the summers, if not quite. Our hallowed routines of morning, afternoon, and evening still held, as they would on Judgment Day, I thought, and reflected again how totally enduring was the glue that held Retreat together, and how totally the product of form and custom. But this time I was glad of it. It gave me a path back to normalcy, and I felt we all needed that more than anything. Oh, Mother Hannah was cooler than usual to me for a couple of weeks, and more distant, but I could hardly count that an injury. And Christina was perhaps a bit quieter in her kitchen, and did not so often sing as she rolled piecrust or washed china, and Micah did not come so often with fresh wood or paint or the shears. But they did come, and neither mentioned that awful afternoon, then or ever. I had not thought they would.

After one anguished apology from Amy, to which I would not listen, hugging her fiercely, we did not speak of Parker or the scene in the cottage again. Helen Potter sent a great armful of iris from Braebonnie's gardens, but no note came with them, and as for Parker, no one saw him for a full ten days after that afternoon. He was, Peter said grimly, off on the *Circe* for an extended tour around the yacht clubs and harbors of the Penobscot.

"I told him if he came back before a week, at least, I'd beat the shit out of him myself," Peter said. "He promised he wouldn't. Said he was going to hole up over at Northeast Harbor with the Fitzwilliams, or somebody else over there, and get himself sober. I don't know about the sober, but I'm pretty sure about Northeast Harbor. I hear he's got a lady friend staying over there with friends."

"Oh, God," I said in utter disgust. "There's just no end to it, is there? I don't see how Amy stays with him."

"What are her options?" Peter said, and I did not reply. There was nothing to say.

But the fact remained that without Parker Potter the colony gradually drifted its way back into the old, lazy shoals of late June.

On the first of July, he came back, bronzed, cleareyed, pounds thinner, and more subdued than I had ever seen him. He came straight from the *Circe* to Liberty, crisp in white ducks and boat shoes, his red hair still damp and comb-tracked. He brought with him an enormous box of chocolates, which he said he had kept packed in ice all the way from Northeast Harbor, for Mother Hannah, a music box that played "London Bridge is Falling Down" for Petie, and a case of extravagantly expensive Bordeaux for Peter. He had nothing for me, he said, because he did not wish to insult me with presents when he knew how I must feel about him, but I did have his solemn promise that he would not abuse the rest of the colony's friendship again.

"And I want you to know that I haven't had a drink since that afternoon," he said humbly. "And I don't plan to. I'm taking Amy home the day after the Fourth. It's time I grew up and began acting like a father and a husband."

After he left, Peter and I looked at each other.

"Do you think he's serious?" I said.

"I think he's sober," Peter said. "That's about as far as I'm willing to go. Whether or not he'll stick to it is anybody's guess. I think he'd be one of the world's dumbest shits if he acted up again so soon up here. Everybody's pretty fed up with him."

"Well," said Mother Hannah, admiring her chocolates, "you can't say he wasn't a perfect gentleman today. He'll straighten up, you'll see. Blood will tell."

"Especially," I said under my breath, starting for the sun porch where Petie had begun to wail once more, "when it's full enough of alcohol to cook a rarebit."

I was not convinced by Parker's contrition. Behind the subdued voice and clear, ingenuous eyes something else, goatish and rank, seemed to prance and toss its swollen neck. If I had known the word then, I would have sworn I could smell the powerful odor of testosterone in the air. I remembered all too clearly Peter's words about the visiting woman friend in Northeast Harbor.

But for the next couple of days Parker was as good as his word. I saw him walking with Amy at twilight in the gardens of Braebonnie, his arm around her, her head inclined onto his shoulder. They were laughing, and once he reached over and patted the bulge in her stomach that was his baby. I turned away from the window then, not wanting to intrude even from a distance. I felt better about Parker Potter at that moment than at any other time since I had met him.

On the Fourth of July, Retreat has for generations hosted an invitational regatta for yacht clubs from Brooklin, Deer Isle, and Northeast Harbor. Thick, bland chowder is served at twilight, and after that, in the early, fast-falling New England evening, there are fireworks from the end of the dock, blooming out over the bay and islands like fabulous flowers. Everyone turns out for the chowder and fireworks, even people who have not set foot on the dock or club porch since the last Fourth of July. Babies sleep in waddings of blankets, children shriek and romp and squabble, young husbands and wives vivid with sunburn and spiked punch laugh on the steps and lawn with their peers, teenagers preen and jostle and flirt, dogs thump tails and sniff comradely behinds in pools of shade, and old ladies in cottons and cardigans and pearls colonize the long porches, accepting plates and drinks and compliments from the young and surveying their domain from the inviolable rockers with the eyes of raptors. Visiting yachtsmen and their wives and crews circulate, greeting old friends, tanned and fair-haired and white-clad, so like their hosts in Retreat that in the dusk I have never been able to tell the difference. They sleep the night over, and the punch off, on their sleek cruising yachts or on the sun porches of friends.

Among them, that perfect day, was a tall, extremely slender young woman with the henna bob and slouch of the flapper we were beginning to read about, although most assuredly without the flapper's flat bosom. She wore white flannels and a taut-stretched striped sailor's jersey, and her teeth were brilliant in the dusk. She flashed them often at everyone, and most often of all at Parker Potter, and I suddenly knew without being told that she was the woman friend from Northeast Harbor. Peter knew it too. I do not think Amy did; when Parker volunteered for kitchen cleanup and vanished into the back of the club and the visiting flapper drawled that she would keep him company, Amy only smiled her old, quick, deep-dimpling smile and said, "Better her than me."

But Peter knew, and his mouth went straight and hard, and he stopped his foolishness on the lawn with Burdie Winslow and Al and Henry Stallings. Others knew too, I think. Many eyes had followed the two figures into the kitchen, though there was no pause in the babble of conversation. Then the eyes pulled away. Better, simply, not to see and not to say. Something hot and bright flared in my chest. How dare he? How dare she? I handed Petie unceremoniously to Mother Hannah in her rocker and went over to Amy where she lounged in a peacock chair on the lawn, covered with a blanket.

"You okay? Want anything? Getting a little tired?" I said cheerfully. I hoped she would say yes. I could then whisk her home and stay there with her. I wanted nothing more of this place and this night, and I wanted with all my heart to have Amy quit of both.

But she said, "No, I'm fine. I want to see the fireworks," and there was nothing I could do to coax her away that would not have drawn all eyes inevitably to her. I sat down on the damp grass beside her, chattering foolishly, determined to keep her from noticing the lengthening absence of her husband and his handmaiden, and for a while I succeeded. Peter sat silently with us, Petie for once asleep in his arms. I do not know when, in the course of the fireworks and the evening, Amy realized that neither Parker nor the woman had returned. By the time she did, most people at the festivities were a couple of beats ahead of her. Heads turned toward the closed kitchen door and then nodded together, and whispers sprang up like a summer wind in the fast-cooling night.

"Come on," I said, getting to my feet and pulling her up behind me. "If it's too cold for me it's too cold for you. I'm going to take you back to Liberty and fix you a cup of hot chocolate, and then I'm going to clap you in bed and you can spend the night with us. Peter will tell . . . your folks. Do, Amy. I'll sleep in the other bed in the guest room. It'll be like a spend-the-night party."

She looked up at me and in her eyes was fathom-less hurt and emptiness and defeat. I almost cried aloud at the force of them. But her face was still, and she only said, "I think I will. I've seen all this before, and I'm pretty tired. Please tell Mother Helen and Mamadear for me, Peter; I just don't feel like arguing with them tonight."

"Don't worry about a thing," he said, kissing her cheek. "I'll take care of it." Above her head, his eyes, meeting mine, were narrowed with anger. Uncon-sciously, I thought, he bent his head to Petie's downy one, on his shoulder, and kissed the soft hollow there, under the spiky dark hair. Pain and love knifed through me. I had never seen him do that before.

Amy did not want chocolate, after all. She said she wanted to go straight to bed, so I tucked her into the little guest alcove over the sun porch and plumped her pillows and smoothed Mother Hannah's silky old family percale sheets and piled blankets and afghans over her.

"I'm going to fix you a plate of sandwiches and some cocoa anyway and leave them beside your bed," I said. "You hardly touched your chowder, not that I blame you. It gets worse every year. You might feel like a bite if you wake up in the night. If you do, I'll be here beside you. I'm just going to wait up for Peter and Petie now. All you have to do is sing out if you want me."

She had rolled over onto her side and burrowed deep into the covers. She did not turn her face from the wall of windows that looked out over a grove of spruce and birches down to the club and the dock and, beyond it, the black sea and sky. Fireworks still arced and bloomed, silently.

"Thanks, Maude," she said, and her voice was soft and level and dead. "If it weren't for you, I don't think I could get through this night."

"Oh, Amy, dear—"

"No. Don't say any more. It's all right. I just want to sleep a little now."

"Shall I pull the curtains?"

"No, I want to see the moon," she said, and her voice had thickened, and I thought that now she would cry. Well, maybe it would be best. Cry some of it out. . . .

"I love you," I whispered, and went out and closed the door.

Peter came in soon after with Petie and his mother. I took my sleeping son from him and nodded good night to Mother Hannah and went upstairs to put the baby down in his crib. I did not want to get into any sort of exchange with my mother-in-law, at least not yet. If she had words of defense and justification for Parker Potter now, I knew I could not bear to hear them.

Peter followed me up and sat down heavily on the bed. He ran his hand hard over his face and mouth, and I heard the whispery rasp of beard growth. It always surprised me. Peter's whiskers were invisible.

"Is she asleep?" he said.

"I don't know. She said she wanted to. It's been an hour or so. Peter, she looked . . . just dead. Like a dead woman. Oh, how could he? How could he?"

"I'd say that for him it was as easy as falling off a log," Peter said. "It's what he does best, after all. It's liquor, of course. He was swigging on a pint in a paper sack all afternoon out on the water. And Burdie says he keeps a stash in the club kitchen. I hadn't heard that, but it must be true. They hadn't unlocked the door when I left, but from the sounds coming out of there they definitely weren't washing dishes. I think several people are ready to set fire to the club and burn them out. I tell you, Maude, I'd light the first match."

"Somebody's going to have to do something about it this time," I said. "She's got to get back home to Boston; that baby could come any time. If he isn't going to look after her, somebody else has to. Did Parker's mother say anything? Or his grandmother? Could they talk to him?"

"How should I know?" he snapped in frustration. "Neither one of them let on by so much as a blink or the lift of an eyebrow that they knew anything was wrong. When they left for Braebonnie everybody at the club was sneaking looks at the kitchen, and those two old trouts just smiled around and cooed their good nights and sailed off for home as if they'd been reviewing the troops. God, his father would have beat the shit out of him."

"Would that he had," I said bitterly. "Then we wouldn't have to go through this. Well, I'm going over there in the morning and tell him he's got to take her home—that is, if he's even there—and that if he won't, you and I will, and we'll stay with her until the baby comes. And I'll tell her mother-in-law and her horrible old grandmother-in-law too. I'll bet you anything they hop to and start looking after her if they think they're going to lose their little handmaiden."

"Let's see what happens," Peter said wearily. "Maybe he's already home. If he's not, I'll round him up in the morning and put the fear of God in him. I promise you that. You don't have to go fight Amy's battles for her. I can do that, and I will."

I kissed him good night, and went in and looked in on Petie, and then went downstairs and read Michael Arlen's *The Green Hat* until I got sleepy enough to drop off. It was after midnight when I tiptoed up to the guest room and inched the door open. Surely Amy was asleep by now.

But she wasn't. She stood by the windows, her bulk wrapped in trailing blankets, her neck heart-breakingly fragile under the weight of her silver-threaded hair, staring out at the woods and the bay. I went up beside her and put my arms around her but said nothing, and she didn't either. Far below us, out on the black water, a light bobbed and flared. I suppose both of us knew, absolutely and viscerally, that it was one of the *Circe*'s running lights, but neither of us said it. There was no need to.

In a moment, I gave her shoulders a little shake and said, "It really is bedtime. And I'm right here. And in the morning, we'll figure out what to do. Peter will help. You'll see. Everything looks better in the morning."

She turned to me and smiled, a small, wounded smile, and started to speak, but at that moment a great spear of pure crystal green lanced the black sky over the water, and then a huge wash of iridescent white, as if someone had flooded the sky with liquid diamonds, and then vast pulsing tongues of pink and purple and aquamarine. I drew a sharp breath, and she squeezed my hand until it hurt.

"It's the northern lights," she breathed. "The aurora borealis. Oh, Maude, look; I've been coming here for six years and I've never seen them. Oh, look; oh, look!"

We stood there for perhaps half an hour, Amy and I, as silent and still as two marble women, watching the entire sky arc and shimmer and bloom. I could not have spoken if I had wanted to. I have seen them several times again, during the long summers in Retreat, those great fires in the heavens, but to me none has ever been as breathlessly, terrifyingly beautiful as that first time from the upstairs windows of Liberty. They ignited the world; they ate the sky and moon and stars and paled the treacherous rocking lights on the *Circe* down to nothing. When finally they subsided, the light was gone. Amy and I were both asleep, this time deeply and truly, within five minutes.

Several years later Amy and I were reading Robert Service's stupefyingly awful poetry aloud together and laughing, and when we came across the line, "Oh, the Northern Lights have seen strange sights, but the strangest they ever did see," we put our faces down into our cupped hands and howled with helpless laughter. We laughed until we could barely breathe, and Amy scarcely managed to gasp, "If he only knew," and we were off again. For Amy's baby was born at noon the next day, in the hospital at Castine as Petie had been, with me and Peter and a fluttering Helen Potter in attendance, and it was not until two days later, when he came limping home in the *Circe* laden once more with contrition and gifts, that Parker knew he had a daughter named Elizabeth Wainwright Potter, and she was forty-eight hours old. I was there when he came in, and when she saw his face, Amy burst into the first spontaneous laughter I had heard from her that summer. Forever after that, the mention of northern lights would set her off, and usually me with her.

But I was to think often, later, as I watched Elizabeth Potter grow, that that eldritch light had not been a benign one.

Chapter Seven

The greatest gift the sea has to give is timelessness. Beside it, if you are able to receive it, that vast blue amplitude of space and time soothes, simplifies, heals. Beside it, if you are very quiet and still, you see clearly that life is and always has been outside time, a thing apart from it, and so you need have no real fear of time's poison fruits. They will still fall in your lap, of course, but beside the sea they do not taste bitter.

It is not a thing you can possibly know when you are young and time is an elusive suitor to be seduced, but the old know it. It is what the old women of Retreat always knew. It is what they labored so constantly and fiercely to preserve. When I first came to Retreat with Peter I chafed under the yoke of that enforced timelessness; I fought its enforcers tooth and nail. But now I am an old woman myself, and I sit on my porch and look out at the eternal face of the bay and taste myself the thick honey of timelessness and sameness, and I say in my heart to Mother Hannah and all those others with whom I did battle so long ago, You were right. It is worth everything.

In this place of sea silence, memories come as

clear as pictures in a book. One book: the book of
Maine. When Petie was about nine, he and Elizabeth
Potter wrote a book on thick, lined Blue Horse tablet
paper, and titled it "The True Story of Maine," and
illustrated it with vivid, lopsided, achingly true drawings of children doing wonderful things in boats and
on beaches and rocks and piers and lawns, and of
spavined adults doing stupid things in those same
magical places. I know every one of those drawings
by heart, and it is the same with the memories that
come to me now, when I sit here in the twig rocker
with the balsam stuffed cushion, both of which were
old when I came to Retreat a lifetime ago. Speak,
memory, Vladimir Nabokov said, and memory did
speak. By the sea, it speaks, often, more clearly than
reality.

Sometimes, in a place like Retreat, where the
same people live for generations in the same way,
years and even decades may seem to pass when very
little changes: when the actuality of life has ups and
downs and ins and outs that might be seen on a sort
of interior seismograph, but the *sense* of that time, its
ethos and essence, remains fixed. Every life has those
hiatuses, but they are only seen clearly, I think, in ret-
rospect. It would save everyone a great deal of grief if
we could see the hiatus midway and know it for
what it is, but that, of course, is not the nature of life.
"It's a poor sort of memory that only works back-
wards," the Queen said to Alice; I remember Petie
loved that when I read Lewis Carroll to him. Carroll's
wisdom speaks far too often only to the very young.

But there sometimes comes a moment, a small,
silent white explosion of awareness, that signals the
ending of one of those long, sweet, suspended times as
surely as the hooting of a great ship as it nears the harbor, and those caught by that awareness feel the great
cold breath of endings and beginnings on the backs of

their necks and prickle with a portent they cannot name. Only then do they look around them and see beyond the familiar inner landscape the shadow of coming change, feel the wind of its wings. These are frightening moments. Nobody embraces them. When they have passed, most people will put great energy into pretending they did not occur. But you cannot unknow the future once you have sensed it, and so forever after you will mark those epochal passages by the first moment you felt their shapes ahead of you.

My first came to me on the dock of the yacht club in late August of 1941, my eighteenth year in Retreat, on a night of icy silver radiance, when the very sea and stars seemed on fire with light. Amy Potter sat beside me, wrapped as I was in heavy sweater and blankets, drinking coffee from the thermos I had brought from the cottage. I had impulsively added a good stout shot of rum to it as we left, and it tasted wonderful in the cold stillness. We were waiting for the Retreat boats to come back from the season's last race, a two-day sortie to Northeast Harbor and back, and we had been waiting for a long time. Priss Thorne had come down to the dock from Mary's Garden an hour or so before to tell us that Tobias had gotten through by radio to say there had been heavy fog off Long Island, in Blue Hill Bay, which had only recently lifted, so we were not worried about Peter and Petie in *Hannah*, or Parker in *Circe* with Elizabeth. Only perhaps just the least bit drunk.

I sighed contentedly.

"If rum tasted as good all the time as it does tonight, I'd be an alcoholic," I said. And then looked over at Amy and grimaced. "I'm sorry. That was not the least bit funny."

She smiled back at me and took a long pull at her coffee. "Don't be. It's been over two months since Parkie's had a drink," she said matter-of-factly. "I really think it might take, this time. The new place has got a good track record, and I truly believe the doctor there put the fear of God in him about his liver. Of course, he's no bundle of joy to live with, but when was he ever? Besides, I know what you mean. I could sit here and drink this stuff all night, just the two of us. When was the last time we sat outside at night with nowhere we had to be? Just us?"

"The last time I can remember was just before Happy was born," I said. "The night Petie and Elizabeth took the dinghy over to Spectacle and were supposed to be home by sunset, and weren't, and Peter and Phinizy Thorne went after them. Remember? We sat right where we're sitting now, wrapped up in blankets just like this, waiting. I know we must have been scared to death, but I can't remember that. I just remember feeling as big as a cow and hoping another baby wasn't going to be born in the Castine hospital."

"I don't think we were particularly scared," she said. "Or at least, not that they'd drowned. Even then Elizabeth could outsail Parker. It did cross my mind that she'd be the first eleven-year-old child in the world to get pregnant, and we could have a Tom Thumb wedding. Do you remember that love affair, Maude?"

"Oh, yes," I said softly. "I remember."

Remember? That summer and the next two were burned into my mind and heart, fiber and retina and viscera, like the unending presence of great pain even after it has cooled. I would never forget that consuming, anguished love of Petie's for Elizabeth Potter, which began when he was twelve, as long as I myself lived. I doubted that many people in the colony would, either. As for Elizabeth, who knew? She was, at eleven, as ardent and volatile and female as she would ever be in her careening life, and she certainly appeared, those three summers, as drowned and witched with love as my poor stumbling son. But

Elizabeth's passions never burnt her up. She might flame with them, crackle and shiver, shower the world around her with the sparks of her burning. But it was never she who blackened and curled. I thought, that night in 1941 on the dock, that Elizabeth, then fifteen and almost terrible in her beauty, no more remembered the conflagration of that first love than she remembered the day of her birth. It was never given to her to count costs.

From the time she could toddle I think I was afraid of her. Elizabeth Potter was somehow born without boundaries, without a capacity for self-governance or moderation. It seems a strange and silly thing, to fear immoderation in a baby; it is, after all, the essence of childhood. But even the most foolhardy child fears something, will flinch and wail at some threat. Elizabeth never did. What she wanted she went after with an awesome singlemindedness—and got. Where she wished to go she went, except when forcibly restrained, and then she simply shrieked until the restraints were withdrawn in exhaustion and capitulation. I have heard her cry like that for nearly twenty-four hours. In the end, no one could keep her off rocks and docks, out of boats and the sea. As graceful as a young mountain goat from infancy, she never seemed to hurt herself beyond an occasional bruise or scratch, to which she paid no attention at all. It was the others—Petie, usually, toiling in fear and desperation behind her—who fell, bled, broke bones. Long before I began to fear she would crush his heart, I was afraid that Elizabeth would kill Petie.

She had the Potter red hair, the color of living flame, and she would never allow anyone to cut it, so that by the time she was four or five it poured down her slim back like lava. Usually it flew free around her narrow head, but sometimes, when it was very hot or she had been in the sea, she twisted it up and pinned it on top of her head; she looked, then, like something Matisse might have painted, much older always than her years. She had Amy's smooth olive skin, and slanted eyes from some piratical Potter mountebank ancestor, and the combination was striking, stunning. It was as impossible to look away from her as it had been, for me, to look away from Peter when he was very young. She had that same quality of absoluteness, that same still impact. Once, at a yacht club tea, when she was still quite small, she and my Peter were standing together drinking cranberry punch, and he was bending down to listen to something she was whispering in his ear, and Augusta Stallings brayed from across the room, "Look at those two. Like as peas in a pod. She should be yours, Peter; except for that red head there isn't God's bit of Parker in her."

There was an uncomfortable silence, in which all eyes turned to my husband and Amy's nine-year-old daughter, and a silvery peal of laughter from Gretchen Winslow, and then the seemly flow of Retreat conversation resumed as if no one had heard her. And probably few people remarked it; Augusta's outbursts were as much a part and parcel of summer Retreat as black flies and no-see-ums. But three people had: Parker Potter's flushed face went a dull magenta, Elizabeth's small face lit with a kind of triumphant joy, and Petie's dark round face went stiff and still with humiliation. I felt outrage and grief for him flood me like hot water. He was ten years old, and he knew that on some essential level he was not and never could be the child of his father's heart. That knowledge had dogged his steps and chewed his heart since he was old enough for perception.

"Why can't you be warm with him? Why can't you play with him and wrestle with him and, you know, mess up his hair and swing him up on your shoulders?" I cried to Peter once, when Petie was little and had lurched away sobbing because his father had told him to take his ball and play with it in the nursery.

"I don't know, Maudie," Peter said, and there was real pain in his voice. "I do love him; God, sometimes I lie awake at night and think, What if something happened to him? What if we didn't have him? But I just can't seem to give him what he needs. Maude, he's the *neediest* little creature I ever saw. Nothing is enough; hug him and he wants to be held, smile at him and he's all over you for the rest of the day. It scares me. I can't fill that bottomless hole in him. You can; sometimes I think you're all he'll ever need in life, and he's all *you* need."

He fell silent, and I looked across at him sitting in his old Morris chair beside the fire in the little den in Northpoint. It was his winter place; I still see him there in the cold months as I do running down the steps of the dock toward the *Hannah* in the warm months, the sun on his fair hair. His face on that night was miserable, and I felt the old stab of pain at his pain, that first and worst source of anguish to me. I have never been able to bear Peter's pain. Even Petie's was always easier.

"He needs his father too," I said softly. "And you must know that it's you I'll need all my life. I had you first. If I lost Petie I don't know what I would do, but if I lost you I would die."

He smiled then. "Did I sound jealous? Maybe I am. I don't think so, though. That kind of frantic, gobbling need . . . I just can't face it, Maude. I have endless love to give him, but not my endless presence. That's a sorry thing to admit about your only child, but I know it's true, and as much as I hate it, I don't think I can change it. I guess I got it from Dad."

I remembered the times Big Peter had simply seemed to vanish from the cottage, often for days and weeks, and the time Peter had done the same thing, when his father died and the entire house of women had toppled down on him. Petie had come to me in his absence; no wonder to Peter he must seem mine alone. Well, I thought, so be it. As long as he loves Petie—and I know he does—I have presence enough for us both. I can supply the thereness. You can't ask what's not there to give.

But Petie did not know that, and the void where his father was not must have ached like a boil throughout his childhood. I wish I had seen it more clearly then. Nothing is ever so simple, I know, but I believe now if Peter could have been closer to his son, we would have had less of the pain of Elizabeth, and perhaps none at all.

For it was absoluteness Petie sought, all his life, until the day when, at age eleven, Elizabeth raised her fiery head and really saw him. Something ungovernable, without conditions and limits; something to complete him. Even my love for him, as empathetic and often terrible as it seemed to me, could not fill him. But the volcano that was Elizabeth Potter could and for a time did, and the consequences were, for him, disastrous. Elizabeth seemed to enter into his flesh and ride him like a succubus; her will was his and he followed without a murmur where she led, and she led him into things that, in the fragile, perfect, small ecosystem of Retreat, went beyond mischief into calamity.

The physical bond between them was powerful and adult. They could not keep their hands off each other. Peter at twelve was still short in stature, and though his shoulders and hands and feet had gained bulk and strength, his face was still round and smooth, and his dark hair fine and silky in his eyes. Elizabeth at eleven was already an arresting woman, and I use the term advisedly. She had only the buds of breasts and her body was as long and slim and quick as a young sapling's, but something looked out of her eyes and soft, volatile mouth that was light-years beyond childhood. But still, she was only eleven, and the constant touching and nuzzling and the long dense looks that shimmered between them would have been inappropriate anywhere. In Retreat, they came near to being pornographic. I warned Petie over and over, and forbade him to spend so much time with Elizabeth, and Peter finally came right out and told him to keep his hands off her or he'd be shipped back to Northpoint to summer school, and I suppose Amy must have said something similar to Elizabeth, because they soon stopped touching each other in our presence. Instead, they vanished together for long hours in the daytime, and that, I thought despairingly, was worse. But Peter said only, "After all, Maude, what can they actually do? They're children. Do you really think they're over on Buck or Spectacle screwing? Do you think Parker is going to come over here with a shotgun and force Petie to marry her? Let it go. They'll wear it out faster if you do."

But I did not think they would. I thought they might well be over on Buck or Spectacle doing just what Peter said. Petie was simply wild with love, blinded and thick-tongued with it. If they had stopped touching in our presence they had not stopped it anywhere else; talk flew like bees in the colony that summer. Mother Hannah, frail and waspish by then, was at me constantly about it. But no matter what I did, it was not enough. I was pregnant, that first summer of the great attraction, with Happy, and tired and uncomfortable and apprehensive about a new baby after twelve years, and whenever I tried to talk seriously about it with Peter, he seemed to melt away like fog to the water. In desperation I went to Amy late that summer and told her I thought we should talk about Petie and Elizabeth, and she burst into tears.

"Please, please," she said, dropping her face into her hands. "I can't talk about it right now. If you think something needs to be done, then do it, but just don't *talk* to me about it! It should be obvious to you that Parker is one step away from killing himself drinking; it is to everybody else, and I never know where he is and who he's with, and that old woman is driving me completely out of my mind with her demands and complaints, and she runs off every housekeeper I can find, and I think I may have had another miscarriage, and . . . there's nothing wrong with Elizabeth! If that damned little goat Petie would stay away from her there wouldn't be any problem!"

I put my hand gently on her curly head, nearly white by now, and went heavily back to Liberty. I should have known Amy could not help me. Everyone in the colony knew her world hung by the most precarious of threads, and Elizabeth was simply and inalterably the joy of her heart. Over the years Amy had lost several other babies, but somehow I did not think those losses had touched her deeply. Elizabeth was, for Amy, always sufficient.

We thought that the winter hiatuses away from Retreat would sap the attraction of its heat, but for two more years they did not. Petie and Elizabeth matured and met in far more than childish passion, and we had cause then, I knew, to worry about what they did in the long hours when they vanished. The second summer Peter took Petie back to Northpoint in mid-July and enrolled him in summer school after he and Elizabeth disappeared in the *Hannah*'s dinghy and did not come home until dawn, and Petie promptly ran away and came back to Retreat. When, in the beginning of the third summer, Ella Stallings found them entwined in each other's arms in her and John's boathouse, two of the three youngest Stallings looking on solemnly, Amy took Elizabeth back to

Boston and ensconced her in the chilly camphor-smelling home of a Back Bay aunt, with a tutor and a governess. She was back within three weeks, having stolen money from her tutor's wallet and caught the train from Boston to Bangor and hitched a ride on an ice truck to Retreat. I had a baby and an ill and impossible Mother Hannah by myself that summer; Peter had stayed behind at Northpoint for the first time in our marriage to serve as acting headmaster after Dr. Fleming's first stroke. When Elizabeth appeared back in Retreat, stained with travel and exuding an invisible musk that my son flew to like a yellow jacket to overripe fruit, I found myself in Lottie Padgett's fusty, chirruping living room in tears, quite literally at the end of my rope.

"What am I going to do?" I sobbed. "I can't lock him up. They can't lock her up. They're too young; it's no good, this kind of . . . of craziness. Everybody's talking, including the villagers. Even if they were old enough, it's no basis for any kind of permanence. This kind of intensity—it can't help but damage their very souls. There's no balance, no lightness, no sweetness. . . . Oh, what does she *see* in him? You can see what he sees in her, my God, but what can she possibly see in my poor awkward Petie?"

Miss Lottie brought comfrey tea and shoved a fat, plumy yellow coon cat off her chair and sank into it. For once the Little House was empty of children, though the smells and sounds coming from the kitchen indicated that something small and wild and orphan was in residence. The room, as usual, was cluttered beyond description. Just being there made me feel young and new and soothed again, made me forget I was sole custodian of a large old house and an ill and angry old woman and a chunky, grave blond toddler and a fourteen-year-old son who had lost his soul to a siren.

Miss Lottie let me snivel myself out, and then she

said, "What does she see in him? Herself. She sees herself whole and complete and beautiful in a man's eyes. She never did in her father's, you know; how would you like to be a highstrung little girl growing up in Parker Potter's house? What kind of picture of women could she possibly see reflected there? So she thinks she's just nothing, nobody, not even there, until she sees an absolute blind adoration in some man's eyes, and it's like a mirror. She sees that in Petie. She feels whole again. Safe. No wonder she's after him so desperately. Without him she just disappears."

"But she's not safe," I said. "Petie can't make her safe; that's ludicrous."

"No," Miss Lottie said sadly. "Elizabeth will never be safe. A lot of people are going to suffer because of that."

"Oh, God, Miss Lottie, our poor children," I whispered. "We try so hard. I know Amy does. But it isn't enough. . . ."

She reached out and smoothed the tangled hair off my face. Her old fingers felt like twigs, warm and dry.

"You've been a good mother to Petie, Maude," she said. "You mustn't go blaming yourself for everything. Some things you're just not going to be able to help. This is a bad place for some children, this colony. A bad place for little wild things. Even though I love it dearly, I've always known that. I've tried to make a kind of safe harbor here for the wild hearts, the different ones. They might be perfectly fine somewhere else, somewhere more in the world, but here. . . . I've seen them go to war against all this before. Not like Elizabeth, maybe, not so destructively, but it happens about once a generation. Sometimes they fight it, sometimes they run. You can't do much about it but try and be there when they fall."

I thought of Big Peter, heading joyously each week for the Aerie, on the cliffs above where we sat now, and of my Peter, heading like a golden arrow to the sea.

"What am I going to do for my boy?" I said.

"I think, give him the gift of his whole pain," Miss Lottie said. "Let him have the dignity of the full brunt of it, without his mama trying to shield him from it. Then it won't be so bad when she's off and gone. He'll have a kind of map to go by."

"You think she's going to drop him, then?"

"It's what Elizabeth is all about," she said, and there was pain in her old voice, but strength and surety too. I came away up the cliff path to Liberty feeling cooled and smoothed and somehow infused with quietness. Perhaps she was right; perhaps there would soon be an end to it. . . .

There was, within a fortnight. Petie came home at dusk one Friday after a day on the water with Elizabeth, looking blind and sick and white-bled, and went straight to his room and crawled into bed. He would not open the door when I tapped on it, and he did not eat the supper tray I left outside his door. When I tried the door again at bedtime there was no answer, and I was not in the least ashamed to go around the side of the house and peer into his room through the gap in the old shutters. He lay mounded deep under the bedcovers, obviously asleep.

In the morning he was gone by the time I was up, and I sent Christina Willis down to the yacht club to see if the dinghy was there. When she said it was gone, I walked over to Braebonnie and found Amy in the kitchen, putting an invalid's breakfast on a linen-covered tray. She looked flushed and pretty again, young.

"Is Elizabeth here?" I said. "Petie's gone in the dinghy, and I thought she might be with him."

"No, she's upstairs packing," Amy said, not quite looking at me. "She said this morning that she wanted to go back to her Aunt Liza's and take lessons at the Art Institute for the rest of the summer. There's a new watercolor class starting Monday. Parker's going to take her down in the morning. You know she's quite gifted with her drawing, but we've never thought she was particularly interested—"

"Did they have a fight, do you know? Petie's in an awful state," I said. "I never saw him like he was when he came in last night."

"Well, I don't think so," Amy said. "She said she told him she thought it would be the best thing for both of them if they didn't see each other for a while, and that she'd always think of him as her best friend. And she said he didn't say much at all about that, so I thought— really, Maude, it's the answer to all our prayers, don't you think? I mean, we've been at our wits' end about them, and now there's nothing more to worry about."

"Except for Petie," I said, rage flaring within me. "Only Petie, who looks like the walking dead. My God, couldn't she have given him some kind of warning, some kind of notice? He literally worships her!"

"It was you who came over here wanting me to keep her away from him, and not so long ago either," Amy said crisply. "Now she's taken care of it herself, and just listen to you. What do you want, Maude?"

"I don't know," I said, turning away. "I thought it was this. But now I don't know."

The next week was a terrible time for Petie, but I think it was just as bad for me. He would not talk with me about Elizabeth, and he ate little and that in his room, and he stayed on the water alone in the dinghy from sunup until long after dark. Only the constant attention that small Happy and Mother Hannah required kept me from dogging his tracks, running him to earth, holding him forcibly to my breast as I had when he was small. Only that, and Miss Lottie's words not long before: "Give him the gift of his whole pain."

And so I sat by, my heart physically hurting in my

chest for his silent white agony, and let him fly to the sea with it as his grandfather and father had before him. And after that first terrible week he came in one night and asked, in nearly his old, froggy adolescent voice, if he might go to Northpoint and spend the rest of the summer with his father.

"I can get a leg up on calculus," he said. "I might even pass it on the first go-round, if I get on it now."

And I watched him off for the Ellsworth train station in Micah's truck with pride and love and pity for him tearing at me like gulls at a fish on the shore, thinking I could see clearly the shape of the man he might be one day, and liking very much what I saw.

"God, let it be over now," I whispered as the truck lurched up the lane and vanished, and when they met again the next summer, the one in which Amy and I sat on the dock watching and waiting, it truly seemed to be. Elizabeth was even more beautiful at fifteen, more a creature of smoke and flame and laughter, and she treated Petie with the kind of lighthearted, bantering affection that old friends have for each other. And he in turn treated her lightly, casually, as a lordly teenager might a pretty child. And only I saw the white pain that simmered in him like a fire in the earth, that would never burn out. I knew, that night as we waited for their lights on the black water, that wherever they were, riding the wind side by side in *Hannah* and *Circe,* Peter hurt for Elizabeth and labored mightily not to show that he did.

"Oh, yes," I said to Amy Potter again. "I remember."

"All those years ago," she said. "Can you believe it? You think when you're up here that time doesn't pass at all, but it does. It does. Oh, Maude! If we could only stop time right now! I don't ever want this to change."

She was silent awhile, and then said, "Maude?"

"Hmmmm?"

"Did you ever feel that way about Peter? That wildness, that burning up?"

I smiled in the darkness, though I did not think
she could see.

"Still do," I said.

"Lord," she whispered, but that was all she
did say.

Presently we saw a light, far out on the water, and
got to our feet and went down to the end of the dock,
but then we heard the soft rumble of a motor and knew
it was not, after all, the returning fleet but a lobster boat,
and a lone one. We watched as its light rode nearer and
nearer, and soon we could see the black shape of it, and
see on its white side the black letters: *Tina*.

"It's Micah," I said to Amy. "What on earth is he
doing out so late, do you think? He usually finishes
hauling by noon. Oh, Lord, I hope nothing's happened to the fleet."

A few yards out he cut the *Tina*'s engine and glid-
ed silently into the dock, and I caught the line he
tossed over to me and said, as he jumped lightly from
the deck to the planks where we stood, "Did you see
the fleet? Is everything okay out there? We heard
there was fog, and they're awfully late."

"Didn't see 'em," he said, his eyes showing white
in the star-pricked night. I could feel the heat of his
body in the cold off the water and hugged myself
with my arms. I watched as he tied up the *Tina*. Who
are you? I said to myself, looking at his silhouette
moving deftly about his mooring. I've known you for
eighteen years, and I still don't know who you are.

Only then did I think to wonder why he was tying
up at the club dock. He always took the *Tina* into the
boatyard harbor, around the point.

"Is something wrong?" I said again.

"Peter up at the house?" he said. "Heard he was
here this weekend."

"No, he's out with the fleet. It's the Northeast Harbor regatta this weekend. Micah, what *is* it?"

"Don't know," he said. "At least, not for sure. Might be something, might be nothing. I wanted to talk to Peter and maybe Guild Kennedy and the Thorne boys about it, seeing they're from Washington. 'Course, there isn't a real brain among them—"

"Micah!"

He looked at me with the white eyes and then sat down on a piling and lit one of the stubby cigarettes he smoked. In the flare of the match his eyes burned blue.

"I was over to the Deer Isle bridge this morning, taking the *Tina* to pick up a pump at Eaton's, on Little Deer. There was an almighty big sailing yacht anchored under the bridge, right in the middle, and traffic on each side of the bridge was stopped. Looked like the sheriff's boys holdin' it up. There wasn't any craft in the water around it, just the big boat, shining in the sun like a wedding cake. Couldn't see her name or her registry, and she wasn't flying her flags. Thought I'd take a closer look, so I cut the engines and kind of coasted on in there toward it, and pretty soon here comes this military cutter out after me like a chicken hawk, Navy, I'm almost sure, motioning for me to go back, go back. I wasn't too fond of that, so I came on, and then I could see she was a gunboat, had a couple of 40 mm Bofors mounted on her deck. Trained right on me. So I reversed and got on out of there, but not before I saw a couple of people on the yacht's deck, sittin' in easy chairs and drinking and smoking like they were anchored off Miami and not Penobscot Bay, Maine. Saw 'em pretty clearly too."

"And?" I said, my brow furrowing. Gunboats, under the old Deer Isle bridge? A coldness that was not of the night crawled up the back of my neck.

"And nothing," he said, stubbing out his cigarette

and starting up the dock toward the colony. "Except that one of 'em was Franklin Roosevelt. I'd know that chin and that cigarette holder anywhere. And I'm right sure the other was Winston Churchill!"

"Oh, surely not," Amy said on a soft little breath.

"I know what I saw," Micah said, and I knew he did.

"What does it mean?" I called after him, not loudly. Somehow I did not want to raise my voice.

"Means war," floated back to me from his retreating shape. "Means we're right before getting in the damned war. And high time, you ask me. We've been letting England twist in the wind by itself long enough."

Amy and I watched him out of sight, saying nothing. I felt fear bloom in a spot somewhere under my ribs and flow like molten lava through my arms and legs; felt my breath stop with it. I felt the change then, the great black pterodactyl shape of change and loss and never-again, off at the edge of the dark. I could almost see the bulk of it. I could almost feel its breath on my face, smell it in my nostrils.

"Oh, my God in heaven," I whispered. "That can't be right. We aren't going to get into this war. Everybody says so."

Amy did not answer, and I did not speak again. In another half hour or so, the women of the colony began to gather on the dock, coming silently out of the black woods behind the yacht club in their cardigans and scarves, rubbing their arms against the chill of the night and looking, as we were, for lights out over the bay. We nodded to one another, and exchanged a few words, but it was by and large a silent group. In another fifteen minutes most of us who could leave their cottages were there. I thought of Petie, out on that black water, and of Happy, sleeping in Petie's old nursery back at Liberty, Christina Willis beside her reading her novel. I thought of Peter coming up the dock, laughing, and a built-up fire and perhaps a snifter of brandy, and deep-piled quilts on the bed upstairs. I did not mention what Micah Willis had seen that morning under the Deer Isle bridge.

Suddenly there were running lights far out on the water, one or two sets at first and then a blossoming of them, far out past Fiddle Head, like a flotilla of fireflies. In a few moments we heard their voices, far away, calling back and forth between boats, laughing. The voices sounded very young, and by some alchemy of night and water and distance, as if they were going away from us, instead of approaching.

And then, as if in a perfect vision, I saw it and knew it with absolute certainty, and nearly fell to my knees under the weight of it: we would have war, and women would gather at the edge of water, as we women were at that moment, and hear over its empty reaches the voices of their men. Voices over water, heard from the edge of water.

Voices going away.

And women watching.

We did have war, of course; Micah had been right about that, even if some of us had our doubts about Franklin Roosevelt and Winston Churchill aboard the yacht off Deer Isle. I myself did not doubt it. Later that month we heard the two met aboard a destroyer in Placentia Bay, off Nova Scotia and very near to Campobello, to begin informal drafting of what became the Atlantic Charter. But even if we had not heard, I would not have doubted Micah Willis's story. He seldom spoke until he knew what he was talking about, and as he said, he knew what he saw.

So when we heard, on a sleepy Northpoint Sunday just after lunch in the dining hall, the terrible news of

Pearl Harbor, it was not shock that struck me white and breathless but the fear that had lain cold and heavy in my heart since that night on the dock the previous August.

"Petie," I whispered, my nails digging into Peter's hand. "I cannot let Petie go to war."

"He's only sixteen, Maude," Peter said, staring at the fretted vent of the big Capehart. "It will be years before he can go even if he should want to."

"But what if it goes on and on?"

"It won't. We'll come in fighting mad now; even old Willie Hearst and the isolationists will be behind Roosevelt. We'll be back home inside a year."

"No, we won't," Petie cried in distress from the rug in front of the hearth, where he was immersed in *Jane's Fighting Ships*. He had been perusing it since Germany had begun to bomb England, sure that the war would take to the seas any day. It was his fondest dream to command a fighting ship. He flung *Jane's* away from him.

"It'll last till I turn eighteen; I know it will! They take eighteen-year-olds in the RAF, sometimes younger, if they don't know. . . . I'll lie about my age. I'll enlist. I'm not going to miss this war!"

"Why don't you just buy a gun and point it at your head and pull the trigger?" I cried, and ran from the living room and locked myself in the bathroom and cried until I could cry no more. When I came out, the living room was empty and the fire had burned low, and there was a note on the gate leg table by the front door saying that Peter and Petie had gone over to Commons to get the late news.

I sat down on the window seat and looked out at the soft gray December campus. Through the diamond panes the quadrangle looked as empty of human spoor as a lunar landscape, totally stopped and still, a place caught outside time. But lights glowed in the mullioned windows of the old Commons building at the far side, and I knew that inside men and boys huddled together, as they had from time immemorial, drawn away from the world of their women, waiting for news of war. All over the country, all those men, all those boys, waiting. . . . Softly, hopelessly, I began to cry again. I did not believe that Petie would not have to fight. I did not, then, even believe that Peter would escape it. It was not the last time I wept during that war, of course, but I vowed then that I would not weep again before my husband and son. And somehow, I did not.

Peter did not come to Retreat that summer. Unlike the summer before, he did not even come for weekends; Dr. Fleming had a second and more severe stroke the day after Pearl Harbor, and with the acceleration of the war and the scarcity of gasoline, there was no question of Peter's driving back and forth to the colony. Petie set his heels and refused to come too; he insisted on staying at Northpoint and taking naval history, and Peter promised to keep an eye on him. If Mother Hannah had not raised such a fuss, I would have stayed too. But she was adamant and Peter backed her up, so I set off with a truculent five-year-old and an ailing old autocrat, now in a wheelchair, on the grinding, swaying Maine Central to Ellsworth. From there we finally found a taxi that would take us as far as Blue Hill, and once there I quite simply bribed the lone taxi driver to bring us the last leg to Retreat. It was after dark when we bumped down the lane to Liberty, and my heart sank into my stomach. Not a single window in any of the cottages we passed showed a light; not an automobile was to be seen in driveways or garages. We might as well have landed, we three ill-assorted and iron-bonded women, on Uranus.

"Are we the only ones here? Where is everyone?"

Mother Hannah said querulously from the back seat, echoing my own swallowed dread.

"I want to go home," Happy whined ominously.

"Ain't many folks here, truth be known," the taxi driver said, I thought happily. "But it's mostly the blackout, y'see. Can't light your lights without you have blackout curtains. Patrol'll get you sure. Up and down these lanes ever' six hours, they are, checkin' on lights. Good thing, too. U-boats all up and down this coast, they say. Been seen off Mount Desert and Stonington, and some says they come in under the water, all the way up Eggemoggin Reach from Frenchmen's Bay to right off your cape here, for a little lookaround. Quiet as death, they say, like sharks; never know they're there. Main convoy route's past Mount Desert. Yup. Heard you folks had you a spy landin' right down there on your yacht club beach month or two ago. No tellin' where else they'll be poppin' up. Must know all the summer men are off fightin' the war and you women are all that's left down here. Don't know why you come, truth be known."

I was shaking with rage and fear as I paid him and struggled to extricate Mother Hannah and her wheelchair from the taxi. At the word "spy" Happy had begun to cry. She was convinced that Adolf Hitler was going to come over and personally dispatch her, and she knew in her dark, quick little soul that spies were his outriders. When I did not move to comfort her the weeping rose to a wail.

"Hope you've got some stores laid in," our driver said, leaning out his window. "Heard they've got no milk a'tall anywhere about, and no eggs or meat neither. Precious few vegetables, too, and flour's long gone. Lobsters and fish too; lobstermen all gone to war, like as not. Might be some clams, though, if you care to dig."

I turned on him furiously.

"Do you think it's funny to scare three lone women

out of their wits? Does it make you feel better?"

"Didn't feel bad to begin with," he said cheerfully, and gunned his lightless taxi back up the lane.

"Get that man's license number and contact his employer immediately, Maude," Mother Hannah huffed. "I will not be spoken to that way, especially by a native."

"I want to go home!" bellowed Happy.

"Both of you shut up this instant," I hissed between clenched teeth, and to my surprise they did, and for the first time in any of our lives we went into a cottage that was cold and completely dark. Peter must have forgotten to write Christina Willis, who always opened Liberty before we arrived and had a fire burning, and the icebox stocked with staples, and something simmering wonderfully on the stove.

"If either one of you says one word, I will walk away from here and leave you," I said, tears trembling in my voice, and I felt in the dark, thick air the nods of both their heads. Shame flooded over my loneliness and fear, and I groped my way to the old writing desk on the sun porch and felt in its top drawer for the matches that always rested there in their little tin. I used nearly all of them lighting the hurricane lamps and candles, but finally we had small pools of shimmering yellow light in the airless gloom, and the living room, its furniture shrouded in white sheets, leaped into life. I whipped the sheets off the sofa in front of the fireplace, and sat Happy and Mother Hannah down on it, and lit some reasonably dry birch logs that had been mercifully left in the fireplace, and looked at my charges. They looked back at me, silenced for the moment, eyes wide and waiting for deliverance.

I know who I want, I thought clearly and fervently. I want Micah.

And as if I had rubbed a lamp, I heard the unmistakable growl of his truck in the lane, and its tires crunching onto the driveway gravel, and his quick, soft steps up the walk. In a moment the front door eased open and he was there.

He was dressed in a dark fisherman's sweater, dark pants, and boots, and his face was smeared with something that looked like a minstrel's blackface. In all that darkness his eyes and teeth flashed bright.

"Evening, ladies," he said. "Thought it might be you when I saw the Blue Hill taxi go past. Couldn't think who else might be . . . determined enough to come up here, way things are."

"You mean stubborn, don't you?" I said, and then felt my eyes fill and my mouth contort treacherously. "Oh, Micah," I said simply, when I knew I would not cry. "I am truly very glad to see you."

"Well, I'll have to ask you to pardon the darky makeup," he said. "I'm the official patrol for this part of the cape, and it keeps my ugly face from shining out and startling the Nazis."

Then, seeing Happy's face, he smiled, and the teeth flashed again. "Figure of speech, dear. No Nazis in these parts, not with me and Bruno on the job. I'll bring him in to meet you in a bit, big old Labrador, he is, not good for anything but riding around in my truck looking official. But he'd scare the devil himself, with those big yellow eyes. You like dogs?"

"Yes," Happy said, staring at him in fascination. "I have a Scottie named Fala. He couldn't come."

"Fala, hmmm? Well, in good company, he is. Tell you what. Why can't Bruno be your part-time friend till you get back home to Fala? Would you like that?"

She smiled, the sudden, sweet smile that had spawned her nickname. I hadn't seen much of it lately.

"Yes," she said.

"Okay," he said. Then, turning to me, "Got some stuff in the truck Tina sent," he said. "Some fish chowder, and a blueberry pie, and molasses doughnuts. And a dozen eggs from her own hens, if you won't tell anybody. We're not supposed to have them. She'll come in the morning and turn the place out, and meanwhile I'll build up the fires in your bedrooms and bring you in some wood. Should be some left in the wood house."

"Micah, I can't begin to . . . thank you," I said weakly. "I didn't realize things were so bad up here until the taxi driver told us about the shortages. And of course the famous U-boats and the spies. We won't lean on you after tonight, I promise. Peter bought an old car last fall and left it in the wood house, so I'll have that to drive for absolute necessities, and I've got my ration cards and things; we'll manage fine."

"Well, about that car," he said. "I'm afraid it isn't in the wood house. Sheriff Perkins commandeered it in April for his patrol; it does the Brooksville to Castine run every night. I do the shore and the village. Wouldn't do you any good anyway. Only gas available is for official vehicles. I can pick up some things for you from time to time, and you can walk to the general store. And I brought Caleb's bicycle for you; it's in the truck. We'll see you have what you need to live, but it isn't going to be much pleasure, I'm afraid. You really shouldn't be up here by yourself."

"Micah Willis, you tell the sheriff to return my vehicle immediately or I will have the law on him," Mother Hannah said coldly, from amid her blankets. "How dare he confiscate it without my permission? And as for being up here, I have never missed a summer in Retreat in my life, and I shall not start now."

"No, ma'am," Micah said, looking at her. "I don't expect you will, at that. But begging your pardon, may I point out that Sheriff Perkins *is* the law?"

He smiled at her, a bandit's smile. And to my great surprise she smiled back.

"In that case, Micah, you may assist me to my

room," she said, holding out her arm, and he came forward and took it and helped her to her feet. I watched as he bore her out of the living room as if he were taking her in to a state dinner and then turned to my yawning daughter.

"Okay, Punkin, let's get you into your jammies, and then we'll have supper by the fire, like a campout," I said.

After my daughter and mother-in-law were settled and we had brought in the groceries and put them away, Micah brought blackout curtains from the truck and put them up for me, and then went to the fuse box and turned on the electricity, and the room bloomed into its familiar soft yellow light. I had made coffee and offered him some, and he stood beside the mantel drinking it. He couldn't stay, he said; he still had most of his rounds to go and another to do in six hours.

"Is it all really necessary?" I said.

"Yes, it is," he said. "What Clem Peak told you about the spies and the U-boats is partly true, though the old fool had no business scaring you like that. Haven't had a sighting in a while, but there've been some off Rosier, and the sheriff's patrol did pick up a spy of sorts down on the club beach one night. Young fellow, said he was Dutch, but that was pure hogwash. So the blackouts are serious, and the patrols and the precautions. You follow them, you should be safe enough. Everybody in the area knows we patrol Retreat regularly now, and you aren't absolutely alone. Miss Lottie is down at the Little House, and Dr. and Mrs. Lincoln at Land's End, and I think there's at least one of the Thorne girls and children down in Mary's Garden. And of course, Mrs. Stallings, over at Utopia."

"Nobody near us, though," I said.

"Well, somebody'd hear you if you hollered loud," he said. "What's the matter with Mrs. Chambliss, by the way?"

"Arthritis, her doctor says," I said. "But I don't know.
. . . She seems to get weaker and weaker. You're right,
this was a bad idea. I hope she sees now that it was."

"Peter's not coming," he said. It was not a
question.

"No, there's just too much confusion at the school,
with so many of the older boys leaving to enlist and
some of the younger instructors gone. It's so sad to
see boys you've known for so long go off to war. I
just hold my breath every day for Petie. . . . Oh,
Micah. What about Caleb? Did he . . . is he . . . ?"

"Went in the Seabees right after the war started,"
he said. "He's in Brisbane now, in the hospital. Got
shot up pretty good in the Coral Sea to-do."

"Oh, God, Micah. But he's going to be all right,
isn't he? Will he be coming home soon?"

"In about a month. All of him but his left leg."

I stared and then put my face down in my hands. I
felt tears start. I shook my head wordlessly and then
whispered, "I'm so sorry. I'm so sorry."

In my mind's eye I saw a small, dark little boy darting across a summer field, his arms full of lilacs, and
felt again in my arms his limp, sleepy weight.

"Don't be sorry," Micah said. "He doesn't need his
leg to haul. At least he's coming home. Some aren't."

I lifted my head and looked at him silently, feeling
my cheeks redden. What he must bear he would bear
like a Down Easter; he would not ask my tears and
would not welcome them. I vowed that he, like
Peter, would not see them again.

"You're right," I said. "Some aren't."

"Well, I'm off, then," he said, and started out, and
then stopped. "By the by, I think you ought to keep
this nearby, just in case," he said, and fished a thick
blunt gun out of his pocket and handed it to me. I
looked at it.

"I don't want a gun in the house—"

"Take it," he said. "Hide it if you want to, but keep it handy. If you can't shoot it, I'll come by tomorrow and show you how. It's loaded now. Be careful, for God's sake; a summer lady over at Sedgwick shot the fishmonger in the arse, thinking he was a spy."

I looked at him sharply, and he smiled. I smiled back and picked up the gun.

"Thank you," I said. "Just be sure to mind your own arse. I can't say I haven't been tempted over the years."

"Don't I know it," he said, and went out of the cottage, and soon we three were alone again in the dark colony. But we slept better that night for his visit, as well as for the provender he brought, though I wrapped the gun in a flannel face cloth and put it under my bed before I climbed into it. Far from making me nervous, it seemed to glow there soothingly like a living coal, and I could sense its warmth through springs and mattress and sheets. I was asleep almost before my head hit the pillow.

After that I felt safe, even though the rumors of U-boat sightings and spy landings and mysterious lights at sea, and cryptic messages intercepted on lobster-boat radios, flew like gnats around the skeleton colony and the village. Somehow the talk seemed, for the first and only time in my experience in Retreat, to bring me close to the villagers; it was as if now, in this time of privation and rumored danger, all shades of nuance were dissolved and all social rules off. Mr. Courtney, who ran the store in the Oddfellows Hall in the village, would send one of his legion of taciturn children down to Retreat with a small sack of whatever he had from time to time, and I would send one of my precious, unusable gas rationing stamps back in return, along with my ration book. Mrs. Fellows, who had the farm up the road toward Brooksville, kept out crabmeat and a few fresh vegetables for me when she had them, and old Trenton Percy in the opposite

direction smuggled me milk for Happy. I heard from
Jane Thorne in Mary's Garden that he kept her two
supplied, too. Micah regularly brought lobsters and
clams, and Christina brought bread whenever she
baked, and once, when his father shot a deer that was
marauding in his green pea vines, Micah brought us an
entire haunch of cured venison. I sent roasts and
chops to the few others who were in Retreat—older
people, for the most part, and a few young mothers
with children, like me.

For my part, I began asking Micah and Christina to
come in the evenings after supper and listen to the
radio with me, or to the old albums of classical music
and operas that Big Peter had cherished and kept carefully shelved in his study. We three sat in the firelight
after Happy and Mother Hannah had gone to bed, cur-
tained against the intruding night, drinking coffee and
sometimes brandy from one of the few dusty bottles
left from Big Peter's prohibition cache, talking little of
the war or of ourselves but much of such unweighted
things as travel and art and music and gardening. I felt
close to both of them in that strange, suspended time. I
felt as if the three of us were voyagers on a small snug
craft in a limitless black sea, unable to see the shore
behind or ahead of us, not knowing our destination,
and therefore somehow content, for the moment, just
to be. It was an oddly pleasant summer: tense but,
below the tension, soothing to near somnolence.

"Strangely enough, I'm enjoying this summer very
much, and so are Happy and your mother," I wrote
Peter in late July. "In a way it's by far the most peaceful time I've had here. I'm glad now that we came. I
haven't heard anything about U-boats or spies since
the week we got here."

"I'd be awfully surprised if Sheriff Perkins caught
himself a live spy," Peter wrote back. "From what I
hear of his extracurricular activities, he's far more apt

to catch himself a wandering agent of the Alcohol, Tax, and Firearms Division. Parker Potter used to buy home brew from him all the time."

The night before Labor Day I sat long on the porch with Dr. and Mrs. Lincoln and Jane Thorne, watching a meteor shower in the black sky above the firs and spruce. All three of them were leaving early on Tuesday, and Peter was coming for us the day after that. I was in the process of closing the cottage. Boxes and bundles and suitcases sat about in the living room, and some of the furniture was already shrouded. I had made a stew from leftover venison and what vegetables I had, and Christina had made Blueberry Fool, and we were sleepy and full of food and nostalgia, all of us reluctant to leave the safe harbor of Retreat and go back into the world, "In harm's way," as Dr. Lincoln put it.

I kissed them all lightly on the cheek, the standard Retreat leavetaking, and told them I would see them before we left, and went upstairs to look in on Happy and Mother Hannah. My daughter slept on her side with her thumb in her mouth; none of Mother Hannah's dictums and scoldings had had any effect on her thumb sucking, and I had long since given up. But she looked sweet and peaceful in the wash of starlight, her brow clear and high, her mouth relaxed around the stubby finger. I pulled her covers up higher and went down to Mother Hannah's room. Sometimes she read late into the night, but tonight her lights were off, and I could see the slow rise and fall of her breath under the cutwork coverlet. When had she lost so much of that imposing bulk; when had she become such a slight, small woman? Awake, she took on substance and presence like a swelling turkey gobbler, but asleep she was simply a sick little old lady in a narrow old-fashioned bed.

I closed her door and tiptoed away and went into the kitchen to pour myself a glass of Trenton Percy's illicit milk. I did not turn on the light, because I had not drawn the blackout curtains. Outside, moonlight poured down on the porch, white on the wide old boards. Not even the normal night sounds of the northern forest pierced the thick quiet, not even the small sucking rattle of the tide on the beach. I'll miss this quiet at home, I thought.

I saw the shadow then. It fell suddenly, grotesquely, across the moon-white boards of the porch, a long, thin, wavering shadow, unmistakably that of a man, unmistakably freighted with menace real enough to prickle the hair at the nape of my neck and draw my lips back from my teeth in a wild animal's snarl. The shadow was still and then took a long, flickering step and held it, and another. I froze, flattened against the kitchen door. My heart hammered. There was no mistaking it: a man who was not in any way one of us was creeping across the porch of the cottage, waiting and listening between steps for some sign that he had been heard. He moved an arm and I saw the grotesque, unmistakable outline of a gun in it. It could not have been anything else. Any thought that it might be one of the sheriff's patrol, or even Micah Willis, left me. No one not intent on harm would steal onto a darkened porch with a gun at the ready. I did not move, and the shadow did not either.

After an eternity, while my ears rang and my heart choked in my throat, the shadow withdrew. I took a long, deep, shuddering breath and moved to the bottom of the stairs, to go up to my child. And then I heard him at the front door, heard him ease the creaking old screen open and slowly, slowly, rattle the old brass doorknob. I had locked it; Micah had made me remember to lock up each night until it became habit, but I knew he could force the old knob if he wished, or simply break out one of the glass panes and reach in and unlatch it. All conscious thought flew out of my head like bats streaming from a cave at evening, and when I came to myself I was standing at the top of the stairs outside Happy's room, Micah's gun in my hand, pointing it straight down the stairs at a dark shape that stood still as death midway up, looking at me. I could see only his outline, but I saw that clearly. His own gun hung straight down by his leg, in his hand. I could not remember running up the stairs and scrabbling the gun out from under the bed. I could not remember hearing the intruder enter the downstairs. I could not remember hearing or seeing him start to ascend. I heard nothing, no sound from him, no breathing except my own, tearing in my throat. Then, behind me, Happy said sleepily, "Mama?"

"Turn around and go back down the stairs very slowly, or I'll shoot you in the head," I said, and my voice sounded as high and pearly as that of a *castrati*. He said nothing, did not move.

"I mean it," I said. "Get out of here right now. This gun is loaded, and I will truly kill you."

He said something, softly, almost under his breath. I could not understand it. He took a step up, and another. I pulled the trigger of the pistol.

The black world exploded into flame; red-shot whiteness battered at my eyes and sound ricocheted around the narrow stairwell and roared in my ears. I did not lower the gun; I could not hear or see, but I felt the vibration of his footsteps stumbling back down the stairs. I shot again, and again, until the gun would not shoot anymore. Then I dropped it on the top step and went into Happy's room and locked the door and pushed her bureau against it, and caught her into my arms and held her. She was screaming by now, the high, thin shrieks of a terrified child. Dimly I heard my mother-in-law calling out from downstairs, over and over, but I did not get up and go to her. I simply sat there holding my child, my eyes closed. I could not have risen if a panzer division had rumbled into the cottage.

Micah was the first one to get there. I don't know how long it was before he came; I do know that Happy had almost wept herself out. Later he told me that Dr. and Mrs. Lincoln had heard the shots and the doctor had run down to Mary's Garden and used Jane Thorne's telephone to phone Micah, who had just been leaving on his eleven o'clock patrol. He called to me through the locked bedroom door, and at his voice I went to it as stiffly as an automaton and opened it, and when I saw him standing there, I said, almost conversationally, "Micah, I think I might have shot somebody," and then sat down hard on the floor, my head spinning. Behind me Happy began to cry again.

The Lincolns sat up with me in the kitchen all the rest of that night, after the doctor had given the outraged Mother Hannah a sedative and Mary Lincoln had soothed Happy back into sleep. One of the sheriff's men stood guard on the porch outside. Micah had roused some of the village men, and they and the sheriff's two deputies spread out through the woods and along the shore with dogs and guns. Dr. Lincoln said, sometime during the long night, while we drank coffee and waited for whatever would come, "I expect they'll have no trouble finding him. He won't have been able to go far or travel fast. There was . . . ah, considerable blood on the floor at the foot of the stairs and on the porch outside. It should be quite easy to track him."

I made a small, wordless sound, and Mary Lincoln patted my arm and said, "Don't you worry, my dear. I got it all out of the carpet with the milk in your icebox. It came right up; milk is wonderful for bloodstains. There're none left at all on the porch."

"Mary," Dr. Lincoln said, "perhaps you would look in on Hannah. If she seems restless, give her another of the powders I left on the night table."

"Oh, Ridley, really," she chirped, but she went.

The doctor looked at me, and I noticed only then that under his overcoat he wore the only real old-fashioned nightshirt I have ever seen. I must have smiled at him, because he said, "That's the spirit, my dear. You need have no remorse for anything that has happened this night."

I thought of telling him that I felt no remorse at all, only horror and weariness and simple disbelief, but I could not make my mouth work. We sat in silence, we three, until the cracks around the kitchen blackout curtains began to lighten, and I got up stiffly and went and raised them. Outside, on a low bough, a blue jay cawed cheekily at me. I rubbed my eyes and, when I opened them, saw Micah Willis coming up the lane with Bruno on his leash, a shotgun in the crook of his arm. I watched as he crossed Liberty's lawn and came into the house and back into the kitchen. We looked at each other, he and I, but for a time we said nothing.

Mary Lincoln poured coffee for him, and as he drank it he told the doctor briefly, "We didn't find him, but somebody will. Lot of blood leading off into the woods; looks like he might have headed for the shore right below the yacht club. Came ashore there, we think. There's marks where a right big shallow-draft boat came ashore and went back out. Must have left him off. If he made it back I'll be surprised."

"Could it have been . . . one of us, somebody from around here?" I said through numb lips. It was what horrified me most, that I might have shot someone who meant me no real harm. But I did not think there was much chance of that.

"No," Micah said. "It could not have been."

Dr. and Mrs. Lincoln left then, and Micah and I sat looking at each other across the old deal table.

"You look like five miles of bad road," he said.

"You look like ten," I said.

"It was a good thing you did tonight, Maude," he said. "I'm proud of you. Peter will be too."

I wanted to say something matter-of-fact, lightly disparaging, fine and ironic, something he would have said, or a Maine woman would. Instead, I put my head down on my arms and cried. Even as I did it I felt contempt for myself, and a kind of dull hopelessness. I knew I would never measure up in Micah Willis's world.

But I could not stop crying. After a moment, he came around the table to me and put his arms around me and lifted me up to him and held me there against him, his hand smoothing my hair back.

"There, now, Maude," he said softly. "There, now."

It sounded as if he were saying, "Theah." I felt laughter bubble in my mouth, hysterical laughter, probably, but laughter, and I raised my face to his, and as simply as if he did it every day of his life he kissed me on my tear-stained mouth, a long, soft, searching kiss. When he pulled away we looked at each other for a long time and then I said, idiotically, "There's something in your shirt pocket that's poking me."

He stood away from me and reached into the pocket and brought out a small dark-brown nut.

"It's a chinquapin," he said. "They're supposed to be good luck. My dad gave it to me; his dad used to carry it. I wouldn't leave home without it."

I took the little nut and fondled it in my fingers. It was smooth and silky, surprisingly heavy.

"At home we call them buckeyes," I said. My voice was dreamy and fluting. I realized I was tired nearly to death. "My brother used to call me Buckeye because I was little and brown and round."

He smiled then, and I saw the fatigue in his face and eyes, too. Fatigue, and something that had not been there before.

"And do you have good luck, Maude?"

"Yes," I said. "I guess I do."

Chapter Eight

In 1950, the United States government closed the tiny post office in South Brooksville that had served Retreat since the colony was established and built a new, larger one. On the last day of business in the old one, Miss Charity Snow, who had been postmistress for more years than most Retreaters could remember, finally and most reluctantly retired. It was said about the colony that it had taken a very stern official letter from Washington to get Miss Charity out of her doll-size post office, and everyone knew she had not spoken to Elsie Borders, the officious new appointee, since April, when the official letter announcing the changing of the guard arrived.

"It's ironic, isn't it, that Miss Charity's death sentence arrived via the U.S. Mail," Peter said. "They ought to frame the stamp and hang it right under Elsie's nose in the new building."

"Don't be silly, Peter; Charity Snow was far too old to handle the mail properly, and her temper was getting really dreadful," Mother Hannah said. "Half the time she wouldn't even speak to me when I went for the mail, and I always had to tell her my name. It isn't as though she hadn't seen me almost every day of her life for fifty years. No, it was her arteries, I'm sure. She knew she was failing. She didn't want to go through a long, undignified decline. Charity was a vain woman."

"Nuts to that. It was being canned," Peter said. "That dinky little place was her life."

And it must have been. I never knew her to have any outside it. A spare, starched, erect maiden lady rooted for generations in the hard Maine earth, Miss Charity lived alone in a tiny white house beside her minuscule post office, both of which sat beside the road and looked over a salt meadow down to the bay. Aside from the tuberous begonias that she grew in the window boxes in the post office, Miss Charity seemed to have allegiance to no living thing; she had no relatives, no pets, and kept no garden. She simply tended her post office and went home to wait for morning, when she could tend it again.

Miss Charity knew three generations of summer people, though she spoke to few of them by name and took pride in never misplacing anyone's mail, be he an original settler or first-time visitor. Her stamps, waiting to be sold, were lined in T-square-edged rows and rolls, and her coin wrappers were dusted every morning after she had swept the faultless floor. She blacked her potbellied stove once a month and solemnly lowered the flag just at sunset each evening, consulting her time-and-tide chart to be sure of the exact moment.

On the evening of her last day as postmistress, as she had done each evening for probably fifty of her seventy-odd years, she realigned her stamps and money orders, swept her floor, consulted her time-and-tide chart, lowered her flag and folded it precisely, and locked the door. The next morning an early lobster-man, heading out at first light to haul his traps, found

Miss Charity's body bobbing gently in the flat calm of the dawn bay, half in the water and half out.

I was just starting breakfast in Liberty's slant-floored old kitchen on the late June morning that it happened, and when Christina Willis came running in with the news, I felt a stab of shock and grief far out of proportion to my connection to Miss Charity. Tina, too, was deeply affected; it was the only time in my life I ever saw her cry. She had not wept when Big Peter died, and I know she was heartbroken about that, and I never even saw a glint of tears in her serene blue eyes on the terrible day that Caleb came home from the war without his leg or during the long bad time after that, when he seemed intent on finding a sort of surcease in liquor and fast driving and fights. When Old Micah Willis, Micah's father, had died on the floor of the boathouse from a swift and merciful heart attack at age ninety-one, it had been Micah, not Tina, who had been unable to speak of his father without his voice breaking. But now tears ran down her brown cheeks and into the corners of her mouth, and her voice trembled.

"It was such a little thing; what could it have hurt to let her keep on until she couldn't any longer? What would it have been, a year more? Two? Her eyes were going; she knew that. She never had anything else in her life, and to fire her, like you would a bad worker . . . it's like shooting a bird, an osprey or an old eagle. It's just pure waste and meanness. I hope Elsie Borders is happy; there's talk that somebody sent the government an anonymous letter saying Miss Charity was getting sloppy and contentious. Well, contentious, maybe, but never sloppy."

She actually put her face in her hands and sobbed, and I put my arms around her, feeling tears start in my own eyes. I had been irritated at Miss Charity's highhandedness myself, over the years, and had not infrequently come home muttering to Peter about her, but Tina was right. The firing was gratuitous and cruel. It was, indeed, like killing a grand old sea bird. It and the subsequent death of the old woman felt wrong, askew, freighted with some sort of import I could not name but felt would cast a long and smoking shadow. It seemed to me a thing that presaged cataclysm, and I came later to think that it divided time as surely as the great catastrophes of history and brought to Retreat not only grief, not only the modern world in the shape of the new post office, but a kind of generic change and loss.

I said as much a few nights later to the family at dinner.

"I thought the war would change everything, but it didn't," I said. "At least not in Retreat. Nothing is different here now, not really. But this is going to change things. I don't know how, but it is. You can feel it up ahead, the change; it's like somebody has poked a hole in the dike, and it's all going to come in on us now."

"What is?" Petie said, pouring wine all around the table.

"Whatever is out there," I said, knowing as I said it that it sounded quasi-mystic and a shade mad, something a dotty old medium might say. But it was as near to what I felt as I could get.

"Shall I get the Ouija board out for you, Ma?" Petie said, grinning first at Sarah Forbes and then at me. He was almost twenty-five and had been in his position as an assistant vice president in the family bank for more than two years, but in the light from the guttering candles he looked like a round-faced, slightly pudgy teenager. He had not had a haircut for weeks, and the dark tendrils were curling around his ears and at his neck, and his white teeth were still nearly as small as baby teeth. He had my teeth as well as my small, round stature and black hair and eyes, and the receding hairline that gave him the look of an ingenuous baby came straight from my father. Kemble had it early, too. Only his chin, thrusting and incongruous, spoke of Chambliss. Mother Hannah had long since stopped remarking on the unseemly peasantlike strength of the Gascoigne genes, but I knew that she felt the sting afresh every time she looked at Petie. I smiled at him across the table for that and many other reasons. I had known he would laugh at my fancy. Peter was, as he had always been, as earthbound as a totem pole. That, at least, he had from his grandmother.

"You know, don't you, that you come from a long line of conjure women?" I said, my grin widening at Mother Hannah's barely audible sniff. She probably thought it was true. Petie laughed aloud, Peter's joyous, rich laugh, and I laughed with him, in pure relief. There was a time, just after the summers with Elizabeth Potter, that we did not hear that laugh for a very long time. Indeed, I had not heard the original much lately. Both were precious to me now.

"Then when are you going to get around to turning Gretchen Winslow into a toad?" he said. Gretchen had given him a rather severe tongue-lashing on the tennis court the day before, and I had seen the old, smoldering anger of his childhood leap in his eyes, though he said nothing.

"Petie, really," Mother Hannah said fretfully.

"Her days as a human being are numbered," I said. Across the table from me Happy pushed lamb chops around her plate, and made mountains of mashed potatoes, and crowned them with peas.

"I hate her," she said matter-of-factly. "I hate that stupid Freddie and Julia, too. They all think they're something. I hope they fall in the bay like Miss Snow and drown. I hope they don't come up till Christmas. I hope their stupid boat sinks, too."

Happy was thirteen that year, square and prickly

and far removed from the bubbling, chattering toddler who had earned the nickname. We had named her Camilla for Peter's favorite aunt, but by the time she took her first steps, stumbling determinedly after Peter and crowing with joy when he picked her up, she was simply Happy, and Happy she remained, even though the sunny temperament had vanished somewhere in her middle childhood, when Peter had begun to submerge himself in the school in earnest. She looked like Peter and his father in some respects; she had the same soft fair hair and skin and the gray-water eyes, but hers were usually wintry with discontent now, and the long bones and slenderness that went with the coloring never materialized. She had my lack of stature and roundness; the effect was of her father somehow foreshortened and broadened, as if he had been squashed by a great weight. She had not lost her baby fat, either; at thirteen, she weighed a bit more, I thought, than I did. I was not sure because Happy had hidden or broken every scale both in our house at Northpoint and in Liberty.

I sighed. It was not easy, I knew, to be a dumpy adolescent in this place of young sun-browned gazelles, and in truth the Winslow children, Freddie and Julia, both years older than she, had snubbed her badly and overtly and refused to let her sail with them when she asked. And her father had left for the summer only days before and was thus out of her grasp for months; that always sent her wild. But still, her outburst was unattractive and excessive, almost shocking, and I knew that Mother Hannah would say something cold and cutting to her if I did not reprove her first. Damn Mother Hannah, I thought wearily.

"Not funny and not allowed, Happy," I said. "Let's not have any more of it at dinner."

"Petie started it. And you said something bad about Mrs. Winslow. If you can, I—"

"I think you can take your plate and finish it on the sun porch," I said evenly.

"Oh, sure, it's okay if you and old Saint Peter there say awful things, but just let me make a little joke—"

"Happy."

She jumped up and blundered out of the room, leaving her plate and banging the door onto the sun porch.

"Daddy wouldn't say rotten, stinking things like that to me," she flung back over her shoulder. I could hear the tears thick in her throat. She would work herself into one of her shrill rages, and it might or might not have subsided by morning. Poor Happy. She was right about her father, though not in the way she wished. Peter would not have reproved her or sent her from the table. Indeed, he would have said nothing at all. That silence was the weight that had smothered the flame behind Happy's smile years before.

"She is badly spoiled, I'm afraid," Mother Hannah said with satisfaction to the table at large. "I've said so all along to Peter. This modern permissiveness will be the ruin of many a child. In my day such an outburst would not have been permitted."

My cheeks burned with annoyance at her, enthroned in the armchair at the head of the table where she had sat ever since Big Peter died, even though for years it had been I who had served our meals and seen to the comfort of guests and done most of the cooking too. To get back and forth from the kitchen I practically had to climb over her, but I knew she would not think of relinquishing her throne to me. Once or twice during every meal I could see that she groped with her toe for the button on the floor that once had summoned servants from the kitchen, forgetting we had disconnected it when I had finally insisted that Tina Willis leave for her own home at midafternoon. Mother Hannah was very old now, and quite ill, and frail to the point of incapacity, and her short-term memory was close to nonexistent. But her autocratic will was unchanged.

"Where is Tina? I've been ringing for five minutes," she would say.

"You remember, Mother Hannah. Tina doesn't come in the evenings now. She hasn't, for almost five years. The button doesn't work. We disconnected it."

"Nobody told me. Why wasn't I consulted? Who took it upon themselves to tell her not to come?"

"I did, but only after you agreed that it was ridiculous for her to come when there were so few of us here. She's entitled to some life of her own, you know."

"Who'll cook for Peter? And Petie?"

"Mother Hannah, I've been doing it for years. It's only you and me and Happy most of the time now; you know Peter and Petie only come for a week or two in the summer."

"No, I don't know. Why don't they come? Did you tell them not to? I want Tina back. Everybody else in Retreat has a cook in the evenings. How will it look, you doing our cooking?"

"Almost nobody has a full-time cook now," I would repeat. "The Winslows are the only ones; everybody else let most of their help go during the war."

"You're being very contrary, Maude," she would say. "You know that is not true. Augusta Stallings has Marjorie, and Mary and Ridley Lincoln have Marva, and Helen Parker has Dorothy."

And I would be silent, because Augusta Stallings and her Marjorie were both dead, as were Dr. and Mrs. Lincoln and their Marva, and Helen Parker was now nearly as old as the fearsome Mamadear had been when I first came to Retreat. In the early days I

would point this out to Mother Hannah, but it had
upset and angered her so I had stopped, and much of
the time she lived among an army of genteel ghosts,
attended by faithful phantoms.

On this night, I did not respond to her remark
about Happy's behavior. Instead, I looked across the
table at Sarah Forbes, Petie's visiting girlfriend,
hunched down in her chair in embarrassment like a
small brown wren fluffed against a gale. Petie had
met her the year before at a dance at the club; her
father was a visiting professor of economics at
Boston University, and they were new to the city. He
had been seeing her fairly steadily, and Peter and I
liked her, though it was sometimes hard to remember her name. She seemed to me indistinguishable
from many of the other young newcomers we had
met in Boston or in New Hampshire since the war:
bright, well-dressed, educated, polite, anonymous.
There was no panache to Sarah, but there was no
overt danger either; I thought on the main that she
might not be a bad match for my stolid son. They
seemed in many ways cut from the same good serge
cloth.

But if Petie was serious about her, no one could
tell; they acted together like comfortable childhood
friends. I thought she was serious about him, though,
very definitely; at times I saw in her round brown
eyes something intense, something so hungry and
devouring as to be almost alarming. I thought that little brown Sarah Forbes, under her chaste Miss
Porter's exterior, literally starved and burned for my
son. It might have frightened me a bit, but it didn't. I
had seen that same desperate hunger in my son's
eyes, hunger for Elizabeth Potter, and it did not dis-
please me that someone now hungered for him in his
turn.

But I was fairly sure Petie did not see it, and even

though he had brought her to Retreat for the first time to meet us all, I did not think she was yet, as the young say today, part of his agenda. I was faintly disappointed and said so to Peter, but he simply shrugged.

"Well, she's certainly no threat to him. That's one good thing. What's that line from the Hippocratic oath? 'First do no harm'?"

"You romantic devil, you," I said. "Don't you like her?"

"What's not to like?"

It was Mother Hannah who did not like Sarah Forbes, and though she did not, of course, say so, her disapproval radiated out from her in small symmetrical waves and I knew Sarah felt in her presence the same outlander's discomfort that I had known, when I first visited the old house on Charles Street. Sarah and her parents had moved to Boston from Michigan. From Grosse Pointe, to be exact, but still Michigan. Sarah might be forgiven much, but not that.

"Forgive us this high domestic drama, Sarah," I said. "Peter has often said that children should be put into cages at puberty and let out the day they leave for college, and he may have a point."

"Please don't apologize, Mrs. Chambliss," she said with a shy smile that slid, even as she looked at me, over to Petie. "My sister Charlotte didn't eat an entire meal with us until she was nearly eighteen."

I smiled at her, and Petie laughed aloud. She looked pleased at his laughter, and blushed, and I felt a surge of affection for her. My son would be safe with this small bird of a girl. He might not soar to dizzying heights in her company, but neither would he plunge into lightless depths. And he would laugh. I had come to know in Peter's dark times what the lighthearted ones were worth, and at that moment, in the old twilight dining alcove of Retreat, I was ready to trade a good part of my life to Sarah Forbes in order that she become a part of my son's. How many mothers, I have wondered since, have wanted just that for their children and labored with all their might to obtain it: safety. I have wondered, too, how many have come to find the victory hollow. There is no safety; of course there isn't. But still, the specter of it powers the world.

Mother Hannah was displeased with the dinner hour in its entirety, I knew. Sarah Forbes annoyed her only slightly less than Happy in a tantrum. I knew also she was tired, and if I could not coax her to bed, her temper would rise until it spilled over onto one or more of us, probably Sarah. She tired very easily now; even though I brought her breakfast in bed and helped her down for a long nap after lunch, she still found it almost impossible to sit up with the family after dinner. But she sometimes insisted, loving, I knew, the quiet, dark hours with music and a book before the whispering birch fire, and so I did not push early bedtimes very hard. But when she did not have them the rest of us usually paid. The debilitating weakness, and the pain from the ulcer her old doctor in Boston had diagnosed two winters before, were constant and, I thought, severe. I could not know for sure because she refused to speak of her stomach trouble and would not let me take her into the new medical center in Castine on the mornings that she woke white-lipped and sapped from a pain-racked night. They were more frequent now, and more than once I said worriedly to Peter that I thought she might have something more serious wrong with her than a duodenal ulcer. The bland foods I cooked were no longer helping.

"He's so old himself; can he possibly have misdiagnosed her?" I would say. "Or know something he should be telling us?"

"He's a good doctor," Peter would reply. "He's been our family doctor all my life and a lot of hers. Let it go. Even if there's something more, she's where she wants to be: at home in her own house or in Retreat. Do you think she'd be better off if she couldn't come to Retreat?"

And so I kept silent. But I worried, and when I could, I got her early to bed. This night was, I thought, one of the nights I would insist. I did not want Mother Hannah's acid to spill over Sarah, and I did not think it would occur to Petie to stand up to his grandmother on her account, as his father had always done on mine. Petie dealt with Mother Hannah by simply tuning her out. I don't think he heard three fourths of the things she said.

To my relief, she did not argue when I suggested an early bed.

"All this talk about omens and holes in dikes and Ouija boards; what nonsense," she said in the breathless ghost of her old imperious voice. "I found a whole stack of Mary Roberts Rinehart novels that someone must have hidden all these years; I've never seen them. She's far better company than gypsy fortunetellers."

"She probably is at that," I said, giving her my arm to pull herself up with. Over her head Petie grinned at me; he knew, as I did, that she had read and reread the Rinehart books in the long summers at Retreat, and he knew also that she sometimes still flicked at me with her oldest whip, that of my dark gypsy coloring. For I had, in all the years in the Northeast, lost none of the ripe, excessive bloom of the Low Country. "Madame Maude," Peter and Petie both sometimes called me, and Peter once observed that his mother must be disappointed indeed that my time in this land of long nights and longer winters had not bleached some of it out of me.

Coming back into the living room after settling her in with her books, I stopped to look at my reflection in the wavery, underwater old mirror over the sideboard. In the dimness, it was indeed a gypsy who looked back at me, eyes black pools, hair still rioting around the dark face in dark laps and whorls, body still round and inelegantly lush, breasts and hips fuller now but waist still small. I smiled experimentally, and small pointed teeth flashed ferally. I picked up a crystal bowl from the sideboard and held it up before my face.

"Cross Madame Maude's palm with silver and she'll tell you a wonderful fortune," I whispered, and then shook my head and went to join the children before the fire. Of course none of them had taken my talk of Miss Charity's death and its portent seriously; who would have?

Micah would, I thought suddenly and clearly. Micah would know what I meant.

But I was not likely to have a chance to speak of it to him, not privately, at least. Since the night of the German spy—or, to be more accurate, the morning of that first and last kiss in the dawn kitchen of Liberty—Micah Willis and I had not been alone together for any length of time. By some tacit mutual consent, we had, in the intervening years, seen each other only in the presence of another person. He came just as frequently to attend to his customary chores around the cottage, and I ran into him just as frequently on my rounds on the cape or in the little Congregational church in whose quiet churchyard we had first spoken at length to each other. But always, since that morning, Christina would be there, or Peter, or Mother Hannah, or one or another of the children.

It was not, I knew, constraint that kept us from being alone together, or any lingering pangs of guilt, or even any dark sense that to be together in privacy would court more than a kiss, would lead to a dangerous and desperate passion. I was not sure what it was: a kind of comfortable accommodation to each other's well-being, I think, and the well-being of others who were dear to us both. I know that with both of us the kiss could easily have become something else, something deeper and fuller and infinitely real. I had, I think, always known that. But it was as if, given that knowledge, we were content to keep the friendship that preceded it intact, each of us knowing in his deepest heart that this lovely other thing hovered always just at our horizons, perhaps not ever to be tasted, certainly not to be hurried. Just there. It by no means changed the love I felt for Peter or, I knew, the quality of the affection and commitment he had to Christina. It was, for both of us, other and apart. There are no limits to our capacity for love; that is the one sure thing I have kept out of a lifetime's scant store of truths. I first sensed it with Micah Willis.

He and Christina came often to Liberty in the evenings, after we had all had our dinners and the washing up was done. These evenings had begun that lonely, uneasy first summer of the war, and we had simply, in the manner of old friends, kept the habit going. We did now what we had done then: we listened to music and talked of anything in the world that intrigued and comforted us, we drank coffee and sometimes a little brandy and ate leftover pie, we laughed and told stories of our childhood and made fun of the people around us who, we felt, merited it. Just as old friends do everywhere. Sometimes, when he was in Retreat, Peter joined us and enjoyed the evenings almost as much as I did. He had always been fond of Tina, saying she was a veritable mother lode of unmined gold, and Micah Willis had long had both his liking and his respect.

The children were fond of the Willises and saw

nothing unusual in the sight of the people who worked for their family in the daytime laughing and drinking brandy in their living room at night. But I have always suspected that the taunts of their colony peers and, less frequently, their peers' parents sometimes found their mark. No one in the collective memory of Retreat, I'm sure, had ever had the hired hands in their homes as guests. I think Petie and Happy took not a little friendly fire over the situation from time to time, especially from Freddie and Julia Winslow, who took their cue from Gretchen. Whenever something snide about me and the Willises made its way back to my ears, it usually had its genesis with Gretchen Winslow. I cared very little about the talk, and in the main I don't think Petie did either. He was already grown up and away from Retreat, essentially, now, a creature of a larger and newer world. But the talk could always wound Happy, sensitive as she was in her very soul to criticism, and I shielded her from the tongues of the assorted Winslows as best I could. In the long run, it did not matter. She heard far worse from Mother Hannah.

It was not that my mother-in-law disliked either of the Willises. In fact, in her austere way, she was as fond of them both as she was of many of her neighbors in Retreat, though in a different way, and probably fonder than she was of a few. It would not have occurred to her that Micah might remember with bitterness her outburst at him on the awful day he found Parker Potter molesting his young niece, Polly, in her living room, and to Micah's credit, if he did, he never showed it.

"Micah and Christina are fine people, the salt of the earth," I heard her say often over drinks, when the eternal colony litany of servants, second only to that of sewage disposal, came up. "I am proud to have them as neighbors."

But not, she might have added but did not have to, since everyone in Retreat understood, as guests. The fact that Micah could play a respectable classical violin and was reading his way through the world's great philosophers, and Christina had a library twice the size of Mother Hannah's back in Boston and was fluent in three languages, cut no ice with her at all. I think she thought of them as idiots savants or laboratory chimpanzees, who could by rote perform wondrous tasks. Amazing, but still chimpanzees. I was used to this attitude and paid little attention to it, since it did not deprive me of the pleasure of the Willises' company. Micah and Tina had delicate antennae for such things and simply did not appear when Mother Hannah stayed up with the family after dinner. I never did learn how they knew, but they did.

But it drove Peter wild. On the evening before he left to go back to Northpoint, he and his mother had had an argument about it. The Willises had been at Liberty the previous evening, and Mother Hannah had simmered and fretted all the following day and then jumped Peter at dinner.

"It's so ostentatious, Peter, such a showy and unattractive gesture. What on earth can you possibly find to talk about with our caretaker and our cook?"

I grinned and crossed my eyes behind Mother Hannah's back, because the showy and ostentatious gesture was so obviously mine. But I saw the familiar dull red come into Peter's cheeks.

"Well," he said, "last evening I believe we discussed Maslow and the nature of peak experiences. And then we moved on to Jung and his notion that the concept of time shuts out eternity. Because, as you know, Mother, eternity is by definition beyond time. Micah was interested in how the image of God becomes the final obstruction to the experience of

God, and I believe it was Christina who pointed out that Jung said that religion was the best defense against a religious experience. Finally, we all agreed that the images of Christ in our culture are very dangerous, because it's so hard to get past the image to the reality of him. You should come to Maude's next salon. You might be intrigued."

Mother Hannah sniffed. Two red spots flamed on her desiccated cheeks.

"That's monstrous," she said. "I thought the Willises were at least good churchgoers."

"Well, now, monsters," Peter went on thoughtfully. "We touched on that too. Micah said he'd read in his philosophy books about the notion that a monster can be a sublime being. That he can be someone who breaks all concepts of ethical behavior. Someone literally beyond ethical judgment, about whom all human concepts of morality are wiped out. The French call those beings *monstres sacrés,* sacred monsters. You may know some of them yourself. I think I do."

"You cannot sit there and tell me that you discussed . . . those things with people we pay to do menial work for us," she said coldly. "I find that impossible to believe."

"Well, we talked about other stuff too," Peter said, beginning to grin. "Micah said some of Caleb's sheep had bad cases of chapped teats, and the lambs' suckling wasn't making them any better. And I asked what Caleb was doing for them, and he said he was using Bag Balm. Cleared those teats right up, it did."

"If you are going to be vulgar, I am going to bed," Mother Hannah said, and when I had settled her in, I came back into the living room and collapsed into Peter's lap in helpless laughter. Finally, unwillingly, he began to laugh too.

"Sometimes I wonder how you've stood her all

these summers," he said. "You're the one who's been stuck with her."

"Now you wonder," I said. "Just when it's getting easier."

"Is it, my poor little Maude?" he said, smoothing the hair off my forehead. "I'm glad. I'd hate to think Retreat meant only drudgery for a sick old woman to you. Even if she is my mother, and I do love her of course, I see every day I'm here how difficult she is. It's funny; for the longest time I didn't see that. I guess I didn't want to. If I'd seen it, I'd have had to do something about it, and that would have meant giving up a few days out on the water or on the tennis court. You've never had it easy up here, have you?"

I felt tears flood my eyes and buried my face in his shoulder so he wouldn't see them.

"I've had other things up here," I said. "I've had Maine itself, the cape, the woods and the fogs and the ocean, the pointed firs . . . that's worth almost anything to me, Peter. And I've had friends. Amy has been a wonderful friend. The Willises, too. And Miss Lottie, and the Mary's Garden girls—God bless them, they finally taught me to play tennis. And the children having their summers here, discovering this magical place for the first time . . . it's more than balanced out.

"And," I added, taking a bite out of the side of his neck, "I've had the supreme good fortune of making love in a bathtub and in the bottom of a Brutal Beast, and just yesterday on a bed of moss that was not only infested with redbugs but an inch deep in osprey shit. Talk about your peak experiences!"

"Well, yes," he said, biting my neck in return. "I can see how those transcendent moments would be worth anything."

We had taken the dinghy out the afternoon before, because the day was as still and warm as August, and the bay was glassy and only heaving gently, like the breast of a sleeping woman, and rowed over to Osprey Head. We usually did this each year in late August, just before we left Retreat, to see how the young ospreys had fared during the summer and to picnic on the deep, silky, acid-green moss that covered much of the rocky little island. It was an immutable ritual with us; I do not think I could have left for Northpoint without my farewell engagement with the ospreys.

It had felt distinctly queer yesterday, though, almost eerily wrong, to make the pilgrimage in early summer. But as Peter said, the weather was too perfect to last; we could be sure of a nor'easter before the week was out. And it might be that he would be tied up at Northpoint at the end of the summer, and unable to come and drive us all back, and Petie would have to do it. So I packed a lunch and a blanket and we rowed the half mile from the yacht club harbor out to the round, green little island, first of the small archipelago that lay off the cove.

The osprey nest stood on the very crest of the island, on the ridge of naked pink rock that always reminded me of a dragon's spine. It was in a dead tree that had somehow withstood the winter gales that howled in from the open ocean out past Deer Isle for as many years as Peter could remember. Some nests, he said, were used for a century, being added to each year by the birds until they reached a diameter of five feet or more. This one looked to be about four feet: an old nest. We stood looking up at it in the warm, insect-buzzing silence, slightly sweated from the climb and the high sun. The young ospreys were there, four of them, almost as large now as their parents but still swiveling their fierce, helmeted predator's heads and shrieking for food. The adults were gone.

"Big babies," Peter said. "Plenty big enough to

fend for themselves, but still sitting there waiting for tired old Ma and Pa to haul lunch to them. Probably won't leave home till their folks kick them out. Not unlike a few youngsters I know."

I smiled and stared at the fledglings. I loved everything I knew about the ospreys of Osprey Head: their clean, lovely grace in flight; the fierceness of their attack on the fish they dove for, sometimes actually being drowned by their struggling prey because of their talons' extraordinary grip; their faithfulness to their homes and their young. Maine had almost lost most of its ospreys in the early years of the century, I knew, because their reluctance to leave their nests made them attractive prey for hunters. But now by mid-century they were back in good numbers, because the state finally moved to protect them and because there was an old and pervading superstition that to kill an osprey brought bad luck. Standing there in that old blue sea silence, looking at the beautiful young birds, I hoped the superstition was true. I felt a pure and shaking rage at the thought of anyone harming them.

"I think I like them better than any other Maine birds, even the eagles," I said to Peter. "They seem so . . . I don't know: willing to share themselves with people. Not that they're tame; they're the wildest things I know. But they don't run away from you. They'll make their homes among you, if you let them. It somehow seems like a kind of blessing to have them near."

"I know," he said, smiling at my fancy. "A good example to their human counterparts. Pity we can't always live up to them. Here's to you, *Pandion haliaetus carolinensis*. May your tribe increase."

We started back down through the dark stand of firs and moss to the little shingle beach where we had left the picnic basket.

"How did you know that? Their Latin name?" I said.

"Dad told me the first time he brought me over here," he said. "He made me memorize it. He said a thing as noble as the osprey deserved to be known by its proper name, and we ought to know it even if we didn't use it."

"Then I'll learn it too," I said, and felt a sudden savage spasm of grief for my father-in-law. My eyes flooded. "I miss your father so much," I said to Peter. "I don't ever stop thinking about him when I'm up here. I can't tell you what he came to mean to me."

Peter dropped down onto the blanket I had spread in the shelter of a huge boulder, a sentinel left on that wild beach from the march of the last great glacier. He was silent for a while, looking out across the still blue water toward the shoreline of Retreat.

"I think I know," he said.

I followed his gaze and saw that he was staring up at the distant chimney tops of the Aerie, just visible in the shimmer of noon light and the haze of heat. I had not been back there since the summer Big Peter died and Petie was born; Sarah and Douglas Fowler had sold it the following year to a family from New Haven, who only came in August, so we did not see much of them. I heard a few years later that Sarah had died, but no one seemed to know of what; it did not seem real to me. It still seemed she must be there, in her wonderful house high in the air and sun and wind; I still had the fancy that sometimes, when she was alone, Sarah Fowler flew triumphantly in the blue air around her home.

"So much has changed," I said softly. "It looks the same, it seems the same, but there are so many of them gone now, and you can feel the holes where they were. What long shadows they cast. . . ."

My eyes fell to the beach below the sheer cliff on

which the Aerie sat. The Little House, that enchanted place of refuge for small creatures ruled over by Miss Lottie Padgett, also stood empty now. Since her death in the first of the war the feckless Frankie, mired in his urban sanctimony, had never set foot in it and, so far as we knew, wished neither to sell nor rent it. It was as if his mother and her sanctuary for the colony's lost had never existed. Several of us had written Frankie with offers, mainly because it was so painful to see the cottage closed and dark and falling further into disrepair, but none of our letters were answered. Of all of old Retreat, except Peter's father, I think I missed Miss Lottie most. I often wonder what might have become of my poor Happy if Miss Lottie could have taken her under her wing. When I think, as I often do, that Retreat and Cape Rosier have the power to heal, it is chiefly of Miss Lottie Padgett that I think.

Many others who were so indelible in my early years in the colony were gone too. Mamadear long ago, of course, and Helen Potter just the winter before, so that Amy was at long last the sole mistress of Braebonnie. Dr. and Mrs. Lincoln had both died, and Land's End was now the property of the still-interchangeable "boys," who alternated summers with their interchangeable wives and children. Miss Isabelle and Miss Charlotte Valentine had left Petit Trianon to a disinterested niece from Mobile, who summered at Point Clear and sold the cottage to the Winslows; Gretchen promptly made a guest house of it, flossing it up with no end of expensively shabby, brand-new wicker and chintz. Only Augusta Stallings, older than Mother Hannah, was, incredibly, still alive and contentious, if bedbound, in Utopia while her aging sons and desperate daughters-in-law and burgeoning tribe of grand- and great-grandchildren burst the seams of the Compound. My mother-in-law was, for all intents and purposes, the matriarch of Retreat. I sometimes thought that fact was keeping her alive.

Peter poured wine and we drank it, and ate our sandwiches, and then lay back and let the sun pour over us like wild honey. Then came that sound I listen for each summer, and hear only once or twice, and only in moments of perfect suspension and stillness: the high, eerie hum I always fancy is the music of the earth itself, or the real old secret of the sea. I wondered if Peter heard it; I was about to break the spell of it and ask when he said, "Dad took you up to see Sarah Fowler at the Aerie, didn't he? The summer he died?"

I lay there for a moment, the weight of the sun red and heavy on my eyelids, and said, "Yes." And when he did not speak again, I said, "I didn't know you knew that he . . . went there sometimes."

"Yes. I knew. I knew that he did, and that he'd gone there for many summers, and why. I knew he was in love with her. I followed him there once, when I was about eighteen, I guess, and watched them through the windows. He never touched her, but you could tell by his face, and hers. I'm glad he shared her with you. She was a special person, and it's a special place. I wish he'd felt he could have shared it with me."

"Peter, you can see why he couldn't . . . I mean, your mother . . . he always loved your mother. This other thing didn't take anything away from that."

"I know," he said, and he rolled over and sat up and looked once more at the chimneys and roofline of the Aerie.

"How did you feel about it?" I said.

"Shocked at first, and angry, and somehow embarrassed, as if there'd been some kind of public disgrace. You know how conventional the young are. But then I came to think—I don't know—that it was sort of his right. That Retreat was always more Mother's than his; that he had a right to something of his own here. I always knew it didn't touch Mother, or how he felt about her, and it didn't threaten me and Hermie. It was just . . . a part of him we couldn't share, or know about, and maybe that was all right; maybe everyone has a right to that. You can love two people and be faithful to both of them, you know. In the end, I came to be glad for him. I think it was a real tribute to you that you're the one of us he chose to share it with."

I sat silent in the sun. I thought of Micah Willis, and my face went hot. Yes, it was true about two people. . . . And then I felt cold. Could it be, was it possible, that he spoke of himself as well as his father? There had been several years now when Peter had not come to Retreat in the summers but had stayed behind at Northpoint; he was headmaster now, and I knew he had very real prospects of going on to a place like St. Paul's or Deerfield or Choate, if he chose to do so. And I knew full well the price he would pay for that in killing hours and sacrifice. I had minded only because he had always loved the summers in Retreat so and would not have them again for many years if he kept to this trajectory; I was proud of him, and willing to have him gone from me as often and long as necessary, if it brought him to a place in his work that he truly aspired to. I had never once thought there might be, somewhere in his summers, someone to whom he went as simply and directly as his father went to Sarah Fowler at the Aerie.

I looked at him, there in the sunlight, and thought, It is not possible, and then thought, But if it was . . . if it was . . . would it be all right? Could I understand with Peter as I did with his father?

And knew that I could not, never could.

But you have feelings for Micah, and they do not even begin to touch the thing you have with Peter, I told myself.

That's entirely different, I thought. And knew that it was, even though I could never explain why, to myself or anyone else. If my husband ever had another woman and I knew about it, it would somehow be the end of me. Something vital that animated and warmed me and enabled me to live in the world would die.

I made a small, stricken sound in my throat, and he gathered me against him, and presently we made love, there in the sun and silence of the beach on Osprey's Head. It was the first time in our life together that I did not feel utterly whole afterward.

After that day, after Peter had gone back to North-point, I could not settle in to the summer. It was not the constant, small tension that accompanied any life in a house with Happy; I was used to that. It was not that I was lonely, now Petie and Sarah had left; I was never lonely in Retreat. It was not even the fact of Mother Hannah's pervasive malaise. She had been disabled for several summers now, and we had managed. It was just that somehow nothing could occupy me totally, fill me. There was an ache, a hollowness deep in the middle of me as if I were literally starving.

Somehow, Mother Hannah knew it. She had never, in all the years I had known her, seemed intuitive, but that summer she sensed the emptiness in me, felt my loneliness herself. And even though she grew perceptibly weaker, and had more nights of pain and sleeplessness, she made a real effort to be kind to me. I have never been sure if she knew the hunger had to do with Peter; we never spoke of him in that respect. But I think now that perhaps she suspected it did, for she spent many hours, over luncheon and drinks or at dinner, and even before the fire on the evenings that she could stay up, talking lightly and fondly of his boyhood. Her voice was softer on these occasions than I had ever heard it, and the Peter she evoked for me was a different child than the one I thought she had carried in her memory; he was funny and sweet and quicksilver, reckless and even foolhardy. I was surprised that sometimes she even laughed at the exploits she told me of. The Peter I had imagined to live in her mind was a far tamer and seemlier one than this remembered Peter Pan. We laughed together at this child, and I was grateful to her as I had never been before.

She talked of her own younger days in the colony too, and that slow, mannered world at the turn of the century came alive for me as it might never have; it gave me a deep and poignant sense of the continuity of life in Retreat that I have never lost, a gift beyond price in a world beginning to flame with change. I think it is among the most valuable of all the things she left me. She never spoke of her own feelings about Retreat, only of its customs and mores and taboos, and anecdotes that made me smile or, far less often, feel tears gather behind my lids. But somehow, in the measured words, in the stilted and homely little stories of her summers by this sea, the ghost of another lost and ill-fitting girl formed in the quiet air between us, a girl who, like me, might have wept in the nights and walked in fear and resentment of a stern and unforgiving older woman. I knew I would never ask her about that girl, but I found I could quite literally love her and, in so doing, come close to loving the old woman who had carried her locked in her breast all these years. After all, she knew. And she had prevailed.

In early July she had a kind of respite from the pain

and weakness and refused the pills her doctor had sent, which I cajoled her into taking four times each day. Nor would she take the sleeping tablets he prescribed.

"I'm really feeling quite well, Maude," she said. "I think I would like to go to the Fourth of July regatta, at least to have a cocktail and a bowl of chowder and see the fireworks. It's been years since I've gone. I do believe the last one was when Erica came and brought her entire dreadful bridge club."

"Mother Hannah, do you really think it's wise?" I said. "You know how the crowd is, with all the Blue Hill and Northeast Harbor people milling around, and all that drinking and yelling. It makes me tired; I hadn't thought I'd go this year."

"I've really an urge to see everybody," she said. "It's been a long time since I've felt like it."

"Then let me ask a few people in, have a little cocktail party. Whoever you like. Guild and Dierdre Kennedy, and Erica, and the Stallingses, and the Mary's Garden girls—"

"No. Please, just for a little while," she said, and smiled. "I think I'd like to see the children, and the dogs, and all of it."

She had not smiled much that summer. My heart twisted. Such an impulse toward life could not be denied.

"Then we'll do it," I said. "It will be fun."

The Fourth of July dawned sullen and misted. I could hear the starting guns for the first race, flat little pops, and knew the air was heavy and we were likely to have fog with the setting of the sun. The humidity made my movements slow and my head ache slightly; outside, the world looked flat and bleached. I thought again how strong the alchemy of the sun was here; with it, the landscape was sharp and dimensional and magical; without it, everything looked, simply, banal.

Happy was snappish and heavy-eyed and announced that she wasn't going to the stupid race. She and Carlton Anderson were going to paint his dinghy and then go up to the general store and play skittles. I did not especially like Carlton Anderson; he was truculent and would not meet the eyes of colony adults when he came to collect his pay for the mowing and painting and trash hauling he did, but he was Micah's cousin's son, and we had known him a long time, and I would have enough on my hands getting Mother Hannah to the regatta without dragging a mulish Happy along with us.

"Fine," I said, and went to wake Mother Hannah. Happy slammed the screen door on her way out. I sighed. I had hoped she would find in her Retreat summers what her father had found in his: days of childhood almost magical in their perfection. Memories to warm the nights of adulthood. But Happy did not want her father's childhood. This summer, as always, Happy wanted only her father.

Mother Hannah was pale and moved slowly, and I knew she had had another sleepless night, though she said she had not and was looking forward to the day. I managed, finally, to get her to agree to cocktails and lunch instead of a long afternoon and evening at the club, but when I went to help her dress I found her breathless and weak-voiced and knew I would never get her down the lane along with her cane and shawl and the hamper of drinks and hors d'oeuvres I'd made the night before. Midge and Buck Fletcher at the general store catered the chowder and slaw and rolls for the race crowd, but lunch-goers historically brought their own cocktails and nibbles, and Mother Hannah had asked for Bloody Marys and crab sandwiches. I knew I would never get the car down the traffic-choked lane. I thought a moment and then went to the telephone

and called Christina Willis. She and Micah were
there in fifteen minutes, talking easily to Mother Hannah as if they dropped in before lunch every day,
dressed like the rest of the colony in open-collared
shirts and boat shoes.

"Micah and Tina are going to walk us down,
Mother Hannah," I said casually, hoping she wasn't
going to be high-handed on this of all mornings.
She arched one of her dark brows but said only,
"That's kind of you, Tina. Micah. I don't get about
as well as I once did. A couple of strong arms will
be welcome."

I breathed a sigh of gratitude to all of them. She's
come a long way, to accept help from the hired man,
I thought. And he's come a long way to offer it, after
that thing with Parker Potter.

We set off down the sandy lane to the yacht club,
Micah and Tina supporting Mother Hannah on either
side, me bringing up the rear with the hamper and
her accoutrements. It took a long while, and we had
to stop frequently to let her catch her breath. Her
face had the sheen of a lit wax candle in the overcast
morning, and I did not at all like the sound of her
breath in her chest. But all along the way colony people
called to her, and came up and embraced her, and
kissed her cheek, and when we came in sight of the
clubhouse, a swell of voices rose to meet us, and several
people broke from the crowd assembled on the
porch and steps to come to her. It was, after all, what
she needed and had missed; I could tell by the light
in her eyes and the strength of her voice. An old
queen had come among her people, and they met
her smiling and calling their allegiance. Over her
head Tina smiled at me, and Micah winked solemnly.

On the porch I saw George motion to us to bring
her up. I waved my thanks. All the other rockers were
occupied by the oldest ladies in the colony, as they

had always been; Erica Conant and her group had many of them, and Dierdre Kennedy was in one, next to Jane Thorne's elderly mother visiting from Providence. The last three, the ones that had the best view of the harbor and the islands beyond it, were occupied by Gretchen Winslow and Burdie and his autocratic old mother, Aurora. Beside them stood their children, the bored and attenuated Freddie and Julia, and a couple of equally equine teenagers I did not recognize, obviously visitors. I was glad Happy had not come with us; Freddie and Julia could not seem to resist baiting her, and Happy could not seem to resist reacting precisely as they planned. No good would have come of it.

Gretchen Winslow looked up and saw us then, and I knew no good was going to come of it anyway. She looked wonderful that morning, seeming to give off light like a pearl in the dull, queer light, dressed in khaki pants and a pale bronze sweater so that she seemed all over a veldt creature, a lioness among cattle. Damn her, would she never age? I thought in irritation. And if she did, would she never mellow? Her light green eyes, as they took in Mother Hannah between the Willises and me bringing up the rear like a native bearer, glinted with malice, and she smiled her slow, pure smile. A lioness among cattle indeed. That blood would run and it would be my own equine red, I had no doubt. I just did not know the occasion of it.

She came to meet Mother Hannah, and kissed her on the cheek, and led her to the vacant chair and settled her in, and took the shawl from me and tucked it around her legs.

"It's good to see you again, Mother Hannah," she said silkily, and my face warmed as she must have known it would, for the smile widened. Gretchen was the only person in Retreat besides me who called my mother-in-law that, and no one, in my mind, had less right to do so. I saw Dierdre Kennedy's head turn toward us, and some of the faces in Erica's group, and knew that I was not the only one who had noticed. Mother Hannah smiled up at Gretchen and took her hand.

"It's nice to see you looking so well, my dear," she said. Her voice was quite strong now. "I've missed your visits this summer."

"We've had our hands full with the children's visitors," Gretchen said sweetly. "Such mobs you never saw."

And of course Peter hasn't been around, I thought, which lessens the incentive to visit cranky old ladies considerably.

Micah turned his head and looked at me, and I saw the amusement dancing in his eyes, even though he kept his face straight, and knew that he knew precisely what Gretchen meant and what I did not say. I rolled my eyes slightly, and he did grin then, faintly.

Still holding Mother Hannah's hand, Gretchen straightened up and turned to me. The lazy green gaze took in Micah and Tina, dressed almost identically to every other man and woman at the yacht club, and then made a slow tour of the assemblage on the porch, to be sure she had their attention. She did; both the presence of the Willises in this veritable Holy of Holies and her carelessly tossed "Mother Hannah" had assured it.

"Well, Maude, I wish you'd let the committee know that you were bringing guests," she said creamily. "We could have held some porch chairs for all of you. As it is, I'm afraid the only seats left are out back. But we're glad you brought your friends. We've all worried that you're lonely these summers when Peter's not here. It's nice to have someone to . . . take up the slack."

There was silence. There could not have been any words. There was simply no mistaking what she meant; she did not even have to let her eyes linger on Micah Willis. I felt fire rush from my neck into my face. The furious heat literally choked me for a moment. All the summers of alienation and loneliness here, of the painfully gradual, hard-won acclimation I had clawed out, of Micah Willis's unfailing courtesy and decency in the face of my mother-in-law's coldness, of Gretchen's gratuitous malice, boiled up in me like a storm tide into a blow hole. I struggled for breath enough to lash back at her; saw Micah's sunburnt face whiten and then go blank and still, and Tina's small, soundless gasp of hurt; saw, too, my mother-in-law's eyes widen and then narrow and her hand disengage itself from Gretchen's.

Before I could speak, Mother Hannah did. It was her old voice, the first one I had ever heard, sweet and precise and stinging.

"As a matter of fact, Gretchen," she said clearly, "Mr. and Mrs. Willis are my luncheon guests. Today is our regular date, and I thought, since it fell on regatta day, it would be a change for them from my dark little dining room. You're sweet to think of it, and we'll accept those chairs with the greatest of thanks. It's getting hot already, don't you think?"

Blue eyes held green for a long moment, during which I fancied that no breath was drawn on all that porch and lawn, and then Gretchen dropped her eyes and murmured, "You're very welcome to the chairs," and turned and went back up onto the porch and gathered up her cocktail things and herded her muttering children before her down the steps. My breath came rushing back. I will love you for the rest of my life, no matter what you do or say to me, I told Mother Hannah silently with my eyes, and thought that her flinty blue ones crinkled just a bit. She turned to Micah and Christina Willis then.

"Micah? Tina? Shall we?"

I looked at the Willises; their faces were as smooth and closed as marble. Oh, please, I pleaded silently. Please. I know it was awful. I know you'd like to spit in all our faces. But please. Just give her this. You don't know what it must have cost her. Give *me* this.

"Nice spot to watch a race," Micah said solemnly, and took her arm and bore her up the steps to the cluster of rockers. I felt as if I would faint with relief and joy. I closed my eyes and then opened them. He was looking back at me patiently, as if waiting for a lagging child, and beside him, Tina was smiling her serene smile. Lightly as a girl, I ran up the stairs and took my seat in the remaining rocking chair, and the day broke and flowed on, as it had, on this old cape, for a hundred years.

And so it was that Micah and Tina Willis had Bloody Marys and lunch on the porch of the Cove Harbor Yacht Club as if they had done it every summer of their lives, and though they never did so again, I know they could have if they had chosen to. For a powerful taboo was shattered that day, and shattered by the only one who could have done it: my mother-in-law, Hannah Stuart Chambliss, doyenne of Retreat Colony on Cape Rosier, Maine, in full possession of all her senses and all that her title entailed. It was, I think, because of her and that one stabbing, diamond-edged moment on the steps of the yacht club that morning that the next year Caleb Willis joined the club as a matter of course and with unanimous approval, and years later his son Micah was commodore.

We did not speak of it, we four. At least not directly. After lunch, Mother Hannah announced that she was tired and wished to lie down for a bit, and we made our stately progression back to Liberty in a wash of affectionate and, I thought, admiring chatter.

I did, when I settled her down for her nap, say to her, after a couple of false starts, "Thank you."

She waved an impatient hand. She was white and pearled with sweat, but her face quite simply shone. I thought, on the main, that the day was as nearly perfect a one as she might have wished for. Not only was she received as a queen; she was allowed the opportunity to pronounce a queen's edict. The triumph shimmered on her like wildfire.

"Well, it was a wonderful thing to do—"

She held her finger up to her lips, and I stopped. She looked at me for a long time and sighed.

"You've not had an easy time up here, Maude," she said. "I know that. And I know how it feels. But you've stayed with it; you've made a life for yourself up here. You could have simply stayed away; I know that too. Peter would have done that for you. Don't think I'm going to change much in my dotage; I'm still going to give you a piece of my mind when I think it's called for, and Happy and Petie as well. And I'm always going to think that Peter . . . your Peter"— and she smiled faintly—"could have married someone more suited to the way he was raised to live. But Gretchen exceeded herself by far today. I will not permit that sort of thing. Not to my daughter-in-law, and not to Micah and Tina Willis. They are good and abiding people, and I have treated them badly over the years, Micah especially. I don't for a moment think one lunch on the yacht club porch makes up for that, but it's the best I can do at this stage."

She lay back against the pillows and was so still I thought she had fallen asleep, and I had begun to tiptoe out of the room when she said, "You could do worse than have Micah for a friend, Maude. Lean on him when you must; you can trust him. Peter is . . . Peter is like his father. Both of them sometimes simply sail away from you, and often they stay away quite a long time. Oh, they always come back, but there are times when you will need an arm, and his won't be there. Take Micah's. A woman alone becomes hard and afraid. I know."

Did she know, then, about her husband and Sarah Fowler? Did she not? What a lot of secrets swirled in this old house.

I started back toward her, thinking to hug her, but she shook her head on the pillow and closed her eyes again.

"Tired now," she said.

And so I did go out of the room this time, saying softly as I shut the door, "Thank you, anyway."

"You're very welcome, my dear," floated after me as I turned away into the kitchen.

Micah was there, piling wood into the kitchen woodbox, but Tina was nowhere to be seen. We looked at each other, and then both of us grinned broadly and began to laugh.

"Micah," I began, "I just want to say—"

"Nothing to say," he broke in. "Had lunch on a danged shingle porch with three middlin' nice ladies, and drank a fancy drink and watched a race or two. I've seen better and worse, and that goes for all three. Haven't seen much better than the way your mother-in-law routed Gretchen Winslow, though. Couldn't have happened to a more deserving lady."

"I know," I said ruefully. "I hope you didn't take it too personally. It's me she was after. She's been at my throat since the first day I met her."

"Ayuh," he said. "She wants what you have and knows she'll never have it."

"You mean . . . Peter?" I said, blushing and hating it.

"No. Well, maybe, but that's not what I meant."

"What then? I can't imagine what on earth I could possibly have that she wants, besides that."

"Maude, you bring a kind of spring to the air around you," he said, looking down into the woodbox. "Gretchen brings winter. She can't change that, but she must be powerful cold all the time. Makes her mean. Makes her hate the spring carriers. . . . You got enough wood to last for the week; I'll bring some more when I come to trim the hedges next Monday. Thanks for the grub and the company. Tell Mrs. Chambliss for us."

And he was gone out of the kitchen, leaving the screen door banging softly on the spring that never quite worked.

Mother Hannah did not want any dinner, so I left a sandwich and a glass of milk beside her bed, and Happy and I ate an early dinner ourselves, and I was in bed rereading *Wuthering Heights* when the telephone rang. I sat down on the top step of the stairs in the dark and in my nightgown and answered it.

"Ma?"

"Petie?"

"Yeah. Me. Listen. I have something to tell you. I . . . we . . . listen, Sarah and I thought we'd get married this fall. Maybe around Thanksgiving, in the chapel at school, if you think you could manage that. Just a little wedding, families, you know. . . . Ma?"

My ears rang. Here it was, what I had come to hope would happen, the call I had listened for half in dread and half in joy . . . and I could not speak. *No,* my heart was shouting in rage. *No.* You're too young, this is foolish, I can't let you go. . . .

Yes, my head said. Good for you. You will be safe with her. *I* will be safe with her. And what in the name of God did I mean by that?

"Ma? Are you there?"

"Yes, darling, I'm here. Well, my old Petie. Married. Oh, my. Let me get my breath."

"You do like Sarah, Mama?" It was a question, tremulous.

"Oh, darling, yes, of course I do. Of course. I'm delighted, really. And of course, the chapel at Thanksgiving, anything you all want. Oh, wait until I tell Gramma and Happy. . . . Have you told Daddy yet? Oh, Petie, what made you decide?"

He laughed, I thought in relief.

"A: wait awhile on Gramma and Happy, until we tell Sarah's folks. B: no, I haven't told Dad yet. We just decided tonight, and he's making a speech in Brookline. And C: Sarah told me that if I wouldn't marry her so she could have you for a mother-in-law and spend all her summers in Retreat she would never speak to me again. What choice did I have?"

I was silent. Of course, Sarah Forbes would not only be Petie's wife, she would be my daughter-in-law. Of course, they would spend their summers here at Liberty, where Petie always had; what had I thought they would do? I saw, suddenly, all the years ahead in this old shingled cottage: two women, mother-in-law and daughter-in-law, only now it would be I who was the former, and this small, brown, determined girl I did not know who would be the latter. Waiting, waiting, for her turn. . . .

I wanted it for myself for a little while, I thought desolately. I wanted it just for Peter and me. Just for a few summers. I do not want this strong young woman coming here to watch me, and serve me, and wait. . . .

"Let me put Sarah on," he said. "She wants to talk to you—"

"Darling, Gramma's calling, and she's really not well," I said hastily. "I'm going to have to run check on her. Kiss Sarah for me and tell her how wonderful I think everything is, and I'll talk to you again after you've told Daddy. Call me tomorrow night and we'll all talk."

"Well, we both love you," he said.

"Me too, darling. 'Bye, now." I replaced the telephone, and for a long time I sat on the top step in the dark, staring at nothing, hearing in the silence downstairs voices that had not yet spoken.

Mother Hannah had not called, of course, but I went to her door anyway and opened it softly and peered in. She lay on her side, mantled with the old Hudson Bay blanket that had always lain at the foot of her bed. The window was open and the faraway sound of the surf was close and clear, like breathing. A little wind, smelling of pine and salt, stirred her hair. Her stationery box lay on the floor beside the bed, and I saw that she had eaten the sandwich and drunk the milk. I shut the door again. Let her sleep. Time enough tomorrow to tell her about Petie and Sarah. I did not know, now, if she would be pleased or not. She would not have, before, but the old woman asleep in that quiet room was not the same one I had known in summers past. She was not even the same one who had come to Retreat this summer. Nor, I thought, trudging back upstairs, the old painted floor sticky and chilly under my bare feet, was I.

When I found her the next morning, going in rather late with her breakfast tray, I was not surprised. Shocked, yes; shaking uncontrollably with shock, and racked with a grief I had never thought to feel, but not surprised. The woman I had known all my married life had left me earlier. The old woman who lay still and lifeless in her bed was in almost all ways a stranger to me. I knelt down beside her and took her hand in both of mine. Cold. It was very cold, and her still face was cold, and so was the loose, silky skin of her throat.

"I wish you hadn't gone," I whispered. "There was so much I had to tell you."

And I got up and walked to the downstairs telephone and called Amy Potter in Braebonnie. And the slow, formal old pageant of death in Retreat began once more, this time for Mother Hannah and so for me.

It wasn't until that evening, with Peter and Petie on the way and Happy farmed out to Priss and Tobias Thorne and their mild-tempered girls, that I found the letter she had left me. It lay inside her stationery box; I had picked it up, finally, from the floor and the top had fallen off, and I saw the sealed envelope with my name on it. Whenever she had stopped breathing, and for whatever reason, she had had time first to write this. I did not think she was in pain when she did it, or felt any reason to hurry; the letter was fairly long, and the handwriting was round and precise and pretty, the confident copperplate hand of her youth.

Maude. I need to tell you this and do not think I can do it in person. I am ashamed of that, but the worm can turn only so much, and we have never taken each other into our confidences, you and I. That is not necessarily a bad thing, but it makes it simply too hard to speak of this to you. So I shall write it, and when it is necessary you will read it.

I have left Liberty and everything in it to you. My will, in Boston, will bear me out. I do not know how Peter will feel about this, but I hope you will not find it necessary to tell him my reasons. They do not flatter him. You are the strong one, Maude; I have always known that, and have not always liked you for it. I wanted Peter to be that. But it is you, and so you must have Liberty, and you must keep it what it is, and see that Petie's wife after you does the same. Take care of all of it: this house, this place, this world. It is all we have, we women.

You will see great change in your life; I sincerely thank God I will not. But I know that you love Retreat and the cape and this house in your own way, and it is only you who will have the strength and so the ruthlessness to keep it as it is, for a while at least. Maybe no one can do that for very long. You are strong, Maude. I could not break you, just as I could not be broken. I salute you for that. I am sorry for much that I put you through, but I had to know that you would endure.

Take care of Peter. Keep this place safe for him, as well as for you. He needs it like air and water but will not always have the strength to stay and guard it. His father did not, either. But neither can Peter leave it, just as, in the end, his father could not.

I think the cottage must go from you to Sarah Forbes. I see in her what I did in you when you were very young, though I can't say I like her very much. Petie can't keep it, and I doubt very much poor Happy can, either. So it must be Sarah, or a woman like her. You will, won't you, see to it that Petie gets around to asking her? You can do that. He will do anything you say.

Thank you for this afternoon and for many things, Maude. Never forget that Gretchen Winslow is not your friend, and I think it would not be a bad idea to kick her in the behind every now and then, just on principle.

The letter was signed formally, *Hannah Stuart Chambliss,* and dated. I read the last sentence over again and began to laugh, and then I put my face into my hands and wept for my beloved enemy.

* * *

Very late that night, after Peter and Petie had come in, and the ambulance from the hospital in Castine had come for Mother Hannah, Amy and I walked down to the yacht club and sat on the porch. Peter had ridden with his mother, and Petie was on the telephone to Sarah.

We rocked silently in the moonlight for a while. Out on the silver-stippled bay the dark bulks of Spectacle and Osprey Head seemed limned in light, and, farther out, Western and Hog islands and Fiddlehead seemed to float on air instead of water. Stars blazed and swarmed. There was no wind, and no sound except the steady creaking of the old willow rockers. Presently Amy reached over and took my hand.

"It's us now, you know," she said.

"Us what?" I said. I was tired to mindlessness, tired beyond surprise and curiosity. The warmth of her hand felt good, though.

"Us on the porch. Us with the right to the rocking chairs. We don't get up for old women any more. We're the ones with porch privileges."

"Oh, Amy," I said, tears starting again as they had first that morning, when I had held another hand, a dead one, in mine. "Oh, Amy. I never wanted to get there."

Chapter Nine

This afternoon, from the porch of Liberty, I heard for the first time in many years the sharp, querulous whistle of an osprey. I heard it quite distinctly, despite the fact that my hearing has for some years been a source of annoyance to me and no doubt those around me. But this piercing cry was clear and close, though as I have said, sound is strange here by the water, and the fog that shrouds the colony this evening had begun to creep in by then, so I could not really tell where the cry came from. Not, I know, from Osprey Head. It has been a long, long time since the ospreys nested there. The eagles who came to take their place are wonderful birds, heart-stopping in their magnificence, and the colony at large is far more protective of them than they ever were of the ubiquitous ospreys, but I have always missed those first fierce and faithful settlers. They endured so much for the sake of their nests and nestlings; they never gave up and never left until it was simply no longer possible to stay. I have come to admire that fierce familial loyalty above everything else. One could live a life for it, as the ospreys do.

The sound made me suddenly and savagely happy, the same dizzying rush of pure joy that I remember from my childhood. I can recall so clearly the last time I felt it: I was standing in a clearing beside Wappoo Creek on an afternoon in October, alone in the peculiar silence autumn brings to the Low Country, bathed in the thick honey gold of the sun through encircling trees only just beginning to turn the muted metal colors of fall. I don't remember what I had been doing, only that I stood very still and closed my eyes. And suddenly such a smashing rush of joy and exaltation shook me that I could only hug myself and hold my breath against the onslaught of that pummeling happiness. Pinwheels of gold arced behind my closed lids, and then tears formed there, and slipped from beneath my lashes, and ran down my face. I don't know what that moment meant, but I was somehow altered by it; after that I had a knowledge of perfect joy against which to measure experience. Nothing else has ever quite met it. Some moments have come close, but none had that quality of annihilation, of obliteration. I have always thought one's knowledge of God should be like that moment, but unless that was mine and I misunderstood it, I have missed that transcendence. I never thought to feel it again, but I did, or something close to it this afternoon, when I heard the osprey call. It was gone in a breath, but I was left both shaken and soothed by it. A great, great gift for an old woman toward the end of her life.

The very old can tell you about peace. They have fought through the black, sinking, visceral knowledge of death—their own death—that heralds middle age and come to the place where childhood meets them once more, and with it that ineffable treasure that only the very young and old know: the tranquillity of the moment. The contentment of living each day as it comes to them, wholly and with all senses. The young do it because they know nothing, yet, of pain and fear and the transience of their lives; the old because they know everything of those things and can bear them only by staying in the moment. *Carpe diem* may be the sum of all the world's wisdom. I have always thought Horace must have been old when he wrote it.

So, yes, the old can tell you about peace, but rarely about pure joy, and it came to me like a benediction this afternoon on the wings of an osprey somewhere in the air above me. I think the sheer, shattering force of it owed all to the fact that it was my child who drove the ospreys from Retreat, all those summers ago.

After Mother Hannah died, the change I had felt in the air around Miss Charity Snow's death was finally upon us. It's funny that I never connected my heavy prescience, early that summer, to the death of someone in my family, but I didn't. Peter still seemed to me, after all the years of our marriage, the most alive human being I had ever known, and one does not think of one's children in terms of hovering death. At least, I didn't. And Mother Hannah had always seemed to me simply eternal, even in her illness and fragility. So it was only later that I could look back and see that the darkness that fell down over us that summer dated from the night of her death. In the midst of it, I could only flail at it in pain and impotence, wondering despairingly what had happened to us and why.

Peter moved through the hours after his mother's death like an automaton, ashen and still-faced and closed. This time it was I who saw to the food and drink for those who came to pay their respects; the entire colony did, of course. I answered the door and the telephone, received the armfuls of cut flowers and the notes and telegrams, patted the frail, spotted hands of the old ladies who had been Mother Hannah's contemporaries, smiled and thanked the younger women and men who had known her all their lives as the fixed star she had been in that small firmament. Christina Willis kept food coming, and Micah brought firewood and mowed and did marketing for me, and even Happy, sullen and clumping in her hated skirts and slippers, did front-door duty for an afternoon or two. Petie came from Boston and saw to the minutiae of death that can be so wearying and endless in a small, faraway place: the death certificate, the notices to the New England newspapers, the calls back and forth from the funeral home in Castine to Fitzgerald's, the old firm in Boston that had handled Chambliss funerals since time out of mind, the services there, the interment.

Peter went sailing with Parker Potter.

When he came home, after almost two days, we fought about it.

"How could you?" I said, near tears from fatigue and my unexpected grief and a real and living anger at him. He was freshly tanned from the time on the water, and the golden stubble on his face and shadowed eyes seemed to me then merely the ensign of carelessness and indolence.

"It was easy," he said tightly. "You just cast off, raise your mainsail, and away you go."

"You know what I mean. When your father died you went sailing. When Petie was born you went sailing. When your mother died you went sailing. If you don't care about us having to do everything for you, you might at least give some thought to your mother's old friends. They loved her too, you know."

"Too?" he said, his eyes suddenly fierce and stormy, like winter water. "What's this too business, Maude? You know you never liked her."

I gasped as if he had slapped me. It was worse than if he had. Tears sprang to my eyes, and I felt my mouth tremble with the hurt and its unfairness.

"I did better than that," I said, trying to keep my voice even. "I loved her, in ways I don't think you ever knew about because you weren't around. And I stayed with her. I took care of her. Maybe we weren't best friends, she and I; maybe I wasn't ever the daughter-in-law she wanted for you, but I was here. It was because of me that you got to go sailing whenever you felt like it."

"Well, thank you, Saint Maude. It didn't help much, did it? She still died," he said, and this time there was no mistaking the pain in his face and voice. It was an older, deeper pain than I had seen there when his father died; that had been pure anguish, leaping like fire. This was dark, dull, endless. Peter would be changed by this. That twisted tie to his mother, which he eluded so long and so determinedly, had held after all; he had fled her all the summers of her life, but in the end she held him fast. My anger drained away. Pain for his pain replaced it; that and a swift cold fear. What would we be now, Peter and I? Who would we be, without her in the world to define us?

"I'm sorry," I said. "It doesn't matter. You're here. I thought we might have a very small service in the morning at the chapel before we go back to Boston. I called the new preacher and he said he'd be glad to do a little memorial, and Petie will call around and tell people—"

"Whatever you like," he said. "I'm going back tonight, though. I want to go home with her. I'll stay at the University Club."

"But . . . I thought we'd all go together tomorrow afternoon on the train. Fitzgerald's will meet her and take care of her. I've asked Mrs. Harris to open the house and get things ready for a little reception after the service, and Petie's gotten tickets for us—"

"I'd rather do this by myself, Maude," he said, not looking at me. "Just a graveside service. I'll call Dr. Constable tonight about that. Everybody will understand about not having people by after the service; I haven't lived in Boston since I left college, and you never have, and most of her friends are dead. Hermie can do something later. It just seems better like this."

I stared at him.

"Peter, she's my mother-in-law. She's Happy and Petie's grandmother—"

"Petie can come with me," he said dully. "He'll have to get back to the bank anyway. It would be better if Happy stayed here with you. I don't know if I'm up to Happy right now, and anyway I've got to get back to school. I'm going straight there from the service."

"But everyone would understand if you took the rest of the summer," I said, my heart pounding with dread, my mouth dry. "You know Charles can handle things just for a month or so. Peter, darling, take some time; you can't pretend this never happened. At least give yourself time to heal a little. You can sail, we can picnic, we can travel around some."

"Now that she's gone and you're free?" he said, and smiled at me, a terrible smile. "I don't think so, Maude. Thanks just the same."

"Why are you doing this to me?" I whispered.

"I don't know what you're talking about," Peter said, and went out of the room and upstairs. When he came down, two hours later, he was shaved and dressed for the city, and he and Petie left shortly after that with Micah Willis, who was to drive them to the train station in Ellsworth, where the body of Mother Hannah had been put aboard a freight car. He put his arm around me when he left, and gave my shoulders a gentle squeeze, but he did not kiss me. It was the first time in our life together that he had left me without doing so. I fought the pain and tears as hard as I could, so that neither he nor Petie nor Micah Willis would see them, and only when the car had jolted out of sight down the lane did I let the tears come. But it did not matter, because Happy saw them and came swooping in from the sun porch where she had been eavesdropping, dressed defiantly in her oldest tennis shoes and dirtiest jeans, face mottled with rage and what I realized only later was pain, primed for attack.

"You ran him off!" she howled. "You ran Daddy off and he said he was going to stay; he promised me he'd stay and we'd do things! We were going to go sailing and clamming, and he was maybe going to get us a boat, just for him and me because everybody knows you can't sail. . . . Oh, I hate you and I hate that stupid old woman!"

I saw that she was quite literally blind with tears, choking on them, and reached for her, frightened and shocked. We were all used to Happy's outbursts, but this was the fury and grief of a much younger child, the words of a preschooler. I had been annoyed with her much of the summer, but I had hurt for her pain and outrage, too, and felt keenly my own inability to soothe and feed her needs. Petie, too, had been a ravenous child, flailing at his own emptiness, but I had always been able to quiet and fill him. From almost the beginning, it was Peter's arms and heart and only his that Happy wanted. And as with Petie, he had simply been unable to give them. I never understood why this man whose love, whose whole being, so filled and completed me could not seem to connect with his children. Perhaps, I thought now, seeking to pull my anguished child into my arms, that was why. The thought flooded me with fresh pain and guilt.

Happy flinched away from me and continued to shriek. She literally danced up and down in front of me in her pain and fury, but she would not let me touch her. The old sinking feeling of rejection and impotence that Happy's vast, unquenchable hungriness always engendered in me welled up again, and I dropped my arms to my side and sank down in the old twig rocker. The abrupt absence in my heart and house—yes, my house now—of the two people who had so filled them for more than thirty years was like an abyss into which I had tumbled; I could not seem to drag myself out to minister to this suffering child. Oh, my children! Why had they both been born so furiously unfillable? Why could I not find food within for this last ravenous one? Why couldn't Peter at least see what his distance from her was doing, even if he was unable to alter it?

I sat still, hoping the tantrum would abate enough so she could at least hear me and be reasoned with. I knew Peter had not promised her his presence this summer or a boat; those were phantom mushrooms sprung from the soil of her need. I knew she was more upset and frightened than she would acknowledge by the sudden death of her omnipresent grandmother. And I knew her need to hurt Peter, to punish him, had been displaced, as it so often was, onto me. She did the same when she was angry and jealous of Petie, whom she perceived as my favorite. Still; I would be still and quiet until she quieted. I closed my eyes.

Presently the crying slowed and lost some of its urgency, and there was a silence, which seemed to stretch on and on. I meant to open my eyes; a moment and I would do so. A moment . . . I was so very tired. . . .

"And you can't even stay awake when I'm talking to you!" Happy screamed, and ran out of the

house and slammed the door behind her. By the time
I got to the front walk she was out of sight, and I
heard her sneakers scuffling down the cliff path to
the beach below Braebonnie. I started after her and
the telephone rang. I paused, torn, and then went
inside to answer it.

I should have let it ring.

She was beyond my control for a long time after
that. She did not act out so much as she simply vanished for long periods of time and would not tell me
where she was. After two or three incidents in which
she came home on her bicycle long after dark, when I
had been out and around the colony in the car, and
had called virtually everyone I thought might have
seen her, and was on the verge of calling the sheriff, I
locked the bicycle up in the garage and hid the key.
After a truly heroic tantrum and three days of black
sulking, she seemed to accept her punishment with a
modicum of the grace I had prayed for and asked me
if I minded if she spent some time with Francie
Duschesne, Christina Willis's niece. Francie was, she
said, learning to quilt that summer and had offered to
teach her.

"It looks like it would be fun," she said. "And
there's nobody in the colony I'd waste a minute on.
Besides, that awful Freddie and Julia said anybody
up here without a boat was a drip, and I guess that
means me."

She cut her eyes toward me, but I refused to be
drawn into the boat debate.

"I think you'd enjoy that," I said, reaching out to
smooth the fair hair off her face. I smiled. She was filling out quickly that summer, sliding rapidly from
child into woman. Peter's high cheekbones were
beginning to emerge from the round pudding of her
face, and my own full breasts were budding, as early
on her as they had on me. I wondered if she minded,

as I had. Surely some equanimity would come with maturity; perhaps this was the beginning of it.

"I thought, if you'd let me, I'd take my bicycle over there," she said. "The quilting frame's in the barn behind the Willises' boathouse, and it's awful hot out there. I won't be late, I promise."

I hesitated. I liked Francie Duschesne; she was the child of Tina's younger brother, Clovis, a stern and old-fashioned parent who kept his daughter close by. At fourteen, Francie reminded me of Micah's niece Polly at that age, though of course there was no relation. She was pretty and capable and bright, though very shy, and I thought she might benefit from Happy's spirit as much as Happy from her decorum. But I did not like her older brother, Jackie. He was sly and sloe-eyed, far too old for his age, and had been in no small amount of trouble around the village: petty vandalism and wildness, mostly. And he worked in the boatyard with Micah and Caleb. Tina had told me at the beginning of the summer that Micah had taken him on as a favor to Clovis and she was afraid nothing good would come of it.

"He's sly and troublesome," she said. "Clovis won't see it and Micah won't have it. I'm some worried about it."

I did not like the possibility of his proximity to Happy. But surely, quilting—and in a barn practically under Micah Willis's eye—was harmless enough. And I knew she was lonely in the colony, and missing her father and grandmother.

"All right," I said. "But please, sweetie, be home before dark. And don't get in the way of the men at the boathouse."

"I'm not interested in the stupid boathouse," she said.

And so she rode off each morning on her bicycle and came home each evening full of talk of stitches

and patterns, and I gradually relaxed and let myself
sink into the silence of the old cottage as into cool
water. I did the things I had done for all those long
summers, either at Mother Hannah's bidding or, later,
under her stern eyes: I gathered food and washed and
polished silver and china; I wrote notes and gardened
and visited about the colony and drove old ladies on
their errands and excursions; I played a little bad
bridge and spent afternoons on the beach below
Braebonnie with Amy; and read, and listened to
music, and went for cocktails in fast-falling twilights
and had people in turn, and once in a while I played
some earnest morning tennis with the Mary's Garden
girls. I cooked small suppers for Happy and me and
sometimes Micah and Tina, and they came in the
evenings as they always had, and we laughed together,
and listened and nibbled and drank.

Only now I did those things for myself. In my
house. And if Mother Hannah was still as immutably
with us as she had been when she lay in her bed only
two walls away, well, that spectral presence would
fade. I might and did miss the woman I had come to
know only this summer, but I hardly missed the one
who had loomed so large over all the others. In
August, I had Micah Willis cut the lilacs far back, and
after that the cottage was flooded with a light that
was both literal and figurative.

"Yes," I said to Peter when he called, as he did
once or twice a week, "we're doing fine. The weather's lovely, and I'm making a routine for myself that I
think I'm going to enjoy. And Happy's made a new
friend of Tina's niece, and she's learning to quilt; can
you beat it? . . . Well, don't laugh; it may save you the
price of a boat. . . . I miss you, too. We both do. We'll
be more than ready to see you for Labor Day weekend."

I had not told him of my troubles with Happy. He

had called the day after his mother's funeral full of apologies for his behavior, and I had been so grateful to have him fully back with me, and so miserable at the grayness of the unhealed pain I heard under his words, that I simply could not add to it. And in my heart I knew I would do anything to avoid hearing in his voice the cold detachment that Happy's behavior so often called up. I could handle Happy. I had already done so.

On the first Sunday in August, at a little past four, the sheriff's dusty blue sedan pulled up in the driveway of Liberty and a still-faced John Gray got heavily out and reached in the back seat and pulled Happy out and marched her up the path to the door. I had been reading on the sun porch, half drowned in Retreat's Sunday stillness and the thick peace that precedes a storm. I met them at the door, my heart pounding in slow, sick, profound thuds. Happy's face was blanched absolutely white, and her nose and eyes were puffed and scarlet with crying.

"What is it?" I could hardly get the words out. "Is she hurt? Has there been an accident?"

"She's not hurt, no," John Gray said. "And no, I don't reckon you could say there's been an accident."

His voice was as neutral as his face, but I could see that he was having difficulty with his breathing, and something that seemed, incredibly, to be rage looked out of his eyes. I had known him for years, ever since he took office from Sheriff Perkins; he was a gruff, jolly man whose voice boomed out often, in greeting to his neighbors and in the choir at the chapel on Sunday mornings. But it did not boom now. I had trouble understanding him. I looked at Happy, who began to wail and covered her face with her hands.

"What?" I said, wanting more than anything in the world not to hear his answer.

"Caught her and Francie and Jackie Duschesne

over to Osprey Head," John Gray said. "Got a call on the radio from a boat passing out in the bay. By the time I got there they'd knocked the nest down and torn it to shreds. Rocks, had 'em a right pile stacked up. Must have finished it with their hands. Birds were gone, except one they got with a rock. Looked like near to grown, but wouldn't have been flying too good yet. I shot that one. Had to. You know, I shinnied up and measured that nest once, when the birds were gone for the winter. Close to five feet, it was, with a circumference at the base of twenty-one feet. Two and a half feet high. Been added on to every year since it was first built, and that's before anybody alive now can remember. I don't know yet what they could be charged with, not the girls, anyway. Probably could have held the boy. Have before. But if somebody around here wants to bring charges, I'm not going to stop them. I took the other two on over to Clovis. If I was you I'd keep this one out of sight. Them birds meant a lot to folks around here."

He turned and strode back down the path, leaving me standing in sickness and horror, looking at my child.

"Why?" I whispered. My ears rang, and the still air buzzed around me.

"They made me," Happy howled. "Jackie and Francie made me. They said they wouldn't be my friends any more if I didn't. It wasn't my fault!"

Rage so freezing and terrible that I thought I would vomit filled me like water. I could have shaken her until she lost her senses at that moment; I could have done anything at all to stop her voice. All that grace and fidelity, all that fierceness and pride and beauty and value. . . .

"Go upstairs to your room and don't come back down," I said, literally having to force the words between my teeth. My mouth shook. "Stay there until

I tell you you can come out. I'll bring your dinner to you, but I don't want to see you for the rest of the day. I don't care who told you what. There is no power on earth that could make a humane person do what you did to those birds. It's the most monstrous thing I have ever heard. I know that we will get past this, but right now I don't see how."

"Oh, I hate you!" Happy screamed. "You made me do it, just as much as they did. I want my daddy; my daddy wouldn't let you talk to me this way!"

"Well, you shall soon have your wish, because I'm calling him right now," I said, and turned away from her.

"No! Don't call Daddy! Don't call Daddy!"

Her voice slid up and up and into hysteria. I could hear the desperation in it, and the terror, and the abject self-loathing that would haunt her all her life. I had said dreadful things to her, things that drew her blood. In that moment I did not care.

"You know what your father told me the day before he left the first time?" I said. "We went over to see the ospreys, and he said, 'I've always heard it was terribly bad luck to kill an osprey, but to me it's purely a sin.' I think he's going to be very sorry he has to come back to this, Happy. Now go."

"Well, he'll come anyway, won't he?" she shrilled as she thumped up the stairs. "Whether or not he wants to, he'll have to come now!"

I went and made the call and then went out onto the sun porch and simply sat there until darkness fell. I shut the terrible sunlit images out of my head and let a swarming whiteness fill it; I heard the telephone ring several times and did not move to answer it. Sometime during the evening Amy Potter came onto the sun porch and stood beside me, and took my hand in hers, and said, "I just heard. I'm so sorry, Maude. I've always thought that Jackie was a little horror. . . . It will pass. The summer's nearly over. Take her home early, and when we all get back next year it will be in the past, and no one will mention it. You know they won't. You know no one thinks it's in any way your fault."

"Everyone knows by now," I said lifelessly. It was not a question.

She was silent for a moment, and then she said, "Yes. I expect they do. Is Peter coming? Do you want me to stay with you?"

"No, thanks anyway," I said, and squeezed her hand. "He'll be here in an hour or so. I . . . need the quiet. Oh, Amy. Our children."

"Yes," she said. "Our poor children."

Peter came in just before midnight. His face looked as if the flesh had been boiled off the bone; I had a sense of how he would look when he was very old or dying. I don't know if he was angry with me as well as Happy or not; if he was, it vanished when he saw my face. It must have been as terrible as his. He made a small sound and came to me and put his arms around me and buried his face in my hair, and we rocked back and forth in our anguish. Finally I lifted my head.

"You'd think somebody had died," I said hoarsely. "Surely it's not that bad."

"I feel as if somebody had," he said. "I almost wish—"

"Peter!"

"Is she in her room?"

I nodded. "Peter, maybe it would be better if you waited until tomorrow. I was awfully hard on her, and she's just terrified of what you'll say. I think, really— she says Jackie Duschesne made her do it."

He simply looked at me.

"Okay," I said. "I don't imagine she's asleep."

I never will know precisely what he said to her. I

heard her scream, once, and had the wild thought that perhaps he had struck her, but of course he had not, would not. I half rose to go to her, then sat back down. It was obvious that nothing I had said, could say, had reached Happy. At least she would *hear* Peter. I listened as hard as I could, but I heard nothing else from the top of the house. I thought of the burbling, trilling, pattering little towhead she had been, trailing endlessly in Peter's wake like a small sturdy dinghy wallowing after a sail yacht. Oh, my baby, I said silently, around the cold salt knot in my throat. What was it I could not give you, and he could not? What would it have taken? What will it?

When he came back down Peter would not speak much of the session with Happy, except to say that she had agreed to several specific things he had spelled out for her. One, she would go in person to each cottage beginning in the morning and apologize. Then she would, of course, never see or speak to Jackie or Francie Duschesne again. She would be taken back to Northpoint as soon as we could pack up and close the cottage, and she would participate in none of her school activities that winter, but come straight home after classes, and would not go out in the evenings. Her allowance for six months would go into a fund to be presented to the Maine Wildlife Protection Agency, toward rebuilding an osprey habitat on Osprey Head.

And finally, she would write a letter of apology to the entire village and mail it herself to John Gray, and Peter would ask him to read it aloud in church the Sunday he received it.

"I called him from Northpoint," Peter said. "I offered to write a check on the spot for any fine or damages he thought would be appropriate. And I told him Happy would be adequately punished."

"What did he say?"

"He said he didn't expect there would be any charges; what good would they do? And he wouldn't hear of my sending a check. I don't blame him. No money in the world will undo it. I doubt the birds will ever come back. They don't, usually, when a nest is gone."

"Oh, God," I said tiredly. "How awful for everybody. What a nightmare. But at least you've said your piece, and she has some concrete things to do, and terribly hard ones, and we can get on with living. You must know how sorry she is. If she can stick with your terms, we can forgive and forget."

"Can you forget this, Maude?" he said.

"I guess not. But at least forgive."

"No," Peter said. "Not that either. We'll go on, and we'll have our lives together, and they'll probably be good ones, but I won't forgive her this."

"You didn't tell her that?"

"I did. Just that."

"Darling, please go back up and—"

"I won't lie to her, Maude. I don't think I can forgive this. Not now. Maybe, after she's done what she has to. Let's see how the apologies go in the morning."

But the apologies did not go at all the next morning. We awoke late to a world flat and white and echoless with salt fog, and Happy was gone.

She was nowhere nearby. By noon I had called everyone who conceivably might have seen her within miles of the colony, and Peter had been out with the car, inching his way the length of the rutted blacktop that loops around the cape, calling and calling, blowing his horn, blinking his light. He was hoarse and soaked when he came in, and shaking with fear as well as cold; the temperature had dropped twenty degrees in the night. By four he and Parker Potter and the Stallings men and even Freddie

Winslow had been house-to-house in the colony and the village, searching attics and barns and outbuildings and boathouses. At five o'clock we called John Gray. By seven there was an all-points out for Happy, and several sheriff's posses, made up of men and boys from our village and surrounding ones, went out into the whiteness. No boats were missing from any of the village moorings or the yacht clubs, so the search did not, that night, take to the sea; in any event, no one could have taken a boat out in the fog. But we all thought of it, that black, silent sea lying just beyond the boundaries of our senses. I know we did. Thought of the sea, and the deepness of it, and the darkness, and the coldness, thought of the endless seas around Osprey Head. The sea ran in my veins instead of blood, that night, black and icy and dead.

Amy came, of course. All the colony women who could leave their children came. Christina appeared out of the fog, serene and tender, with a great basket of food and her altar guild's enormous coffeepot, and all through that first night she kept hot coffee and sandwiches coming to the men who went out and the women who waited. Micah brought in wood and built up the fire and came and squatted down before me in the wing chair that had been Mother Hannah's and looked intently into my face. He did not touch me.

"She isn't in the water, Maude," he said. "She can't be. We'd know; she'd have taken a boat. So we'll find her. It might be a spell, but we'll find her. She couldn't have gotten far. Fog will lift by dawn."

I looked into the dark face and could say what I could not to Peter or any other living being that night.

"I did this. I did it with my tongue. I wouldn't tell her it was all right, and I didn't make Peter do it. I never have loved her like I do Petie, and she knew it and it killed her."

He did touch me then, lightly, on my cheek.

"You didn't kill her. Peter didn't kill her. She's not dead. Don't say that again. We can't help who we love, or how much. It isn't your forgiveness she needs, or even her dad's, it's her own. That'll come along with the light, and then we'll find her or she'll come on back by herself. Wait for the light, Maude."

The light came with the morning; Micah was right. The fog was gone. But Happy did not come with it. At seven all the sailboats that had skippers went out, and all the power launches, and the Coast Guard came, in three sleek blue-and-white cutters. Micah went out with the first of them. Peter and Parker went out with the second and third. Peter and I could not seem to speak to each other; we could not even meet each other's eyes. In his I saw only the unforgiveness that had sent Happy out into the fog. For the first time I understood how the loss of a child could tear a man and a woman apart. I had never understood that before. We will not withstand this, he and I, I thought clearly. We will be dead to each other if she is.

By noon the numbness that the first fear had brought with it had worn thin and I felt hysteria rising in my throat and behind my eyes, threatening to close over me like the dark-blue cold sea outside Liberty, and I knew if I once went down into it I would never come out. I looked wildly around the room and the crowd of women gathered there, blindly seeking something to anchor myself to. The first face I saw clearly was that of Gretchen Winslow. She took one look at me and crossed the room rapidly and grabbed me by the shoulders and dragged me up onto my feet. I saw Amy frown and start toward us, but Gretchen shook her head at her, and Amy stood still.

"Listen, Maude," she said sharply. "This is what

you're going to do. You're going to hold on for fifteen more minutes. You can do that. Anybody can hang on for fifteen minutes. And then it'll make an hour, and you'll say, 'I'm going to hang on for one more hour. Anybody can do that. I can do that.' Do you hear me?"

"Yes," I said. And that is what I did, through that endless bright killer of a day. I held on for an hour. And then I did it for another. And then another. At one point, I remember saying dazedly to Gretchen, "Why do we fight?"

"I don't know," she said.

At seven o'clock the sheriff came to say that the boats were coming back in but would go back out at dawn the next morning. At eight Peter and Parker came back, white and mute, and the women gave them coffee and sandwiches and brandy, and some of them finally went home to their own families. At nine Micah came by to bring more wood and hug my shoulders wordlessly and fetch Christina.

"We went as far up as Castine and as far down as Haven," he said. "Didn't see anything. That's the best sign, Maude. Tomorrow we'll scour Islesboro and Deer and Little Deer. But we're not going to find her in the sea. We would have by now, if she'd been there."

I could only nod, mutely. One more hour, one more. . . .

Micah left to go and look in on the boatyard. Caleb had been seeing to things alone all day. I knew that Jackie Duschesne would never set foot there again.

He was back inside of thirty minutes, holding a filthy, sobbing Happy in his arms.

"Found her under the tarp over that great walloping beast of Freddie Winslow's I've got in for restraking," he said, his voice thick in his throat. Happy had her head thrust into his neck and would not look up.

Micah looked at me and at Peter and then put Happy down. She stood wavering and blinking, her face wet and streaked and ashen, her clothes covered with filth. She started toward me and I held out my arms, feeling my knees begin to go; then she veered and ran toward Peter. The floor rose up then, and wheeled over me, and I felt Micah Willis catch and hold me as he had done twice before in times of terrible trouble, and just before the sick, buzzing darkness crawled up my wrists and dragged me down I saw Happy reach up with her dirty arms for Peter, and saw him turn silently and walk out of the room and up the stairs. The last thing I heard, after sight left me, was the sound of Happy's lost wail as he went.

After that we tried harder with her. We took her home to Northpoint early, and though we were adamant that she observe the terms of the punishment Peter had set for her, we spent as much time with her as possible. Both of us cut our duty rosters back to the bone to do it. The headmaster of a large flourishing private school wears more hats than anyone else I know; he must involve himself fully in the life of the school, the alumni corps, the faculty, the community, and the larger corporate world from which funds and largesse might be coaxed. Peter delegated as much as he could to Charles Corwin, his assistant, and put in at least an hour or so with Happy almost every evening after dinner, though he grew harried and distinctly gaunt trying to manage it. And I curtailed my endless round of committees and school-related social functions and hallowed Northpoint rituals and managed to be home each afternoon when she returned from her school. It was a private country day school nearby, with many extracurricular activities to accommodate its privileged students, but Happy had never involved herself in them to any extent, and I do not believe she missed them. She did not say. Happy in that autumn and winter was silent and withdrawn as she had never been in her volatile life.

I oversaw her homework and fixed snacks for her and took her shopping and to matinees and movies in Laconia, and I took her to get the fine, thick, white-blond hair cut that autumn so that it swung at chin length in a shining bob, distinctive and becoming to her. I bought her a bit of makeup and her first—and long overdue—bra. Peter gave her several twin sets of lovely, thick cashmere sweaters for her birthday, and paid for riding lessons in the village when she said she might like them, and bought her a beautiful tweed riding jacket and shining English boots for Christmas. She looked so grown up in them my throat closed. She had not had much appetite since we had come back from Retreat, and was much thinner by Christmas than she had ever been before, so that her heavy breasts and rich hips stood out sharply in contrast to her small waist. With Peter's newly emerged cheekbones and the new haircut she was, I realized suddenly, a striking young woman, if not a pretty one, arresting in a lush and somehow troublesome way. Her expression was usually impassive or sulky, but it did not seem mulish and maddening now, as it had when she had been a pugnacious child. It was simply challenging. Peter and I looked at each other over her head the night she modeled the riding habit for us.

"I almost feel like locking her up until she's twenty-one," I said that night, getting ready for bed. "She looks like she's twenty-one already. We'll be beating boys off with clubs."

"She hasn't shown any interest in them so far," he said. "I wouldn't worry. What kid her age would risk making a pass at that stone face of hers?"

"I'm not worried about kids her age," I said. "We

can run those off. I'm worried about old lechers age eighteen and up. Look at that body; it looks like what we used to call jail bait."

Peter grinned.

"It looks like yours when I met you," he said. "In fact it looks not unlike yours now. So you may be right at that. Here's one old lecher who means to crawl all over you inside five minutes."

"Wait till you're invited. So you think there's no need to worry?"

"At least not until she starts sending out signals," he said. "I'd say you had ample time until you have to fret. Am I invited?"

"You're invited."

When the appointed six months were up Happy wrote and signed a brief and, I thought, dignified letter to the Maine Wildlife Protection Agency on behalf of the ospreys and enclosed a check for the amount of her allowance for that period of time. Her father took her to the village to mail it and bought her a soda at the drugstore in celebration, and then we three had a celebratory dinner at the Northpoint Tavern.

"I'm very proud of you, Happy," Peter told her over the lobster dinner that had always been her favorite. She only picked at it that evening.

"Thank you," she said, not meeting his eyes.

"You've behaved like a trooper and a very grown-up young lady," I said. "I think we can lift the restrictions on your time now."

She raised her head and looked at me with Peter's eyes, and then at her father.

"Have you forgiven me?" she said.

"Oh, darling, of course we have," I said quickly and warmly, and Peter nodded.

"You've handled yourself very well, Hap," he said.

"And have you forgotten about it?" she said. She was not looking at me.

Peter gave her back the look, and for a long time he did not speak. Oh, please, I said silently.

"I'd be lying if I said I had, Happy," he said finally. "It's not the kind of thing you forget. Isn't forgiving enough?"

"No," Happy said. "I don't think it is."

We spoke no more of it. Happy was quieter than ever. Near the end of February she came to us as we were having a drink before the fire and told us she wanted to transfer to Miss Cawthorne's School in the suburbs of Providence.

"They have the best riding facilities in the East," she said. "You can have a horse there if you want to. I thought I'd save up for one; by the time I'm sixteen I should have enough if it isn't a very good one. I hope you'll let me. I really want to do this."

"Well, gosh, honey," I said, nonplussed. "I suppose we could think about it. Fall term's a long way off."

"I want to go for the spring one," she said levelly. "It starts in less than a month. They have an opening, I know, and I think they'd take me, with Daddy's being a headmaster and all. I've already written them about it. I know it's more expensive for me to board, but there are jobs I could take. In the school store, and as a waitress in the Commons. . . . I've looked into that, too. You wouldn't have to worry about me. It's all girls and very strict. I wouldn't have any choice but to behave."

My heart gave a painful plunge, and I looked quickly at Peter. His eyes closed involuntarily.

"You haven't been a worry this year at all, Punkin," he said. "No complaints."

"And I wouldn't, you know, be in anybody's way," she went on. "I know you've both stopped doing a lot of stuff to stay with me. I don't want you to have to do that any more. It makes me feel awful."

"We've loved being with you, baby," I said.

"A changed woman, you are," Peter said, smiling painfully.

She simply looked at him. Then she said, "I hope you'll let me know soon. I really want to do it."

And she went back to her room.

In the end we let her. I was against it; she was so young, and I was worried as well as gratified at the change in her that autumn and winter, beginning to think we had been far too hard on her. But she was undeniably handling herself better than she ever had, and she did adore horses and riding, and Miss Cawthorne's School had a grand old luster to it. As Peter pointed out, she was practically a shoo-in for one of the Seven Sisters with an undergraduate degree from that august academy. And as he did not point out, but I well knew, Happy out of the house and in a chaste fortress of rectitude hundreds of miles away was the answer to Peter's prayers. He could go back to his duties with a lighter heart and a clear conscience. Happy out of sight was for Peter, I am afraid, Happy out of mind.

And so she set off on a blue, wind-booming day in early March for Providence, with me and a trunk full of new clothes and riding gear and her radio and phonograph in the station wagon and Peter behind us in the Volvo pulling a trailer containing a newly purchased mare, a light hunter named Quicksilver. Both the school and Quicksilver had cost more than a headmaster could afford, but Peter and Hermie had shared Mother Hannah's estate equally, and our portion was, to me, an astounding amount of money. Even though we had bought a sprawling old Dutch Colonial in the village at Christmas and contracted for extensive and much-needed repairs to Liberty, and Peter had promptly turned the balance of the estate over to the discreet old man in the trust department of the bank who had always handled his family's investments, we could afford the school and the horse. There was little else to spend money on. Peter had given the family house in Boston to Petie and Sarah for a wedding present and set aside a sum to be held for its management, and nothing else except the bank, which was running well under its own momentum, claimed our allegiance.

"It's well worth it if it makes her happy," Peter said on the way back to Northpoint the day after we had settled Happy in at Miss Cawthorne's. "New friends and new experiences and a horse of her own. What more could she ask?"

I thought she could have asked for her father to protest her decision, beg her to stay, tell her he would miss her. But I didn't say it. I knew his work had piled up, and this moratorium on strife of Happy's probably could not last. Instead I said, "I feel like I'm seeing the last of her childhood. I feel like she's going to be someone I don't know when she comes back."

"I doubt it, since she's coming back in two months for the summer," Peter said, smiling over at me. "Relax and enjoy it, Maude. We haven't been alone in an awfully long time. She'll be the same old Happy; you'll see. How much can she change in three years?"

It wasn't long before we found out how much.

In November of the following year Happy was discovered to have spent the night in the apartment of a young instructor of mathematics and, when charged with her sins by an appalled Miss Cawthorne, said defiantly that it wasn't the first time by any means; she had been sleeping with him for weeks. The instructor was dismissed immediately and Happy was, of course, expelled. To Peter and me she said nothing at all for a long time, merely smiled and went up to her room and closed the door. She would not let either of us in at first, and when Peter finally got her to open it, to ask her in low, cold tones of anguish for God's sake *why,* the smile only deepened.

"At least I got his attention," she said.

Within a month, by dint of what cajoling and calling in of old debts I will never know, Peter had enrolled her at the French School in Boston, known far and wide as the institution of last resort for recalcitrant young women, a forbidding pile of red brick that lacked only crenellations and arrow slits to complete its air of medieval fortification. She went there for the winter term, saying scarcely a word to Peter or me and without Quicksilver. There were no horses, no town privileges, nothing at the French School to distract or seduce its charges.

"Looks like it could use a little livening up." She grinned at us when we drove into the driveway of the French School. It was not a smile I wanted to remember.

"I wouldn't advise that," Peter said, smiling the awful smile back at her.

"Wouldn't you, Daddy? That's a shame. A girl only wants to have a little fun now and then."

She was barely fifteen on that day. On the silent drive home I wondered bleakly what the next trouble would be, and how long before the call came.

"We shouldn't have sent her away again," I said. "We should have kept her at home; I should be looking after her, not some blueblooded warden."

"I'm not going to have you spend all your time being a jailer for Happy," Peter said tightly. "Barbara French can do that better than anybody else alive. Happy needs a firmer hand right now than you could give her; probably than I could, either. This is best," Peter said.

"I don't think we really know what she needs," I said miserably. "I wonder if we ever did."

"Let there be an end right now to the dithering

over Happy," Peter said. "She's where she should be and where I want her to be, and that's all I want to hear about it for a while. Say about a year."

"Oh, the children," I had said to Amy Potter on the night Happy had stoned the ospreys' nest.

"Yes, the children," she had replied, and I knew she had been thinking of the heart-wrenching, careening course of Elizabeth's life. Through her teenage years, Elizabeth had given Amy no end of grief, and the stories of that beautiful, flame-kissed girl had floated back to us at Retreat: of drinking, of experimentation with drugs, of flagrant affairs with an astounding range of men, of her eventual flight to Paris and subsequent involvement with what came to be called later the jet set. There were whispered accounts of this infamous yacht and that notorious house party and the publication in foreign newspapers of scandalous nude photographs on a white Greek beach that included Elizabeth, and of a long string of titled and unsavory men. Parker would not discuss his daughter, and Amy grew drawn and completely white-haired, and the rich laughter did not float from Braebonnie on the morning wind often any more.

And others of our friends had had heartbreaks with their children. We were not alone. Albert and Louise Stallings's son Gus had refused the family patent medicine business and struck out as a jazz saxophonist; we had heard terrible stories of heroin addiction and degradation in the slums of the Lower East Side of New York. Marie Conant's daughter Ceile, Erica's cherished only granddaughter, had had a baby out of wedlock two summers before and had vanished after giving it up for adoption, lost for long months to her anguished family. And Micah Willis's Caleb had, I knew, spent years in a darkness of his own after coming home without his leg from the war. Micah had spoken little of him to me in those years, but stories of the drinking and fighting and nights in jail, the drifting and disappearances, the midnight phone calls from sheriffs' offices in small towns all over the coast, reached our ears in the colony. After my first attempt to speak to him of it, Micah's frozen face warned me off, but his face was blanched and drained throughout those years, and Christina's was often blotched and swollen from her tears. Oh, yes, the children. None of us had really escaped, it seemed.

But the other children came home again, one by one, if only metaphorically. Elizabeth Potter abruptly renounced her freewheeling life and went back to Paris to study art at the Sorbonne; Amy had been as radiant as a candle when she told me, lit from within with relief and joy. Elizabeth met a wellborn young Frenchman in Paris, the son of an old banking family much like the Potters, and married him quietly in a small ceremony in the chapel of Notre Dame at Christmas time two years later. Now she was pregnant with her first child and glowingly happy. Even in my pain for Happy I had felt real joy for Amy's joy. I needed her caroling laugh myself in those years, and had missed it as one misses the sun in a season of rain.

And Gus Stallings was back in harness at the family's offices, I heard, free of all his addictions but that to the saxophone. And Marie Conant's Ceile came home. And Caleb Willis had some years before met a forceful young woman from Bucksport and been entranced and changed by her, so that finally, in his early thirties, he married her and stopped his carousing and settled in a new house on Cove Harbor that Micah and his Duschesne cousins helped him to build himself, and now he worked side by side with his father in the boatyard his grandfather had begun. I saw him often, as I had not in the years he spent in his wilderness; he was now a quiet and soft-spoken young man with his father's thick dark hair--though his was receding as

Micah's never had—and his mother's enduring serenity. He smiled and spoke whenever we met, and I could still see in his dark face something of that brown, darting child I had held in my arms on that endless drive to the doctor so long ago, on the day he cut his foot in the front yard of Liberty. He had, I knew, children of his own now, two small dark daughters who looked uncannily like he had at their age.

"I'm going to keep after him until he gets us a boy," Micah would say, looking after his pattering grandchildren. Grandchildren! Micah? "Drownin' in women, I am."

But I knew he adored the little girls. How could he not? They were the visible proof of his prodigal son's return.

Yes. The children had come home. And so, I thought—hoped, prayed—would Happy. In her own time, so would Happy.

And she did. In the late spring of 1953, after slightly more than a year of incarceration without incident in the French School, Happy came home to Northpoint with a red-haired, extraordinarily handsome Irishman fully ten years her senior in tow and announced that she was planning to marry him as soon as possible and wanted to have the wedding in the Northpoint chapel, with a reception following the ceremony in our drawing room. She introduced him to Peter and me as Thomas O'Ryan and said he had been employed until recently as a bus driver and mechanic by the French School, but that he was eager to expand his horizons and try his hand at something that was more suitable to his talents. Happy was sure Peter could find more challenging work for him, either at Northpoint or the bank. The bank would be best, she thought. Tommy O'Ryan was a native of Boston, as was Peter, and he'd feel more at home there. She hoped he might stay in one of our guest bedrooms until the wedding, but if that did not suit he would be happy to find lodgings in the village.

Happy was still sixteen on that tender green day in June. She was also two months pregnant. The swift, cold quietus Peter started to deliver to her plans died in his mouth when she told us that. He stared at her in shock and disbelief, the sharp angles of his face leaping into relief as if flesh were actually draining away from bone. I felt the breath leave my body and could not seem to regain it. Happy smiled a beatific smile; she seemed in every way that evening a woman, ripe and totally contained and indolent in her glowing skin. Tommy O'Ryan gave Peter a practiced smile both obsequious and familiar. He did not even look at me.

"So what do you think?" Happy said, and only then did I hear the tremor in her voice and understand that she was terrified and trying to bluff it through. "Can Tommy stay with us or not?"

"Are you out of what passes for your mind, Camilla?" Peter said in a low, terrible voice. Even I, shocked and horrified, flinched instinctively from it. It cut like a lash. "He may not stay with us, nor may he remain in this house. He will leave this instant and you will go to your room and wait until your mother and I have had a chance to think, and then we will tell you what we are going to do next. How in the name of God did this happen? The school *bus* driver? The school *mechanic*? How on God's earth did this *happen?*"

Happy's face contorted. It rearranged itself into a smile that had nothing in it at all of childhood or innocence. I shut my eyes against that smile.

"It's easy, Daddy," she said. "You just drop your pants and he puts his thing into your thing and sooner or later there'll be a baby. I thought you knew. I've heard you and Mother often enough."

I thought he was going to strike her and moved swiftly between them. Tommy O'Ryan, still smiling, moved back a step or two. Peter stopped and scrubbed his face with his hand.

"Go upstairs," he said. "There will be no marriage. Mr. O'Ryan will leave us now and be thankful that I do not shoot him. Whether or not I have him arrested remains to be seen. We will decide later what to do about your . . . child. I don't want to see you again until we have worked this out. If Mr. O'Ryan still entertains any ideas about staying in this house I will call the police right now. That goes for this town, too. I assume he cannot go back to the school, so he may go wherever he wishes and he had better start this instant."

"If he goes, I go with him. I'm sixteen. You can't stop me," Happy said, and her face was almost as white and old as Peter's. I looked from one to the other in anguish. What would become of us now?

"Then do it," Peter said, and turned and went upstairs.

The three of us stood in the twilight in the foyer of our home and looked at one another. I still could not speak.

"Mama?" Happy said, and suddenly my child was back behind that woman's face. "Mama? We don't have any money. We don't have any other place to go. Can you talk to Daddy? If he'd just give Tommy a chance I know he'd like him. And he'd have a grandbaby. . . ."

Tommy O'Ryan spoke for the first time, in a rich, musical tenor that faintly charmed me even as I recognized in it the practiced lilt of the born charlatan.

"I'm not such a villain, Mrs. Chambliss." He grinned. "I'm on the ropes temporarily, but I mean to better myself and make a home for Happy and our babe. I'm a hard worker and I can make myself handy at anything. This was all a bit hasty, I suppose, but I do love your girl, and everything can still come right."

I looked at him. Nothing would come right. Everything Tommy O'Ryan seemed and was and ever could be was total anathema to Peter. I knew that viscerally. But, oh, Happy!

"Mama?"

"Wait a moment. Wait and be quiet," I said, and went into the kitchen where I had left my handbag. I took out the week's grocery money that I had in my wallet and gave it to Tommy O'Ryan.

"Go down to the inn and get a room," I said, my mouth numb with pain and shock. "I'll talk with my husband. I can tell you now that I think it will do no good at all, but I can't have my daughter out in the night with no place to sleep, and I think it would be better if she weren't here for a while. Wait in your room until I call you in the morning. We can't resolve this now."

"Mama," Happy began again, and made a small movement toward me. Tears formed in her eyes and began to spill over the white-gold lashes that were Peter's. I said nothing, and she came and put her arms around me and pressed herself against me. I held her loosely, feeling the hard new swell of her breasts, the rich, used curve of her young hips. My own tears overflowed.

"Go on now. I'll call you," I whispered, and watched as my child, my last baby, went out to spend the night in a hotel room with a man who would, I knew somehow, haunt our lives for perhaps the rest of our years. Then I went upstairs to talk to Peter.

It was a terrible night, awful past anything I had ever gone through with Peter. Even now I cannot remember much of what he said, and what I did; I have all these years later only a sense of anguish and finality, of hopelessness, of ending. I was not sure then what it was that was ending. Now I know it was any chance that Peter might ever truly connect with his yearning, destructive daughter. Poor Happy, she destroyed in that one night everything she had ached and burned for all her life. She always did that. Somehow, for Happy, the need was the death sentence of the fulfillment.

By dawn we had hammered it out. We would allow them to marry, since I knew they would elope to Maryland or somewhere and do so anyway if we did not. Peter would do what he could to help Tommy O'Ryan find employment; I knew he could do that. We would rent an apartment for them close to Tommy's work and pay the rent for a year, so he could put aside his salary for a nest egg. We would pay Happy's hospital bills if Tommy O'Ryan could not, when the time came. We would see that Happy had a nurse for the baby for the first year.

Happy would visit us at home no more than twice a week with the child, preferably when Peter was not there. Tommy O'Ryan was never to come to the house in Northpoint again. Neither of them was to come to Retreat.

The terms were hard. They were hard past, I thought, my ability to enforce them, but I would worry about that later. I knew I was fortunate to have gotten any terms at all from Peter. I have never seen him so furious, so implacable. There was, that night, nothing at all in him of the funny, tender, luminous young man who had danced with me in the moonlight on the banks of Wappoo Creek. Oh, he still burned, but it was a cold fire.

Happy began to cry when I told her her father's conditions the next morning, but I cut her off.

"Give him some time," I said. "Try and do this without making a fuss, and give him some time. It was an awful shock, Happy. This is the best I can do, and I don't think you have any alternative."

"It wouldn't have mattered if it was Jesus Christ I brought home to him," Happy sobbed. "He hates me, and he'd have hated anybody I wanted to marry. I should have known he hated me. I guess I did and just didn't want to admit it to myself."

There was nothing to say to that. Peter had never hated Happy, of course, but she had caught the essence of the truth about her father: he had never really loved her either. Not fully, not wholly, not without condition or boundary. It was that she sought and wept for on that morning. No, there was nothing to say. I did not answer her.

Two days later I stood in the shabby offices of a justice of the peace in a small village outside Laconia, rain falling steadily, and watched as my daughter became Mrs. Thomas Sean O'Ryan, and then I took the newlyweds to lunch at a little lodge near Lake Winnipesaukee, where Peter and I had spent the night once when we had first come to Northpoint. I remembered that we had sat, that evening, on the shore of the great lake and talked of the upcoming journey to Retreat, my first. I had not, I remembered, wanted to go, sensing ahead things that would alter me, change my life forever. We had made love in the pine-scented twilight, under the trees; we had laughed. My poor child, no laughter for her on this day. But for her, too, a journey ahead that would change her life. And ours.

We did not see much of them that summer and fall. Peter did not speak often of Happy, and I did not push it. When the baby came, I thought, maybe, maybe. . . . Once in a while Peter was at home when Happy, vastly pregnant, came to visit and was neutral and pleasant with her. He refused to see Tommy O'Ryan. He refused to speak of him at all.

Happy's son, Sean Williams O'Ryan, was born in January, and I held him and felt again that sweet, milky-smelling solid weight, and touched the silky-swirled crown of the red-gold head, and was for a moment blissfully, blindly happy. Now, surely, Peter could not deny the existence of this child. The baby was a portrait in blood. There was the unmistakable

Chambliss chin cleft, and the same whorl of hair at the crown of the head. And the eyes: Peter's gray instead of Tommy O'Ryan's watercolor blue.

But Peter would not come. And Happy would not bring the baby to him.

"He can avoid seeing him for the rest of his life, if that's what he wants," she said coldly. "He's mine and he's all I need, he and Tommy. The hell with Daddy."

"Fine with me," Peter said, when I told him Happy would not bring his grandchild to him.

I looked at him, sunk now for so long in the chilly stillness, the flat grayness that his father before him had gone away into from time to time. Peter that winter was with me in body only, and then not often. He stayed late and long at Northpoint and went in early. We did not often talk beyond desultory, carefully channeled conversations, and we had not made love since the autumn before. I wondered often in those days if our lives would end like this, flash-frozen years and years before death. It was the unhappiest period of my life; after all these years, I can still say that.

One day in early August, as we sat with our books on the sun porch of Liberty, we heard the noise of a car stopping outside, and footsteps on the walk, and Happy walked silently through the cottage and onto the porch and put her baby into Peter's arms and stood and looked down at him. She did not speak. Peter whitened and stared up at Happy and then down at small Sean. The baby looked solemnly into his face, his great gray eyes fastened on Peter's, the titian curls on his head blazing in the late-afternoon sunlight. Then he smiled, and then grinned, a wicked and completely enraptured grin, and put his finger into Peter's mouth and crowed with delight. Peter shut his eyes, and when he opened them he was back with us as completely and unreservedly as he had ever been. His whole face radiated his presence;

his old fire flamed; his eyes crinkled with something that had never been there for his own children, and his smile reached out and wrapped the baby in.

"Well, by God," he said to the baby. "What took you so long?"

After that Sean became, simply, his heart. Peter's delight in him was endless, bottomless, almost ludicrous. It lit the cottage and spilled over me and trickled over Happy, and even reached out, tentatively and fleetingly, to Tommy O'Ryan. There was, at least, a moratorium on his cold contempt for Tommy. He did not go back to Northpoint as he had planned; he stayed on in Retreat and did all the summer things that he had once done: he sailed, and played tennis, and read before the fire at night, and took me for trips to Castine and Blue Hill and Bar Harbor, and once even down to Camden for two entire days.

And wherever he went, even sometimes out on the *Hannah,* small Sean went with him in the crook of his arm. Tommy, who had driven Happy and the baby to Retreat in the old Ford he had bought, had to return to his job as head of maintenance for the Northpoint motor fleet and left two days after he came . . . just in time, I thought, to spare him considerable grief, for in two days his insinuating manner and bluster and gaudy flamboyance of dress and manner and enormous ignorance of all the rituals and nuances that held the colony together had become painfully apparent, and thunderclouds were gathering in Peter's gray eyes. But Happy stayed the rest of summer, and later in August Petie and Sarah and five-year-old Maude Caroline came for three weeks and stayed down on the beach in Miss Lottie's newly refurbished house that we rented for them. The Sunday after the last regatta we christened Sean at the little chapel on the shore, and all of Retreat turned out for the small champagne reception I had at Liberty afterward. Peter carried

Sean in his arms all afternoon, and everyone exclaimed over the baby and praised him to Happy, and there was, just for that moment and that summer, nothing in my child's face of want or need but only what was, for her, joy. If, when they looked at her, my friends and neighbors saw, instead of a young mother, a troublesome, malicious child and heard again the long-vanished cry of the ospreys, they did not by so much as a flicker of an eyelash let on.

Bless you all, I said to them silently, loving them, and to Peter, aloud, after the last guest had left and Happy had gone to put Sean down for his nap, "Bless you. You've made me so very happy this summer. I didn't think I'd ever have you back again."

He put his arms around me and held me close and rested his chin on the top of my head, as he used to do.

"Bless you, my dearest Maude. It isn't you I leave. It never is. Don't you know that by now?"

"Oh, Peter. Don't leave any of us again," I whispered into his neck. "We're all here, every one of us, all together in this place I love more than any other on earth; that you love. Nothing on earth could be better than this; this is what I used to dream of, all those summers . . . just this. All of us here. But it would be less than nothing if you left us."

"Then," said Peter, "I won't."

Chapter Ten

There's something rather pretty and Norman Rockwell about us this morning, isn't there? Three generations all together for a day at the beach?" Elizabeth Potter Villiers said on a radiant, restless day in June of 1961, on the little shingle beach below Braebonnie.

I shaded my face against the high noon sun and looked up at her. Against the lead-foil dazzle of the bay she was all silhouette: long legs sliding up into narrow, canted hips, the sweet line of her waist flowing unbroken to the deep swell of her breasts. She seemed outlined with silver light, as things do on our coast just before a storm breaks. She also seemed naked and nearly was; she wore one of the new French bikinis that were only that year beginning to be popular on American shores, and then only on those far to the south of Retreat's. Only the flash of her white teeth and the copper gleam of her sleeked-back hair broke the skin of the dull silver dazzle. I laughed aloud. Even in outline, there was nothing at all of Elizabeth that spoke to me of Norman Rockwell.

"Lord, sweetie, that makes me feel as old as Methuselah's mother," Amy Potter said, but her dark eyes, as she looked at her daughter, gave the lie to her rueful words. Her white curls were covered with a huge red straw sun hat Elizabeth had brought her from Italy, and with her face and eyes flaming with joy she looked younger than I had seen her in years. Elizabeth could have told her she looked like Whistler's mother, and she would have laughed her delicious, rich old laugh. Despite the strife and illness in Braebonnie, above us on the cliff, Amy was happy this summer. Elizabeth was home from Europe for the first time in nearly ten years, and back in Retreat for the first time since she had left college and fled to Paris, when she was barely twenty. Amy's was, I thought—by no means for the first time that summer—a dangerous joy.

Elizabeth dropped onto the towel beside her mother, showering us with droplets of water. They burned like acid or ice. I knew the bay must not have reached sixty degrees yet, but she had been in twice that morning, this last time swimming far out into the dazzle until we lost her in its radiance. My skin shrank from the icy pinpricks, but Elizabeth did not seem cold. She sat cross-legged beside her mother, the bikini barely containing her deep, coffee-cream breasts, reached up and coiled the wet sheaf of her hair into a severe knot at her nape, and fastened it with an ivory skewer that looked like a poultry lacing pin. She was all over tawny that morning, the shades and colors of the veldt. A predator among us, I thought. A predator among adoring sheep.

She had changed in all the years since I had seen her, of course, and yet somehow she was the same. How long had it been? Probably the end of that awful summer when she had gone back to Boston and left Petie skewered and bleeding on his desperate love for her. She had been fifteen then: a child, but somehow as fully a woman as the one who sat on this morning beach and sleeked back her wet red hair. All that had changed was the degree of the womanliness. What had been promise was now ripely fulfilled, and Elizabeth Potter Villiers was as beautiful and vivid and somehow implacably and sensuously innocent as a great predator.

And predator, I thought, was the right word. Behind her, I knew from the scraps Amy had given me and the colony gossip that had floated through those summers, lay a string of the dead and dying, both literally and figuratively. There had been two or three abandoned relationships in Paris and Greece and Spain in those first years abroad; a middle-aged French banker and his wife dead of murder-suicide and a crumpled note with young Elizabeth's name in it; an abortion in Athens and Elizabeth herself near death from sepsis; more broken love affairs back in France, and a brief and savage flirtation with heroin in Paris, until young Toby Villiers met and married her and fathered the dark five-year-old who pranced naked in the shallows of Penobscot Bay this morning, chattering in silvery French.

And finally, the violent death of that marriage, and the flight to Italy and the sheltering hills of Tuscany, where Elizabeth found refuge in the arms and country villa of a Florentine baron of astounding wealth and charm. Unfortunately, the baron had, in the classic tradition of that worldliest of cities, a handsome wastrel son and a formidable feline wife. Both had dropped in unexpectedly at the villa while Elizabeth was there with the baron, and after a couple of titillating but tense weeks in which the baron and baronessa fought in hissing seclusion in the master suite and Elizabeth and the young baronet amused themselves in the taverns of the nearby hill towns and in other, more private places, Elizabeth had grown sufficiently intimidated by the baronessa's increasingly murderous ire and fled home to her mother with her child. As always, when catastrophe had fallen on her head as the result of her own actions, she seemed genuinely bewildered and wounded by this latest contretemps. It had always been Elizabeth's vulnerability, the slight, sweet odor of the victim in her powerful musk, that gave the final piquant twist to her attraction. Even when you most wanted to shake Elizabeth Potter, somehow you wanted more strongly to protect her, if only from herself. Even I felt that.

Except for dark little Warrie Villiers and Petie and Sarah's fat little Sally, we three women were alone on the beach. Happy would not come near Elizabeth Villiers and had made that fact elaborately clear to everyone in Retreat. I never saw such instant antipathy, even in my emotionally naked child. She would not even allow Sean to be in small Warrie's presence, a fact that bothered Sean not at all, especially given the gap in their ages. He was, that summer, learning to sail his first Beetle Cat, the *Osprey,* and totally absorbed in it and the waiting sea. He was all light and length and sinew, like his grandfather, and all boy; there was never even a trace of the feminine about Sean, as there is about most other small boys. He scarcely had time for his mother and me, and as for Warrie Villiers, he only said dismissingly, "He's a baby and a sissy. A frog sissy. He flutters his fingers, and his eyelashes are too long."

I spoke sharply to him when he brought out the "frog," after waiting in vain for Happy to do it. She would not discipline her son and never had, and I knew Peter would lift neither a finger nor an eyebrow at anything the boy did. I caught the slow, small smile of satisfaction on Happy's face at her son's careless little epithet, and my face burned. Sean was nearly a perfect prototype of everything Peter and I loved in children; I would not allow him to be indulged in such ugliness.

"Whether or not you like Warrie Villiers is your business," I said crisply. "What you call him in my house is mine. That's an ugly and prejudiced word, and I don't want to hear it again, Sean, is that clear?"

He looked at me with his brows level over his gray eyes and his mouth twitching with the impulse to sass me. But he didn't. He only said, "Yes, Grammaude. I'm sorry." And my heart melted, even though I knew he was not sorry at all.

"Come on, Slats," Peter said to him, avoiding my eyes. "We've got a couple of hours before dinner. Let's take the *Hannah* around Osprey Head and back. It's calm enough, I think, for you to take the tiller."

And they were off, the screen door banging behind them, before Happy or I could say a word. Even through my annoyance at Peter's undercutting my discipline of Sean, I had to smile at the image of the two of them, loose and tanned in their khaki pants and polo shirts, hair flopping over their eyes, loping down the dock to the dinghy. Behind me, Happy said, "It's really a lot of fun to play second fiddle to a child with your own father. Daddy *never* asks me out on his precious *Hannah.*"

Her voice was so childish and thick with spite and yearning that I simply did not turn to confront her. Though things were better with Happy during the years that she came to Liberty with her son than they had ever been before, there were small flashing moments like this one when I knew, wearily, that she would never be healed of her devouring need of Peter, and he would never meet it. I was tired to my very marrow of trying to mitigate, smooth, compensate. Sean was Peter's heart and Happy was nowhere near it, and there was nothing I could do.

I could see, this morning on the beach, what Sean had meant about Warrie Villiers, though. There was indeed something feminine about the child, something knowing and accommodating and almost sly. It would not have seemed awry in a little girl; one would have smiled at the miniature woman hidden in the child flesh. But you noticed it in Warrie. He did flutter his long dark lashes a lot, and look sidewise under them, mostly at his mother, and his long, supple fingers did indeed dance in the air, and flutter, and hover, their tips almost vibrating, over this object and that, without actually touching them. His voice was a fluting treble, normal in a small child, and the rapid French that spilled from his pursed pink mouth was only natural for a child born to a household where French was the first language. But somehow in Warrie those things lodged in the consciousness just a shade unpleasantly, casting just the smallest of shadows. I might have thought he was edging dangerously toward the irreversibly feminine but for his manner with his mother, and hers with him. It was more that of man to woman than child to mother; his hands were on her breasts and flanks and hair and nape as often and casually as they were on the shells and pebbles that he collected, and hers smoothed his silky brown nakedness all over with conscious delectation whenever he was near. I found that, even knowing the profound difference between Latin ways and those of this cold northern shore, I could not look at Elizabeth Villiers and her son after a while. And I saw that, try as she might to notice nothing, Amy could not either. Otherness clung around them, mother and son, like a miasma. Otherness and a kind of danger. It was the danger I had tasted in Amy Potter's joy that morning, the danger that charged any air where Elizabeth was, and always had.

I remembered Miss Lottie Padgett's words, twenty

years before, when I had fled to her in pain and desperation over Petie and Elizabeth: "Elizabeth will never be safe. A lot of people are going to suffer because of that."

And so they had, already. And so, I thought, more would. But not Amy. Oh, please, not my poor reborn Amy. I did not think Amy could take much more pain, not from this quicksilver prodigal daughter who was at the core of her heart. There had been enough pain already, from Parker. After more than a quarter of a century of warnings from doctors, scenes, crises, alarms, heartaches, and humiliations, Parker Potter seemed finally and truly to be near death from the drinking he could neither tolerate nor stop, and it was to stand by her mother in this last and worst siege that Elizabeth had ostensibly left Italy and come to Retreat. But day melted into summer day and Elizabeth spent far more time on the beach below Braebonnie than by her father's side. Most mornings she managed to coax Amy to sit beside her, and Amy grew smoothed and sun-flushed and lightened with love and laughter, even as her husband swelled like a mordant toad with the toxins his liver could no longer fight. I thought Parker drank, now, with a new and bitter defiance since his daughter had come to beguile his wife, and the storms and tantrums and outrages that issued from Braebonnie increased in number and severity. Scarcely a day passed that Peter did not drop what he was doing and dash over at some frantic telephoned summons from Amy or Elizabeth, and I had gone a couple of times, too, to no avail. Parker drank and stormed on. But Amy had her girl and her mornings in the sun, and so far they had been more than enough.

Sally came toddling to me, pink-nosed from the high sun and howling from a careless blow from Warrie, who was both older and bigger. I caught her

warm, wriggling little body into my arms and rocked
her, glaring at Warrie. Was it only I who had seen the
sly, sidewise little kick from his monkeylike brown
foot? No, Elizabeth had seen too; she shook her head
at her son, but she was smiling when she did it and
made a little silent kiss to him. He sent one back. I
turned the glare on her.

"She should just kick him back," Elizabeth said,
stretching so that one rose-brown nipple escaped the
dull black of the bikini top. Warrie giggled and she
tucked it back in, expertly. Her slicked-back hair
shone as if lacquered, and she wore many gold and
jeweled rings on her long fingers. With one of them
she reached out and lifted Sally's furious little red
face up to the sun.

"Just kick him back, *chérie,* preferably in his little
brown balls," she said. "It's never too soon for a girl
to learn what makes a young man sit up and take
notice. Lord, but she's the image of Petie, isn't she?
I'll bet he looked just like that when he was her age,
all fierce and determined and stubborn as a little
mule. I wish I remembered him then; the first clear
memory I have of him is running after me yelling that
he was going to tell if I jumped off the dock into the
water. And I did, and he did too. Scared to death and
furious, but he did. We must have been eight and
nine."

She laughed, and then let Sally's face go and turned
to me.

"I wish he hadn't felt he had to leave, Maude," she
said lazily. "I had no intentions of gobbling him up
this summer."

I felt my anger swell, and even Amy stared hard at
her daughter, a blush staining her face. Petie and
Sarah had left the Little House and gone back to
Boston only a few days after Elizabeth had come. The
entire colony knew they had planned to spend the

entire summer in the little cottage, which Peter and I had bought for them when Miss Lottie's feckless son finally put it on the market, and I knew there had been a groundswell of gentle buzzing when they pleaded Sarah's father's sudden ill health and went back, leaving Maude Caroline and Sally with Peter and me. Most of Retreat would, I knew, remember the days of Petie's desperate love for Elizabeth and put two and two together, or think that they had. Only Peter and I knew it was Sarah, her face white and set, who had insisted on leaving. I still did not know what had decided her, and I hoped I never would. If anything sufficient to send my son and daughter-in-law away from their long-planned summer had passed between Petie and Elizabeth, I knew as certainly as I knew the sun shone overhead that it had not originated with Petie. And I knew Amy Potter knew it, too.

"It just may be that one or two people in Retreat have plans that do not in any way concern you, Elizabeth," Amy said crisply to her daughter, and Elizabeth laughed aloud, a rich, plummy, liquid sound. Light seemed to gather around her, thick as cream. She had lost none of that quality of luminous presence she had as a child; she remained, with Peter, one of the only people I have ever known who had it.

"I'm sure that's true," she said, and then, tilting her head and squinting at me, "Maude, I'd love to try you in one of my bikinis. You're as lush as a ripe peach; you'd drive the guys up here berserk with those boobs of yours showing, and that tiny waist, and those hips—you wouldn't last a minute in France or Italy. A Tintoretto, you are, or a Velázquez, with that black hair and those eyes. And just the right age for Europe. You should come back with me when I go."

"Oh, but honey, you said you thought you'd be staying for a year or two at least!" Amy's voice was almost a wail.

"Of course, Mommy. And I will. But sooner or later I'll have to go get my things, and then there's Warrie's schooling. . . ."

"Warrie should stay right here and go to Miss Dawson's, and then to Choate and on to Harvard, or maybe Yale, like a proper Potter," Amy said firmly.

"Somehow I can't see Warrie's dear papa letting him do that," Elizabeth said, amused. "His family honor would be stained beyond repair. And he's going to have to foot the bill for this chick, because I haven't a sou. I had to literally pay ransom to get out of France, and then I had to sneak Warrie out in the dead of night. It was all very exciting, wasn't it, Pippin?"

And she reached out and fondled her child's hard little buttocks, and he squirmed against her in pleasure and complicity, and I picked up the sniveling Sally and said, "I think this pippin has had enough sun for the day. Her nose is on fire," and turned to leave the beach. Behind me I heard Amy say something, sharp but unintelligible, and heard Elizabeth's languid answering laughter. Enough of sun and indolence and flesh, I thought in sudden disgust. I wanted a bath and cool, starched, clean clothes for Sally and me, and a nap in a white room with a sharp little salt wind blowing through it. And then I smiled into my grandchild's sweaty neck. I was, myself, a creature of sun and indolence and flesh; Charleston was surely a city of all those things, fully as much as Cap Ferrat or Rapallo. What a very long way I had come from home.

The house was empty when Sally and I got there. Sean was, I knew, down at the yacht club, where Caleb Willis was schooling the colony juniors in the new Beetle Cats. The club had bought a fleet of them from a broker in Boston, small, tippy little catboats to replace the aging and nearly unsalvageable Brutal Beasts in which generations before had learned to

sail, and we had all cheered when Caleb came into
sight around the dark bulk of Little Deer on a misted
June morning the summer before, his father's lobster
boat towing a long line of Beetles down the bay. Peter
and I had taken one, for Sean and Maude Caroline and
whoever came along behind them, but Maude Caroline
had my inherent loathing of imbalance and cast her
lot with tennis and swimming. She was twelve this
summer and had, for the past four years, gone to day
camp over on Rosier Pond, at Camp Four Rivers.
Many of Retreat's youngsters did; the wallowing
yellow camp bus called every morning at the top of
the lane, and the chorus of "Yay, Camp," rising from
sturdy young throats in the still dawns was so frequent
and loud that most of us had forgotten the camp's
true name and called it simply Yaycamp. I knew
Maude Caroline was there today, probably knifing
like a brown minnow through that blue lake water
her great-grandfather had loved . . . and died in. Peter
would be out on the *Hannah,* and as for Happy, I did
not know where she was, only that she was gone.
She took the car most mornings and drove away
about ten, and returned at perhaps three or four, in
time to supervise Sally's bath and afternoon bread
and butter and to have drinks on the porch with
Peter and me.

If we asked where she had been she would say
only, "Around. To a yard sale here and a bake sale
there. I like to keep moving."

And so we seldom asked any more. My dear
Happy; she did, indeed, like to keep moving.

Sometimes, if we were going for drinks to one cottage or another, she would come with us, but not
often. There were few households in Retreat where
Happy had friends. I did not insist when she did not
want to come with us on those evenings; Happy
when she had had one or two drinks too many was as

formidable as she had been when she was a tantrum-prone teenager. There was no telling what would come out of her mouth. I disliked those evenings, and Peter hated them; he would be cool and distant for days afterward, and Happy would be wretched. So she did not often come with us.

When she had not drunk a bit too much, she was good company that summer, for the most part. Peter's delight in Sean spilled over her, and if she was jealous of the attention her father paid her son—as I knew she was—she wisely did not show that jealousy to Peter. Sean himself was offhandedly affectionate with her, as he was with everyone else except, I thought, his father. The few times I saw my grandson in the company of Tommy O'Ryan, there was an ostentatious boisterousness in Tommy's manner, as if some savage competitiveness boiled just below the surface of his rough joie de vivre; I thought him just as jealous of his son as was Happy, but for different reasons, and felt contempt and uneasiness in the presence of that deep undercurrent. Except for his blazing strawberry-blond hair and the two deep vertical dimples in his cheeks, Sean was every inch a Chambliss, every inch his grandfather, both in looks and manner. He walked surefootedly and without thought where his father never could. I knew Tommy O'Ryan hated that, even as he beamed upon it and used it as his most effective wedge into the world of his wife's birthright. That unspoken hate frightened me badly. It would, I thought, come home to haunt us one day. For his part, Sean was quiet and closed and unreadable in his father's presence, at least around Peter and me, and of their times together in the smallish house we had bought them in Saugus, where Tommy's latest job had taken them, Happy would only say, "He and his father don't really get along. Tommy needs a little girl to adore him like

Seanie does Daddy. He's after me all the time about that."

And she would smile, a deep and secret smile.

Lord, Tommy O'Ryan. How that handsome mountebank has haunted us, even in his absence; I was
right about that, the first day I set eyes on him. He
was as much a presence, in his way, as Peter was, or
Elizabeth Potter. No one in a group that included him
could look away from him. Until the last day I ever
saw him he remained one of the handsomest men I
have ever known. I have seen strangers, men and
women alike, turn to look after him on the street, and
at times when you saw him at close range, laughing
his beautiful tenor laugh, say, with his white teeth
flashing and his shining red head thrown back, or listening intently to you, with his blue eyes fastened full
on you and that head cocked to one side, he simply
took your breath. I could see, at those times, why
Happy actually shivered sometimes with pure physical ecstasy in his presence; even when things were
worst between them, there was that warm, invisible
steam of flesh about the two of them together that
spoke of night and bed, and even at my angriest with
him I could understand why my child could not leave
him. Had I not felt that way about Peter ever since
the first night I met him? What, I thought often,
would I have done if Peter had been a Tommy
O'Ryan? I could not have walked away from him, any
more than Happy could.

But he could not sustain any good feelings he gen-
erated. Tommy O'Ryan had no boundaries and no
sense of them in others; given any time at all in any
group, he seemed devil-driven to exceed the bounds
of taste and sensibility and often even common sense,
and his appetite for what he called, often and loudly,
the good life, was bottomless. He bragged and boasted
and assumed airs when he visited us at Northpoint or

Retreat until Peter refused him both houses. He alien-
ated the colony with his loudness and familiarity, outraged even Parker Potter with his drunkenness and
language, and made flagrant passes at almost every
woman under sixty in Retreat, with the exception of
Gretchen Winslow, whom he called a frigid bitch—in
her presence.

When he heard from an embarrassed Guild
Kennedy that Tommy had cheated at poker during
the hallowed Men's Wednesday Night at the Yacht
Club, Peter threatened to cut off Happy's inheritance
if he ever came back to Retreat. And so, except to
deliver Happy and Sean to Liberty and fetch them, he
did not. We saw little of him, I almost none. Peter, I
knew, saw him periodically, since Tommy tossed
away job after job, and another introduction would
be required of Peter.

I believe he would have simply ceased to work at
all, and lived off what he referred to as Happy's
birthright, if Peter had not tied Happy's portion of
Mother Hannah's estate up into an unbreakable trust
and arranged that only a middling income from it be
sent her each month; he had done that upon meeting
Tommy O'Ryan, long before Happy reached her
twenty-first birthday. As for cash gifts to her, he simply would not make them. He would, he said grimly,
continue to find jobs for Tommy O'Ryan as soon as
he lost them, and was prepared to do so until hell
froze over, and he would educate Sean and provide
housing and an automobile, and medical care if it
was required. But as long as Happy was married to
Tommy O'Ryan, she would receive her inheritance
in the form of gifts to fill particular needs. If that did
not suit, she was free to divorce him. Otherwise, she
would simply have to wait until Peter and I died to
provide Tommy with the lifestyle to which he
aspired, and even then there were ways to keep

much of her so-called birthright from falling into those strong, shapely Irish hands.

Happy stormed and sulked and raged, but Peter held firm. And so, for several years, Tommy O'Ryan was with us largely in the hair and dimples of his son, the checks Peter sent for medical and dental bills, the inevitable calls from the latest of our old acquaintances who had employed him, and the shivering flesh and softly loosened mouth of his wife and our daughter. But with us he was.

"Is, was, and ever shall be," Peter would say, closing the soft old leather check portfolio that had been his father's after meeting still another demand from Sean or Happy's doctor or dentist. "World without end, amen."

"It could be worse," I said once in the middle of this summer.

"How?"

I did not answer.

That was on a day in July, just after the Fourth of July regatta, the very same day Elizabeth Potter Villiers came pounding into the cottage sobbing that her father was trying to kill her mother with a poker, and please, Peter, please come quick. And once more, Peter took her hand and ran for Braebonnie, with me behind them, my heart frozen with dread that this time Parker might actually succeed.

When we reached Braebonnie we found Parker on the floor before the cold fireplace, vomiting, and Amy trying vainly to pick him up. The poker was still sheathed in its iron stand. Peter gave Elizabeth a swift look of query but said nothing. She flushed and turned away. Peter put his arms under Parker's armpits and hauled him to his feet and marched him, stumbling, toward the downstairs bedroom. Even monstrously swollen from the poisonous fluids that had collected in his belly and extremities, Parker was so desiccated that Peter lifted him as lightly as a bag of dry sticks. Amy pushed the white hair off her tear-splotched face and tried to smile at us.

"Sorry you had to get involved again," she said, and her voice was remarkably steady, if deeply weary. "I told Elizabeth not to go running to you. It was only a stage two or three alarm this time. I don't think he could have gotten the poker out of the stand, much less hit anybody with it."

I hugged her briefly, and said, "No problem. That's what we're over there for."

"Absolutely," Peter said, returning.

"No," Amy said, "it's not. Nobody should have to do what we've called on you to do. It was a mistake to bring him, but the doctor said he probably wouldn't have another summer."

"I hope he doesn't," Elizabeth Villiers said in a low, cold voice. "I hope he doesn't have another week. He's not even a man now. As for a father, forget it. He was never that."

"Lizzie—" Amy began, but Elizabeth burst into tears then, and turned into Peter's arms. He held her gently and patted her on the back, looking helplessly at me over her shaking red head.

"I know it was silly of me to come running to you, Peter," she sobbed into his shoulder. "But he said he was going to kill Mother with the poker, and I knew that he would if he could. . . . I'm afraid of him. I don't feel safe in the house with him."

"Honey, Daddy's way past hurting you," Amy said softly, but Elizabeth just shook her head. How could she not feel safe with this poor scarecrow? I thought in brief annoyance. She had apparently felt safe with some of the most dangerous men in Europe. But then I thought of what Miss Lottie had said—"Elizabeth will never feel safe"—and I thought that what Elizabeth said about safety had less to do with the physical threat Parker was to her than the primal bond of father to daughter that had never been there. She was right; Parker had never been a father to her.

As if picking up my thoughts, Amy said, "She's never really known a father. He was past that when she was born. I think maybe that's what she's been looking for all these years. . . . I'm sorry she's leaning so on Peter this summer; I think he's become a kind of substitute for Parker. I'll speak to her. It's just too much a burden to impose on you two."

"I'm sorry too," Elizabeth said, raising her head and looking up at Peter and then over at me. In that moment her face was scoured of everything but loss and yearning and fear, and pity swept me. She looked like a frightened child. As, I thought, she was.

"No need to be," Peter said, tweaking her nose. "I haven't been able to play Galahad in a very long time. My two women are tough cookies."

I looked at him, shaking my head in mock reproof. But I felt a small shock. Did he really think that of me? And as for his precarious, starving daughter, how could he?

"Let me give you a drink, then, as a peace offering," Elizabeth said, but I declined.

"Sally will be waking up and Maude Caroline will be coming in from camp, and I don't think Happy's back," I said. "Rain check?"

"I'll have a quick one and see that your dad is settled down," Peter said, and Amy and Elizabeth both smiled gratefully. I thought it had probably been a long time since either one had had a pleasant social drink with a man who was as whole and comfortable in his skin as Peter.

"Good idea," I said, and kissed Amy and Elizabeth and went back to Liberty. Behind me, as I stepped over the stone wall, I heard Elizabeth's restored laugh and Amy's full rich one. Thank you, darling, I said to Peter in my head.

*   *   *

In mid-August I gave a cocktail party for Elizabeth
Potter Villiers. It was what one did in Retreat, when a
close friend had visiting family or friends, and
besides, I knew Amy had longed to do it herself, to
reintroduce Elizabeth to the colony, and had not
dared, with Parker in the condition he was.

It was a large party. I even bit my tongue and
asked the Winslows. Young Freddie had been an
admirer of Elizabeth's when they were both
teenagers, I remembered, even when the wildfire
between her and Petie was at its most desperate, and
she had had other light friendships with colony
youngsters her age. They would want to see her. So
I simply asked everyone. Most came, whether out
of curiosity about Elizabeth or loyalty to Amy, I did
not know. I was simply glad, for Amy's sake, that
they did.

It was a pretty party, with late wildflowers and
Japanese lanterns, and it spilled out over the lawn.
The sunset over the bay that evening was a conflagration of blood-red and orange and deep, gold-edged
purple, I remember: unforgettable. It was an autumn
sunset, and everyone lingered outdoors until it faded,
despite the gathering chill. I did not think we would
have many more perfect days like this one had been.
Even Micah Willis, who had come with Christina and
Caleb and his Bucksport wife and their small toddling
son Micah—the last and clearly most beloved fruit of
that marriage, and a carbon of his grandfather—
remarked on the dying of the sun.

"Haven't seen a bonfire like that one in years," he
said. "My dad used to say the devil was burning his
trash when we got a sunset like that. The old-timers
used to think that one of those red and purple
doozies used to summon up the aurora borealis.

Wouldn't be surprised if we didn't see it one night before long."

"Oh, I hope so," Elizabeth said. "I can't remember ever seeing it."

"Well, I have, lots of times," Happy said. She was holding what appeared to be a glass of pure amber scotch, and I tried to catch her eye to warn her to go slow. But she was looking at Elizabeth. "Daddy used to take me out on the boat to see them better," she said. "They're nothing like as pretty on land as they are on the water."

Peter looked at her neutrally and smiled. I knew he had never taken Happy out on the *Hannah* to watch the northern lights.

"Oh, Peter, if they come this summer will you take me out?" Elizabeth cried. "I'd so love to see them. I don't think we get them in Europe."

"Well, Lord, Elizabeth, Scandinavia is their very home." Happy snorted. "What a stupid thing to say."

Elizabeth flushed, and Peter said, "Of course I will, if they last long enough. Sometimes they just flare out and are gone."

"We saw them the night you were born, your mother and I," I said. "Didn't she ever tell you? You were literally born under the northern lights."

"Well, scotty-wotty doo-doo-doo," Happy said sarcastically.

"No," Elizabeth said. "I don't think she ever did."

When we went back into Liberty, Parker Potter was there, half sitting, half lying on the wicker sofa, dressed in a gaping bathrobe and nothing else, drinking scotch out of a half-empty bottle. The assemblage fell silent. He looked dreadful, corpselike, sick unto death, obscene, with his shrunken flaccid penis and testicles showing and the monstrous stretched belly shining fish-white beneath the robe. Amy gasped and ran toward him, and Elizabeth made a sound of horror and nausea deep in her throat. Peter started for him behind Amy. No one else moved.

"God damn him to hell," Elizabeth said in a deep, shaking voice. "How did he manage to get over here? Sonny Norton was supposed to be watching him."

Just then Sonny Norton, the large young man who was assistant postmaster that year and who had long helped Amy with Parker and chores around Braebonnie, came stumbling into the room. There was a rapidly swelling cut over his eye, and blood had dried on his face and shirt.

"Jesus, I'm sorry, Miz Chambliss," he gasped. "He hit me with the liquor bottle, and by the time I got my wits back, he was gone."

Parker looked at the room full of his friends and neighbors, and up at his hovering wife and Peter, who was attempting to pull the robe together over his stomach, and smiled, fully and dreadfully. And then he drew the scotch bottle back as far as he could and hit Amy across the face with it. She went straight down, without a sound.

The living room erupted into horrified noise and motion. George Stallings caught Amy just before she hit the floor and pulled her onto the sun porch. Micah Willis and Peter pinned Parker's arms behind him, scotch from the flying bottle splashing them. The crowd surged toward the struggling group like a tide, and then stopped, wavering, as Caleb Willis held his arms up for silence.

"You folks go on home, please," he said in the deep voice that was so like his father's. "If Frank Stallings is here, maybe somebody could run get his bag and he could see to Miz Potter. Doesn't look like she's much hurt, but we ought to see. I know Miz Chambliss would appreciate it if things could quiet down, like. She'll most likely call around and tell everybody how Miz Potter is in a while."

"Thank you, Caleb," I said over the fading babble, trying to wade through the crowd to Amy's side. Micah and Peter had taken Parker into the big bedroom behind the kitchen that was mine and Peter's, and George Stallings had Amy on the sun-porch sofa. I could see she was moving her hands, feebly, and her eyelids were fluttering. There was a dull red spot high on her cheekbone, and only a thin runnel of blood cut her white skin.

Happy stood motionless beside the bar, drinking her drink, watching Elizabeth.

Elizabeth stood in the middle of the sun porch, looking down at her mother, and began to scream.

Frank Stallings, Albert and Louise's visiting physician son, came running back from the Compound just then with his medical bag and dropped down beside Amy.

"Somebody give Elizabeth a smart slap," he said, "and then I'll get her a sedative. The rest of you move back and give us some air. Better still, go on home, like Caleb said."

People began to move away and straggle out the door, talking among themselves in low voices, and Elizabeth continued to scream almost abstractedly, like a machine. Her eyes were closed and her face was paper-white. Happy put her glass down and walked over to her and slapped her so hard she rocked back on her heels. Elizabeth took a great, gulping breath, stopped crying, and opened her eyes. Then they narrowed to slits. It was, suddenly, the face of a Medusa, a Chinese were-tiger. I drew in my breath and Happy slapped her again, as hard as before, smiling a small, casual smile.

"Through crying, Elizabeth? I'd love to do that again," she said. Elizabeth made a sound like a teakettle beginning to whistle and drew her own arm back, then stopped, looking over Happy's head. Following her gaze, I and the others left saw Peter standing in the kitchen doorway, staring at Elizabeth and his daughter.

Elizabeth's frozen, chalky face crumpled into tears, and she ran straight into Peter's arms. He held her and looked at Happy. For a long moment, there was no sound but Elizabeth's choking sobs.

"Did you have to hit her so hard?" he said to Happy.

His voice was quiet and awful. I did not remember ever hearing it before. Happy's face began to melt as if a candle had been held to it.

"Dr. Stallings said to," she quavered, her voice that of a small child.

"I trust he didn't say to knock her out," Peter said.

"Oh, Peter, take me home, I want to go home," Elizabeth wept, and when he did not answer she looked up into his face. For some reason the sight of those two heads so close together, those two faces only inches apart, struck me like a fist in the stomach. They looked . . . one of a piece, sculpted from the same radiant rock. A scene out of Elizabeth's childhood flashed into my mind, perfect and living. Peter at the yacht club, drinking punch and bending down to whisper something in nine-year-old Elizabeth's ear, and the voice of old Augusta Stallings saying loudly, "Look at those two. Like as peas in a pod. She should be yours, Peter; except for that red head there isn't God's bit of Parker in her."

"Then you shall, sweetie," Peter said now to Elizabeth, and started with her toward the door, his arm tight around her. Breathless with dread and something I could not name, I looked mutely after them. Everyone else did, too. I heard Gretchen Winslow murmur, "Looks like Peter has another high-strung daughter on his hands this summer, doesn't it?" and then I heard Happy laugh. It was an ugly sound. "Daughter?" she said. "Is that what you think, Mrs. Winslow? She's in Daddy's hands, all right, but I wouldn't exactly call her a daughter!"

The silence in the room had the quality of deafening sound. Peter stopped and looked back at Happy.

"Go upstairs to your room, Camilla," he said, in the cold new voice. "I'll speak with you later."

"You can't order me around any more," she shrieked. "I'm a grown woman with a son; you can't tell me what to do!"

"Go," he said, and turned and walked out the door, still with Elizabeth crying quietly in the curve of his arm. No one spoke.

Happy turned and bolted up the stairs and slammed the door behind her.

Everyone left after that, of course. Frank and George Stallings took Amy home, and soon only Micah and Christina Willis were left. I thought miserably that I could not have imagined a more destructive and appalling scene, from start to finish, if I had tried. No one would mention it to me, of course, but no one would forget it either. It would become one of the ugly, livid threads in the tapestry of Retreat, a story told and retold over the years, losing some of its heat, perhaps, but none of its clarity. I raised my head and looked at Micah and Christina, who had brought a tray of coffee and set it before me on the tole tray table.

"The Chamblisses have just added their hieroglyphics to the others on the cave wall," I said heavily. I was so tired I thought I might simply never get up again. Christina poured coffee and Micah handed it to me. He regarded me silently for a moment and then said, "I reckon it's not exactly your hieroglyphics, Maude. More likely Mrs. Villiers's doing. Peter's too, come to that. Nobody's going to read your name up there."

"Happy didn't exactly acquit herself wonderfully," I said.

"Nope. Don't reckon she did," he said. "But it isn't Happy the colony's going to talk about, if that's what's bothering you. Happy's guilty of nothing but wanting her daddy. Bit old for it, maybe, but it's not unnatural. The sooner Mrs. Villiers puts some water between her and Retreat, the better we're all going to be. Don't be too hard on Happy. And for God's sake, don't be hard on yourself. If you got to sling mud, point it toward the right person."

"Micah's right," Christina said, putting her hand on my hair and smoothing it off my face. "It doesn't take a genius to see who's selling the snake oil around here. Get some rest and let Mrs. Potter tend to her own. Peter doesn't need to do it, and you sure don't."

I stood up and kissed her cheek gratefully and pressed Micah's hard brown hand, and they left and I sat down again, heavy and empty. Presently Sean came back from the young people's square dance at the yacht club, looked warily and silently at me, got himself a glass of milk and a piece of cake, and came back into the room.

"You okay, Grammaude?"

"Go on to bed, darling," I said dully. "I'm not very good company tonight. There was an awful scene with Mr. Potter, and your mother and grandfather had words. Grandpa's gone to take Mrs. Villiers home, and it would be better if I could talk to him alone when he gets back. Things will be back to normal in the morning."

He looked, all of a sudden, desolate, stricken.

"Oh, Grammaude," he said in a low, tight voice, "Mother's going to make me go home. I know she is. She threatens to do it every time she and Grandpa have a fight, or she thinks he's been mean to her. Last time she said next time it happened we were going home and never coming back to Retreat again. Oh, jeez. . . ."

Tears stood in his gray eyes, and he turned his head away. I reached over and took his hand.

"Darling, your mother wouldn't do that," I said. "We wouldn't let her. Your grandpa wouldn't let her. All of us know what these summers mean to you. This is your place; there just couldn't be any summers up here without you."

He looked full at me then, a skinny, sunburned child with fine gray eyes and a hurt almost too heavy to bear on his face. It was at that moment far too old a face for a young boy. I felt tears start in my own eyes. He blinked and looked away again. When he spoke it was to the middle distance.

"You don't know," he said. It was almost a whisper. "You just don't know what the winters are like, Grammaude. I hate them. I hate every minute I'm not in Retreat. Mother and Dad . . . together, they're . . . I don't know. Not like other people's folks. You don't see them, but they're not. If I couldn't come to Retreat and be with you and Grandpa in the summer, I think I would die. I wish . . . I wish I could just stay here forever."

His face twisted.

"And so you shall," I said, pulling him to me so that he could not see my own tears. Damn Happy, damn Tommy O'Ryan, they did not deserve this large-hearted boy. Why had I never wondered what his winters in the dingy little house in Saugus were like? Why had I never thought about his coming to us to live or starting at Northpoint?

But I knew the answer to that. Tommy O'Ryan would not have it, and he was, after all, Sean's father. There was nothing we could do. Well, then, we would just have to make the summers even better, Peter and I.

"We love you very much, darling, your grandpa and I," I said.

"I love you, too," he said, his voice muffled against me. Then he gave a great rattling sniff and hugged me hard and pulled away.

"I better hit the sack," he said. "Grandpa said we'd go over to Little Deer tomorrow, if the weather holds. That is . . . do you think he'll still want to?"

"Are you kidding? Wild horses wouldn't stop him," I said, smiling, and he gave me a little salute and galloped up the stairs toward the sun porch where he slept, taking them two at a time. I sat back down to wait for Peter.

He came in barely five minutes later.

"That ought to hold everybody for a while," he said, sitting down heavily on the sofa next to me and reaching for the coffee. "Frank's given all three of them a sedative, and he's going over first thing in the morning to check on them. I will too. Amy's going to have to have Parker hospitalized. She can't take any more of this, and neither can Elizabeth."

I waited for a moment, and then I said, "Peter, I think you're going to have to stop going over there every time Elizabeth calls you. Somebody else is going to have to do it, after tonight. It's just . . . too costly to all of us."

He looked at me.

"You buying into that stuff Happy was spewing, Maude?" he said finally, and his voice was edging close to that cold, dead new note I had heard earlier.

"You know I'm not," I said. "You *know* that. But darling . . . it's a small place. People misunderstand. People talk. Your mother once told me that in Retreat, as nowhere else on earth, appearances are everything, and I can finally begin to see the truth of it. You don't want your friends talking behind your back about your . . . relationship with Elizabeth

Villiers, for Happy's and Sean's sake if no one else's. It's terrible for Happy; you know she's jealous of Elizabeth. Why rub her face in it? And I just found out tonight that Sean bears the brunt of it when you fight with her. Let me tell you—"

"I'm not going to discuss it," he said, and rose. "I can't believe you're saying this. Elizabeth is . . . a child. A child, Maude. Would you have me turn my back on a child that needed me?"

I stared at him.

"Peter," I said, "you've been doing exactly that with Happy all her life."

I thought he was going to be very angry with me, but then he sat down again and took my hands in his.

"Maude, let me see if I can tell you how I feel about this, about Happy," he said tiredly. "It's like it was with Petie; I can love them both, and I do, but I simply can't hold up under all that *need*. It's too heavy and too constant; I can't fill them up and still breathe myself. I feel sometimes as if that . . . *wanting* will just smother me. I have to step back or I'll die. They have you; they don't need all that much of me, not all the time. . . . My mother always held me lightly; she didn't hang on me. You don't; you never did. You love me, but you don't *need* me to death. . . ."

I sat looking at him. There was nothing to say. I do need you, my heart wailed silently. I always have. I always will. I love you and need you both; don't you see? Why don't you see? You're always here to love me, but you often don't even notice when I need you. It isn't your hands that bear me up then. . . .

I thought of whose hands were there, always had been, and shut the thought away from me. There was a line I loved in a poem of Robert Frost's: "Only where love and need are one, and the work is play for mortal stakes. . . ."

Peter would not like that poem. It would sit too heavily on his heart.

Oh, Mother Hannah, I thought bleakly. You crippled your son in your awful strength. He spent his life running from the power of your grasp; it's the sum of what he learned from you.

"Well," I said, "see if you can't make it up to Happy in the morning. You were terribly hard on her, in front of everybody. Do it for Sean if you won't do it for her, or me. He's going to suffer if you don't. I found that out tonight."

"What do you mean?" he said.

And dear God, I did not tell him. I sat there and said, "Later, please, darling. I'm about to die right here."

I did not tell him.

We woke to gray, scudding clouds and a tossing bay. Micah, coming in with wood for the fireplace, said he had heard on the radio that there was a gale coming up the coast, first of the autumn storms, and none of the lobster boats had gone out. It should, he said, hit with rain and high winds about midafternoon.

"Good day to sit by the fire and read a book." He smiled at me, as if the night before had not been limned in destruction.

"That's just what I'm going to do," I said. "Why don't you and Tina come share the fire with us after dinner? Peter brought some Courvoisier back from Ellsworth."

"Done and done," he said. "Is everybody okay over here?"

"Seems to be," I said. "Peter's gone over to Castine to get something or other for the *Hannah* from Pengallen's, and Happy's sleeping in, I think, and I heard Sean leave at dawn. He wanted to go sailing with

Peter, but I expect he met him on his way back from the yacht club and rode over to Castine with him. It's surely not a day to be on the water."

"It's not, and that's a fact," Micah said, and went out of the kitchen, and I went back to the old book of English gardens I had found in the bookcase. Except for the lingering frisson of hurt and anger that stood like stale smoke in the air of Liberty, it was my favorite kind of day.

Happy came creeping down about two, looking swollen-faced and sheepish.

"Is Daddy here? I thought I'd apologize right quick and get it over with," she said.

"Gone to Castine with Sean," I said. "That wouldn't be a bad thing to do, Punkin. He will too, when you do, and then we can put it all behind us."

"Huh!" She snorted. "Until the next time Elizabeth calls." I looked at her, and she said, "Sorry," and went to fix herself a late lunch.

About four Peter came stamping into the kitchen, dashing rain off his hair and clothes. The wind outside had risen to a howl, and I could see the lilacs thrashing in the front yard.

"Daddy, I'm sorry," Happy said instantly in a small voice.

He hesitated, and then said, "No harm done. Where's Sean?"

Happy and I went still, looking at each other. My heart began to pound. Happy's face blanched.

"I haven't seen him, but I heard him go out early this morning, and I thought he'd caught up with you," I said through stiff lips. "Have you not seen him at all?"

He did not answer. His face was still and blank.

"Happy?" he said.

She shook her head back and forth, no, but she would not meet his eyes or mine. She looked down at her hands. Her face reddened and then whitened.

"Happy," Peter said. It was not a question.

"I haven't seen him, really," she whispered. "But I . . . I think he might have, you know, run away or something."

"Why?" Peter said. It was almost casual.

"Well, I told him—it was after you were so awful to me, Daddy, last night, you know, in front of everybody when you made me go—"

"Happy!"

"I told him we were going home today and never coming back," she whispered, and then she began to cry. "But he's heard me say that before; he knows I don't mean it. He knows I just say it. . . ."

Peter wheeled and ran out of the cottage. I stood in the kitchen, my head buzzing, the room seeming to revolve slowly around me. Happy ran out of the room, and I heard her pound back upstairs and slam her door. I caught up my own raincoat, then, and ran out after Peter. I knew he would head for the yacht club.

The wind was so strong I had to fight against it. The rain blew past in horizontal silver bands. I could not see far ahead of me. I met Peter in the lane in front of Camp Corpy. He swept me around and dragged me toward the cottage, head down, not speaking.

"The boat?" I screamed. "Peter, is the *Osprey* there?"

"No," Peter called back, and I began to cry. I think I knew then.

It was Caleb Willis, in Micah's lobster boat, who found him. He told me much later that his father had said, when Peter's call came, "You go, Caleb. I'll man the radios to the fleet this time. I can't go to her and tell her the sea's got that little boy."

I knew when Caleb told me that Micah had not meant Happy.

Caleb found him almost immediately. There was no anguished, two-day ordeal for us; I have always been thankful for that. It was almost as if Caleb knew just where Sean would take the *Osprey,* and he went straight there: to the rocky near beach of Osprey Head.

"I taught him in the *Osprey,* remember," he told Peter sometime during the haze of red pain that wrapped us that night. "I knew and he knew that he could just about make Osprey Head alone, if he was careful—on a sailing day, of course, not . . . like this. We used to joke that his was the only Beetle Cat with its very own home port. I'd have made for there if I'd been him. But in this sea—"

In that angry sea Sean had never had a chance. How he had gotten as far as he had was something that will haunt my nights for all the time I have left to me, as it did Peter's. I know that. I used to waken at night in a sweat, seeing the wave that finally took him over and wondering what those last moments must have been like, and then I would hear Peter groan and stir, and I would know as if a red cord bound our two minds that he was seeing it all too.

Caleb found the *Osprey* beached on the near rocks of Osprey Head. Sean bobbed nearby, in the shallows, the long halyard that must have taken him and the flying little boat all the way across that crazed stretch of sea to the haven of Osprey Head wrapped firmly around his foot. He must have gotten tangled in it within sight of the head, and fallen, and the little cat, without its taut sail and a hand on the tiller, had flipped. Caleb had taught even the smallest juniors how to right a Beetle Cat if it flipped over, but he had taught them in the gentle water of Cove Harbor, under the sweet high sun of summer.

Except for the abrasion around his ankle, Sean seemed merely asleep. Even his tan had not faded. I supposed stupidly, when Caleb pulled the tarpaulin back from Sean's face, his own face tracked with tears, that the cold sea had seen to that.

Peter turned at that sight and pulled himself up the stairs of Liberty. Happy, more crazy and senseless in that moment than ever before, started after him.

"I'll have another one for you, Daddy," she screamed, as I caught her around the waist and held her fast. "I'm pregnant now, three months; I'll have another one for you—"

"Hush, darling, hush." I wept, holding her. "You don't know what you're saying. Hush. . . ."

Peter turned and looked down at her.

"You can't seem to keep one alive, Camilla," he said, almost pleasantly. "Please don't honor us with another."

And he went into his bedroom and closed the door. For a long terrible time, while the storm boiled itself out and the cottage filled and the ambulance from the new South Brooksville medical center came howling in, and Happy screamed and screamed and screamed, I did not see him.

Finally, at midnight, when I was at last dozing in front of the fire, with Christina Willis sitting quietly across the room knitting, he came back down. He was dressed in his oil clothes and carrying his ditty bag.

"Have the arrangements been made?" he said. His voice was formal.

"Yes," I said, past surprise and almost past grief. He wasn't, could not, be going sailing. The wind had died, but the rain still pelted down.

"Tommy is coming in the morning," I said. "They're going to . . . there will be a service and an interment here, in the churchyard. I told him we wanted to take him home to Boston, that Happy would want that, but he won't hear of it. I couldn't talk him out of it, Peter. Sean's not our child, he's Tommy and Happy's, and that's what they want. Or at least, Happy does. She was adamant. She's out of it now; Frank gave her a triple dose of sedative. Tommy said . . . he said they'd do it day after tomorrow. He wants us to ask the new minister—"

"Fine. You ask the minister," Peter said. "I won't be here. You all do whatever you like with . . . him. Let Tommy O'Ryan have an old-fashioned wake, with all the trimmings, if he likes. Dance a jig."

"Where are you going?"

"Where do you think?" he said, and walked out the door and shut it behind him.

I leaped off the couch and ran after him, out into the rain. I caught him just as he cleared the path and turned onto the lane toward the yacht club. I spun him around by his shoulders.

"Peter," I said, "if you go off on that boat now, I will leave you and never come back. Do you hear me? If you go off on that boat now, I will not be here when you get back. And I never will again. And I mean that, before God."

"And where would you go, Maude?" he said. I could not see his face under the brim of his slicker hat.

"Home to Charleston," I said instantly, and in that moment knew I would. I had not called it home for many years, not even in my heart, but some long tap root must have remained; Belleau rose before my eyes, dreaming in the silence of the summer swamp, golden and whole and eternal. Kemble had not wanted it, after our father died, and had rented it to a doctor and his wife from Connecticut after he and Yolande Huger had moved into her parents' great old house on Legaré. I could go to Belleau, and I would; I was a creature of those swamps, that water, long before I became a creature of this bay. I might come near death from grief and loneliness without Peter, but I knew Belleau would sustain me. I would have no compunctions at all about ousting the Yankees from my old home.

"Would you do that?" Peter said wonderingly. "Would you, Maude?"

"You just try me and see," I said.

And so it was that on a bright-washed cool August day in the year 1961, Peter sat beside me in the little church overlooking Penobscot Bay, with all the colony and much of the village behind us and a stunned Happy and a white-faced Tommy O'Ryan in the pew ahead of us, and heard the new young minister pray.

"O merciful Father, whose face the angels of thy little ones do always behold in heaven, grant us steadfastly to believe that this child has been taken into the safekeeping of thine eternal love, through Jesus Christ our Lord, Amen."

I lifted my streaming eyes to Peter and saw his lips form the words, Mother, take care of him, and then he put his head in his hands and cried aloud. In all my life, I had never seen Peter do that, and I never did again.

Most of the congregation left after the service. Only a few remained with Happy and Tommy and Peter and me—Micah and Christina Willis, and Caleb, and the young minister, I think—when Sean Williams O'Ryan went down into the summer-warm earth beside Penobscot Bay, there to stay, as he had wanted to, forever.

Chapter Eleven

We all left Retreat after that. Though there were a couple of weeks of summer left, and Maude Caroline's camp was not over for another few days, Peter was gone from beside me the morning after Sean's funeral when I finally woke, aching and heavy and stiff as if I had been beaten, and I found him in the driveway loading the car. I took two cups of coffee and went out, the grass dew-sharp and cold on my bare feet. I saw, suddenly, what I had not noticed before: that somehow, in the week past, summer had died. There was a new steel-edged blue to the bay and the sky, and the barberry hedge was going scarlet in clumps, as was the rowan down the lane on the Compound lawn, and the bracken at the edge of the little birch wood behind the tennis court had turned its pale Florentine gilt. It would be an early winter on Cape Rosier, and a cold one.

"Are you going back to school, or are we all?" I said. I really did not know. After the funeral Peter had taken the *Hannah* out, and I had been finally fast asleep, fathoms deep in deathly weariness, when he returned. We had not talked since.

"I thought you'd probably want to come with me, and I can't stay," he said. He looked dreadful, gray all over, bloodless. His old mythic fire was out.

"No," I said. "I don't think I can either. It'll be better next summer, but this one is over. Let me go wake everybody and tell them."

"Happy and Tommy left an hour ago," Peter said. "I saw the car turning out of the lane when I came downstairs. Just as well. I couldn't have spoken to either of them. I've already called Petie and Sarah, and they're going to come down to Northpoint and get Maude Caroline and Sally. Let's just throw our clothes in the car and get out of here. Micah and Tina will close up, and I'll call about getting the *Hannah* wintered when we get home."

"Peter," I said hesitantly, "about Happy. . . . You can't cut her off now. Surely you see how badly she's hurting. Let's just try, darling: reach out some way, let her know she's not alone."

"She's not alone," he said. "She has Tommy. She has this brand new fruit of her singular womb. She has you. She's a long way from alone."

"Peter . . ."

"All right, Maude," he said, and his voice was dead and level. "I'll try. I'll do my best with her. But I've got to have some time first."

As if sensing the tenor of things with her father, Happy stayed away from us that fall. She did not even phone, which she had always done on weekends. When I called the little house in Saugus, she was polite, if subdued and weary-sounding, and did not mention her father except to ask after him perfunctorily. When I asked if she was all right she said yes; when I asked how her pregnancy was coming she said fine; when I asked after Tommy she said he was doing as well as he ever did. She did not ask to come for Thanksgiving or Christmas, and she did not mention any plans she and Tommy had for the holidays. When I asked when her child was due, she said only, "February," and when I suggested coming to be with her then, she said Tommy's sister from Chicago had volunteered to take her in her little city flat, and Tommy wanted that, so that's what she planned to do. Knowing a little of Tommy's malevolently ignorant clan on the South Side of Chicago, I cringed at the thought of Peter's and my grandchild coming into their superstitious and mean-spirited world. But I held my tongue. There was time to think what to do about that. I would figure a way.

It seemed to me that fall and winter as if we were proceeding with our lives via some prescribed set of external imperatives. It was as if there were some universally accepted manual for those who lived on after the death of a loved child, and we were trying our best to follow it as scrupulously as we could, all the while resolutely stopping our ears to the screams of rage and tearing pain and grief that flew about inside us like bats. I threw myself into my duties as chatelaine of Northpoint as I never had before, finding a kind of anodyne in motion and involvement, escaping anguish by the oiled wheels that seemed to bear me, machinelike, through the shortening days. Peter began, that autumn, a long-planned and often-delayed book, a memoir of his decades of ministering to the orderly boyhood of New England's privileged sons. It had a wry, graceful lightness to it, an affectionate but entirely unromantic vision of the boys who trooped and whooped through its pages, and I thought parents all over the Northeast would love it. Peter was a good writer, as he was most everything else he set his hand to, and nothing in the steadily mounting pile of pages that kept him late in his study every night would wound or threaten. It was as if, by holding many boys lightly in his mind and heart, he could

exorcise the pain of the one boy who lay heavily at
its core. Both of us worked prodigiously. After a few
weeks, both of us, I think, slept fairly well once
again. Our lives went forward, and if we did not hold
each other close for comfort, at least we stood shoulder to shoulder and looked outward. It was serving;
it would serve.

But sometimes . . . oh, sometimes, a pause would
come to each of us, and we would find ourselves still
and empty and caught without occupation, and we
would stop and stare blankly at nothing at all, and
we would have to think consciously then: What
next? What is the next step here? What would the
next action, thought, feeling be for someone whose
heart had not been burnt dead and cold with loss?
And when an answer came to us, that is what we
would do.

I did this many times that cold, dark autumn. I
know Peter did too. I saw it on his face and in his
stance, just as he must have in mine. In this way we
made our way toward Christmas.

On the sixteenth of December the telephone rang
late in the evening. I was sitting in front of the fire in
the den, feet up on the cracked old leather hassock,
reading over the guest list for the Christmas open
house following the choir's Festival of Carols and
Lights two days later, putting off leaving the warmth
of the small room and climbing the stairs into the
chilly dark of the second floor where our bedroom
was. It had been gray and marrow-chillingly cold for
weeks—I had been right about an early severe winter—
but so far no snow had fallen. Somehow the iron-
jawed dry black cold was worse than our customary
felted white winters. We had had a hard time heating
the big old house this year. I began to struggle out of
my nest of afghans to get up and answer the shrilling
bell, heard Peter pick it up, and sank back gratefully.

It would be for him anyway; the telephone pealed endlessly just before the long holidays.

I was frankly nodding over the *J*s when I heard the door to the den open, and when he did not speak, I looked up. He stood in the doorway in his old cardigan, holding on to the frame, his face bleached and stiff. I felt my lips make the word *what?* but heard no sound.

"That was Elizabeth Potter in Boston," he said, and his voice was thin and slow. "Amy died an hour ago. They think it was an aneurysm. She said she had a headache and lifted her hand to her head, and then she just . . . fell. She was dead when Elizabeth got to her. She wants us to come."

I began to cry. I got up and went upstairs and began to pack my bag, and then I packed one for Peter while he made the necessary telephone calls and arrangements, and I changed and sat on the side of the bed while he showered and dressed for the trip, and all the while I cried. I cried for the vibrant young woman with the wild curls and flushed cheeks who had borne me up through my first days in Retreat; I cried for the woman with the rich laugh who had had, in later years, precious few reasons to use it; I cried for the slender white-haired woman who had so recently sat on the beach in a red sun hat and laughed once more in pure joy for the love of her daughter. And I cried for myself, because who was there now in Retreat who would laugh like that with me, who would understand and grin when I made a face at the oldest ladies who colonized so fiercely the rockers on the clubhouse porch, who would understand, and smile an answering secret smile, when the sky over Penobscot Bay bloomed with the great fire of the midnight sun? Amy was dead, and with her a great slice of my personal history. Peter was my heart, but Amy was my girlhood.

We got to the town house on Endicott Street where Amy and Parker had moved, once they sold the huge old family house, just as a red dawn was flaming over the Charles. Elizabeth was out the door and into Peter's arms before we had mounted the hollowed marble steps. He held her silently while she wept, and his face was empty of everything but pity and a kind of focused calm. We had not talked much on the long drive from Northpoint, only a little about the early days of our marriage in Retreat, and Amy and Parker's, before things had gotten sad and frantic and ruined. But once he had said, "I'm going to have to do what I can for Elizabeth, Maude; you know Parker isn't going to be able to. She's probably going to lean on me. Are you going to mind?"

"Of course not," I said, and meant it. "It was only this summer, when everybody was starting to talk. . . . Oh, darling, of course not. If you can help her, do. Parker may not even know yet. But surely there are other relatives; I know Amy has family in Vermont somewhere, and it seems to me Parker had a brother who left the mill and went out west somewhere, and there are some cousins in Salem—"

"And when they get there, I'll be glad to let them take over," he said. "But please, until they do, just be patient. She's still very much a child under all that European froofraw."

And I smiled weakly and said, "Well, maybe *way* under," and he chuckled softly.

But when she came rocketing into his arms and buried her face in his neck and scrubbed it back and forth as I myself sometimes did, in affection or passion, something old and cold curled in my stomach and I had to force myself to put my own arms around her and gently disengage her from Peter and walk her back into the house. She was dressed only in a short peignoir of some green seafoamy stuff, over an even shorter nightgown, and her pink-brown nipples stood up in the cold. Her face was swollen and streaked, and her eyes were slitted with grief and a kind of desperate glitter, a wild anguish, almost a craziness.

"Come in the house, darling, and let's have some coffee and get a warm robe on you and see where we are," I said, and when we had wrapped her in her bathrobe and I had sat her down on the sofa in the living room and Peter had built up the fire, I wiped her face with a warm washcloth and smoothed back the wild red hair.

"Now," I said. "How is your father taking it? And what did the doctor say officially? I know you haven't had time to call any of your people, so we'll do that for you, I imagine your family uses Fitzgerald's; most of the old Boston families do. Can I call them for you and tell them what hospital she's in?"

Elizabeth looked at me, then at Peter. She got up from the sofa and went over to Peter, where he sat in a great Hepplewhite wing chair by the fire, and sat down on the floor beside him and wound her arms around his knees and laid her head on them.

"She isn't in any hospital," she said, and her voice was that of a small child, muffled and singsong. "She's in there on the floor in the den. I didn't call the doctor yet. I don't know any doctors here, and I didn't know what you were supposed to say. Daddy's still upstairs asleep. Or maybe drunk. Or maybe he's dead too. Warrie and his nanny are in the nursery on the third floor. They won't get up for hours. I waited until Peter got here; I knew he'd know what to do. I put a blanket over her, though. It's cold in the den, and I don't know where the thermostat is."

Peter and I looked at each other over her bent head. Amy must have lain there for hours; the call had come to Northpoint close to eleven.

"Sweetie, what have you been doing all this time?" I said. "Somebody has to know about your mother, you know that."

"Well, Peter's here now, and you," she said, still muffled in Peter's knees. "I didn't think anything would happen until it got light. I sat with her for a little while, but I got cold, so I came in here. I've been reading a little bit. And I had the radio."

I shook my head in despair and looked at Peter. He simply shook his head too. Then he lifted Elizabeth up and walked her to the sofa and sat her down beside me.

"Go up with Maude and get some clothes on, Punkin," he said. "I'll go tell your father, and then we'll get the doctor. We have to have her taken care of now. You know that, don't you?"

"What do you mean?" Elizabeth said, looking at him with her oblique eyes.

"The doctor will have to take her to the hospital and declare her—deceased, and then Fitzgerald's will have to get her ready for the services. We'll take care of all that, don't worry. All you need to do is tell Maude where your mother keeps her telephone and address book. You and your dad can tell us who to call, and we'll do that for you."

"You mean they're going to take her away?"

"They'll have to, darling, for a little while," I said. "It's the law."

"But then they'll bring her back?"

"Well . . . no, they'll let Fitzgerald's come and get her, and they'll handle things after that."

"You mean drain all her blood out and put make-up on her," Elizabeth said. Her voice was shrill.

"Honey," I began. It was hard to remember that this was a thirty-five-year-old woman.

"No," Elizabeth said.

"For her sake, Elizabeth, let us take care of her

decently now," I said. "You don't want people to come and see her lying on the floor."

"No!" Elizabeth cried.

"Elizabeth, this would distress your mother very much," I said, struggling to keep my temper. There was nothing in this fragmented child of the fearless, flame-touched sprite who had shimmered through those long-ago summers in Retreat.

"She of all people would want things to go smoothly so they didn't cause undue pain to other people. And I know she taught you that too."

She was on her feet in one fluid motion, the sheer layers of nylon swinging back from the supple nakedness that was still browned from the sun of the past summer and many others. She ran across the thick old Aubusson and planted her feet apart only inches from mine and looked down into my face. She was much taller than I; she had to bend.

"She never taught me that or anything else," she cried. "She never taught me how to live, and now she'll never teach me how to die! I hate her! I'm scared and I hate her! I don't know who's going to take care of me now!"

I reached up for her and she slapped me, hard, on my cheek and fled back to Peter and wrapped her arms around him once more.

"Don't you touch me!" she screamed. I stood shocked and numb, but I could hear the hysteria rising in her voice. I could not seem to move. Peter's face had whitened at her slap, and he held her away from him with both hands and looked intently at her.

"You are not to slap Maude ever again, Elizabeth," he said. "You have had a terrible shock and we understand that, but you will not slap anyone again. Now get hold of yourself and go with Maude and get some clothes on. We have a lot to do this morning, and your son will be waking up soon."

"No!" she shrieked. "I won't go with her! I won't go with anybody but you! I don't care about Warrie; his stupid nurse will take care of him. I want you, Peter! I want you to stay with me . . . stay with me . . . stay with me . . ."

The shrieks had fallen into a regular rhythm, and her face was bone-white, eyes closed, mouth squared like a wailing child's. Peter took a deep breath and slapped her smartly across the face, once on both cheeks, and the shrieking stopped on a long indrawn breath. She opened her eyes and looked at him.

"Now go with Maude," Peter said in a normal voice. "And stop this foolishness."

She stared at him for a long time, her chest heaving, and then turned and came to me and put her hand into mine and stood waiting.

"I should go to Amy," I said.

"No," Peter said. "Better let me do that. You'll want to remember her the way you said you saw her this summer on the beach, laughing in her red hat. Not like this."

"No," I said. "Not like this." And I took Elizabeth's hand and led her upstairs, so blinded by tears that I had to grope my way along the banisters with my free hand. I have always been grateful that Peter spared me that last sight of Amy Potter. He told me much later it was dreadful, but he never elaborated.

It was a very long day, endless. While Elizabeth dressed I went up to the nursery on the third floor and woke Warrie Villiers's mamselle and told her what had happened, and waited while she fluttered and chattered in her rapid-fire French, no doubt imprecating these barbarian New Englanders who had the audacity and sheer bad manners to die while she was under their roof. When she had dressed herself in layers of black silk and gone in to see to her small charge, I went back down to the second floor and looked in on Elizabeth. She was fully dressed, in a short, simple column of cream jersey that looked as if it had been poured over her from a pitcher, but she stood in her stocking feet, holding her pale kid high heels in one hand, staring out over the bare traceries of the treetops of Beacon Hill. I could hear that she was humming, tunelessly, and shut the door softly so that I would not disturb her and went in search of Parker Potter's room. I found him lying naked on his back, covers spilled onto the floor, motionless and pale and distended as a bloated fish in a tide pool and breathing with such stertorous gargles that I thought he too might be dying. An empty bottle of cognac lay on the beautiful thick carpet, stained now with the dried blood of many such bottles. The room smelt powerfully of liquor and sickness and unwashed body, and I walked back out and closed the door. Peter or some male relative was going to have to deal with Parker Potter. I knew I was looking my last on him, and that forever after that when I thought of him, it would not be that grinning, sly-faced young man with the flying red hair I had first met, but this husked, living corpse.

"Goodbye, Parker," I whispered, and went downstairs, where Peter was settling in at the tall Hepplewhite secretary for the first of the telephoning.

"You can count Parker out," I said. "Someone's going to have to put him in the hospital. I don't think he can get through today, much less a funeral."

"Dear Jesus," Peter said wearily. "What on earth is going to become of them? Who's going to look after Elizabeth and Warrie?"

"I suppose we could take them back with us for a while," I said reluctantly.

"No," Peter said, not looking up from his list. "That's not a good idea. Some of Amy's people will be here soon, or Parker's."

"But Peter, I don't think she even knows any of her relatives," I said. "She's been away since she left school. I never heard of any who were close to her."

"We are not an option for Elizabeth," he said, and something in his voice told me to drop it. I did.

A stooped old doctor came soon, and went into the den where Amy Potter lay, and came back out shaking his head.

"Aneurysm, sure enough," he said. "May have been there all her life. I'm sorry. I loved Amy Potter like a daughter."

And after he had been up to see Parker, he shook his head again and said, "I'm admitting him to Silver Hill this afternoon. The daughter signed the consent forms. It's very likely he won't come out. And he may never know Amy is gone. Will the daughter be staying on here, do you know? If she is, she'll need to see about setting up some kind of permanent arrangement with them for maintenance . . ."

"I doubt if she's up to that," Peter said. "When his brother and sister get here I'll turn things over to them; for now, I'll take responsibility for whatever has to be done. Our families were old friends. I'm Peter Chambliss—"

"Know who you are." The old man smiled. "Got a little dab of this and that stashed in your father's bank. I'll tell the hospital and Fitzgerald's and the Silver Hill people to talk to you."

All that day people came in and out of the narrow old house, while the pale lemon sunlight of that cold December gradually faded and snow clouds gathered. The dark, deferential young men from Fitzgerald's came and took Amy quietly away with them; I took Elizabeth into the kitchen, while they did that, and watched her pick at the toast and coffee a weeping cook prepared. Small Warrie, looking very French and formal in dark short pants and knee socks and a dark jacket, hovered silently beside his mother, his hands always somewhere on her flesh, his dark, slanted eyes fastened on her face. He was polite and silent and only spoke once in my hearing: "Are we going back to Paris, then, Mama?"

"No, hush, I don't know," Elizabeth said, smoking one cigarette after another, her eyes roving restlessly.

"Is it the end of our money?" he said.

"Certainly not, Warrie, don't be tiresome," she said dully. "Grandpa and Grandma have lots and lots of money. We certainly won't starve."

"But who will write the checks now that Grandma is dead?"

"I said we'll be all right. Go somewhere with Mamselle, why don't you? Go to . . . oh, go to the park. Ride the swan boats."

"Mama, it's cold out there."

"Then go upstairs and listen to your records! Mama is tired of your chatter and she is sad! Don't you know that Grandma is dead?"

"I'm sorry, Mama," the boy said softly, and my heart hurt for him. There must seem nowhere in this tall dark house—indeed, in this whole strange country to which his mother had fled with him—where a thin dark boy with too-old eyes was welcome.

"Maybe, when things calm down a little, you could come and play with my grandchildren," I said. "They live not far from here, out in Brookline. You met them last summer, up at your grandmother's house in Maine."

As soon as the words were out of my mouth, I wished them back. The likelihood of Sarah allowing Elizabeth Potter's child to play with small Sally was practically nonexistent. I had simply, in my fatigue and grief and pity, forgotten all that lay between Elizabeth and Petie.

"I really doubt that Sarah would find that appropriate,"

Elizabeth said, and even in her distraction and grief she smiled with something near enjoyment.

"I thought that boy fell into the water," Warrie Villiers said. "Mother said he did, and I would not see him any more."

"That was my other grandchild," I said through pain. "I have two more."

By late afternoon all the Potter and Bartlett kin were gathered in the drawing room, and arrangements for a quiet funeral were under way. Elizabeth sat in her cream and gold, nestled as close to Peter as she could get, and listened remotely as the talk of the orderly tending of the privileged dead washed around the room. Night drew down, and the old servants closed the curtains and brought the drinks tray and answered the softly chiming doorbell, to receive the cards and armfuls of hothouse flowers and the occasional friend close enough to mingle with the family. To all of them, Elizabeth bent her sleek red head and murmured her thanks and suffered her high cheekbones to be kissed, and said no, she did not yet know what her plans were, and yes, it was a mercy her mother hadn't suffered. She did all this from Peter's side. When he got up to go into the kitchen, she followed him; when he went into the downstairs bathroom, she followed him with her eyes. After several hours of this, I saw eyebrows began to rise and a few swift looks exchanged among the women, and once I interrupted a whispered conversation in the conservatory. Weariness and a kind of dull resentment weighed me down. We had been up all night and all this day; both of us needed sleep. We needed to get out of this dim house of death and go out to Petie and Sarah in Brookline and sleep long and deep in the vast upstairs bedroom they kept for us. But how to disengage Peter from Elizabeth Potter's bottomless need?

I was just about to broach the subject aloud when I saw Elizabeth's head go up, and something like deliverance flare in her brown eyes, and an actual radiance flood her face. Following her gaze, I saw that Petie and Sarah stood in the doorway to the drawing room in their coats and boots, a powdering of new snow on their shoulders and the soft-footed old butler behind them. Sarah, her dark hair ruffled from the scarf she had flung over it and her snub nose reddened with cold, smiled faintly and waved at Peter and me, and then started toward Elizabeth. Petie stood still, staring across the room at her. I read his face and felt cold fear flood me. It was the old look, the one I remembered from that awful time in their adolescence: pure, naked, living wanting. Elizabeth jumped up from beside Peter and ran past Sarah and her outstretched hands and straight into Petie's arms, and I saw rather than heard her lips form the words, into his neck, "Oh, Petie, help me," and felt in my very bones, rather than heard, his answer: "I'm here. I will."

After that, through that evening and the next day, through the morning of the funeral and the funeral itself, through the small gathering in the town house afterward and the night after that, through Peter's and my frowning looks and then admonitions and then outright warnings and Sarah's white-faced silence and then inconspicuous departure from the Endicott Street house, Petie tended his old love with his whole heart and his constant presence, and nothing—not the tears in Sarah's voice on the telephone that I could not help overhear, not the closed faces and lifted brows of all Elizabeth's kin, not the hissed, whispering argument with his father that I heard from the kitchen of the Potter house—could move him. When Peter and I went to his and Sarah's house in Brookline to spend a final night he was not there, and Sarah was shut up in her room and would not talk to us, and when we got up the next morning he had not come in. I got breakfast for the children while Peter, grim-faced, went over to the town house on Endicott Street to have it out with his son, only to find Petie getting into a taxi with a pale, fur-coated Elizabeth and a silent Warrie, and when he asked where they thought they were going, it was Elizabeth who said, "Back to Italy, Peter. Petie is taking us to the airport." Petie said nothing at all. Elizabeth kissed Peter softly on the mouth.

"Thank you," she said. And then they were gone.

Peter came back to the Brookline house to wait for his son, and presently, when Petie got out of the taxi and came into his silent house his round face was so drained and blasted that Peter had not the heart, after all, to excoriate him.

"Sarah is upstairs," he said quietly. "She's not in very good shape."

"I know," my son said. His voice was dead. "I'm sorry, Dad, Mom. I'm going to fix it now, if I can."

"Is it over?" I said. I was beyond feeling.

"Yes," Petie said.

But it was not over. Just after the New Year dawned, Sarah called us in Northpoint, her voice so thick with crying that at first I could not understand her, and told us that Petie was up in Retreat with Elizabeth, holed up in Braebonnie. She found out when Micah Willis saw lights in the Potter cottage and called Peter and me to see if we knew who might be in residence there and, failing to reach us, called Sarah and Petie in Brookline and talked to Sarah. Sarah knew instantly and viscerally that Petie was not at an American Bankers Association meeting in New York, as he had said; she called Braebonnie and got Elizabeth Potter, who laughed but did not deny that Petie was with her. Petie himself would not come to the telephone. He had been gone three days by then. She was certain Elizabeth had been drunk when she called.

"Please, please, Grammaude," Sarah sobbed. "Please go get him. He'll listen to you when he won't anybody else. He's drunk, or crazy, or something. If you don't I can't stay with him any more, and what will happen to my children? Please help me."

We went. There was never any choice about that.

My heart had always lightened as the car turned east from Northpoint, onto the wandering little blacktop that would take us, ultimately, over the border into Maine. But on this bleak, ashen morning it lay stonelike in my chest, as if Peter and I were driving to attend a dying. And perhaps we were, I thought; the dying of my son's marriage, and his place in the world our family had always known: the world of orderliness and rules, the world of accountability. Outside that world lay wildness. I knew about that wildness, perhaps better than anyone in Petie's ken, but Petie himself knew virtually nothing of it except those brief years so long ago when he had stumbled after Elizabeth Potter in her molten wake, and he had been burned so badly by it I had thought he abjured it forever. Poor Petie, perhaps he had thought so too. But Elizabeth was wildness itself, and when he had come within her range, even after all these years, she had toppled his towers with one sentence. I had no idea, on that long and largely silent drive through winter-locked Maine, whether I could prevail against that power.

Peter drove steadily, so locked within himself that I rarely spoke to him. What, after all, was there to say? Once, he turned his head to me and said, "What is going to become of our children, Maude? Is all of this our doing? What could we have given them that we didn't? What can we give them now?"

There had been snow, finally; it lay in great gray-blue banks along the highway, where the plows had pushed it, and on fields and rocks and the boulder-strewn shore below the Camden Hills. The islands were all blue and black and white, and the small bays and inlets themselves were blue-shadowed white: ice beneath snow. I have never seen such a blue as the snow blue of Maine. The cold light threw Peter's face into sharp relief and backlit the networks of fine lines around his eyes and mouth and on his forehead. His fair hair was more silver in that northern light than gilt. Peter was sixty years old that year, and looked to me, for the first time, every moment of it and more. I felt tears come into my eyes.

I had some ideas about what we had not given Happy and Petie and what we might attempt to give them now, but I did not speak of them. Now was not the time, not with the man I loved most and longest in the world beside me in his pain and defeat. If we could win Petie back, then would be the time for Peter and me to talk of compensatory palliatives for him. As for Happy, I did not think anything could heal or change her. I reached over and touched Peter's cheek.

"There are a great many things our children must do for themselves, that they have not or cannot do yet," I said. "They either will or they won't. Don't go borrowing guilt, darling."

"I wonder if anything could have made a difference to Elizabeth," he said.

"Nothing but Parker, and it's decades too late for that," I said. "Peter, dearest, when we have Petie back—and we will—you're going to have to cut Elizabeth loose from our family. There isn't any help for her in us, and there's nothing but grief for us in her. You do know that, don't you."

"Oh, yes," Peter said. "I know that."

We came to South Brooksville at midafternoon. A new little inn had opened there the summer before, and though it was closed in the winter months, Peter had called ahead and obtained the promise of a room to be opened for us and a fire lit in the fireplace. The innkeepers, an interchangeable pair of chic middle-aged men in narrow blue jeans and sweaters that spoke of Abercrombie and Fitch, said our room was at the top of the stairs, there was a space heater and some additional quilts, and we might share their early breakfast of tea and toast but no other food could be provided. They were, they said, on their way to an estate sale in Castine and would see us, perhaps, in the morning. Otherwise we could leave payment on the kitchen table.

"Are you always so trusting?" I said pleasantly.

"Hardly ever," one of them said. "In fact we wouldn't have opened for you at all except that Micah Willis came by and put a deposit down. Everyone around here knows the Willises."

"Most know the Chamblisses too," Peter said tightly, and the pair tossed their heads in tandem and went out, leaving us to the chilly comfort of a small, low-ceilinged room with a sputtering fire, three thin gray blankets, a scuttle of coal on the hearth, and a bathroom at the opposite end of the hall. But the view out of the small-paned window over Bucks Harbor was breathtaking, a woodcut in blacks and grays and smoke blues and the white of fine rag paper. A white ghost of a quarter moon hung in the tender blue over Harbor Island.

"Cold Comfort Farm," Peter said, piling coal onto the fire. "I'd counted on something hot to eat. We'll just have to nip instead."

And he produced a bottle of good old brandy from his suitcase, and poured some for me into the tooth-brush glass, and took a neat swig himself from the bottle. I sipped, and warmth curled into the cold hollow at my core.

"I'll bet Tina and Micah would feed us," I said. "I'll call them from downstairs. We can't go over to Retreat on empty stomachs. Lord, Peter, it's a totally different world, isn't it? I didn't expect it to look like it does in the summer, of course, but this is . . . implacable. Outside human ken, somehow. It's almost frightening."

"It's beautiful," Peter said, staring out at the fast-falling blue dusk. "I never thought much about insulating the cottage before, but it would be something to be able to stay up here occasionally in the winter. The Potters used to do it, you know."

I thought of Braebonnie, and how it must look in all that empty blue: a lightship, a fortress lit against the cold and endless night. A fortress where two errant children played corrupted games in a world of pure inhuman white. . . .

"We should go," I said. "We'll stop at the Willises on the way. Let's just get it done."

"I don't want you to come with me, Maude," Peter said, not turning from the window. "I want you to stay here where it's warm, at least until I see the lay of the land. I want to handle this myself; I've let you carry the load with Petie far too long. This may be very unpleasant, and it's mine to do."

"Do you think I've never handled unpleasantness?" I cried, stung. "He's my son; I know him better than anyone else—"

"Precisely," Peter said. "He is now going to get to know his father."

"Are you going to be hard on him?" It was a stupid thing to say. Did I expect that we were up here to coax and coddle Petie home?

"Hard enough to get done what has to be done," Peter said. "Hard enough so that he knows once and for all that I care very much what happens to him. Don't fight me, Maude. I'll call on you if I need you."

"All right," I said weakly, suddenly hating the thought of the empty hours ahead of me in that stark room, hung in the air over no landscape that I knew. And then, "But let me call Micah. He could go with you."

"No." Peter looked levelly at me, two hectic red spots on his high cheekbones. "He could not. Call him if you like; he and Tina will give you some supper. But I don't want Micah Willis to help me get my boy home."

He kissed me on the cheek and went out the door and closed it. I heard his footsteps echo on the old steps, and the front door of the inn open and shut again, and, in a moment, the car engine start. And then there was silence. I brought the brandy bottle and glass and put it on the bedside table, and wrapped myself in the three blankets, and stretched out on the bed to read my paperback and wait for my husband to bring my son to me. I have seldom felt so alone in my life. I have seldom felt so heavily, hopelessly sad.

I must have dozed, despite the discomfort of the thin mattress and the scratchy blankets, because when the knock at the door waked me, the fire had all but burned itself out, and the square of the window was full black and pricked with stars. The room was cold; the floor numbed my stockinged feet as I ran across it and threw the door open. Peter, I said with my heart and head, but it was not Peter who stood in the door. It was Christina Willis, and she was smiling and holding out her arms. I ran into them with a little wail of disappointment, mingled with sheer gratitude at her solid, comforting presence. Her heavy sheepskin coat was cold from the night air, and her cheek, as she pressed it to mine, was icy, but her arms and voice were warm.

"I'm some mad at you for not letting us know you were here," she said, pulling me up to the guttering fire. "Sitting in the dark and cold when I've had a leg of lamb roasting for you and Peter for hours, and good red wine open. . . . Come on, get your coat and boots and let's get out of this disgraceful garret and home by the fire. I wonder those two fancy boys ever make a dime, the way they treat their guests."

"Tina, I can't leave, Peter could be back any minute—" I began, and then stopped. How much did she know about what was transpiring at Braebonnie, or how much had she guessed? There was little that Micah and Tina Willis did not know about us by now, but this . . . this was a special pain, a special shame. I did not think Peter would want me to speak of it.

She looked at me, her smooth face as serene as ever, but her eyes were soft with pity.

"Peter called Micah a little while ago," she said gently. "He asked us to come get you and give you some supper and a bed for the night; he's going to stay at Braebonnie until morning. I gather Petie is . . . he doesn't want to leave, and Elizabeth is pretty drunk and near hysterical. Peter said he could handle it, but it's going to take a good while yet."

"Oh, Tina, I'll have to go," I cried, reaching for my coat.

"No. He said absolutely not. He made us promise, Maude. And we agree, Micah and I. It's no place for you tonight. What needs to be done in that house needs to be done by Peter and his son. Please let it be that way."

I started to flare up; what did she know of me and my son, of the long bond between us and the pain of this terrible winter rendezvous? And then I thought of the years of pain that she and Micah had borne while Caleb wandered in his own wilderness, and of the hard peace to which they had won through. Christina Willis knew. Tiredness and a kind of heavy peace flooded into me.

"All right," I said. "Okay. I'll be very glad to get out of here. I've felt like the Snow Queen in her prison, up here above all the cold and the blue."

"I feel that way from November to April." She laughed, and we went out together into the vast night.

Tina and Micah Willis lived in a neat, pretty Dutch Colonial directly on the road a half mile above the entrance to Retreat. Behind it lay a garden and salt meadow, snow-covered, and then a small stand of fir and birches, and beyond that the boathouse and the beach and the bay. Everything was silent, silvered by the thin young moon.

I had always wondered about the houses of the natives of Cape Rosier; with all the empty and spectacular shoreline, they invariably sat within three or four strides of the pitted blacktop road, with their great barns connected by covered walkways beside or behind them. But on this night I understood. The new snow, three or four feet deep and even more where it drifted against houses and piled stone walls, was impassable except where it had been shoveled. No one down on the shore, once snowed in, could dig their way to the road. They would be imprisoned until a plow could come, or a thaw. I thought of the narrow lanes of Retreat and wondered if two cars sat on the road in the moonlight, at the entrance by the weathered oar, and if two sets of footsteps had broken the diamond-white surface of the snow, along with those of partridges and foxes and hares, until this last fall had buried them? How would Peter get in?

As if in answer to my unasked question, Christina said, "Micah took Peter in on Caleb's old snowshoes. He's okay. Micah came back as soon as he saw Peter clear the porch. He's going to send Enoch Carter with the plow in the morning. Then they'll all be able to come out."

"*Will* they all come out, do you think, Tina?" I said.

"Oh, ayuh," she said calmly. "I reckon they will."

"There's not much you don't know about us, you and Micah. I wonder sometimes you bother with us."

"You're worth bothering about, Maude. You're one of the few who are," Tina Willis said, smiling at me. She must be older than me by a decade, at least, I thought, but in the green light from the old Volvo's sturdy dash I could see clearly the young wife I had first known, the fair girl, as placid and deep as a pond of clear water, that Micah Willis had married.

"If you can say that after tonight, you're a better woman than I would be," I said, sudden bitter tears in my nose and throat. "My son isn't much of a man tonight."

"My son is alive because of you," she said. "He had his bad patch, just like your Petie is having, and he found himself a snug harbor. But he wouldn't have been alive to do it if you hadn't been there the day he cut his foot so fierce. It's not the least of the reasons I think you're worth bothering about, but it's the first. I think you may be the only ones of the summer complaints I do think that about, though, you and Peter. There were a few others, but mostly they've died."

I reached over and squeezed her hand on the wheel, and she took it off and squeezed mine back. The door of the great barn was open and we drove in, and she shut the door and we ran through the dark connecting hallway, piled with boots and snowshoes and trunks and lawn furniture, and into a great terra-cotta-tiled kitchen where a fire roared on an open hearth, and cherrywood chairs stood around a polished table in the center of the room, and a deep-cushioned sofa and chairs made a grouping in a corner by the fireplace, and Micah Willis in a handsome icelandic sweater and corduroys stood at a modern range carving a crusty brown joint of lamb into thin pink slices. I could have wept at the warmth, and the smell of garlic and basil and red wine, and the sheer dark safe bulk of him. He held out one arm and I ran into it and he kissed me on the cheek, still brandishing the knife in the other hand.

"Come in the house, summer lady," he said, in the rich voice that, it seemed, had stood in my ears since last summer. "Do you know that you've never been here before?"

"Oh, Micah, I must have, in all those years," I said.

"Nope. We always came to Liberty. It didn't matter then and it doesn't now; your mother-in-law could only bend just so far. But I'm glad to welcome you. It's our turn and some past."

He poured red wine for us into thin old crystal glasses, and we sat on the sofa before the fire and drank it and I looked around the room. It was the room of cultivated people; I had been in many like it at Northpoint and in Boston: rich with books and beautiful, fragile things on shelves, and warmed by firelight dancing on polished old wood and brass and silver. Oriental rugs worn thin and silky stood in pools on the floor, and plants and flowers, kept carefully away from drafty doors and windows, stood on tables and in deep Italian pots. A small spinet stood in a corner, with Christina's violin lying on top of it, and a good phonograph and what seemed hundreds of records occupied its own wall unit. I remembered that Micah had said that both his and Tina's fathers had been in the China trade; relics of that rich era stood all about the room. It was much more than a kitchen, it was the heart of this house, and the heart of what was, I saw suddenly, a rich and complicated and very complete life that Micah and Christina lived together. A thing entirely separate from what I knew of their summer lives; another universe entirely. I could not name the feeling that drifted like smoke to the surface of my consciousness: a kind of envy? A wistfulness?

"This is a glorious room," I said. "I don't know

why it's such a surprise: I guess I'm used to thinking of Maine in terms of Retreat, of summer, wicker and rattan and shabby old porches. It's a very shortsighted way to look at it. I always thought of Retreat as the real world; I'd wait all year, through all the seasons in Northpoint, to get back to the real world. And I never knew, all that time, that when the summer was over, there was still, for you all . . . all this."

"For us," Christina Willis said, "the real world starts when all of you leave. This is our real world."

She looked over at Micah and then at me and smiled.

"You can have two real worlds," she said. "You just can't have them at the same time. My real world and yours . . . they can stand side by side, but they can't mingle. It doesn't make either of them any less real or valuable. Only separate."

She knows, I thought suddenly. She knows about Micah and me—whatever there is to know—and she always has. I wonder if she minds. Somehow I don't think so. She said it herself: *They can stand side by side, but they can't mingle.*

Micah's eyes were on me, dark and unreadable and steady, the look I had seen a hundred times before, the look on which I had leaned over a score of summers, that had borne me up as surely as a rock or a tree.

"Peter is doing the right thing tonight, Maude," he said. "He's got the strength for it, and it's his to do. Not yours this time. Lean back and let him do it and let us take care of you for a spell. It'll come right. There isn't much that doesn't look better in the morning."

I thought, suddenly, of that long-ago dawn after the endless night of the intruder that we still thought to be a German spy. Micah Willis had come that morning too, and things did indeed look better when he did.

"Do you still have your chinquapin?" I said.

"Ayuh." He grinned. "Wouldn't part with that."

"You two are demented," Tina Willis said equably, and brought the platter of lamb and browned potatoes to the table, and I was surprised to find, after all, that I was very hungry indeed.

After supper we watched a little flickering, utterly inane television from Bangor, and Micah played some records—the Brandenburgs, and the Goldberg Variations—and Christina played a few old French folk songs on her violin. But we did not talk much. Until the knock came that brought Peter and Petie with it—or brought whatever there was to come out of Braebonnie—there simply did not seem anything to say. I had thought I would stay awake, would sit up on the couch and wait, would not, could not sleep, but at midnight Micah leaned over and touched my hand and said, "It won't help either of them to have you dead on your feet, and they can't come out until dawn at any rate. Come on to bed, Maude. I promised Peter we'd see you got some sleep. Tina's made up Caleb's old room for you. You'll see the prettiest sunrise in the world over the bay."

"Peter might call—"

"He said not. He said to tell you not to expect a call. And not to call there either. You don't want to talk to Elizabeth, I can promise you, Maude. From what he told me, she's not got hardly an oar in the water right now. Never did have, if you ask me. Bad trouble she is and was, bad trouble for somebody she always will be. I doubt if it will be the Chamblisses after this night, though. Peter had a look in his eye I'd not like to meet on a dark night. Come, now."

And he took my hand, and I rose and followed him down the hall to where Tina was folding back drifts and shoals of down comforters on a pretty, carved sleigh bed, in a room that looked as if it might have been a page torn from a book of old Scandinavian woodcuts. I undressed and stood still and let Tina drop one of her long full-yoked flannel nightgowns over my head, and when I had crawled under the covers, both Willises kissed me on the cheek and bade me good night.

"Call me if anything happens," I mumbled, feeling sleep rising to take me under like a tide.

"I will," Micah said.

And Christina said, "Pancakes and maple syrup for breakfast," and they turned off the lamp, and the room and I slid together into darkness. I did not turn, and I did not dream.

I opened my eyes when I felt a weight fall on the edge of the bed, and it was full morning. Snow light stippled the ceiling. Peter was there. His face was stubbled with fine gold, and his clothing was rumpled and stale, and he simply sat, staring, his gray eyes focused on nothing at all. Haunted eyes. He felt my eyes on him and turned to me.

"Peter," I whispered. I was terribly afraid. His eyes were terrible.

"Petie is on the train from Ellsworth," he said, and his voice was hoarse and weak, as if he had been speaking, or shouting, all through the night. "I put him on it myself, at five this morning. Sarah will meet him. Elizabeth is in our room at the inn. Micah will drive her to the train in an hour or so. She's going back to Boston, and then to Italy."

"Peter, how—"

"Later, Maude," he said. "Later. Please."

"Is she really going back to Italy?"

"If I have to put her on the plane myself."

"Peter . . . do you really think it's over now?"

"Yes," he said.

Chapter
Twelve

The weather was wild and strange the year my granddaughter Darcy was born. If I had been a wiser woman, or the wild one the colony thought I was when I first went there as a bride, I might have read the portents. But I was neither of those. I never was.

It was mid-February when tiny Darcy Chambliss O'Ryan came roaring into the world, but the air outside the window at Brigham and Women's, where she lay with her mother, was as soft as May and freighted with the smells of spring. I opened one of Happy's windows halfway, to let in the strange freshness, and caught the unmistakable smell of the Low Country river swamp in first bloom; I could not imagine what sly green wind had borne it all this long frozen way. I closed my eyes for a moment, transported, giddy and homesick. It was like a benediction on my new granddaughter's red head, a blessing from my faraway people to her. Poor mite, she had need of blessings.

A nurse came bustling in and tut-tutted and closed the window.

"February air on a newborn? Really, Mrs. O'Ryan,"

she said to Happy, who merely looked back at her dully. Happy had hardly moved since they had brought squalling red Darcy to her, and she had not spoken at all. She could not or would not nurse, either; Darcy got her first sustenance in life in strange arms, from a bottle. And when the baby was put into Happy's arms, she merely let her lie there. If Tommy O'Ryan had not leaped to catch his daughter, I think she would have rolled to the floor. I knew then that something was badly askew with Happy, but it was not until she looked dreamily out at the bare winter branches outside her window and said, "The fall colors are really pretty this year, aren't they?" that her doctor grew alarmed and brought in a psychiatrist. Happy went into the psychiatric wing of the hospital with severe postpartum neurosis that afternoon, and Darcy, when she was able to leave the hospital, came home with me and a nurse to Northpoint. And Tommy O'Ryan, for once subdued and visibly worried about his child, came each weekend and stayed in our guesthouse at the bottom of the garden, to be near her. Even Peter could not object to that. He simply went in on Saturdays and Sundays to his office at the school, and Tommy prudently arranged his hours with his daughter during the daytime and spent his evening hours bragging about her in the taverns along Water Street. I don't think he and Peter met more than once that entire winter and spring.

Tommy O'Ryan had done many things that disgusted and outraged me, and he would doubtless do others, but he went a long way, that strange soft winter, in redeeming himself in my eyes. He sat for hours in Darcy's nursery, rocking her and singing to her in a silvery Irish tenor that proved to be as irresistible as his speaking voice, and he could soothe and quiet her as no one else: not me, not her phlegmatic German nurse, and not Peter, on the rare occasions that he picked her up. He was the first to point out that except for her silky thatch of curly, blazing red hair, she was the image of me, and after that, even I saw it and could not help being charmed by it.

"It's powerful blood you have, you and Peter," Tommy said. "First the boy, who was the picture of Peter, and now this scrap, who is you all over and no mistake. All there is of me is the hair, and just as well. I'm only hoping this one has your kindness, Maude. And your backbone."

"Oh, Tommy, there's more of you in her than that," I protested, laughing. "Listen to her voice. Pure Irish blarney. Even when she cries you can hear the Aeolian harps. None of that Chambliss New England *whonk* through the nose, for which I am eternally thankful."

"And I am that for you," he said, and I thought he meant it. "I couldn't have handled the baby by myself. I don't even know if I can look after Happy when she comes home. I never meant my family to be a burden on you, and that's the God's truth, even though I don't think Peter is ever going to believe that."

"Give him a little time, Tommy," I said. "He had a bad time with his son this winter, and now his daughter's in a psychiatric hospital. There's always been a kind of darkness in Peter's side of the family, and it frightens him when he thinks he sees it in one of his children, let alone both. When he sees that this thing with Happy is hormones and not heredity, he's going to feel a lot better. And I think he likes having Darcy here, whether or not he lets on."

And I think that he did. The first thing Peter did when he came in on weekday evenings was to go upstairs to Darcy's nursery and look in on her. She would have had her bath and her bottle by then, and was fresh and dewy and flushed, with her gold-red hair peaking in damp little whorls on her head and her great pansy eyes wide with interest. I would follow Peter and take Darcy from Fräulein Schott and send her down for her dinner, and would settle with the wriggling little bundle into the old rocking chair that had been Mother Hannah's, beside the nursery fire, and rock and sing to her. Darcy would crow and pump her arms and legs, and Peter would laugh and touch her silky cheek, or the soft spot on her head and go down and make us cocktails, and we would have them there in the gathering dusk, with the newest of the Chamblisses. "The next of us," as Peter put it. I could see that Darcy charmed Peter with the same tools that Sean had employed: laughter, fearlessness, a sort of cockeyed baby wit that burst out at odd intervals. And there was a plus: "It's like looking at you when you were a baby," he said. "It's like being given the gift of all of you, not just you from seventeen on."

But he would not often hold her or rock her. And he did not stay long in the nursery after he had checked in with her. Peter had given his heart away to one laughing baby. He was not going to do it again.

Happy came home from the hospital in an April week that was as gray and bone-sucking as February should have been, with no tender green haze at all on the trees and the cold of iron in the earth. I pleaded with her to come to us and let us and Fräulein take care of her and Darcy for a while longer, but she was implacable. Tommy took Darcy home the next weekend, his handsome face furrowed with doubt and worry, and the best Peter and I could do was insist that Fräulein stay for a week in the little house in Saugus and pay her ahead of time for that. I wept when Tommy took the baby from me, wrapped like a little Chinese child in layers of lacy-knit white, and handed her in to Fräulein in the clunking, fin-freighted Plymouth Fury he had bought years before. It was like handing away a piece of myself, a portion of my own flesh. Even Peter's eyes glittered, and he turned abruptly away.

"Take care of her, Tommy," I whispered. "Please, if you need us at all—"

"I'll do my best, Maude," he said, and there was nothing in that moment of bravado in his voice. Only worry, only doubt. "Maybe when things settle down Happy will see that she needs some help. . . ."

But Happy did not. Whether she settled down we could not say, for we did not hear from her for a long time after that, but Tommy called to say that she had dismissed Fräulein after two days and hired a woman from down the street with whom she had become friendly to come every day and help her tend Darcy.

"I'm not liking the smell of it, Maude," Tommy O'Ryan said. "Florrie Connaught has a kind enough heart, but she's big as the side of a barn and not on the best of terms with soap and water, and she and Happy watch television from the time she comes in in the morning to the time she leaves, just before supper. And I don't know for sure, but I think she nips a bit. I've smelt it on her when I come in. At least, I hope it's her. I can't have Happy nippin' along with her, not with the little one in the house."

"No, of course not," I said, and after that I kept tiny tiny Darcy O'Ryan in my heart as I had not had another child since Petie. Her gamin face and three-pointed kitten's smile and flaming head were never out of my mind, nor was my worry for her.

"I wish we could get her away from Happy somehow, just until she's old enough for school," I said to Peter once that spring.

"You really think your own daughter can't raise her child?" he said.

"I wish I thought she could, but I'm just not sure."

"Relax, love," he said, kissing me on the forehead. "Kids are tougher than you think. They're more resilient than adults; I see it every day."

There was a time you didn't see it at all, I thought. You didn't see that famous resilience in your own children, because it wasn't there. What do you think we're talking about now?

But I let it go. Peter was nearing the end of his book and was more distracted and fragmented than I had ever seen him before. When it was over, perhaps by midsummer, he could relax, and we would have the long, sweet days in Retreat, and then we would begin to sort it out, this endless dilemma of our children and theirs. . . .

For the first time in my life, I went to Retreat alone that summer. I had known for weeks that I would and had not been bothered by the prospect. I often stayed alone in Liberty, now that the children were grown, and Peter sometimes came only for weekends or a week or so at summer's end. I had not thought I would be lonely. There had never been a time that the wildness and grandeur of Cape Rosier, the wild, rich life of the woods and fields and ledges and the cold sea itself, the sheer intricacy and primal smoothness of the rhythms of each summer day, had not engaged and filled me. I could not imagine a time when all that was Maine would fail to sustain me.

But that summer I was lonely. It took me almost a week of restless wandering and broken sleep to figure it out: there was no one within hundreds of miles who needed me. Peter was fully occupied with the closing pages of his book and the summer life of the school and was cared for by Mrs. Craig, our housekeeper, and Craig, her husband. Petie and Sarah had parked the children with the doting Forbeses at their Santa Fe retreat and gone off for two months' healing

hiatus in Jamaica. Happy would not part with Mrs.
Connaught and her soap operas and bring Darcy to
Retreat, and Kemble and Yolande, who had long
planned a visit from Charleston this July, bought
instead an old house on Sullivan's Island and began a
lengthy renovation there. Amy was newly gone and
Braebonnie stood shuttered and dark for the first time
in my memory, and Peter's *Hannah* and Sean's
Osprey lay shrouded on blocks in Micah's boathouse,
and even Gretchen Winslow had gone abroad with
Freddie and Julia and their families. I had waited all
my adult life for this moment of perfect freedom in
Retreat, and now everywhere I drifted in that foggy
green June, only the soft footsteps of my dead went
with me.

Even Micah and Christina Willis were absent. It
was their forty-fifth wedding anniversary that June,
and Micah had taken Tina on a long-promised trip
across Frenchman's Bay, in Bar Harbor, out into the
wild blue Atlantic and east to Nova Scotia, where she
had Duschesne kin she had not seen since she was a
child. Caleb had sent his stepdaughter from Bucksport,
a thin, closed-faced teenager named Ruby, to open
Retreat and "do for me" if I wished, but I soon felt her
dark presence in Liberty like a low-lying cloud, and
paid her for the month and sent her on her way,
assuring her that I could perfectly well attend to my
own small wants. And after that I was as alone, even
with the usual summer back-and-forth visiting for
cocktails and the meetings at the general store, as if I
had no kin upon the face of the earth.

This is what it would be like here if I were a
widow, I thought, seeing in my mind's eye the frail
old ladies at whom Amy Potter and I had giggled,
clinging together in their fierceness and fussiness in
the prized rockers on the porch of the yacht club. I
would never, I thought, laugh at them again.

I kept my voice light when I talked to Peter most evenings, but finally one Sunday, when we had had five straight days of fog that pressed itself against the windows like a great, blinded face and I had seen no one and heard nothing but the incessant booming of the fog buoy off Head of the Cape, I broke down.

"I'm so lonely I think I'm going to die, Peter," I half wept. "I'm ashamed of myself, but I am. I never realized how much of the magic of this place rode on you and the children."

He was silent for a moment, and then he said, "Maude, what would you think about a place on Winnipesaukee? There's a great old house on Weirs Beach coming on the market; Gordon Wells told me about it. I thought I might run up and take a look. It's at most two hours from our front door; I could get there after school in time for a sail before supper every day, and you could run in to see the kids whenever you wanted to. It's making better and better sense, with me working the hours I do."

"Oh, Peter . . . leave Retreat?" I could not take in his words.

"It just seems to me we're drifting away from it," he said slowly. "It's harder and harder for me to get there, and the kids aren't coming so much, and you're feeling so lonely and blue. . . ."

"Peter, it's . . . a part of us," I said. "Retreat is part of who we are. I don't think we could just—what, sell it? Rent it?"

"There's not much for me there now, Maude," Peter said in a soft, dull voice, and I knew he was seeing again the empty slip in the storm-tossed harbor where Sean's *Osprey* should have bobbed, and did not, and winter lights in Braebonnie where no lights should have shone.

"There will be again, darling," I said. "Just wait until the book is done and you're back and out on the

Hannah in the sun, with all the time in the world ahead of you. I shouldn't have laid all this on you. It's just the damned fog; we've been socked in for days."

"Well, think about it," he said. "Will you do that for me?"

And I promised that I would, and I did just that. I took a sandwich and a glass of milk and went to bed, closing the shutters against the face-pressing fog and the banshee weeping of the buoy, and I thought about summer nights on another shore. Could I leave Liberty and Retreat? In the middle of that long white haunted night, it began to seem to me that perhaps, after all, I could, if Peter went with me.

I woke to a blazing blue morning and a rattling in the big fireplace that meant a fire being laid, and smelled fresh coffee, and ran in my flannel nightgown into the living room, to find Micah dusting birch bark off his hands and whistling "The Road to the Isles." He wore the striped jersey and old white pants that meant he was going sailing, and I could have wept with the rightness of him, solid and brown as ever in my cold living room. Flames leaped on the hearth and steam coiled out of the mug of coffee that he held out to me, and I simply grinned at him and took the coffee.

"Did you bring the sun, or did it bring you?" I said, after I had drunk half the mug. The world had transmuted itself again in an eye blink, and the thought of leaving Retreat was as ridiculous as the notion of colonizing Saturn. Why had I thought it was necessary to be needed incessantly to be content? Surely, simply *being* was enough.

"Followed it all the way west from Grand Manan," Micah said. "I think all the fog in the world makes up in Nova Scotia. Can't think of a crowd that deserves it more."

"You can't be speaking of your long-lost in-laws, can you?" I said. "Shame on you, Micah Willis."

"Puts me in mind of something I read about Verrazano, who fell on those parts looking for the Northwest Passage," he said. "Said something to the effect that they found the natives to be a discourteous lot, and when they ran out of gewgaws to trade and left, the natives 'made all signs of scorn and shame that any brute creature would make, such as showing their buttocks and laughing.' And I quote. Old Verrazano called it Terra Onde di Mala Gente on his map. Means Land of the Bad People. I always did think it was Tina's tribe he was referring to."

"I trust you haven't shared that insight with Tina," I said, laughing.

"Nope. You're the first I've breathed it to. If you tell her, I'll tell the tribunal at the general store that you receive gentlemen in your shimmy of a morning."

I looked down at my nightgown. It covered me from chin to ankles, but I was as aware of my naked flesh beneath it as if I had not worn it at all. I blushed, and he laughed aloud.

"Go put on something you can sail in," he said. "I'm going to show you something."

"You know I hate sailing."

"You'd hate missing this more."

"You promise to be careful?"

"No need to fear today's sea, Maude," he said gently, and I knew that he too sometimes saw the empty slip in the yacht club harbor and its small occupant dashed on the rocks of Osprey Head.

"I won't be a minute," I said.

Micah had been right; there was no need to fear the water off Cape Rosier on that diamond morning. We went in Caleb Willis's slender new wooden sloop, which had just come off its blocks in the Willis boatyard that April, and the Beth slid across the glittering water as if her keel had been oiled, listing hardly a foot in the light breeze. As we rounded the headland out of Harbor Cove I could see we were headed for Osprey Head, and I drew in my breath slightly in pain and surprise that Micah would take me there so soon after Sean's death, if indeed at all. He caught the sound and looked over his shoulder at me.

"I can't change what happened out there, Maude," he said, "but I can make it bearable for you again, I think. Or at least introduce you to some souls who can."

"I never wanted to see it again," I said softly.

"You couldn't stay in Retreat and not see it," he said. "It would mean never looking out to sea, and sooner or later you'd do that or you'd leave."

I was silent, watching the quick grace of his still-compact body, and the cat-footed ease with which he moved in the *Beth*. Like Tina, he must be sixty-five or past that now, but the young man who had pulled me out of the cold sea still lived very close to the surface in him. Only the white grizzle of hair at his temples and neck, and the cross-webbing of lines in his dark face, spoke of work and weather and pain and the passing of time. We had none of us slackened in age, I thought, looking down at my own body in sweater and pants. Not Tina and Micah, not Peter, not me. We had, instead, hardened and gone sinewy, weathered, corded. Cured with the cold like aging Inuits, I smiled to myself. Maybe Ponce de León was wrong, and the Fountain of Youth was up here in these cold bays and inlets all the time.

Micah began a long beat over to Osprey Head, and the sun's dazzle was behind us, and I saw for the first time that a low, spidery bridge, perhaps a pontoon affair, stretched from the long finger of Loon Ledge to the rocky beach of Osprey Head. You could not see it from Liberty or Braebonnie, but I could tell now that it would give access to Osprey Head to anyone who could make their way through the dense undergrowth of Loon Ledge. I felt alarm tighten my stomach.

"Micah," I said, "when did that bridge go up? Who put it there?"

"Thought you'd never notice," he said, grinning at my tone. "There's a wicked good story behind it, if you'd care to hear."

"You know I would! Has somebody bought it, then? Oh, Micah, don't tell me somebody's going to put a house on Osprey Head!"

"Not going to tell you anything unless you hush and listen," he said, letting the mainsail fall slack and gliding to within a few yards of the shore. Then he heaved the anchor overboard and turned and faced me, arms resting on his knees, eyes squinted against the brightness.

I waited.

"You know that the Fowlers up to the Aerie owned Osprey Head and sold it along with the big house to those folks from wherever, the ones we don't see much of. Well, late last fall they put it up for sale without telling anybody, and it was bought on the sly, if you will, by an outfit out of New Jersey who planned to put a sardine cannery here. Water around the outside of Osprey Head has always been so thick with sardines you could walk on 'em, almost. It's what brought the ospreys in the first place."

"Oh, God," I whispered, stricken, but he raised his hand and grinned and I fell silent.

"Well, the word got out around here about Christmas, as it was bound to do, and a group of us went to the national parks boys. We knew if we could get the parks people to buy it we'd at least be safe from development. And they were interested enough to make a good offer. But the sardine people weren't interested, so we formed ourselves a little committee and went to them and told them that not a man or boy Down East would work on the construction. Now that gave 'em pause, sure enough, because they were counting on cheap native labor, as they put it. Couldn't bring in their own crews anywhere near as cheap. Finest word a New Jerseyite knows, seems to me, is cheap, and the men around here don't know how to work any other way. But we all agreed; we wouldn't touch the damned construction if it turned to gold in our hands. Well, that put a crimp in things right enough, because the sardine folks had jumped the gun and brought in a whole fleet of their bulldozers, ready to go—tore hell out of the county roads, I can tell you—and the foreman was so mad he said he was going to start his dozers next dawn if he had to do it himself. Didn't look good for Osprey Head, I tell you."

"What happened?"

"Well, funny thing," he said, looking off toward the horizon. "Foreman scraped him up a crew from a couple of bars in Ellsworth and got out here at sunrise, and damned if every one of his dozers hadn't just broke down in the night. Missing cog here, broken teeth there, busted gear somewhere else. Damned fool. Should have known what cold salt air does to machinery when you leave it out overnight."

"And so?"

"So he stomps back to the New Jersey bunch and tells them they owe him for a bakers' dozen of dozers and he's out of there. And the owners saw the wisdom, finally, of accepting the Park Service's offer and did just that, and all that's going to happen, looks like, is that bridge. Just so the Park Service can get in and out with a four-wheeler occasionally, to clean up the coastline after storms and replenish some of the mussels and clams and quahogs. I don't like it either, but it seemed the best of a bad situation."

"And you wouldn't have any idea who—er, helped the salt air along a little bit with those dozers," I said.

"I couldn't really say for sure," he said. "I'd hate to think any of my friends and neighbors had such calumny in their hearts."

"You damned fool," I said, starting to laugh. "You could have landed in jail for years and years. Why would you risk your stubborn neck like that?"

He looked at me steadily. His face was calm.

"There are eagles there now, Maude," he said. "I saw the nest last fall, and the eggs at the beginning of mud time. I think there may be more than one pair. I'd risk a lot more than my neck to have eagles come where the ospreys haven't been able to."

I felt the hair at the base of my neck begin to prickle and my forearms shiver as with cold.

"Is that what you brought me to see? The eagles?"

"Ayuh," he said, looking away. "They aren't a trade for the boy you lost there, but it's mighty grand to have that kind of life back on the Head. I thought it might . . . ease you a bit."

"Then take me to see them, Micah," I said softly.

We rowed ashore in the *Beth*'s dinghy, to a different part of the beach from where Peter and I had come ashore all those years ago for our picnic and Sean had gone off the *Osprey* into the water. This was wilder coast altogether, sown as thick with rocks and boulders and twisted roots as a lunar stone garden and inches deep in brilliant neon-green moss. It was still wet from the days of fog, and so slippery we often went on all fours, pulling ourselves up the face of the near-vertical cliff like rappellers on a mountainside. The cliff was rock; the great shrouding firs and pines and spruce began farther up, on the crown. We did not speak; there was no sound in all that great expanse of salt-scoured air and high sun and dark blue sea except the call of the gulls and the slap of the small waves on the beach below us and the soft grunts of our breathing. Occasionally Micah reached a hand back to me, but always I shook my head, determined to come to this healing, if healing there was here, alone and on my own. It seemed, that morning, the most important thing I might ever do.

Near the crown of the cliff Micah Willis said, almost under his breath, "Look up," and I did, and the impossible, incredible shadow of an enormous bird soared across my face and his, and then the bird itself rode in on a current of air and dropped onto a branch of a dead fir, perhaps blasted many years ago by lightning, beside a huge rough nest that clung in the crotch of the tree. The tree sat atop the rock that capped the cliff; nest and bird could not have been more than ten feet above us, and the bird could not have failed to see us. But it did not move, and we did not either. For a long moment we stared directly into the cold yellow eyes of a great bald eagle, the largest, Micah said later, that he had ever seen, and time and sound and sensation stopped as if all life save that of the eyes had gone out of the world.

The eagle's head was white and shone in the sun, and in its great hooked yellow beak, almost as long as the head itself, a fish flopped feebly. The eagle turned its head from left to right, regarding Micah and me frozen to the rock, and then dropped the fish over the lip of the enormous nest. It was both wide and deep; it might have sheltered two or more adult humans, but from the shrill clacking clamor from within I knew it sheltered eaglets. I stared, breath still held; a downy head, all gaping yellow beak and pink maw, appeared over the rim of the nest, and another, and another, and the eagle spread its vast wings in a flash of white tail and underbelly and lifted off again into the blue, and we felt on our faces the wind of its passing. In the air above us it screamed, and far away and

below us, the scream of another eagle answered, and
the babies' *kik-kik-kik-kik* grew more frantic, and I
knew the other parent was on its way to the nest
with more food for the young. I laid my cheek
against the stone face of the cliff and wept. The surge
of joy and strength and fierce, singing love that
shook me was nearly monstrous; I could have flown
away into the pure air on it as the eagle had, as I had
fancied Sarah Fowler doing in the air above the Aerie,
all those summers ago. I knew in that moment that I
loved this wild place, this Cape Rosier, with a passion and power that was all engulfing and all my
own, independent of Peter or Micah or Petie or anyone and anything else on earth. I clung to the cliff
and wept, as strong as the rock in that moment, as
whole as the island. I knew that I would never leave
Retreat.

It never occurred to me that we had been in danger on the cliff face until much later, when Micah
told me, tears not yet quite dry on his own face, on
the sail home.

After that, the tide of the summer turned toward
joy, and in all the summers at Retreat I remember
now, that summer of the eagles was, until its end, the
most golden.

Just before the Fourth of July, Peter finished his book
and sent it to his Boston publishers and received
such an enthusiastic reception from those august
personages that I believe he could have flown to
Retreat on the wings of their praise. As it was, he
came careening down the lane and into the driveway
of Liberty nearly a week early, in a sleek, growling
foreign roadster I had never seen before. He
slammed to a gravel-spurting stop, took the front
steps in one leap, and caught me up from the porch

where I was potting begonias and swung me around like my father used to do when I was a small child. Then, before I could get a word out, he kissed me full on the mouth so hard and long that my breath vanished, and Jane and Fern Thorne, on their way to the tennis courts, clapped, and Phinizy Thorne put two fingers to his mouth and whistled. Peter released me and bowed deeply.

"It's an Austin Healy," he said a bit later, showing me the creamy leather interior of the little car. "British Racing Green, they call it. You wouldn't believe how fast it is, Maude; it's like driving a missile of some kind. And the way you can feel the road!"

"I can just imagine the way you can feel the roads on Cape Rosier, Peter," I said, smiling at him. "Sixty-year-old spines are not designed for that."

"Speak for yourself," he said. "My spine feels about twenty. My legs and arms, maybe fifteen. And you wouldn't believe how young my—"

"No, I probably wouldn't," I interrupted hastily, seeing Erica Conant and her bridge club approaching on the lane, bound for the yacht club porch. "But you could probably convince me by showing me."

"My very deepest pleasure, if you'll pardon the pun," Peter said, grinning in the sun of that enchanted afternoon, and I hugged him fiercely, Erica or no Erica. Peter was back, Peter without shadows; all light and as young, to me, as when he had waltzed with me on the moonlit banks of Wappoo Creek. I did not care to whom or what I owed the gift of this joyous, burning Peter; if it took a successful manuscript or a new sports car or was simply the product of sunspots or positive ions, so be it. Peter for the rest of that summer was Peter as I had always thought he would be, and me with him, when the two of us were finally alone in Liberty, with a purse full of blue days to spend as we wished. I had, I remembered, looked far ahead out of that early fortress of rules and duties and reprovals and seen precisely this summer.

Looking back, it seemed to me that it never rained, and yet the grass and wildflowers in the salt meadows were more brilliant than I had ever seen them; that it never grew hot and muggy; that the fog never came crawling back to press its hungry face against my window; that the black flies and mosquitoes and no-see-ums never bit. Crystal-blue days followed one another in a stately procession, a string of perfect weather breeders that spun on through July and August and yet never bred any weather but ringing bronze days and star-bright nights. Petie and Sarah came back from Jamaica renewed and redeemed and closer than ever and opened the Little House, and both Sally and Maude Caroline went happily each day to Yaycamp, and when we did see our son and his small brown wife, it was briefly: for cocktails or a cold Sunday supper or a picnic on one of the inner islands—for that was a summer spent on the water, even for me—and always they were wrapped in a quilt of deep, quiet love and content that sometimes brought tears of thankfulness to my eyes. My boy had weathered his great storm and found his harbor, just as Peter had apparently, found his own. If we owed that to Elizabeth Potter Villiers, Sarah and I, I believe we would both have heaped our gratitude on her red head with no reservations. Whatever had transpired in that cold, awful night scarcely seven months ago, it seemed to have drawn Peter and Petie together as nothing before had been able to do. They sometimes sailed together, far out into the bay, and more than once I saw Peter drop a hand on Petie's shoulder and leave it, and Petie smile up at him with nothing in his round brown face but simple content. Elizabeth had gone back to France late that past January and moved back into the chateau of her husband; Gretchen Winslow heard it in Paris and told us when she and her children arrived in Retreat. I often thought, that summer, it was Elizabeth's final and definite leavetaking that so lightened and charged the air around me and mine.

Peter and I roared around the cape in the Austin Healy so often and so giddily that twice the new sheriff reluctantly ticketed us, and once we actually ran out of gas in the twilight atop Caterpillar Hill, where we had gone to watch the sunset over what is still, to me, the most spectacular vista of sea and islands and sky in all of Maine. We were far from home and probably would have spent the night miserably in the Healy, except that Micah and Tina Willis knew where we had headed and came with a full gas can and takeout clams from the Bagaduce Lunch.

"How'd you know it was gas and not some gruesome catastrophe?" Peter asked Micah, for Micah had said that Peter drove the little car like a lunatic out on a pass and refused to ride with him.

"This is not a summer for catastrophes," Micah said equably. "But it sure was past time for you to run out of gas."

We saw a good bit of Micah and Tina that summer, sitting before the fire in Liberty and talking and drinking good brandy. Those nights were as comfortable and companionable as they had always been, and if I sometimes thought of that glorious kitchen of the Willises where I had been only once, I put the thought away. Our worlds could not mingle; Tina had told me that. It was enough for me that she and Micah share ours.

We made love, Peter and I, like the insatiable children we had been in those first days in Northpoint; almost everywhere in Liberty we could think of, and once or twice out of doors, on nights when the moon was down and the wind off the sea was high. I insisted on the wind; the sounds we made were past indelicate and into the fringe areas of obscenity. Always, they finished in laughter. We laughed as we had not since we were newlyweds in Liberty, stifling the rich, vulgar sounds of love from Mother Hannah's pitch-perfect ears with our hands, blankets, whatever we could reach in that final transport. Once we went upstairs to the little room that had been our first bedroom in Retreat and Peter's before that, and made love on the spavined little bed, and it collapsed under us as it had threatened to do that long-ago night, and we nearly choked on our laughter. We climbed off the floor and Peter pulled me into the bathroom and threw the musty old Princeton blanket down into the tub, and we did there, those decades later, what we had done on that first night, and finished up as we had then, weak and breathless with release and laughter.

"I'll never throw that blanket out," Peter said, sitting naked on the side of the old claw-footed bathtub. "When we're ninety-five some poor bride of one of our grandchildren will be up here getting it on that blanket, and we can pound on the ceiling with a broom and ask if anybody is sick. What goes around comes around. Lord, Maude, just look at you, an old lady with gray hair, and those boobs and butt are still as round as they were then, and they still bounce like rubber, and you still holler like a Comanche."

"How perfectly elegant," I said lazily, stretching out in the bathtub on the ubiquitous blanket, feeling the rich wetness of him still inside me. "And you, my dear old fool, are *years* older than I am, and you still look like a stork with a hard-on. What goes around comes around."

"Sail with me this summer, Maude," he had said when he first arrived, and I did. For the first and only time in my life I got up with Peter in the chill dawns and followed him down the echoing steps of the yacht club dock and into the dinghy, and we rowed in that motionless pink mirror water out to the waiting *Hannah*. At first we did not go far out; Peter knew the profound tilting of the deck as the lee rail rode under still sickened and terrified me, and he kept to the shoreline and made only for the near islands. I had told him about the eagles on Osprey Head, and I think he was truly overjoyed that they had come back, but he did not suggest taking the *Hannah* there and, when I did, said only, "It would be a shame to startle them when they're just getting established. Next summer I'll go."

And I knew the healing I had found there would not happen for him and was deeply sad about that. But I did not push it. The one thing Peter simply would not speak of that summer was Sean.

Gradually I grew, if not to like, then to accept the rolling movement of the *Hannah* and the cant of the teak deck, and we went farther out into the glittering bay. Way out on the water, with the shorelines of Rosier and Islesboro and Deer Isle only cloudlike smears on the horizon, it was better for me: the rush of all that wind-scoured blue and white around exhilarated me to near drunkenness, and I could begin to understand the old, old spell that drew Peter out on the sea again and again. With him at my side, it was a fine sorcery. But alone . . . I knew that I would always hate and fear the thought of being alone on that sea. Not for Peter; he was as good a sailor as there was on the cape. But for me. For me, to be alone in a boat on the seas of Cape Rosier would be to be alone in the hands of my oldest and most implacable enemy. Even in those light-spilling days of July and August, that sea remained, in its cold heart, my foe.

On a day at the end of August, when the light

around the cape seemed so clear and blue and radiant that the entire world seemed carved of crystal, Peter took the *Hannah* out past Western Island and dropped anchor off Green Ledge. The wind was down and the sun high and honey gold, and the *Hannah* rocked on the empty sea like a cradle. We ate our sandwiches and drank our wine, and then we stripped and made love on the deck, twice and then three times, and I really think if Peter had not braced his bare feet against the coaming we might, the last time, have simply thrashed and rolled into the sea.

"I'm not even going to speculate what anybody sailing past us would think if they'd seen that," I said, lying still and letting the light breeze dry the sweat off my body.

"Nobody out today but the lobster fleet," Peter said. "And the natives are pretty pragmatic about this kind of thing. You know the old joke about the lobstermen out off the cape who saw a rowboat pitching like a rearing horse with nobody in it, and when they got closer they looked down and saw Clem and Mary doin' it, and they just nodded politely and hollered down, 'Nice day for it!'"

We laughed all the way home to Retreat, and when, as we were tying up, stately silver-haired Guildford Kennedy said, from the club porch, "You children been cruising? Nice day for it," we doubled up on the dock and were unable to speak for a matter of some minutes. "It's not you, Guild, it's just . . . a boring old family joke," I gasped finally, sure that the unworldly Kennedys would not have heard it. "It was, indeed, a nice day for it."

"One of the last we'll have, looks like," Guild said serenely. "Saw on the television this morning that there's a hurricane coming up the coast from North Carolina and Virginia, and it looks like it might smack us one in two or three days. Andrea, it is. The first one this season. At the very least we'll get a good soaking. Not that we don't need it."

"I've never heard of a hurricane on the Maine coast," I said, frowning at Peter as we trudged up the lane toward Liberty lugging ditty bags.

"I've heard of them, but I've never seen it happen," he said. "There's a theory that we rarely get them because of the Humboldt current, or some damn thing. And the ones we do get land on the open shore. The bays hardly ever get more than a blow; too far from open water, and too sheltered by all the islands. I don't like to think of the outer islands getting pounded, though, and I hate like hell to see this weather end. But at least it'll be easier to leave if the weather's nasty. I always used to hope for rain on the day we left for home, when I was a kid."

"I wish we could stay on awhile this year," I said.

"Me too, but it's just not possible. Next year, after the book's out and I've found a new assistant, we'll stay. That's a promise."

The Humboldt current cut very little ice with Andrea. The hurricane ground its way inexorably up the coast; we watched as blurry black and white images of spuming storm waves and thrashing trees flickered on the screen of the disreputable old television set Peter refused to replace. It dealt Long Island a smart but glancing blow, flattened portions of the seafront on Cape Cod, took a swirling feint at York Beach far to our south, and then veered right and headed vaguely for Nova Scotia.

"Looks like Tina's kinfolks are going to get a little taste of Andrea," I said to Micah, when he came in with a double load of wood the morning before Labor Day. It was gray and misty, and the wind was behaving queerly: running spiderlike along the surface of the bay and dropping to a dead calm and then doubling back on itself and eddying around the chimneys of Retreat. There was a hollow moaning high in the tops of the firs that I had never heard before, but it was low and not particularly ominous. The buoys off Head of the Cape and Little Deer called, and flocks of silvery seabirds, gulls mostly, wheeled overhead and then headed inland in clouds.

But still, the earnest weatherman from Bangor asserted that morning, Hurricane Andrea would miss the Maine coast and glance off Nova Scotia before blowing itself out over open water.

"I'm not worried about Tina's tribe," Micah said, dumping the wood into the bin beside the fireplace. "They can roost in trees like the gulls; started out that way, I reckon. I wouldn't mind seeing you folks head on out of here, though."

"But the TV said it's going to miss us," I said, troubled.

"Might be right, might not," Micah said. "I don't fancy the feel and smell of that wind, and those gulls know a dite more than that pegpants little fella over in Bangor. Peter button up the *Hannah* good?"

"That's where he is now," I said. "I'll tell him you think we ought to go. But Micah, it takes me two days to close up Liberty—"

"Go on and leave Liberty open," he said. "Tina and I'll close her up later. It isn't as if we hadn't done it before."

"I just don't think I can get Peter to budge," I said. "He's ridden out his share of blows all these summers, Micah."

"Didn't figure you could persuade him," Micah said. "That's why I brought you a double load. We'll likely lose power, but you can cook on the fireplace, if you have to, and heat water. I'd get those kids of yours up here from off the beach, though."

By noon the sky had darkened to a kind of white twilight, and spume rose off the surface of the bay like smoke. The moan of the wind had risen to a shriek. Rain blew in sheets across the harbor, stopped, and sheeted in again. Peter went to the phone, to call Petie and Sarah and tell them to bring the children and come on up the cliff path to Liberty, but got no tone.

"Line's down somewhere," he said. "I'll go get them. Back in a minute. Why don't you heat up the clam chowder we had last night? Mother always had it for lunch on storm days."

He vanished out into the flying gray day in his yellow foul-weather gear, and I went into the kitchen and put the iron pot of clam chowder on the stove to heat. On impulse, I poured myself a glass of tawny port. I don't know why; I've never liked it, particularly.

"Here's to you, Mother Hannah," I said, raising the glass. "Clam chowder for a storm lunch it shall be. And any old port in a storm."

I giggled at my own cleverness, and at that moment the lights flickered, sank, flared up again, and died out.

"Shit," I said, and went to throw another log on the fire Micah had lit. We lost power fairly regularly out on the cape; almost any sizable wind could topple a rotting pole or snap one of the ancient lines that Bangor Hydroelectric kept promising to replace and never did. I had coped with meals in the dark, sometimes for a day or two, and could certainly do it again. But I did not like the moan of this wind; it prowled the sky like a mad thing, and the pointed firs just outside were thrashing nearly to the ground and back, and I could not even see the little birch thicket off behind the tennis court. I hung the iron pot on the old swinging arm in the fireplace and got out candles and oil lamps and sat down and waited for Peter and the children.

They came in presently, in a swirl of rain and a howling of wind, soaked through and pinched-looking. I found towels and blankets and they went off to change into dry clothes from the trunk of assorted castoffs and left-behinds we kept in the pantry, and Peter came and sat down on the sofa and looked at me.

"The bay down there looks like Thunder Hole," he said. "And the water was up on the porch. I never saw it like this. I think we may really be in for something, Maude."

"Could we make a dash for it in the big car, do you think?" I said. "Get into the village, at least, off the water?"

"No," he said. "There's a monster spruce down across the lane. That's what took out the power, I think. We couldn't get out, except on foot, and nobody can get in until it's over and the county gets a crew in here. I think we'll be safe enough; you can tell a big difference in the wind up here from down on the beach. It's lots stronger down there. Braebonnie is shielding us directly, and the trees look like they're holding. The old spruce that's down has been dying for two years now. There's lamplight in most of the cottages, and smoke from the chimneys, so nobody much has left. We'll just keep the fire going and maybe play some parcheesi or something. There's a whole box of old games around here somewhere. Who knows, maybe we'll sing. The one thing I wish we had is a battery radio; I kept meaning to get one, and I just never did."

"Well, if it doesn't get any worse than this, I think we can manage," I said. "It's almost an adventure, isn't it? At least it is until the roof flies off."

"This old pile has stood for a hundred years," Peter said. "It's not going anywhere now. That chowder getting hot?"

It was not an unpleasant afternoon and evening, looking back. The dark fell early and was total, and the wind prowled and howled, and smoke blew back down the chimney, and once or twice we heard a heartbreaking creaking and snapping and then the long dying crash of a tree going down, but that was mainly in the birch grove, among the fragile silver army I had always loved. The larger trees held, and the wind did not seem to get any higher, and by six o'clock that evening its keening had become a kind of white noise to us, a sort of wild lullaby that underlay the waterfall rush of the rain.

I fried bacon and eggs on the iron griddle over the fire for supper, and Sarah made toast on the old toasting fork, and we made what Petie called Pioneer Coffee, and in the lamplight, with the flickering of the firelight and the shadows playing over the old living room and the faces of the five people on earth closest to me, I felt a sudden surge of love and gratitude so strong that it was almost an epiphany. There seemed more of us in the room than there were, and my love reached out and overpoured them, too. I saw the brace of heavy old crystal decanters in their silver cradles that had been Big Peter's; Petie was pouring brandy for us from them. Peter sat on the swaybacked old sofa that his grandmother had brought from Boston by packet, with a cracked leather volume of fairy tales that had been his as a child; he was reading them to Sally. Maude Caroline wore the vivid Spanish shawl that had been Mother Hannah's, which she had wrapped me in that first summer when I had received the colony on the sun porch, after the incident with the fawn. Sarah poured coffee from the old blue speckled pot Peter's grandmother's housekeeper had brought from Boston, refusing to use the heavy silver one that so quickly went black in the damp. Over the mantelpiece, on the brick chimney breast, the firelight danced on the varnished transom from Sean's *Osprey*. Peter had hung it there in silence before we had left last summer, and I knew it would remain there until Liberty itself was no more.

Thank you, Mother Hannah, I thought. It was for

this, wasn't it? So that all of us could come together in Liberty and ride out the storms—all of us, the living and the dead. Somebody has to know how to do it, don't they? And they have to teach the next ones, and they in their turn teach the next. . . .

"I love you all," I said into the fire-shot darkness.

Everybody laughed, and Petie said, "We look pretty good by firelight, don't we?"

And we laughed some more.

"Mother." Maude Caroline's voice came from the back of the house, where she had ventured to the bathroom. "Come here a minute. There's smoke coming out of Braebonnie, and a kind of light . . . I think maybe it's on fire!"

We looked at each other for an instant, and then Peter and Petie leaped to their feet and grabbed oilskins from the coat rack and dashed out into the storm, pulling them on. Sarah and I and the children ran to the back windows that overlooked Braebonnie; we could see it ourselves, the smoke pouring through the slanting rain and the leaping shadows in an upstairs window that meant a flame. Dear God, I thought, there's no way to call the volunteer fire department, and they couldn't get in anyway; why doesn't the damned rain put it out? How in the name of God could it have started? There's been no lightning—

The front door opened and banged shut, and I ran into the living room. Peter and Petie stood there, dripping on the rug, their faces white as death.

"Peter?" I whispered.

"Get your rain things and come, Maude," he said. His voice was very low and even. There was white around the base of his nose. Petie looked like a dead man propped on his feet. My heart froze.

"What? What is it?"

"Come. For God's sake, just come. Hurry," Peter

said, and he and Petie turned and went out again, into the screaming dark.

I scrambled into my own foul-weather gear and shouted for Sarah. She came running.

"Is it a fire?"

"No, I don't know what it is, but it's not dangerous to us. Peter wants me to come. Please, Sarah, stay with the children and don't let them be frightened. Keep them away from the back windows. I'll come tell you all about it when I can."

"I can't stand not knowing—" she began.

"You damned well can, if you care anything about your children," I shouted. "I don't know what it is, but it's nothing that could hurt any of us or Peter wouldn't have called me over. Just do what I say this one time and don't *whine,* Sarah! We don't have time for that."

"Yes, Grammaude," she said in a level voice, and I knew that in that moment she hated me as I had hated Mother Hannah, and though I might try the rest of my life to make it up to her, I would not entirely succeed. I ran out into the wind and rain, my heart dead as a stone. I knew as if Peter had told me what I would find in Braebonnie.

Elizabeth lay in the upstairs bedroom that had been Amy and Parker's. She was as white as paper; even her eyelids looked bleached, even her lips. The room was cold; the fire she had tried to get going spat and billowed smoke into the room, and there was only the light from that and one guttering candle, on the table beside her bed. But even in the flickering low light I could see that the sheets beneath and over her were soaked with blood, and that the baby she held against her breast was blood-dappled too, and whiter and more transparent than the petals of a narcissus. The baby was, I thought in a curious calm, almost surely dead; it was simply too small and too still to be anything else. It might have been a tiny china doll.

Peter and Petie stood side by side across the room, simply looking at me, and Elizabeth raised her head and smiled.

"Dreadful weather for a call, isn't it?" she said, and her voice sounded as if there was not enough breath to push the words out. The white baby made a sound like a seagull, very far away. I moved then, fast.

"Peter, go downstairs and build a fire and heat me some water and find a hot water bottle, and do it fast," I said, and he turned and strode from the room. "Petie, go get all the blankets you can find in the house, and find the whiskey and bring it up here," and he, too, vanished. Neither he nor his father had said a word.

I went over to Elizabeth and looked down at the baby. It was premature, even I could tell that, so small it would have had little chance even in a hospital. Here, in this dark, cold house, in this storm? I pulled the bloody blanket back from the tiny face, and the mewling wail rose a bit higher. My blood turned to ice in my veins, and I really think that for a moment my heart stopped.

There was the unmistakable arched nose that I had looked down upon in the face of my own newborn son and the tiny delicate cleft in the chin that was unmistakable Chambliss. They looked as if they had been carved in that waxen little face by a miniaturist.

"Oh, Petie," I said to my son, who had come in with a load of blankets and was looking down in horror a twin to mine at the fading baby. "Oh, Petie. What have you done?"

"I didn't know," he said, and his voice was none that I had ever heard. "I didn't know."

Tears welled in my eyes and spilled over and ran down my cheeks. I took the baby and wrapped it in one of the clean blankets—so light, so very light, so little—and laid it on the bed and lifted Elizabeth's head up from the pillow. It lolled in my arms as if there was no spinal cord. She winced.

"Are you still bleeding?" I said urgently.

"No. That stopped a while ago. I'm just so . . . sleepy, Maude. So very sleepy. The baby . . . it's too early, isn't it? I know it is. . . . I didn't know it was coming when I left Boston. It wasn't until I was nearly to South Brooksville that . . . it started. I thought I could make it here and get somebody . . . maybe Frank Stallings or somebody from the village who's a midwife . . . but it came by the time I got upstairs. It was real fast. I almost didn't feel it, it's so small, you see. Only there was all this blood. . . ."

"Elizabeth, how did you get to Braebonnie?" I said idiotically, as if it mattered. I was packing clean towels around her crotch and legs as I talked, trying not to hear the sound of the baby's breathing. It sounded like a tiny bellows, rasping, stopping, rasping. . . .

"I parked the car on the road where the tree is down and walked," Elizabeth said.

"Dearest God in heaven," a voice behind me said, and I turned, and Peter stood there with a steaming kettle and a hot water bottle, looking from Elizabeth to the baby on the bed.

I took the kettle and hot water bottle and put them down, and took my husband and son by their arms and literally dragged them to the door. They stumbled behind me like automatons, like victims of a terrible disaster. They were, of course. We all were.

"Go back," I said. "Go back. Get out when you can and bring help. Go to Micah, send Micah and Tina, and if there's a doctor in the village bring him. I know there's no one in the colony. . . . Go now. Don't come here again."

"Maude . . ." Peter said, his face awful.

"Get Petie out of here, Peter," I said. "Get him away, him and Sarah and the children, take them to

the Stallingses, or to the Willises and tell them—oh,
God, I don't know, tell them whatever you have to
and don't let Petie talk about this."

"Maude . . ." Peter said again.

"In the name of God, Peter, go!" I screamed, and
Peter took Petie by the arm and they went. I turned
back to the woman and the baby on the bed.

"Why, Elizabeth?" I said, holding whiskey to her
lips. I had laid the swaddled baby on the hot water
bottle, and it thrashed feebly for a moment and then
was still. I found I could not look at it.

"Because the colony will have to accept a little
bastard if it's born here," she said. "Otherwise, I
knew he'd never be acknowledged in Retreat. Where
you're born is very important in Retreat, especially if
you're a bastard. And besides . . . he has kin here.
That's important too. It *is* a he, you know, Maude."

I closed my eyes, and when I opened them she was
looking at me with those tilted eyes, and there was a
terrible calm in them, a kind of serene madness.

"He isn't going to live, is he?" she said.

"I don't know," I said, and picked the baby up and
held him, hot water bottle and blanket and all, close
against my breast. I walked with him to the rocking
chair by the fire, where Amy used to like to sit when
Elizabeth was born, rocking her, rocking, rocking.

I sat there with the baby for a very long time,
warming him with my body and hands, singing to
him songs I cannot now remember, feeling rather
than hearing the ragged, thready breath fighting on,
and on, and on. I think I sat that way with him until
near dawn.

But the baby died in the earliest hours of that
morning, before help could come.

Chapter
Thirteen

Just before Easter, Peter's publishers had a letter from President John F. Kennedy—to whom they had sent an advance copy of Peter's book, expecting little but hoping against hope—praising *Commons* for its insight, humanity, and unsentimental wit. Jack Kennedy, himself a product of Choate and a participant in the same pageant of privilege and rehearsal for power that spawned the book, understandably could not endorse it with a promotional blurb, but he let it be known via one of the firm's editors who had been at Harvard with him that he would not be unhappy with media reports that *Commons* rested on his bedside reading table. This tidbit hit *The New York Times* scarcely a day later, and *Commons* went back for an astounding second printing within the week. The publishers promptly arranged a national author tour for Peter. When he replied that he didn't wish to do that, his editor responded, not with the carrot of personal glory or a place on *The New York Times* bestseller list—Jack Kennedy had pretty much taken care of that—but with the request that the royalties be assigned to a scholarship in Peter's name, and of his choice, at Northpoint.

"So," Peter said to us at Easter Sunday luncheon, where he told us about the proposed tour, "I don't see any decent way to get out of it. It would be like using Northpoint to feather my nest and then refusing to share the booty. It wouldn't be more than a month or two. You could come with me, Maude; in fact, Martin suggested it. What do you say? First class all the way, to Pocatello, Idaho, and Scranton, Pa., and so on?"

"Oh, Peter, when?" I said. My heart was straining with pride in him, and relief that the film of dead dullness that had seemed to lie over him all that winter and spring had lifted a bit. His gray eyes were spilling a little of the old luminosity that had been there last summer, before the awful night of the hurricane. I would have given anything in my power to see those fires lit once more, anything but what I suspected I was being asked to give.

"They want to start in June and finish up in late July," Peter said casually. But his eyes were intent on me.

"You mean, not go to Retreat," I said.

"I guess I do, not until maybe the middle of August, anyway," he said.

I was silent for a while, looking down, and then I said, in a low voice, "Peter, I have to go this year. Of all years, I have to be there this one. And you do too. We all do. Can't you sort of make your base there and travel out of . . . oh, Bangor, I guess?"

"No," Peter said. "I can't. And to tell you the truth, Maude, I don't think I was planning on Retreat this summer, anyway."

"What?" I said, looking up at him. He was not looking at me now, but at the green-velvet limbs of the old willow that stood just outside our dining room windows. Easter was late that year, and it had been a warm spring.

"I guess you should know that we aren't coming this summer either," Petie said in a formal voice from across the table, and I swung my eyes to him. There were spots of color on his cheekbones, but he held his dark eyes resolutely on mine. Sarah bent her head over her plate. She did not speak.

I felt something akin to panic start up in my chest and had to take several deep breaths before I could say, "Why?"

Peter said nothing, and Petie finally said, in the same cool, formal tone, "There doesn't seem to be anything there for us, Mother. We've talked about it and we agree."

I looked from my son to my husband, heart hammering.

"Peter?"

He lifted his hands and let them fall and then shook his head slightly.

"I guess that's it, Maude. There's just . . . not anything there."

I could not seem to get a deep breath or control the ridiculous racing of my heart. This was absurd. I forced level words out over the breathlessness.

"If any of you are afraid Elizabeth will be there, you can rest easy. She won't. I very much doubt that she ever will be again," I said.

"How do you know?" Sarah said. Her voice, too, was level, but I could read the cost in the white-knuckled hands that were knotted in her lap. The girls had finished their lunch and gone out to the guesthouse that doubled as their retreat when they visited us; otherwise, I knew, Peter never would have broached the subject of the tour.

"I know," I said. "Trust me; I know."

And I did know. After the ambulance had finally gotten through to Retreat the morning after the hurricane, I had gone with Elizabeth to the South

Brooksville medical center while Peter packed us up
and closed Liberty and Petie and Sarah readied the
girls and their station wagon to go home. I had told
Peter in the thin, watery dawn that had broken after
the storm that I wanted it that way, and he had nodded his agreement. I wanted, too, I told him, to stay
behind with Elizabeth until she had been judged fit
for travel and someone had come from Boston to see
to the arrangements about the baby, and he had not
argued about that either. He was white and remote
and still-faced, and moved with a leaden stiffness I
had never seen before. I did not know, and never
will, what passed between him and Petie and Sarah
after they returned to Liberty and left me at Braebonnie that night. I know only that somehow Peter handled it; Petie and Sarah stood together and in full
knowledge of what had transpired, and I loved my
husband for whatever he had given his stricken son
that had enabled him and our daughter-in-law to do
that. I knew that Petie and Sarah would not part
now; the bond that lay between them was almost visible. I would ask no more of Peter.

I stayed at the inn in Bucks Harbor where Peter
and I had stayed that past winter, and from there I
called the guardian of Elizabeth's trust at the bank
and told him the situation—or what part of it he needed to know—and he agreed to send a junior trust offi-
cer with money and papers and power of attorney to
act for her. And where, he asked, would she want
the baby to be buried?

"In Boston in the family plot, I'm sure," I said, and
he said he would arrange it with Fitzgerald's.

And would she be staying on at the family home in
Boston?

"No," I said pleasantly, "I feel sure she'll be going
back to France. The house will only need to be
opened until she's made her travel arrangements."

He would, he said, see to the opening of the Beacon Hill house too. And he thanked me for my kindness and concern.

"You're very welcome," I said, and went to the medical center to see that all of it would transpire.

Elizabeth lay perfectly still in a white room in which cold blue light from the harbor danced on the walls and ceiling. Her red hair was as lusterless as a dead crow's wing, and an IV tube snaked from a metal stand into her arm. She did not turn her head when I entered, but she said, "Maude. I knew you'd be here. I want you to see what we need to do to get the baby buried in the cemetery up here. Is it the preacher we ask, do you know?"

I sat down beside her.

"The baby is going to be buried in your family's plot in Boston," I said pleasantly. "That's being arranged. Charters Cobb is sending someone to handle it from here and see that you get properly discharged and back to Boston safely. He's opening the house for you and will make your travel arrangements when you've decided about that. He'll go over your financial situation with you and make sure things run smoothly, both here and in France. You won't lack for money, I'm sure. I'm going to stay with you until the man gets here."

She turned her head and looked at me then. A ghost of that first Elizabeth shimmered over her white face for a moment and then flared out and was gone. She smiled, a small, weary, cynical smile.

"You're running me out of town, aren't you, Maude?" she said.

"If you want to put it that way," I said. "Make it easy on yourself and go, Elizabeth. There's nothing for you in Retreat any more. Not at Braebonnie and not in the Little House and not in Liberty. Simply . . . nothing. And there won't ever be."

She was silent, and after a long while she said, "No. There won't ever be. I can see that. But I'll tell you one thing: my baby is staying here. Here with . . . his family."

And she smiled the smile again.

"No, he isn't, Elizabeth," I said, smiling back at her as easily as if we were chatting about the weather. "Your baby is going to lie at home, with his family. You said you loved your mother more than anyone on earth; how do you think she'd feel, seeing her daughter use her dead grandson as a little football, a little club . . . to bludgeon people with? How do you think your mother's friends will feel?"

I did not say *would feel*.

After another long silence, she nodded her head weakly against the pillow and closed her eyes.

"You're right," she whispered. "There's nothing here for me any more. And maybe nothing in France either, but we'll have to see about that. All right, Maude. Is this how it's going to be? I leave and never come back to Braebonnie, and this just . . . ceases to exist? It didn't happen? To me, or you, or Petie?"

"That's right," I said serenely.

"And it's all for . . . him?"

I nodded.

"God Almighty," she whispered. "The awful power of your love can alter reality. I never knew that about you. You're such . . . a little thing. Such a little, soft woman."

"Go to sleep, Elizabeth," I said. "The sooner you get your strength back, the sooner you can leave here. Things will look better to you then."

She closed her eyes. "I should thank you, Maude," she said. "Without you I'd probably be dead. But I'm not going to. I wish I *were* dead, and I hope I never see you again."

And I knew that she would not, nor I her.

"Even if that's true, and she never comes back," Petie said now, all these months later, "things can never be the same again in Retreat. Not for any of us."

"They can if you make them the same," I said.

"Mother," Petie said with the cool patience that used to infuriate me when he was a teenager, "no matter how much you'd like to live happily ever after in that perfect little dream world you've made of Retreat in your own mind, the reality is that for the rest of us Retreat is not the same place after what happened, and if we don't think we can bear to go there again you should respect that. You know people are going to talk, even if—"

He stopped and looked at Sarah and reached over and patted her clenched hands, and she gave him a brief, tight smile. Peter seemed miles away, gone from us all.

I thought quite clearly, It's coming now, and only then realized that ever since we had all come home from Retreat in September and begun studiously avoiding talking about the night of the storm, to each other or anyone else, I had had the awful malignant feeling that I was poised on a precipice, waiting to be pushed over. I did not know whose hand would do the deed, but I knew that at the bottom of the cliff lay loss. Loss of Retreat, and possibly loss of everything. I looked at my stiff, miserable son, and though my heart wrenched with love and pity for him, I knew that I would fight him like a tigress to avoid that precipice.

"Who do you think is going to talk? Nobody knew anything about it," I said. But I knew as I said it that the words were futile; people would know, and they would talk. Retreat has always had a positively eerie system of what Peter calls jungle drums.

This time it was Sarah who spoke, in a furious little rush of words.

"Oh, for God's sake, Grammaude, of course people will talk; they probably started the day we left last year. The ambulance driver talked, and the doctor talked, and those two adorable innkeepers, and the doctor's nurse, and the man from the bank who came to get Elizabeth, and maybe even Elizabeth herself; she'd love to get some dirt on us started, you know that. If there's a person who goes to Retreat left who doesn't know about it, I'll be astounded. How do you think that's going to be for me and Petie and the girls? Even if it doesn't bother you—"

She stopped and dropped her eyes again. I was looking at her as if to memorize her face, and something in my own must have been difficult to countenance. I could feel the terror and pain and anger looking out of my eyes.

"Then do it for me," I said, my voice shaking and near to cracking. I could feel tears start down my cheeks. What on earth was the matter with me? Who was this speaking?

"If you won't do it for yourselves, do it for me. Just . . . just go! Live! Do whatever you do every summer in Retreat. Pretend it never happened and people will go along with you; you'll see! That's the way it is in Retreat. It always has been. No one is going to so much as mention it—"

"Mention what, Maude?"

It was Peter's voice, speaking for the first time, and it was soft and conversational and elegant: his public classroom voice. Fear and fury erupted together in my throat.

"That that baby looked exactly like us!" I shouted.

There was silence. They all stared at me, faces white and frozen. I had thought the unthinkable, spoken the unspeakable. On your head be it, then, their eyes said.

"Don't you see?" I tried to shout again, but my voice was a strangled whisper. "If you don't go back, all of you, and go for the whole summer, it's over and you can never go back again! And then it will have been for nothing, all of it."

"All what?" Peter said, again in the pleasant school-room voice.

I will not say it, I thought. You cannot make me. Anger flooded me, drowned me.

"God *damn* it," I shouted. "All this garbage about yourselves. About your pain, your tender feelings, your can't-bear-thises, and nothing-left-thats. *What about me?* You've never once in all your lives, any of you, asked me what I wanted! I gave up a whole . . . a whole *life,* a whole *world,* and I came up here and worked like a slave and waited for years to make Liberty and Retreat a place where . . . where we could all be together and be *safe,* our place, the *Chamblisses'* place . . . and now I've come to love it more than any other place on earth, and you're all prepared just to throw it away over one night out of one year in all your lives. *Do it for me!* If you can't see that it's for you, then *do it for me!* Maybe you'll come to see later that it was for all of you, all along."

I fell silent, because I had run out of breath. My head spun and my ears rang. How'd you like *that,* Mother Hannah? is the only clear thought I can remember. I looked down at my plate and waited for what would come.

Petie was the first to speak. It seemed a very long time before he did. Coolly, coolly.

"Then of course we'll go in early June as we always have, Mother, and stay until the day after Labor Day. We had no idea you felt that we . . . did not think of you."

"Of course," Sarah murmured. "Forgive us for distressing you."

I have behaved abominably, and they truly hate me for it, I thought bleakly, but I could not apologize. I must not let up on this.

I lifted my eyes to Peter, who had not spoken.

"I will come," he said, "in August, as soon as the last speech is over. I can't refuse to tour, but I will come as soon as I can."

"Thank you," I said. "All of you."

And I got up and began to clear the table. The ugliness of that Easter meal would live with all of us, all the days of our lives. There was nothing I could do about that.

As they were leaving, Sarah pulled me aside, in the foyer.

"I want you to know, Grammaude," she said, her voice trembling, "that we will come to Retreat as long as Petie wants it, and we will stay as long, each time, as he wants. But after you are gone I will never set foot there again. Petie may if he wishes, but I will not. Your precious Liberty can be sold to a tribe of aborigines as far as I'm concerned, and will be, if I have anything to do about it. So you may as well plan to leave it to somebody else. I don't know you any more; you've turned into . . . you've turned into Mother Hannah! And if you don't remember how she treated people, especially you, her daughter-in-law . . . well, I do. I remember."

And she turned and followed Petie and her daughters out into the tender green afternoon.

After they had gone, Peter kissed me briefly on the forehead and went into his study and closed the door. I was in bed, the lights out, long before he came into the bedroom. I think that neither of us slept. In the morning, everything was as it had been all year: pleasant, suspended, smoothed, and even. I had, I sensed, somehow won the victory of my life, but I did not feel remotely as a victor should. Only a trifle guilty at making a scene (but really not very guilty at all); only dull and heavy. And underneath it, still, the quelled panic, waiting. The panic that should have abated but had not.

It came to me as I worked in the tulip bed one afternoon in early May, clearly and roundly and seemingly out of the air, that the source of that deep-buried, seeping fear was Sarah's words in the foyer on Easter afternoon: "After you are gone I will never set foot in Liberty again."

Who, then? Who would take up our standard in Retreat? For whom would I keep Liberty in trust, to whom would I teach those narrow life-giving rules? Not Happy; my poor wounded and wounding Happy could never be a chatelaine, even of her own life. Who?

I threw down the trowel and sat down directly on the still-cold earth and squinted up into the sun, and it was as if the answer was there, burned into the heart of brightness: Darcy. Somehow, I would bring Darcy Chambliss O'Ryan to Retreat each summer and give her the whole gift of it, and she would give it the whole gift of herself. It was purely a deliverance. I laughed in the sun at the simple rightness of it.

And as if summoned by an epiphany, a call came the next evening from Tommy O'Ryan in Saugus. Happy had left that morning, taken a bag and some clothes and all the money in the emergency cash envelope and simply . . . gone. It was the first of the disappearances that were to mark the rest of her life, but no one knew that then; Tommy was truly distraught and had begun calling all Happy's sparse acquaintances and haunts in the neighborhood. He would contact the police next. In the meantime, could I possibly come? Huge, shambling Florrie Connaught, Happy's confidante and household helpmate, was gone too—undoubtedly with Happy—and there was no one to stay with Darcy.

"My job's hanging by a thread, Maude," Tommy said heavily. "I can't miss any more time. We'll be done for if I lose this one. I'll find somebody for the baby as soon as I can, but until then could you—"

"I'll be there in the morning," I said. "Don't worry about the baby. Just concentrate on Happy and your job."

"Bless you, Maude," Tommy said.

Peter sat beside the fire in our bedroom that night, sipping scotch, as I packed. He said little, but it was clear that he was deeply disturbed and unhappy at my going to Saugus.

Finally I stopped folding clothes and came and put my arms around him from behind and kissed the top of his fair head. I could feel his cool white scalp with my lips now; when had that happened?

"It might help if you talked about it, darling," I said. "We've turned into the original family of monkeys: hear no evil, see no evil, speak no evil. How can I not go? That little girl has never had any stability to speak of in her life. Tommy says she's cried for her mother all day. It's only going to make it worse if he brings in a stranger to look after her."

"I know," he said. "We've got to do right by this child. It isn't that. It's Happy. I think—Maude, sometimes I'm so terribly afraid that I've passed something . . . dark and sick and fatal . . . on to her. You know how my father was, those times he went away. I know I've got that same thing in me; sometimes the world just looks dead to me, finished and cold, and I have to get away from it—and I wonder, what if it's on its third generation now, in Happy, only in her it's growing into a real madness, real illness? The seeds have always been there in her, you know that. I know you think that spell she had after Darcy was born was mostly hormones, but I've always felt there was something else."

"Well," I said, taking a deep breath, for the same fear had plagued me since Happy's hospitalization, "we'll just have to deal with it. Find the right kind of doctor for her, or medication, or hospital, whatever it takes, or take care of her ourselves if Tommy can't. Keep Darcy with us, if it comes to that."

He reached up and covered my hand with his, still looking into the fire.

"My tough little girl. My tiny titan," he said, and I could hear the smile in his voice. "You've always been the staunch one, Maude; throw the book at you and you come out fighting. And I've always let you and leaned on you. We all have. You were right to lambast us the other day. But a real madness . . . could you handle that?"

"Of course," I said. "If I had to. And so would you."

"My God, though, Maude, craziness . . . madness . . . it's always seemed so abhorrent to me, so awful, so final. And to think I might be some kind of carrier—"

"Peter," I said, "many other things in the world are worse than madness. Any Southerner knows that. We're comfortable with eccentricity and craziness; most of us lived with it in some form or another for years. We don't lock our crazy folks up in the South. It's a rare family that doesn't have a strange aunt flitting around the top story, or a notorious drinking uncle, or a cousin or grandpa who preaches on street corners, or an odd nephew at the table on Thanksgiving and Christmas. It's sad to us, but it's not tragic, and it surely isn't shameful. We work it out and take care of our own. And so will you and I, if there's anything badly wrong with Happy."

He laughed.

"The thought of the Stallingses or Guild or Dierdre Kennedy preaching on street corners is past imagining," he said.

"Well, just because they don't think there isn't strangeness and trouble and pain in their families," I said.

"No," Peter said. "I'm sure sad and scandalous

things happen everywhere. But they don't seem to happen in Retreat."

And I knew then that for Peter the stormy night last September would never end, never be eased or mitigated. His terror and disgust at madness and outrage went too deep, and his horror at its happening in his own family in that place of his perfect boyhood was insurmountable.

"Then Happy will simply not come to Retreat if and when she's out of control," I said. "I know what it means to you. I'm not going to let it be spoiled."

"I'm going to miss you more than I can tell you," Peter said, and got up and drew me into his arms, and we slept that night enclosed in each other, seeds in a single pod, two halves of a whole. I lay awake after he had fallen asleep, and it seemed to me that our very breaths slid together, as if one entity lay sleeping in the old bed with the pineapple finials that had been my mother's, that I had brought from Charleston. We had slept that way from our very beginning, Peter and I.

I stayed in Saugus until near the end of June. After the first week or so it was agony for me. Tommy O'Ryan worked late most nights, and the little house was dark and soiled with a kind of effluvium of the soul that resisted all my attempts to scrub and air it away. And the thin, ferret-faced neighbor woman Tommy found to help me with Darcy proved to have a spirit to match her demeanor. Millie Leary was sly and ingratiating with me and virulently curious about my clothes and the books I read and my life and family; she was also as God-ridden—or perhaps I should say God-riddled—a human being as I have ever known and justified herself with the holy Bible, the passage about sparing the rod and spoiling the child, when I caught her slapping Darcy smartly across the face for upsetting her orange juice for the second time that morning. Darcy was cowering in her high chair, white-faced except for the red imprint of Millie Leary's hand and silent as a stone. That was the final horror to me; a fifteen-month-old child should be shrieking her lungs out in outrage and pain if slapped. But Darcy rarely cried or spoke. Mostly she clung. I fired Millie Leary on the spot and stood in the door-way with Darcy pressing into my neck while she went, fairly spitting with virtuous fury. And then I called Tommy O'Ryan at his job, something I would ordinarily never think of doing, and said, coldly and without preamble, "I want you to tell me if anyone is in the habit of striking this child."

His beautiful Irish voice began its familiar cajoling carol of denial and then, abruptly, stopped. We listened for a moment to each other's breathing.

"Happy does sometimes, I think, Maude," he said. "Not when I'm around, of course, but I've come in when Darcy was still crying a little, and there was . . . maybe a wee mark or two on her face. But," and he added it hastily, as if it explained everything, "only when she's had a mite much to drink. When she's sober and I tax her with it, she cries as if her heart would break. Ah, Maude, things are going to be differ-ent when she gets home this time. I know it. She's a good girl, our Happy. You know that."

I put the telephone down without answering, my heart jolting with anger, and sat and rocked Darcy until she loosened her deathlike grip on me and slack-ened into sleep. And I thought, I'm going to take her to Retreat tomorrow, and I don't care what Tommy or Peter or that muddleheaded doctor say. She is not staying another night under this roof, nor am I, and I am not at all sure she ever will again. Not until I am sure past any human doubt that Happy will never strike her again.

And I went to call Micah and Christina Willis, the

sleeping child heavy in my arms, to ask them to open Liberty and see if they could find someone to help me with Darcy in the daytime. And then I went once more to pack. I laid Darcy on the bed beside me as I did, and every time she stirred I sang snatches of nonsense song to her and she mumbled and stretched and slept again, a flushed pixie, a small, tawny animal deep, finally, in the sleep of safety.

I felt a savage rush of love for her, an impulse for her safety so primal and deep that it might have sprung from my womb.

"Going to Retreat," I singsonged to her under my breath. "Everything's okay 'cause we're going to Retreat."

Two weeks after she had disappeared, the police had traced Happy to a motel near South Yarmouth, a stale anonymous place with hourly rates and slovenly housekeeping units at the back, overlooking the mud delta of the Bass River. Happy was in one of them, dead drunk at two o'clock in the afternoon, her flesh saffron with old bruises and shrinking off her bones, her reeking clothes lying in heaps on the sticky linoleum floor entwined with the underwear and soiled blue jeans of a very large man. We never did know who he was; the police thought he must have driven in, seen their car with its blue light spinning, and simply driven out again and away. The motel manager reported that he never did come back to pay the bill or collect his things. Peter went up to fetch Happy, taking our family doctor with him, but she was in such a state of shouting and thrashing alcoholic dementia that they took her instead to the emergency ward of the Hyannis medical center. From there, in two days' time, Peter accompanied her to the small, carefully rustic and stunningly expensive hospital for psychiatric and addictive disorders our doctor recommended in Vermont. She had been there since, allowed visitors only recently and then only Tommy O'Ryan, who went on Sundays and came back telling us how pretty she looked and how eager she was to please us all and get home to see her baby.

But her doctor there said otherwise; Happy needed long-term psychiatric therapy as well as continuing medical management for her alcoholism, and her support group, as he put it, needed family counseling ourselves so as best to bear her up when she got out. I went dutifully to the earnest young man recommended to us in Boston, with Tommy and Darcy. Peter had begun his tour by then and refused to curtail it to join us. I could not really blame him; when he had found her, Happy was so abusive to him, physically and verbally, that he could not, even now, speak of it.

"But it's you she needs most, Mr. Chambliss," the young psychiatrist said to Peter on the phone after our first visit. "It's you she's looking for in all those beds and bottles."

"I devoutly hope for all your sakes that she will think to look elsewhere," Peter said from Washington, where he was speaking that evening at the Folger Shakespeare Library. "Send your bills to my office in Northpoint; my secretary will see that they're paid."

Across the doctor's office I heard him slam the telephone down, and I stifled the impulse to laugh, inappropriate as I knew laughter was at that moment. I could tell from the doctor's pale face that Peter had been using what we always called the official Chambliss voice. Few souls prevailed against that. It was not suggested again that Peter join us for counseling.

And so we went, all that spring and early summer, hearing about childhood traumas and repressed sexuality and regressed ego states and alcoholic psychosis, and still Darcy started and clung to me, her huge gentian eyes almost white-rimmed, her red-gold curls seeming the only living thing in the whiteness of her too-thin little face. She had been toddling when I arrived, but she soon stopped that and began creeping about on her hands and knees, and the fluid, joyous, birdlike chatter I was used to hearing slowed to whimpers and then to silence. I would have taken her away long before, since her father spent so little time with her and we two were alone in that dark little house, but the doctor said she needed the continuity of familiar surroundings more than anything.

"The surroundings she's familiar with would oppress Old King Cole," I said to Peter when he called that night. "I'm taking her to Retreat in the morning and the hell with continuity. Tommy professes to be concerned about it, but even I can hear the siren call of McNulty's tavern down on the docks through his protests. To hell with all of them, Peter. She needs Retreat and so do I. And I'll bet you do too. When can you come?"

"Oh, Maudie, not for a while," he said, and I thought he was truly contrite. "Martin wants maybe another month; they've asked me to do a southern leg, and I really ought to. The scholarship is almost assured. And after that, a city or two in Canada—"

"Oh, Peter," I said softly, disappointment searing me. I had seen us all together so long in my mind, playing on the beach with Darcy or sailing with her, her little head aflame in all that blue.

"But I promise I'll come when I can," he said hastily. "Listen. How'd you like to meet the President? Not to mention Jackie?"

"Peter! When?"

"Sometime around Christmas; Martin says JFK wants us to come to one of the state to-dos during the holidays. Dinner and a concert or something. I said I'd love to, but of course I'd have to coax you."

He laughed. He knew I loved the tall young President with a fierceness to match that red head, and my joy and pride in him had gotten me into not a little hot water at Boston and Northpoint dinner parties, where Republicanism flourished like tomatoes around a hog pen, as Aurelia used to say so long ago on Wappoo Creek.

I laughed too.

"Boy, are you going to have to dish out for a new dress," I said. "Okay. We'll see you when we see you. But August, Peter. By August. Promise."

"I promise, Maude," he said.

Retreat did, indeed, start to work its magic on Darcy from almost the instant we arrived at Liberty. Micah had engaged Caleb's capable wife, Beth, to mind her in the mornings and early afternoons, on the condition that small Micah Willis III could come along, and from the moment Darcy laid eyes on that square, brown, darting three-year-old the healing began. Darcy stretched out a finger from the safety of my arms and touched his nose and said, "Funny," and both children stared at each other and then began to laugh, that glorious, froggy belly laugh of childhood that sweeps everything before it into joy. After that, her robust bloom came creeping back, and she began to walk and then to run after him wherever in Liberty and on the lawn and beach and down at the yacht club that Beth took them, and in the space of two days they were inseparable, almost twinlike in their closeness.

"I never saw anything like it," I said to Micah on the afternoon of the second day, when he came to pick up Beth and little Mike. "She's as shameless as a camp follower. Oh, Micah, this is such a place for children; I wish every child could have a dose of

Retreat. It's practically healed her already, when nothing else we or the doctor did helped."

I knew he would understand my allusion. I had told him about Happy and our visits to the family counselor when I called, and he had merely snorted.

He looked speculatively at me, now, and I read something in his dark face that stopped my tongue. I waited. He did not speak.

"What's bothering you?" I said finally.

"Nothing that won't wait."

"Tell me now. I've got Petie and Sarah coming for supper, and whatever it is will just hang over me until I know. Tell me so I can enjoy my evening."

He sat down on the edge of the kitchen table and picked Darcy up and held her over his shoulder, absently fondling the red curls while she patted him all over, head and face and shoulders, mouth and nose, babbling softly to herself.

"I reckon Petie and Sarah aren't going to tell you, at least not right off, so I will, because you should know. It isn't apt to amount to much, but this is a small place. . . . there's been a smart bit of talk around the colony this summer about last fall. About the hurricane, and Elizabeth and the baby, and all. It's not so nasty as it could be, but bad enough, and it's gotten back to Sarah and Petie and the girls. I hear the girls had some things said to them at camp. Petie and Sarah have gotten so they won't go out, and people have gotten so they're kind of scared to ask them, thinkin' they won't want to come—you know the damn fool kind of social things that go on up here. So now I think Petie and Sarah feel that everybody's avoiding them. It's good you're here. They've been holed up in the Little House for two weeks, like they were under siege. Truth is, everybody'd be glad to see them, but I think they're past seeing that. Nothing you can't fix, I'm sure."

My heart dropped coldly, and then anger flared up, red and blinding.

"What talk, Micah? Who started it?"

"Talk about who the baby might favor, and one thing and another," he said levelly. "You were bound to hear it, Maude, and it was bound to start. Place small as this, and the drama of it, and then most everybody knew about Petie and Elizabeth being up here that time two winters ago, and most of 'em can count. It would have flurried around a little and died out, but Gretchen Winslow got it early from those two little fairies up at the inn—thick as thieves they are this summer, those three; goin' to open a collectibles shop, I hear—and is amusing herself by keeping it spinning right along. Doesn't take much, a word here and a little eyebrow raisin' there. If Petie and Sarah had laughed at her, or told her to shut her face when they first heard it, it'd be over now. But they didn't. Just went into the Little House and shut the door."

"I would like to kill her," I said, tears stinging. But I did not cry.

"Wouldn't be a bad thing, actually," he said. "But you'd do better by getting Petie and Sarah to come out and settle her hash. Wouldn't be hard to do. They could just have a few folks in and not invite her. I took Petie sailing last week and suggested just that, but I guess by now they're afraid nobody would come if they asked them."

"Well," I said, "I can do better than that. I'll have a party and ask everybody in Retreat but Gretchen. Every single living soul. A party for—let's see—Petie's birthday. An early birthday party. I'll do it next week. It's going to be the biggest party anybody ever had in Retreat, and they're going to talk about it for *years*, and Gretchen Winslow is the only breathing soul who won't be there. I'll send the invitations tonight."

"Sounds like a good idea," Micah said, and began to laugh.

"What's so funny?" I glared at him.

"You. You remind me so much of your mother-in-law."

"Well, thanks so much, Mr. Willis. If I can ever return the favor, do let me know."

"No, you remember the year she died, when Gretchen Winslow popped off at her and you because you'd brought us to the yacht club, and she asked us to sit on the porch with her in front of the entire colony and took Gretchen's chairs to boot."

I began to laugh too.

"Punishment by porch privileges," I said. "A form of social retribution unknown except to the female of the species."

"Ayuh," Micah said. "And the thing was, she didn't like us worth a damn, but she did it anyway. I guess she figured an afternoon with us was preferable to a minute of Gretchen Winslow's tongue. Stopped it too, if I recall. Don't know if it would work now. Gretchen's acting this summer like she runs Retreat and the village both. No bounds on her tongue. She's hurt a lot of feelings. Guess she figures she's the doyenne."

"Gretchen has a great deal to answer for," I said. "And she's just about to answer to me."

"Good huntin', Maude," he said, and jerked his thumb up in the old World War II airman's salute, and went out of the kitchen, still grinning.

"Absolutely not," Petie said that night when I told him and Sarah about the party. His face was mottled with anger and what looked to me like fear. Micah had been right; he and Sarah had not mentioned the talk around the colony, but they were both thinner, and their faces were strained and pale, faces that had rarely seen the sun. I was glad I had sat down to write notes of invitation to the colony the instant Micah and Beth and little Mike left, and had hurried to the post office to mail them only minutes before my children came to Liberty. There was no going back now.

"It's going to be a wonderful party," I said. "You've never really had a birthday party in Retreat, and you're the first Retreat baby I know of. It's past time."

"It's monstrous," Petie said. "It's a vulgar outrage and worse; it's a bribe to everybody up here. We're absolutely not going to consider it."

Sarah said nothing but looked at me speculatively.

"I think you'll have to consider it, darling," I said. "The invitations have already gone out—to everyone but Gretchen, of course; I really didn't think she'd add a lot to the festivities."

"Then you'll have it alone, because we will not come," my son said, the mottling fading to white.

"Yes, we will," Sarah said. "Thank you, Grammaude. It's a lovely idea."

"Sarah," Petie began, but she turned on him, her eyes sparkling.

"Hush," she said. "Don't you know when your hide is about to be saved?"

Petie hushed. We had a pleasant nightcap before the fire, and I watched Sarah in its light. There was a power about her that I had not seen before, and it eased my heart. Petie might be the undisputed lord of that marriage, but I saw that Sarah had become, sometime during the difficult past year, its rock. I smiled at her and she returned the smile, fully.

"Thank you, and I mean it, Grammaude," she said softly to me, while Petie hunted for a flashlight to see them down the cliff path to the Little House. "It's a stroke of genius," she added, bursting into laughter. "If you're going to break the rules, break them big. I'll remember that. Even if it doesn't work, this party is the most wonderful go-to-hell thing I've ever seen."

"It will work," I said, kissing her cheek. "You wait and see."

"What in God's name are you thinking about?" Peter said, when I called him late that night. He was in Atlanta and would be heading to New Orleans the next day. His voice was tight and irritable; Peter hated heat.

"I'm thinking about a birthday party for our son, nothing more and nothing less," I said. "I called to see if you might not slip away and come for it. You're back in Boston that weekend, before you go to Canada. I've got your schedule right here. You could drive over just for that night, if nothing else. Peter, you must. You're the only missing piece. You really must."

"I think it's a ghastly idea, Maude," he said. "Probably the worst thing you could do, under the circumstances. Spare us all and cancel the goddamned thing."

"Under the circumstances, Peter," I said, "it's the only thing I can do."

He was silent, and then he said, "Things are bad there."

"They have been. Gretchen, of course. They're looking better, though. And this will cinch it for good and all. But you've got to be here. That's vital."

"This could blow up in all our faces, sky high," he said urgently. "What if nobody comes, or only a few? What kind of game are you playing, Maude?"

"A game for mortal stakes," I said softly.

"'Only where love and need are one,'" Peter said after a moment, and I could hear the smile in his voice, "'And the work is play for mortal stakes,/Is the deed ever really done/For Heaven and the Future's sakes.'"

"Robert Frost couldn't have said it better," I said.

"So you think the deed has to be done for Heaven and the Future's sakes."

"Yes, I do."

"Then I'll try to come," Peter said. "I can't promise, but I will try."

"Try very hard, darling," I said, and hung up.

That weekend I took Mike Willis and Darcy, in her stroller, down to the yacht club. It was late afternoon, and the fleet was straggling in after the Saturday regatta, and much of the colony had gathered on the porch to see them in and have tea. That had not changed since Mother Hannah's day.

It was a glorious blue-edged day, warmer than most, even nearing August, and the porch and steps were crowded. My heart began to pound as I rounded the last curve in the lane and came into view with the dark little boy at my side and Darcy bobbing and crowing in her stroller. Her hair blazed in the sun, and there were pink-bronze roses in her cheeks. I had, on a whim, put her into a blue T-shirt and white trousers, miniatures of what I wore myself. I took a deep breath. I had seen none of these people since before the storm last September. It was a gauntlet of sorts and I knew it, even if woven of my oldest friends. And I knew Gretchen Winslow would be among them. Well, that could not be put off any longer. Get it done.

There was silence, and then a few tentative smiles broke out, and a soft murmur, and Dierdre Kennedy called from one of the rockers, where she sat with the female elders of the colony, "Well, look who's here! We've missed you, Maude, dear. Bring that baby here and let's have a look. We've all been dying to meet her."

Bless you, Dierdre, I said to myself, and lifted Darcy out of the stroller and took Mike's hand and went up the steps to the group of rockers. More smiles and a flutter of greetings followed me, and hands reached out to pat Darcy, and my breath eased a little. Then it quickened. Gretchen Winslow sat in the last chair in the group, years younger than any of the other occupants but looking as regally at ease as if she owned the entire club by sheer force of being, and there was in her splendid water-green eyes the look of a lioness crouched for the kill. There was no mistake about that.

"Hello, Gretchen," I said. "And Dierdre, and Erica, and all the Stallingses. This is Darcy, Happy's little girl. She's spending the summer with us; we bribed her mother and father liberally. Can you say hello, Darcy?"

"'Lo!" Darcy shrieked, and everybody laughed, Gretchen loudest of all.

"And who's your handsome boyfriend, Darcy?" she said, looking at Mike Willis out of the long eyes. "That's a Willis, or I miss my guess. Keeping it in the family, sweetie?"

I looked at her. She smiled into my face. Beautiful; she was still simply so beautiful. And as dangerous to me and mine as a madwoman. There had scarcely been time for replies to begin coming in to my invitations, but I knew Gretchen would have heard about the party. I was going to begin paying for that today, and so were those close to me. Micah had said there were no bounds on her tongue this summer. He had been right.

"We hope so," I said, grateful that dark glasses shielded my eyes. "Every time I look at Mike I wish parents still arranged marriages."

"Oh, but they do—at least, if they're lucky," Gretchen said, and there was just the smallest murmur on the porch. The old ladies present would remember perfectly how discontented Mother Hannah had been at her son's choice of a bride.

"Not always, or many of us would have different surnames, wouldn't we?" I smiled at Gretchen, and her smooth coffee-tan face darkened. The old women would remember, too, that Gretchen had set her cap publicly for Peter all the years before me.

I turned to Dierdre Kennedy and hugged her, and she reached out her arms for Darcy. Darcy went into them, gurgling and smiling.

"What a darling she is!" Dierdre said. "It's really so good to have you back, Maude. When is Peter coming? We're all so thrilled about his book."

"*Be*-dar!" Darcy crowed, and everyone laughed.

"Yes, darling, Peter," I said. "Granddaddy. He's coming next weekend, as a matter of fact, Dierdre. And looking forward to seeing everybody."

I did not need to look at Gretchen to know that she understood precisely where Peter would see everyone. The party throbbed in the air between us like a sunspot.

"You know," Frances Stallings said, tilting her head at Darcy, "she is the absolute image of you, Maude. Not the coloring but everything else: the shape of her face, and the smile, and that compact little body. It's uncanny."

"Isn't it," Gretchen Winslow said.

I knew what was coming, and that it would be bad. I tensed my muscles, waiting.

"And isn't it a shame about Elizabeth's baby," she murmured. "If it had lived, Peter would have had a perfect little miniature Chambliss to take around with him, just like Maude has a Gascoigne. A matched set of look-alike grandchildren, as it were."

This time there was no gasp, only silence. It was far beyond the pale; even Gretchen seemed to know that. She opened her mouth to speak further and then did not. She looked away from me and down.

Help me, Mother Hannah, I said silently, entirely spontaneously, and then I leaned down slightly, so she would have to meet my eyes, and said, "You might as well give it up, Gretchen. Peter didn't marry you when he could have, and he hasn't gone to bed with you any time since then—and boy, could he have!—and he isn't going to, any time in the future. If I were you I'd cut my losses and get out of the game."

And I smiled, and took Darcy back from Dierdre Kennedy, and went down the steps and put her in her stroller, and we went back up the lane toward home, Mike Willis capering ahead of us. Behind me, just as we turned the curve that would hide us, I heard, as distinctly as I heard it every summer day in Retreat from the little tennis court, the soft pattering of applause.

I knew then there would be no refusals to Petie's birthday party.

"And there aren't, not a single one," I said to Peter at midweek on the phone. I would not, I decided, tell him about the ugliness with Gretchen. I knew there would be no more of it—not, at least, that would be likely to touch us. "Everybody's coming. I even asked those strange people from Los Angeles who're renting Braebonnie this summer, and *they're* coming. Everybody says they're actors, Peter; isn't that wonderful? Just what we need in Retreat. It's going to be the party of the century."

"I'm glad, love," Peter said. "Then you really don't need me, do you? Maude, just the thought of it makes me gag—"

"More than ever I need you, Peter," I said urgently. "You just don't know; it's imperative that you be here. There's no choice. I can't understand what bothers you about it now; everybody's coming, don't you see, it means that everything's all behind us, the prodigal son is forgiven, we can go on like we always have."

"Can't you see it's a total charade, Maude?" Peter said. "That's what bothers me about it. It's a lie. Petie's not the prodigal son—"

I cut him off in desperation. I would hear no more of this.

"Darling, that's just a figure of speech. I meant—all right, Peter, I didn't want to tell you, but if that's what it takes to get you here, I will. Someone would anyway, sooner or later."

And I told him about the incident at the yacht club the weekend before. All of it, from start to finish. When I was done there was a long silence on the line, so long I took a breath to speak, but then he did.

"God damn Gretchen to hell," he said. "All right. I see. You're right, I don't have any choice. I'll drive up from Boston that afternoon, but I'm going to be late getting there. Martin's got some kind of lunch thing for me that I can't cancel."

"Oh, darling . . . thank you! It'll be wonderful, you'll see. Nobody will ever mention that business with Gretchen; that's over. And simply everybody's asked about you. Darcy asks three times a day."

"Give her a kiss for me," he said. "I miss her. I miss you, too. Maude—"

"What, love?"

"Do you remember Wappoo Creek? Do you remember what we sang that night?"

"As if it were yesterday," I said, laughing.

He sang softly, over the wire from a long way away. "It's three o'clock in the morning . . . we've danced the whole night through. . . ."

"It doesn't sound a bit better now than it did then," I said.

"It doesn't at that, does it? It's been stuck in my mind lately; I've been singing it for days," he said.

"Well," I replied, "put the top down and sing it all the way up here Saturday, and hurry up!"

"I will. Listen, Maude. If anything else happens—anything unpleasant—call Micah. Will you do that? You can depend on Micah."

"I don't need to call Micah," I said, puzzled. "I can take care of Darcy and myself. Don't you see? That's what that sad, silly scene at the yacht club was all about. I can take care of things."

"I know you can," Peter said. "I know you can. But I want you to promise me, anyway, about Micah."

"Then I promise," I said. "Get here soon, darling. I need hugs."

"I love you, Maude."

"Me too."

It rained the day of the party, but an hour before time for it to start the rain stopped and a spectacular sunset broke through the storm clouds over the bay. The entire bulk of Islesboro and the Camden Hills flamed with it. Over it all hung the white ghost of a new moon. I went outside in my wrapper, face still unmade, to watch it. Micah and Tina stood beside me; they had come early for a quiet drink and to help me with last-minute details. There did not seem to be many; from the very beginning, this party had taken on its own charmed life. The flowers I ordered were the prettiest I had ever seen; the hors d'oeuvres Tina and I spent the week making looked festively elegant; the Japanese lanterns that were a Liberty party tradition looked magical in the sunset and fading storm light; Darcy had been an angel all day and was having her supper with Beth and Mike in the upstairs nursery without so much as a whimper.

"Remember when you said that a sunset like that meant the devil was burning trash?" I said to Micah, and he nodded. He looked fine in his gray slacks and dark blue blazer, indistinguishable from any of the men who would come this night, as Tina, in her pastel linen and cashmere cardigan, did from the women. As, now, they were.

"And you said this kind of sunset sometimes brought the northern lights," I went on. "Wouldn't that be perfect? Just the right finishing touch, a grace note."

"Wouldn't be surprised," Micah said, and we went into Liberty, and I ran upstairs to dress. I heard Micah greet Petie and Sarah and smiled. They would remember this night.

I was just coming down the stairs when a knock sounded at the door, tentative, soft. At the same moment a howl from the nursery announced the end of angelity.

"Get that, will you, Petie?" I called. "It'll be the boys from the inn with the shrimp; it's too early for anybody else yet. I'll see what's going on up here."

I started back up, and then I heard Petie say, "Mama?"

I turned slowly and came back down the stairs, staring at him. Petie had not called me Mama for years. I stopped. His face was oddly fragmented; it looked as if it might fall away, feature by feature. Behind him stood the new sheriff, the one who had stopped Peter and me those times, when the Austin Healy was new. Last summer. I could not remember his name.

"Mama," Petie said again, and took a step toward me. I stepped back. I began to shake my head, back and forth, back and forth.

"Mama. Dad, it's about Daddy. . . ."

I took another step back, staring, shaking my head. Petie came on toward me with his awful face.

"He . . . the car went off Caterpillar Hill," Petie said, and began to cry. I stepped back again. I felt as if there was nothing in the world but space, cold and limitless, behind me. Here it was, then: the precipice.

"That can't be right," I said, shaking my head. Stepping back.

Hands caught my shoulders then, and held them

hard, and I felt a body behind me, a body that held
me still as I tried to step back once more. Micah. I
stood still in his grasp.

"I'm so goddamned sorry, Miz Chambliss," the
new sheriff said, his voice trembling. "Some folks
from over to Penobscot was parked at the overlook,
watchin' the sunset, and the car just come straight
up the top and veered off and . . . went on over. They
called me from Bagaduce Lunch; we got a car right
on down there. We . . . the car was at the bottom,
not far from where those woods around Walker's
Pond start. We found some papers with his name on
'em in the glove compartment, but we haven't
found—we haven't found Mr. Chambliss yet. We got
backup comin' in from Brooksville and Castine,
though. . . ."

"Go back and look, then," I said. "Do it now. He
could be hurt; you might not hear him call."

"Ma'am, he . . . the top was down," the sheriff
said. "It's a drop of a thousand feet there at the overlook."

I shook my head. Micah's hands tightened on my
shoulders. I tried to make a picture of it come into
my mind, but there was nothing but blankness,
whiteness. I could not see Peter. Something was
wrong about all this.

"What was he doing on Caterpillar Hill?" I said
wonderingly. "This is all wrong; that wasn't Peter.
Peter would have turned right for Brooksville. Caterpillar Hill isn't on his way. . . . This is all wrong. . . ."

"Maybe he wanted to look at the sunset," the sheriff
said in a low voice. "Lots of folks do from up there. I'm
sorry, Miz Chambliss, I surely am. But it was his car."

And still I shook my head. No, no.

Petie cried quietly in Sarah's arms. Tina came in
from the kitchen, her face bleached the color of long-
dried bone. I shook my head.

Micah turned me around with both hands and looked down into my face. His was still and intent. I noticed that he had cut himself just below his ear, shaving. There was still a tiny trickle of dried blood.

"Peter does that," I said, reaching up to touch it.

"Peter is gone, Maude," Micah said. "You've got to know that."

I looked at him. I felt his hands and his arms. I could not make a picture come; I could not find Peter in my mind.

"Micah," I said, "I always thought it would be the sea."

His face wrenched and crumpled in pain then, and he pulled me against him, and I shut my eyes and the pictures came: the panorama of hills and ponds and inlets, islands and ledges, and finally the open sea, burning in that sunset, burning; the little green car hanging in that lambent air for a split moment; a man—had he been singing, had he really?—a man with fair hair spinning up and out, and out, and out, and then down. . . .

At some point, I thought, blackness beginning to slide in at me from the sides of my vision, at some point, it must have been almost like rising to meet the young moon. The figure fell, and fell, and the blackness slid in, and I followed it down, and I heard myself crying aloud into Micah Willis's chest as I, too, fell, "Micah, I don't want to go to the porch! I don't want to go to the porch!"

Darcy Chambliss O'Ryan

Chapter Fourteen

I went back to Retreat in a rusted 1979 Pontiac Firebird with a bumper sticker that read SHIT HAPPENS. I had admired that sticker enormously the entire time I was in the hospital; so much that Leroy Greene, whom we called Mean, suggested I drive it the two thousand miles to Maine when I was discharged, instead of flying as I had planned to do.

"Give you a little breather before you get there to take up your life of ladyhood." Mean grinned. "Go roarin' in there flyin' all your flags. Wear your heart on your bumper."

"Oh, Mean, what a great idea!" I said. "It really might be just the thing. But I couldn't just take your car."

"Go on," he said, turning back to the pool table in the day room as if the subject held no more interest for him. "I ain't likely to drive the fucker again in several lifetimes."

That was true. In addition to being treated at Peachwood for chronic long-standing alcohol and drug addiction, Mean was prohibited by the State of Georgia from driving in the foreseeable future. Mean collected DUIs as frequently as he had collected yardage for the Atlanta Falcons in his short but splendid career as a running back. He himself saw the car only when his brother Errol drove it up from Zebulon, Georgia, to visit Mean once a month. Mean had two or three other cars, a Mercedes and a BMW, I think, on blocks in a garage near his condominium in Buckhead. But it was the twelve-year-old Pontiac he asked Errol to bring. I knew it was a real love with him, and I did not think he had any others. Mean was enormous, black, singularly uncharismatic for a sports hero, and . . . mean. I was the only person at Peachwood he spoke to on a regular basis. I have always been proud and honored by that.

So in the end I did take the Pontiac, promising to return it in the fall when I came back to Atlanta, and, pocketing the substantial sum for airfare that my grandmother had sent to see me to Maine, I set off on the long three-day drive that would bring me, finally, to Cape Rosier.

For a full day I felt splendid: indomitable, tough, and free. Part of my euphoria, I knew, was the result of the red and yellow Xanaxes with which I had left the hospital—a month's supply. I had taken them three times a day in the hospital, and they had put the panic at a remove I could tolerate. I loved those pills. And on that first day, I felt as if the world streaming by just beyond the interstate was one pane of glass away from me. I did not have to do anything at all about it but drive. Maybe I never would.

But another and very potent part of the well-being undoubtedly came from that bumper sticker. SHIT HAPPENS. What an admirable, cool, hard-edged sentiment: just the one I wanted to take all those miles and flaunt in the face of that beautiful place that had so nearly killed me. What a fine, supple statement of control and contempt and wellness. The new Darcy O'Ryan. Don't fuck with me.

"It might not be a bad idea, at that," my shrink said when I told him about driving the car to Maine and the bumper sticker. He was young and shaggy-haired and a little overweight; I liked him as well as I liked anyone, which was not much. To let my defenses down enough to admit full-blown liking was also to let the fear in; I knew that. But I thought he was less full of shit than anyone else in that absurd place, and I knew he cared what happened to me. He also kept the Xanaxes coming. I would have cooperated with Charles Manson for less.

"Why?" I said. "I thought you wanted me to fly. Didn't you say the stress of driving all that way wasn't a good thing right now?"

"Yeah," he said, polishing his glasses on his shirt cuff. "But you'd be going under the protection of your own personal amulet. And it's a damned good statement of condition for you right now. 'Shit happens' is an angry statement. It's the closest you've come in nearly a year to admitting you're pissed off. And now you're proposing to go right up there into the teeth of the enemy and say it, even if you say it on your bumper. Excuse me; Mean's bumper. Not bad, Darcy."

"How many times do I have to tell you I'm not angry?" I said. "I've never once felt angry; what I've been feeling for more than two years is fear, plain and simple. I don't know why you can't understand that. Are shrinks afraid of fear?"

"You're nothing if not angry," he said. "And you should be. Anybody would be. If you could just once feel it and admit it, you'd have been out of here months ago. You're mad at your mother, you're mad at your father, you're mad at that feckless jackass of an ex-fiancé of yours, you're mad at yourself and the world, and you're mad at the very place you're about to go. If I could have found another place to take you for three months I'd have refused to consider this

Retreat place, but I couldn't, and the rules say you have to be in someone's care for three months after release, and you're ready to get out of here, even if you don't think you are. Keeping you would be worse than sending you to your grandmother. You're getting way too attached to this little demi-paradise. Incidentally, you're mad at your grandmother too. So, all in all, confronting everything at once may not be as bad as I thought at first. At least you're ready to admit how you feel via bumper sticker, if not head on."

"Why do you think I'm mad at Grammaude?" I asked, and realized that this was the first time in nearly twelve years I had called her by that childhood name. He noticed it too, and I flushed with annoyance.

"For not protecting you that last summer," he said. "What else? You were only seventeen years old. She should have done better by you."

"She tried," I said, surprising myself profoundly. I had not remembered that my grandmother had tried to stay my course that summer in all the years since. I had thought of her little at all. "She didn't know I was sleeping with him," I added softly.

"Did she not?" the shrink said. "I think she did. How could she not? Okay, Darcy. I approve. I'll okay the car. Go on up there and tell her how you feel. Think about it on the way. Get it straight in your mind, once and for all, and tell her. You won't really start to heal until you do. And may the shit be with you."

And he grinned, the full, sweet child's grin that I saw infrequently and loved, and I hugged him, and on the duly appointed day I said goodbye to Mean and the few other people who meant something to me, loaded the Pontiac, and rolled out of the Peachwood driveway in the sunshine of a hot June day, my purse full of Xanax and SHIT HAPPENS riding with me, as my shrink had said, with all the power of an ancient clan amulet. And the first day was good.

But on the evening of the second day, as I pulled into the Holiday Inn I had chosen just outside New Haven, I saw that something dark and as impervious to fingernails and even a metal nail file as Krazy Glue had splashed over the bumper sticker so that it read, IT HAPPENS, and my well-being vanished in an instant. IT HAPPENS was not the same thing at all, not at all. IT HAPPENS was a sort of powerless mental shrug, a free-faller's fatalism. I had spent two years trying to pull myself out of free-fall. I went into my room and ordered a hamburger and a martini for dinner and took three Xanaxes before the nibbling edge of the terror shrank back. Before I did, I counted out my remaining Xanaxes on the bedspread. Enough to last, at this rate, for ten days instead of the thirty I had bargained on. I knew my shrink would send me another prescription, but not until this one had been taken as directed. Twenty days in Retreat without either my drug or my SHIT. Well, then, I would just have to find a way to get more of the former. I should be able to convince some country doctor I needed Xanax. Providing, of course, any doctor on Cape Rosier would have heard of it.

Either that or I could die. It was not that I had not thought of it before.

It was three o'clock in the morning before the lonely, swishing hum of the passing big rigs faded, and I slept.

It is about an eight-hour drive from New Haven to Retreat. I left at six, my eyes grainy with fatigue, the Xanax humming in my blood like music. The familiar hammering of my heart was not so pronounced at first, but after I left I-95 in Boston and picked up old U.S. 1, which snakes its way up the entire coast of Maine, it began to pound once more. With each passing mile, each glimpse of harbor and village and weathered gray shingle, each breath of pine and salt, each wedge of pure June-blue sea and sky, the fear carved out another inch of conquered territory, so that by the time I reached the Camden Hills I was dry-mouthed and light-headed with it. I took another pill with my Wendy's lunch in Rockport, and another when I reached Orland and turned south on 15, toward Cape Rosier and Retreat. Always before, when the fear was at its worst, it shut off outside sensation and perception like a petcock, but now color and fragrance and sights and sounds and resonances dove at me like sharp-beaked birds.

"Expect more of the panic attacks, and maybe worse, before they ease off completely," my shrink had told me. "Panic disorder doesn't ever just roll over and give up. It'll come back for a sneak attack or two or three. And you're going back to a place where there's a trigger every half mile. You're in charge now, though; remember that, even when it feels as if you aren't. Now you know you can just wait them out, and when they're over you'll still be you on the other side of them. You *know* that. You didn't before; that's the difference. And you can always call me if it gets too bad."

So I knew to expect the fear, but still, just past Brooksville, as the familiar green and blue waterscape of Spruce Head and Walker's Pond loomed up on my left, I stopped and found a pay phone in a general store and called Peachwood. The terror was just too great, the free-fall unbearable.

"I can't do this," I said into the phone when the front desk operator answered. But when she said, "With whom did you wish to speak, please?" that fifties-modern plastic-palmed reception room with its soothing motel abstracts of green and blue—soothing colors for the entering beasts—and its antiseptic stench bloomed whole and awful in my head, and I hung up. I could not go back there. I bought a Coca-Cola and took two more Xanaxes with it, and rode onto the cape with my blood fizzing like charged wine.

Past the village, just before the place where the old gray oar stood on its post at the turning into Retreat, I saw, suddenly, the little cemetery where Mike Willis and I used to go and smoke cigarettes and tell each other stories; go when we had sinned flagrantly, to escape retribution; go when the sheer outsideness of the two of us became oppressive. It seemed empty from the road. I slowed the Pontiac and rolled down the window. Summer and quiet and the ghosts of cigarette smoke and gull cries and laughter vanished many years before washed over me in the cool wind off the bay, a benediction. Without a conscious thought I wheeled the car sharply in between the stained marble pillars and parked and got out. Here was peace, if peace there was for me in Retreat. I would sit here for a while, under one of the great spruces, until my heart ceased its deathly galloping and I knew I could go on to Liberty, where my grandmother and all those long-ago summers waited for me.

I sat for a long while against the big spruce at the top of the hill, Mike's and my favorite place. From here we could see the entire business of the harbor and bay spread out before us: the white triangles of sails out from the yacht club, the comings and goings around his grandfather and father's boatyard, early lobstermen coming in to the village docks on a bad day. From here, too, we could see, behind us, anyone approaching through the gateposts and so avoid capture, if we had misbehaved, and mere adult intrusiveness if we had not. Immediately beyond us lay the graves of all his Willis and Duschesne ancestors, and beyond them and to the right, the grave of my older brother, Sean, who had drowned off Osprey Head before I was born, and beside it the grave of my grandfather, Peter

Chambliss, who had been killed when I was far too young to remember it, in a car crash from the top of Caterpillar Hill. I had, I remembered, envied Mike the sheer numbers of his dead clansmen, and he had envied me the exotic manner in which mine had died.

"Far as I know," he said once, "all of mine died in bed from something you catch or just being old. None of 'em died in a special way, like yours. My folks still talk about the way your brother and grandfather died, but they don't ever talk about any of our folks. Not that I hear, anyway."

"Well," I had replied, thinking to comfort him, "maybe some of them died in ways so awful and disgraceful that nobody talks about them. Why don't you ask your grandfather?"

I did not even think to suggest that Mike ask his father. Caleb Willis had only one leg and was dour and dignified, unlikely to share glittering skeletons with his son. And his mother, Beth, who had cared for me and continued to, after that, until I no longer needed caring for, and whom I loved, was nevertheless the absolute soul of practical rectitude. There would be no enlightenment there. But Mike's grandfather, Micah, was another matter. Dark and blackbrowed and stern though he might be at times, his white teeth sometimes flashed in laughter, and he told stories with my grandmother; I heard them often, after I had been put to bed in the big back room. He was around Liberty a lot, and I adored him, as Mike did. He spent considerable time with us, when we were small, on the water in our catboats and in Liberty or in the Willises' wonderful, cluttered house on the road, and there seemed no end to the stories he would tell us, if we asked.

"My grandfather doesn't like to talk about our dead relatives," Mike said. "I don't think he ever did, not after my grandmother died. I don't want to ask him."

I did not remember Mike's grandmother Christina, but my own grandmother often told me about her, a beautiful, serene woman with fair coiled hair, who played the violin magically and came to Liberty more often even than her husband.

"A wonderful friend, Tina was," I remember Grammaude saying often, a soft smile curving her mouth.

"We could ask Grammaude," I said to Mike that day. "You know, there's nothing you can't ask her."

And that was true. For as long as I could remember, my dark little grandmother had been Mike Willis's strength and refuge, the port of absolute safety in the frequent storms of his small life, the binder of bruises, the baker of cookies, the teller of truths and the recipient of them.

"I don't much think she'd know," Mike said. "Summer people don't know anything about us, not really. My father says that. Mother, too."

And now, perhaps twenty years later, I still did not know if any of Mike Willis's ancestors had had the glory of colorful and violent deaths.

And would not find out now. Mike and I had parted in bitter, searing anger that last summer; he had not said goodbye and I had not been back. He had not written, and I had not. For all I knew, he was married and had children; Grammaude had written me a few times in Atlanta about him, but I had torn the letters up, wanting nothing in my life of him and little of her. I did remember, though, that he had become an architect and had an office someplace on the water. But it was, I thought, far away from Cape Rosier and Retreat. I was not even sure I remembered what he looked like. Dark, solid, blue-eyed—but what else? An odd lapse. For sixteen summers he had been the other half of me.

The sun was beginning to lower straight out across the bay when I got up, cramped from sitting on the ground and light-headed from hunger and the waning drug. It had been a good idea to come here, though; peace hung in the air like smoke. I must remember this place. I looked out over the bay once more, shading my eyes against the diamond-edged glitter on the sea: a weather-breeder day, I thought suddenly, the phrase rushing at me out of my childhood. I was nearly blinded with the silver-foil dance of light on water.

"Maude?" The voice came from behind me. I turned but in the glare could see only the dark shape of him, a solid, square man sitting down. But the shape of the head, and something in the way he held it to one side . . .

"Mike?" I said. And, when he did not answer, "Is it you?"

"No," the man said. "Come closer, so I can see you. The light's in my eyes."

And I knew who it was then and ran to him in joy. "Mr. Willis! Micah!"

And, on reaching him, stopped. The low line of blackberry brambles along the stone wall broke the glittering light, and I could see that it was indeed Micah Willis, but he was old. Very old, and ill. He sat in a wheelchair, and only his head and the hand and arm on one side moved. Stroke, I thought. His slack, lined face and filmed eyes and lank white hair all spoke of it: illness, helplessness, age. He must be very old; he was older than my grandmother, and she was . . . what? In her mid-eighties? I felt such grief that my eyes filled with it. He had been the most vital, forceful man I had ever known.

"So," he said, looking up at me. "Darcy O'Ryan, isn't it? Maude said you were coming this summer, but I thought it was tomorrow she was expecting you."

His voice was thin and frail; petulant, almost. And then he smiled, and it was as if the years spun away from him and backward, like something in an animated movie. He was there after all, Micah Willis, under the wreckage. It spoke in his smile, if not in his eyes and voice.

"You're the image of her," he said. "Thought you were her, for a minute, there under that tree, silhouetted against the bay. Take away that red hair and blacken those blue eyes, and you'd be Maude Chambliss when I first knew her, when she was younger than you by maybe ten years."

"And I thought you were Mike," I said, smiling at him. "Sitting there with your head cocked. He used to look at me like that when he thought I'd done something stupid, which was most of the time. So we're even."

"Not much of Mike in the rest of me," he said matter-of-factly, looking down at his thin body in the chair.

"I'm sorry," I said awkwardly, "was it . . . ?"

"Stroke. Three years ago. Don't be sorry. I get on pretty well. One of the younger Duschesne girls stays with me except when I sleep—my wife was a Duschesne, you know—and Caleb and Beth look in every day and bring my groceries. And take me over to see your grandmother once or twice a week too, so I'll be seeing something of you as well."

"Good," I said, wondering if he knew why I was in Retreat this summer. I could think of nothing else to say, and so said, "Grammaude told me about your wife. I'm sorry."

He looked out over the water, and then to the cluster of graves, and sighed.

"Ayuh," he said. "Me too. Well, you better get on down to Liberty if you're going; your Uncle Petie and Aunt Sarah will be coming to get your grandmother for supper, and you'll miss her if you don't get along. I'm glad you're here, Miss Darcy. It's your place,

Retreat is. You be gentle with her, now. She was like somebody with only half a heart when you left, and she trembles like a bird with happiness that you're coming this summer. Whatever way you left her, try to make it a good time now. She's been alone a long time, and she's not young any more."

"I'll try. Can I give you a lift?"

"No, Caleb'll be back directly. He drops me off here every afternoon or so and comes and gets me on his way back to the boatyard. Thank you, though."

"Well, then, I'll see you," I said, turning to walk back to the Pontiac. I wanted, suddenly, to ask about Mike but somehow could not. Let it lie, let it be. . . .

I had opened the door of the car when he called after me, "Nice car. Interesting coloration. What is this ɪᴛ that happens?"

I squinted back up at him and saw that he was grinning his old white grin.

"You darned well know," I called, and he laughed aloud, and I drove out of the cemetery with, for the first time in two days, a heart that was not devouring itself in fear.

The fear returned, though, diving and stabbing, when I came to the rotted old post and the skewed oar. The white lettering on the blade of the oar was completely worn away now, but it still meant Retreat to me as no other symbol did, and I had to stop the Pontiac and lay my head on the wheel before I could go on.

"Shit happens," I whispered to myself finally, and turned in and drove down the lane into the colony. My hands gripped the wheel so hard I thought they could not be pried off, and it was a good thing; the lane was still not paved, and the potholes sent the car springing and careening. I knew the county would not have filled them this early in the season, and the frostline here lay fourteen inches deep. The Pontiac gave a grating, drunken lurch and I heard metal scrape rock and muttered "Cheapskates" under my breath. Only then, after my treacherous car had announced itself to all comers, did I dare look around me. Pure, stinging sensation flooded in.

There was no one on the tennis court, but to my eyes it thronged with figures in wrinkled white, mine and Mike Willis's among them. I could feel the slant of the low summer sun; taste my own earnest sweat and the bitterness of defeat at the hands of some tanned young Retreat royalty; smell the pine and spruce and salt and the dark, secret dampness of the birch grove beyond the court; hear the nasal prep school jibes at my Irish clumsiness and reddening face. I swung my head to the right; the row of old gray- and brown- and white-shingled cottages began, and each one was as familiar to me as a chamber of my own heart. There did not seem to be anyone about. Tears and terror mingled in my throat: the first spoke of innocence and love and remembrance; the second of the death of all those things. I did not look around again. I drove on to the driveway of Liberty, still sheltered behind tall barberry hedges, and turned the car into it. I did not want to look up at the tall, sprawling old house before me—surely it would be altered, darker, smaller, shabbier—but then I did. It seemed not to have changed since the day I left it. It stood as it had for more than a century, and it said to me as it had all those years ago, "Safe. I will keep you safe."

"You lie," I said aloud, and got out of the car and walked into Liberty.

I walked through the living room and the dining room and into the kitchen: empty, spotless, unchanged. Ghosts beckoned and capered; voices called and cajoled. I would not see or hear them. There would be nothing of me in this house this summer except what I granted. And that would be little and fleeting. Three months. Three months of necessity, and not a day more by choice. I put my head into the big back bedroom that had always been mine, but it too was empty, fresh and shining and waiting. My grandmother was nowhere to be seen: good. Perhaps she was at Uncle Petie and Aunt Sarah's, as Micah Willis had said. It would give me time. . . .

I walked out onto the sun porch, and she was there. She lay on the old wicker chaise that had been her afternoon reading spot for all the summers I could remember, and she was asleep, wrapped in the soft, thin folds of the old Spanish shawl she had always kept there for cover against the cool twilights. Its colors were faded now, so you could hardly tell what they had been, and against her still body and hands it seemed, suddenly, a shroud, a wrapping for the dead. The thought came whole and clear into my mind: my grandmother is dead.

When I had left her she was vivid and dark-skinned, her curly hair streaked black and silver, her face soft and tanned and crisscrossed with tiny lines, like old silk velvet. Her dark eyes danced and her small pointed chin was sharp and firm, and her body was still curved and quick in the pants and sweaters she always wore. She refused, except for evening cocktails and dinner out, to wear the print silk and linen dresses the other older women wore and wrapped herself, instead of in silk-bound cardigans, in shawls. She always wore the same pair of dangling gold earrings in her pierced ears, and I always thought of her as a secret captive of this place, a gypsy brought and kept here by some unbreakable spell. I told her that once.

"I am." She laughed. Grammaude laughed a lot, a rich, throaty laugh. "I am indeed. And," she went on, "I'll wear the little dresses and little sweaters when I apply for porch privileges at the damned club. And not a minute before."

But she wore a dress now, a navy print shirtwaist

that seemed to swallow her frail body in its starched folds. She seemed to have shrunk in on herself; her tiny bird's bones showed plainly, and the slack skin draped and folded around them like stretched fabric. She was still dark, but now it seemed the dry, dead golden darkness of long mummification. Her mouth was a thin bleached line, the mouth that had been full and soft and quirky, and there was not an inch of her face and hands and arms that was not as finely etched with wrinkles as something long cured and dried. Her closed eyes were sunken in dark pits that seemed to claim half her small face, and the bones of her forehead and cheeks were those of a beautiful small skeleton. Her eyelids, drawn down over the round marbles of the eye orbs, were bruised-looking, fine as crumpled tissue. Old: dear God, she was so old! My breath seemed to simply stop. This fragile old mummy with the pure-white dandelion hair and the silk-tissue skin could not possibly keep me safe.

Only then did I realize that I had thought she could, and that the thought had brought me all those trembling, dry-mouthed miles from Atlanta. I closed my eyes against the terror. I tried to get a breath and failed; I stood on the sun porch of Liberty in the presence of an ancient and possibly dead woman and knew I could not go on living.

"*Prrrow?*"

It was a soft, throaty, trilling little sound of inquiry, and I knew it in my bones and heart. My eyes flew open. A huge Maine coon cat raised its head from the folds of the shawl, its cloud of tawny-striped fur almost invisible against the same-color pattern, and stretched its legs and kneaded huge paddle feet in the air.

"Oh, Zoot!" I said softly, and began to cry.

I picked him up from the chaise and held him over my shoulder and buried my face in his fur as I used to do. It still had the same smell: of dry silk with the sun and a bit of dust trapped in it. He was light on my shoulder; I remembered that most of his bulk had always been the luxuriant gold and brown tabby fur. He lay patiently under my grasp, and I remembered that too. Zoot had always been a phlegmatic animal. It belied his exotic appearance. Named Zut Alors by the young man who had given him to me my last summer in Retreat, he quickly became Zut and then Zoot for my grandmother, who claimed that his full leggings looked a great deal like a zoot suit. We had looked at her blankly, and she had shaken her head in mock irritation.

"You children know absolutely nothing," she had said. But he remained Zoot. It suited him better. He was never a French cat.

"I thought you would have died," I said to him, wiping my nose in his fur. "I'm so glad you're still here."

"Darcy?" a thin voice said, and I looked up. Grammaude was awake and staring at me. She seemed almost afraid. Her dark face had blanched. Her eyes, though, were those I remembered: dark and liquid and shining. And then I saw that tears stood in them.

"It's me," I said. "Hello, Grammaude. I didn't mean to wake you."

My voice sounded silly in my ears, high and childish.

"Is it really you?" she said, and the tiny voice strengthened a little. Some of the soft richness of the Low Country, which she had never really lost, clung in it.

"It's really me. I decided to drive, and I got here a day early, and I didn't think to call. I'm sorry if I startled you."

She shook her head as if to clear it and smiled. More of the old Grammaude came flushing back into her face.

"I dream of dead people a lot these days, and sometimes I can't remember who is and who isn't," she said. "And I can't always be sure when I'm awake. I was afraid I was seeing a ghost."

"Me too," I said, smiling tentatively.

I put Zoot down and he floated back onto her lap in the chaise and began to clean his behind. I remembered what Grammaude had always called that leg-over-head posture: playing the cello.

"I'm so glad he's alive," I said.

"I'm so glad you are," she said, and tears began to roll silently down her fissured cheeks. I made a small sound of distress, and she shook her white head impatiently and dabbed at them.

"Don't pay any attention," she said. "Old people cry like other people belch. Or fart. It's entirely unconscious and serves to relieve a little pressure. That's all. But it has to be the most unattractive thing to watch. . . . Oh, my dear child. Here you are at last. And still you, except much too thin. And you've cut your hair; I like it. You look like a redheaded elf."

Her voice was like my own blood beating in my veins. It warmed and eased me; it always had. I did not want to be warmed and eased; I wanted only white, seamless peace. I wanted control and distance.

"They made me cut it in the hospital," I said. "They won't let you have curlers or scissors or dryers or anything you need to take care of long hair. After a woman committed suicide by taking her hot curlers into the shower with her, they made everybody have short hair, even the guys. Some of them were gay and minded a lot more than I did."

She looked at me steadily, smiling just a bit, and I felt as I had as a child, when I had tried to shock her and failed.

"So you have a car," she said. "Wonderful. I can stop depending on Sarah or Petie or one of the Willises to do errands for me, and we can do some serious running around. I sold the big car several years ago when my hands got just too bad to drive—arthritis; it's a monumental bore."

"I don't think you're going to like this car," I said. "It belongs to a black drug and alcohol addict, and it's rusted all over, and it has a bumper sticker that says SHIT HAPPENS. Or it will again when I get some stuff to clean it."

She looked at me in silence for a little longer, and then her mouth twitched and she began to laugh. There it was, bleached and diminished, but there: Grammaude's old laugh. I smiled too, unwillingly.

"Perfect," she said. "Let's take every old lady in Retreat to lunch. We've had SAVE THE WHALES and BABY ON BOARD, and I believe one of the Conant children had a RUGBY PLAYERS EAT THEIR DEAD last summer, but to my knowledge we've never had a SHIT HAPPENS. Come on, dear, give me a hand up and I'll point you toward your room, and then I think I'll call Petie and Sarah and tell them no thanks for tonight and make us a martini. Maybe two. There's enough crab to do for dinner."

I helped her off the chaise, wincing to myself at the stiffness of her gnarled hands and stooped body and the way she had to lean on me. She was as weightless as a child, but I remembered the straight spine and quick steps. Now she clung and hobbled and her breath came in laboring, wheezing gasps.

"Grammaude, are you okay?"

"Perfectly," she said with effort. "It just sounds grisly. Low blood pressure or something about the circulation, I think. Mainly age. I've got you upstairs in my old room; I'm sorry to switch you, but I just can't manage the stairs any more. Will it do?"

"Of course. I never could figure out why you gave me the big downstairs room all those years. A child in the best bedroom . . . I know it had been yours and Granddaddy's."

"That's why," she said softly. "I never could sleep

there again, somehow. But I find it's perfectly all right this summer. I guess I should have moved down there long ago."

That night my grandmother and I got drunk. I took a bath in the old claw-footed bathtub upstairs and changed into clean jeans and a sweater, and when I came downstairs she was in the kitchen in a bright Indian cotton caftan, a bit of lipstick on her mouth and a cloud of Caleche enveloping her, mixing martinis in a pitcher. A bowl of crab and mayonnaise salad sat on the old oak table that had always occupied the precise center of the kitchen. We took the pitcher out onto the porch and sat drinking, looking at the sun sliding down behind the Camden Hills. Everything that had happened for twelve years and before lay between us: too much. Somehow I knew we would not speak of it, not this night. And we didn't. We had one drink, and then two, and then I poured us another. Calm dropped down around me like a glass dome. We talked a little of my trip up from Atlanta and who was in the colony this summer, but mainly we looked at the eternal blue of the bay and the orange sun. And we drank. I could not ever remember my grandmother having more than two drinks. The calm deepened and thickened.

Later we sat at the dinner table in the light of two candles in the old faience holders, looking across at each other. Spots of color stood on her cheeks and her eyes glittered. My own face was warm.

"I haven't had this much to drink in I can't remember when," she said. "It's wonderful. I don't know why I don't do it oftener. I'll know in the morning, though."

"You look twenty years younger than you did when I saw you this afternoon," I said. The calm was profound and wonderful. I felt I could say anything to her.

"So do you," she said.

"I haven't had anything to drink since I left here," I said. "Twelve years, as dry as a bone. Tranquilizers have been my addiction of choice lately. I've been missing out. I feel better than I have in years. Booze is the answer. You know, this is what I remember most about this place. This . . . certainty of safety. This peace. I hope it's not all liquor."

"Not all of it," Grammaude said. "It's what Retreat does best. I'm glad you feel it. I hoped you would."

"My shrink said it wasn't good to lean too much on places or people," I said. "I'm supposed to be learning to trust only myself, lean only on my own strength. Isn't that a laugh? But I know what he means. Places change, or you lose them. People go away, or they die."

I looked away from her. She would die soon, I thought. She was silent for a long moment, playing with her fork in the crab salad, and then she said, "Was it so bad, this fear? I've never quite understood what panic disorder is. But sometimes I think there are many, many worse things than fear."

Anger flared, far below the martini calm. She knew nothing.

"It was horrible," I said. "It *is* horrible. It's nothing at all like ordinary fear, not even like honest terror. It's like . . . imagine that you know you're about to die awfully, horribly, and magnify that a thousand times, and let it go on and on for months and years. Sometimes you want to scream with it. Sometimes you do: scream and scream and scream. . . ."

"When did it start?"

Her voice was calm, but there were tears in her eyes again. I was perversely glad to see them.

"I'm not really sure. Gradually. Sometimes I think it was when I first graduated from college and went home and Dad wasn't there. I mean, I knew he had gone to

Nevada; we'd talked about it and decided I'd keep the apartment, since I'd need one anyway. But we thought maybe Mother might be home from the hospital by the time I graduated, only of course she wasn't. There wasn't anybody at all. I don't know why it was so bad, or so different, being there alone. He'd been gone often while I was growing up. I never had anybody staying with me after I was sixteen or so. I was used to taking care of him and myself. Her too, at first.

"But it *was* different. I began to be afraid; my heart would pound and I'd feel like something awful was going to happen. I couldn't keep still. So I went out and practically knocked on doors and took the first job I was offered, at a public relations agency, as a receptionist. And I got myself a smaller apartment and a roommate, and I worked nonstop, day and night, for the next six years and got to be a senior writer at a regional magazine, and was really very good at it too, and for a long time I didn't really think about the fear. It was just when I was alone and not busy, like a long weekend, that it came back.

"And then I met Hank, and he was so perfect—old Atlanta family, money, charm, wit, prospects: the whole nine yards, old Henry Chiles Taliaferro had—and we got engaged and thought we might be married in June. This was in January, when I was twenty-seven. . . . Well, I had the first full-scale panic attack the night his parents were announcing our engagement to all their buddies. Instead of the Piedmont Driving Club, I went to the Piedmont Hospital emergency room. They diagnosed it as fatigue and hyperventilation, and we told everybody it was food poisoning, but it kept happening, oftener and oftener and worse and worse, and finally even I saw that I had to have some help or I'd just . . . die. By that time I was afraid to leave the apartment, afraid to be alone for even five minutes. My roommate moved out and I lost my job, of course. Hank said he couldn't spend any more time babysitting me, so I signed myself into Peachwood Hospital. I paid my own bill for the first month and then had them call Dad in Las Vegas. I didn't hear from him for nearly three months; I know you must have paid for all of it. It's supposed to be a very good hospital, by the way; you got your money's worth. Hank's mother picked it out herself and came along when Hank drove me there. I never saw either of them again after that night."

We sat in the candle-flickering silence. There was only the peace and a kind of sighing hum, like white noise. I listened contentedly to it.

"Was he special, this Hank?" Grammaude said presently.

"I can't even remember what he looked like," I said.

We both began to giggle.

"I can remember what his mother looked like, though. W. C. Fields. She was not enchanted by the prospect of a mentally ill daughter-in-law. Try telling that lady about childhood trauma and delayed reaction and repressed anger and all that jazz. She, by God, knew it ran in the family. I think old Hank told her about Great-Granddaddy and Granddaddy's little spells, and about Mother's big ones, before he stopped the car that night they put me in. He married Luanne Ormsby the next year, I read in the society section. Nothing running in that family but Republicanism and money and maybe a little hookworm, way back."

"You think this . . . whatever it is, fear . . . comes from your Chambliss blood?"

"Who knows?" I said. "Even my shrink doesn't. It sure as hell couldn't have helped."

"Well," Grammaude said, "you've got just as much Gascoigne blood in you as Chambliss, and I'll tell you, there's not sturdier or more constant blood on the

East Coast than that. Eccentric, maybe, but the lot of us are hopelessly sane and doomed to stay that way. So put your mind to rest on that score."

I finished my martini and poured another. It felt like perfume on my tongue: lovely stuff. Grammaude seemed to have a limitless supply. I decided to stay just a bit drunk for the entire three months I would be in Retreat.

"Tell me about Mike," I said, ready now to hear anything.

"Well, Mike. Let's see. He's a very good architect in . . . I think it's Portland, or maybe Portsmouth, I can't ever remember. He wins awards and has his designs in magazines. He was married briefly, a long time ago, right out of MIT. They split up after a year or so, and there weren't any children. I think she was awfully rich, and he wasn't, and one or the other of them cared too much about that, and one thing led to another. . . . He doesn't get home much, but when he does, he comes to see me and spends hours and hours talking, just like he used to do. He's a much more attractive man than he was a boy, but he really hasn't changed a great deal. I'm terribly fond of him. He never got over you. I don't think he ever will. You needn't worry, though; I don't think he plans to be here this summer."

I was silent. For just a moment Mike Willis stood in the shimmering air beside me, dark, solid, the odd light-blue eyes gleaming, the thick lock of straight black hair down over his left eyebrow. I could see the peppering of dark freckles across the bridge of his nose and the gap between his two front teeth.

"When did his grandmother die?" I asked. "I realized today that I never actually knew."

"Tina died the summer after your grandfather," Grammaude said softly. "She had cancer of the colon; she must have had it the summer before, and they didn't know, or I didn't. . . . I didn't come to Retreat the first summer without Peter; it was the only summer since we were married that I didn't, but . . . I didn't, and so I wasn't here when she died. Micah called me in Charleston. It was very quick, I think. It's always been one of the few real regrets I've had in my life, that I wasn't here when Tina died."

"I saw your boyfriend today," I said, grinning at her, the wine humming in my ears.

She smiled at me inquiringly.

"Your old boyfriend. Micah Willis. I stopped in the cemetery for a minute on the way in, and he was there. I'm sorry about his stroke; it must be very hard for him. He's failed badly, hasn't he? But the old Micah is still in there."

She was quiet, and I looked at her across the table and saw something that had not been there before.

"He *was* your boyfriend, wasn't he? Lord, Grammaude, I was teasing you, but he was . . . something to you, wasn't he?"

Dear God, part of me thought, what are you saying? You can't say things like that to Grammaude. But she only smiled at me.

"Yes," she said. "He was something to me. He *is* something to me. But not a boyfriend. Not . . . a lover. Only your grandfather was that, always."

"But you loved him . . . Micah."

"I needed him."

"It's the same thing."

"No. But in a way, a very real way, I loved him too, just not in the way you meant."

"You mean you never . . . had an affair with him? Oh, why, Grammaude? You always were together, the two of you; I can hardly remember a day that didn't have Micah in it. It could have been such a good thing for both of you, I mean, after all those years when you were alone, and then he was. . . . Was it because he was a native?"

She smiled. "Never that. It was . . . I suppose it was because of Peter—your grandfather—and Tina."

"But they were gone."

"Oh, no."

"You mean, you and Micah felt you had to be faithful to their memories?"

"If you like. Gracious, what a conversation to be having with your granddaughter. It can't be proper," she said, and I knew she would talk no more today about Micah Willis. Well, there would be time for that. The white peace swirled and hummed.

"I don't see a thing of my mother in this house," I said, looking around the dim old room. The warm smoke gold of the walls had not changed since I was small. There were amulets of family all about, all familiar to me. But I realized for the first time that I could not see my mother here.

"I see a lot of her," Grammaude said, "but not the woman who became your mother. Only the little girl who was my daughter. She's everywhere. Your mother never came here after you were born."

"Because of the way Grandfather felt about my father?" I said.

"I suppose so, yes," she said. "That and other things."

"I'm supposed to get therapeutically angry at them," I said serenely, "but I just can't seem to feel it. I never have."

"How can you?" Grammaude said. "It would be like getting angry at a couple of abstract ideas. You can't get angry at your mother because she was never a mother to you. She was never anything to you, really; the running away and the drinking and the craziness started in earnest before you were old enough to remember her. She's been in hospitals most of your life, and when she wasn't, you were more like a mother to her than vice versa. And she's been away in this last one for . . . what, seven years now? Eight? I don't think she'll come out this time. She's just gone too far past healing. And your father . . . dear God, what was he to you? All over the country, from one job to another, broke most of the time, hardly ever home, you in those awful boarding schools he picked out, never even letting you come to me except here in the summers . . . and the few months at a time you were both home you were taking care of him like a little wife. You can get angry at the *idea* of what they both were to you, or were not, but not at them as parents, because neither ever was. No wonder you can't feel anything."

She stopped, breathing hard, coughing a little, and drank off her wine. I stared at her. I had never heard her speak so of her daughter or the man she had married. I knew only that she paid my bills wherever I was, both before I left her that last summer and after, and that for most of the seventeen summers of my life she was its sole and very present polestar. I had never considered how she might feel about Happy Chambliss O'Ryan, though I suspected what she thought of my father.

"I think maybe we're both drunk," I said. "And you may be right about all that. But somehow it seems to me very important that I feel the anger. My shrink says I really must, or I'll never be well."

She made a small noise of disgust. "What can he possibly know about you, this shrink? Let them go. That's something the old always want to tell the young and seldom can; one of the few true things we've come to know in our lives. Just . . . let them go. You can't get them back as parents; they're gone from you. Let go. Save your splendid anger for something worth it."

"What is, Grammaude? What's worth it?"

"You'll know," she said, "when the time comes. Don't worry. You'll know. And it will be a fine anger, one that can blow up the world. It means nothing that you don't feel it, except that there's been nothing yet really worth it."

"My shrink says I'm supposed to get angry with you too."

"I rather thought you had been, all those years."

"No," I said in a low voice. "Not angry. Afraid to think of you, I guess; certainly afraid to be in touch with you. Afraid I'd run straight back to you and end up here. And now I have. Dear God, Grammaude, how can I just let twenty-nine years go?"

"Darling, I really think you haven't any choice, if you want a life."

I looked off into the darkness beyond the circle of the candles' guttering light.

"I can't see ahead," I whispered. "I can't see what comes next. Only white, like on a broken TV set: snow. I can't see."

"Why do you have to?" she said, reaching over to touch my hand. "Why not just rest in the moment? It's what Retreat is for, exactly that."

"I have to know."

"Nobody does, darling. That's one of the other true things I know. Nobody knows what's ahead."

"How can they stand it?"

"By taking nothing for granted," she said fiercely. "By being willing to dare anything, everything. And then . . . by letting it go. T. S. Eliot said it better than anybody: 'Teach us to care and not to care. Teach us to be still.'"

Later, after I had helped her back to the big bedroom and watched her smile at me and close the door, I went back and lay on the sofa before the dying fire. I knew I should get up and go upstairs to bed, but my head was spinning and the fire was hypnotic, and I was afraid I would lose the fragile envelope of white peace if I left it. I pulled the old Hudson Bay blanket that was always kept on the back of the sofa over me and lay in the fire-leaping darkness. I felt alone on the planet but somehow sealed in a cocoon of warmth and timelessness and nowhereness.

"I let you go," I said to my mother and father into the darkness. "I do."

Zoot came padding in sometime later and leaped softly onto the sofa and curled into my side, and I drifted, the fire whispering on one side of me, Zoot's light steady breathing on the other.

"I let you go," I whispered, and slept.

Chapter Fifteen

The next morning, those two malignant ghosts were gone. I was sure of it, for the drumbeat of fear that had festered viruslike in my blood for the past two years was gone too. Not muted, not in abeyance, but gone. I sat on the edge of the sofa in the chilly room, staring at the dead ashes in the fireplace and testing deep breaths, and then I leaped to my feet and ran to the porch and put my head out the screen door and sucked salt-sweet, spruce-sharp air into my lungs until I felt my heart would burst with it. Only then did I realize that I had not dared draw deeply of the air of the world for many, many months. I could have wept, shouted, flown off the earth with the joy of it. There is no way to tell how the absence of fear feels to someone who has not known it for a long time, someone who has been sure they would never know it again.

The bay and sky shimmered with the satin blue of early morning, and the water lay as still as a mirror, misted off at the point where it washed Islesboro and Little Deer. I could not see all the way to North Haven and thought we would have weather of some sort later. Not, though, until twilight at least; that left all of this perfect day to run through the colony: down to the water, around to the yacht club, in and out of the birch thickets, up to the lips of the cliffs—everywhere I had run as a child, tasting it all once more, feeling once again its benison. I would look in on some of the cottages and see who was there; I would say hello to the people I had known before. . . .

The fear smashed me like a breaking wave. I literally staggered back under it, and sat down on the edge of the chaise, and hugged myself, fighting for the breath that had come in deep drafts only a moment before. I put my head down on my knees and rocked, waiting it out. Waiting it out. I don't think I ever felt so hopelessly certain—even in the hospital—that there was nothing ahead for me but death.

There is a certain smug conventional wisdom that says suicide is an act of supreme cowardice. Even the impulse to it, many say, shows a singular lack of character, of moral fiber, of plain old-fashioned gumption. Brave people don't do that. We used to laugh grimly at that in the hospital. The bravest people I have ever known, I knew there: the ones who got themselves through another day without ending their lives. Don't think it isn't possible to kill yourself in a mental hospital. There are quite a few ways, and by the time you have been inside a month you've heard them all. They are just about the only gifts the patients have left to give one another. It is easier to stay alive there, though. You are surrounded by people who are doing it with you. Outside . . . outside is dangerous. I sat on the screened porch of Liberty in that tender morning and knew I was in grave peril of my life.

And then the monstrous fear began to ebb, and soon it had slunk back to its familiar post-hospital level: simmering but on low. If I took my Xanax, if I moved slowly and lightly and did not breathe deeply,

I could manage this day. But only with someone beside me.

It is nearly impossible to explain, also, how terrible the anticipatory fear of the fear is: almost worse than the main event. It is this foreshock, which shimmers around you like the aura of a migraine before it begins, that drives you to seek company, to avoid being alone at all costs. In the company of people there is a sort of shadowy baffle between you and it. It will have to go through them to get to you. Before the hospital I used to spend whole days in a mall, or tagging after an exasperated Hank on weekends when he did errands and played golf or tennis. I even once invited a Jehovah's Witness lady into my apartment and pantomimed fascination; she stayed for hours and came back many times, and such were my straits that I was always overjoyed to see her. She must have wondered where she had failed when at last she knocked and found me gone. I would have let anyone in, bought anything, in those days.

Now I hauled myself up off the chaise and padded in to wake Grammaude. My shrink had said it might come back; well, here it was, and I would see it out, but I would do it in company. It was, after all, the deal: I would wait it out in Retreat, and Grammaude would provide the company.

I heard her coughing before I reached her door and knew she was awake, but when I came near I saw she had taped a message to the closed door. *Darling,* it read, *I'm going to have a day in bed. The wages of sin. Can you manage? Food in fridge.* And it was signed *MGC.*

I stood outside her door taking careful breaths, eyes closed, struggling not to wrench the door open and go in and beg her to stay with me. And then I got a pencil out of the old Royal Copenhagen mug that stood beside the telephone and wrote beneath her initials, *Booze is the answer. I'll see you at dinner.* I signed it *DCO* and went downstairs and dressed and forced myself out into the day.

I decided on the shingle beach in front of the Little House where my aunt and uncle summered. Grammaude had said they were going to Bar Harbor this morning; that meant a full day, I remembered. And my older cousins were not in Retreat this summer. I don't think they came often; girls who married out of the colony usually did not. I would probably have at least a part of the beach to myself. I could watch people that way, and dash into their midst if I had to, but unless things got too bad I could be apart from them too. It was no morning to meet the colony.

I sat on the top step of the Little House and watched brown children playing in the cold shallows. Like children in my time here, they had a sameness about them: square, towheaded, possessed already of long faces and definite chins, dressed in faded, unfashionable bathing suits with Yaycamp T-shirts over them against the bite of the sun. I could almost see my mother and my Uncle Petie among them, and my older brother, the legendary Sean. Even, if I stretched it, small Mike Willis and myself. When I first came to Retreat, according to Grammaude, I was laughing and fearless and gregarious, the darling of the colony. That was in the days before my remembrance began, before the disappearances of my mother came too often and lasted too long, before the screaming and the slaps and tears and rages started in earnest when she was home, before my father began to go to other cities and then other states "for interviews" and not return. Before the trickle of coarse, middle-aged Irish "companions" for me became a steady stream; before the green-walled, linoleum-floored convent boarding schools that taught me guilt and self-disgust and patience. A very long time ago indeed.

My own child would be here now, if I'd amounted
to anything, I thought, and realized that no matter
how bitterly I had come to hate this place later, I
would still, if I could, give my child the gift of Retreat
summers. There was still, despite everything, a quality
of timelessness and indelibility on this beach. It
would be a powerful amulet for a child.

Then why had it failed me? Or had I failed it?

A tiny child, smaller than the rest, tagged after the
larger children as they sprinted up the beach after
their bored teenage au pair. At least that had
changed; in my day it had been nannies or doting
grandmothers. For me, it had usually been Grammaude. The older children looked back and laughed
at the small one, and she sat down on the pebbles
and wept bitterly, until the impatient girl came back
and scooped her up, chiding her. The sting of tears
surprised me.

That's me, I thought.

And it *was* me: the child I could remember, at any
rate. By that time I was not a popular child in Retreat.
Not like the small spawn of the families who had
summered there for generations. Oh, there were the
Boston Chamblisses on one side of me, but one had
only to look at my fiery hair and listen to my novena-
thickened speech to realize what was on the other
side. And the children knew it and, unlike their
elders, were not slow to tax me with it. Over my furious little head the raffish shade of my mad mother,
Happy, hovered, and the loud Irish presence of my
father, Tommy; and there was still the pale ghost of
my Uncle Petie's dead baby, for the colony still talked
of that at their dinner tables all these years later, and
their children talked of it with alacrity to me. The
weight of all those specters was too much for me.
Volatile by nature, I became fierce and truculent; I
got into fights and blacked aristocratic blue eyes and

blooded aristocratic small noses when some child called me the grease monkey's daughter or pointed out that my mother slept with anybody at all, and spent half her time in the crazy house, and had just the past winter tried to kill herself by cutting her wrists with the night nurse's nail scissors.

I swore too, with a proficiency that only my mother could match and from whom I had learned it, and was given to long spells when I simply vanished into the woods or sneaked out in my older cousins' Beetle Cat and could not be found for hours. The wildness and the solitude of Cape Rosier were its earliest and best gifts to me, and I went out into them like a wild thing and stayed until someone hunted me down. It was usually Grammaude.

I was a born tomboy; by the time I was six I could swim like a fish and was learning to sail like a native child under the tutelage of old Micah Willis, and there was not a tree in the colony I had not climbed, not a slanting roof, or a rock, or a cliff. I sassed old ladies who were syrupy to me, ignored old gentlemen who were debonair and charming, would not pass canapés at parties or go to square dances at the yacht club or wear anything but blue jeans. I was the only child in colony memory who hated Yaycamp. The children thought I was queer and unfeminine and common, and the adults thought the same, and in time it was decided that my manners, despite the best efforts of my grandmother, were nothing they wanted their offspring to emulate. If it had not been for Grammaude, who seemed simply not to notice that there was anything wrong with me or to hear any of the talk about me, and for Mike Willis, I would have spent all my time alone.

But there was Grammaude. And there was Mike.

I am told that I played with him the entire summer that I first came to Retreat; that even though he was almost four and I was not quite one and a half, we were instantly and almost uncannily inseparable. I don't remember that summer at Retreat, of course. But I remember the next one—or at least I remember one incident from it.

It was two summers before I came to Retreat again; my grandmother did not come the summer after my first one, and the next summer my mother was spending her last long stay at home and was savagely and crazily protective of me, letting no one near. So I was four and a half when I came the next time. After that, I never missed a summer again until the last one, when I was seventeen.

At four and a half, a child remembers the things that divide its life. What I remember is Mike Willis.

I think it must have been the first day he came to Liberty with his mother, Beth, who had taken care of me that first summer and had been persuaded by Grammaude to do it again. As he had that first summer, her son Mike came with her. She was always rather protective of him. It was far too early for him to help out in the family boatyard, and there was no one else to leave him with. Having him at Liberty was no problem; Grammaude always loved Mike. She has told me over and over that on the morning when he and Beth came into the kitchen, I looked up from my cereal and grinned as though I had seen him only the day before and said, "Where you been?"

I don't remember that. But I remember something else. I remember something about the day that puzzled me; I could not figure it out, and then, at the end, when Grammaude was reading to us from *The Jungle Book* and his mother called to him that it was time to go home, I said, "Why are you going home with that lady?"

"I have to. She's my mother," he said.

"No, she's not either," I said, troubled and uneasy.

"Well, she is too. Who else would she be?" Mike said.

"I don't know. But if she's your mother, where does she go?"

"What do you mean?"

"You know, go. Mothers go away. Where does yours go?"

"She doesn't go nowhere," Mike said, scowling. "She just comes here and goes home, and I go with her."

"Well, then, where does your daddy go?"

"What's the matter with you? He goes down to the boatyard and then comes home," he said.

I began to cry. "You lie," I sobbed. "You lie. They go away!"

My grandmother reached down and gathered me into her arms, and through my tears I saw Beth Willis lean down and whisper something to Mike, and he came over to me and put his hand on my shoulder, tentatively.

"I ain't gon' go off and leave you this summer," he said gruffly. "I'll come every day, if you want me to."

"I don't," I sobbed. "I hate you, and I don't want you to come over here any more."

But I did want him to come. And he did, most days after that, for the entire summer, and all the summers that came afterward. From the very beginning, Mike Willis was with me. He even went into exile with me. If it cost him much, I never knew it.

He was not an outcast when I first remember him. He was a tough, cheerful, sweet-tempered little boy with a wide, gap-toothed white grin and his father and grandfather's crow-black hair—like theirs, usually in his eyes. He did not boast or show off, but something about him drew the eye and commanded attention. I think it was his sheer competence and his innate self-confidence. Mike could do almost anything with his hands, play any sport, outswim and outsail even the older colony boys, hold his own in any fight. Even though he was a native—and that still mattered in Retreat then, and probably still does now—he was something of a leader for the young people. He was a native but with a difference: his grandfather was the confidant of one of the colony's acknowledged doyennes, Maude Chambliss, and his father was not only a member of the yacht club but had been commandant only a year before. The Willises were village, but they were different too. I always heard that they had been thick with the Chamblisses since my grandmother and grandfather were young. It had something to do with the formidable old woman who had been my great-grandmother, but I could never remember what.

So Mike Willis was not, before I came back to Retreat, a pariah. He chose that role himself, and he did it for and with me, and I remember well the summer that he did it. Indeed, I remember the day and almost the hour.

I was seven that summer and he was nearing ten. He had watched my steady descent into disreputability with an equanimity uncommon for a boy his age, championing me when I got myself in too deep, consoling me gruffly and matter-of-factly when I was hurt or angry, spending more and more time with me alone because I refused to stay around the others on the beach or at the yacht club. But still, the other children flocked around him like chattering birds when he would let them, and on this day we were the center of a small flock, he and I, sitting on the dock of the Willises' boatyard in sweaters and long pants because of the chill fog that had becalmed that morning's Beetle Cat regatta. All of us were restive and cranky because of that and were playing a desultory game of mumblety-peg, strictly forbidden by all adults we knew, on the soft silvery wood of the dock, simply because Mike's father had gone to Ellsworth and his Grandfather Micah was inside caulking a Winslow dinghy. I thought sourly that there were too many Winslows in the colony; there were three in this group around Mike, and I liked none of them. They were handsome, autocratic, and uniformly mean.

One of them, Gretchen, named for her grandmother, who was keeping her that summer, cut her slanting green eyes at Mike Willis and said, "Let's cut our wrists and be blood brothers and sisters. I bet you're scared to do it, Mike Willis."

She was a year older than he, but she followed him everywhere that summer with those eyes. I saw her do it; I watched her all summer, watching him.

"Not," Mike said, deftly flipping the pocket knife off his ear and into the wood, where it quivered upright.

"Are," Gretchen said.

"Not," Mike said, and pulled the knife out of the deck and made a swift, deepish cut in the little blue delta of veins in his brown wrist. Blood welled up and spilled over, spattering on the gray wood. My stomach heaved and my head spun, but I did not look away. The others gasped and murmured, and Gretchen Winslow gave a little shriek of surprise. Mike stared at her levelly.

After that, of course, all of them cut their wrists. No one would dare not, after Mike had. Most only scratched the skin enough to produce a beading of blood with much squeezing, but everybody did it. Then Mike handed the knife to me.

"Want me to do it, or you want to do it?" he said.

"Wait a minute, I didn't mean her," Gretchen Winslow said. She was having a hard time keeping the bright little drops forming on her wrist. Mike's still pumped blood right along.

"Naw, not with her." Another of them took up the cry.

"Why not?" Mike's voice was pleasant, and his hair was, as usual, in his eyes, so I could not see them. Queasiness warred in me with rage and despair. I wanted to be away from there more than I had ever wanted anything in my life, but I would not get up and run in front of them. And I would not cry.

"Because you'd get garage grease in your veins, not blood," said the oldest Winslow boy, grinning, and all the others except Mike laughed.

"Maybe she ought to cut hers, after all," Gretchen said in the slow, rich voice that reminded me of her grandmother. "Maybe the sickness would run out then. Maybe the craziness would just run right on out. But nobody better touch that blood, though. Yuck. Sick blood."

Mike raised his head and looked at her. "You wanna tell us what you're talking about, Gretch?" he said.

"Well, everybody knows her mother cut her wrists in the nuthouse last winter," she said defensively, hearing in his voice something she did not often hear. "Everybody knows there's sickness in her mother's blood; hers too, probably. Everybody talks about that. Sickness and craziness, it's in the blood. My grandmother said so. They must have been trying to get it out of her in that hospital."

Everybody laughed.

"Darcy, hold out your wrist," Mike said.

I did, and he cut it, neatly and swiftly, and reached over and joined it to his own. I watched as if hypnotized as the blood mingled and washed over our wrists. I could not look away. I never did feel the pain of the cut.

"Now, you go on home, Gretchen, and take your little friends with you," ten-year-old Mike Willis said in the voice of a man. "I wouldn't have Winslow blood in me, or any of the rest of yours, if I was bleeding to death in the desert."

"I'm going to tell on you," Gretchen said, furious, scrambling up from the dock and starting off.

The others followed her, mumbling uneasily. None of them would look at me.

"I'm going to tell my grandmother you tried to make me cut my wrist and all kinds of other awful things," she shouted. "I'm going to say you pulled a knife on me. You're almost as bad as she is: Chamblisses and Willises, both trashy. My grandmother says so. She'll make your mother and father punish you for the rest of your life."

"I sincerely doubt that, young lady," Micah Willis said, coming out of the boathouse and staring down the dock at her. "If I hear that you've said a word about Mike or Miss Darcy here I'll tell your grandmother what *did* happen, and make no mistake, Mike won't be the one gets his hide tanned. Your grandmother knows which side her bread's buttered on, believe me."

Gretchen flounced away, and the others melted off into the birch wood that linked the boathouse with the Retreat tennis court. Micah Willis ambled over, hands in his pockets, and stood looking down at us. Mike looked steadily back at him, his finger pressed over the cut in his wrist. I stared down at the dock, watching slow drops of red splatter and dry.

"Know you're not supposed to be playing that game, don't you?" Micah said.

"Yes sir."

"Know what your father said he'd do, next time he caught you doing it."

"Yes sir."

"Well, don't do it again."

"No sir."

"And go get Mrs. Chambliss to fix those wrists, both of you."

Micah turned back toward the boathouse.

"Grandpa, you goin' to tell?" Mike called after him.

"Reckon not," his grandfather said, not looking back at us.

"You goin' to tell on Gretchen?"

"Don't need to. Just being a Winslow is punishment enough," he said.

Mike and I began to laugh, there on the dock, with the fog gathering like smoke off in the birches, already whiting out the nearest islands.

"I now pronounce you an honorary Willis," he said. After that, in the summers, we were not often apart.

There seemed little change in him for the next few years. Oh, he went through a relatively trouble-free puberty, growing tall and lanky where he had been square and low to the earth before, the smooth brown of his thin arms and legs sliding into ropy muscle, his round face squaring up and taking on the high planes of his father and grandfather's faces. And he was moody sometimes where he had been open and cheerful before, vanishing for an afternoon or even a day in his Beetle Cat or on foot into the woods or along the high, wild cliffs beyond the Aerie. But I did not mind; the essential Mike remained, and from early childhood I had done the same thing, spending long, suspended, timeless afternoons just lying on my back in the soft green moss of the birch thicket, staring into the canopy of leaves overhead or dreaming out to sea on the lower cliffs beyond Braebonnie, where, when she had first come to Retreat, my grandmother had tried to rescue a fawn trapped in the rocks of the ledge. Mike's and my togetherness was the spine in the skeleton of those summers, but our twin needs for solitude were the sinews that supported it.

I changed though, or at least the outside of me did, and I hated it. At ten I had a spurt of growth that

brought me to just below five feet and lengthened my
wiry body into budding curves and softness. I loathed
both the new body and the height, thinking despairingly that if I had been conspicuous before among my
peers in Retreat, I was downright grotesque now:
taller by half a head than many of them and shaped like
a miniature woman, the whole sorry edifice crowned
with a mane of burning red ringlets. That summer,
after enduring a spate of clumsy innuendo from most
of the boys and one or two of the girls, I took Grammaude's sewing scissors and cut off my hair. After that
there was no doubt about it: I was as conspicuous as a
balding female midget among all the shoulder-brush-
ing, ironed-straight hairdos of those post-Woodstock
days. I literally hid from everyone, even Mike, until late
summer, when my hair had grown back enough to
feather around my face in a cap of curls.

"It's sort of nice," Mike said. "It looks French."

"How do you know?" I said. "You don't know anything about French people."

"Well, I do too," he said. "My grandmother's people are French, aren't they, Mrs. Chambliss?"

"Indeed they are. Duschesnes from Nova Scotia
and before that, I think your grandmother said, from
Brittany. A wild coast something like this one. They
were seafaring people even back in France."

We were sitting around the fire in Liberty in the early
morning, dressed in sweaters and heavy socks against
the chill white fog that refused to burn off. Mike had
been working that summer in the family boatyard, so I
would not have seen much of him had I wanted to, but
I had not wanted to, before. And then suddenly I did,
and as if summoned by sorcery he appeared out of the
fog with a plate of still-warm molasses doughnuts from
his mother and a volume of Thoreau's essays he wanted
to discuss with Grammaude. He did that a lot; I can't
remember a time that Mike and my grandmother did

not talk about books and writers when they spent time together. I thought he looked even taller than I remembered, and I blushed for some unfathomable reason. I had not seen much of him since the middle of June, when I had cut my hair.

When we had gorged ourselves on doughnuts and dipped into and back out of Thoreau and Grammaude had gone upstairs to dress, he said, "Get your oils. I want to show you something."

And as naturally as if we had left off our association the night before, I got my yellow slicker and hat and followed him out into the fog.

"Where we going?"

"Osprey Head," he said, and I smiled. I had first been taken to Osprey Head in his company by his grandfather when I was very small, and we went at least once each summer after that, Mike sailing his own catboat when he was adjudged old enough. We did not go often; it was Park Service land now, and they did not encourage foot traffic on it because of the nesting eagles. But Cape Rosier natives and some of the summer people did go, quietly and infrequently, and though they undoubtedly knew of the visits, the service did nothing to stop them. Those pilgrimages were just that: gentle voyages to pay homage. The colony of eagles was flourishing now, and seeing the huge purse-like nests and the great wings against the sky never failed to make the hair on the back of my neck prickle and tears come to my eyes. Osprey Head: it was a wonderful idea, a celebration of wildness and freedom. It would signal an end to my self-imposed exile.

We did not go down to the dock where Mike's catboat swung against its mooring, though. We cut through the dense spruce and fir wood that spilled down the rocks to the beach below the Aerie. I knew you could get to the bridge that way, the wooden one that connected the long thin finger of Loon Ledge to

Osprey Head, but I had never crossed that bridge and had been to the little secret half-moon beach only once, when Grammaude had taken me and Mike there long ago, for a picnic. We had had our lunch and paddled in the flaccid little wash of surf, and then she had told us of the beautiful solitary woman who had lived in the big house above the beach, who had been a friend of my great-grandfather's, and how she herself had come there to sun and dream while she was waiting for my mother to be born. It was an enchanted spot, but somehow I was not comfortable there. It seemed too much the property of others, and I did not mean the Park Service. They merely owned it. It belonged to people who were dead now, yet somehow lived vividly in the quiet air. I had not asked to go again, and Grammaude had not suggested it. Perhaps she had felt those presences too.

I knew Mike would explain why we came this way today in his own time. He did few things without a reason. I was content, that misted morning, to clump along behind him in my sucking boots, one hand affixed to the back of his sou'wester. I could not see far beyond the path and the closest trees and clumps of white-dropleted bracken. We often went without talking for long periods of time on our rambles. There was no need. By that time we could finish each other's sentences and not infrequently catch each other's thoughts.

We slogged through the ferny undergrowth that led out to the tip of Loon Ledge, and only when we approached the water did I make out ahead of me the bulldozers squatting on the beach like prehistoric animals at rest in a misted dawn, and the piles of lumber under tarpaulins, and the raw yellow beginnings of a much more substantial bridge beside the spidery old one. It seemed to reach out into infinity, vanishing as it did in the white fog about ten yards out. I could not see Osprey Head at all.

"Well, shit, what's this?" I said. "I didn't know this was down here."

Mike grinned at my language, but then his face went sober again.

"Nobody else did either, until it was well under way. Seems like the Park Service is going to build a pedestrian bridge and let people pay to go over to Osprey Head and have picnics and gawk at the eagles. Going to put a parking lot right here and sell tickets and everything. Granddaddy said they're going to make a right fair bit of money with it."

"But Mike, the eagles!"

"I know," he said, bitterness thick in his voice. "They'll leave. The Park Service says they won't, but Granddaddy says different."

"What?" I was near tears. "What does he say?"

"He says some damned fool did a study that says eagles will acclimate to people, so they're going to haul fools in and sell 'em eagle views by the carload."

"Can't he get them to stop? Can't he talk to them?"

"He tried, Darcy. He and some of the men went all the way over to Augusta to talk to the parks people, and took a petition and everything, and even wrote to the national headquarters in Washington. The Augusta folks wouldn't even talk to them, and nobody in Washington answered the letter. Granddaddy's trying to find out who to call now. My dad called this guy he knows at the *Ellsworth American*, to see if he'd write an article about it, but the guy said he was sorry about the eagles and all but it really wasn't news. He said as soon as there was some hard news, to let him know. Dad asked him what he'd consider hard news, and he said when the eagles filed a petition in Augusta, that'd be news. And he laughed. Dad was pretty mad, and so was Granddaddy. But they both said there wasn't anything we could do about it."

"But you think there is," I said. It was not a question.
"Yeah."

He turned to face Osprey Head, staring off into the
fog as if he could see the island through its swirling
density. Then he turned back to me.

"I think we ought to give 'em some hard news," he
said.

That night after Grammaude had gone upstairs to bed
I got up and put on my jeans and a sweater and went
out on the porch to wait for Mike. My heart was hammering, but it was not precisely fear I felt. It was
more the enormous, profound sense of an appointment with some irrevocable destiny, something that
was mine alone to do and must be done but that
would change me for good and all. It was solemn and
exhilarating at the same time, an important feeling,
powerful and adult. I hugged myself in the thinning
fog and stared into the darkness beyond the barberry
hedge, but I saw nothing of Mike yet. There were no
other lights on this lane. It was past midnight.

Mike had told me why I had to do this thing with
him, and after he did I could see that he was right.

"It was your own mother and my aunt and uncle that
ran the ospreys off," he said. "They did it back when
they were younger than we are now—or than I am, anyway. They killed a young bird and tore up all the nests.
Nobody knows why. The ospreys have never come
back. I know it's got nothing to do with you and me—
Granddaddy told me so when he knew I'd found out
about it—but it seems to me like somebody's got to do
something for those eagles now, and it ought to be us.
Try to make up a little for what our kin did. Do you see?"

"Yes." I was horrified and ashamed. I had never
heard the story. There seemed no end to the things
my mother had broken.

"We could get in trouble."

"I don't care."

"Me either. Okay. Here's what we'll do."

I saw the soft yellow glow from Grammaude's upstairs window go out, and as if in answer to a signal Mike stepped out from behind the barberry hedge and motioned to me to follow him. He wore dark clothes, as I did, and sneakers, and in each hand were ditty bags containing the things we would need. I took a deep breath and followed him off into the dark.

By the time we gained the beach on Loon Ledge, the fog had mostly dissipated and pinpricks of stars studded the high, milky sky. There was no moon, but we could see clearly. The sighing, rolling bay and the islands seemed to give off a luminous white light of their own, and we could make out the machines and the tarpaulined lumber piles and the bridge easily enough. I have seen that light many times beside other seas than that one. I have never known what it is.

Mike stood still, looking out toward Osprey Head as he had that morning, and then I saw, rather than heard, the deep breath that he drew.

"You can still back out," he said.

"No way," I said fiercely. "You think I'm chicken? I'm not chicken. You made me an honorary Willis, remember? If I'm chicken you're chicken."

"Okay. Then let's do it."

And he took a kerosene can out of the ditty bag and gave me another, and we walked past the bulldozers and out onto the span of scaffolding of the new wooden bridge, anointing the floor planks with that raw breath of destruction. When we had gone out as far as the bridge went, Mike took out a box of kitchen matches and handed it to me.

"You want to do the first one?"

"Sure."

My hands were shaking, and it took three matches,

but I eventually got one lit and stood looking at him. He stared back. I tossed the match to the floor planks and we watched for a moment as it fizzed and smoldered futilely, our very breathing stopped, and then, when it budded and flowered and bloomed into flame along the railings and the planking, we thudded back to the beach followed by flame.

We stood on the cold beach for a small space of time, watching as the fire fed and grew and drew back on itself and then boomed along the bridge toward the beach, the skeleton of the planking blackening and shriveling in the white heart of it. Then we scrambled back up the cliff path and through the woods to the boathouse and called the fire department and the editorial departments of every newspaper and television station on the mid coast; Mike had prepared the list that afternoon. We even called Portland and Augusta and Bangor. This time the man at the *Ellsworth American* listened to us.

And then we went to wake my grandmother and Mike's parents and grandfather and wait for what would come.

We had thought we were prepared for recriminations from the Park Service and punishment from our parents, but it is the nature of children to see themselves as both heroic and invulnerable, and in our hearts I am sure neither of us thought the furor would be unmitigated by admiration for our daring and our passion to save the eagles. But the wave of official outrage that broke over our heads was swift and cold and very adult. Almost before the fire had burned itself out under the helpless noses of the volunteer fire department, representatives from the Park Service in Augusta were knocking on the door of Retreat, where Grammaude and Mike's parents and grandfather had incarcerated us. The unamused sheriff and a couple of his deputies were there too, and a few of the older men and women from the colony who were especially close to Grammaude. They were drinking coffee and murmuring among themselves, and occasionally they would look over at Mike and me, where we sat side by side in front of the fire on the sofa, but no one spoke to us. Grammaude looked a million years old, bleached and ill; the thought occurred to me as I sat in my isolation—for we had been told to sit down and be quiet—that this was the second time one of her own had been brought home in disgrace over Osprey Head. Shame flooded me.

"I didn't want to hurt Grammaude," I whispered to Mike, sniffling. He squeezed my hand.

"It was the right thing to do. She'll soon see that."

"Hush over there," Mike's father said in a voice that froze my blood. We hushed. Mike's grandfather got up at the knock and went to let the men from Augusta in.

It was an awful night. There was cold, muted talk of legal ramifications and punishment; voices were raised; angry talk flew. Once Caleb Willis raised his fist at a colorless, vulpine Park Service man who seemed to be the most adamant about punishment and his father silently caught it, whispered something to him, and led him out to the kitchen. Beth Willis went out to join her husband, and after that things were quieter. But still no one talked to us. Grammaude sat in the big twig rocker that had been my grandfather's, rocking silently, not speaking, while Micah Willis argued with the Park Service. Despite our misery Mike and I dozed; dimly we heard talk of remuneration, and court orders and probation, but none of it seemed very real. Just before dawn the park people left, and Micah Willis came and sat down heavily beside Grammaude on the rocker's hassock, rubbing his eyes.

"Can't do anything much to them because of their

ages," he said tiredly. "Can press charges against them as juveniles and get 'em put on probation, and still may do it, but it's more likely they'll just ask for damages."

"How much do you think that would be?" Grammaude was nearly whispering.

"Don't imagine Park Service bridges come cheap," Micah Willis said.

Mike got up and went over and stood before his grandfather. I followed him and stood looking down at Grammaude. She was looking not at me but at Mike. I did not see anger in her eyes, but I could not read what I did see.

"I'll work and pay for it, Granddaddy," Mike said.

"Then you'll be working for a good part of your life," Micah said. His face, too, was grave and still but not angry.

"I can work too," I said, struggling not to cry. "I can get jobs babysitting after school; the sisters let us do that."

"Oh, Darcy," Grammaude said, finally looking at me, "it's not the money. We'll find the money. It's just that . . . oh, darling, it's happened before. Your mother, when she was a little girl—"

"I know," I said, the tears spilling over in spite of me. "Mike told me. That's why, Grammaude. We thought . . . we thought if we did something to save the eagles it would help make up for—"

I couldn't go on without sobbing aloud, so I stopped, my face screwed up furiously with the effort to repress outright weeping.

Grammaude began to cry too, softly, her face still. I could not ever remember her crying before. It hurt my heart.

"You could have been killed, darling. You could have so easily been hurt or killed, and then what would I do? You simply can't do things that put you so at risk."

"Yes," I sobbed. "Yes, you can! You have to do

them! You have to do anything it takes, if it matters."

Grammaude reached out and pulled me to her and held me against her for a long while. I could hear Mike's breathing, and his grandfather's, but neither of them spoke. Finally Grammaude put me off at arm's length and looked at me and smiled faintly.

"Maybe you do," she said slowly. "Well, of course, maybe you do."

In the end, no one brought any charges and there were no repayments required from the Park Service, for the simple reason that the state media picked up "the heroic efforts of two young Hancock County residents to save a colony of bald eagles being threatened by a proposed Park Service bridge that would open their habitat to pedestrian traffic," and even though Grammaude and Mike's parents would allow no interviews and no contact with the media, we became, for a brief moment in that age of growing environmental awareness, something of cult heroes. Indeed, the outcry fanned itself and grew so raucous that the embarrassed Park Service reconsidered its notion of opening Osprey Head to the public, tore down the charred remains of the bridge, and spent an additional several hundred thousand dollars in restoring the old narrow bridge, posting KEEP OUT signs on the beaches of Loon Ledge, and mounting a discreet public relations campaign via an agency in Portland.

Mike and I enjoyed little of our fleeting fame, however. He was put to work in the boatyard all day and until noon on Saturdays, and I was kept under house arrest in Liberty for the rest of the summer. We were forbidden to see each other and we did not, until the next summer, when he was even taller and I was even rounder and softer and more loathsomely feminine, and everyone had forgotten that we had ever laid siege to the bridge to Osprey Head—or, if they had not, did not speak of it—for such was the way of the colony. And the summer flowed on as all the ones before it had, and we were together again, and though the outsides of us had changed, nothing else had. And it was enough.

In the end, it was not enough, and it was Mike who ended it. Or perhaps it was me, but it was assuredly Mike who precipitated it. At the end of his seventeenth summer and my fourteenth, when he was preparing to go away to MIT to study architecture in the fall and I was determinedly pretending that nothing had changed and nothing would, he took me in his new still-nameless sloop over to Osprey Head for a farewell picnic, and there he abruptly pulled me up from the rocks where I had been sitting and put his arms around me and kissed me hard. It was a long kiss, and a seeking one, and it felt as if I had swallowed fire down into my stomach.

When he raised his head, I drew back my arm, blinded with panic, and slapped him. He simply looked at me.

"I thought you might feel the same as I do now," he said. His voice caught in his throat, and his eyes were dark with shock and pain. The print of my hand was livid on his tanned face.

I began to cry. "Why did you have to spoil it?" I wept. "Why did you have to change everything? Don't you see we can't ever be the same now? Don't you see what you've done?"

"It couldn't have stayed the same, Darcy," he said.

"Yes, it could! Yes, it could have too! But it can't now; now it will have to end! It's what happens when people start kissing and being in love and all that stupid business . . . it ends! It ends and they go away!"

"I won't go away."

"Well, you damned well *are* going away in just two weeks," I wailed. "You're going all the way to Boston, and you'll be gone for five whole years, and when you get back I'll be nineteen and you won't even remember me!"

"I'll be here summers, just like always," he said. "I'm going to work in the boatyard; nothing will change, you know that."

"Yes, it will! It already has!"

"You want me to pretend I don't feel any differently about you from when we were kids? Okay, I will. But it's not true. I feel . . . awfully different. You're not a kid. I'm not either. I want something else for us now. I thought maybe you did too."

"I want you to take me home. I want to go home. And I don't want to talk to you any more. I don't want to see you any more."

We did not speak on the sail home, and when we docked I jumped from the sloop and ran up the dock and back to Liberty. I locked myself in my room and would not come out, and I cried and cried and cried. I did not know what I wept for, and I did not know what had so frightened me. I have never been entirely sure about that. But it did not matter. He left three days later for MIT, much earlier than he had planned, and for the next two summers he did not come home to Cape Rosier but found construction jobs in Marblehead or on Cape Cod.

No one, not Grammaude, not Mike's parents, not Micah Willis, mentioned him to me after that. Once only, the first summer he did not come back and I had taken to spending all my time in my own new catboat, did my grandmother say, "Is everything all right with you, darling?"

"Yes, ma'am," I said. "Everything's fine."

And such was the power of the sea and the solitude wrapping me that summer that for a long time I thought everything was.

*　　*　　*

"What did you do with yourself today?" Grammaude said that night, after I had come up from the beach and she had finally gotten up and dressed and made our supper. I thought she looked as insubstantial as a moth, nearly transparent, and her breath was still short and fragile in her chest, but her eyes shone and there were two spots of color in her cheeks. We had wine with our chowder, but no more of the lethal martinis.

"I sat on the beach and watched ghosts," I said.

"Oh, dear. I hope they weren't threatening."

"No. These were nice ghosts. You'd have liked them."

"Maybe I still do," she said, and smiled.

I slept that night, for the first time, in the little upstairs bedroom that had always been my grandmother's, and found to my relief that it was as small and enfolding and comforting as a cocoon or a womb. I could see the stars and the silhouettes of the pointed firs outside, but I could not see the great restless glitter of the bay. I could hear it, though, a sweet sussuration, an endless soft sighing. I thought I could sleep here, and I was right: I got into the narrow little white bed and pulled up the silky old cutwork linen sheets that smelled of cedar and lavender and slid fathoms deep into that lightless, dreamless sleep that the sea gives. Sometime during the night Zoot sailed up onto the bed with me, and I pulled him into the curve of my arm without really waking and slept on.

And when I woke in the morning it seemed that, for just an instant, I was seventeen again, and the summer was new, and in a moment I would be running across the dew-cold grass to Braebonnie to meet my love.

Chapter Sixteen

On a Sunday morning in my second week in Retreat, the year I was seventeen, I came stumbling barefoot out of my room with my hair falling uncombed into my eyes and the oversized Cove Harbor Yacht Club T-shirt that I slept in slipping off one shoulder and found Grammaude sitting at the kitchen table drinking coffee with a young man I had never seen before. I turned to rush back to my room, seeing in my grandmother's face the picture I must make, but he smiled at me and said, "Don't run. I was looking at *La Primavera* in the Uffizi just last week, and here she is in the flesh."

And I stood still, smiling tentatively at him. I had studied the Botticelli painting in art history the winter before and knew he had given me a double compliment: one on my looks and another by not explaining the allusion.

"Providing she had six million freckles," I said.

"And a T-shirt down to her ankles," he said, in a soft voice tinged with something . . . what? Not a foreign accent, but the shadow of one. "Never mind. The look is the same."

"Warrie, this is Darcy O'Ryan, my granddaughter," Grammaude said, looking from me to the young man. "Darcy, this is Warrie Villiers. Warren, of course. His grandmother was my best friend, and his mother owns Braebonnie now. I haven't seen him since he was a very small boy. He's lived abroad all his life, and this is the first time to my knowledge he's been back to Retreat since he was about five. He popped in on me just a minute ago and I knew him immediately. He's the image of his grandmother Amy."

"That's nice," the young man said. "Most everybody thinks I look like my mother. Almost nobody thinks I look like my father. I can't really remember him—or my grandmother either. Hello, Darcy O'Ryan. There are all the fires of Ireland on your head, but the rest of you is very French."

I felt myself blushing and ducked my head.

"I don't think so," I mumbled. "Mostly Irish and whatever my mother's side of the family is. English, I guess."

"Well, there's a touch of French Huguenot way back," Grammaude said. "My surname was Gascoigne before I married your grandfather. Though I can assure you that those good gray souls were not the ooh-la-la French you might imagine."

"Too bad. It's what we do best," Warrie Villiers said, and smiled again. It was a small smile, soft on his full red mouth, and had a hint of sadness in it. His whole face did, somehow. He was dark, and had a head full of dark curls cut longer than the fashion that year, with threads of silver through them, and his eyes were hooded and nearly black and tilted up at the corners: gypsy's eyes, I thought. His nose was high and narrow and long, and he was very tan. Even if Grammaude had not told me he had lived all his life abroad, I would have known it. There was something ineffably foreign about him, a difference so powerful it was almost

palpable. He was smoking a short brown cigarette
without a filter, holding it between his thumb and
middle finger, and there were very fine white lines
webbed around the extraordinary eyes. He was older,
on second look, than I had first thought.

"Well, let me fix you some breakfast," Grammaude
said to him. "If you got in past midnight last night,
I'm sure there's nothing to eat in that kitchen. Are
the covers even off the furniture? I haven't seen anyone over there airing. Darcy, go put something on."

"Nice to meet you," I said, still mumbling, and
crossed my arms across my breasts and tiptoed out of
the kitchen as if by doing so I could keep them from
bobbling extravagantly. It was useless; the growth
spurt I had had at ten had not been repeated, so that
I still stood just at five feet, but the early promise of
breasts and hips had been amply kept. I was, I knew
from looking at old photographs, shaped exactly as
my grandmother Maude had been when she was only
a few years older than I. I heard Warrie Villiers
chuckling softly as I went and blushed again, not
knowing if it was at the mutinous, animated lushness
beneath my T-shirt, my discomfort at it, or simply
something my grandmother had said. I put on the
tightest bra and the loosest oxford cloth shirt I had,
and cut-off blue jeans, and dragged a damp comb
through my wild mop and came back into the
kitchen. Grammaude smiled at me and handed me a
cup of coffee, but she did not speak to me, and the
smile was an abstract one. Her attention was fully on
this strange young man, and she seemed of more
than one mind about him. Her mouth smiled at him
and said warm, gracious words, but her eyes on him
were uncertain, troubled. Grammaude was seldom of
two minds about anything or anyone. The kitchen
and the morning felt strange, displaced in time.

I slid into a chair opposite Warrie Villiers and

buried my nose in my coffee, looking at him through steam. He smiled at me again but did not speak to me. He leaned loosely back in his chair, balanced on the back two legs, and drank his coffee and watched my grandmother moving about the kitchen making breakfast. He seemed completely at home for someone who had not seen Grammaude since he was very small and perhaps did not even remember her. It was that quality of total self-possession that struck me first about him, and it is the last thing I remember of him. He seemed utterly at home in his dark skin, profoundly sure of his place in this kitchen and this colony and this world. It did not seem to me a quality born of conceit: more, perhaps, of control. He seemed to exude control like a body scent. I was powerfully drawn to that. I had spent my short life in search of it.

"So what brings you to Retreat?" Grammaude said, stirring eggs, not looking over her shoulder at him.

He laughed, a short, sharp laugh. "You might ask, rather, what sent me. Or who," he said. "I'm here because my mother has a new prospect on her line, and the presence in her life right now of a twenty-three-year-old son does not, I suspect, exactly jibe with the age she's hinted to him. He's going to be at the villa all summer, it seems, and since I was supposed to be at home working on my senior thesis, it struck Maman that Retreat and Braebonnie might be just the place for it. Peace and quiet, you know. Isolation, healthy living, no distractions. I gather that the gentleman in question, who, I believe, drives racing cars or something, is hardly ten years older than I, and Maman's last overhaul in Switzerland was superb; she looks younger than he does. I told her I'd say I was her little brother, but she was adamant. Adamant is Maman's forte. So here I am, and she's right. It's going to be just the place to think and write; I can't imagine that the night life is terribly distracting. It's really beautiful; I've seen pictures, but I didn't really remember the house and the sea and all that. Very different from the sea I know."

"Where's that?" I said, feeling a pang in my heart for him, unwanted by his mother. I knew that feeling.

"Sardinia. Maman has a villa there from her third husband, the Yugoslavian greengrocer king. It's beautiful too, all hot pinks and reds, and rocks and sand and blinding blue and white, but it doesn't sit softly on your heart like this place does."

I smiled. That was just what Retreat did.

"Where do you live in the winter? Where do you go to school?"

"We live in a flat in Trastevere, in Rome. It's the old section, very old, very picturesque, very expensive, if you live where we do. Maman got it from her fourth and last husband, the importer of Taiwanese 'antiques' and perhaps a few selected controlled substances. She's set now, as far as primary and secondary dwellings go, and can shop for more—transitory pleasures. I think my father's family paid her enough to leave France—and them—so she can live as she pleases if she's very careful. Of course, she seldom is. I'm not in school this quarter because she's forgotten to send them my tuition again, and she's neglected to wire me the money for the cottage and food and a servant this summer, so I'm probably going to be grazing on the lawn like a cow. But I'll get a check from my trust fund next month—that's done out of Paris; she can't get her hands on that—so I'll be fine. And I'm used to managing. I've lived alone since I started school."

His words might have sounded bitter if he had not been so at ease in our kitchen and his smile had not been so quick and free. As it was, he merely sounded amused by his mother and affectionate toward her. But my heart gave another fishlike leap in my chest.

Controlled perhaps, resourceful maybe, but Warrie Villiers was like me, a child abandoned by its parents. Well, of course I had Grammaude, and she had made all the difference—but still, I had walked in that wilderness too. I wanted him to know that, but I did not know how to tell him.

"I've been alone a lot too, except when I'm up here," I said. "It's really not so bad."

"Not by half," he said. "But I wish I'd had this place when I was growing up. What a difference it could have made."

Grammaude put a plate of eggs and bacon in front of both of us and sat down. I was surprised to see a glint of tears in her eyes.

"You'll have your dinners with us until your check comes," she said, "and no arguments. And I'm going to send Sukie Duschesne over with a few things for the house this afternoon. She's the young woman who helps me out this summer; her parents have been friends for many years. I'm sure she can spare a few hours a week to help you with the cottage or will know someone who can. You can't get any work done and keep up that huge old house by yourself."

Most of the young men I knew would have automatically protested that Grammaude really mustn't put herself out on his account, but Warrie Villiers didn't. He simply said, "I would greatly appreciate that, Mrs. Chambliss. My mother said you were an extraordinary woman, and she's right. Unlike Tennessee Williams's lovely Blanche, I have not always been dependent on the kindness of strangers, but I am grateful to be dependent on you for a while. You will, of course, permit me to run errands for you in return and perhaps see to your lawn, or whatever else I can do."

"Nonsense," Grammaude said. "I have someone to do that. Let me feed you dinner strictly for the pleasure of your company. As I said, your grandmother was the best friend I ever had, and your mother is one of the most vivid memories I have of these summers."

He smiled. "She says the same of you. She says you taught her a great deal. I believe she was a special friend of your son's?"

"Yes," Grammaude said, getting up. "Pass me your plates, you two, and I'll give you a refill. Your father, Warrie: are you in touch with him?"

"My father is dead," he said neutrally. "He died in an auto crash in the Dordogne when I was seven. His family—my grandparents—are not so fond of my mother, nor, I think, of me. We do not see them. They send money under the terms of my father's will. I think it causes them great pain to do so. I don't quite know why; it's not a lot, and they are very rich. I do wish Maman could have gotten along better with them, but there you go. It was not necessary to please when she was that age, and now that she is . . . more mature, shall we say, she only cares to please adolescent racing car drivers. But I think she has not given up on the Villiers lucre; she has me studying finance and hopes that I will become a banker and be taken into both the family firm and the family bosom."

"And do you like finance?" Grammaude said.

"About as well as I like . . . what do you call them? Root canals," he said. "Finance! *Zut alors!*" It was the first French expression he had used, and he used it with such comic wryness that Grammaude and I both laughed aloud. It became a watchword with the three of us in the weeks that followed. *"Zut alors!"* we would cry when something surprised or delighted us. Much did, that summer.

I fell in love with him on that first day, of course. Looking back, it seems inevitable that I would. Untouched as my heart might be, except for the cold void where Mike Willis was not, which I simply refused to look into, my mind and body were ripe for involvement and intensity, and my shuttered heart was hungry for it without my awareness. The time had come, had had to come, when Grammaude's nurturing love was not enough. I had tended my tomboy persona with something near desperation that summer; I had applied for and gotten a position as assistant steward at the yacht club and spent long hours every day doing the sort of scutwork the senior steward would not touch. But all the traffic with boats and lines and tarpaulins and tide charts and kitchen trash and storm debris could not mask the kind of supple, budding greenness that clung about me. I can see it now, looking back. I could not, then. It must have been a bad time for Grammaude. Nothing had ever come easily to me. She must have known that this first love—for she could not but have known that it was—would not either. And no matter how he charmed her and made her laugh, and how much the vulnerability under his cool matter-of-factness touched her, and how deeply she felt that this estrangement from this place of his birthright was her fault—though I came to know this only much later—there was much about Warrie Villiers that troubled her. I could read it in her eyes all summer, though she spoke of it directly to me only toward the end.

It wouldn't have mattered what she said. Older and wiser women than I would have found it nearly impossible to withstand that combination of vulnerability and sensuality. I didn't have a chance and didn't want one. Physical readiness aside, Warrie Villiers did with that first conversation what no other young man of my acquaintance could have possibly done precisely because he was unlike any young man of my acquaintance. He was the very antithesis of all the boys in Retreat whose companionship I had so fiercely abjured; he brought with him from Rome no baggage of the kind I had learned to fear. When I looked at him and listened to him I saw no ghosts and felt no frissons of recognition and heard no old resonances at all. I saw only him, Warrie, as new as morning to me, with no sharp history between us.

He was as far removed from Mike Willis as it was possible for a young man to be. None of that grief and loneliness could spill over me from Warrie. Nothing of Mike could live in his aura.

At first he talked mainly to Grammaude. He came, as she had asked, almost every evening and shared supper with us, and we talked . . . or they talked and I listened, content simply to sit in the fire and candle light and watch and listen. He did not stay long; he went back to Braebonnie by nine, and I went to bed in the big back bedroom and lay watching the light in the window upstairs that I knew was his, feeling his presence on my very skin, there just over the piled stone wall. He worked late those nights, and worked the whole of the days, or I assumed he did. I never saw him down around the yacht club, and the over-heard talk from the old women in the porch rockers told me that try as they might to lure Amy Potter's handsome French grandson for cocktails or lun-cheons, he politely refused them, saying he was swamped with work on his thesis but expected to finish up sometime later in the summer and hoped he might accept their kind invitations then. I learned he was adjudged a catch.

"It's too bad, Maude, that Darcy is so young," old Mrs. Stallings said to Grammaude at the Fourth of July tea; I heard her from the kitchen. Grammaude had gone to the yacht club as her guest; she had not kept her club membership after my grandfather had died. She would not, she said, sit on the porch and rock as a matter of policy. I learned to sail in the little Beetle Cat she bought me, but I used my Uncle Petie and Aunt Sarah's membership. Grammaude went near the club only once or twice a summer, and then usually on the arm of old Micah Willis and in the company of his son, Caleb, and Caleb's wife, Beth.

"How do you mean, Marjorie?" Grammaude said that afternoon.

"Well, of course I mean that with him right there it would be a match made in heaven if she weren't too young," Mrs. Stallings said. "After all, you're the only people he'll talk to. And such a sweet irony, him Amy's grandson and all, and really so much more suitable than the Willis boy. We've all said so. Of course, I know how you've always felt about Elizabeth—"

"No, you don't, Marjorie," Grammaude said sweetly. "You've really no idea. And of course Darcy is too young; she's only seventeen, and he's twenty-three. It's much too big an age gap. Thank goodness he doesn't feel that way about her at all, and I don't think she pays any attention to him."

By that time I paid nothing but attention to him, and my grandmother knew it. My face burned in the kitchen of the yacht club as it burned at night during dinner, when he smiled over at me. As it and my whole body burned in the nights when I lay awake watching his upstairs window.

But all his talk was for my grandmother, and most of his attention went to her. The six years' difference in our ages and the vast gulfs of difference in our experience lay palpable between us.

Gradually, though, his talk reached out to include me, and his attention lay lightly and softly on me, and the evenings around the dinner table in Liberty became something else. Now I was part of a circle of three that laughed together, told irreverent stories about colony people, talked of the small world of Cape Rosier and the larger one outside it. The gap in our ages narrowed. He teased me about the Irish; I teased him about the French. We both teased Grammaude about being a southern belle. Though I changed each evening from my disreputable steward's togs and bathed and dressed as carefully as I could, and began to experiment with makeup, I was dizzyingly careful not to reveal how I felt about him, and he gave no indication at all that he thought of me in any way except as the pleasant third person he had dinner with each evening. I really believe Grammaude came to be lulled and soothed as the nights passed and no evidence of catastrophe presented itself. Once she let us wash dishes and went upstairs to bed, and within a week or so it became standard practice. And still nothing changed between Warrie and me. And still I lay in the dark, in the nights, and burned all over.

One evening in mid-July he came for dinner with a great tawny puff of a young cat in his arms. It was wearing an enormous red bow made from yarn, and it had on its face such an expression of delighted surprise that Grammaude and I cried, together, *"Zut alors!"* And so Zut he became, later, as I have said, changed to Zoot because of his extravagant leggings.

"Is that creature for me?" Grammaude said that evening, a smile tugging at her mouth in spite of her efforts to be stern. Nobody could be stern around Zoot when he was a teenage cat. He was simply too cheerfully, rambunctiously pleased with his world and everything in it. He never met a human being he didn't like, and the sentiment was usually reciprocated. Grammaude, not a natural cat fancier, was kneading the moss-soft fur under his chin as she spoke, and Zoot was smiling in transported pleasure.

"No. That creature is for Darcy," Warrie said. "I saw him sleeping on a shelf at the general store, and he looked so much like Darcy O'Ryan that I burst out laughing on the spot and then had to explain because Mrs. Sylvester was working up a real snit at me. I said I had a friend who looked just like that, and she said she hoped my friend was a better mouser than that cat; he was doing such a bad job she was going to take him to the county animal shelter. I couldn't have that. It would be like having Darcy put to sleep. So I had no recourse, don't you see? It's fate."

"It's blackmail," Grammaude said, but she was laughing. Zoot reached out a fat paw and patted her cheek in little butterfly pats. She held him out to me.

"Go suck up to your mommy," Grammaude said. "I'm on to your wicked ways. Honestly, Warrie, I'm glad you didn't get besotted with a pig or something."

"Moi? Un cochon?" Warrie said, wiggling his eyebrows. I reached out my arms and Grammaude put Zoot into them; he felt as light as a bag of feathers under his flamboyant coat. He nuzzled up under my chin and closed his eyes and began to knead my arm with his huge soft paws.

"You silly cat," I said in joy. "I love you."

Grammaude went upstairs, shaking her head, and Warrie and I started on the dishes. I ran hot water into the pan and he scraped, and neither of us looked at the other. Something was fizzing up like ginger ale in my chest, and I thought I might laugh or cry or simply shout aloud with happiness.

Zoot sailed up onto the sink and sat immobile and imperial, regarding us with enormous bronze eyes. Then he reached a paw into the pan of water and solemnly flicked a spray of it across Warrie's face. We both dissolved into laughter, and I threw my soapy arms around Warrie and hugged him. He stood still for a moment, and then he put his arms around me and pulled me to him so hard I felt my breasts flatten against him and felt his ribs under my fingers. He was tall; my face fit just into the hollow of his throat. I could feel a pulse hammering there, and the heat of him through his shirt.

I lifted my face up and he kissed me, a long, slow,

open-mouthed kiss. It was not the kiss of a friend. It was unlike anything I had ever felt, or dreamed of feeling. I remembered only much later that I had only been kissed once, and then by Mike Willis. This was not like that.

Finally he lifted his head and looked down at me. I thought I could still see the print of my mouth on his. My heart was hammering so fast that I could feel it in my throat.

"You just aged five years," he said huskily.

"Is that old enough?" I whispered.

"For what?" His voice was just as low. It sounded . . . dark.

"For anything. For everything."

"Be careful, Darcy," he said.

"I don't want to," I said.

He went home soon after that. We finished drying the dishes and attempted to be light with each other once more, and on the main did pretty well, but of course something else, this whole other thing, lay trembling in the air between us. He touched me on the cheek and started to say something and then didn't and went out of the kitchen. I stood staring at the closed screen door, Zoot cradled purring and kneading in my arms, and then took my cat and went to bed. I even went to sleep, Zoot curled along the length of me, purring in the dark.

But I might have known I would not sleep the whole of that night, and I didn't. I woke about two hours later, and knew without knowing how that he was outside my window; when I got up and tiptoed to it, I saw that the close velvet darkness was broken by the red tracery of his cigarette. He sat on the stone wall that separated Braebonnie's lawn from Liberty's, and he was so close I could smell the pungent smoke of his Player's and almost feel the displaced air from his body.

I ran on tiptoe through the kitchen and out the

back door and around the house and came up to him.
He said nothing, but opened his arms, and I went into
them silently in my soft T-shirt and nothing else. He
held me close but loosely, tracing the line of my body
from waist to thigh absently with one hand. I trembled all over as if with a chill.

"You'll have to ask," he said presently. "I don't
rush women. I won't rush you."

"I'm asking," I said, drunk on his touch.

"Are you sure?"

"Oh, yes!"

"Then . . . what?"

I put my face into his chest and held on for dear
life, feeling as though I were stepping off the face of
the world into a bottomless abyss. Terror and wanting shook me as a huge wind would do.

"Show me . . . something French," I whispered.

And he picked me up in his arms as if I had been a
child and took me into Braebonnie and laid me down
on the big sofa before the dead fireplace, and he did
just that. And it tore and savaged me, and flamed me
from my mouth to the soles of my feet, and turned my
bones to jelly and my muscles to sponge and my blood
to lava, and lifted me shrieking to the top of the highest
hill in the world and swooped with me down into red
nothingness as if a great bird had me fast in its beak. I
cried and sobbed and shouted and laughed aloud; I
pounded him with my fists and grasped him with my
legs and ground at him with my hips, and once bit his
mouth until blood ran, and when he came pouring into
me and I exploded in fire and nothingness, I heard
myself shouting aloud, "I am too old enough! I am!"

Presently he lay beside me, sweat drying on our
bodies in the chilly wind off the bay just beyond Braebonnie, smoking one of his cigarettes. He had not
spoken since we finished, but I could still remember
the things he had said to me, and I to him, and I went

hot with embarrassment at the memory of them. There was no moon, and except for the light from his cigarette, when he drew on it, I could not see his face. I wondered if I had bored or disappointed him; he must have known it was my first time and I had not known what to do. Finally, in a voice that sounded, in my ears, impossibly young, I quavered, "Was I . . . okay? Was that right?"

He took a long drag, and then he laughed.

"Right?" he said. *"Zut alors!"*

After that I was lost.

"I will never rush you," he said that night, afterward as he had said before. "I will never push you. Tonight shouldn't have happened; you're only seventeen. They probably have laws against that here. And you should have told me it was your first time. They probably have laws about that too."

I did not reply. Could he not tell? I thought men could, somehow. There had been blood. Was there blood every time, then? And could he really think I had done that awful, glorious thing before and he couldn't tell?

"So we won't do it again?" I said in a small voice, not looking at him.

He laughed, and ruffled my hair. "You are a little *cochon*. I didn't say we wouldn't do it again. You are delicious, and I am besotted with you. But if we do, you're going to have to ask. As I said, I don't push."

"Then I'm asking."

"Not tonight. Go home and think about your sins. Oh, God, I didn't mean it like that," he said, for I must have looked stricken. I know I felt it. "It's no sin when it's that good, Darcy. God made us as we are, and I believe he meant for us to enjoy it. But enough is enough. I'll walk you to your house. You must be very careful going back in. Your grandmother would put you in a cage and shoot me."

I did as he said. I knew he was right about Grammaude. Guilt rose and flickered, but it was very faint, and it did not last. Surely, surely, she must know this glorious fire. She had, she had told me over and over, been very much in love with my grandfather, and she had been just my age when she met him. But somehow I did not think they had done . . . this . . . until they were married.

At the stone wall he stopped.

"I'm not going to come any farther with you. If she sees you, you can just say you couldn't sleep and went for a moonlight stroll," he said.

I looked at him. All I could see was the white flash of his teeth and a white glint that must have been his eyes.

"Are . . . will you still be coming for dinner?"

"Of course. Nothing has changed. A man still has to eat. You mustn't act any differently, though."

"No. But . . . Warrie?"

"Yes?"

"What will happen next? I mean, how will we—"

He put his arms around me and held me close and traced a line with his finger from my forehead down over my breasts and to the hem of the T-shirt. His finger felt as if it had been dipped in fire.

"If you're serious about wanting this to happen again," he said, "just come knock three times on my door. Any night. I'll hear you."

And for the next week or so, I did just that, and we went on laughing and sparring across the dinner table, and teasing Grammaude and Zoot, and later in the dark night I crept out of Liberty and knocked at the door of Braebonnie and we did those things that he was teaching me, that set me afire and burned me to ashes over and over and yet never consumed me.

He knew a great many. I assumed they were French.

On our second night he used a condom, wryly and with distaste.

"I feel like a sixteen-year-old," he said. "You can't imagine what I went through getting these. I had to go all the way over to South Brooksville to the drugstore; Mrs. Sylvester almost fainted when I asked at the store. I have a feeling she thinks the Cape Rosier sheep are in great danger."

I almost rolled off his bed laughing. I could just see it.

"Warrie, you didn't ride your bike all the way over to South Brooksville!"

He had no car, but he had found an old Schwinn in the shed at Braebonnie and resurrected it and used it jauntily for his small errands. When I commiserated with him about the bike, he had just grinned. "I don't mind," he said. "Everybody rides them in France and Italy. It's very chic. I'm actually bringing a touch of continental class to this oh-so-Yankee Cape Rosier. I wish I could find a baguette to put in the basket, though."

"No," he said that night. "I hitched a ride with Caleb Willis. Told him it was an errand of mercy. And so it was. But I can't abide these things. I know it's ridiculous to think you could get your hands on pills up here, so I've called a friend in New York and there are some on the way. You must take them. They're much safer, and they won't hurt you."

"All right," I said dubiously, and when, in a few days, the little packets came in to the post office, I did take them. But I never liked doing it. It felt . . . contrived. Cynical, somehow. I could no longer pretend to myself that I was being swept off my feet night after night.

One evening near the end of July, Grammaude was waiting on the sun porch for me when I came in from the yacht club. Her face was strained and pale, and she did not smile.

"Come sit a minute, darling," she said. "I want to talk to you."

Oh, God, she's found out, I thought, heart beginning to pound. Somebody saw me. I sat down silently on the hassock to the big willow rocker and looked at her, small and erect on the chaise. Beside her Zoot grinned his Etruscan grin up at me and turned over on his back, his big feet sprawled in the air. I did not speak. I waited.

"I heard something today that upsets me very much," she said finally. It was obvious that the words were costing her. "Mrs. Winslow's granddaughter— well, you know little Gretchen—met Warrie in New York just before she came here, at some party or other, and she told her grandmother that . . . that his mother had sent him over here because there was a very ugly business in Rome earlier this spring with the daughter of one of our embassy people. The child was only sixteen, and there were drugs involved, and an abortion that nearly killed her. I believe it could have been a criminal matter because of the girl's age, but her father agreed not to press charges if Warrie . . . left. I think you will see we cannot have him here for dinner any more. And I cannot let you associate with him in any way. I know you're fond of him—so am I— but this is way beyond the acceptable."

"I don't believe it," I said calmly, around the ringing in my ears. Ice was forming around my heart.

"Darling, I know it's hard. I was inclined not to believe it either, at first, because he's been so dear to us, and there's been no evidence of anything, and it did come from the Winslows, but I had to check. You must know that. I called . . . I made some calls. Petie knows a good many of the embassy people in Rome through the bank, and he told me who to contact. It looks as though it's true. I'm terribly sorry."

"It's a lie. Somebody's lying. People always will, about a man that attractive," I said numbly. "I can't believe you'd just . . . take anybody's word for it . . . without asking him. Go on, ask him. I dare you."

I could hear my voice rising. I fell silent. This was not real, of course. She would talk to Warrie and he would put it all right, and the dinners would go on. My life would go on.

"I intend to," she said, looking closely at me. "I wouldn't take any action without doing that. But until I do, I mean what I say about your not seeing him. You must obey me on that. I would hate to send you home, but I will if I have to."

"And just where do you think I'd see him if it wasn't here at dinner?" I said bitterly, daring her with it. "Do you think we make mad love down at the yacht club on my lunch hour? Or in the dark of night in his little white bed?"

And my heart gave a great lurch, for he did indeed sleep in a narrow white iron bed, with white sheets and a white cotton plissé coverlet.

But she only shook her head tiredly and said, "Of course I don't think any such thing. I just . . . I want so much to keep you safe, my dear Darcy. I wasn't able to do that with my daughter. I hoped I could with hers."

My anger faded. Numbness flooded back in. Soon it would all be well.

"I know that, Grammaude. But Warrie wouldn't hurt me. Go ask him. Just do that."

She did do it, almost immediately. I waited on the sun porch, cradling Zoot in my arms, while she went around the house and over the stile to Braebonnie. Around the great humming in my ears I heard her call, "Warrie? It's Maude Chambliss. May I come in a moment?" and after that I heard nothing but that profound, faraway *shushing* roar that always seemed to me to be the very music of the earth. You could hear it on Cape Rosier when the air was very calm. I sat still and waited. Soon, now, and then a gear would slip forward and life would flow on.

She came back and her step was heavy, and I knew he had not convinced her that the story was a lie.

She stopped before me on the porch and said, "Warrie will not be coming for dinner any more. The story may or may not be true—I believe it is—but he is a danger to you. His mother has always been unstable and a danger to others, and I believe the same is true of him. It's a terrible, terrible pity; growing up the way he did, he probably could not be otherwise. But I cannot change that. We will not speak of it again. If you disobey me and attempt to see him I will send you back to Saint Anne's immediately."

"I don't believe you!" I shouted.

"I cannot help that," my grandmother said, and turned and went up the stairs. She was halfway up before I saw her thin shoulders slump. I didn't care. In that moment I hated her as much as I have ever hated anyone.

We ate our dinner in silence. His absence was stronger, more vivid, than his presence had ever been. He shimmered and danced in the air between us. I did not mention him, did not speak except to reply to the few sentences she directed to me. I tried not to sulk or cry, to keep my back straight and my face calm. Hers was as still as a death mask, and near-ly as white. We did not speak of him again. She went to bed directly after the dishes were done, and the moment I saw her light go out upstairs I was out the door and over the wall to Braebonnie.

He was waiting for me by the door. We did not go up to his bedroom then; we simply did it on the floor by the closed door, as if to keep our bodies apart for an instant longer would mean death by starvation.

Only afterward did we go up the black stairs, and only when the door to his little bedroom was closed did he light a small lamp and a cigarette and look at me, smiling slightly. The smile did not reach his eyes.

"You don't believe it, then," he said.

"My God, of course not," I said. "I could never believe such a thing about you. But who on earth could have started it? It isn't like Grammaude to be so judgmental. You should stop it if you know where it started."

"There was a girl in Rome," he said calmly, and my heart shriveled in pain and fear. "She was at the embassy. But she was twenty-five, not sixteen, and she was a telephone operator, not an official's daughter. And I never forced her. I told you I don't do that. I did, however, leave her. She was incredibly jealous and possessive. I cannot abide that. She told me I'd be sorry. Believe me, I am. I was very fond of your grandmother. And I'd be more than sorry to lose you."

"You won't lose me," I said, putting my arms around him. "We'll just keep on like this until . . . until the summer is over."

I wanted more than anything to say, Until we go away together after Labor Day, but I did not. What he had said about jealousy and possessiveness rang in my ears.

"If you really want to. But you can't come through the house any more," he said. "Why don't you just take the screen off your window and put it back in when you go back? That way you'd be right at the wall and only a few steps from my front door, and you wouldn't have to go through the house and around it."

"I will," I said. "Her room's upstairs and at the front of the house. She'd never hear me if I went out the window. Aren't you smart to think of it, and to use this room where she can't see your light? I wondered why you picked this little one, with the other big ones empty."

"It was my mother's room," he said. "I liked the idea of sleeping here too."

Later, when we had made love again and it was almost time for me to go home—there was the faintest hint of lightening in the black over the bay—I said, "Warrie, what did you tell her when she asked you about the story? Did you tell her about the girl at the embassy?"

"Yes," he said. "I thought she might have believed me, but then she said I mustn't come for dinner any more, or see you. She seems to think I'm a danger to you."

"What did you say to that?"

"I said I was no more a danger to you than my mother had been to her," he said.

"I can't understand it," I said. "Could your mother have been some kind of threat to Grammaude, way back?"

"A girl not yet twenty? I can't think how, can you?"

"No," I said. "I really can't."

For the next couple of weeks we simply kept on doing what we had all summer. His check did not come but was promised, now, by late August, and so he had little choice but to keep to Braebonnie and work on his thesis. I had little choice but to go about my tasks at the yacht club as if the waiting nights did not sear at me like live coals caught in my clothing. Grammaude and I ate our solitary dinners and gradually began to resume, at least on the surface, something of a normal relationship; she smiled and talked of her usual summer interests and my next and last year at Saint Anne's, and what I might like to do after that: what college, what plans for the future. But her voice was frail, and she seemed to fight tiredness all the time, like someone convalescing very slowly from a bad illness.

I answered as lightly and noncommittally as I could, outlining elaborate college and career plans that would never happen, because, of course, I would be somewhere with him. I never doubted that. We had made no definite plans, but we had talked about it. It was enough to sustain me through anything.

I had broached the subject one night, my heart sick and high in my throat because of the risk I was running. But I could live no longer without knowing that we would go on. Summer was ending. There was a new slant to the sun now, and the barberry hedge outside Liberty was tinged with red. I had seen my first ragged V of wild geese against the grape-flushed sky only the night before.

"I saw wild geese going south last night," I said lightly, lying naked in his dark arms. "You'll be flying off with them pretty soon. I'll be a lost sheep when you're gone."

"Maybe not," he said, reaching his dark head down to nibble at my breast.

"Maybe not what?"

"Maybe you won't have to be a lost sheep."

"Why? Shall I come to France?"

I said it lightly, but my heart was pounding so hard I thought he would hear.

"You'd hate that, you little puritan," he said lazily. He put his hand between my legs, and I pressed hard against it.

"Italy, then?"

"That's even worse."

"Then how will I not be a lost sheep? How will I see you?"

"I'd sort of thought I might stay over here," he said. "See something of the country. Maybe finish school somewhere. I've only got a quarter more: that is, if my courses will transfer. How about Atlanta? Have they got good schools in Atlanta? Could I learn anything that would make me a good living in the land of *Gone With the Wind?*"

"Oh, of course," I caroled, my heart singing. "Georgia Tech has a great school of finance, and so does Georgia State. We could . . . you could go to school and I could work and help you finish—" I stopped, reddening. It was a big leap from school in Atlanta to a life shared there.

"I don't let women support me," he said. "There are a lot of young French and Italian men like me in New York who do that, just hang around and live on what their women bring home. Eurotrash, I think they call us. I will not do that."

"It wouldn't be for long, just until you finished."

"No. I want you to go on to college and get your degree; that's a must. That's not to say I wouldn't come and be with you while you did it. You just can't support me. I'll manage that."

I heard only the "come and be with you while you did it." Joy swept me.

"I was so afraid you thought I was too young or too boring," I whispered into his neck. "All those exotic foreign women you see all the time."

"Darcy, you are anything but boring," he said. "You're right; I see exotic foreign women all the time. But I don't often see a living Venus on the half shell. You're the first."

"And the last?"

"I wouldn't be surprised."

"Oh, God," I breathed. "I want . . . Warrie, let's tell Grammaude. Let's go wake her up and tell her. She'll see that none of it was true, that you had . . . honorable intentions—"

"No," he said. "She isn't going to believe me, Darcy. You'll have to take my word on that. She'll send you home—or worse, cut off your trust fund—and I can't follow until my check comes. Don't say anything yet. When the check comes, in September, we'll tell her."

I had no trust fund that I knew of, but it mattered less than nothing to me.

"Tell her . . . what?" I had to hear it.

"Tell her whatever you want, love."

And so I sat at the dinner table in Liberty and told my grandmother great, sensible, and considered lies and waited for the coming of autumn and the check that would set us free.

In the last week before Labor Day my period did not come. At first I thought nothing of it; I simply could not connect the absence of that clockwork red tide with what Warrie Villiers and I did in the nights at Braebonnie. Hadn't I taken the pills? Hadn't he said it would all be fine?

But I had never been late before. And there was a strange rich feeling in the pit of my stomach, and a kind of quickening when I touched my breasts. Dear God, could I be pregnant? All the shame and terror that the nuns had implanted in me rose boiling to the surface, but I pushed them down and thought about it. Pregnant. A baby. Warrie's baby and mine: a small real person with, perhaps, my red hair and his strong features, my white skin and his gypsy's eyes. A baby, something we had made together that was ours alone, mine alone. Mine. A very grown-up thing indeed, to have a baby. He would be overjoyed, of course he would. A son. All men wanted a son, didn't they?

But somehow I did not tell him. The week wore on and my period did not come and I grew surer and surer, and I did not tell him. We made love longer, harder, more often in the nights than ever before, and I did not speak of it.

Labor Day, I thought. I'll tell him then. After my last day at the yacht club, after his check is here, while Grammaude is packing us up to go home.

We'll have to make definite plans then anyway. That's when I'll tell him.

And on the night after my last day at the club, after the debris of the last regatta had been cleared away and the commandant had given me my last pay envelope, and Grammaude and I had eaten our hasty supper, surrounded by half-packed boxes and suitcases, and she had gone to bed in preparation for our next-to-last day in Retreat, I went out the window and over the wall to Braebonnie to tell my love about his baby.

There was a car in the driveway, pulled around to the front of the house so no one could see it from the lane. It had New York license plates, and it was long and sleek and low, obviously foreign, though I did not know what it was. I saw no evidence of anyone, but the light burned in his bedroom upstairs. Could his check possibly have come and he had bought this sleek machine with it? Where on Cape Rosier could he find such a thing? I knocked, the three knocks that were our signal.

He did not come. I knocked again. He did not come. I knocked and knocked, puzzled, and finally he did come, jerking the door open abruptly. He was damp and naked, and wore a towel knotted around his lean waist. His hair was wet and his face was closed, impatient.

"I got you out of the shower," I said. "I'm sorry."

I made as if to enter, but he put an arm across the door and stopped me.

"It's not a good night, Darcy," he said. "I have company. A friend from New York, unexpected. I'll see you . . . later. Tomorrow night, maybe."

"But . . . I'd love to meet your friend," I said doubtfully. What was the matter with him? Why was his face so distant and cold?

"I said not tonight. It's late and I'm tired. Go on home now. I'll see you when . . . I'll see you later."

"I had something to tell you," I whispered.

"It can wait," he said.

"No."

"Warrie? Where are you? Come back to bed, I'm freezing," a voice called down the stairs. It was a woman's voice. It was, like his, faintly foreign. I looked at him. The world wheeled and rang; my vision blurred.

"I see you know about Eurotrash first-hand," I said.

He shrugged. "It's nothing. I'm sorry you found out. It doesn't change anything. Go on home. I'll see you tomorrow; she isn't staying. She's just passing through."

I turned and went back across the stone wall and through the window and sat down on the side of my bed. Zoot made a small trilling sound in his throat, and I picked him up and buried my face in his fur and then put him back down. I sat and watched Braebonnie; in about an hour the upstairs light went off. In another, a fog-white dawn came up over Penobscot Bay. By first light I was halfway across the stretch of shrouded water to Osprey Head. The morning was cold and a wind had come up, stirring the water to a chop. I knew it would be frigid with the coming of winter.

Off the rocky beach I let the sail drop and tossed over my sea anchor. I looked back at the shore and could not see it; I looked down at the cold green water. I could see only a small stretch of it. My little brother had gone into this very water and Grammaude still sometimes wept for him. All right, then. So would I go into it. So, then, might they weep for me. Or not. In that moment I did not care about that or anything else. Taking a great, despairing breath, I dove off the bow into the bay.

It had been my thought, if one could have called it that, to go down and simply let myself drift, so that the cold would take me before the drowning did. I had heard that in a few seconds one went so numb that there was no sensation but sleepiness, a dreaming green peace. That was what claimed you, not the choking water.

But it was not true. The water was terrible, fire and pain and darkness and an aching beyond pain. I choked and my lungs seared, and I fought and arched and kicked and knew that this was death, not a green peace, and I feared it more than anything on earth, even the loss of Warrie. I struggled for the surface far above me, hobbled by my wet blue jeans and sweater. Just as I thought my lungs would burst, I gained the surface. The little catboat bobbed, waiting. I swam heavily and clumsily for it and struggled aboard, nearly capsizing in the process. Then I set the sail for the yacht club. As it materialized out of the fog, I felt a terrible cramping begin in the pit of my stomach, and the warm rush on my legs that meant blood, and knew that if there had been a baby there no longer was. By the time I gained the harbor I was shaking all over, so hard that Caleb Willis, who was there alone taking the young Thornes' catboat out of the water, had to row out and tow me in. It was he who carried me, wrapped in blankets from the club and racked with tremors and sobs, up the lane to Liberty.

Even in my pain and the floating, buzzing beginning of the pneumonia that nearly took me away with it, I could see over his arm that the car was gone from Braebonnie and it was closed and shuttered. I turned my face into his chest. I was not surprised by that or anything else.

I was very ill in the hospital in Castine for two weeks after that. Grammaude stayed to nurse me, along with Beth Willis; I remember the first week only in vivid snatches, as you remember something from a fever dream. After clarity came back, I was simply too tired to talk, so I did not. There was nothing to say.

Grammaude seemed to know that. She sat beside me, reading aloud or just knitting and watching me, until someone made her go home, and then Beth Willis or a night nurse would take over. I said nothing to any of them. I think that Mike came, from MIT in Boston, but it might have been an image born of the fever; I did not speak to him either. He did not come back. I never asked if he had been real or a specter.

On a cold blue morning in the first week of October, Grammaude and Caleb and Beth Willis drove me to Bangor and put me and my luggage aboard a Delta jet. I would go straight to the infirmary at Saint Anne's; my father was in Lima on business and could not be reached, and the matron Grammaude had spoken with had agreed to let me begin some tutored lessons from my bed. I was well enough to study a bit, but so weak I could not sit up for more than three or four hours at a time. I slept prodigiously, endlessly. Grammaude worried about letting me go, but she thought it was more important that I not lose any more of my senior year.

I thought nothing was important. I would as soon be at Saint Anne's as anywhere else, so long as I was not in Retreat.

As I turned to go aboard the jet at the Bangor airport, she hugged me hard, her tears warm on my cold face.

"Take care of yourself, my darling," she whispered. "And forgive me for not doing better at it. We'll make up for it next summer, I promise you."

But I knew there would not be another summer, not in that beautiful killing place, not for me. And I thought that morning she knew it too.

In any event, it did not matter.

Chapter Seventeen

Y̶ou should have told me he was here."It was three weeks to the day from the Sunday I had arrived in Retreat in Mean Green's old car. I was standing on the sun porch in a pool of butter-yellow July sun, looking across the stone wall to Braebonnie. A black foreign touring sedan with an international license plate stood in the driveway, and I had known when I saw it that morning that Warrie Villiers was back.

When I spoke of it to Grammaude, I saw by her face that she had known too. She freely admitted it. He had been in Retreat since the end of April, she said; Micah Willis had told her so. He was here when she arrived. He had been downstate in Portland and on down to Boston and New York since a day or so before I came; he had told her this himself. Seeing to some business details, he had said. Warrie was back with apparently substantial financial resources, and he was in the process of buying property in Retreat.

He had already made several purchases, mainly from the old widows, Maude's friends, the ones with porch privileges. Many of them, frail, burdened with spiraling taxes and insurance costs, unable to find full-time help to tend the big old cottages, their children uninterested in the colony, thought Warrie Potter Villiers was an answer to their prayers. In all instances he had assured them that they might stay on for their lifetimes. And if he resold the cottages at all, it would only be to buyers who loved the colony as it was. Their families and friends, in fact, would have first refusal. What, they said to one another, could it hurt? His prices were wonderful; he was, after all, a Potter; and he had said, over and over, that his only purpose in buying was to keep Retreat as unspoiled and protected as it had always been. All over Maine, the old colonies and cottages were being sold to encroaching tides of outlanders, new people who cared nothing for the quiet, spare old ways, who seemingly wanted to make of Maine and this wild cape new versions of Palm Beach, Southampton, Cape Cod. If Warrie Villiers could prevent that, he was indeed the Word made flesh.

"He's quite the darling of the colony this summer," Grammaude said. "Part of it, anyway. A great many of the older people remember him when he was a little boy, and that's a very disarming thing up here. Family is everything. He's probably going to own us all before he's done."

"I don't care if he owns Retreat and Bangor to boot," I said. "You should have told me."

The old fear, that I had thought was beginning to be smothered under the weight of Retreat like a fire beneath damp leaves, leaped and licked once more.

"I know," she said. "I really should have. But I was afraid you'd leave before you saw how little he can hurt you now. There's almost nothing there of . . . the young man you last saw. He's quite fat, and he's got a bald spot, and I think he's drinking rather a lot. I hear he's divorced from his second wife, the Italian one; a lot of his money is some sort of settlement from her. The rest is an inheritance from his mother, I suppose. She died last year, in a nursing home in Nice. Hepatitis, we hear, but of course it could be anything. The point is, he just doesn't have all that power any more. At least, not physically. And I wanted you to see he didn't. If I'd told you when you first came, you'd have simply gotten in that car and driven away."

I was silent.

"Are you going to be able to handle it?"

She stood beside me on the porch, her arm around my waist, but she did not look up at me, and her voice was small, nearly inaudible. I had not heard it so frail since the first days I was here.

"Grammaude," I said, "I don't think I've thought of him three times since the day I left here, until I got back. He's history. He'll stay history."

She did look at me then. Her dark eyes were misted, far away.

"I was very wrong that summer," she said. "I'd always felt bad about Warrie. He seemed such a lost little soul. To be her son was a terrible thing; you could see the damage in him even when he was very small. But I should have stopped it. I was wrong even to let it get started, much less go on. You were just no match for him."

"You could no more have stopped it than an avalanche," I said.

"Yes," and she looked at me, fully back in the moment now, "I could have. I stopped his mother."

"His mother? How?"

She looked back out over the stone wall and the foreign car, out at the glittering bay.

"Just a figure of speech. She was always trouble, Elizabeth was. I was finally able to convince her to . . . stand on her own feet."

"She must have been very beautiful," I said. "He

said . . . that summer . . . that she had red hair like mine."

Grammaude turned away.

"No, not like yours. Yours is like a living flame. Hers was . . . the red of old blood. Elizabeth was not on the side of life."

"Well, anyway," I said, "I wish you'd told me. It would have been awful to just run into him."

"I wouldn't have let that happen," Grammaude said. "I just wanted us to have a little fun together first. And we have, haven't we, darling?"

We had. Despite the racking onslaught of the fear—or perhaps because of it—the three weeks had been oddly peaceful. Looking back I could see how hard Grammaude had worked to make them so; an enormous effort on her part had bought that sense of seamlessness and open-ended time. I spent a good part of each day alone, roaming my old paths along the cliffs and in the woods, rowing my Uncle Petie's dinghy in the cool early mornings, or just sitting on the rocks below Braebonnie staring out at the cloud shapes of Islesboro and Little Deer. But some part of almost every day was given to an expedition of Grammaude's devising. Remembering her dislike of what she termed "running around" in the summers I had spent with her, and seeing now how diminished and fragile she was, I could only wonder what these past days had cost her. And yet, I knew that in some way they had nourished her as they had me. I could read that in her face, see it in her step.

It had been three weeks spent largely in the company of old women. I drove small shoals of them, every day: to lunches in little towns up and down the coast, where they knew of restaurants they wanted to try or had old favorites; to antique and junk shops as far as Bar Harbor; to have their hair done and keep their doctors' appointments and have a Bloody Mary

and lunch afterward; to see the galleries and muse-
ums and sights that had been part and parcel of their
lives in this place for half a century. I took them to
the library to change their books, and to chamber
concerts over in Blue Hill, and once Grammaude and
old Mrs. Thorne from Mary's Garden and near-blind
old Mrs. Stallings, the last of the old ladies at the Compound, and I went over to Castine and had an afternoon of shopping and then dinner at the wonderful
old Pentagoet Hotel, spending the night there and
coming home the next morning singing like children
from Yaycamp as we soared up and over Caterpillar
Hill: "I been working on the railroad, all the livelong
day. . . ."

But at the top of Caterpillar Hill, Grammaude
turned her face away and closed her eyes, and I could
have kicked myself for choosing that way, remembering only then that it was just here, out into all
that amplitude of space and wind and water, that
my grandfather had soared in his little green
sports car.

"I'm sorry," I whispered to her, and squeezed her
hand on the seat beside me. It was as cold as ice, as
death, the claw of a dead bird.

"Don't be," she said. "It's a beautiful spot. One you
would choose, if you had to choose."

In the evenings I took Grammaude to other cottages for drinks, or we had a few people to Liberty.
Most were old. Several times old Micah Willis came
and sat before a fire in the living room and had coffee
and brandy with Grammaude, and I would hear them
laughing together from upstairs where I lay reading
old Mary Roberts Rinehart novels, hear their voices
rising and falling like frail birdsong, hear the comfortable cadence of more than half a century's affection,
like an old phonograph record long since worn into a
groove. I heard the chink of china as Grammaude

poured more coffee, and the ring of crystal from the old decanter where she kept the brandy, and sometimes little spills of music from the phonograph or the radio, but usually only the talk. They asked me to sit with them, and I might have, for I was fond of Micah Willis, but somehow the most comforting thing for me in those long nights, when the fear still nibbled and raked at me sporadically, was simply to lie under piled quilts in the circle of light from the reading lamp and listen to those two voices rising and falling in concert, like the twin threads of a sonata. They were anchors, those voices, anchors to my childhood summers here, anchors to the very earth. I slept deeply on the nights I slid into sleep listening to them.

More than once in those weeks I thought ruefully that I was doing what young women had done in Retreat since time out of mind: tending the old. But instead of finding them oppressive, I felt this time that the company of old women was soothing. They did not fuss and twitter nearly so much as I remembered, or at least the ones Grammaude spent time with did not. And they were not autocratic. They were funny, these old women; they may have talked constantly of the past, but it was a past full of particular and often eccentric people doing things that charmed and amused me. I remarked on it once to Grammaude.

"When you're old," she said, "you have a lot to pick and choose from in your memory. If you've lived an interesting life, the things you'll want to keep will be rather wonderful. I think only bores talk about boring things. There are some awful bores in Retreat, but I've never hung around with them if I could help it. I heard too many dishwater-dull stories from old people when I was your age. I vowed I'd have good things to remember and talk about."

"Well, you have," I said.

"Oh, yes," she said. "And when you've been here a little longer I'll tell you some even better ones."

"Like?"

"Like 'What I Did for Love.' You remember that song? You liked it, the last year you were here." She stopped. "I'm sorry, Darcy. I keep forgetting it was such a bad year for you. This one has been such a good one; for me, anyway."

"For me too, Grammaude."

"We haven't driven you to distraction, we old ladies?"

"No. I forget the difference in our ages, I really do. Sometimes we all might be teenagers together. And my car hasn't shocked a single soul. I'm terribly disappointed."

She laughed. "After what we've all lived through, a little shit happening isn't going to matter one way or another. I'm glad you've gotten to know them a bit, darling. I think it's maybe your time to get to know the old. You couldn't have, before, but you've been through enough now so that you can begin to understand the . . . the impulse toward simplicity that a lot of people think is senility."

She was right. In those three weeks, with the old ladies of Retreat, I had tapped into an odd richness; they were, literally, the past, the provenance I had always felt denied me. Retreat's timelessness had begun to work its old magic. The moment, the moment was all and would sustain me. The moment had been, would always be.

And now, into it, Warrie Villiers had come. I leaned against the old rattan writing table that had been my great-grandmother Hannah's and looked at Braebonnie, lying quiet and shuttered in the bright morning. Upstairs. He would be upstairs, perhaps still sleeping, perhaps just waking. . . . I felt heat start in my chest and climb my neck to my face. Did he still sleep in the little white iron bed that had been his mother's?

That had been ours?

I held myself very still and closed my eyes and looked as deeply inside myself as I could, to see what I was feeling. I had not done that since before the hospital in Atlanta; to do it after the onset of the fear would be to open myself to devastation. I was a past master at closing off those deep places where old feelings lay. But I did it now. I needed to know if, after all, I must get into Mean's old car once more and run away. I did not know where I would run to; Retreat was my last refuge. Back against the wall, I held my breath and looked.

I felt only mild disgust and a kind of sadness, a pity for all things young and vulnerable, all things still unbroken and waiting, unaware, for the first inevitable great smashing. Disgust and pity. That was all. It was all right, then. I could stay. He could not touch me again.

Grammaude came onto the porch with a tray of coffee and blueberry muffins. She looked at me keenly and then nodded faintly and set the tray down on the desk.

"Beth Willis sent these yesterday," she said. "First of the season's blueberries. She picked them herself. Butter one while it's hot. Did I tell you Warrie's been over to talk to me about selling Liberty?"

My heart gave a queer twinge, as if a small pellet of some sort had struck it, a tiny barb.

"You know you didn't. What did you say?"

"I told him no the first time. And the second, and the third. The fourth time he came I'm afraid I was really quite rude. He hasn't asked again. I hear he's been nosing around Petie and Sarah, though, to see if they can persuade me to sell. I don't know how firm you need to be with Warrie."

I knew she came near to hating Warrie Villiers for the way he had treated me that last summer, though she had never said so. It must be cruelly painful for her to have him next door now, to see the old cottages of her girlhood friends promised, one by one, to him.

"Well, I hope he'll leave you alone," I said. "I'll roust him good if he tries it again; I'd love the chance. But you know you're going to have to do something about Liberty one day, and you say Uncle Petie and Aunt Sarah don't want it. Maybe you ought to see what kind of offer he'll make you."

"I'm saving Liberty for you," Grammaude said, looking up at me. Her face was serene.

"Oh, Grammaude . . . don't, please," I cried in distress. Why had I not foreseen this? "I don't want Liberty. I can't handle it. You know I'm only here this summer because there was nowhere else and because you're here. You won't care who has it after you're gone. Let it go. It could be good money for you—"

"I will care," she said, and smiled, but she said no more.

He came the next day. I only realized I had been waiting for him when I looked up from the sofa on the sun porch, where I had been reading in the late afternoon while Grammaude napped, and let a long trembling breath go when I saw him coming over the stile in the stone wall. I knew then I had been walking lightly, as on unstable earth, and breathing lightly, as you do when you are trying to be very quiet, ever since Grammaude had told me the day before that he was in Retreat. All right, then, I told myself. Here he is. You have a few moments. Look inside and see what this silly business with the breath is. Yesterday you thought you felt only disgust and pity. What has changed?

What has changed is that he is here in front of me and I have not seen him for twelve years, and he hurt me nearly to death, I thought clearly. I am afraid he can do it again. The fear blazed up into panic, and my heart began the dreadful half-forgotten pounding, and I struggled for breath even while I made my lips curve into a rigid smile as he came up on the screened porch and looked in at me. The sun was behind him, and I could only see his silhouette.

"Hello, Warrie," I said, and clenched my fists so hard that my nails bit into my palms. I thought my voice sounded all right, but I knew I could not manage another word. I sat smiling, waiting.

"Hello, Darcy," he said, and the panic gave way to plain fear. It was not the voice I remembered, which had sucked my breath from my body and turned my bones to water. It was still his voice, rich and soft and with that hint of other shores in it, but it did not touch me anywhere except in my ears. I felt the iron band around my chest ease a little, and my heart slowed.

"May I come in? I know your grandmother sleeps about this time. Otherwise I wouldn't intrude. I know she doesn't want me here. But I wanted to say hello. I won't stay long."

It should have been a disarming little speech, humble and dignified at the same time, but it wasn't. There was mockery under it, and something else under that: what? A kind of obsequiousness, a smack of the mountebank. I had never heard it before. The fear leaked out like dirty water, and I knew I would be all right.

"Please do," I said.

He came into the sun porch and I could see him plainly. Despite what Grammaude had said about him, I was genuinely shocked. What had I ever seen in this man? What was there here that had made me abandon myself so totally to him? This man was soft and slack through the belly and shoulders, a roll of flesh spilling over his belt under a too-tight black T-shirt. He was deeply tanned, but there was a grayness under it, and his face, that had been a young hawk's, was blurred and pouched now, and webbed with tiny lines. The hooded gypsy eyes were deeply sunken and red-veined. I knew that Grammaude was right; he was a drinker. I had seen that stigmata every day in the hospital. He had a neat round bald spot, like a tonsure, tanned to leather, on top of his head, and the thick black hair was streaked with gray and still worn long around his neck and ears. He was . . . old. I knew he must be only thirty-five or so, but still he was far past youth. I felt profound, crawling shame at the thought of what we had done together, this man and I, and a faint nausea, and that was all, except to wonder if I looked as used and worn to his eyes as he did to mine.

"Sit down," I said finally. "Can I get you something? I was just thinking I might have a glass of wine."

He sat down on the edge of the chaise and smiled at me. I smiled back, unwillingly. Fragments of him were still there, then, under the wreckage. It was almost his old smile.

"Thanks, no," he said. "I'm doing my best to quit. That's one reason I'm here this summer. I don't think it will come as a surprise to you that I've had a bad problem with liquor; I can see that in your face. But some coffee or iced tea would be nice. Only if there's some made, though. I really won't be staying."

I went into the kitchen and brought back a tray with iced tea and some of Beth Willis's blueberry muffins. I thought of a truism we heard frequently at the hospital: admission is the first step toward healing the addict. Warrie Villiers admitting a weakness was unimaginable. It was a step I would admire in anyone else. The least I could do was give him the benefit of the doubt.

"Well," I said, passing tea and muffins to him, "Grammaude tells me you're interested in Retreat property. That surprises me somehow; I never thought you cared a lot about the colony."

"I can see why you thought that," he said, looking down into his glass. Then he looked at me, a long, serious look. "I was pretty snobby about meeting people and joining in that summer, wasn't I? I don't know; I guess I changed somewhere along the line. Europe will do that to you; in the circles I ran in, you get old and cynical pretty quick unless you're very strong. I wasn't, obviously. There came a time when I realized I wanted and needed . . . permanence. Quiet, real things that don't change, people who remain constant. And when that happened, I thought about Retreat. I hadn't, in years. So I came over this spring to open the cottage, and I found that a lot of the old places were in danger of going to outsiders with ideas something like the ones I used to have, and it struck me all of a sudden as a really awful thing. I had some money from Mother—I suppose your grandmother told you she died last year—and some from my second wife. I'm not particularly proud of how I got that. And I thought, What better thing to do with it than try to keep this place like it's always been? I know that must sound fatuous to you; this has been part of your family's heritage for three generations, and I've only been here one summer that I can remember. But this place really gets hold of you, Darcy."

He pronounced it "Daircy," as he always had. I looked steadily back at him. It sounded reasonable, even admirable. It also sounded absurd in that soft, exotic voice. What could this man, this product of so much sinuous slackness and corruption, know of permanence and quiet? But a memory, buried all those long years, surged into my mind, something he said the first time I ever met him: "This place sits softly on your heart."

"So they say," I said neutrally.

"But you do not think so?" he said, leaning back on the chaise, still looking keenly into my face. "No, I don't think you do. I could always read that little cat's face. Yet here you are."

I flushed. The allusion to my face was gratuitous and familiar; it presumed far too much.

"I don't care about Retreat one way or another," I said. "I'm here this summer because I haven't seen Grammaude for a very long time and because she's failing and I'm between jobs. It seemed a good time. I doubt that I'll come again."

"That's too bad," he said. "It would be pleasant to have a friend nearby in the summers. I think I am no longer that to your grandmother. I really regret it."

My face burned and I stared at him. Could he really not remember, not understand, what had happened that last summer? Could he possibly have thought I would be a friend to him, or be surprised that Grammaude no longer was?

"I'm sure you'll find friends, Warrie," I said. "I understand quite a few old ladies up here already think you're the chosen one. With the old ladies on your side, you can't lose."

He laughed, his old nasal laugh.

"They are charming, my old-lady friends," he said. "I'm truly sorry your grandmother isn't among them. I think she thinks I'm trying to hustle her out of her cottage, but nothing could be further from the truth. I only wanted to assure her it would stay as it is. I thought, since you had not been back for such a long time, you were probably not interested in Liberty, and I know her son and his wife are not. I still hope she'll reconsider my offer."

"If she says no, she means no, Warrie. You must respect that. Whatever she wants to do with her cottage is her business," I said.

"And yours?"

"None of mine. You were right about that. I don't want Liberty. I just want her to be able to decide what she wants to do with it without pressure. And I plan to do whatever I can to see that happens."

He grinned again, faintly, and raised his iced tea glass and saluted me.

"The old fire still burns," he said. "You have grown up, haven't you, Darcy? A formidable woman, and a very handsome one. I'm glad to see that; I was afraid my unspeakable behavior that last weekend might have damaged you somehow."

"Not in the least," I said, anger quickening my breath. "Not an iota. Not even the ghost of one. Now, if you'll excuse me, I need to go start dinner. Grammaude likes to eat at six."

He got up and picked up my hand and bowed over it, very slightly.

"Might I tempt you to come and share dinner with me sometime soon?" he said. "Your grandmother too, of course. I've turned into quite a good cook."

"No," I said levelly. "I don't believe you could tempt either one of us. We're living very quietly this summer, Warrie. Grammaude is very frail. And you'll forgive us, I know, if we don't entertain."

"Well, in any case I shan't give up on you," he said, moving to the door. "You were my first two friends in Retreat. I'm not going to let you go so easily."

"I don't think that's your decision," I said, heat and redness flooding up my neck to my cheeks. His eyes tracked them, and he laughed.

"Not everything about you has changed," he said,

and went out, closing the screen door softly. I stared after him, dizzy with anger. He was beneath contempt; I would not receive him at Liberty again. I would hook the screen doors and refuse to talk to him if he called; I would not sit on the sun porch again and risk his seeing me there. Grammaude was right. There was nothing left in Warrie Villiers that could hurt me.

I got no chance to refuse him the house, though, because he didn't come again, and he did not call. I did not even see him from the window of my room, which gave onto the roof of Braebonnie over the stone wall; I had been keeping the old orange shade down so that he could not see me inside, but when days and then weeks went by and I saw nothing of him but his figure, getting in and out of the black sedan in his driveway and twice from a distance at the post office, I raised the shades again. By keeping them lowered, I had only flooded the room with hot red light. By tacit agreement Grammaude and I began to have our predinner cocktails on the sun porch once more. Neither of us had spoken of Warrie Villiers since the day she told me he was back. I thought she knew nothing of his visit.

On the second night we sat on the sun porch again, however, she smiled at me over the rim of her martini glass and said, "I gather the fort is still secure."

"I'm sorry?" I said, knowing full well what she meant.

"Warrie wasn't able to melt you with his rueful smiles and protestations of change."

"No," I said, grinning. "You were right. He's pretty awful, isn't he? How did you know, by the way?"

"Saw him come over the stile and came out and listened, like any reasonable woman. I don't know what I'd have done if you'd let him suck you back in. I'm having a hard enough time with some of these old fools who think he's the savior reborn. He goes somewhere to drinks every night."

"You don't believe him, about the alcoholism and the change of heart and all?"

"I believe him about the alcoholism, and I'm sorry," she said, her fine-etched face growing grave. "He's never had an easy moment in his life. I'm sure of that. It's just that he's responsible for most of it and will never see it, and that's the part that's dangerous. As for the change of heart—well, it happens, I suppose. I just don't believe it in his case. I think he's here to punish us in some way, not to save us. I think that's probably why he came the time before."

I stared at her. It shot through my mind that she had had a sudden small stroke, or something similar, the words were so bizarre and spoke so obviously of paranoia. But her dark face was as it had been all summer, alive and quick with intelligence. Only now a shadow of worry lay over it.

"Why would he want to punish us, Grammaude? Nobody here has ever done anything to him; he's never even been here except that summer, and then it wasn't we who harmed him, if you recall."

"I recall better than you can possibly know, Darcy," she said. "But you forget, he was here when he was very small, with his mother. He'll have remembered that, I think, no matter what he says. And there was harm done to her, or at least I imagine he would see it that way. He would think it grievous harm, and it was I who inflicted it. I cannot imagine what she might have told him, but I feel sure it is me—and, because of me, you—whom he wants to punish. I think Warrie has had only one great love in his life, and it was neither of his wives and none of his other women. His love died last year, of the life she led. If it were not for me, she might have led a far different life, perhaps in a far different place. Perhaps even here in Retreat. And so here he is, determined to lead it for her. More than that, even. Determined to own it, as she never could."

"You mean his mother? Grammaude, what on earth could you possibly have done to her? She was a grown woman when she left here the last time."

"No." She shook her head, looking out at the satiny mauve of the sunset bay. "No. Elizabeth was never a grown woman."

"You said you only convinced her to . . . stand on her own feet, was it? I wish you'd tell me what you meant."

"I will, darling, when it's time. One day soon, I promise. It's not important because he's not a threat to you any longer. That's all I ever cared about. And I can tell he's not. He can't get his hands on you and he can't have Liberty, so he's simply . . . not important. Let's enjoy having the sun porch back and have maybe one more of these before dinner. And then I think I'll start that new Martha Grimes. I've been putting it off until a night there was nothing on TV."

As July faded into August, I became gradually aware that the colony was neatly split over the matter of Warrie Villiers and his avowed mission in Retreat. With the coming of August, traditionally the busiest month in summertime Maine, the luncheon and cocktail parties escalated, and there was a regatta and tea every weekend afternoon at the yacht club, and dances and card parties and movies almost every evening. Everyone who had been putting it off all summer had an enormous pay-back cocktail party, and it was possible, if one wanted, to go out every noon, twilight, and evening for the entire month. Neither Grammaude nor I wanted to, but we ventured out to the ones she felt we could not refuse, and at each one Warrie was the subject of heated conversation. With her undetectable but infallible social antennae, Grammaude invariably knew ahead of time which gathering he would not be attending that evening, and it was to those that we went, and it was at those that the war—for it was that, a little war—was waged.

"It's just not right for one person to own so much property up here," the younger people would say. "It's dangerous; he could do anything with it. We don't really know him, after all. Who knows where that money comes from? You know what his mother was."

"It's not you who has to pay the taxes and insurance on these old barns," the indignant older ones would retort. "It's not you who lives on a fixed income and can't do the upkeep and can't find help. What would you have us do? We've known his grandparents and some of us his great-grandparents; his family has been here longer than almost anyone's. This way we can keep our cottages and have the money to keep them up, and not see them sold to just anybody. Do you want people from Florida or Texas to come here and put in *swimming pools,* for God's sake?"

"No, but how do you know he means what he says?"

"How do you know he doesn't? What could he do but resell them? We'd have to do that ourselves, or you would when we're gone."

And so it went, night after perfect amethyst night, for it was one of the loveliest summers I have ever seen on that coast. Cool, bright, blue-edged, crisp—and salted with the faint corruption that was Warrie Villiers and his foreign money. I hated the thought so much I simply stopped listening to the never-ending debate, which in any case went nowhere. I sipped my drinks and went out onto porches or terraces and looked at the still twilit bay and smelled the ripe pine-laden smell of highest summer, that absolute pinnacle that was like a jeweled gear frozen in the moment just before it ground forward again toward autumn. It filled me up and smoothed me out and sang in my blood and ears like wine, and I was determined to let nothing and nobody spoil it. Warrie Villiers was so far from my thoughts in those few perfect days that he might as well not have existed.

But then I came home from the hardware store in Blue Hill one afternoon and found him leaning over my grandmother as she lay on the sun-porch chaise, striking his palm with his forefinger as he drove home point after point to her, and saw her white, still face looking resolutely up at him, and I whirled on him like a dervish.

"Out!" I said furiously. "Out this minute! What do you mean coming over here waving your finger in Grammaude's face like that? You know she doesn't want you here, and neither do I. I want you to leave this instant. Look at her, she's white as a sheet."

He got up and nodded to Maude, his face flushed. He looked crestfallen and contrite. I stood between them, my hands clenched into fists at my sides. He turned away and started out, and then turned back.

"Mrs. Chambliss, I'm truly sorry," he said. "I didn't come here to hound you, and I can see now how I must have sounded. I just . . . I wanted you to know that I have arrangements with about half the cottages along this side of the shore now, all the way down to the yacht club and around the other way up to the Aerie. I thought you'd feel more comfortable about what I'm doing if you saw that your oldest friends and neighbors trust me. I've even got a promise from your son that he'll think about my offer. I really am on your side—"

"Warrie!" I shouted.

"I'm going," he said quietly. "I'm sorry. I won't come again." He bowed to Grammaude and left the porch. I strode along behind him, following him over the stile to the yard of Braebonnie. For an instant, old sensations, old memories, dove and shrieked at me. The dark lawn, the dark porch, only moonlight on the face of the bay, only starlight, and above, against the night sky, one yellow-lit window. I had not stood in this yard for twelve years.

He turned to face me, in the late sun again, his hands in his pockets. His full, dark face was flushed, and there was perspiration at his hairline.

"I really am sorry, you know," he said. "I truly thought she'd feel differently if she knew about the others. I only meant to reassure her."

"Well, you didn't," I said hotly. "You bullied her; you were bending over her shaking your finger at her. I wish you could have seen yourself. Goddamn it, Warrie, why is this house so important to you? You have all the others. Why aren't they enough? How much of Retreat do you want?"

"It's just that I don't want to see it go to the developers after she's gone. After all, how long can she last? And I know you don't want it."

"Well," I said, glaring at him, "maybe I do, after all. Maybe I've changed my mind. You said yourself people do. So there's no more reason for you to bother her again. And if you do, I'll get . . . I'll get a restraining order or whatever I have to get."

He laughed and held up his hands, palms out. "No need. Though the idea of anyone on Cape Rosier being able to produce a restraining order is piquant, I must say. No, if you want the house yourself, that's the end of it, of course. I'm only interested in helping out the old ones who don't have heirs. I apologize, Darcy, to you and your grandmother. I wish that we might have been . . . friends. Just that."

"Well, if that's what you wanted, you picked a hell of a way to go about it," I said, and turned and went back over the stile to Liberty. But I felt oddly ungracious. Somehow I knew that he would not approach Grammaude about the cottage again.

"That's the end of that," I said, sitting down on the edge of the chaise and taking her hands. They were cold, but the color was back in her face, and her eyes sparkled.

"That was wonderful, darling," she said. "I couldn't have done better myself."

"Was I yelling that loud?"

"You know how sound carries down here by the water. He did sound sorry, didn't he? I wonder about what? Probably that you want Liberty after all."

"Grammaude—"

"I know. It was only to get rid of him. Still, I'd like to think . . . oh, well. You know, it bothers me terribly that those poor old fools along the shore have signed their cottages over to him, and as for Petie . . . well, I'll deal with Petie later. I could simply threaten to disinherit him—"

"You wouldn't! Petie is your heart!"

"No, I wouldn't, of course. And you're right, he's much of my heart, but I really suspect you have a bit more of it. The thing about Petie is that he's never really known it. Now you, my dear redheaded minx, must surely know."

A great wash of fatigue flooded me. I slumped on the chaise. The scene with Warrie was only the culmination of the small, continuous subterranean drumbeat of tension that had pounded me over the past few weeks. But it all had its genesis in him.

"I know," I said. "I do know that if I don't know anything else, Grammaude. Tell you what, if you're as tired as I am, let's have chowder on trays in front of the fire and go to bed right after. I really don't think either of us needs to sit up with a shotgun across our knees tonight. I think the old homestead is safe."

"I hope so," Grammaude said. "I hope so."

The next afternoon twin bunches of roses came for Grammaude and me from the florist in Blue Hill. Mine were yellow and hers were a wonderful rose-coral. The cards read, simply, *I am truly sorry. Warren Villiers.*

"I'm throwing these right out," I said.

"I'm not," Grammaude said. "They're my favorite color. I wonder if Mark Graham told him? They must have cost him a mint. Don't throw the baby out with the bathwater, Darcy."

And so for the next week, we went about the slow, symmetrical business of the colony with War-rie Villiers's roses glowing in the background like amulets. By the time they had faded, he had made no other move toward Grammaude but to nod pleasant-ly to her and to me when he saw us on the sun porch or at the general store or the post office, and once, when she had a cold and stayed in bed for two or three days, he brought a small terrine of chicken and artichokes over and left it on the porch with a note that said, *This is the Gallic idea of comfort food. I hope it lives up to its name.* It did; it was delicious, and she and I ate all of it at a sitting.

"Maybe he could open a restaurant," I said, licking my spoon.

"Maybe he will," she said.

I took the washed casserole back on a day that the black car was gone, thinking I would not run into him, but when I opened the screen door at Braebon-nie to go up on the porch, he was there on the old glider. His foot and ankle were wrapped in an Ace bandage, and a pair of crutches lay beside him on the deck-painted boards.

"What on earth?" I said.

"Sprained it stepping off the curb in Castine yesterday, right on Main Street," he said. "It'll be okay in a week or so, they tell me."

"Where's your car?"

He grimaced.

"I hired a kid at the gas station to bring me home and take it back. It needed tuning anyway. He's going to work on it and bring it back in three or four days. Somebody will follow him and take him back. At least I hope he brings it back. He looks like a fledgling repo man to me."

I laughed. I knew that station and the young man in question. He had leered so covetously when I stopped one day for gas that I almost spoke sharply to him, until I realized that it was Mean Green's car he coveted and not me. He did indeed look adept at spiriting cars away in the dead of night.

"I know," I said. "I dare not take my car back there. I could tell he lusted after it."

"No wonder," Warrie said. "It's a wondrous machine, that car. This IT that happens, it is—ah, *merde,* no?"

I laughed aloud. I had forgotten how funny Warrie could be. "It is. Are you going to be able to manage?" I said.

"Oh, sure. I'm getting good with the crutches. And I need to drop some flab, anyway. I've stocked up on tuna fish. I'll be skinnier than old Mrs. Stallings by the time I'm off these things."

I was silent for a moment, and so was he. Then I said, "I'd be glad to—" and he said, at the same time, "Listen, Darcy, I wanted to—"

We stopped, smiling.

"I could bring you something for supper till you can get around better," I said tentatively, wondering what possessed my tongue. But what sort of enemy, what sort of danger, could he possibly be, flat on the glider and unable to move around? I'd offer the same to anyone.

"I'd be very grateful," he said. "I'll be able to manage after a bit, but I'm on pain medication now that makes me woozier than hell, and I'm afraid I'll set the place on fire if I light the stove. I've meant all summer to get a new electric one in here. This old job must be thirty years old."

"Get gas," I said. "Everybody has it. We usually lose power up here at least five times a summer, when it storms. I wonder that we haven't before now. At least you'll be able to cook when we do."

"Good idea," he said. "Thanks for thinking of it. Listen, Darcy, I just wanted to say again that I'm sorry—"

I shook my head and got up, preparing to leave. I did not want another apology.

"No, I want to say this, and then I'll drop it," he said.

I waited.

"I know that I hurt you terribly that last summer," he said slowly. "I've thought of it often. I wish I could undo it, but I can't. You were . . . you were a small miracle, and I just threw it away. I've never stopped regretting it. I don't want anything more from you or your grandmother, though I'd have been very proud to have you as my friends. But I did want you to know that."

"Well, thank you for telling me, Warrie," I said, aware that the flush was creeping up my neck again and hating it. "You needn't have, but it was . . . a nice thing to do. Now. I'm making chicken pie from a recipe my great-grandmother had, and I'll bring a plate for you. You needn't come to the door; just leave the screen unhooked and I'll put it on the table by the door where the keys stay."

"Thanks," he said. "I probably won't come down. I'm going to try and sleep some now."

He wasn't on the porch when I brought the pie, and he often wasn't during that week when I came with food. But he was occasionally, and when he was I would sit and talk a little, and once or twice I made us iced tea in the familiar and yet unfamiliar kitchen and we sat drinking it and looking out at the sweep of sea and islands and sky that Braebonnie commanded. It was a spectacular view; I wished afresh on those evenings that Liberty had that direct water frontage. But I was glad, too, in a way, that it did not. You would have to live up to that magnificence. Liberty simply let you sag when you needed to.

We talked, on those evenings, of nothing in particular, nothing in the past. We were careful about that. He told me a little about France and Italy in these opening days of the new decade, and I talked a little of Atlanta and the blaring, sun-punished new South. It was light talk, and I did not stay long. Mostly, we laughed. I had not laughed much that summer, and before that, not at all for a very long time. The laughter felt good.

Grammaude said nothing when I left with the plates of food each evening. I know she was uneasy at my going, but I knew too that she would have done it if I had not. It was unthinkable, in Retreat, to let a neighbor lack food because of illness or injury. Mostly, I knew, she disapproved of and somehow feared the laughter. She could not help but have heard it. Her window gave directly onto the piled stone wall and the lawn of Braebonnie. I noticed, each evening as I came back across the stile to dinner, that the shades in her bedroom were drawn once more.

At the end of that week I took her to Donald and Marie Elliot's enormous lawn party at Fir Cottage. It was the loveliest of a string of preternatural nights. My grandmother's old friend Erica Conant was gone now, but her legendary rock garden rioted and tumbled

down the cliff face, and her Japanese lanterns, like
the ones in Grammaude's shed, glowed magically in
the dark branches of the great firs for which the cottage was named. Fireflies winked, and the darkening
bay breathed and sighed like a great dolphin, and the
thin pure curve of a young moon hung in the green
sky over the Camden Hills. I looked at the handsome
people in flower prints and linen and madras on the
lawn and veranda. How little this place had changed
since I was small; how much had happened! It struck
me that there should be, in every life, a place like this,
a kind of Brigadoon, where you could come and visit
your past, and the past of your people, and know that
whatever happened outside, here timelessness lived.
But few lives can claim one. I knew myself blessed, in
that moment, by Retreat, and wondered for the first
time if perhaps there might be more for me here than
the enforced healing of this one summer. But at the
thought the fear, dormant now for weeks, coiled and
struck sharply as a snake, and I pushed it away. No.
Not for me. Not any more.

I got up and went up to the bar to get Grammaude
a refill, and listened closely for the first time in many
days to the talk in the group milling around it. Then I
began to laugh. I was still laughing when I brought
Grammaude her drink and sat back down. She smiled
up at me inquiringly.

"Sewage," I said, motioning with my head toward
the bar. "Everybody's talking about septic tanks and
sewage disposal. Come to think of it, they've been
doing it all summer. I'll bet Retreat is the only place
on earth where people routinely talk about shit over
drinks."

Grammaude smiled and looked down into her gin
and tonic. Then she looked at me. "Shit, as you put it, is
a real dilemma up here. Most of the cottages on our
side of the main lane sit on a rock ledge; dig down

about nine inches and you'll hit it. They can't have septic tanks in their yards. For more than a hundred years—maybe for as long as the colony has been here—the only septic field available to them has been that big old meadow that runs alongside Liberty and behind Braebonnie down to the water. We own part of it, and the Potters own the rest—Warrie, now. Both families have always been glad to let the other cottages channel their septic lines there. I don't know how many do; probably about half the cottages in Retreat. Otherwise, they simply couldn't be used. You can see that people are concerned about . . . shit."

She smiled again and looked away.

"You mean," I said slowly, "you mean that if . . . somebody . . . owned Liberty and Braebonnie he'd—they'd—have the only septic field in this half of Retreat?"

She nodded, her eyes on the bay.

"And if they chose, they could deny all those people the right to use it? But then they couldn't come here."

Grammaude said nothing.

"Grammaude, he would not do that," I said.

She looked at me then, but she did not speak.

"I know he would not," I said.

"Oh, Darcy," my grandmother said, and her voice was tired and old. Soon after that we went home.

"He would not," I said aloud into the salt-cool air that night, after I had turned off my light. And there was such a simple, solid truth to it that I slid immediately into sleep on the hardness of it and did not dream.

Chapter Eighteen

When Warrie graduated from his crutches, I borrowed my cousins' Beetle Cat and took him sailing. It was the first clear day we had had after nearly a week of cold, thick-felted white fog, for the perfect weather had finally broken the day after Donald and Marie's party, and I was restless and dull-minded and needed the fresh, sharp-edged blue of the sea and sky.

I asked Warrie along because, after being housebound in the gloom with Grammaude for so long, I needed also to laugh. She had been distant and preoccupied ever since our conversation about the septic field in the great meadow shared by Liberty and Braebonnie, and I had finally given up trying to get back to our old easy footing. In another woman I would have put the silence down to simple sulking because I had defended someone she thought indefensible, but Grammaude did not sulk. I knew she was deeply troubled and strongly suspected that she was trying to decide what to do about my seeing Warrie the little that I did.

I could have put her mind to rest about that, I thought; I wanted only simple lightness and the thoughtless companionship of someone near my own age, after a summer spent with the old. But I did not. For one thing, her unhappiness at the situation made me perversely annoyed; I simply did not want the weight of it on my head, not now, when the years-long cloud of misery and fear was finally giving way to a frail normalcy. For another, I knew on some level that my seeing him had more to it than a way to pass the time. Every woman who has been in love with a man long before and lost him wants to retest those waters when she meets him many years later. She may be supremely happy with her current state of affairs, and usually she has no wish at all to resume the relationship. She simply wants to see if she has the power to make him the slightest bit sorry. I think it is so universal a trait with women as to be genetic. I recognized a small streak of it in myself and did not admire it. So I did nothing to ease her pain. I did not admire myself for that, either.

She hadn't spoken of Warrie during the week after the party, when I left in the evenings with his supper plate. But when I told her where I was going and with whom that morning, she put down her coffee cup and said, "Oh, darling. I do so wish you wouldn't. I know you're twenty-nine years old and all that, but I didn't really speak up that last summer, and look what happened. Taking his dinner over to him is one thing, but a day on the water alone is quite another. You're still very fragile, and I don't think you see him plain even now."

"I see him as plain as day for the rat he was twelve years ago and the ass who's been annoying you all this summer, and I can handle that as well as you can," I said a bit sharply, for she seemed very old and diminished that morning, almost as faded and used as she had when I found her asleep on the sun porch at the beginning of the summer, and that frightened me. I did not want to feel guilty about Grammaude.

"Then why not cancel today? Spend it with me instead of a rat and an ass. We could go somewhere: Bar Harbor, maybe."

"For God's sake, Grammaude, we're only going sailing, not . . . to a motel or something," I snapped. "I'm not going to get involved with Warrie Villiers again; I don't even particularly like him. I just want to spend a few hours with somebody who makes me laugh."

She turned back to the coffeepot, but not before I saw the hurt in her face. She had made me laugh quite often that summer, so my words were thoughtless and hard. I should have done what she asked; the sail was nothing to me. But I didn't. I just kissed her wrinkle-etched silk-velvet cheek and said, "Back before drinks time. Want to have Mrs. Thorne and Mrs. Stallings over? I'll get some crab at the store if you do."

"I don't think so," she said. "Maybe I'll take P. D. James and go back to bed for a little. This is an elephant day."

A small dart of worry pierced the impatience I felt; occasionally Grammaude had days when it was hard to draw deep breaths and there was a sensation around her heart that felt, she said, as if an elephant were sitting on her chest. These attacks had frightened me at first, but she said she had been checked over just before she left Northpoint, and her doctor had said there was nothing critical there, just the expected weariness of old muscles and long-used lungs. She was simply to rest when she felt the elephant, and it would be gone in a few hours. And it always had been, at least by the next day. But usually, also, she would follow her announcement that the

elephant was back with a wry smile and the statement, "A very small elephant." This time she did not.
Even that annoyed me. Could it be possible that she
was feigning illness to keep me from seeing Warrie?

"'Bye," I said breezily. "I'll get the crab anyway, on
our way back. We can have salad for supper."

"Goodbye, darling," she said. And I went out into
the diamond morning to meet Warrie, who was
standing in the lane outside the barberry hedge in
white pants and a striped shirt looking decidedly
international. He had a string bag with a real French
baguette in it and bottles of red wine and Perrier.

"Good God," I said, grinning. "*Matelot, matelot* . . .
remember the old Noel Coward song? You're far too
exotic for Retreat. I ought to take you over to Northeast Harbor or somewhere rich. Where on earth did
you get the French bread?"

"Bribed the baker in Castine to make me some," he
said. "It's probably made with brown flour and
Crisco, but the shape's right."

The yacht club was practically deserted, and I
could see from the number of empty floats that
almost everybody had had the same fog-spawned
yearning for open sea that I had. One or two small
boys were still wrestling with their Beetles, and a
small knot of women sat on the porch, taking a
breather from the preparations for that afternoon's
tea. It was Saturday, one of the last regattas. I had forgotten. I felt my throat tighten a bit; I had not wanted
to meet anyone I had known before in Retreat this
summer, except Grammaude and her old friends. But
I had been bound to do it sometime. Looking at them,
I could not tell if they were old acquaintances of
mine or people I had never seen before. They looked
almost exactly alike to me, in tennis dresses or white
shorts and shirts, and no one looked familiar. I wondered if twelve years had altered me as much in their

eyes, or if it was my own eyes that had changed their way of seeing. I lifted a hand and smiled toward the group in case they were known to me, and a chorus of polite greetings floated back: "Hello, Darcy. I heard you were here." "It's nice to see you; you've cut your hair or something, haven't you?" "Come and say hello, when you get back, and have a cup of tea."

I called back that I would, meaning to do no such thing. I did not take Warrie up to be introduced. I never even considered that he might know these women, but when one of them called out, "Warrie! Wait up!" and got up and started down the steps toward us, I wondered why I had not. Of course he would have met them; he would have met almost everyone by now. He'd been here since April, after all. It was I who had been sequestered.

The woman came close, and I saw she was about my age or perhaps a bit older, and startlingly beautiful. Familiar, too, in a way that brought the old fear out of hiding to snap at me briefly. Who was she? Why the stab of anxiety? Then I knew: Gretchen Winslow, my grandmother's old enemy's granddaughter. Her grandmother had been a beauty too, and her mother, I had heard, and fully as mean as Gretchen. What a pity to waste those genes on Winslow women, I said to myself peevishly, remembering the ugly little scene on the Willises' boathouse dock all those years ago, when she had jeered at me about my mother's madness and nymphomania in front of all the colony children. It had taken Mike Willis to shut her up, Mike and his grandfather Micah.

"Hello, Gretchen," I said. She smiled sweetly at me and reached up and kissed Warrie lightly on the mouth.

"You rat," she said. "You never called after Southampton. I waited all the rest of the weekend. If you think you're getting your sweater back, think again."

"Hello, Gretch," he said, disentangling himself and patting her on the rear. "Keep the sweater, by all means. You do it far more justice than I. When did you get here?"

"Day before yesterday," she said. "I was going to come over and see if you wanted to sail with Corky Stallings and me this afternoon, but I see you're spoken for."

"I'm not regatta material," he said. "Darcy's going to show me about this fabulous creature called a Beetle Cat. I'm only familiar with power boats, I'm afraid."

"Too bad," she said, turning away to resume her place in the group. "I'd have bet you were world-class material. Regatta, of course. We'll have to work on that." She smiled again and went up the steps, and we went down the dock gangway to the dinghy, to row out to the Beetle Cat.

"I didn't know you knew Gretchen," I said. "I didn't remember your knowing her that last summer."

"I didn't," he said. "I met her at an extremely silly house party in Southampton early this summer, before you got up here. She hadn't brought any warm clothes with her and I lent her a sweater, which, as you'll have guessed, she still has. Gretchen is a beautiful woman, but a bit . . . hard-edged for my tastes. No subtlety or nuance. She hasn't been divorced six months and she's already been through New York's finest. Or so I'm told."

"And were you . . . one of the finest?"

I was laughing, but my face began to redden too. Oh, Lord, why on earth should I care? In truth, I didn't.

"Not fine enough, obviously," he said, grinning.

"For all her talk she went home from Southampton with a gentleman in a Rolls-Royce who, I understand, made a killing in insider trading. My modest inheritance couldn't stand up to that."

I brought the little boat about. The wind was light and soft and steady. I had us on a long beat over toward Eggemoggin Reach and Little Deer Isle. In the opposite direction lay Osprey Head. I did not want to see those waters again.

When we were under way, I said, "I thought somehow that you'd come straight here from Italy. The way you talked—"

"I was in New York for almost two years before I came to Retreat," he said neutrally. I was silent; so was he, for a long moment. There was only the low rushing of the wind and the little liquid spill of quiet water past our bow. Then he turned to me and said, "I was in a hospital outside Manhattan for almost fifteen of those months, up the Hudson Valley past Sneden's Landing. It was a hospital for alcoholics and other addicts. My wife's parents picked it out and sent me there, and paid the bills, and rented me an apartment in New York when I got out. That and a rather substantial cash settlement were the price they paid for getting me out of Giulia's life. I think they considered it cheap at the price. By that time I was an outrageously bad husband and probably a dangerous one. My mother died while I was in the hospital, and then there was nothing left for me to go back to and a good bit of money . . . so I stayed around Manhattan awhile, seeing bankers and finance people about this project up here and going to AA. The Winslow bank was one of the places I contacted. Gretchen's brother runs it now and remembered my name. He and his wife and Gretchen had me for dinner. That's how I know her. That's all. Just that."

The heat in my face roared into full flame.

"Oh, Lord, Warrie, I wasn't prying," I said. "It's certainly none of my business where you've been and who you've seen. You don't have to report to me."

"No, I know you thought I came here from Europe," he said, looking out to sea. His face was grave. "I let you think so. I didn't want you to think—I remembered the last words you said to me, before. About Eurotrash. I didn't want you to think I was that."

Pity flickered, pity and perhaps the smallest taste of triumph. He remembered then, those last words of rage and pain I had spoken. But, oh, dear God, the hospital; I should have known. I should have sensed it. There is a fraternity of us, those of us who have been inside such places. We know one another on meeting, as if by some scent on our skins. Why had I not picked it up?

"I'm sorry about the hospital," I said. "I was in one too. I just got out to come here. Not for addiction, but for what they call panic disorder. I can usually tell who's been in one, but I've been pretty wrapped up in myself lately. It must have been bad, all alone and sick in a strange country, and then losing your mother."

"Yes," he said. "That was bad. That was the worst part. She died before I could get home. Hepatitis. She'd lived a hard life, but she was still very beautiful."

We sailed in silence for a while, and then he said, "Actually, I knew about your . . . illness. Your grandmother told me before you came. Not what it was, precisely, but that it was quite severe and emotional in nature. I can see now that she was warning me off you. Maybe she was right."

"She was not right, and I'm very angry at her," I said. "Not that she told you—I'm not ashamed of it—but that she'd take it on herself to do that. She had no right."

"I think," Warrie said, "that she probably had every right. I also think you're better now," he said. It was not a question.

"I am. I didn't expect to be, and I find myself really sort of surprised that I am. When you're in the middle of those things you don't think they're going to end," I said. "You think in terms of living the rest of your life in accommodation to the . . . whatever. The fear, in my case. Of finding a way you can live out your years without just dying of it or killing yourself. You think in terms of what you'll have to do to keep it under control, how and where you can live with it. It's like some huge, awful, inevitable animal or something, that's chained to you for the rest of your life. You only look for places that will take huge, awful animals. It's a terribly minimal way to live. I'm sorry, Warrie. I didn't mean to make a speech. I am better. The animal is a much smaller one now, and shrinking every day. It's about down to poodle size. It surprises me."

He reached over and put his hand over mine on the tiller, briefly.

"I know," he said. "I do know. I know every syllable of what you're saying. It's hard, and there are so few people you can talk about it to. I won't, to you . . . but it's very comforting to know that I can, if I need to, and I hope you know that you can, to me. Always."

"Yeah," I said, and smiled at him. "I know. Let's don't . . . but let's hold it in reserve."

After that we did not speak of our pasts again. We found a little cove off Herrick's and dropped anchor and ate our lunch with the high noon sun pouring straight down on us, and laughed a lot about things I cannot even remember now, except that Gretchen Winslow and her New York set were part of it, and we came sailing home in the afternoon just before the fleet came in, at that hour when everything stops still in a kind of dreaming lull before it flows forward into evening, and we were still laughing when we docked. We went straight up the dock and the path to the main lane of Retreat without even looking toward the clubhouse, and when someone— Gretchen, I think—came out onto the clubhouse porch and called after us, "But you said you'd come have some tea," we joined hands and ran up the lane laughing like two children with a delicious guilty secret between them. I dropped his hand when we turned into the lane, and he straightened up and walked decorously beside me carrying the empty wine bottle in the net bag, but the secret still lay there in the air, whole and living.

"See you," he said, and ruffled my hair, and went on down the meadow path past Retreat to the turnoff to Braebonnie.

"Yes," I said, and went into the cottage.

When I came into the living room the fire was lit, and Grammaude sat before it in her Spanish shawl talking to Mike Willis. For a moment I stood in the doorway, still unseen, and simply looked at him. He was sitting on a hassock leaning forward with both of Grammaude's hands in his, and she was talking intently to him. Firelight threw dancing planes and pools over their faces and picked out the glint of his white teeth and something—could it be tears?—on her face. If it was, she was smiling faintly through them, looking at him with the old mixture of fondness and careful attention that I remembered as if on my very flesh. I had seen them sit so, talking by the fire, since my earliest memories in Liberty. He looked so utterly familiar and natural there in the firelight that I realized I had carried just that picture of him with me through all the years since I had last seen him, closed out of my sight like an old photo in a wallet but never away from me.

Mike, I said soundlessly, and then, aloud, "Mike."

He turned his head and looked up at me, and I could see then that there were indeed twelve years of wear and weather and care in the dark face, and wires of silver in the rough hair that still hung over his brown forehead. But he was still Mike and no one else on earth, uncannily, like his grandfather Micah in that light. No wonder I had mistaken them in the cemetery, the day I had come. The likeness must give my grandmother a turn whenever she looked at him.

He smiled and said, "Hello, Red," and I ran across the room and threw my arms around him. He half rose, hugging me back, smelling of salt and soap and Mike, and then lost his balance and we both sat down heavily on the hassock, me in his lap. I sat there for a moment, my face buried in his shoulder, feeling all the summers flood back over me like a runaway reel of movie film, and then I leaned back and said idiotically, "I wish you'd let me know you were coming home. I must look like a mess; I've been out on the water."

"So I hear," he said, standing and pulling me to my feet. "You look pretty good to me, though. A sight better than the last time I saw you, and that's the truth."

Only then did I remember that we had parted in anger and misunderstanding, with me running from him up the dock to Liberty and him running after, not knowing what he had done except kiss me once. I felt shame and pain. Another memory swept in behind that one: Mike leaning over me in the hospital, talking softly, me with my face turned away. Or was it a dream? I could not remember much about those few weeks.

"Did you come to the hospital that time?" I said.

"Did I ever. Hitchhiked all the way from Boston, only to have you turn your face to the wall. Yep, this is a decided improvement. I always thought you'd look like this."

"Like what?"

"Like a ginger cat. A reasonable assumption, when you consider you looked like a ginger kitten before. Stripe you up a little and you'd look like old Zoot here, with his plumy hair and big fat tail."

Zoot came eeling out from under the sofa and coiled himself around Mike's leg, purring creamily.

"Thanks ever so much for the bit about the tail," I said. "I see you two have met."

"Oh, ayuh. Zoot and I have shared many a can of sardines in mustard on my visits to your grandmother. He insists on the mustard. About the tail . . . it looks good on you. A little skinnier than I'd have thought, but still substantial. Glad to see you haven't taken up anorexia."

"I will, after this discussion of my tail," I said, leaning over to kiss Grammaude on the cheek by way of hello and apology for my behavior that morning. It was wet. They had been tears, then.

"What's the matter?" I said, looking from one of them to the other. It struck me suddenly that it was odd that he was here. Hadn't Grammaude said he would be downcoast all summer and fall supervising a seaside house he had designed for a wealthy summer resident?

"My grandfather had another stroke last night," he said, the laughter leaving his face. "He's in the hospital in Castine. It doesn't much look like he's going to make it."

"Oh, Mike," I said, feeling tears start swiftly. "Oh, Grammaude . . . oh, I'm so sorry. Oh, Lord. . . ."

"Well, darling, I am too, but my poor old Micah . . . he hasn't enjoyed these last few years," Grammaude said. "It's going to be better for him presently."

Her face was white and worn, but calm. I felt a palpable shiver along my arms and legs. What must it feel like, to be her age, so very near to the other end of life herself, watching everyone she loved go, one by one, through a door that was even now half opened to her? What did she think came next? Why would it be better for Micah Willis on the other side of it? I knew she was not a conventionally religious woman, but I did not, I realized, know what she did think about life and death and what lay beyond. I'd have said my grandmother was solidly on the side of life; life was the force I connected most with her. But here she sat, speaking with a kind of approval of death. I remembered that when I had thought of it myself in the past few years, the death of a suicide, I had thought only of a surcease of pain, an ending, not the beginning of anything. When this is over and she has grieved a little, we must talk about this, Grammaude and I, I thought.

"I know how much you'll miss him," I said, and, looking at Mike, "and I know how much you loved him. I did too. I do, rather. I always thought you were more like him than like your father."

"That's nice," he said. "I hope that's true. There aren't going to be any more like him. I think his time in the world is past. What we'll have ahead will need lesser men than he could ever be."

Grammaude laughed aloud, almost a gay sound, almost girlish. "Oh, how he'd growl about that, and how proud he'd be to hear it," she said. "He always was the worst man about accepting thanks or a compliment I ever met. I think I'll go sit with him awhile and just pump him full of flattery, gush all over him, while he can't yell back at me."

"Good idea," Mike said, grinning himself. "I really came to see if you wanted to ride over with me. I was there all morning, and he was sort of in and out of a coma, but just before I left he rallied a little, and I think he'd like to see you. If you're going, it ought to be now. Will you come, Darcy? I'd like it if you would."

"Of course," I said. "Just let me run change—"

"Better come as you are," he said. "I don't much think he's going to hang around."

I sat in the back seat of his mud-spattered Cherokee on the trip to Castine, not talking much, listening to the soft talk between him and Grammaude while the sunset miles unrolled and the pink-flushed panorama of sea and sky and woods flashed past. They did not talk much, mainly about his project down at Wells, and how his design firm was doing, and a little about the changes in the village and the colony. Neither of them mentioned Warrie Villiers and his purchases in Retreat, and neither spoke directly to me.

Mike drove fast and well. Only once did he half turn to me and say, over his shoulder, "Where did you go today? Over to Osprey?"

"No," I said. "Down off Herrick's and on over to the mouth of Eggemoggin and then home. The fleet was out but we . . . I didn't see them. I think they must have gone the other way, toward Osprey."

"Ah," he said.

"Why?" I asked.

"Just wondered. I haven't been over to Osprey this entire year. I thought I might take Dad's boat over one day while I'm home. Want to come along?"

No, I almost shouted, but did not, of course. But Osprey Head, those deep waters, that killing cold, bottomless and black . . . I did not know if I could go back. I did not know if the sleeping fear would let me. I did not even know if I cared any more about the little island whose bridge to the mainland I had helped burn so long ago. Once I had thought of it as my island, mine and Mike's, but there had not been anything there for me for many years but pain and loss.

"Maybe I will," I said. "Let's see how it goes."

"Right," he said, eyes on the road. He did not speak to me again until we reached the hospital. By then full dark had fallen. It came faster now, at the end of this lovely August.

On the third floor Mike stopped at the nurses' station. There seemed to be no one about, so he went around to the open door at the side and stuck his head in and called softly, "Millie?"

A stocky woman in starched white with a tightly frizzed permanent came into the enclosure from a back cubicle. She smiled when she saw Mike and then frowned.

"Boy, am I glad to see you," she said. "I've been calling you."

"Is there any change?"

"No. Well, a little. He's not really any better, but he's said a few words pretty clearly. I don't think it means anything, and neither does Dr. Elton, but he's alert and we don't think he's uncomfortable. No, the reason I called is that preacher. The new one at the church in the village, that fundamental charismatic fool. He's been hanging around all day, pestering your grandfather about being saved and being anointed and all. Your dad ran him off once and I did again, about an hour ago; you could hear him praying and carrying on all the way down here. Somebody told him your grandfather had never joined the church, and he thinks he's got to baptize him or he's headed straight for hell. I think that's where your dad told him to go himself. The minute your mother and dad left to get a bite he snuck back up here. He's in there now. I was just headed down, but you'll probably want to take care of it yourself."

"I will be exceedingly happy to," Mike said grimly. I smiled in spite of myself, and Grammaude did too. I knew she was thinking what I was: Micah Willis had no more to do with the rules and rituals of religion than he did with cities and nightclubs. I thought he was probably one of the most completely good men I had ever known, but it was not the kind of goodness that could be legislated by dogma.

"By the way," Mike said to me, "this is Millie Prout. I went to high school with her. She runs this place now, and I'm some glad of that. Millie, you know Mrs. Chambliss, I think, and this is her granddaughter Darcy. Darcy and I grew up here together summers. She's an old buddy of Granddaddy's too."

"It's nice to see you again, Mrs. Chambliss," Millie Prout said. She looked at me. "Nice to meet you, Darcy. You're the image of your grandmother, aren't you? You go on down there now and roust that fool, Mike. I've got some fresh coffee going, and I'll bring you some in a minute."

She nodded at Grammaude and me and went back into her cubbyhole. Mike strode off down the hall, his heels thudding on the white tile. Grammaude and I sat down on orange Naugahyde chairs in the dim little waiting area. The alcove was a dreary affair, with tall dull chrome ashtrays overflowing and a coughing, wheezing vending machine. A pile of magazines with covers that dated back three and four years sprawled on a scarred and burnt table. There was no one else present.

"I can't imagine you're comfortable," I said to Grammaude, after trying to find a hollow in my chair that would accommodate my bottom. "I can ask Millie if she's got a straight chair back there."

"No, this is fine," Grammaude said, smiling at me. "I think it still fits my fanny perfectly. I spent a great deal of time in it the summer you were here. I'm positive it's the same chair. I recognize the cigarette burns."

"Poor Grammaude," I said. "This place can't have very good associations for you."

"On the contrary," she said. "This place got you well again, and they're taking very good care of Micah. I can't think of another place he'd want to be, or I'd want him to be, but here close by home, with a local girl to look after him and a view of the harbor if he lifts his head."

I looked away from her great dark eyes, like coals in sugar-white sand in the pallor of her face. We both knew Micah Willis was not likely to lift his head again. We fell silent, holding magazines in our hands but not reading them. Waiting, waiting. . . .

In a few minutes a door down the deserted white hall flew open and a man came scuttling out. He was tall and cadaverously thin and wore a shiny dark suit and a dark tie whose width I had not seen the likes of since the seventies, and he held a Bible in his hand. It looked from my vantage point to be the sort you find in motels, put there by the Gideons. He had a very small head atop a long neck, and lank brown brush-cut hair crowned one of the highest foreheads I had ever seen. He had a curious face; all the features were very small and close together in the middle of it, giving him the look of an ill-made old-fashioned Kewpie doll. He kept his eyes on his lace-up shoes as he came past, walking with small steps so rapidly that we could practically feel the wind of his passing. There was a scowl on his face, but it looked the sort of important, assumed grimace a child employs when it wishes to be thought adult. He jabbed at the elevator button with a finger of astonishing length and whiteness and then turned and made for the stairwell and vanished into it. He had not said a word. Grammaude and I looked at each other.

"Mike one, Christians nothing," I said, and she laughed, a delighted small sound.

"Good for Mike," she said. "The idea, trying to convert Micah Willis. Even flat on his back and not able to move a muscle he's more than a match for that kind of drivel."

"You think it's really drivel?" I said, only half teasing her. I wanted, suddenly, to know.

"Of course it is—his kind is," she said. "It's simplistic. I don't mean simple, either. It dishonors a complex man like Micah. Whatever salvation, if you want to call it that, he finds for himself won't be a matter of saying he's sorry about anything and hopes to do better in another life. All I wish for him is that he might be able to do the very same things he did in this one a little better. I think he'd settle for that."

I looked at her curiously. I started to ask her if she'd tell me what she meant, but then the door to the distant room opened again, and Mike came down the hall toward us. He had a strange expression on his face; it was suffused with red, and his eyes brimmed with tears, but I could see that he was struggling with laughter too.

"I don't know what you said to him, but it must have been good," I said. "He came steaming by here like the Jesuits were after him."

Mike shook his head.

"It wasn't me," he said. "Oh, I laid into him good, and I was about to grab him by the collar and throw him out, but in the end it was Grandpa who got him."

"Micah?" Grammaude said.

He nodded.

"I haven't heard him say a word the entire time I've been home, although I could tell at times he was trying to," he said. "But after about five minutes of back-and-forth between me and that asshole, Granddaddy said, as clear as he's ever said anything in his life . . ."

He paused, covering his eyes with his hand, and his shoulders twitched. I thought he was crying, and put my hand on his arm helplessly. But then he raised his head and looked at me and then Grammaude.

"He said, 'Eat a shit sandwich,' and that preacher was out of there."

Grammaude and I burst into laughter, and Mike did too, and then he turned abruptly and walked to the wall of windows and looked out, and I saw from the harder shaking of his shoulders that he was weeping now. I started to get up and go to him, but Grammaude stopped me.

"Let him be," she said. "He needs it, and if you're there he won't."

Presently he came back to us, his face clear once more, though stained and reddened.

"Ah, God," he said. "I didn't have any idea how bad this was going to be. Darcy, he wants to see you for a minute, and then Grammaude."

"Are you sure?"

"Yeah. He was running out of words, but I understood that. Go on in."

I had never in my life wanted less to do anything, but I went down the hall and opened the door very softly and went into the dim little room. Micah Willis lay in a high narrow bed, its sides raised to keep him from falling out, tubes and monitors snaking from a stand into his arms and nose. He lay perfectly still, and he was whiter and older than any living human I had ever seen, a marble effigy of a man. Against the pallor his white-streaked black hair looked almost grisly, vivid with life, like that of a vampire. Black stubble stood out on his jaw. His hawk's nose jutted from his shrunken features, a thin blade of bone, and his lips were slightly parted and papery white. His breathing sounded as if it were coming from a subterranean cave. I thought of the poor, awful minotaur trapped in his labyrinth. His eyes were closed and he might have been dead except for the breathing. I turned to leave, but he opened his eyes then and looked at me. I went to the side of the bed and sat down in the chair.

He could not move his head, but he turned his eyes to me and looked at me so intently that I knew he was trying to tell me something. The eyes probed and pierced. I took his hand and held it between mine, thinking I had never felt anything so cold and lifeless. It was as if all the life had left his body to live in those extraordinary dark eyes. They burned with life, sparked with it.

"I hope you're going to feel better soon," I said, and wished I could bite out my tongue. There would be no soon for this man.

He lay looking at me for a while, and then, very slowly, the lips parted and he struggled to say something. It was such an awful, agonizing attempt that I said, "Why don't you just rest now, and I'll go get Grammaude for you?"

"Stay," he said. It was very clear, though faint and without breath behind it.

"I really shouldn't," I said. "I'm tiring you too much. You shouldn't try to talk. I'll come back later."

"Stay."

I sat still. What did he want of me?

"Stay . . . Maude," he breathed after a bit. I thought I understood.

"I will," I said, pressing his hand. "I won't go off and leave Grammaude here. I'm going to be with her until she goes back to Northpoint."

He closed his eyes and then opened them again.

"Stay . . . Liberty," he whispered. Then his head lolled over on the pillow, and except for the breathing he made no other sound. I understood that he could not.

I closed my eyes to keep the tears from spilling over and leaned over and kissed the cold white cheek.

"All right," I said, in a whisper not much louder than his. "All right. I'll stay in Liberty."

What could it hurt? Micah Willis would never know.

In a few minutes I got up and went out and down the hall to Mike and Grammaude.

"I think he'd like to see you now," I said to her, and she nodded. Mike walked with her down the long hall; she leaned heavily on him, a small, frail, very old woman, going to say goodbye to a long, long love. I thought, on the whole, that she was bearing it much better than I.

Mike came back and sat down beside me, but he did not speak, and I didn't either, not for a long while. After a bit, absently, he picked up my hand and held it in his, turning it over and over. I did not think he even realized that he was doing it. Presently he put a finger out and traced the thin white crescent of scar that ran across the underside of my wrist, and turned his own wrist up so that I could see the matching crescent on his. It was like a white curl of fine wire against the tan of his skin. I could see the pulse beating there, slowly, strongly.

"Am I still an honorary Willis?" I said.

"Long as you want to be," he said. "Did he say anything? Grandpa?"

"Not really," I said. "Not that made any sense."

After a long time we heard the door open once more and my grandmother stood in it, looking back through it into the room. Mike went down to get her. They walked back together toward me in silence, and I thought that her back was straighter and her step lighter. In the dim white corridor she looked, for just an instant, much younger; I could see, as in a kind of pentimento, the woman she had been when she and Micah Willis were in their primes.

"Want to stay awhile?" I asked when they reached me.

"No need," she said. "I think he's going to sleep now. Caleb and Beth will be back in a minute, and they should have the rest of the time with him. You too, Mike. I hate for you to have to take us all the way back to Retreat."

"I don't mind," he said. "I've said what I came to say to him."

"So have I," she said, and smiled.

I rose and took her other hand and noticed that she had it curled fast around something. I looked at her questioningly, and she smiled again and uncurled her fist. A round, dark, satiny object lay in it. I had never seen anything like it.

"It's Grandpa's chinquapin," Mike said, smiling down at her. "Isn't it? He always kept it in his pocket."

She nodded. "Only at home we called them buckeyes. My brother used to call me that, because I was round and dark. They're supposed to bring you good luck. He said . . . he told me he wanted me to have this one, but it probably really ought to go to you, Mike."

"No," he said, closing her fingers back around the buckeye. "You keep it. You were his luck. You always were."

She laid her head briefly against his arm. It came just to the top of his shoulder. "Thank you, dearest Mike," she said. "I *will* keep it. A dose of the Willis luck is just what I need right now."

By the time we reached the turnoff to Retreat, she had fallen asleep in the front seat, her head resting gently on Mike's shoulder. In the white light of the late-rising moon she looked as young as she had for that instant in the hospital. Oh, Grammaude, I thought. Together you and he must have been something to see.

He died just before dawn. I came downstairs at first light, cold and muddled from a thin sleep and dreams of falling, to find Mike with Grammaude before the fire again, drinking coffee. I did not need them to tell me; they were laughing, and it was the soft laughter of remembrance.

She did not want us to stay with her that day. I would

have, gladly, for I was hollow with loss and in need of company myself. But she was adamant about that.

"Go on out somewhere, you two," she said. "It's going to be a perfect day and the weather's due to change. Go sailing. Take her over to Osprey, Mike, and show her what you told me about. Fix a lunch and take some wine and hoist a glass to him, if you insist on memorials. He'd far rather you did that, out on his bay, than sit around here chafing the hands of an old lady who doesn't need them chafed."

"Are you sure?" Mike said. "I don't like to think of you totally alone on this of all days."

"My darling children," she said, and smiled a smile that just missed being a grin. "I'm going to be less alone on this of all days than any other I can think of."

Tears started into my eyes again, and she said in real, if mild, exasperation, "Oh, for God's sake, Darcy, go on and let me be. There's far less reason to cry today than there was yesterday. Save your tears for them as needs them."

And so I let Mike Willis take me out onto Penobscot Bay in the wake of a soft following wind, on one of what I thought would be the last great days of this summer. But instead of his father's sleek sloop, he came around the point from the boatyard to the yacht club dock where I waited for him in his grandfather's old lobster smack, the *Tina.*

"I thought both he and you would like this," he said, when I had rowed my uncle's dinghy out and climbed aboard. I looked at the stubby, wallowing old boat, its brass salt-pocked and its teak deck stained from years of rubber soles and the sea, and felt the solid sweetness of the straking under my feet in the slight chop, and I did like it. Mike ran up the jib to take us out into the bay, and I saw that the *Tina* had a set of newish Dacron sails. But other than that, I could imagine Micah Willis taking out his *Tina* just as it was today, on a sweet day fifty summers ago.

"I feel badly about taking you away today," I said. "There must be a million things your family needs you to do, and you can't have really taken this in yet."

"Don't," he said. "For some reason, it's better today. I feel like being on the water. And Dad told me to get lost until tomorrow or the next day." He squinted out into the dazzle where water met sky. "Every Willis in Maine will be congregating at the house today, and a good many of them drive me nuts. There aren't many arrangements. He'll be cremated. And Dad wouldn't let that fool of a preacher near him, so there's not going to be a funeral per se, just a memorial maybe day after tomorrow, and that's going to be on the boatyard dock. My cousin Seth from Machias is a Unitarian minister, and he's going to come do it. Dad and I are going to take Grandpa's ashes out on the *Tina* after that. He told Dad a long time ago he wanted to go into the bay."

A thick clot of cold salt lay at the base of my throat. It had been there since I had kissed Micah Willis goodbye the day before, and it neither went away or grew larger. It did not feel like the fear, or even grief; I did not know what it was. I swallowed around it.

"Where are you going to take him?" I said.

"Osprey Head," he said. "That's what he asked for. We're going to go over and pick a spot this morning. I'd like you to be part of that, and he would too."

"Mike," I said, my heart beginning to pound, "I can't go to Osprey. Please don't take me. I can't . . . you don't know."

"Yeah, I do, if you mean that's where you did your swan dive that last summer," he said mildly. He wore khaki shorts and a faded old MIT sweatshirt and Topsiders without socks, and he looked so much like the Mike Willis I had last seen out on this bay twelve years before that I could not even be angry with him for the little meanness of his words.

"I guess Grammaude told you too," I said wearily. "She's been the Mouth of Maine this summer."

"I've known since the day you did it," he said, looking over his shoulder at me. "Don't forget it was my father who pulled you off your boat and carried you up to Liberty, shaking like a leaf in a gale."

"Then don't you see why I can't go there now? I've been awfully sick for the past few years, you might as well know that too. Sick like in a psychiatric hospital. I just got out this summer and my dad wouldn't take me; otherwise I wouldn't be up here. My therapist said I needed to avoid conflict as much as I could—"

"I know all that too," he said. "I don't think your therapist meant you couldn't go sailing on a calm day with an old friend. I'm sorry about the hospital, Darcy; you don't know how much. But your dunking yourself in the bay off Osprey didn't make it holy water. It's water like any other around here, and there's something on that island that could make up for what happened here back then. I'm sure of it. So we're going."

Over my head the mainsail bellied out with a great snap, and the *Tina* dropped her lee rail and lifted up and soared off toward Osprey Head like a toy paper boat in a breeze. I closed my eyes and clenched my fists on the rail and took a deep breath. I could feel the fear coiling itself like a serpent deep within me, but the cold knot held it down. At that moment I couldn't have spoken if I wanted to.

But the steady sun on the top of my head and the peculiar rushing silence of a quiet day under sail soon loosened my fists, and I opened my eyes to find Mike leaning back against the wheelhouse, drinking wine from the bottle and looking at me. He handed the bottle to me, and I took it and drank. It was lovely wine, soft and full of flowers.

"I thought I was going to die for a long time," I said. It seemed necessary that he recognize my pain.

"Kill myself, I mean. I really did think that, and I'm still not sure I won't someday. You can't possibly know how strong the pull is sometimes. My family does that, you know. My mother told me that my great-grandfather did it by swimming out too far in cold water up here, and my grandfather went off Caterpillar Hill in his sports car. And she's doing it too; it's just taking longer. You feel almost like it's an obligation, sometimes."

"So you think you'll get it, like a virus?" Mike said. "What your family has a history of is running away, your grandmother excepted. You don't catch that, you learn it. And you're getting a good start on it, seems to me."

"How dare you say a thing like that to me?" I said, anger boiling past the knot. "You don't have the slightest idea what my life has been like or how I feel. What about you? Grammaude said you were married for a little while but that you couldn't take the idea that she had a lot of money, so you split. What do you call that if it's not running away?"

"If you think you're going to make me mad by throwing M'Lou up to me, try again," he said, reaching out for the wine bottle. I passed it over to him. "Your grandmother was absolutely right about that. I did run. If I hadn't I'd be a southern society architect today, designing cutting-edge barns for pampered horses, with weathervanes on the top of them. Probably a bourbon drunk, too. I didn't say running away was necessarily a bad thing. Not for me, anyway. I don't think it's the answer for you, though."

"Well, you shit. Why is it right for you and not for me? That's hypocritical crap."

"No, it's not. I was running from a clear and present danger, a person with the power to do me real harm. You're trying to run from a place. Places can't hurt you. They can heal you sometimes, but they can't hurt you. Only what you bring to them can."

"Thank you, Dr. Willis," I said sullenly. I would have been angrier with him if my shrink back in Atlanta hadn't said substantially the same thing, many times. But I was still angry, and the thought of Mike with a wife, no matter what sort, suddenly rankled sharply.

"What sort of precious adorable name is M'Lou?" I said.

"Just the right one for precious, adorable Mary Lou Campion of Nonesuch Farms, just outside Lexington, in the heart of Kentucky's fabled blue-grass country," he said. "Lots of honey-blond hair. Lots of white teeth. Lots of charm and softness and lots and *lots* of money. I met her at Wellesley. Her folks named her M'Lou because they were friends of the Whitneys. You know, the horse Whitneys? Marylou Whitney?"

"I know who the horse Whitneys are," I snapped. "Why didn't they just name her Sea Biscuit and be done with it?"

"Wrong stable. I know, though. I think the pre-ciousness of her name, and all that it implied, got to me long before the money did, and what they all wanted to do with it and me. Or anything else. When it really started to bother me, I said I wanted to come back up here to live and practice. She said Maine was a toy place for rich people and I said what the hell did she think she'd been living in all her life. She said real people didn't live up here. And I realized then that, to me, no place and no people on earth are real-er than here on the cape. After that, I just . . . couldn't stay. There wasn't any real bitterness on either of our parts, I don't think. We both knew we married in a hurry. She hadn't even finished Wellesley. It was the spring after you left the last time."

There was nothing to say to that, so I said nothing. The salt knot was back, but the anger had faded. So had the fear. I put my face up to the sun and closed my eyes and leaned back. I was very, very tired.

"Darcy, what are you going to do now?" he said.

"I don't have the slightest idea," I said. The sun on my eyelids felt heavy and hypnotic. I wanted to lean there forever, rocking on the pillowy sea under the sun.

"It's four days until Labor Day. Everybody goes home then. Your grandmother always goes back to Northpoint the day after. Are you going with her? Going back to Atlanta? What?"

"I have plenty of time to decide," I said drowsily. "Why does everybody have to plan everything ahead of time? You sound like Grammaude. She wants me to come back with her to New Hampshire this winter and stay. Can you imagine what I'd do in a tiny little place like that all winter with nothing in it but a boys' school?"

"I imagine it's coed now," he said. "Most of them are. I don't know. It sounds like a good idea to me. I think she's going to need you this winter. She's grown awfully frail since I saw her last. And it would be easier for you to get her back up here next summer. Maybe you could teach at the school. Most of them have very good communications curricula nowadays. They'd for sure waive the advanced degree requirement for Peter Chambliss's granddaughter."

Teach? I had not thought about that. Teach. . . . In my mind I saw classrooms with sun coming through tall mullioned windows, and young faces serious about receiving what I had to give. . . . What I had to give. I had not thought in terms of giving for a very long time.

"I'm not coming back here next summer," I said.

"It will kill her not to come."

"She has Uncle Petie and Aunt Sarah," I said. "She can come if she wants to. She can hire somebody to do the housework and tend to her; she's always done that. She doesn't need me to come to Retreat."

"Yes, she does," he said. I did not answer. He did not speak of it further.

"I'll probably move my office back here," he said minutes later. "Grandpa left me his house. Dad told me this morning."

I did open my eyes, then, and looked at him. He was looking at the green bulk of Osprey Head, coming up fast on our bow. He had busied himself with the lines.

"Oh, that wonderful house," I said, meaning it. "I always thought there was something magical about it. Will you live there too?"

"Yep," he said. "I've wanted it since I was five years old. I didn't know he knew that, though. I thought he'd leave it to Mom and Dad. But then they built the new one."

We slowed and stopped, and the *Tina* settled into the water like a proper New England matron.

"Come on," he said. "Roll up your pants legs. It's shallow enough here to wade in."

"No! I can't!"

He jerked me up by the hand, and before I could even protest he had leaped over the rail and pulled me after him. By the time I got my mouth open to scream at him, the cold green water had closed around my legs at mid-thigh and pebbles rolled under my sneakers. I stood gasping for breath, glaring at him. He was already going ashore, picking his way over the rocks.

"Not a ghost or a corpse or a ha'nt in sight," he yelled back. "Come on. You'll get frostbite."

Taking a deep, shuddering breath, I looked down into the clear, vivid green water. I saw pebbles and coarse sand, and snaking scarves of green seaweed, but nothing else. Nothing. I hitched my sopping pants legs up and sloshed ashore after Mike.

We were on the other side of the island from the bridge and the eagles' nests. I wondered why we had not sailed around and gone ashore there. We could have put in at the bridge and tied up and not gotten wet. On this side, toward the body of the bay, nothing was visible but the distant bulk of Islesboro and, beyond that, a smudged blue smear, the Camden Hills. A line of white sails dotted the calm bay like children's toys back toward Western and Green ledges and Hog Island, but none were near Osprey. We had the island and the sea to ourselves. Mike dropped the basket with our lunch and the wine in the shelter of a leaning glacial boulder and held out his hand to me.

"Come on. It's not a long climb."

"Is it the eagles? I don't remember them over this far," I said.

"Nope. They're here, or the nests are. . . . Dad told me the young ones are hunting for themselves now, so there aren't usually any around the nests this time of day. No, this is something else. Something new. You're going to like this."

We climbed for about five minutes, up through immature stands of fir and spruce, over flat rocks set flush into the earth and shawled with the hectic green, cloud-soft moss I remembered, through yellowing blueberry tangles and bracken going white-gold, and once through a perfect little stand of adolescent birches, their bark just beginning to roughen, gleaming like silver in the green gloom. He held his hand out behind him and I clung to it, feeling the rough place on his middle finger where the drafting pencil had worn a callus, stumbling on the loose shale and over deadfall limbs in my slippery wet sneakers. I had been trembling with cold when I came ashore, but by now my pants were drying, and sweat had begun to run from my hairline into my eyes, and no-see-ums bit like little points of fire.

"If I meet one mosquito I'm out of here," I called.

"I don't care if you've found the Holy Grail up there. How much farther?"

"Here," Mike said, and we broke out of the undergrowth to a clear space about halfway up the dome of the island, a place of gray stone that had a blasted look of great age, as if a monstrous bolt of lightning had struck here in the dawn of time. Mike pointed silently.

On the other side of the clearing stood a dead fir, or the trunk of one. It had been broken off about halfway up. In the space where the first branches had begun, a sort of bowl had been formed, and in it a large nest was cupped, as in two sheltering hands. It was not the size and depth of the eagles' nests, but it was larger than anything else I had seen. The sun, directly overhead, dazzled my eyes, and I put my hands up to shade them. And then I saw them clearly against the cobalt of the sky: four of them, elegant flat raptor's heads hooded in black-brown, cold yellow eyes staring, curved beaks and white throats and bellies shining. One of them lifted powerful white-speckled wings and beat at the air, and they all gave shrill, angry cries: *cheereek!* I stared, feeling the air vibrate with the wind from the wings, seeing the patches of black on the cheeks that I had read about. Ospreys. Not fully grown, I did not think; their wings had not achieved the four- to six-foot wingspan I knew the adults had. But almost grown. Ospreys. For the first time in colony memory since my mother had destroyed their nest and sent them into exile, ospreys on Osprey Head.

"Oh, Mike," I breathed. "Oh, Mike!"

We stayed there, being as still as we could, for nearly half an hour. The ospreys made short circling flights around the nest but did not leave it. They shrieked and flapped at us, too, but still did not go.

"Folks are out getting lunch," Mike said under his

breath. "These big spoiled brats aren't about to leave when grub's on the way. We'd better go now. The adults are bigger and fierce as hell when something gets near the nest."

We scrambled back down to the beach, slowly now, my eyes dazzled with the wild power and beauty of the young birds, the salt knot swelling until I could scarcely swallow. I knew I would remember the sight until the day I died.

"Thank you for making me come," I said, when we had sat down in the shade of the boulders and uncorked the wine. "It would have been terrible to miss this."

"Does it change anything?"

I shook my head slowly. "No. But it makes things . . . better."

"Did you know that the parents virtually never leave the nest?" he said. "They'll stay through anything: storm, fire, drought, direct attack, gunfire even. You can kill them. They'll stay until the nest doesn't exist any more."

The knot spread swiftly up my throat to the base of my tongue. I actually put my hands to my neck. I thought I was going to . . . what? Scream? Choke? Weep? The ospreys, who would stay until the nest didn't exist any more, stay through anything with their children, die there with them. . . .

"I've always thought they were far better to their young than most humans," Mike said, watching me.

I could only nod.

"I wanted you to see them before they're gone," he said. My heart stopped, still and cold. Then it jolted and shuddered on. I watched him but could not speak.

"Your great good friend Warrie Villiers owns Osprey Head now," he said. His voice had not changed; he might have still been talking of the birds. "He bought it from the Park Service late this winter. It's tough to do, but it can be done, if there's enough money. The island never was anything but a drain on the service, and Warrie had enough money to make it a done deal within a day or two. Still does, I hear. Yep, old Warrie has great plans for Osprey Head. There's going to be a yacht club and marina the likes of which even Northeast Harbor hasn't seen, right here. He'll have to dredge, of course, but hey, that's nothing. Around where the bridge is, on the side that faces Retreat, you'll be able to see the whole project. Going to be a resort to end all seaside resorts along there, with condos and shops and tennis courts and maybe a nice little nine-hole golf course. And a marine repair facility. And all kinds of pretty things. Right where the old cottages are now. Going to take up the whole waterfront half of Retreat, it is. He's calling it Cape Villiers. A nice international touch, don't you think?"

I stared at him, saying nothing.

"It isn't going to take him long to get all the property he wants," Mike said. "He's got a good start now. I don't know what he's been telling all the old ladies who've signed on, but he wouldn't have to tell them much. They know his folks, don'tcha know. Magic words up here, always have been. And as for money, he's got enough to buy the rest of the colony if he wants it. Though he probably doesn't. Just the half on the water. Of course, the other half won't be quite the place it's always been."

I still did not speak.

"Where did he tell you he got the money, Darcy?" he said. "From his wife's family? From his dear mama, dead so tragically before her time of hepatitis? Bullshit. He might have gotten a little from the girl's folks, to get him out of the family and out of Italy, but I know for a fact his mother died of AIDS in a charity hospital without a penny. He got a lot of it from Gretchen Winslow personally, along with a lot of Gretchen, and he got the promise of the rest from her family's bank. Good business, it is. Cape Villiers will sell like hotcakes. Best location on the East Coast."

"That is a lie." All I could do was whisper. My throat was monstrously swollen. I thought it would burst.

He scrubbed his face with his fingers and spoke through them.

"I wish to God it was. It's not. I checked. Anybody could have; the site and project plans are on file in Augusta, and I got the rest from a private detective in Portland. I hired him after Grandpa called me late this spring and told me Warrie was up here buttering up old ladies and buying up property. Grandpa paid for the detective. It didn't take long. Any one of the folks in Retreat could have found out at any time; your uncle Petie could have done it without even hiring a detective, the circles he moves in. It was just that nobody did. They all knew his family, you see. It's all true. I have the report, and photocopies of the site and the plans. He doesn't know I have them, of course. I don't know what I thought I was going to do with them. I guess I was going to use them if I needed to. And maybe I still will. I think it depends on you, whether I need to or not."

I looked at him mutely, fighting cold salt bile and the awful swelling in my chest and throat.

"He can't do it without Liberty," Mike said. "He won't have septic access without Liberty's half of the meadow. Your grandmother is the only holdout he's got; when she's gone, if someone doesn't keep Liberty, he's as good as got it. He could pay millions for it; in the end almost anyone would sell. I just don't think he figures he'll have to."

I thought of the laughter we had shared on the water—was it really only yesterday?—and his soft voice telling me about the hospital and his mother, and the feel of his hand in mine as we ran up the lane together, laughing. The feel of his hand on my hair. . . .

"No."

"Stay, Darcy," Mike whispered. "Stay and fight him. Without Liberty he can't do any of it. Stay on after she's gone. All you have to do is accept the cottage. She wants you to have it, she's told me that."

"I can't, oh, I can't. . . ."

High above us, in the thin, hot blue air above the clearing, the scream of a young osprey rang. I lifted my eyes from the beach and looked up. Far away out over the sea, the pure line of great wings slashed the sky, angled in the characteristic dip that only ospreys in flight have. The parents were coming home with food for their young.

"Then do it for them," he said.

The knot in my chest exploded, and I felt a great primitive surge of grief and fury pour out behind it. My ears rang as if there had been some awful cosmic cataclysm; I could not hear the noise I made. But I could feel it, flowing up from the very pit of me and out into the still air, feel the force and fury of it. I don't think I ever made words, but the sound doubled me over physically, jerking me as if I had been thrown. Mike held me hard on the beach as I half lay, half knelt on the loose shingle and shrieked and vomited all the endless red rage I had never been able to find, in all those years in the hospital and even before, out into the air of Osprey Head.

When I finally stopped, my throat was as raw as if I had a bad illness, and my ribs and lungs and stomach hurt. Tears still pumped from my eyes over my face and down onto my hands and Mike's arms. The world seemed too bright and too sharp, and everything was thick and queer and soundless. It took almost half an hour for my breathing to slow.

"Stay," he said again, finally, holding me to him, my body boneless with depletion. "Stay."

I spoke against his shirt. It was as wet from my tears as if he had been in the sea. I could feel his heart beating, and his ribs under my clutching fingers. I let my hands and arms go loose.

"I can't stay here," I whispered. "I was never strong enough for this place. You have to fight too hard to stay here, Mike. I'm through fighting. I can't fight any more."

"You're never through fighting, Darcy," he said into my hair. "Nobody is."

"No. Not in this place. This is not my place. There is no one of mine here."

"Yes," he said softly. "There is."

I did not answer him. Presently we waded back to the *Tina* and he set the mainsail for the long beat home. I did not speak the rest of the way; my throat felt flayed and bloodied, and every muscle in my body ached as if I had been beaten. Hot water and then bed. Sleep. Just that.

We tied up at the boatyard dock.

"I'll run you home," he said.

"No. I'll cut through the woods. I want to walk."

"You'll have to decide now, Darcy," he said.

"Then," I said, turning to look at him as I stood at the edge of the little wood, "I'll decide. I'm going home. I'm going as soon as I can pack and get out of here. Uncle Petie and Aunt Sally can take Grammaude back. They always do."

He stood looking at me and then turned away and walked down the dock toward the boathouse.

"Have a nice trip, Darcy," he called back over his shoulder.

Chapter Nineteen

She came into my bedroom as I was finishing packing. I had not brought much with me, just what I had had in the hospital. It did not take long. I had glanced out onto the sun porch when I reached Liberty and seen that she was asleep there on the chaise, Zoot around her throat like a muff, and had not wakened her. It was going to be hard enough to tell her later. Let me have a little time. The sight of her, still and small under the Spanish shawl, her face so very old and defenseless, hurt me like a hot poker on naked flesh.

"I wish I could have been more use to you," I had said very softly, and went upstairs.

"Darcy," she said from the doorway as I closed the suitcase, and I turned to look at her. I had not heard her come. She held on to the doorframe, and all the life seemed to have drained from her, even from the black eyes. I thought she would simply sink to the floor, and went and supported her by her thin, knobbed arm and led her to the bed. She was trembling all over, like a small half-frozen animal. She sat on one side of the suitcase and I sat on the other. Across it, she said to me with bloodless lips, "What has happened?"

I told her. I told her everything I could remember of what Mike had said, and when I could remember no more, I simply stopped talking and waited. She would see, must see, why I could not stay.

"Well," she said after what seemed a very long time, "it's good to have it out on the table. It's better, really, than I was afraid it would be. This can be handled. You'll have to stop him, of course. It's yours to do, but you can do it quite easily. All you have to do is hang on. I was afraid too much would be asked of you, but you can handle this."

Some of her color came seeping back as she spoke, and her voice strengthened until, by the time she finished speaking and sat looking at me, it was quite strong. She smiled.

"What do you mean, it's mine to do?" I said. The high, silvery ringing started again in my ears, and I could feel the rage building once more. I thought I had spewed all that out, back on the beach at Osprey Head.

"Because you're my granddaughter, and my daughter's daughter," she said. "Because you're the great-granddaughter of the woman who taught me this: it's what we do, we women. We hold this place."

The rage exploded and I heard myself shouting at her: "Granddaughter! Great-granddaughter! Daughter! What is this shit? What are you talking about? The hell with this place, the hell with holding it! I'm not anybody's granddaughter, or daughter either! Neither I nor my poor crazy mother ever had a real mother! She never loved me in her life, and you never loved her; she told me! She told me! You simply would not be a mother to her, and she would not be one to me; you loved only Petie, Petie and Granddaddy, and Mama never loved *anybody* but Granddaddy! All those men, only those damned men. . . . Always and only the great, perfect, walking-dead Chambliss men!"

Grammaude sat still, stricken.

"I never told either my son or my daughter that I loved him best," she whispered. "And I am certain your mother never told you or anyone else she did not love you just as much as she did her father—"

"She didn't have to, and you didn't either," I cried furiously. "You spent a lifetime showing them and everybody else! They didn't have to hear it from you, those men; they *knew* they were enough. This whole place up here, this whole little paradise, is for them; men are emperors here! It's the girls who need so desperately to hear the words, and they never do! Not up here! Not in this place. . . . Grammaude, damn you, you should have stopped him that summer!"

"Oh, God!" my grandmother cried softly, and I stopped shouting and looked at her, and I saw anger in her white face. Real anger, hot and living. I had never seen it, not even at my most outrageous childhood excesses, not even at Warrie Villiers. Not this kind of anger.

Grammaude took a deep breath and let it out.

"Oh, the sheer, ignorant tyranny of the young," she said as if to someone else. "Just listen to you! 'You should have stopped him. Be my mama. Be only what you can be to me and nothing else. Have no life and no reality but the part *I* can understand, the tiny bit that applies to me. Me, me, me. Be a fraction of a woman, or I will not love you.' God. You know nothing of me. None of you do."

I put my hot face into my hands once more and cried. Her words called out a grief so old and simple and pure that I knew instantly it was the heart, the crux of everything. She was right. I had fought and flailed my way through the world, demanding a parent from it, a parent of her, and had found only . . . people. And except for her, that was all I ever would find. I cried and cried. After a long time, I felt Grammaude get up and come around the bed and sit down beside me and put her arms around me. Without looking up I turned into them and laid my head on her shoulder. I had to lean over to do it. Still I cried; the tears would not stop. Who would have thought the human body could hold so many tears?

After a long time, Grammaude said, in a different voice, her own again, "You're right, of course. Men have always had the overt power in Retreat, but it was we who gave it to them. So it was really ours all along. I think I must have always known that. Look at us, a world ruled by old women for men children. And our daughters die for lack of love."

She raised my chin with her hand and kissed me on my wet cheek.

"I love you, my dear Darcy, with all my heart," she said. "I always did. I always will. You owe me nothing and you owe this place nothing. I will not make you pay with any more of your life for my loving you."

I held on to her as hard as I could, unable to stop the child's tears.

"I love you too, Grammaude," I sobbed. "I wish I could have helped."

"You have," she whispered. "You will."

Neither of us wanted supper. Neither of us wanted to talk any more. I did not even want to think about the next day. I simply wanted to sleep. She must have known that, for she came back up after I had had my bath and pulled the old thin-worn Princeton blanket up over me and turned off my light.

"Go to sleep now," she said. "Are you old enough to know that things always look better in the morning? I think you are. I hope so. It will get you through a lot of nights. This will look better too. You'll see. Go to sleep."

And I did. As swiftly and weightlessly as a very small child, I fell into bottomless blackness, unlit by dreams. I don't think I even turned over until near dawn.

I dreamed she was calling me. I dreamed that I was very small and lost somewhere down on the shore—for I could hear wind, and water moving—and she was looking for me, calling me over and over from far away: "Darcy! Darcy!"

I struggled up through the heavy layers of sleep and still she called: "Darcy . . ."

I sat still in the lightless darkness for a long moment, breath held, and then leaped out of bed and ran downstairs toward her voice, switching on the overhead stair light as I ran.

She lay at the bottom of the first stair, her arm thrown up over it as if she had been trying to pull herself up. She wore only her long white cotton nightgown, and her white-streaked black hair was wild around her head. The gown had pulled up around her legs, and I could see that she was still moving them feebly, still trying to climb. Zoot circled her, trilling low in his throat. Her flesh was blue and white and threaded with veins and knots, and the old bones showed through as if she were lit from inside. Birds' bones, dry sticks. She did not seem to be able to move her head, but her eyes found mine and held them. Her face was as white as old snow. When she saw me she smiled, very faintly.

"Can you help me?" she whispered.

I knelt down beside her, feeling for her pulse. My own seemed to be trying to shake my flesh apart at my throat and wrists and temples.

"What hurts? Can you tell me?" I said, my voice trembling.

"Chest," she said, on a shallow little sigh. "The elephant. A big one this time. Listen, I want you to light the fire . . ."

"Hush, Grammaude," I said, whimpering with fear. "Lie very still; I'm going to call the ambulance. Just lie still."

"Darling, the fire . . ."

I pulled blankets and throws from the couch and threw them over her, and then ran to the phone and dialed the South Brooksville rescue squad. When they had assured me they were on their way, I went back and knelt by her again. Zoot had dug himself into the blankets beside her.

She stared up at me, the whole force of her being in her eyes.

"Make a fire, Darcy, and turn me so I can see it, and do it quickly," she said, gasping a little with each word, and I stumbled obediently to the dead fireplace and fumbled with the matches, beginning to cry again, silently. The flame finally caught, and the fire leaped up. I watched its shadows prowl on the old smoke-blackened, gold cedar planks of the walls, thinking suddenly that they looked like the walls of firelit caves. Even through my terror, even in my stupid haste, I thought, Fire is the medium. Fire is the element that passes everything on. Not blood and bone, not the pages of history books, but fire. All those stories, all those lives, all those *truths,* down through all of history from the caves to Retreat, borne on fire.

I went back to Grammaude.

"Lift me up a little," she said.

"Please be still—"

"Lift me up! I need to talk to you. . . ."

I lifted her head and put it in my lap and looked down into her face. I could see her heart, bucking like a wild thing in her chest. Oh, dear God, would they never come?

"Do it for me," Grammaude whispered, looking into my face. "I said I wouldn't beg, but I can now, and I will. Do it for me. Take Liberty. Fight for Retreat. Retreat needs you. Liberty needs you. You're the only one I have now."

"Uncle Petie—"

She shook her head slightly, weakly. "Only you."

I began to cry again, harder. I saw my tears fall on her face, and brushed them away. They kept falling. "I can't," I said. "I can't, without you."

"You *can!*" It came out on a long, trembling sigh. "You only have to love it enough. The power of love is everything. *Everything.* And you do love it enough. You always have. I know."

"Oh, God, Grammaude, the power of love almost killed me up here twelve years ago!"

She smiled and shook her head again and then coughed. It was a deep sound, dreadful. Her thin fingers worked against her chest. I put my fingers against her lips, but she turned her head.

"You know absolutely nothing about the power of love," she said presently. Her voice was weaker. The thrashing of her heart against her chest wall was threadier. "Listen. I'll tell you about the power of love. I'll tell you . . . what I did for love. You remember. We both liked that song. Do you remember?"

"I remember. Oh, Grammaude, please don't talk any more. Tell me later. I'll stay, you know I'll stay; I won't leave you. I'll keep the cottage, of course I will, if you'll just be quiet now, and be still. . . ."

She reached her hand up and touched my wet face, very gently, and then let it fall back.

"Hush and listen," she said softly. "I don't think I have a whole lot of time. . . ."

Chapter Twenty

From where I sit in this September dawn—on the dock of the yacht club, looking out toward Osprey Head—the whole world seems frosted with autumn. The old clubhouse and the deep spruce and birch woods behind it are blurred and dreamlike in the white salt fog. I can hear the soft little slappings on the pebble beach as the morning tide turns toward the full, but I can't see the water. It is a ground fog. Only the delicate tips of the pointed firs pierce it. It lies over the bay and shrouds all but the fierce cock's comb of Osprey, lying like a prehistoric water beast half a mile out. But the sun will burn it off by midmorning. Then I will see the buoys, bobbing gently in the pink-foil water. Most of them are empty now. Was it only three weeks ago that tanned families worked to decant their boats from the nourishing sea and ready them for the boatyard or the long trip home behind station wagons and big sedans? I suppose it was. It seems only an eye blink, a heartbeat, since Labor Day. But it is irrevocably past and gone. I have never been here so late. Summer is long over.

I think about the boats, especially the Beetle Cats. They will hibernate in dim garages, and little boys, rushing through the black weight of the coming cold

to the haven of warm kitchens, will catch from their
fiberglass pores the salt sweat of this northern sea and
stop for a moment, hands on the dried-out flanks of catboats, and be plummeted again into endless summer.

Remember, I say silently to them. Remember. It
will not last long. Nothing is forever. I was one of you
once, and I know.

It is now, on these black, lengthening nights, the
dark unbroken by cottage lights except the ones from
Liberty, that we might get the aurora borealis. I have
not seen it for a very long time, but I remember that
occasionally we did, late in the summer. I remember
that the word seemed to fly from cottage to firelit cottage, and sweatered families would stream out into
yards and look up, pointing the faces of us children to
those great flickering washes of fire in the sky. Green,
violet, pure white, tender lapis blue. . . . What are
they? I asked Grammaude when I first saw them.

"Promises," she said.

Perhaps they are. Promises of the long sweet summer kept, promises of the slow bronze autumn to
come. The dot over the "i" of summer, the final
covenant to those of us who watch. Oh, if that could
be true; if there could be promises kept and
covenants in this place. . . .

Even after everything, all the anguish and pain and
worry, I am not sorry I stayed on. The cottagers who
leave after Labor Day miss the absolute pinnacle of the
year here, the supernal quintessential moment of pure
being and beauty. Mornings are brilliant, sharp-edged,
fizzing with diamond light on the water. In the long
afternoons some of the heat will come stealing back,
but the red bite is gone from it, and the drone of the
cicadas in the birch woods lulls me when I drowse on
the sun porch. The barberry hedge has gone pure scarlet, and the mountain ash trees burn like wildfire at the
fringes of the pine forests. Along the roadside and in

the salt meadows and beside the gray piled-stone walls, goldenrod and Queen Anne's lace shimmer. Windfall apples are sweet in the long grass along the road to the general store. Collards in farm gardens stand like great silver-green sea anemones. Almost every time Mike and I came back from the hospital along the coast road during the last weeks our headlights would cast up white-tailed deer, bounding ghostlike across in front of us. I never saw many in the summers. Occasionally, a porcupine or red fox froze in the wheeling lights and then was gone. We have already seen the wild geese sweeping out of Canada toward the south, an epiphany against the hanging white moon.

"Why didn't you ever tell me about this?" I said once to Mike.

"We never tell the summer complaints about it," he said. "What if they decided to stay on through the fall?"

"So what does this make me?"

"That's for you to figure out, Darcy," he said.

I sit here, trying to do just that.

The fog silence is broken now by the muffled chugging of a lobster boat putting out. The little deep-water harbor begins to emerge from the whiteness like a photograph in developing solution. There are the buoys, like seals' heads in the water. Suddenly I miss the bustle and confabulation of hard, brown, knee-scabbed little boys pounding down the dock and thumping down the rickety stairs to the dinghies, to row out to their Beetles. I miss their yelps and laughter. The jeers of the gulls sound lost and metallic, like winter. I suddenly feel the cold of this morning through my sweat pants and heavy socks, and get up reluctantly, and walk back along the dock and up the fern-fringed lane toward Liberty. Cold dew and cobwebs sparkle icily in the birch grove. The *twang-thud* of tennis balls from the court is stilled, and so is the banging of screen doors. Somewhere off beyond the woods a dog barks, but it does not sound like one of the summer spaniels and retrievers I know. They have gone, gone with the caravan of cars and boats and children back to the cities. Retreat is empty, and sleeps.

I turn into our lane and see white smoke climbing into the deepening blue vault of the sky, and I know that Grammaude has lit the logs from last night's fire and put the coffee on to perk and will be frying bacon and scrambling eggs. Mike brought new brown ones last night. I begged her not to bother; she is still terribly weak from the hospital and so frail as to be almost transparent. We brought her home only yesterday. She slept most of the rest of the day and through the night, and I had hoped she would sleep in today. But she insisted about breakfast.

"Who knows who'll cook the next batch of brown eggs here?" she smiled.

Oh, my Grammaude. . . .

She told me, finally, while she lay swaddled in blankets on the floor and we waited for the ambulance that night. I don't suppose they were any longer than they had to be, but it seemed to me, clutching her icy hands and trying to stop crying, that they took forever. It was, at any rate, long enough. I know it all now: about Elizabeth's baby, about that whole awful storm-wrecked night and what happened then and after. My God, what a woman she is, this dark little grandmother of mine. What a love affair it was, hers and Granddaddy's. I simply had no idea, and am ashamed that I did not. Now she has shown me the whole of her life, I see how true it was that, as she said, I never knew her. I hate that. She was right, too, when she said some kinds of love have an awful power to diminish. A child's does; mine for her did. I spent so much of my life, and hers, demanding that she be . . . only my grandmother. And all the while, she was this other magnificent woman.

I told her that, when we brought her home.

"I'm going to spend whatever time we've got getting to know that woman now," I said. "I hope it's years and years."

She smiled. Then she said, "So you will stay, then? Keep the cottage? He really mustn't have it. You'll do that?"

And I told her I would. But I truly don't know if I can. The woman who went to Osprey Head with her rage and terror that summer afternoon is not the woman who came back, but I do not know yet who this new woman is. I do not know yet what she must do, or what she can.

Was the lie bad? She'll probably never know. She's failed so much. But while she lives . . . at least that.

I hear the engine of Mike's Cherokee. After breakfast we'll take the *Tina* and go over to Osprey one last time. We'll go under sail, very quietly. I want to spend this last day there, check in with the young ospreys; Mike says they're fishing for themselves now. I'd love to see that, those great dark shapes plunging headlong into the sea. They're the only raptor that does that. We'll visit the eagles too, I think. Mike teases me that theirs was the first of the bridges I burned. He knows, as I do, that there will be others. Neither of us knows which ones they will be.

We'll drink wine and eat the lobster salad I made last night, and maybe we'll go for a swim. The water off Osprey Head seems warmer, somehow, than it ever did before, and clearer. Perhaps it is just that I do not fear it any more. We should be back at nightfall. Then we'll pick up Grammaude and her bags and Zoot in his carrier, and we'll make Bangor by nine, and she and I and old Zoot will stay over at the Airport Hilton and fly on to New Hampshire in the morning.

And from there . . . we'll see. We'll see.

Maude Gascoigne Chambliss

Epilogue

Darcy asked me before she left with Mike this morning if I was afraid to stay here by myself. I think, if I had said yes, she would have stayed with me. Her attention to me since the hospital is nearly total and touches me deeply. So I would have said no, even if I had been afraid, but I have never been less so. There has not been enough time in this long day to remember all I wanted to.

I really think I am the only person in Retreat at this moment. It is a lovely feeling; as if for just this instant I truly do own it. It used to be a fancy of mine that I did, owned this place all by myself.

"Greedy guts," Peter would say. "Black eyes, greedy guts, eat the world up. What would you do with it if you did own it?"

"Put up a chain across the lane and lock the world out," I would say.

Or was it Micah I said it to, and did he say that back to me, about greedy guts?

It scarcely matters. Both of them would have understood what I meant. And now, for just this twilight moment, I do own Retreat. What a gift solitude can be when one is old. It is a thing the young simply cannot know yet.

There has been no one in Braebonnie for some days now, Darcy tells me. I don't know if Warrie Villiers has gone to New York for the winter, or simply to tap into more of the Winslow money and come back here. Darcy and Mike say he cannot possibly have any idea she means to keep Liberty, and so he still must have plans to court her, if that is what the dull, sly little lies he told her that day she took him sailing can be called. He knows she has been devoting all her time to me at the hospital; it must have disappointed him no end when he heard that I was still alive. I don't know what he makes of Mike Willis's being with her so much. Nothing, probably. Men like Warrie simply can't imagine women would prefer . . . another sort of man.

I am just as glad that she'll be out of his reach for a winter, though. She will spend it with me in Northpoint, or at least those are the plans. I hope it happens. It will be like summer, having her there. When next summer comes he'll see for himself that she is going to fight him, and Mike will stand with her. I don't know what they can do about Osprey Head; Warrie does own that outright. But at least no monstrous clubhouse affair will sit there. Mike said last night that he planned to take the matter of the island up with the environmental protection people as soon as we left, to see about getting some protected status for the birds. Warrie would probably sell it then. He has no need of ospreys or eagles.

"And if he does," Mike said, "before God, I'll find a way to buy it."

"It seems a lot of trouble to go to, all that fooling around with bureaucrats," I said.

"But worth it, don't you think? Besides," he said, "it'll give me something to do until you two get back next summer. It was looking like a long hard winter."

Oh, yes, infinitely worth it.

I heard an osprey call earlier this afternoon. There is no sound in the colony to compete with the birds now, and the sea might well have carried that shrill cry all the way from Osprey Head to my sun porch. I like to think it came from the island, and that they heard it, my two children, at the same time I did, perhaps even saw the bird itself. Osprey Head, through all those years, as solid and immense, in its way, as Gibraltar. She has gone there with Mike and been healed, just as I went there all those years ago, after Sean's death, with his grandfather and found healing of my own. Looking back, all this long day, I have seen afresh how often I ran to Micah Willis. . . .

Oh, Micah. Do you remember the last time? The first summer I was back in Retreat after Peter died, back in despair because Retreat was closed and bitter to me without him, and yet I could not stay away, because all I had of him was anchored here on this old cape? I was alone in Liberty that summer; Happy would not let Darcy come to me and would not come herself, and Amy was gone, and Parker, and Christina, and you seemed lost to me too. You had buried yourself in the boathouse, Caleb and Beth told me. Locked yourself up there with your loneliness as I locked myself into Liberty with mine. You even slept there most nights, they said. Brought a cot from the house and set it up in the sail loft. That broke my heart more than almost anything, Micah Willis, that even that wonderful house held no comfort for you then. But I knew that feeling too. I moved, that summer, up to the little upstairs bedroom because I could not sleep in the big one downstairs, where Peter was not.

Do you remember the night I came to you? Just got up out of bed, ill and finally nearly wrecked with loneliness, and put a raincoat on over my nightgown and walked through the dark, dripping birch woods to the boathouse and saw the light up in the loft and climbed the stairs in silence to where you sat on the cot, reading by lamplight? You remember. I think the long healing began then, for both of us, though of course it was not, could not ever be, complete. But what we did then enabled us to live on and stay here, even to laugh. To be, again, whole people, if wounded ones. I have always loved you the more for it.

The love we made on the narrow cot was as simple and without forethought as my coming to you in the night. You did not speak, and I did not either, until it was over. It was lovely love, my old Micah. Tender, fierce, sweet, funny, enduring. A covenant. You asked me after, when I lay still in your arms—and I always knew that they would be hard and brown as they were, and taste of the salt of the sea—if I was disappointed. Oh, not for a minute, not for a second.

"On the contrary, you are some stud, Micah Willis," I said then, and you turned a dull red to the roots of your hair. Imagine you blushing, a man going on seventy. It was the first time I had really laughed since Peter, and the first time you had, I am sure, since Christina. So we did begin to heal each other. Didn't we, my other love?

But when you said, "Will you come again, Maude?" I said "No." And you were silent then, and finally you said, with a half smile that hurt to look at, "You see? I told you about the summer people. The distance between us is too far after all, isn't it?"

"I'm waiting for Peter, Micah," I said, and you looked at me in slight alarm, as if I might have gone gently off my head.

"He's gone, Maude," you said. "You're here."

"No. He's not really gone."

You shook your head.

"What a waste," you said. "You need a living love, Maude."

"I have one," I said.

That first time was also the last. I wonder if you have been sorry? I still do not know, all these years after, if I have been.

I did not tell Darcy about that night. She has it all now, she has everything of mine . . . except that. I am not ashamed of it; it is simply that it is not something she can comprehend yet, not really. "Only when love and need are one," I would have had to tell her. Only with Peter alive, and Tina, could Micah Willis and I have had a complete and living love. We both saw that, Micah and I, the night we tried it, no matter what he said. Darcy cannot know that yet; it is not a thing you can tell the young. If they are lucky, they will learn it. Many never do, but I believe she can. . . .

She was very still while I told her about Elizabeth's baby. About seeing instantly, in the light of that guttering candle, that it was not my son's child but my husband's. It was premature and already doomed, but it was Peter's child. There could be no mistake about that; Peter saw it too. Petie, bless him, did not; only Peter and I, but we knew. . . .

Darcy sat motionless, holding my hands and dropping her poor tears down on my face while I told her about holding that beautiful, blue, even-then-dying child in my arms, rocking, rocking and weeping, until my hand over its nose and mouth finally stopped the terrible struggling breath. Told her about the sacrifice of my own son, Petie, when I let the entire colony go on believing that the child was his. Most who remember it still do, I suppose. I know Petie still thinks it, and his Sarah.

When I stopped talking, and lay there trying to breathe around the elephant, her tears stopped. She looked at me in simple wonder.

"And all these years you've let them live with that?" she said. I did not think there was censure in her words, and I heard none in her voice. It was hard to talk, but I wanted her to understand about this.

"Well, darling, you see," I said, "Petie had always been a little arrogant. Very much the male Chambliss. And he always had Sarah. I didn't think a little humility would hurt him as badly as having people know . . . the truth . . . would have hurt his father."

"And what about Sarah? It must have hurt her terribly, Grammaude."

"Petie always did need a dash of salt, Darcy," I said. "He was in danger of becoming a very dull middle-aged man, very closed to possibility. I always thought a little salting of sin . . . a little doubt . . . was what drew him and Sarah so closely together afterward. It was a big risk, I know, but one I felt fairly sure of taking."

"But Granddaddy knew the truth, and you did," she said. "And yet you never even thought of leaving him, you protected him all those years."

"Elizabeth Potter was a sickness," I said to her. "She was both sick and a sickness in herself. I could never blame any man for a sickness. As it was, Peter almost could not bear what he did. His whole world was in ruins. It was my job to make it whole again. Petie's world was safe by that time."

She stared into the fire, still holding my head, and I lay still, hoarding breath. I knew we were not done talking.

"What if it had been Gretchen Winslow in that room?" she said. "You told me she'd been after Grandpa all her life."

"Then I would have left him instantly and never looked back," I said. "Gretchen was simply . . . bad. Elizabeth . . . Elizabeth was death."

"I guess she was, in the end," my granddaughter

said, starting to drop her tears again. "She was death for Grandpa, at any rate. Wasn't she?"

I closed my eyes. *Were you singing, Peter? Oh, were you?*

"Hush," I said. "I'm tired now."

She was silent for a long time. I lay listening to the snicker of the fire, feeling Zoot purring softly against my neck, feeling the elephant press down, press down.

Presently she whispered, as if to herself, "Mother Hannah was right to be afraid of you. She was right. You came in here and broke every rule in this place; you changed this whole little world, didn't you?"

I opened my eyes again and looked up at her. I thought she was about to laugh.

"Someone would have," I said. "Just as someone will this one. It's not important that this little world is changed; what's important is who does it. That's what you have to look out for. This one . . . this one could be changed by someone like you, or someone like Warrie Villiers. Do you see? Don't forget that, about who does the changing. I've always thought Retreat was really rather lucky it was me."

She did laugh, then, and put her face down to mine and kissed me.

"Grammaude," she said, "you really are one hell of a woman."

"Us southern girls are wild at heart, my dear. Don't you forget that, either."

"I won't," she whispered against my hair. "I won't."

The ambulance came then.

She has promised me she will fight. Keep Liberty, fight Warrie Villiers, make a place for herself here in Retreat. I know she is lying, but I also know the depth of her love for this place, and its hold on her, and perhaps the depth of her love for Mike, though she does not really know that yet. What she knows now is her need for him, but it is a good start. "Only when love and need are one. . . ."

And yes, I know even the depth of her love for me. So the chances are good that she will keep her word to me despite herself. She is a good child or, I should say, a good woman now, and quite a different one from the wrecked child who came to me at the start of the summer. Something happened to her out on Osprey Head the other day; she left something behind and brought something new back with her. Interesting; it would be interesting to see who this woman is.

Whoever she turns out to be, my blood runs strong in her veins. I think, if she will let it, that strength will carry her home.

I hear Mike's jeep crunching down the lane now. Good. It's full dark, and I am tired, so very, very tired. . . . Oh, listen. Mike is singing that old song that Peter sang to me that first night on Wappoo Creek: "It's three o'clock in the morning . . . we've danced the whole night through."

Fancy, those children knowing that old song. . . .

I rise and run lightly down the steps. The screen door bangs behind me. Mother Hannah will be furious; she hates it when I do that. There is laughter from the tennis court, and applause. The air is crystal blue and sweet with lilac. I hear the Potters' screen door bang too, and Amy calls, "Maude. You there? Maude?"

The car stops at the foot of the driveway.

"Maude," he calls. "Over here, Maude."

The heavy door opens and he is there, smiling, his sleeves rolled up on his tanned forearms, the flaxen hair, as usual, in his eyes. Gray eyes, eyes like sea water. The sun burns on his face and hair. He is all light, all flame.

"Peter, my dearest heart. Peter. Hello, love. You see? I did wait. . . ."

Author's Note

There are still a few old summer colonies left in Maine, places where for generations the same families have come each summer, to leave the present-day world behind and immerse themselves in an older, simpler one. The present world, however, has other ideas and leans close around these enclaves now, in many cases literally knocking on their doors. I have often felt that after this generation of elders is gone, there will be few left who remember what slow, sweet summers those in the old colonies were like. Families will still return, but the "real" world will come and go with them. This is inevitable, and on the whole, a substantial loss.

Retreat Colony does not exist, though in feeling it may perhaps come close to some of the older and more isolated ones Down East. Neither have I intended that any of the characters in this book have their counterparts in colony-goers anywhere, living or dead. The Chamblisses, the Potters, the Willises and their peers in Retreat exist only in my mind and heart, and now, I hope, in yours as well.

Cape Rosier does indeed exist, pretty much where I have set it, and is still, to my eyes, one of the wildest and most beautiful parts of the Maine coast, though that, too, is changing as developers discover what natives and summer people have known for a long time. As novelists are wont to do, I have changed some of the geography of the cape and surrounding territory, and moved some of its landmarks around, and relocated some of its roads and harbors, and even added a few of my own. But I hope lovers of this wild and lovely place will recognize the spirit and substance of it.

I am grateful to many people who have touched *Colony* in its making, either directly or indirectly. Some of them are:

Virginia Barber and Larry Ashmead, agent and editor, who cleared the jungle and laid the roadbed, as they always do . . .

Martha Gray, who processed these words and kept perfect track of many disparate threads . . .

Sunny Toulmin and Jane Hooper, who lovingly collected the memories of a score of members of our own Maine colony in one enchanting little book, from whose ambience I have borrowed liberally, if not its facts . . .

My friend Sue Dawson, beautiful in every way, whose memories of wartime colony summers I have appropriated and transmuted into Maude Chambliss's . . .

Connie and Bill McCornick, gone now, who made Maine literally magical for me in so many ways . . .

My mother-in-law, Annalee Hagerman Siddons, who has loved being "at Maine" for sixty-five summers now, and passed that love along to me with both hands . . . and my husband Heyward, who took me there twenty-five summers ago and is, in that place as well as this, both anchor and wings.

Thanks and love to all of you.

ANNE RIVERS SIDDONS
Atlanta, Georgia
January 5, 1992

Here is an excerpt from
Anne Rivers Siddons'
John Chancellor Makes Me Cry,

Published by HarperPaperbacks.

Introduction

SINCE THIS BOOK WAS FIRST PUBLISHED IN 1975, SO much has changed in the rather small world it concerns that my first thought, when I knew it was to be rereleased, was to go through it with a blue pencil and update feverishly. But when I reread it for the purpose of doing so, I found myself simply unable to cut and amend. The prospect was nastily like that of editing one's children . . . wiping out what they had been simply because of what they have become now. The grown child does not devalue the young one, and I don't feel that the 1992 perspective on this book devalues the 1975 one. On the main, I think these essays have held up pretty well, and that pleases me no end.

The world that surrounds us in this year of the Lord 1992 is a vastly different one, of course, and if the truth be told, not all that much better. The passage from Watergate to the Iran-Contra affair does not represent a great deal of progress, and the blithe little skip from supply-side economics to the S&L scandal and the insider-trading caper should, I suppose, surprise no one. We have come limping home from an unpopular war and marching home from an enormously popular one, but behind us we have still left death and destitution and loss. The poor, as it is pointed out in the New Testament, are always with us, but now they are largely homeless as well. Terrorism has become a way of life and AIDS a way of death, and the anchormen who present them all to us each evening are not, with a very few exceptions, a patch on the ones who made us weep each evening back then.

But there have been some spectacular candles lit in the darkness of this last decade of the century, and they truly light up the skies. Is it possible that that great twentieth-century bugaboo, Communism, was defanged practically overnight? Is there anyone on the planet whose heart did not lift and sing when the Wall came tumbling down? Has there ever been anything quite as gee-whiz-holy-cow-wonderful as the 1991 World Series?

Looking back, I see with surprise and a jot of chagrin that the woman who wrote these words is still, in many ways, the same woman. Shouldn't there have been some progress here? Isn't that what growing older is about . . . growing wiser? But no, eighteen years later, here is that Atlanta woman who still weeps copiously over the seven o'clock news, even if it's Peter Jennings who sets her off now, instead of Walter Cronkite. The woman who is still foolishly in love with the misfits and sociopaths of the animal kingdom, even if the original three miscreants have been gathered to the Big Catnip Patch and a new crew of wackos moved into their places. The lady who is still afraid of tornadoes and still loves reunions in Princeton and does not love New York in June. The stepmother who still dotes, if ineptly, on her four stepsons, even though they are mostly all married now and have introduced three visibly perfect grandchildren into the family stew.

And I think that is the point of this little book, and always was . . . that somehow, no matter what goes on around us during the gallop of time, we still manage to stay . . . us. I don't know about you, but to me that's a source of considerable comfort. I may not necessarily approve of the woman I find looking back over these pages, but I know her. She's the one I started out with. She can't fit into her cheerleader uniform anymore, but she certainly hasn't been sidelined yet.

And John Chancellor, bless him, still makes her cry.

Anne Rivers Siddons
January 10, 1992

The Seven O'clock Syndrome

I CRY OVER THE SEVEN O'CLOCK NEWS.

At least three evenings a week, and in a prime week every evening. Sometimes it's just the familiar walnut-at-the-base-of-the-tongue, accompanied by an eye-sheening wash of tears which I can usually hide behind the *National Observer* or the round dome of the cat's back. (*He* spends the seven o'clock news crouched on my chest, tail in my face—from this angle he is a perfect series of ellipses—blinking serenely at God knows what inklings and oddments of his own.)

But at other times, the tears catch me unaware, a flood tide that rises up through my throat, reddening my eyes and corrugating my face truly hideously, spilling out in a guttering runnel of Revlon, prompting me to strangle and snort and rush into the bedroom for a Kleenex and my husband to sigh. He isn't callous, only accustomed. This briny ritual is my evensong, as the brief, neck-crippling, head-on-chest nap before dinner ("I am not asleep, I am merely resting my eyes") is his.

It didn't start until a couple of years ago, this peculiar affliction of mine. Leaving the hermetically sealed dome of an Alabama college campus in the late fifties, I found the shining, murderous sixties a shattering enough experience, but it was with more or less normal bemusement and judicious, abstract outrage that I reacted. As a reporter for a city magazine during this decade, I found enough in my own backyard to mourn or decry, but somehow, it didn't unglue me. Some things came close; the fire storms of Selma and Cleveland, where my own friends in the news media stood to lose more than their cameras and tape recorders and half a nation stood to lose it all, wrung tears of fright and frustration from me. But others wept then, too. Those were the years when a whole generation of placid young sheep learned how to howl like starveling wolves. And there was the anguished jungle lying just beyond the world I knew, that bloomed, mature and perfect and terrible, when the bullet that shattered John Kennedy's head also cracked the skin of my world to reveal it. And the snowballing horror of watching them go, one by one—Medgar Evers, Martin Luther King, Bobby Kennedy. I cried then, furiously, blindly, for days— but so did everybody else. Almost.

Later in that decade, and into the next one, there were things that merited—and received—the cathartic ceremony of grief. Appalachia, Biafra, Vietnam,

Bangladesh; ritual murder in California and bloodied, near-human seal pups in Alaska; the crippling of a man I feared and loathed, but whose life I affirmed, in a Maryland shopping center; earthquakes, fire, and the incredible, unspeakable image of a girl child half a world away, naked, arms outflung, running down a road in Vietnam. *On fire.*

Things, truly, to cry about. And sane people eating their dinners all over the world did.

This seven o'clock thing of mine is different.

It generally starts when our local news hits, at six-thirty. I've probably just come in from work and switched on the set in the den. First, the local big stuff: A member of the police aldermanic committee has been nailed for accepting a bribe from a creamy, smiling restaurateur and club owner who happens to live down the street from me. Two mayoral candidates are calling each other names. The sanitation workers' strike is waxing ripely into its second week. A black man in one of our yeastier ghettos—slated for urban renewal nine years ago—has shot his common-law wife and her three young daughters. A local supermarket survey has shown that meat prices jumped eleven percent this past week. The Falcons have lost—again. It's going to rain—again. The smirking station ombudsman, the one with the Frankenstein-like hairpiece, whose task it is to preserve, protect, and defend the small consumer by publicly shaming his corporate malefactor, silkily announces that the Ed Fleag family of Sweet Harmony Drive, this city, is indeed going to get a refund on the chemical toilet that blew up their camper on the interstate last month. The appallingly young critic-at-large, who resembles a cadet Cuban pimp, blasts a visiting symphony conductor to shards and mispronounces "Moussorgsky."

Except for the murdered family, surely not the stuff of tears. Rage, maybe, but not tears. Nevertheless, they begin to nibble at my sinuses like demented mice.

Then the national news, and out come the big guns. John Chancellor, chanting like a Druid who knows a dirty joke, is telling us about Watergate. No inherent grief there, for me, anyway; I fiercely love every new morsel and can't wait for the whole suppurating mess to be laid out cleanly, like the seed mass of a rotting pumpkin spread on newspaper, so we can throw the damned thing away. But the traitorous muscles around my mouth quiver.

Mr. Kissinger has done a good day's work on the Middle East imbroglio; gallant, cliff-faced Mrs. Meir smiles her smile of lopsided grandeur. One sinus pings shut like a butterfly valve.

An oil slick from a wounded tanker has slimed a section of coast, but area conservationists and kids, working together, have managed to capture, clean, and save most of the affected sea birds ... close-up of saved sea bird. I whiffle, drawing an apprehensive glance from my husband, who had innocently thought tonight's news was the best we'd had in days.

David Brinkley says something so utterly sane, acid, and funny about the energy crisis that I wish I'd said it—or written it to my congressman. And a burping sob comes skittering up from behind my rib cage.

And then the news is over and the Hamm's Beer commercial comes on—the one with the shambling, trusting clown of a bear—and I am back scrabbling on my dressing table for a Kleenex.

I thought for a while that I was probably having some sort of nervous breakdown. I had always believed that to grow older was to lose the hurting edge of perception—a keen loss, a sad one, but mitigated by some measure of equanimity, a *little* wisdom, one or two scraps of tranquillity. Or, failing those, just a tougher hide and atrophied lachrymal glands. The process, I thought vaguely, was something like the change medical students undergo, which enables them to function in a world of idiot pain. But here was my hide, growing daily older and stretching daily thinner, like a squeaking balloon. Here were my tear ducts blooming wetly like ferns in El Yunque. Here I was, in the middle of my thirties (you're not getting older, you're just getting better), and on the fine edge of sitting down on the floor of the city's largest department store and wailing for somebody to come and get me because I simply couldn't *cope* anymore.

Nut City. No doubt about it.

Then one day, at the advertising agency where I write copy for resorts, real estate developments, and computer software, my friend Loraine, who has always been my grudging candidate for the best-dressed, coolest, chic-est, most unflappable and hung-together woman in the world, said, "I think I'm losing my mind. I burst into tears in the middle of *Cactus Flower* last night and had to leave the theater.

And not only that, I heard on the radio, driving in this morning, that Lindbergh Drive was closed from Piedmont to Peachtree for repairs, and I started hyperventilating."

I loved her in that instant like the sister I don't have. Because it wasn't war, famine, pestilence, or death that got to sweet Loraine. It was *Cactus Flower* and street repairs. My own territorial madness.

Since the onset of my seven o'clock sniveling syndrome, I have thought a lot about why everything is getting under my skin. Loraine and I talk about it between agency crises, over agency coffee. My husband and I talk about it over sleeping cats and sodden Kleenex. Sometimes he leans to the theory, probably a reasonable one, that the Watergate malaise has crept into the fabric of the nation like a disease and corroded the connective tissue, and that we're all going to end up, in time, blubbering along with Walter Cronkite. I just got it earlier than most. At other times, he simply thinks that some small, vital element, as yet unidentified by medical science, has been left out of my body chemistry. Which makes me, I suppose, an emotional hemophiliac. Loraine alternately inclines to sunspots, positive ions, UFOs, and something in the soil or water, an opposite of the lithium in the soil of the town in Texas where everyone is gently and sweetly happy all the time. Alvin Toffler tells me I am suffering from future shock; Robert Coles and R. D. Laing have some interesting theories. Transactional analysis helps me refrain from screaming at my own nearest and dearest, at least some of the time.

But John Chancellor and Walter Cronkite won't transact back.

I think that's it. I think I've had a bait, as my grandmother used to say, of other people's problems—without a chance to talk back. They live in a walnut veneer box behind a screen in my den; they posture on a screen in my neighborhood theater; they lurk behind the dashboard of my car or inside coats of newsprint-and-ink armor. They come in and out of my life and bang the screen door, every *day* of my life—to anger me, touch me, amuse me. But I can't get to them—to rebut, comfort, or laugh with them. There are all these people in my den, in my head, in my life, and they are all asking for my time and my attention and my *self,* and we haven't even been introduced. Their lives are laminated away from me.

And so I run for comfort to my own life like I run to my refrigerator for Rocky Road ice cream when I can't balance my checkbook. I know what it tastes like. That's all I do know, really . . . the taste of my life. It is, God knows, a disorderly thing, arrhythmic, skittering, blatting around like an irregular pulse. But it is orderly in its ordinariness, it is reassuring in its familiarity, and it is mine. I own it. I can keep my finger on it. I can tot it up and leaf through it. Nobody can fool around with what there's been of it so far. My life is built of sequences. Hinged pieces that fit together like a vertebra—that simple, that intricate. Days. Months. Seasons. They are as comforting to tell as a rosary. They are talismen; I am a bead rattler. A kisser of elbows. A don't-stepper-on of cracks. It doesn't matter. These days, months, seasons, serve me well.

A year is a fine thing. Anybody's year. Here is one of mine. I dedicate it to everybody else who cries at the seven o'clock news.

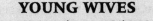